Freedomland

Books by Richard Price

The Wanderers

Bloodbrothers

Ladies' Man

The Breaks

Clockers

Richard Price

Freedomland

Broadway Books New York

I would like to thank the following people for their generous help on this book: Calvin Hart, Jose Lambiet, Larry Mullane, Mark Smith, and Donna Cutugno.

BROADWAY

FREEDOMLAND. Copyright © 1998 by Richard Price. All rights reserved. Printed in the United States of America. No part of this book may be reproduced or transmitted in any form or by any means, electronic or mechanical, including photocopying, recording, or by any information storage and retrieval system, without written permission from the publisher. For information, address Broadway Books, a division of Bantam Doubleday Dell Publishing Group, Inc., 1540 Broadway, New York, NY 10036.

Broadway Books titles may be purchased for business or promotional use or for special sales. For information, please write to: Special Markets Department, Bantam Doubleday Dell Publishing Group, Inc., 1540 Broadway, New York, NY 10036.

BROADWAY BOOKS and its logo, a letter B bisected on the diagonal, are trademarks of Broadway Books, a division of Bantam Doubleday Dell Publishing Group, Inc.

Library of Congress Cataloging-in-Publication Data
Price, Richard.
　Freedomland / Richard Price. —1st ed.
　　p.　cm.
　ISBN 0-7679-0024-3
　I. Title.
PS3566.R544F74　1998
813'.54—dc21　　　　　　　　　98-10527
　　　　　　　　　　　　　　　　　　　CIP

FIRST EDITION

Designed by Ralph Fowler

98 99 00 01 02 10 9 8 7 6 5 4 3 2 1

Grateful acknowledgment is made for permissions to quote from the following:
　True Love Travels on a Gravel Road, by Dallas Frazier and A.L. "Doodle" Owens. © 1968 (Renewed) Unichappell Music Inc. and Acuff-Rose Music, Inc. All Rights Reserved. Used by Permission. Warner Bros. Publications U.S. Inc., Miami, FL. 33014.
　(Your Love Has Lifted Me) Higher and Higher, by Gary Jackson, Carl Smith and Raynard Miner. © 1967 (Renewed) Chevis Music, Inc. Warner-Tamerlane Publishing Corp. and Unichappell Music Inc. All Rights Reserved. Used by Permission. Warner Bros. Publications U.S. Inc., Miami, FL. 33014.

To Judy, Annie, and Gen
with all my love

A broken and a contrite heart,
O God, thou wilt not despise.

PSALMS 51:17

Freedomland

The Convoy brothers, hanging in the soupy stifle of the One Building breezeway, were probably the first to spot her, and the spectral sight seemed to have frozen them in postures of alert curiosity—Caprice, sprawled down low in a rusted dinette chair, his head poked through the makeshift bib of a discarded shower curtain, and Eric, standing behind him, four fingers stalled knuckle-deep in a wide-mouthed jar of hair-braiding oil.

She was a thin white woman, marching up the steep incline from the Hurley Street end of the projects, appearing head first, like the mast of a sailing ship rounding the curve of the earth, revealing more of herself with each quick, stiff step across the ruptured asphalt oval that centered the Henry Armstrong Houses. That sloped and broken arena, informally known as the Bowl, was usually barren, but tonight it lay planted with dozens of new refrigerators awaiting installation, resting on their backs in open crates like a moonstruck sea of coffins.

"Where she goin'," Eric said mildly.

The woman was carrying one arm palm up, cradled in the other like a baby.

Caprice leaned forward in the chair. "Bitch on a mission," he said, laughing.

"Huh," Eric grunted, faint, tentative. It was a quarter past nine in the evening, the grounds mostly deserted because of the rally being held at the community center to solve the double homicide of Mother Barrett and her brother. But despite being in the wrong place at the wrong time, this white lady didn't seem right for a fiend—wasn't looking at them, looking *for* them. In fact, she was ignoring them, coming off neither dope-hungry nor afraid, just taking those brisk little steps and glaring at the ground in front of her with an expression somewhere between angry and stunned.

Tariq Wilkins, scowling in the swelter of this end-of-June Monday evening, came hunkering out of One Building, his hands crossed and buried in the armpits of his Devils jersey.

"That meeting over yet?" he drawled. He took in the still-lit windows of the community center, made a clucking noise of annoyance.

Tariq, like Eric and Caprice and just about everybody else, knew who had killed the two old people exactly one year ago to the day. But also like everybody else, he was keeping it to himself, because what goes around comes around.

"Look like a cemetery out there," Tariq said, gesturing to the mute field of refrigerators. Then he spotted her climbing the asphalt Bowl and reared back. "Dag . . ." His mouth hung open, his hands moving to the back pockets of his hang-dog jeans.

She wore dungarees with fresh dirt stains at the knees and a black T-shirt sporting the naggy legend IT TAKES A WEAK MAN TO DISRESPECT THE STRONG WOMAN WHO RAISED HIM. Her hair was shoulder-length and lank, her face pale and thin. She had no lips to speak of, but her eyes— the building-mounted anti-crime spotlights picked them up as a startling electric gray, like a husky's, so light and wide as to suggest trance or blindness.

She came within conversational distance of them, and Tariq stepped parallel, sizing her up. "What you lookin' for . . ." he said. Then, just as Eric snagged his sleeve and pulled him back, he caught the reflection of something both bloody and glittering in her upturned palm.

Without so much as a hitch in her stride, the woman sailed right past them and was gone—out of the Henry Armstrong Houses, the heart of that section of the city given the side-mouthed tags Darktown, D-Town, and into the world.

"What you be pulling on me . . ." Tariq snapped, without any real heat, jerking his elbow high to free himself from Eric's grip.

Eric didn't answer, just got back to working on his brother's head. A withdrawn silence came down on all three of them now, each having caught sight of that cupped bloody dazzle, each of them pulling in, as if to be alone with his abrupt and mystifying discomfort.

The woman marched through the city of Dempsy on a determined diagonal, with the same pinched yet rapid stride with which she had climbed the Bowl, up and out of the Armstrong Houses. Cradling her arm, she tramped through red lights and green, the traffic next to nothing at this hour of the workweek. She walked through the parking lot of a Kansas Fried Chicken and across a deserted basketball court named after a local projects kid turned pro, the sodium lights casting her shadow thin and twisted to the Powell Houses behind the backboard. She marched across the diamond of a Little League field resting atop a fifty-year-old chromium dump, her face sullen yet tremulous, her light eyes fixed on the ground in front of her.

The fashion wave rippling through Darktown that summer was fat strips of metallic reflector tape slapped on jeans, sneakers, and shirts. As she approached the dingy yellow sizzle of JFK Boulevard—all storefront churches, smoke shops, and abandoned businesses—the agitated boredom of the dope crews brought the street corners alive with restless zips of light.

A patrol car slowed to profile her as she passed under a crude mural of a fetus with a crucifix sprouting from its navel. She raised her eyes, opened her mouth, and took a step in the car's direction. "Give a saliva test to this one here," the driver murmured to his partner. But then she seemed to change her mind, quickly giving the cruiser her back and evaporating into a side street.

In a few more minutes she was striding across another ball field, this one also atop an old chromium dump, and then she was facing the Dempsy Medical Center, vast, Gothic, and half shut down, the emergency room entrance shedding the only eye-level light before the city hit the river. She finally came to a halt just outside the cone-shaped perimeter cast before the entrance like a spotlight on a bare stage.

She hesitated on the edge of the pale, one foot in, one out, her face taking on a sparkle of panic as she eyed the full-up benches of the waiting room through the gummy glass of the automatic doors. For a moment she froze but then seemed to get a grip, decisively rolling off to her left, turning the corner of the building, and descending to a more shadowed entrance at the bottom of a ramp. Walking through a partially raised roll-down gate, she stepped inside an empty, garishly lit room, the silence and stillness such that the buzzing of a fluorescent desk lamp could be heard twenty feet away.

At first, as if disoriented by a sense of trespass, she appeared not to notice the overweight young black man on the gurney directly across the room from her. But once she caught sight of him, she seemed unable to look away. He was barefoot but otherwise fully dressed—dead, the fatty tissue billowing out from the box-cutter slash under his chin like a greasy yellow beard. She stared at the pale-skinned soles of his feet as if hypnotized by this hidden whiteness, stood there staring until a stainless-steel freezer door opened directly across from her. A yellow-eyed middle-aged man in a hooded parka came into the room, instantly rearing back from her presence.

"You a relative?" he asked, removing his coat. His eyes rose to something directly over her head.

She looked up to see a digital readout blinking "115," then down to see that she was standing on a gurney-sized weighing platform set into the floor. When she looked back at the morgue attendant his eyes were on her hands.

"You in the wrong wing."

Standing by the nurses station that fronted the medical center's ER, the security guard, a goateed, nose-ringed kid tricked out in a uniform like a full-bird colonel, eavesdropped on an overnatty detective. He was on the phone to report a shots-fired situation—one dead Rottweiler, the shooter getting his face resewn in one of the trauma rooms. "A good shooting. Just thought you needed to know." Twenty feet down the corridor a sad-faced Pakistani leaned patiently against the wall, a bloody bath towel swirled tightly around his head, his ear in an ice-filled Ziploc bag.

There was an abrupt rapping against the glass doors of the ambulance bay, and the guard turned to see the woman outside, trying to push her way in. His mouth in a twist, he brusquely signaled her to walk around to the main entrance, then resumed watching the free show in the hallways, zeroing in on a mush-mouthed drunk reclining, fully dressed, on a slant-parked gurney. The guy lay casually on his side, propped up on an elbow like a Roman senator, his head resting on the palm of his hand. Earlier in the evening, the story went, he had bitten down on a shot glass and added a three-inch extension to one side of his smile.

"I'm a alcoholic," the drunk said, having caught the guard's eye. "I got me a big problem with that. Not a little problem, a big problem. A goddamn *Shop* Rite–sized problem. I ain't gonna lie about it."

The guard snorted and turned his attention to a bored correction officer on escort duty. He was doing half-assed push-ups against the wall while waiting for his charge to get the rest of his thumbnail removed.

A nurse's aide, a round, bespectacled, almost elderly black woman with a bemused set to her mouth, slapped a blood-pressure cuff on the drunk.

"I need me something for the pain. I told you that, right?"

"Right."

"I got to get some Percocets or something 'cause I can*not* stand pain and I got to get to work at 6:00 A.M. in the morning."

"Yeah? What do you do." The nurse smirked.

"You don't want to know."

"Well, I hope you don't drive no school bus."

"Mommy, I got me a forty-thousand-dollar car, cash paid. I'm telling you, you *don't* want to know."

"You *don't* want to know," the nurse said, mocking him. "I can*not* stand pain," she added mincingly. "You want to know about pain, you have yourself a baby, then come talk to me about pain."

"Hey, I had six—"

"No, *you.*"

"Well, I was in the vicinity."

The security guard, laughing now, hands behind his back, took a spacey 360-degree spin on one heel, then came alert with irritation as that lady outside the ambulance entrance renewed her rapping on the door. He began to wave her around again but saw the blood smearing the glass and what looked like a palm full of jewels pressed against the pane.

The ambulance bay doors were opened by remote to let a uniformed cop out, and suddenly the woman was in the house.

Eyes unfocused, teeth chattering, she floated down the hall, ignoring the irritated shout "Miss! Miss! Ex*cuse* me," a reproachful singsong from the nurses station.

She wandered down the hallway, past the examination rooms—surgery, trauma, medical, X ray—then, as if remembering something, abruptly wheeled around, inadvertently stepping into the startled embrace of the goateed security guard.

"You got to go out to triage just like everybody else," the kid lectured awkwardly, wincing at the sight of her upturned palms, the things growing there. He steered her back past the nurses' station to the dented, paint-chipped double doors that led to the waiting room. She went willingly at first but then suddenly, with an expression of disgust, twisted out of his grasp. Her supported arm fell from its cradle, the hand hanging from the wrist like a dead goose.

An East Indian doctor, petite, slender, and almost prim in his self-possession, strolled down the hallway eating a sandwich. His face registered a look of grudging interest as he noticed the floppiness of the hand.

"What happened to you," he asked flatly, between bites, taking in the glassy dislocation of her eyes, the labored workings of her chest. His identification tag read "ANIL CHATTERJEE."

"He threw me down. I couldn't even get the *words* out." Her voice was smoky and deep, vibrating with a kind of retroactive panic.

"Down where." He lifted her limp hand, gently felt the outer wrist bones.

She ignored the question, her head jerking like a bird's.

"What happened to you."

Still no response.

He gave his sandwich to the security guard and took both her hands. Her palms were embedded with shards of glass, clear and beer-bottle green, bits of gravel, some rusted wedges of tin, sharp fragments of various colored plastic, and in one hand a fine, small coil of metal, the inner spring of a cheap ballpoint pen—all of it implanted in the red-and-blue rawness of abraded flesh.

"I want you to answer my question," he said sternly. "What happened to you."

"He threw me out of the car . . ." Suddenly she stomped her foot like a child, her voice soaring. "I couldn't get the *words* out! He didn't give me a chance! I tried, I swear to God!"

"Threw you out. Was the car moving?" Chatterjee gripped her above the wrists to prevent her from flailing and complicating the damage.

She turned away, her face bunching, tears popping like glass beads.

Casually bypassing the screening drill, he walked her directly to the surgery room, escorting her in an awkward sideways scuttle, still holding her in that double-handed grip. The guard followed tentatively with the doctor's sandwich.

The surgery room was crowded, the floor sticky, littered with torn gauze wrappers. Along the walls, patients sat quietly. A frazzled doctor with a Russian accent held a bouquet of MRIs, CAT scans, and X rays to his chest and read out names, mail-call-style.

"Salazar?"

No answer.

"Vega?"

Two men, both wearing blood-drizzled shirts, cautiously raised their hands, then, noticing each other, simultaneously lowered them.

Chatterjee sat her on a backless stool and took her pulse, which was racing like a hummingbird. He strapped a blood pressure cuff on her arm, holding himself still. Ninety over seventy, the blood somewhere in her feet at this point.

"I need to know what happened to you. I cannot treat you if I don't know what happened to you," he said, locking his eyes into hers, staring into that dazzling lupine gray.

She looked away again, exhaling in graduated shudders, trying.

"I was lost," she began, in that smoky, stunned vibrato. "He said, he said he could help me get through the park. The guy, he didn't . . ." Her voice fluttered away. "He didn't even—I got out of the car, OK? He didn't even let me get a *word* out. He threw me down." She looked off, clenching her teeth.

"Were you raped?"

She balled her impaled palms into white knots, blood dripping. Chatterjee quickly backed away to save his pants, then, leaning forward from a safe distance, forcibly pried her fingers open again. The security guard placed the doctor's sandwich on a stack of X rays and left the room.

"Listen to me. I speak six different languages. Just answer in human range. Were you raped."

The triage nurse, a woman in her fifties with frosted red hair and a giant button reading "#1 NANA" pinned under her collar, slipped in behind Chatterjee. She held an admissions form on a clipboard. The doctor waited for an answer as the young woman looked at both of them with a pleading muteness. His gaze compulsively returning to those eyes, he nudged her stool with his knee, moving it along on its casters to a sink. He worked on a pair of latex gloves, then took one of her palms and began to wash it gently.

"Listen to me. I'm going to tell you something to calm you down, make you think about something else, OK? Then we'll talk again." He cleared his throat. "Besides Americans, do you know who're the most dangerous people on earth?"

He removed a shark fin of green glass with his fingers. The woman didn't even flinch, her gaze roaming the walls.

"The most dangerous people on earth are the educated middle-class men of the Third World. Do you know why?" He scowled in concentration, plucking a piece of rusted tin. The triage nurse, still behind him, rolled her eyes.

"They labor under the illusion that their education will allow them to rise to the upper class of their homeland, OK? But the class system is too rigid. Are you following me?"

The woman hid her eyes behind her free forearm.

"So they come to America thinking anybody can rise to the top in America, but here they run into the skin game like running into a wall, so at best they get to be professionals, own a few tenements on the side. So what do they do, eh? You know what they do?" He teased out the tiny coil of metal, the woman's knees running like jackhammers. "They go back to the country they came from and they start a peasant revolution to overthrow the upper classes in the name of the people. And in *this* way, they finally get to the top of the chain, the new elite. What do you think about that, huh?"

"It's not my fault," the woman said distractedly.

"What isn't?" he asked, his tone registering true confusion. She wouldn't say.

"OK." He shrugged, reaching for a soap solution. "So. That's my story. Tell me yours. What happened to you tonight?"

The woman opened her mouth, but her throat caught and her juddering spine jerked her into a hunch.

The doctor's eyes strayed to a matted tangle of hair slightly to the side of her head. Still holding one of her injured hands, he reached out and fingered the crusted ridge of a scalp laceration.

"Is this from tonight too?"

"No," she muttered.

He glared at her for a long minute, as if challenging her reticence with his own. Finally, letting loose with an ostentatious sigh, he carefully laid her hand on the edge of the sink, said "Don't move," and walked out of the room.

A dazed, disheveled black woman drifted in from the hall, one eye closed as if by a punch, her blouse buttoned all wrong. She had a dollar bill in one hand and a business card in the other.

"You got change of a dollar?" she asked no one in particular. "They said I'm supposed to call this detective." Before anyone could answer, she drifted back out into the corridor.

"What's your name, hon," the triage nurse asked easily.

Behind the nurse's back, the Russian doctor interviewed a man on a gurney. "High blood pressure. Anything else?"

"Yeah, well, I hear voices . . ."

"What's your name," the nurse repeated.

"Brenda Martin," the woman answered distantly, watching another East Indian–looking doctor, a woman, extract a roach from a child's ear with a pair of long dogleg scissors.

"Brenda? Do you know your Social Security number?"

Before she could answer, Chatterjee reappeared, a uniformed cop in his wake.

"C'mon, Doc, I'm backed up the yin-yang here."

"Then radio for another unit."

Chatterjee gave the woman a sour look from across the room. "You talk to him," he said, chucking a thumb at the cop over his shoulder.

Brenda Martin shot to her feet and stood there as if about to make an announcement. Her sudden uprightness made the two men hesitate. She opened her mouth, and both of them, seemingly reading her eyes and coming to the same conclusion, made a tandem lunge. It was a heartbeat too late. Sliding through their grasping hands, Brenda Martin hit the floor hard.

One Monkey
Don't Stop
No Show

1

"You know, life, life and death, you hear the kids; life and death are so, *flippant* to them. Death is no big thing. Death is, *life.*"

Pacing back and forth across the stage decked with two pictures of Mother Barrett and her twin brother, Theo—enlarged photos framed in black construction paper with white doily trim—the Muslim cleric, a local black man in *kufi* and dashiki, was winding up his appeal, the people giving him a kind of slouched-down, half-guilty look of attentiveness. There were about a hundred tenants seated on folding chairs in the hangar-shaped community hall, but not many of them were under fifty or more than children. Six uniformed housing cops, flat-faced, arms folded across their chests, stood at the rear because of rumors about some kind of trouble.

Detective Lorenzo Council, sporting black rumpled jeans and a positive-message T-shirt, sat on a window ledge to the side of the stage, waiting for his turn to speak. Everywhere Lorenzo looked there was something to piss him off. Out the window was that field of crated refrigerators Housing had neglected to secure with some kind of lock or seal. Lorenzo knew that tomorrow, or maybe even tonight, some of the kids would most likely try to find a way inside those death traps and make little clubhouses for themselves. Housing had laid the things flat on their backs, fearing that the kids would start tipping them over, but no one had had the additional brains to lay them door-side down. And what made it even more ominous was that every refrigerator had its destination chalk-scrawled on its side, like "12G 14 Hurley." Like "This coffin's for you."

Lorenzo also got hot on seeing the Convoy brothers out there, them and that bonehead Tariq Wilkins, hanging in the breezeway of One Building. Even though most of the guys their age were avoiding this meeting, avoiding that tap on the shoulder, the others at least had the decency to refrain from rolling outside tonight, a gesture of respect for the people who did show up. But these three . . .

And this crowd in here, just what he would expect—mostly seniors like the murdered couple, showing up out of a lifetime reflex of heeding the call. But they were scared. You could see it in their lack of verbal response, in how they looked off or down, looked anywhere but at the memorial photos or the speaker.

"The, the cowards, the coward, no . . . The *thing;* 'cause whoever did this ain't even human, so I'll call it a thing, a punkified thing."

The people nodded soberly, stone-faced, a tear here and there, a baby crying, a whiff of sweetish liquor. But it had been a whole year. Although this first-anniversary memorial rally had been Lorenzo's idea, he was skeptical about anything tangible coming out of it. And this cleric was straight-up boring him to death.

Nine-thirty. He had arranged a split shift for tonight with his partner, Bump Rosen, who would field all jobs from four o'clock to nine-forty-five. Lorenzo would return the favor from nine-forty-five to midnight so that Bump could race home in time to catch his twelve-year-old son's acting debut on *Law and Order.*

Nine-thirty. Fifteen minutes to go, and he hadn't even got up to speak yet.

One of the purposes of this "rally" was to get the murders back in the news, to keep the crime warm if not hot, but only two reporters had shown up—the runner from the *Dempsy Register* and some intern with the *Jersey Journal.* Neither the police nor the press could throw much energy into two homicides committed in a county that had since tallied up 59 fresher ones.

Lorenzo eyed the street reporter from the *Register,* Jesse Haus. He'd known her going on eight years, this small, overdenimed, overmascaraed, fine-boned young woman sitting on the aisle and scowling at her nails, reminding him, as she always did, of a race car stuck in traffic—crossed legs pumping, untended notepad bobbing in her lap, a nervous flicker in the eye, as if some of that mascara had gotten under the lid.

A few months earlier, she had spent some time with Lorenzo, writing a profile of him for the *Register* that had landed him on the Rolonda Watts program. Now, absorbing her oddly vacant yet alert expression, Lorenzo found that her frenetic impatience was intensifying his own, making him feel more keenly that this whole show was slipping out of his control. Telepathically he beamed to her: Wait.

Anxiously caressing his shaved head, Lorenzo studied the portraits of the elderly Barrett twins—both faces heart-shaped and genderless, each topped with a short iron-gray crop, the old lady's eyes beady and disapproving, her brother's equally narrow but impish. Uncle Theo, in his seventies, had still favored tight continental slacks and, even in the hottest months, turtleneck sweaters. He had retired as a bookkeeper at the Apollo but remained a fey smoothy who addressed everybody as "Baby"—everybody except the great entertainers he had been introduced to over the years. He referred to them as "Mister" Billy Eckstine, "Miss" Dinah Washington, "Mister" Sam Cooke, and "Miss" Sarah Vaughan. Uncle Theo was a "character" who had enticed decades of projects kids with ice cream and pizza, suckering them into digging Lionel Hampton jive his way through "Hey Ba Ba Re Bop," Joe Liggins work out on "The Honeydripper," Billy Ward and the Dominoes go on about a "Sixty Minute Man." He always asked the boys if they knew what that meant, Sixty Minute Man, but that was as far as that kind of stuff ever went with Uncle Theo. Hundreds of Armstrong kids over the years, Lorenzo included, sitting on that plastic-sheathed couch, trying not to laugh at him. A character, Lorenzo thought, a singular individual who is no more—a loss honestly felt in him, one that justified this extra effort tonight.

As far as Mother Barrett went, Lorenzo had never really liked her, although, given her brother's flamboyant sexuality, her memory would be the smarter of the two to invoke at a rally like this. The hell of it was that Lorenzo, just like everybody else in the room, knew who had committed the murders, but no one, neither clergy nor cop, could speak the name in public, because the actor had never been charged.

It was the grandson, Mookie, a die-hard crackhead—huge, explosive, semi-intelligent, not all there. Lorenzo was sure he'd done it, because Mookie had been homeless except for the times his grandmother and granduncle had taken him in, let him sleep on the floor, raid the refrigerator; and whoever had committed this monstrous act had afterwards laid neatly folded blankets under the victims' heads, as if to make them comfortable—a gesture of remorse. The apartment hadn't been trashed, just that one drawer left open in the bedroom, a scatter of food stamps and pocket change still in it: whoever had done this had known just where the money was hidden. But the Homicides had fucked up, had failed to get Mookie's statement down on tape last year, so there was nothing to pin his contradictions against. After a few agitated sit-downs, the kid had simply refused to talk anymore, then had left the city for Brooklyn, where, unbelievably enough, he had "family" to take him. Without a murder weapon and without a witness, without someone's stepping forth and saying, "Yeah, I saw him going in, I saw him coming out, I heard his voice raised in anger," there was next to nothing Lorenzo or anyone else could do. And even though no one was talking—out of fear of payback, fear of involvement—all of Armstrong was raw and testy tonight, suffering through the first anniversary of one of its most shameful hours.

"You know," the cleric said, smiling and adjusting his horn-rimmed glasses, "I could muster a hundred men with one phone call. Raise me a army, go out tonight, and it would be nothing for me to execute this, this *creature* right on the spot. Nothing." The cleric grinned at the cops in the rear of the room, a few of whom grinned right back, softly bouncing their spines against the glaze-tiled wall.

"But what we have here in this country, as, as flawed as it is, is a system, a judicial system . . ."

Everything was rubbing Lorenzo wrong—like the arrest this morning of Supreme Griffin, the kingpin of the minute. The knockos had popped him coming off the George Washington Bridge, finding a baggie of chronic right up on the dashboard. Word had it that Supreme had simply stepped out of the car and, without prompting, casually told them about the half ki in the hubcap, the fifty bundles of heroin in the fake Benzi box. Running into him at the intake unit before coming to the rally tonight, Lorenzo had asked him why he had rolled over on himself like that. Supreme's response, offered to a detective who liked to describe himself as "an old narco man," made him sadder than hell:

"I'm just so tired of it, you know what I'm saying? Just motherfuckin' tired."

These days people were fond of saying, "Crack's whack, heroin's back." Yeah, well, Lorenzo was thinking, the stats might be down, the body count, but there was a tangible sadness out there, a resignation and surrender that was like death itself.

"We are sometimes"—the cleric, speaking softly now, smiled forgivingly at the sullen folks below him—"sometimes a frightened people. And with good reason, good reason. A young black male growing up in this, this cesspool of a city has a greater chance of meeting a violent death before he reaches his majority than did the average GI overseas in World War II. And that is according to the *New York Times,* the *New York Times.* But I am here to tell you something, and that is that there is *nothing* and *no* one to fear in this world but God himself. For we shall all die, and then comes Judgment, then comes Judgment." He bowed to his audience. *"Asalaam alaikim."*

As he moved off the stage, a thin murmur of *"Asalaam alaikims"* came back at him, most people here a little too old to have tossed off Jesus in favor of Muhammad.

On the sidelines, Lorenzo rubbed his face as the audience politely turned to him, dutifully awaiting their next pounding. He looked out the window, eyeing the Convoy brothers one more time for a hit of anger, took in that eerie geometric garden of refrigerators, then hauled himself to his feet.

"We call ourselves a community. We call ourselves a family," Lorenzo declared in a cracked bellow, his usual tone of voice when addressing a large audience. "But we don't want to be known as a *snitch,* so we are paying our allegiance to the wrong people."

He lumbered back and forth across the stage like a big cat in a cage, gazing heavy-lidded at the squirming tenants, the impassive housing cops. He was a big man—six foot three, 240 pounds—with a royal gut, a pendulous and chronically split lower lip, and thick glasses. In situations like this, loud and angry usually did the trick.

"I have heard, I have heard someone say that if this was a *white* area, the police would have caught the guy already. If this was a white . . . No! No! That would only be true if the *white* people, the *blue* people, the *polka-dot* people would have stepped up and said, Yes! I saw who did it. Yes! I had heard those shots. Yes! Yes! Yes! . . . It's time to get *real* with yourselves!"

Lorenzo glared at them, his anger fueled by the fact that he knew he was castigating the wrong people, the ones who at least showed up.

"But in this project it's, No, no, no, don't mention my name, no, no, don't, don't, no, no, what goes around comes around. So!" He reared up. "It has been a whole *year.* These people were shot a total of *eight times.*

Eight explosions at nine o'clock in the *morning*." He prowled the stage, spotting Miss Bankhead in the crowd, the elderly lady who had lived next door to the Barretts.

"But nobody heard nothing, nobody heard nothing. Now how can that be, if I know that if I turn on my radio too loud on the *fourth* floor someone on the *first* floor's gonna be complaining about the racket. How can that be, if I know that if I drop a, a juice glass on the *second* floor someone from the *third* floor is gonna be running to the housing office complaining about the party in my apartment." Lorenzo paced, furious, pushing up his glasses. "We have lost two of our loved ones."

He pointed to Mother Barrett's photo. "Look at her. Look! *Mother* Barrett. *We* gave her that name. She was *our* mother. *Uncle* Theo." Lorenzo hesitated, knowing "Uncle" hadn't the same visceral tug as "Mother." "*We* called him that. How many of you here have gotten phone calls from him saying, Your kid's at my house listenin' to records. Is it OK I feed him dinner, feed her dinner, give him a book, buy her a, a ice cream cone."

There was some solemn nodding going on out there now, a pickup in the weeping.

"They were *old*-school folks!"

"That's right," someone said amidst a rising mutter.

"Old school! The best people in the world! They were here back in the day! Back when everybody in this project looked out for each other!"

People nodded more vigorously, peppering him with responses.

"*Tell* it, Big Daddy!"

He eyed old Miss Bankhead, suffering in her chair, rocking with her secrets. She'd been ducking him for a solid year now. There was a crackled report on one of the police radios in the back.

"When I was a kid here growin' up? If I messed up on one end of these houses, I got my butt kicked all the way home. My mother had her *fifty* pair a eyes back then!"

People laughed a little, wary, Lorenzo wincing for them, for what he was about to do to them.

One of the cops yawned audibly.

"If, if I played hookey or smoked me a cigarette, I had *fifty* mothers to yank my ear. Old school!" He was still pacing. "Old school! Mother Barrett—" Then he stopped, making himself laugh like he had lost his train of reproach. "Mother Barrett, one time, when I was a kid? I stole some chocolate sprinkles from the Chilly Willy truck. You remember that truck came around in the summertime?"

"Oh yeah."

"Yes-s."

Jesse Haus of the *Register* quietly collected her stuff and crouch walked up the aisle to the exit. Lorenzo was slightly stung by the bad review—he was just getting started.

"The Chilly Willy truck," he repeated, having momentarily lost his place. "Had this, like, a, a service tray hanging out the side, had all the toppings in it, the sprinkles, chocolate, blue, green, rainbow, dip your ice cream cone in there, kids' eyes gettin' all, you know." Lorenzo bugged his eyes, licked his lips.

The laughing came easier now. Even a couple of the housing cops were smiling, heads turned to the windows.

"One time, in what I call my pre-po-lice days, I couldn't help it, I just got so greedy crazy I just, just snatched me a fistful, *two* fistfuls. The *hell* with the ice cream cone!"

Lorenzo acted it out, and people were throwing back their heads, laughing at the ceiling. Miss Bankhead was still rocking, a hand over her mouth, the burden of her knowledge making her oblivious to the show.

"Man, I just run like the devil, got all up behind One Building." Lorenzo thought of those damn knuckleheads out there. "Chilly Willy man didn't even know what hit him. I turn around, gettin' ready to scarf me a mouthful . . ." Lorenzo was doing Cosby now, turning, then freezing, his eyes popping with fear, staring up at some invisible gigantic adult. "Turn around, there's ol' Mother Barrett give me that *eye*. You remember that eye she had? Kind of, kind of *freeze* you in your tracks."

"Tell it!"

"That old lady, she don't even ask for my side of the story, don't even let me prepare a *lie* for myself. She gave me a whack on my behind? I swear, people on the benches was pickin' sprinkles out their hair for a solid week! That lady done pro*pelled* me home that day!"

People were jerking back and forth in their folding chairs as if someone had them by the scruffs of their necks—hissing with glee, backhanding one another on the arms, Lorenzo laughing with them, one of the cops looking right at him now, grinning like, "OK, you win."

"*Old* school!" he bellowed amiably, waiting a beat for them to come down and then saying in that same pleasant tone: "Yeah, ol' Mother Barrett. You know when I got called into her apartment this time last year? There was so much blood on the floor that I slipped and fell flat on my back. Yeah."

Lorenzo smiled at his sneakers. The air had gone dead and heavy now.

"She had been shot so many times and at such close range—" And then he just stopped himself, thinking, They got the message. Just let them know you're here.

"And don't tell me the police ain't doin' their job. *We* are the police in our area." He thrust a finger at the cops in the rear. "*They* are not here twenty-four hours a day. *We* are. We got to stand for something. We got to walk upright. If somebody's doing wrong, they're doing *wrong* and we got to stand *up*. In our homes, in our families, in our hallways, our buildings, our courtyards, and our projects—*we, we* are the police."

A patrol radio crackled again back at the rear wall.

"Yes-s," came forth the disembodied response.

"We lost two in one day. Two beautiful old folks, watched over all of us, year in, year out."

Lorenzo prowled the stage, shifting his Glock out from under his gut.

"There are people in these houses that *live* in their windowsills." He was speaking softly now. "The world's biggest TV, right? That's what you call it, and you know who you are. I ain't gonna point you out by name." He shifted his gun again, hitched up his jeans, and smiled down at the crowd. "People, I just might be *this* far away from a lockup, and that little bit you got for me might be all that I need.

"You know me. I'm here twenty-four, seven. All it takes is a phone call." He scanned the beat-down faces, trying to make eye contact with the windowsill crew—all the seniors living in the two lowest floors of Three Building, the area designated for the elderly by Housing and known by the creepers as the Lamb Pen.

"All it takes is a phone call." Lorenzo avoided looking at the Barretts' old neighbor Miss Bankhead, gracing the room with a respectful half bow instead. "And I thank you for having the courage to come to this here meeting. Allah, Jesus, Jehovah, or Muhammad, God bless each and every one of you."

As the rally broke up, Lorenzo lingered in the community room small-talking, looking for that furtive I-got-something-for-you-but-not-here eye, slowly working his way to the exit, people saying "I hope you get him" and other useless shit.

He tracked Miss Bankhead as she toddled from port to starboard on her three-hundred-pound arthritic bulk, pacing himself through the hugs and tears so that he could catch her outside without looking too obvious about it, but one of the housing cops snagged his arm.

"Yo, Big Daddy, you hear about your boy there, Supreme?"

Lorenzo stopped, half smiling: Your boy. "Yeah, he got himself locked up again."

"Big time, Mo," the cop, Eight-Ball Iovakas, said. He went up on tiptoe to let another heavy woman exit between them.

Eight-Ball's radio crackled.

"*East 202.*" The dispatcher's call-out was as flat as a dead man's EKG.

"*Two-oh-two. Go,*" the responding unit answered in kind. Lorenzo and Eight-Ball were barely listening in.

"*Report of a bowling ball dropped from the roof of 15 Weehawken, Roosevelt Houses. Please respond.*"

Eight-Ball turned the volume down. "I heard Supreme just gave it up, like, '*Whoop,* they it is.' "

"I heard that too," Lorenzo said distractedly, still trolling the crowd for eye contact. The room was lined with children's self-portraits from the day-care program, big crude faces in poster paint on oak tag, each one entitled, I AM SOMEONE.

"So how's this going here?" Eight-Ball nodded to the enlarged memorial photos, now being carried out under the arm of a maintenance worker.

Lorenzo shrugged. "People scared. You know how it is." He started to peel off, eager to catch Miss Bankhead, but Eight-Ball's radio came to life again.

"*South 111.*"

"*One-eleven. Go.*"

"*One-eleven, please respond to medical center emergency room. See female vic of a possible carjack at that location.*" Both of them were eavesdropping more intently this time, since South District was their territory.

Lorenzo peeked at his watch: ten-fifteen, batter up, Bump Rosen sitting at home now watching his kid play a preteen homicidal skinhead on prime-time TV. Lorenzo's beeper went off, as if to confirm the favor swap. The carjack would be his once the uniforms took the preliminary report.

"Awright, boss." He tilted in the direction of the exit, but Eight-Ball touched his arm again.

"Lorenzo." Eight-Ball nodded toward the cleric, who at the moment was talking to the assistant on-site housing manager. "You better tell Abdool Ben Fazool over there to go easy on this 'Raise me a army' bullshit. Somebody might believe him."

"Tell him yourself." Lorenzo smiled thinly, then moved off, looking for Miss Bankhead. But she was nowhere to be found.

As he pulled the Crown Victoria out of his parking spot, Lorenzo's headlights caught a tall woman clutching an armload of dry cleaning. She was standing in the path of his car, rocking slightly from foot to foot.

Lorenzo rolled up alongside her, laughing. "Hey, baby, what you doin' in the middle of the street? I run you down you ain't gettin' dime one off me. I'm indemnified."

"So I'll sue the city," she said, and moved closer to the car door. Ruth Raymond was a forever tenant, born in the Armstrong Houses some thirty-five years ago.

On a sultry night like this one, the plastic sheathing over the folded clothes adhered to her bare arm like cling wrap. Lorenzo wondered where she got ahold of dry cleaning after ten in the evening.

"I like what you said in there, Daddy." Ruth's face was like putty. She had been drinking heavily since her son died six months ago, shot for his shearling parka. "You know who you should talk to? Miss Bankhead. You *know* that lady knows something."

"I believe she does."

"You know she's been down to North Carolina must be like nine or ten times in the last year—just going up and back on the bus, as heavy and old as she is? I swear, Big Daddy, something's eating her to death. She can't even sit still in her own living room, watch TV no more."

"I'm on it."

"*All units wanted for carjacking in the South District. Nineteen ninety-one Toyota Camry, four-door, color beige, New Jersey reg 665 Gamma Delta. Roger.*"

Lorenzo lowered the volume on his radio.

"Yeah, I heard that she was the first one walked in the apartment, found the bodies," Ruth said, seeming to retreat slightly from the coconut-scent deodorizer hanging from his rearview.

"Yeah, she was." He nodded solemnly.

"Must of put the fear of God in her, seeing that," Ruth said, getting teary now.

"Must've."

"She *knows* something, Daddy." Ruth grabbed his forearm. "Please make her say it."

"I'm tryin'."

He had gone as far as grabbing up Miss Bankhead's grandson on an old unexecuted warrant, offering to swap the kid's freedom for her information, but even the kid had said it—"My grandmother gonna take that to her grave"—forcing Lorenzo to go through with the arrest.

"All units, further information on South District carjack. Vehicle occupied by black male, five foot ten to six feet tall, shaved head. Last seen driving west on Hurley."

"How 'bout you, Mommy? You got anything to help me out with?"

Ruth looked right, left, then pressed her dry cleaning up against the driver's door.

"Give me a card," she said, low and urgent.

He produced one from his cup caddy, holding it upright in his lap. Ruth reached in through his open window, crumpled the card in her fist like tissue paper, and slid it under the dry cleaning, Lorenzo thinking that it must be the fiftieth card he'd given to this woman since her son died.

"I'll call you, all right?" Ruth said out the side of her mouth, eyeing the buildings.

He nodded, not holding his breath over this announcement. "Ruth, you get yourself some sleep. You look tired." Then he slowly rolled off.

"Sleep, that's all I do," she called after him. Then, louder, "And tell Housing to get them damn refrigerators out of the Bowl. They give me the creeps."

Lorenzo drove to the emergency room musing on the call: carjack, female victim, Hurley Street. It was an unlikely crime for the location, a potholed cul-de-sac at the bottom of the Armstrong hill, a broad strip of asphalt canyoned between the high-rises climbing to the east and a sloped Conrail retaining wall to the west, ending in a grubby pocket park that straddled the city line with neighboring Gannon. Hurley was more of a half-assed parking lot for the tenants than a bona fide street. The combination of murky desolation and a spongy borderline made it a good dope spot and, by extension, no place for a violent crime that would only draw police and shut down business.

Lorenzo entered the ambulance bay of the medical center with a wave to the guard, the grinning and glad-handing starting immediately. Everybody knew Lorenzo "Big Daddy" Council in this city, and vice versa. He pointed and laughed at the personnel behind the nurses station, greeting six people at once while scanning the room for Penny Zito, the triage nurse, and shaking hands with the goateed guard, a kid he had once arrested for possession with intent. He had secured this job for him when the kid came back out.

Given Lorenzo's effusive and tireless presence, his social ability to bat from either side of the plate, it was inevitable that there existed word, mostly pie-in-the-sky, 4:00 A.M. diner talk, that if his buddy Michael Hooks, director of the Urban Corps, made a successful run for mayor, Big Daddy Council could become the new police commissioner.

"Mister, Mister," Lorenzo said, beaming down at the guard, taking in the pierced nostril, the stumpy ponytail. "How you doin'?"

"Hey, you know, one day at a time, right?" The kid almost blushed with pleasure.

"I hear you," he responded, in an Amen singsong.

Penny Zito entered the hall from the waiting room, most likely returning from an outdoors cigarette break. Lorenzo sought her eyes over the guard's head, looking for a quick eyeball read on the carjack victim: Bullshit or for real.

Penny coughed loose and crackly into her fist, shrugging in response to Lorenzo's raised chin: Tough call. She was a good reader who could give him an accurate thumbs down for a whacked-out lush screaming bloody murder or cock her head toward the examination room, meaning, "You better get in there."

"How you been, Pen?" he called out loudly, already laughing in anticipation of whatever she would say—not that she was so funny but because that's the way Lorenzo was. "Number one Nana, huh?"

"I'm telling you . . ." She coughed in her fist again, the breakup sounding like radio static.

"Yeah, I hear you. Where's she at?"

"In twenty-three, with the most dangerous man on earth."

He laughed hard, staggering forward as if the wisecrack had whacked him in the small of his back. "Che Guevara, huh?"

"*What?*" the question came from right behind him, like a throwdown challenge. Lorenzo wheeled around.

"I said put out the *smoke*," the security guard snapped, up on tiptoe, going in the face of a black man with a shaved head, a cigarette hanging from the corner of his mouth.

The guy glared one-eyed through the ascending drift of his own smoke at the much shorter guard. "Get the fuck out my goddamn face."

He would have smacked the kid down if it hadn't been for the infant lying in his arms. "The fuck is *wrong* with you," he said, the squinted eye narrowing, his other one a reddening homicide beam.

Lorenzo thought the baby might be dead.

"Put out the smoke," the guard snapped again, reverting to jail head—inching up closer, his ear to his shoulder, doing the D-Town matador dance.

Lorenzo leaned in between them, crooning "Army, Army," carefully taking the cigarette from between the guy's lips while blocking out the guard with his body. Army reared back, ready to deal, baby or no, until he saw who it was.

"Lorenzo!" Army gestured with his chin to the baby girl in his arms, then to the guard. "Get this Swiss Navy nigger out my face before he ends up in one a these *beds* here."

The guard opened his mouth, but Lorenzo gave him a look: I got it covered. He put a hand to Army's shoulder and eased him around until he was facing the nurses station.

"She all right?" Lorenzo peered down at the infant swaddled in a yellow bath towel, her tiny heart-shaped face exuding an unnerving stillness, nothing akin to natural sleep.

"Naw, she ain't all right." Army twisted his mouth in derision. "What the hell you think I'm doin' here?" He turned his head to glare at the guard. "They gave her this MRI thing this morning? She ain't come out of medication all day. They gave her too much, or some damn thing."

A nurse came by and took the baby; they had been waiting for her. Army hunched over a clipboard and signed his name, straightening up as Lorenzo nodded to the guard.

"She was, I don't know, like, born with something wrong. Doctor says she had a stroke in the belly."

Lorenzo jerked his head. "The baby's belly?"

"Naw, the *mother*. You know, when she was carrying her? We brought her in. Doctor says to my wife, 'Were you doing drugs when you was pregnant?' My wife says, 'She's my *grand*daughter,' but, you know, yeah." He looked off, sighing. "My daughter, when she had this one? She just cut out, ain't seen her since, and you know, like yeah, she wasn't, taking care of herself, my daughter, so . . ." Army sucked air through the side of his mouth, shook his head, Lorenzo thinking, What goes around comes around, volume 99. "Now this one's mine too," Army muttered. "Like starting all over."

Lorenzo kept his mouth shut, thinking anything he said right now would be too much like rubbing it in, with Army Howard being, among other things, an on-again, off-again midlevel dealer since the seventies.

"Yeah, go on an' say it." Army lit another cigarette.

"I ain't said nothing, Army." Lorenzo smiled soberly, his eyes subdued and level.

"No, huh? Well, you can say it anyhow because you ain't wrong."

"C'mon, brother, put out the cigarette."

"Naw, I want Captain Crunch to put it out." Army glared at the guard across the floor. The kid ignored the taunt, having had time to think about things.

Lorenzo shrugged, stepping away. "I hope she's OK."

"Yeah, me too," Army said through his teeth, still staring down the guard. "Captain Crunch motherfucker . . ."

Heading down the corridor to Room 23, Lorenzo greeted another security guard, an X-ray technician clutching a dozen fresh transparencies for the surgery room, and a drunk brought in by cops after taking a beating at the bus terminal, his face a bounty of lumps. The drunk looked at Lorenzo and said almost sweetly, "It's OK, I'm all right. Thanks, thank you."

"Yo, Pops, you gonna stop gettin' oiled now?" Lorenzo was just saying it because you had to say something.

The drunk smiled sheepishly. "Most likely not."

"Young man." Chatterjee's elegant monotone rang out as the doctor floated toward Lorenzo now, his trim collegiate threads spattered and soiled, from his oxblood loafers to his blue broadcloth shirt and gold silk grenadier's tie. Lorenzo knew that this disarray was a nightly state of affairs for Chatterjee that usually came less than halfway through his shift no matter how long the hem or how high the buttons of his examination-room whites.

Chatterjee extended a petite hand, which disappeared into Lorenzo's oversized mitt.

"Papa Doc, what's up. She being admitted?"

Chatterjee shrugged. "Won't even let me take an X ray."

"She good to talk?"

"I think, I think she's not . . . she's lying about something, leaving something out. She got a little roughed up." The doctor thrust his hands straight out, palms facing the floor. "Got knocked down pretty hard. Broke her fall with, like this." He shot out the heels of his palms again, arched his fingers backwards. "Might have fractured . . ." He took Lorenzo's hand and ran his thumb and forefinger along the outside bones flanking the wrist. "She won't let me X-ray, so . . . and she picked up half the parking lot or wherever. I had to force her to take a tetanus shot. Also, she's got a nice little contusion up here." Chatterjee reached up and tapped Lorenzo's crown. "You can't fall forward on your hands and cut the top of your head, correct?"

"I hear you."

"So, I don't know. My feeling? I think she might have gotten raped, but she won't go upstairs." He shrugged. "Or maybe she knew the guy who attacked her, you know, like an outdoors domestic."

"Maybe she just don't want anybody knowing she was in a dope spot that time of night," Lorenzo said dryly, unconsciously voicing why he had taken his sweet time getting over here. "Could be just that."

Chatterjee took him by the elbow. "Talk to her," he said, gently launching him toward the examination room. "Youth wants to know."

Room 23 was smaller and more private than the general surgery room—three fixed gurneys ringed with plastic curtains, a view of the Hudson. Brenda Martin, sporting a shiny goose egg high on her forehead from her earlier fall in the ER, sat slumped and disheveled on the edge of one of the gurneys. Her legs dangled lifelessly, and a mahogany spray of Betadine solution ran in a comet tail from her jeans to her chin, as if she had struggled with whoever had tried to disinfect her wounds. Both her palms were fat with bandages, and one wrist sported a Curlex splint.

Lorenzo eased into the room, not wanting to step up until the two uniforms who were squatting below her, bouncing on their haunches, found a natural break-off point in their interview. Hands folded across his belt buckle, he lay back in the cut, like a soloist waiting for his cue, and attempted to size her up. Thin and colorless, she struck him as one of those people whose fervent desire to be unnoticed, to be invisible, makes them disappear before your eyes. Picking up only an honest aura of emotional distress, he would just have to see what else developed.

The only other patient in the room, a fat, unkempt white man, sat in a corner reading *Moby-Dick*. One bare, diabetically bloated foot was propped up on a chair in front of him, an IV drip ran into his left arm from a stand, and under his right arm, nesting on the chair beside him, three yellow semitransparent Foodtown bags bulged with clothing and paperbacks.

The two other gurneys were unoccupied, one piled high with a wild rumple of bedsheets, the other stripped to its rubberized surface.

"You say black," one of the cops said softly, shifting his weight. "Black, like, darker than me? Lighter than me?"

Brenda held a Diet Coke between her bandaged palms and brought it to her mouth with both hands, as if she were a bear trying to get honey out of a jar. "I told you, I don't want to say. It was, you know, night."

Her voice was small, her eyes stark yet avoiding direct contact. Lorenzo wondered if that was about deception or shame.

"OK, fair enough," the cop said. "And you say five-ten, six foot, about?"

"About."

"One eighty, two hundred pounds? You still feel that?"

"Guessing." She saw Lorenzo and quickly took him in, head to toe. Lorenzo tried to throw her a smile, but her eyes were moving too fast to catch it, now staring down at her bandages, then across the room to the slovenly diabetic.

"*Moby-Dick,*" she said hoarsely, looking again at her lap. "That's a good book."

The diabetic eyed her for a moment before returning to his reading; Lorenzo thinking, Miss Peekaboo.

"Anything else you can tell us?" the other cop said, shifting his weight in obvious discomfort.

Lorenzo assumed that they had both positioned themselves below her because they were black, like the carjacker, and wanted to adopt a nonthreatening posture to make her feel as relaxed as possible. But why the hell didn't they just pull up some chairs?

One cop tapped his partner on the shoulder and they both turned to him, then stood upright, somebody's kneecaps popping.

"Hey, boss," he addressed both of them, using his business smile. "Can I . . ." He left it hanging, nodded to Brenda.

"You gonna write the report?" one of the uniforms asked hopefully.

Lorenzo shrugged: No problem.

"Brenda?" the same cop spoke up. "This is Detective Lorenzo Council."

Lorenzo smiled at her again, took another half step forward.

Brenda's eyes went up as far as his chin, and then she did something that threw him: she extended one of her bandaged hands, saying, "Hi," almost inaudibly. Warily Lorenzo made physical contact. Her fingertips were like ice.

"How you doin', Brenda?"

The other cops began to back out of the room.

"Not good."

He pulled up a chair, thinking, Six-foot, two-hundred-pound black man knocks her around, here comes me—she should be jumping out the window. Shaking my hand . . .

"Brenda, anything I can get you?" He tried again to catch her eye. "Anything you need?"

She raised her soda can. "They got me this," she said, nodding to the doorway where the cops had exited.

"You comfortable?"

"No."

"OK, listen. I know you're upset, all right? And I know you're probably real tired right now." He waited for a reaction, but she just stared at her soda. "But the sooner we go through this the faster we can make something good happen, OK?"

She looked like she was about to cry, her face bunching up again, but all that came out was a vibrating sigh, Lorenzo thinking, Something else.

"Brenda? Would you like a female investigator here? Would that make you more comfortable?"

She compressed her lips, eyes on her hands. "I wasn't raped, if that's what you're driving at."

"Good." He studied her. "I'm glad to hear that. Now, the other officers? They already put out a description of the car and the actor; everybody's already looking for him, OK? But if you can bear with me, just tell the story one more time, so I can—"

"I was trying to get from Hurley Street to Gannon," she said, cutting him off. "I live in Gannon."

Lorenzo had guessed as much, Gannon being the mostly white blue-collar town bordering the so-called Darktown section of Dempsy. The city line ran right up against the Armstrong—or, as some preferred, Strongarm—Houses. One of the main jobs of the Gannon PD was to keep an eye on the high-rises, see if any Gannon junkies were scoring dope over there and attempting to hop the fence back into town. That and eyeing the Armstrong youngbloods, watching for four kids on two bikes riding into Gannon and returning a half hour later, four kids on four bikes. The Armstrong teenagers were scared of getting popped over there too, because the Gannon PD liked to make a lasting impression: "Keep our city clean."

"I was on Hurley Street, right? And I had heard that—where the street ends? That you could just keep going, you know, drive right through that park—what's that . . ."

"Martyrs Park?"

"Right, Martyrs."

Some park—a half acre of garbage, trees, and benches dedicated to the memory of Martin Luther King, Malcolm X, and Medgar Evers, the Gannon-Dempsy border running right through the middle. Gannon maintained a twenty-four-hour post, informally known as the Watch, a permanent patrol-car presence on their side of the line, directly across from Martyrs, in the parking lot of a bankrupt mini-mall.

"Martyrs Park," she went on. "See, I had heard . . . I had heard that you could drive right through and come out on Jessup in Gannon, right?"

"Yeah, you can," Lorenzo said, not writing yet, holding a notepad in one hand, a radio in the other. He took in her lank hair, her thin, sloped shoulders, that T-shirt and its public-service announcement.

He found himself growing somewhat cool to her. Armstrong was always taking shit, but half the customers were from Gannon. Keep our city clean . . .

"So I got halfway into the park and, like, where's the . . . There's no road. It's like a forest, just trees. So, I was starting to back *out* of the park? Go the regular way? And this guy appears in my headlights. It's like he just came out from behind a tree or something, and I couldn't, I didn't want to deal with him, but I couldn't see that well where I was going in reverse, right? And before I know it he comes up to the window, says to me, 'You trying to cut through? You off the path. Path's over there.' " She was using a black inflection, but lightly.

"And he's pointing to, like, between the trees, and I can't see where, and he says, 'Just through *there*,' and he's laughing, but not—I mean, he's friendly, like, trying to help out, and he says, 'Just . . .' and he opens my car door, says, 'Look where I'm pointing,' like I should get out of the car, stand up, and . . . I *knew* better, but I wasn't thinking or something. Next thing I know the guy, like, yanked me out, and I went . . ." She held up her hands, palms out. "He, like, shoved me down so hard I hit the ground like I fell off a *build*ing or something."

Lorenzo nodded, glancing at her knees to see if there were dirt stains consistent with the throw down she was describing. There were.

But she still wasn't making eye contact.

"And I, I got up and he was climbing into the car and I yelled, like, 'Hey!' and I went to—I grabbed his arm. He came out and this time he tossed me, I landed, like, 'Whoof.' I couldn't get my wind, but I tried. I got up, I *tried* to, but I couldn't get the *words* out." She was hyper now, Lorenzo just taking it in. "I mean, he was just flying out of there, and I . . . You don't know, I just . . ." Faltering, she shrugged, a small gesture of retreat. Lorenzo was only half listening. He was thinking about a Gannon woman's getting beat up in Armstrong, in Strongarm, in Darktown Park, hoping he wouldn't have to deal too much with any of their people—then drifting off even further, dividing their PD into the hotheads and the steady hands, the negotiators and the hard-asses.

Brenda raised her bandaged hands to her eyes. The sudden movement pulled him back into the room.

"You OK?"

She didn't answer.

"Brenda?"

"What."

"He took your car and reversed all the way out of the park?"

"Right."

"And then drove away on Hurley?"

"Right."

"You possibly see which way he was headed?" Lorenzo thinking, Toward Newark, where else, stolen-car capital of the free world. "Brenda? You see which way he turned off Hurley?"

Before she could answer, he cut her off. "Excuse me." Then, into the radio, "South Investigator 15 to base."

"Base. Go."

"Yeah, on that carjack in the South? Make sure Newark PD is notified. And please reach out to Bump Rosen, have him start a canvass for witnesses in Armstrong." Lorenzo hated to have to do that. He checked the time: ten-forty-five. *Law and Order* was still on, Bump's kid probably only halfway through the courtroom part of the show. He hoped that Bump would dally out the door, wait until his kid was sentenced, at least.

He turned down his radio. "I'm sorry," he said to Brenda.

"You don't know," she said, glaring at the far wall, her head jerking. "I tried. I tried to run after him. I tried to tell him."

"Tell him what?" Lorenzo hunched forward, elbows on knees.

She carefully placed the soda can next to her side, on the table. "I don't want my mother to know about this."

Lorenzo nodded, thinking, Buying dope.

"Brenda, I have to ask you this, but I want you to know that whatever your answer's gonna be, all *I* care about is getting the guy that hurt you, OK?"

"So what was I doing there, copping rock?" Her mouth went tight.

"I don't really care, but if that was the case, then that helps me know who to reach out to. You're not in no trouble. I just need to know who to hit on. You're the victim, plain and simple. Your mother, nobody needs to know nothing else, you understand?"

"I'm clean almost five years. I don't even think about it."

"Good, good." Lorenzo was not particularly convinced. "So—"

"And my brother's on the job."

"Oh yeah? Where at?"

"Gannon. He's a detective."

"Huh." Shit. "What's his—"

"Martin. Danny Martin."

"Oh yeah." He nodded as if pleased. "He's a good cop." The guy was decent enough but a hothead. A real mess shaping up. "Do you want me to call him?"

"Not really," she said in a desultory mutter, as if she shared his vision of things to come.

"OK, no problem." He said this easily, but he'd have to call the guy anyhow—professional courtesy. "So, Brenda, tonight—"

"What was I doing there if I wasn't buying drugs, right?"

"I got to ask."

"I work there."

"Where."

"In the houses. I work in the Study Club for the Urban Corps."

"The Study Club's in the Jefferson Houses, isn't it?"

"We just opened up a second club in the basement of Five Building."

Lorenzo hesitated, things coming a little fast now. "OK, yeah, yeah, I heard about that, OK, OK," he finally said, nodding. The Study Club was an afterschool program set up to keep preteens off the streets and, in some cases, out of their home situations as much as possible.

He read her T-shirt again—IT TAKES A WEAK MAN TO DISRESPECT THE STRONG WOMAN WHO RAISED HIM—thinking, Maybe she's the goods. Maybe. "Yeah, I had heard you were coming in there. OK. OK."

His tone of mild enthusiasm made her lean forward, her speech speeding up as if she had a fixed amount of time to win him over. "See, we just moved some of the stuff over from Jefferson yesterday, and I was home tonight? And I couldn't find my glasses, so I thought maybe they got packed by mistake, so I went over to Five Building, you know, to look through the boxes? But I didn't have the right key and I couldn't get in and then—So I was just trying to get back quick to Gannon, and—" She suddenly pulled up short. "I told you the rest."

She was working it too hard—no eyes, hiding her face, hiding. Boyfriend? Black boyfriend? Rape? Dope? What . . .

"OK." He rubbed his palms, marking time, the two of them sitting in silence, an expectant vibration in the room.

The diabetic sneezed, flipped a page, yawned.

"How you feel about coming down looking at some mug shots now?"

She gave him a small shrug, not answering, making no move to stand up or conclude, knitting her fingertips, waiting.

Lorenzo cocked his head, trying to raise her eyes from her lap. "Brenda?"

She grudgingly flicked him an agitated glance.

"Brenda." He leaned forward, twisting his head so that his face was in her sight line. "What are you not telling me . . ."

She shrugged again, trying to find somewhere else to look, a bandaged hand flying to her mouth.

"Brenda." Lorenzo's voice was soft. "I can't help . . ." He faltered, hit with a wave of dread, a distinct fear of finding something out that he'd rather not know. "I can't help but feel like something else is bothering you, you know what I'm saying?"

She nodded vigorously in confirmation, withdrawn but alive to the moment, as if waiting for a first kiss, the right question.

"I'm gonna ask you again. Do you want a female investigator in here?"

She shook her head no, still waiting, her chest visibly rising and falling with each breath.

A movement caught his eye: one of the seemingly empty beds erupted in a flurry of sheets. Someone had been lying under the rumple all this time and now was coming to life with a musical moan, making the diabetic sigh loudly and mutter, "Jesus Christ."

"Brenda. Did you know the guy?"

She slowly hit herself in the forehead with the Curlex splint. Then she did it again, clenching her teeth and keening. Lorenzo read the tune as fear and frustration.

He pressed in closer, stayed on her, almost touching.

"Who's the guy, Brenda."

She glared at the wall, her eyes iridescent with tears, the keening kicking up a notch.

He touched her knee. "Brenda, this is your lucky night. I *own* Armstrong. There isn't nobody I don't know. Who's the man, Brenda. Who did this."

"My son . . ." she said to the wall.

"What?" Lorenzo was thrown, reading her as around thirty years old. "Whoa." He put out a hand like a stop sign. "Hold on."

Brenda packed up, her body jerking involuntarily, once, twice, as if cold.

He moved to touch her again, get her back, then decided to keep his hands to himself.

"Your son what . . ."

She raised her forearm to mask her eyes, knocking the soda can to the floor. The hollow clatter made the diabetic cluck his tongue.

"Is in the car." The words came out of her in a tremulous hoot. Lorenzo sat up as she finally stared at him straight on, no more peekaboo, her eyes terror-blasted, as if she expected him to rise to his full height and beat her to death.

2

At ten past ten in the evening, the stains that dappled the cement steps of the D-Town tenement stoop were still vivid, uncongealed, and Jesse Haus's first thought was that her timing was off, that she had made the scene too early. On the other hand, although a Dempsy police cruiser was still parked next to her brother's Chrysler, the crowds were gone and the bright plastic crime-scene tape lay in a discarded tangle atop a balding shrub.

She had heard about this shooting over an hour ago, but if she had shown up as soon as the call had come over, the cops would have been too cranked to talk, too shut down; the neighbors would either be in the dark or, if they knew anything, talking to the cops themselves; and she would have had to play human bumper pool with the handful of other reporters who had probably overheard the same radio squawk she had. Besides, there was no rush. It was long after the six o'clock deadline so, short of a mass suicide or an assassination, everything was for tomorrow night's edition anyhow.

Back at the rally in the Armstrong Houses, she had barely heard one word of what Lorenzo Council or that Muslim cleric had said, having just dropped in to kill time as she waited out the initial hubbub on this double shooting, like someone ducking into a shop to wait out a sudden shower.

In fact, all she could recall of that exercise in civil futility was the cleric calling the killer "a thing, a punkified thing," a tag that reminded Jesse of her roommate. She had just found out that the woman, a lawyer or a broker, had been charging her seventy-five percent of the total rent. Jesse was forking over nine hundred dollars a month for a don't-tell-management bedroom created by bisecting the living room with an unpainted sheet of Masonite.

Since she had moved in eight months ago, responding to an ad in her own newspaper, Jesse had always paid her portion of the rent to her roommate, the tenant of record, and had never actually seen the monthly invoice from the building. But earlier today, she had come on it by chance while making her midday breakfast in the kitchenette, the mingled aromas of Jean's or Jane's collection of International Blend instant coffees making her queasy as she stared at the tab: twelve hundred dollars, not eighteen hundred like she had always assumed. Seventy-five percent, and that slick bitch had the real bedroom too.

But even at six hundred a month the place was a dump, a hastily built waterfront apartment house featuring starter pads for young professionals, the hallways reeking of canned air and the construction so tentative that her roommate's never-used mountain bike, which hung suspended from ceiling hooks in what remained of the original living room, swayed every time the PATH train rumbled underneath the ground-floor health club. The interior walls of the building were so porous that, when Jesse had gone next door to complain about the *Greatest Hits of the Eagles* one day, she had discovered that, in fact, the music was emanating from the *next* apartment down the hall. Her own Masonite wall was, of course, no better: she awoke every morning to the sound of wet, smacky chewing from the kitchenette, her roommate a nine-to-fiver.

The only aspect of her current living arrangement that she enjoyed was the view from her bedroom, the broad expanse of the Hudson River and, at the far shore, the West Side skyline of Manhattan, a vista she found both potent and serene, so much so that she had pushpinned a tourist poster of basically the same sight alongside her view of the real thing. That odd, redundant wall hanging was the only effort she had made in the last eight months to decorate, personalize, or somehow soften the ten- by fifteen-feet makeshift cell that she called, for now, home.

Jesse had left the community center in a fog of agitation, but she was not so distracted that she didn't register the look of mild dismay Lorenzo Council had thrown her way as she began crouch walking up the aisle. And not so distracted that she didn't hear the momentary fumble in his delivery as she headed out the door.

He was a good guy, fighting the good fight, as her father would say, but vain and touchy about his reputation and popularity in the community.

Thinking about Lorenzo as she finally began climbing the steep, narrow tenement stairs to the third-floor crime scene, she found herself once again wishing that she had never written that profile of him for the paper a few months ago. There still seemed to be some requirement for appreciation around him that made her feel more like a publicist than a reporter. The high, funky, crumble-textured hallways of the tenement had last been painted a glossy maroon and mustard, and the claustrophobic colors, combined with the dense waft of cauliflower and fried meat, made the hike to her floor an oppressive experience.

A young cop stood spread-legged before the open apartment door. As she rose to the landing, Jesse could see behind him, triangularly framed by his ankles and legs, an overturned dinette chair and a large spatter of creamed corn on a rug.

"Hey, how you doing?" She made herself sound exhausted.

"I'm sorry, you can't go in." The cop sounded polite, bored.

"But I was sent here," she said vaguely, huffing now, going for the Oscar.

"I'm sorry." He crossed his arms like a genie.

Then Jesse saw the other cop, inside the apartment.

"Willy!" she called out, the uniform at the door now null and void.

"Hey, Jess, what's up?"

Willy Hernandez came out smiling, having grown up with Jesse in Dempsy's Powell Houses—her family had been one of the last white families, the Hernandez clan among the first of the Puerto Ricans.

"What happened here?" Jesse asked, sounding personally dismayed.

Hernandez shrugged. "Guy comes in, pop, pop, the old lady, the kid, then into the night."

"They're gonna make it?"

"I think so." Hernandez shrugged again. "I hope so."

"Where'd they go, the OMC?"

"Saint John the Divine."

"Who's catching?"

"Cippolino and Fox."

Jesse nodded, knowing Cippolino, knowing that whatever she

couldn't get here in the moment she'd get from the detective later on over the phone.

"You know the actor?"

"We're looking."

"Who is he?"

"So how's your folks doing?" he said, stonewalling her. "They still in the projects?"

The Hernandez family was long gone from Powell, the Haus family, her parents, still hanging in. Jesse was desperate to get them out, but her father saw their moving as an act of racist capitulation. Sometimes Jesse wished that someone would just come along and do them in, get it over with.

"Comrade Haus!" Hernandez announced, saluting her father by his nickname. "Your pops was *down*."

"Yup," Jesse said quickly. "Can I come in?"

"I can't, Jess. You know that."

"Willy, I'm batting zero all day. C'mon, do it for the comrade." She forced herself to smile, as if the memory of the few friends she had had in Powell—a clique of Dominican girls in junior high, a Jamaican boyfriend in high school, an odd mixed crowd of Filipinos and Guyanese for a few months after that, all lectured on racism by her white Commie father anytime they were foolish enough to come into the apartment— was a fond and rosy recollection. The dumb kids had felt bored, the bright ones bored and patronized. Her father never understood, or refused to accept, that most immigrants—white, black, brown—came over for the same reason they had always come over, not to embrace the struggle but to embrace the brochure, to have a good life. That meant, first and foremost, to get cash money paid. But you could never tell that to the last man on earth to call Russia "the workers paradise."

"C'mon, Willy, I'm not going to touch anything."

Hernandez sucked his teeth, about to relent, when a photographer from another in-county paper, an overweight wheezer trudging up the stairs, joined them at the door. "Can I get some pictures, boss?"

"No, no." Hernandez waved him off, then looked at Jesse with regret. This guy had tipped the scales; no one was coming inside now.

Loitering in the shadows of the third-floor hallway until she was sure the fat bastard had left the building, Jesse walked down one flight and hit the apartment directly below the crime scene.

Responding to Jesse's crisp raps, a fiftyish black woman wearing a quilted housecoat and a short coppery wig came to the door, the humid aroma of stewed meat escaping out into the hall from behind her. Taking one look at Jesse through eyeglasses the diameter of drink coasters, the woman said, "No, I don't talk," and attempted to close the door. Before she could retreat, Jesse blurted, "But they said I should talk to you," and gestured to the floor above, to the cops.

"No." The woman shook her head, her hands entwined in a dish towel. "I don't do that."

Jesse played through. "Did you know the child?"

"No, I don't know nothing."

"Your kids didn't play with him?"

"My kids?" The woman smiled, touched her fingers to her chest. "My kids is *grown*. That's a child."

"How old?"

"I don't know." She started to close the door again.

"How do you have grown kids?" Jesse slid her foot a few inches over the threshold. "You look too young."

"No, they grown now."

"That lady up there was a friend?"

"No, she was old."

"So the child was a grandchild?"

"I don't know. I keep to my own business."

"You see anything?"

"No. I don't do that."

"No?"

"I just heard . . ."

"What you hear?"

The phone rang from inside the apartment.

"Excuse me." She attempted to close her door yet again, but Jesse's foot was over the line. The woman gave her a long, pointed look, and Jesse had to withdraw.

"I'll wait for you here," Jesse announced, pretty much knowing that the woman wouldn't come back. She gave her two minutes before knocking again, then knocked louder, then finally tramped down the stairs. When she reached the front door of the tenement, Jesse spotted her brother outside, sitting in his car, sipping coffee, and rereading the paper. On seeing her, Ben quickly opened his door, ready to help, but Jesse waved him off.

No one really seemed to care about this stuff these days, but as red-diaper kids growing up in Dempsy during the early sixties Jesse and Ben had been known as the Khrushchev kids, treated by most of their peers as two walking KICK ME signs adorned with hammers and sickles and, for those who wanted to see them, the faint outline of skullcaps hovering over their heads like halos, like cherries on top.

Jesse, four years Ben's senior, was his self-appointed protector for the first decade of his life, once half carrying, half dragging him in her arms five blocks to the hospital after some little patriot hurled a can of string beans at him, opening up his right eyebrow like a zippered purse. With adolescence, they had reversed roles, the newly six-foot-six Ben declaring himself his sister's shield. This oath of fealty held right into adulthood, where Ben's flexible and vaguely shady schedule allowed him to chauffeur his sister night or day, through the beat-down streets of her job. Jesse, reluctant to cut free from the bond of their wretched childhood, expressed that conflict by way of a graceless and surly demeanor toward him. Nonetheless, she always seemed to take him up on the escort service, whether it was needed or not.

At Jesse's feet now, a portly young black man sat on the bloody stoop gazing out at the quiet street and smoking a blunt.

"You know what happened up there?" Jesse asked mildly.

He leaned back, half turning to see her. "Nope."

"Two people were shot."

"Yeah, well, I knew that."

"You know them?"

"Naw, well, yeah." He offered her the fat joint but she waved it off.

Her brother was only pretending to read, flicking glances at her through the windshield, pissing her off.

"That ol' lady and the child . . ." The man on the stoop shook his head. "Fuckin' asshole."

"Who."

"The, you know."

"The shooter?"

He responded to the question with a languid cluck of the tongue, the sound conveying both reproach and disgust. "I *knew* that was gonna happen."

"What's his name." Jesse took the joint, took a tiny hit, exhaled before it could work on her.

"Damn. I come by, that old lady, she be out here, sit right here on this step, blood all over her ches', just sittin' here. I come over, she say, 'Get the baby, the baby's shot too, get the baby.' Then she like falls over, so I go upstairs." He made that clucking noise again. "Baby's all laying there on the floor, *blood* all over."

"Crying?"

"Hell, yeah. So I go call, the amalance come, cops come."

"Who did it?"

"The boyfriend, who you think?"

"Of . . ."

"The, you know, Chantal."

"Chantal . . ."

"The mother."

"The baby's mother?"

"Man, she wasn't even home, so he goes and . . ." He clucked and waved again.

"Goes and shoots the grandma and the baby?"

This time he made a noise like escaping steam.

"What's his name?" Jesse was writing all this down using her thigh as a desk, writing without looking. "What's his name?"

He hesitated, took a long toke, slowly twisted around again. "How you know it wasn't me?"

"Was it you?" Jesse wished it was. That would be fucking aces. She flicked a return glance at her brother. "Was it you?"

He turned around to face the street again.

"Tiger."

"It was Tiger?"

He didn't answer.

"Tiger what."

"Just Tiger."

"They know that?"

"They lookin' for him now."

"The cops?"

"Hell, yeah."

"Tiger, Chantal's boyfriend?"

"Was."

"Tiger the baby's father?" Jesse was getting impatient.

"Could be."

"Tiger the old lady's son?"

"Alls I know is Tiger."

"Where's Chantal right now?"

"I don't know."

"She at work?"

He didn't answer.

"How come Tiger did it?"

"She kicked him to the curb."

"Chantal did?"

"Yup."

"The cops know this?"

"The ones talked to me does. But you could ask anybody on this street. Tiger's a asshole. I just hope Miss Delano pull through. The baby too."

"Where's Tiger live?"

"Used to live upstairs. *Damn,* I can't believe that shit. I jus' come back from giving my father a driving lesson with the car, Miss Delano sittin' out here, bleedin', *God* knows how long she sittin' there, *rockin'.*"

"You just come back from giving your father a driving lesson?" Jesse was slowed down by that, touched, thinking maybe she liked people after all.

Trudging back up the stairs, Jesse found the door of the crime scene closed. She had to ring the bell for close to a minute before the cop she didn't know would open up.

"Hey there." She smiled, her fatigue now only half faked.

"You can't come in. I told you that."

"Who's Tiger?" She asked like he owed it to her.

"What?"

"I hear Tiger did it."

"A tiger did it?" Fucking with her. "Hey, I'm just safeguarding the scene."

"You didn't hear anybody talk about Tiger?"

The cop just looked at her.

Heading down the stairs again, Jesse ran into Cippolino, the catching detective. He had once held a damp paper towel to her forehead after she'd thrown back a few shots too many at a Saint Patrick's Day open house. It was at some bar two, possibly three years earlier. Tommy Cippolino, as of this moment her oldest friend in the world.

"**Jose.**" Jesse sat in the shotgun seat of the Chrysler, cell phone to her jaw, and glared at her own scrawl. Ben was halfway down the street, making a few business calls of his own.

"Yo."

"I got two shot."

"OK."

"Infant."

"OK . . . Where."

"In the chest."

"No, *where.*"

"D-Town, 440 Firpo."

"OK."

"And I got a grandmother."

"OK."

"D-E-A. No, D-E-L-A-N-O. Esther."

"OK."

"Baby's Damien, Foy. F-O-Y."

"Damien?"

"Yeah, like *The Omen.*"

"OK. Age?"

"I'll get that. Shooter's maybe the father."

"There you go."

"But it looks like they're gonna both pull through."

"Huh. OK."

"The grandmother comes out, shot."

"OK."

"Just sat on the stoop, like in shock, I guess."

"OK."

"Neighbor comes by . . ."

"OK."

"Aaron P-A-R-M-A-L-E-E."

"OK." Jose's responses were soothing and rhythmic as he simultaneously took down her words and edited them on the fly, the two of them getting into a familiar call-and-response rhythm that they had cultivated over the years.

"Parmalee comes by. Lady says, quote, 'The baby's upstairs, get the baby,' end quote." Jesse thinking, More or less.

"OK."

"Goes upstairs, sees the baby on the floor, bleeding."

"OK."

"Parmalee calls the *ama*lance," Jesse said, putting the guy's spin on it.

"OK."

"Aaron says to me, quote, 'I knew that was gonna happen,' end quote."

"Good."

"Says the actor's a guy named Tiger."

"Last name?"

"Yeah, right. Parmalee says Tiger done got kicked to the curb by the baby's mother, Chantal. I don't have a last name yet."

"OK."

"Police say, 'Tiger? Who's Tiger?'"

"OK."

"But she kicked him out."

"Neighbors say?"

"Neighbors say."

"OK."

"Neighbors say . . . they had been known to quarrel."

"OK. Police won't confirm?"

"Not . . . I have an ongoing dialogue with the detective here, but no, not yet."

"So the kid's gonna make it?"

"Well, he was crying, right? So I guess so."

"Grandma too?"

"Don't know yet. So what else is going on?"

"Forty-four Forest in Gannon, a shooting. Sounds like one friend shooting the other."

"Gators?"

"Don't know, it's pretty fresh. Hang on . . . Here we go. Fifteen-year-old male, thirteen-year-old male."

"Who shot who?"

"Don't know."

"What, playing with the father's gun, showing off?"

"Wait up, here we go. Fifteen shooting thirteen and . . . It's a graze wound. Fuck it."

"Maybe it's a brother act."

"They're under sixteen. We couldn't use the names anyhow."

"What else . . ."

That was Jesse's theme song. Jesse was the type of journalist known as a runner, a stick-and-move artist covering the six incorporated cities and towns of Dempsy County, living off the police scanner, hitting the scene, getting the names, a few quotes, a little local color, dumping all of it into a cell phone to Jose or someone in rewrite, and then asking what else was going down out there—perpetually asking what else.

She could have as many as two or three bylines a day, but the price she paid was that the pieces would rarely read deeper than a snapshot.

"What else, Jose."

"We got a possible carjack in Strongarm."

"I was just there."

"Female being treated at DMC."

"Black or white?"

"Don't know. Fuck it, never mind."

"What else?"

"What else." Jose paused for dramatic effect. "Someone hit the Dutchman."

"There you go."

Impatient to roll, Jesse hit the car horn. Halfway down the block, Ben, still on the phone, gestured for five more minutes and she had no choice but to hang in, respecting the fact that, although her brother's money gigs could come in at any hour and at a moment's notice, they also tended to run in a pattern of feast or famine.

Having grown up as two moving targets, brother and sister had both developed an unconscious lifelong commitment to staying light on their feet. Jesse converted journalism into a track-and-field event, and Ben became what he called a "freelance expediter," a top-of-the-line odd-job man, intelligent and temperamentally stable enough to do anything, night or day, in light or in shadow.

As she restlessly watched her brother pacing under a streetlight, Jesse had no clue as to whom he was speaking with, the nature of the work involved, or the amount of compensation. She was reasonably sure that he would be paid either in cash or in goods, since Ben had no charge cards, no bank account, and most likely no Social Security number.

The Dutchman was fifteen feet tall and bronze, standing there in front of City Hall since 1904, clutching his deed and musket, goateed, pot-bellied, and stern. His seventeenth-century big-buttoned tunic and breeches made him look vaguely like Oliver Hardy in *Babes in Toyland*.

His name was Jan De Groot, and he was the first settler of record in what was to become Dempsy County. For the last ninety-odd years, De Groot's gaze had been directed straight down Division Street. But tonight he seemed to be scoping out the midblock 7-Eleven. The Coptic

Egyptians who worked there were standing in the doorway staring right back.

The Buick that had knocked the Dutchman off-kilter was still on the scene, its grille crumpled against his big bronze ass. The driver, a gaunt middle-aged man sporting a thin pompadour and glasses, leaned against his passenger door, arms folded across his chest, looking both miserable and utterly alone.

On the ride over, Jose had called back to tell Jesse that the car was supposed to have been driven by someone high up in City Hall, someone drunk, and that the statue had been knocked over, but she could tell from twenty feet away that this guy was stone sober. He projected more the harried and downtrodden air of a ticket taker at a multiplex than that of any kind of political player. Apparently the police had already come and gone and the poor bastard was just waiting on a Triple-A tow truck. This was a total bullshit run and Jesse was pissed.

"What happened?" She slammed the door of the Chrysler, making her brother flinch and approached the scene of the crime with that look and tone of personal dismay that she always used for openers.

The guy's first reaction was to move toward her, as if Jesse were here to rescue him, but then he saw the notepad and wound up simply sinking back into himself, seeming, if possible, twice as dejected as before.

"What the hell did you do to the Dutchman?" Jesse squawked, keeping it light.

"Aw, now see, you're putting me on the spot," he said, shaking his head, talking to his shoes.

"What do you mean?" Jesse eyed the pedestal, the statue having pivoted maybe six inches to the left—big fucking deal.

"You wouldn't want me to put *you* on the spot, would you?" He sounded nervous, in unfamiliar terrain.

"Somebody said they saw beer cans rolling around in there." She nodded to the car.

"How can they see the floor of my car? I'm *driving*."

"That's what they said."

Rising from the Chrysler, Ben lumbered toward the scene. The driver eyed him apprehensively, giving Jesse the impression that if her brother announced he was here to take him off to jail the guy would go without protest.

"You weren't a little bozoed?"

"The accelerator got stuck." He stepped away from the car. "Look for yourself. I don't even drink coffee, I swear."

Jesse took him up on it, opening the rear door, seeing nothing in there but some unused envelopes with a Board of Education return address. Bullshit. Jesse wanted to go, move on.

When she straightened up, she saw her brother squatting in front of the Dutchman surveying the damage, as if he were about to pull a Hercules here and realign the statue with his bare hands.

"So what's your name?" she asked.

"I can't really say." The driver hugged himself again.

"You don't know your name?" Jesse said, experiencing a wave of fatigue.

"See, there you go, putting me on the spot again."

"C'mon, I'll make you famous."

"I don't want to be famous."

"Everybody wants to be famous."

"No."

"The girls'll go crazy."

"No. I'm too old."

"Nobody's too old. What's your name?"

"No."

"You work for the Board of Education?"

Emitting a loud, fluttery sigh, he got back into his car, locked the door, reached for the air conditioner, realized the engine was off, turned the ignition. The car refused to kick over, so he just sat there sweating, staring straight ahead.

Hoisting up the knees of his pants, Ben actually tried to slide the statue back to its original position. Jesse watched him, marveling at his every-ready willingness to pitch in, wherever he went.

"What are you doing," she snapped. "Are you brain-damaged?"

Exasperated, Jesse walked back to the Chrysler, to the cell phone. Her brother, unable to move the Dutchman, was now trying to pop this poor mope's hood, pinpoint the problem. Momentarily comforted by the plush and musk of big-car leather, Jesse closed her eyes and brailled her way over the phone to the paper.

"Yo."

"Jose." His name was as natural in her mouth as a cough.

"Yo."

"It's bullshit."

"Yeah?"

"It was an accident."

"Drunk?"

"No."

"Who's the guy?"

"Won't give his name. Nobody."

"I want a picture. Wait for the photographer."

"Aw, c'mon, what are you gonna do, shoot the statue's left foot?"

"It's the Dutchman."

"He's still standing. What else you got."

"Still got that Strongarm carjack."

"What else."

"Hold on . . . 125 Division Street. Over in Tunnely. Got a body."

The body was a stinking, gas-filled balloon yielding neither sex nor race, the skin marbled, stretched taut, the color of smoke. There was no trouble getting past the door on this one, since the two uniforms charged with preserving the scene were almost grateful for company and Jesse had known one of them from back in the day.

The cops, Jerry Bohannon and Tony, she thought, Siragusa, had lit some incense they had found on a desktop next to the burned spoon—maybe a dozen sticks jammed into the door frame and around the bed—but it was a basement apartment, the sole window halfway below street level, and the scented smoke only added a sweetish element to the overall stench.

"Live by the spike, die by the spike," announced Jerry Bohannon, a milk-white Irishman with a pale, almost transparent moustache. He was gesturing to the needle still stuck in the left forearm.

"No ID?" Jesse asked, exhaling through her mouth to avoid the smell. "Jesus."

"The old lady upstairs, I guess she owns the house. She's not home, but the shoes tell me it's a him."

"As does the 'stache," Siragusa added, holding his nose as he leaned over the body. "Hair's kind of straight, so I'd say white, Hispanic."

"I don't want to start going through his shit," Bohannon said. "Wait for Crime Scenes."

Jesse looked around the bedroom, fairly neat for an overdose: some old pop-culture stuff lying around, airplane models, World's Fair buttons, a Howdy Doody doll hanging from a noose, some *Mad* magazines from the sixties, the body something of a nostalgia buff. She wandered into the bathroom: a mildewed shower curtain, a stack of fuck books on one side of the toilet and a kitty litter tray, soiled, on the other. Quickly, quietly, she opened the medicine chest, trying to find a name on a prescription bottle. A vial of Fiorinal gave up Michael Jackson, Jesse thinking, Good one.

There was another room, an eat-in kitchenette with nicer shelves and surfaces than those in her own. She grunted distractedly, wheels turning. One of the perks for a runner was occasionally getting to know, before anyone else, that an apartment was about to go on the market.

"You see a cat around here?" Jesse asked, reentering the bedroom. The cops were sharing a cigar now, to further mask the smell, Bohannon using his cupped palm as an ashtray.

"A cat?" Siragusa said.

"What do you think he pays here?" Jesse asked.

"Rent?" Bohannon made a face. "Three, four hundred?"

"I'd say four, five," Siragusa said.

"Yeah, huh?" Jesse looked around again. She'd miss the view of the river, but she could be alone.

"Jess." Bohannon offered her the cigar, which she declined. "If you're thinking about making a move on this, you should go for it, like, *now,* right now, 'cause I'll bet with this smell in here? They'll let it go for a song."

"I ain't afraid a no ghosts," Siragusa said, vamping Ray Parker.

"It's the live ones that's the problem." Bohannon puffed away.

"I need a name," Jesse said to him. "Can I look in the drawers and stuff?"

"I kind of wish you wouldn't. They're bitching about sloppy preservation."

"Whatever." Jesse shrugged.

Siragusa poked the Howdy Doody doll, making it sway in its noose. "What do you think this goes for? It's kind of like a rarity, isn't it?"

"Michael Jackson!" Jesse almost shouted, making both cops jump. Suddenly the name had rung a bell beyond the obvious. "I *know* this . . . Aw, Jesus." She flapped her arms. "I *know* him, I went to school with . . . Aw, Jesus. You know who this is?" she asked Bohannon, who, like Willy Hernandez, she had grown up with, gone to high school with. "You remember Mrs. Jackson? The English teacher? Remember she had a son? Michael Jackson?"

"Wait." Bohannon's face was working.

"You got to remember. He was in special ed. Everybody used to make fun of him because of his name."

Bohannon looked at her blankly.

"C'mon. Jerry—Michael Jackson, Mrs. Jackson."

"I remember *Mrs.* Jackson," he said cautiously.

"Don't you remember that time she had that big fight with Marko-witz in the hallway, screaming about how the school was treating her son, saying he didn't belong in special ed, the kids were torturing him, she was gonna quit teaching there, sue the city, sue Markowitz . . ."

Jesse saw the memory hit Jerry Bohannon, pushing him back two steps like a buffet of wind.

"Fuck!" he hissed. "This is . . . She still around, Mrs. Jackson?" He grimaced as if hoping she was dead.

"I think she's retired," Jesse said, feeling the same way and hoping that if she *was* still around, Bohannon here wouldn't be making the noti-fications. The notion of one of Mrs. Jackson's former mediocre students coming to tell her that her son was dead was intolerable.

"Aw, man," Bohannon said heavily, then looked at his partner for a long moment. Siragusa, having grown up in Gannon, not Dempsy, wasn't in on the Jackson family's tribulations. He returned Bohannon's pointed look with what to Jesse seemed like an artificial blankness. But Bohannon wasn't having it, continuing to stare down his partner until Siragusa nodded, a gesture of surrender. Jesse felt like she was witness-ing a telepathic conversation.

Bohannon took a handkerchief from his rear pocket and used it to carefully pull out one of the desk drawers. Then both he and Siragusa emptied their front pockets into the open drawer, tossing back two rub-berband-bound stacks of furry-edged baseball cards, a nickel-plated Zippo lighter, a fat swirl-textured fountain pen, and a Swiss Army knife.

A great crash from the dining room had both cops spinning around, Bohannon with his gun out front, Siragusa sliding to the wall, his Glock held down along his leg, Jesse praying, Make my night here.

The cat walked in, took a look, and ran out again. All three of them exhaled. Siragusa inched forward to check the dining room, his gun still drawn, Bohannon mumbling, "Just shut the goddamn drawer."

Jesse's cell phone rang. It was Jose. "Jess, you remember that carjacking?" His voice carried a certain restrained edginess that she hadn't heard in weeks—a good sign.

"Carjack?" Then, going bandido on him, "I don't need no stinking carjack."

"Hey," Jose said sharply. "Don't fuck with me on this."

Jose losing his cool; a *great* sign.

3

Lorenzo found himself out in the corridor, without any memory of leaving the examination room. "My son," Brenda Martin had said to him, "is in the car."

Maybe he hadn't heard right. Closing his eyes, fending off the hall's astringent reek of alcohol, the cologne of panic, he saw her face again, those stark, expectant eyes, and began to dread his next question: How old . . .

When he finally walked back inside Room 23, Brenda was as he had left her, perched on the edge of the gurney, trembling like a fountain. He approached the diabetic, needing to get him out of there, but before he could open his mouth, the unseen presence in the mound of sheets cut loose with another moan. Lorenzo wound up simply raising the flinching woman by the elbows and escorting her across the hall to the doctors' locker room—swiftly and quietly, as if he were already trying to keep this Red-Ball under wraps.

Placing Brenda in a folding chair at a snack-strewn card table, he closed the door and pulled up another chair, across from her, for himself. She sat with both hands covering her face, her knees fanning back and forth like bat wings. Lorenzo took a moment to breathe deep, trying to expel the clamor that had shot through his chest like an arrow over the last few minutes.

"Brenda." He swept a half-full bag of Doritos off the table and onto the floor, clearing a space for his radio. "Boy, right?" He flipped his note-book open, the pen quivering in his fingers like a polygraph needle. "How old . . ."

"Four," she said, from behind her bandaged palms.

Lorenzo dug his fingers into his eyes, pushing his glasses up to his forehead. Then, without ceremony but not quite roughly, he reached out and brought her hands down from her face to her lap.

"Four. How old . . ."

"I just *said.*"

"Slow down, slow down," Lorenzo told himself out loud. "What's his name . . ."

"Cody."

"Was he in a car seat?" Lorenzo felt his chest getting tighter.

"No."

"Seat belt?"

"No."

"Front or back."

"Of . . ."

"The *car,*" he said, snapping, passionately telling himself he didn't want this, didn't ask for this.

"The back."

"Hang on." He reached for the radio. "South Investigator 15 to base. Stand by for emergency transmission."

"Base. Go."

"Advise all units that, that carjack in the South District? That, there is a *child* in the car, four-year-old Caucasian . . ." He stopped a second, looking to her for verification. "Caucasian male in the backseat."

"He was asleep," she said, hunching forward, bringing her hands down on her legs. "He was sick. I tried to *say* something—"

Lorenzo stopped her with a raised palm. "Child is, or was, asleep in the backseat, might not be visible to pursuing officers." Lorenzo worried about cowboys going for some kind of run-and-gun apprehension on the car—shots fired or a broadside ramming, the kid caroming around the interior like a bullet in a steel drum. "Stand by for further description."

"I couldn't get the *words* out." Brenda was still in that jack-knife crouch, begging, Lorenzo chanting to himself, Why me, why me, why me.

"Brenda, what was he wearing." He watched as she shoveled her face into her hands again.

"Brenda! Your *son.* What was he *wear*ing . . ."

"He had a blue shirt on."

"Dark, light . . ."

"Light. A T-shirt. It said, 'GANNON NARCOTICS, MIDNIGHT MADNESS.'"

Lorenzo shut his eyes, thinking, Shit, the woman's brother. His notes flew across the page in a jittery scrawl.

"Hair?"

"Black, like, short in front and long in black, *back*—like some wrestler he watches on TV. I don't know who."

"Pants? Jeans?"

"Jeans."

"Blue? Black?"

"No. No. Pajama bottoms. He was sick. With Ren and Stimpy on them."

Lorenzo struggled over that last bit, not knowing who Ren and Stimpy were.

"Shoes?"

"Slippers, big slippers with dinosaur heads. They had batteries in the heels so that they growl when you take a step." Brenda was suddenly animated.

Lorenzo scribbled away, mumbling, "Hang on, hang on," hitting the radio again, repeating the details, adding, "And please notify Port Authority PD in case he makes a run for the tunnels." Taking a breath, his lungs even tighter now, his asthma coming on, he tried to be on her side, this lady staring at him all of a sudden with those white-wolf eyes, like she couldn't get enough of his face; this lady putting off the child part of things for God knows how long.

"Brenda." He leaned forward, contemplating his own outspread hands. "Your boy's asleep, right?"

"He's asleep." She nodded, repeating his words avidly.

"OK, now." Lorenzo massaged his chest, trying to get at his miserly lungs. "OK, this knucklehead? All he wants, is your *car*. He just wants to sell that car, OK? If he meant to hurt somebody, he'd of hurt *you*, all right?"

"He *did* hurt me." Her voice was fruity with conviction as she held up her hands.

Shit. Lorenzo arched his back. "OK, but I'm telling you. He's gonna see that kid? He's gonna pull up to a street corner and put him on the sidewalk. He don't want *no* part of that kid, all right?"

She curled back from him a little, crossed her arms over her chest, fending something off, making him angry again.

"Now I'm gonna ask you one more time. What were you doing there."

"I told you."

"You told me *what*. Tell me again." Lorenzo patted himself down, looking for his inhaler.

"I went to get my glasses."

"So you took your sick son out at nine o'clock in the evening—"

"I don't have a baby-sitter!" she said, almost shouting. "I can't afford one! What are you trying to do, punish me? Believe me, you don't have to." Her voice was raw, Lorenzo fucking up big time now.

"Base to South Investigator 15," the radio goosed him.

"SI 15," he responded in a subdued tone.

"Can you get us a better description of the actor? We're light on details here."

"Stand by." Lorenzo felt chastened, the dispatcher having to tell him how to do his job now; giving this lady the third degree like that . . .

"Brenda." He sounded contrite. "Let's do the bad guy again."

She exhaled heavily, her shoulders dropping with a "Huh."

"He didn't show you any weapon?"

"He didn't need to."

"Black—"

"Black, bald, about five-ten, two hundred pounds." She rattled off the specs in an exasperated litany as Lorenzo scrawled.

"Face hair?"

"I don't know."

"No moustache?"

"Maybe, I don't know."

"Jewelry? Scars?"

"I don't know."

"What was he wearing. Shirt, sweater—"

"Sweatshirt."

"What color . . ."

"Gray?"

"Any words on it?"

"No. Maybe. Wait. Michigan. Michigan? Michigan."

"Just Michigan? Not Michigan State? Not, not Michigan University, University of Michigan, no teams, no mascots?"

"I don't know. Just Michigan."

"Hang on." Lorenzo sent it out on the radio as Dr. Chatterjee walked in. Lorenzo saw, heard, through the half-open door, a cluster of cops—word going through the city already.

Chatterjee headed for his locker, eyeing Brenda hard. Lorenzo snapped his fingers to get the doctor's attention, then mimed an asthma attack—acted out labored breathing, the winking mouth of a landed fish—as he fed details to the dispatcher.

Brenda abruptly wheeled in her seat to face the doctor. "What if my son wakes up?"

"Talk to him," Chatterjee said sullenly, jerking his head toward Lorenzo. Seized by this terrible question, she wheeled back. "What if my son wakes up?" she asked, barrelling over Lorenzo's feed to base.

"Stand by." He leaned toward her. "Then that's all the sooner he's gonna get, you know, let out the car."

"He's gonna be so scared," she said, her voice taking wing. "I'm never not there for him. Never." Something was sinking in, Lorenzo feeling her move into a colder, more frightened place. He made himself slow down for her again.

"Brenda, this is hard, I know, but I'm telling you, we'll get him back. This is like a fluke. Nobody wants a kidnap tag. Nobody." He even smiled for her, as Chatterjee nodded to him on his way out, Lorenzo knowing that the doc would fix him up good, his asthma already lifting with the anticipation.

"Now stay with me, OK? This is important. Did anybody see you. Was anybody around when this happened . . ."

"I'm never not there for him. When he wakes up, he'll know." Her voice was calm, certain, almost prophetic, Lorenzo getting the sense that she was preparing herself for a long, perhaps lifelong, bout of self-laceration, and that her value to him as a source of hard information was coming quickly to an end.

"Brenda," he said, going for every squeezed drop. "Think on it. You walked all the way back through Armstrong, OK? Straight up the hill, right through the Bowl. You remember all those refrigerators? Somebody must have said something to you on the way—somebody asked what you wanted, what you were *doing* there, asked you—"

"I should have fought harder."

"Hey, look at you." He sat up and gestured to her wounds. "You did what you could."

"No," she said with that same self-sentencing iciness, "I let him down. He's my world and I let him down. He's worth ten of anybody else. He's worth ten of *me."* Her face contorted with self-loathing. "He's everything."

Lorenzo leaned back, thinking, Family time. He hoped this lady was from decent people.

"SI 15 to base, I need a reach out to Detective Daniel Martin, Gannon PD. Please have him contact me at the MC." Then, remembering her saying she didn't want to deal with her brother, he eyed her for a reaction. She was too far gone for his words to have registered, so he just signed off.

Before he could get into pushing her for witnesses again, Chatterjee came back in holding a loaded spike. Lorenzo heard the cop buzz out in the hall; it had grown in volume since the last time the door was opened.

"Brenda, I'm gonna tell you something that's true." Lorenzo hiked up his T-shirt sleeve without losing her eye. "Somebody saw what happened. They saw you, and you saw them."

"What's that." She watched the needle go in through a tattoo of his wife's face, directly beneath his shoulder.

"Adrenaline," Chatterjee murmured. "Straight, no chaser."

"Maybe somebody in a window." Lorenzo was thinking of Armstrong's Lamb Pen, even though most of them were at the rally. "Maybe . . . Hold on." He called for a quick time-out as the adrenaline took him for a three-second spin. He was missing half of what Brenda was saying now, something or other about her own childhood, as near as he could tell.

". . . So she put me out on the side of the road and drove off. I mean she just, like, circled the block to teach me a lesson, but . . . Can you be*lieve* that? That somebody would do that to a child?" Her voice started to break apart. "See, we all say we'd never do to our kids what was done to us—we all say that, right? Well, if you want to make God laugh, tell him your plans. I should have thrown myself in front of the car—you don't need words to do that, right?"

Lorenzo just watched her, trying to size her up, this lady who had taken so long to come across on the kid end. But those injuries—no way she wasn't suffering right now. He glanced at her hands again, thinking, If she's faking this, she's in the wrong line of work. But also thinking, Check out her house—bloodstains, signs of struggle, chaos. Thinking, This one's a bear.

"He's my heart." She swallowed half of each word, her knees fanning again. "My heart and soul."

There was a knock at the door, and a fat baby-faced cop stuck his head in. "Detective Council? Somebody on the horn, says you called him?"

Lorenzo got to his feet, tried to take the kid's measure quickly. "Can you stay with her?"

"Sure." The cop smiled, sliding into the room, hat in hand. Lorenzo saw a five-by-seven color photo of a girl in a confirmation dress crimped and crammed inside the roof of the cap.

"Is that your daughter?" Brenda said even before the guy could take Lorenzo's seat. Her voice was hoarse and tinkly with tears. "She's beautiful."

Lorenzo took the call at the nurses' station, having weaved his way through a mob of cops and even a few police-scanning stringers from some in-county papers, giving everybody the same no-comment, averted-eye smile.

"Hey, this Danny Martin?"

"Big Daddy Council, how you be, what you need." The guy was chewing something, kids shouting in the background; off-duty. Lorenzo pictured him on the job: knotted temples and quick hands.

"Yeah, Danny, I got—I'm here with your sister, Brenda, over in the Medical Center?"

A long silence. "What happened," he said, in a flat, almost angry way, the response slightly throwing Lorenzo; then, finally, "She OK?"

"Yeah, well, she got jacked at the Armstrong Houses. She's kind of roughed up but she's all right. But her son, Cody? We think he's still in the car."

Silence. "In the car . . . Guy's still out there?"

"Yeah."

"From Armstrong?"

"We're on crash alarm. He ain't gettin' far."

"Where in Armstrong."

Lorenzo heard something in the tone that made him regret the call.

"I think she needs some family right now. You think you can come down here, you know, like, be with her?"

"Where in Armstrong."

Lorenzo palmed his face again, the adrenaline giving him the jumps.

"Below the Bowl."

"On Hurley?"

"Yeah."

"Which end, Three Building or Five."

"Hey Danny, I know where you're coming from, but we're on it. I think she needs you *here*, OK? We'll wait for you, OK?"

"Three or Five."

"Danny, you know Chuck Rosen? Bump? He's got it covered, OK? I would like for you . . ."

But Danny Martin had already hung up.

Lorenzo stood there by the nurses' station, the receiver still in his hand, knowing that he'd just fucked himself good, knowing he had to get over to Armstrong before Gannon tore it up, but he was stuck with the mother. Maybe he could dump her off with the state police artist or get her home. No, he didn't want to give her an opportunity to clean anything up. Maybe he should get her with other family members or . . .

The hospital continued to fill with cops, some escorting victims but most coming by to eye her, a mob of alert loafers angling for a way to get in on the action.

Lorenzo picked up the phone again, paged Bobby McDonald, his boss, who was over in Hoboken at some kickoff dinner for a charity golf tournament. Then he called Bump Rosen's house to give Bump a heads up on the impending Gannon offensive into Armstrong. Despite his panic, there was a small sober part of him that was loath to cut in on the son's big night, but at least it was after eleven—*Law and Order* would be safely on videotape—and Bump just had to be there. Lorenzo did too, anxiously high stepping in place, chained to the vic, going nowhere.

"Hey, Jeanie." Lorenzo reflexively smiled into the phone, as if Bump's wife could see him.

"He already left, Lorenzo," she said with a whiff of reproach.

"He's headin' to Armstrong? So how was the show?" He hung up a few seconds later without having absorbed her response.

Lorenzo took it for granted that if Cody Martin was still missing twenty-four hours from now the job would be taken away from him. It would either be given to a more senior investigator or turned over to the prosecutor's office or perhaps even the FBI, and he was half ashamed to admit to himself that he would have no problem with that if that's the way the world turned.

Meanwhile, all of Dempsy was out there humping on this. He had gotten as much information from the woman as she was willing to give, and if he could only keep Gannon from trashing Armstrong, he could work those houses better in one night than anybody else taking a week.

Looking back down the corridor, Lorenzo saw a small crowd of cops standing in the open doorway of the doctors' locker room talking to the fat kid who was supposed to be guarding Brenda. He responded to this wrong picture by covering the distance from the phone at the nurses' station to the doorway in a half-dozen long strides.

"Where she at . . ." Lorenzo slid through the uniforms and ducked his head into the empty room.

"She had to go to the bathroom," the kid said.

"What?" Lorenzo got in the kid's face; the other cops reared back slightly.

"She had to go," the kid said, his voice climbing defensively.

Lorenzo stared at him.

"What was I supposed to do?"

She was in neither of the women's rooms in that sector of the hospital. Lorenzo had recruited two nurses to do the search, then taken off on his own into the less populous, more shadowed hallways connected to the ER wing.

After a few minutes of bobbing his head into doorway after doorway, he finally found her standing motionless in a six-bed examination room, one bandaged hand gripping the doorknob of a private john. She was making no effort to enter, just standing there as if entranced, her eyes fixed on an encounter taking place at the far end of the otherwise deserted room, where two men, partially obscured by a plastic curtain and apparently unaware of her presence, were talking in loud, hyperactive gulps. Lorenzo quietly stepped over the threshold, but then, catching the nature of the conversation that had seized her, silently retreated. He stood just inside the doorway, sensing the damage that could take place if either of these men were to become distracted.

"Thomas, hear me out." The speaker was a flush-faced detective in jacket and tie; Lorenzo tried to remember his name: Mallon, Mallory. "The doctor says to me, 'The child has bruises around her genital area, there's some tearing of tissue down there,' OK? You do the right thing, you bring her in, OK? But then you tell me your wife works nights, your daughter gets scared, so you sleep with her. Isn't that what you told me? OK. So. You be me. What am I to think?"

"No, no, no, no," the other guy said, pop-eyed with agitation. "No, I *sleep* with her. In the bed. Not, you know—I'm *sleep*ing."

"Thomas." The detective laughed, like the guy was nothing more than a rascal. "You say she wakes you up crying, it's just you and her in the house."

"And I rush her here. You saying I shouldn't have?" Thomas arched his chin to the ceiling and vigorously scratched his stretched throat.

"You did the right thing. I told you that. But what *I'm* asking you is, maybe you did something in your sleep, like, you were sleeping, you know, and you couldn't *help* it. You didn't realize. Do you think that's a possibility?"

"No, no, no. I want to tell you something. There's no *way* that could be, because I'm very careful. I wear four pairs of underpants to bed, just in case, OK?"

"Four." The detective nodded.

"See?" Thomas unbuckled his pants, pulled them down to reveal a pair of boxer shorts stuffed with three other pairs beneath, the waistbands staggered from directly beneath his rib cage to below his hips.

The detective finally noticed Brenda standing there, one hand on the bathroom doorknob, and his face went blotchy.

"What are you doing there." He glared at her, livid, all of his carefully contained anger prematurely exposed; a jagged row of cigarette-stained teeth slanting above his lower lip.

Brenda ignored the detective and his rage. She stared at the father— his staggered pairs of shorts, his taut and hairless belly.

"You should burn in hell," she said, then turned to see Lorenzo in the doorway. He signaled her his way impatiently.

"Don't you *touch* me," she nearly hissed as she pushed past him, marching back toward the ER. No problem, Lorenzo thought, imagining himself free of her, losing himself so deeply in the wish that, by the time she collapsed, a slow-motion, rickety, hands-out descent, she had gotten far enough away from him that he had to fight his way through a crowd.

Ringed by those who should have known better, Brenda sat on the floor, the nurse Penny Zito squatting before her, talking in a comforting gravelly murmur and holding one of Brenda's hands in both of her own.

Brenda was sobbing, her mouth locked open, braying over and over, "I woo-want to *be* with him, I woo-want to *be* with him," a nasal hiccupy lament, inconsolable and childlike. Lorenzo felt for her, knowing that if her kid was awake, if her kid was alive and awake right now, that's exactly what she should be feeling. In her despair and loss the woman had become her own missing son.

Lorenzo dropped down alongside Penny and was quickly joined by Chatterjee. The three of them eased her upright, Chatterjee murmuring in Lorenzo's ear, "Either we put her in psychiatric or you leave with her now. It's only going to get worse."

Lorenzo carefully steered her down the hall, his fingers lightly planted between her shoulder blades. "I'm taking you out of here, OK?"

"All right." It came out high and broken. She put one foot in front of the other as the doctor slipped Lorenzo a packet of codeine tablets, then retreated, calling out, "Get her back here for an X ray on that wrist."

As Lorenzo shepherded her toward the ambulance-bay doors, the goateed guard walked backwards in front of them in case he was needed. A gurney came flying through from the street, three medics racing it like a bobsled, almost upending the guard. Lorenzo caught the glazed, dying eyes of Miss Bankhead, the next-door neighbor to the murdered Barretts, her red underrims exposed by the downward pull of the oxygen mask.

Out of habit, he looked toward the nurses station, but he didn't really need Penny Zito tapping her heart from across the room to know what had happened. Lorenzo corkscrewed with frustration, flinging his hands over his head, that Armstrong double homicide now a triple in his book. Then Brenda jerked him back into the world, her words coming out choked and grievous: "I dreamt my son is dead."

As Lorenzo guided Brenda out through the ambulance bay, he saw that the summer night had cracked open, the overhang outside the doors crowded with people unhappily eyeing the parking lot a wet fifty yards away. The crime scene was probably a mudhole by now. The red-faced detective, Mallon or Malloy, gave her the once-over—pitiless, acidic— then abruptly flapped out a borrowed examination gown and, holding it over his head, made a run for the lot, the force of the downpour instantly swamping his shoes and battering his makeshift canopy into a sodden shawl.

"What do you mean you dreamt—" Lorenzo cut off his own murmured question. This wasn't the place, but eager to hear what she was driving at, he hustled her out into the rain, racewalked her to the lot, and deposited her in the passenger seat of his Crown Victoria. Brenda looked up at him.

"When I was on the floor in there? I saw him. I saw my son—"

"Hold on, hold on." Raindrops were springing off Lorenzo's shaved dome. "Just . . ." He whipped around to the driver's side and slid in, drenched, a residual tremor in his hands from the adrenaline. "What you mean you saw him. You dreamt? Or you saw."

The ignition wouldn't catch in the downpour, Lorenzo thinking, City-owned piece of shit. Turning to her, he repeated, "You dreamt or you saw."

"When I was sitting on the floor. He was right there in the hallway. He was like halfway down the hall. But he was upside down."

He tried again; it still wouldn't kick over. Lorenzo worried about flooding the engine, then went off thinking about Miss Bankhead. She had barely been able to get out of her TV chair, yet she had had a cash crop of five foster children last time he counted, none of them over six years old. Those kids would be going back to the recycling plant now.

"He was upside down, like a playing card, like a jack or a king. It was like he was dead."

The ignition finally caught, Lorenzo feeling overvictorious about it, playing back her recounting of the dream or vision or whatever it was.

"Brenda, what are you trying to tell me."

"What I saw."

"Brenda." Lorenzo forced himself to be all there. "Do you know where your son is right now?"

She looked at him with starred eyes. "If I did," she said slowly, each word distinct and paced. "I would be *with* him right now."

Lorenzo watched those eyes brim, then spill their dazzle.

"OK," he said, nodding, too tense to truly get inside her, to gauge her realness. "OK." Gingerly he gunned the engine, studying her as she struggled with her bandaged hands to work the seat belt clasp.

"Why'd you wait so long to tell me your son was in the car?" He leaned over and locked her in, thinking, Seat belt time is way over. "Huh?" he asked again.

"Because . . ." She stared straight ahead, her shoulders jerking as if she were freezing. "Because I didn't, don't want it to be true."

Before Lorenzo could pull out, a car came flying into the lot, slamming itself into a space. The driver popped out while the car was still rocking and slipped a plastic patient's bracelet on his wrist as he jogged to the emergency room. Lorenzo grimaced—that bring-your-own-bracelet bit was an old reporter's trick for getting around unchallenged inside a hospital.

His pager came to life: his boss, Bobby McDonald. Lorenzo reached for the radio, then pulled back, knowing Bobby would have him take her to the Bureau of Criminal Identification to look at mug shots.

"I'm taking you back to Armstrong now," Lorenzo said, as he finally pulled out of the lot. "I just want you to walk me through the scene, all right?"

"No. I don't want to do that. He's not there." She took a swipe at her bedraggled hair.

"Most likely not, but . . ."

As they pulled onto JFK Boulevard, the accumulated strips of reflector tape worn by the dope crews and others strobed the way for him as far as the eye could see.

"What do you think of my dream?" she blurted, then abruptly twisted around, as if someone were hiding in the backseat.

"What do I think?" Lorenzo was balking, associating dreams more with Bible stories than with analysis.

"Is it true? You think it's true?" She twisted around again.

"Brenda, you got to have a positive attitude."

He had seen that swivel-hipped body language before—adrenalized helplessness, people chained to a clock with no hands.

"I want to go look for the car," she announced.

"No, I can't do that right now." He shook his head emphatically. "Because if we run up on it? I can't get involved in an apprehension with you sitting next to me. But see that?" He leaned forward over the steering wheel and pointed out a helicopter heading north toward the marshes. "Look up there. Now, unless that guy put your car in his pocket, he ain't going far." Lorenzo was just guessing that the whirlybird was looking for the kid.

"I don't want that dream to be true," she said, ignoring the copter. "It was just a dream."

She rattled the envelope of codeine tablets against her parted lips. Lorenzo had no memory of handing them over.

What else. What else. "Do you want me to notify the father?"

"The father?" she whispered with alarm.

Father, mother, brother—those who would have to be told. Brenda clutched her stomach.

"What's his name," Lorenzo said.

"Ulysses."

He scribbled it on an empty paycheck envelope propped on the steering wheel. "Ulysses what."

Stopped in traffic, he saw one of his snitches detach himself from a street corner and head for the car, most likely looking for a little money hit. Lorenzo casually ran a red light to avoid that conversation. "Ulysses what."

"I don't even . . . Maldonado."

"You know where he is?"

"Puerto Rico, Florida. I don't know."

They were almost sideswiped by a white van with New York plates cutting into the oncoming traffic to pass them.

"Don't waste your time," she said. "It wasn't him."

The across-the-river tags and the heedless speed gave Lorenzo a bad feeling.

"I want to see mug shots." She shook the envelope against her lips again. "I should see mug shots now."

"Just walk me through the scene real quick." Lorenzo looked away. "Then we'll set up some trays for you, OK?"

Armstrong jackers—Lorenzo flipped through his head file. Hootie Charles? But Hootie was a little guy with a full crop up top. But victims make the worst witnesses. But Hootie had switched over to stealing lawn furniture in the last year, just strolling across the city line into Gannon, hopping fences and walking off with lawn mowers, deck chairs, barbeques—rolling those Weber grills and Toros down the street in the general direction of home and selling whatever he had for twenty, forty bucks to whoever happened to be out sitting on their porches.

"You said this guy had a shaved head?"

"A shaved head."

He couldn't tell if she was repeating the question or answering it.

It just didn't sound like an Armstrong-based crime.

"Are you related to Lorenzo Wilkinson?" she asked, with a dislocated chattiness.

"Lorenzo who?"

"I just thought because you had the same . . ." She closed her eyes.

"Brenda. That cut on your head. How'd you get that?"

"I banged it." Unconsciously she fingered the crust on her scalp.

"That part of what happened tonight?" He drove four blocks before adding, "Huh?" Then another two.

"No." It sounded defeated, minute, and from far away.

Parked in the gravel bed of the elevated Conrail tracks opposite the Armstrong Houses, Lorenzo looked directly down at Hurley Street, the rubbled cul-de-sac that lay beneath the low end of the great sloping refrigerator-strewn Bowl.

This potholed stretch of asphalt, which served as the access road to the bottom-end buildings—Three, Four, and Five—was littered with city vehicles: Gannon's blue-and-white cruisers, Dempsy's red-and-cream ones, a motley collection of unmarked Crown Victorias and confiscated dope cars. There was even an ambulance, the paramedics sitting on the hood and smoking, watching the play develop, somebody in the dispatcher's office having gotten their wires crossed. Lorenzo had a feeling that, even if they weren't needed now, sticking around tonight might not be a bad idea.

The Armstrong residents, kept out of Hurley by the cops, had retreated to the elevation of the Bowl, the refrigerators now serving as bleacher seats. The slope had taken on the gap-toothed aspect of a ruined and ancient amphitheater.

It had stopped raining, but the occasional sweep of headlights bucking their way over the potholes to Martyrs Park at the closed end of the street caught the residual droplets that clung to the gritty foliage there and momentarily graced what remained of the crime scene with a gauzy spray of diamonds.

As they sat above the action, Lorenzo's right headlight nuzzling the razor-wire-topped fence meant to keep Armstrong off the tracks, the sputter and squawk of radio transmissions, the bellow and bark of stressed-out cops and tenants floated up to them. Brenda absorbed the soundtrack with what he interpreted as honest horror, blindly reaching out with a bandaged hand to slap down the pop lock on her door.

"He's not *here*," she said, with teary insistence.

"Just . . ." Lorenzo raised a staying hand and began to roll, driving along the track bed above and parallel to Hurley, then down an embankment, curving around to the action.

At the mouth of the cul-de-sac, they found themselves behind the white kamikaze van that had earlier cut them off, now humming in neutral. The van veered left to park, one side up on the curb, revealing a slant-parked Camaro—a confiscated dope car—blocking the Hurley Street entrance. An older Gannon detective, Leo Sullivan, was standing on post, arguing with the driver of a station wagon hitched to an old sky-blue camper that was attempting to exit the houses.

Gannon was sealing off Armstrong—no one in, no one out. Brenda groaned.

Lorenzo, knowing Sullivan, muttered, "Wait here." Struggling to achieve a smile, he left the car.

"You're going to South Carolina *now?*" Leo grinned at the apoplectic driver. "It's almost midnight."

A cameraman with a shoulder-mounted Betacam topped with a sun gun erupted out of the passenger side of the van and disappeared at a run, into the shadows of a train trestle underpass. Lorenzo guessed the guy was going to make an end run around the border patrol by scampering up the embankment to where they had just been parked, overlooking the play. Then he would climb over the train fence, clamber down the sloped, easily scaled retaining wall, and drop into Hurley Street somewhere closer to the crime scene and well away from this checkpoint.

"Mr. Leo." Lorenzo came on grinning like a pumpkin, seething with rage. "You guys taking over Dodge?"

"It's that funny fuckin' city line, Council," Leo said, making a slithering gesture with the side of his hand. "Goes through that park like Snake Hips Tucker, you know?"

The city line was famously tortured, at one point cutting through a bowling alley—three lanes in Dempsy, twelve in Gannon.

"We think the deed might of been done on *our* side of the park, you know what I'm saying?"

"Huh." Lorenzo felt the chest tightness again.

Whenever Gannon took a beating along the border, the line always wiggled a little so that they could pursue and punish the D-Town–bred perp themselves.

"Lorenzo!" The white-haired driver of the camper stuck his head out the window. "Tell this . . ." he said, clenching his teeth and chucking a thumb at Sullivan, "I got to go!"

The guy had his wife sitting next to him and two sullen teenage granddaughters in the backseat. It's starting, Lorenzo was thinking, knowing he'd be pulled to pieces by aggrieved tenants every step of the way once he got out on the playing field.

"Why don't you go in the morning?" Leo said, trying to be friendly about it; then, turning to Lorenzo, "Guy's got a long trip"; then, back to the driver, "Get a good night's sleep. You drive all night, pull over to sleep in that metal box you got back there with that southern *sun* coming up? You'll cook like an egg."

"I'll go any got-damn time I want," the driver said, getting buggy. Lorenzo knew the guy was heading down there to drop his granddaughters off for the summer, pick up a few hundred dollars' worth of firecrackers, get back to Armstrong before the Fourth of July. It was coming up in a few days, and he'd make himself a little money.

"Hey." Leo's lips disappeared. "I'm trying to be respectful to you."

"Then respect my *got*-damn wish to *go.*"

Lorenzo quickly turned to check on Brenda, who was still in the car, hands to her face. He had no business bringing her here, he thought, then returned to the conflict before him.

"C'mon, Leo." He made himself grin again, eyeing the Convoy brothers over Leo's shoulder. Through the gap between Four and Five Buildings, he could see them standing on refrigerator crates back up in the Bowl. Lorenzo remembered spotting them from the community center window earlier, knew they had to have seen her, but no way was he sharing that information with Gannon—risk their getting a little slaphappy with the Convoys and shutting down the lines of communication.

"C'mon, man," Lorenzo said, exasperated at the pettiness of this shit.

"Now he's leaving town?" Leo muttered. "Why now?"

"He works nights at the hospital. This is when he's up."

Leo shrugged unhappily, then saw Brenda in the car, his eyes registering recognition. Before he could approach her, he was distracted by the driver of the white van, who came up with business card in hand and yet another Betacam, held under his arm like a football.

"Hey guys, I'm with National—"

"I know who you are." Leo went thin-lipped again and turned to the camper. "All right, get out of here," he said, like the words cost blood; then he turned back to the man with the Betacam. "This is a secured crime scene. If I catch you or the other guy in there, you're both going to jail and I'll throw so many fuckin' Denver boots on that van it'll *sink,* you got me?"

Lorenzo pegged them as freelance scavengers, trolling both sides of the Hudson with a police radio, responding to crimes and fires, phoning the local networks, who shut down their own roving crews at eleven, to try to get a precommitment on the footage as they tore ass to the scene.

The video hustler retreated to his van and drove away. The antique camper, exuding an odor of burned hair, sputtered past the blockade. Both Leo and Lorenzo, alone now, turned to the Crown Victoria: Brenda was gone.

Lorenzo wigged for an endless moment before he spied her sitting on the curb, doubled over, her injured hands palms-up, resting on her knees.

"You OK, Brenda?" Leo asked, down on one knee, his voice gentle but level. Lorenzo heard some kind of subtle withholding in his tone, and apparently Brenda did too, curling her chin into her shoulder.

"We'll get him back. Right, Big Daddy?"

"Hell, yeah," Lorenzo said, a little tightly. He didn't like the sound of his tag in a white cop's mouth; he was always braced for an unindictable tinge of mockery in the air.

Leo got up and headed for the seized dope car, moving it to let them drive through to the scene.

Once Lorenzo had parked inside the Hurley cul-de-sac, pulling in along the base of the Conrail retaining wall, Brenda had to be coaxed out of her seat. If he was going to go through with the charade of bringing her back to the scene, to jog her memory or whatever, he would have to play it out all the way. But from the moment Lorenzo stepped out of the car, he saw at least three things wrong from the jump.

He saw Danny Martin, Brenda's brother, standing in the middle of Hurley talking to Bump Rosen, the both of them trying not to argue in front of the customers. Danny was high-chested and raw, wild-eyed and stubble-chinned, wearing rubber flip-flops and baggy shorts, which meant he had dashed out of his house with his head not right. Bump was himself, plug-squat, bald and bearded, wrestler-thick, but the strain of trying to be diplomatic made him seem even more condensed than usual. Then Lorenzo saw Teddy Moon, a Gannon detective on loan to the Dempsy County sheriff's office, distributing a sheaf of papers to Gannon and Dempsy detectives both, who fanned out and hit the buildings. Lorenzo guessed the papers were unexecuted arrest warrants on Armstrong residents, mostly bullshit complaints: motor vehicle violations, possession, the odd robbery or assault. And lastly, he saw two cruisers, one Dempsy, one Gannon, blocking the driveway exits at the high end of the projects above the Bowl, the Gompers Street end— Gannon, with the cooperation of their Dempsy brothers, locking down Armstrong like East Berlin.

Brenda stared at her brother, Danny, all hot-eyed and knotty, and responded by retreating from the middle of the street to the safety of the shadows under the retaining wall. Lorenzo backtracked along with her, taking a moment to get the lay of the land.

Eyeing Three Building across Hurley, he scanned the lower-floor Lamb Pen windows that hung directly over the park. He knew who lived in each of them—who was legally blind, who was hard of hearing, who knew more shit from sitting in that row of geriatric box frames than the CIA. Lorenzo wasn't planning to share any of that with the Gannon detectives.

Directly above their heads, at the top of the Conrail wall, a powerful light jerked erratically, up, down, then laterally. Lorenzo returned to the middle of Hurley, looking up and seeing that first video commando, the passenger from the white van, the Betacam held upside down between his legs now. The guy was using his sun gun as a high-powered flashlight, searching for burrows under the razor-topped train fence, any place he could crawl through, dragging his camera after him, and start making some money.

If it was mostly video freelancers so far, they still had a little time to get this over with before the big guns rolled in from across the river. The satellite trucks, the newscasters, the tabloids—the vision of it moved Lorenzo out onto center court.

"Lorenzo."

He turned to see Bobby McDonald, looking dapper in a wash-and-wear, color-coordinated kind of way but slightly wobbly, having just been pulled out of that golf dinner over in Hoboken.

"What you got?" Slightly built, gray, rumple-faced, Bobby immediately infected Lorenzo with his chronic inability to panic.

"I don't know." Lorenzo took a long breath, shifting a few feet in an attempt to block Brenda from Bobby's sight lines. "I got to tell you, nobody around here's jumping out in my mind, you know what I'm saying?" Then, tilting his head toward Danny Martin, "He got no business being here."

"I can't keep him out. He's off duty."

"C'mon, Bobby, he's family. Call the chief over there. Shit's gonna happen."

"I know what you're saying, but—"

"And that paper they're running around with? That best be Gannon-based warrants."

"We're trying to work it out here," Bobby said, finally noticing Brenda up against the wall. "So how'd she do with the mug shots?" he asked with an edge, as if knowing that Lorenzo hadn't been to BCI yet.

"He's not *here*," Brenda called out tearfully to Bobby, to everybody. "I just *know* it."

"Hang on." Lorenzo quickly walked away to avoid the subject and headed toward Bump and her brother, Danny. Bump was holding a steel ring heavy with the keys to all the unoccupied apartments in Armstrong, rhythmically banging it against his leg like a tambourine, his chest rising to his teeth with the strain of trying to contain his anger.

"No, no, no, Danny, Danny, I understand, I understand, but what *you* got to understand is that this is *our* house. We got to *live* with these people, you see what I'm saying?"

Another Gannon cruiser rumbled past—more cops—the headlights catching in Bump's oversized Buddy Holly glasses, causing them to flash white fire.

"No problem, no problem." Danny Martin was not even listening, his eyes, light gray like his sister's, surveying the scene. He wore a wrinkled U.S. Olympic soccer team T-shirt, Gannon being the hometown of the goalie. And he had that same pro-wrestling hairdo that Brenda had described on her son—crew cut in front and long enough on the sides and in back to look like some kind of hairpiece. Lorenzo wondered if Danny and his nephew were close. He hoped that they were not.

"Danny." Bump touched Martin's arm, speaking with a soft urgency. "It's like, you go in, you don't know who to bang, how to bang 'em, shit's gonna shut down so fast around here you're gonna think you're in a cemetery, so what I'm saying is, let's just team up on this, my guy with your guy, put our *heads* together."

"I have no problem with that," Danny said, still not listening, eyeing Teddy Moon, who was continuing to hand out warrants; Dempsy and Gannon lining up for them. Lorenzo saw Dempsy cops who hadn't been in this project in years, everybody wanting a piece of this.

Something or someone had flushed Brenda out from the shadows, and looking back over her shoulder as she fled the wall, she wound up crashing into Lorenzo. The mild collision distracted both Danny and Bump, causing them to turn around. Danny studiously ignored his sister for the moment. "What you got?" he demanded, glaring at Lorenzo.

"I'm working on it," Lorenzo said, noticing that Danny had some kind of slice across his shin. Blood was dribbling down to his rubber flip-flop.

"What was she doing here?" Danny asked, speaking to him as if his sister were not among them, then abruptly turning his beam on her before Lorenzo could respond.

"What, were you out of your fucking *mind?* What were you *doing* here, Brenda?"

"Danny, I work here." She tried desperately to stand her ground but unconsciously dipped into a pleading crouch.

Stepping in front of her, Lorenzo forced another smile. "C'mon, Danny, she's been through some shit here."

"Hey!" Danny snapped, hand on his chest, "I don't see no *ax* sticking out of her head." Then he stepped around and, hunching down a little to be at her level, pointed at his eyes, almost poking himself. "What were you *do*ing here, Brenda."

The five of them were abruptly blasted with light, the video shooter from the van having made it down from the wall. Brenda crouched even lower, her fingers splayed in supplication.

"Danny," she whispered, fresh tears popping from behind crushed lids, matted lashes. "Danny, I swear from the death of my heart . . ."

The brother raised a forearm to shield his face. "Get that . . ."

The shooter cut his light and bolted into the shadows before anyone could grab him.

"You call Mom?" he asked sharply.

"No."

"*Don't.*"

Lorenzo stepped in front of her again.

"Danny, you shouldn't even be here now."

"Well, you shouldn't've called me then."

"Some of your people here I understand, but—"

"Hey! Reverse the situation. Would you or would you not be over in Gannon *right* now, shaking our tree."

"No, no, I hear you." Lorenzo was starting to do Bump's dance. "Just don't break nothin', OK?"

"I'm just here. So you're on point for this, huh?" Danny asked dimly. "She telling you everything?" He turned to his sister with that same withering tone. "You telling him everything?"

"God!" Brenda bellowed rawly. "He's my *son,* you motherfucker!"

Unimpressed, Danny gave her his back.

"So who's the actor?" he asked Lorenzo.

"I said, I'm working on it."

"What, you don't know who's runnin' hard around here?"

"Not like this."

"Not like this," Danny repeated, scanning the Bowl, the endless windows.

"We got any kind of crime scene up there?" Lorenzo asked Bump, nodding toward Martyrs Park as he blindly fished behind him for Brenda's wrist, to keep her from wandering.

"Are you kidding me?" Bump pushed up his glasses, adjusted his Knicks cap. "It looks like a freakin' tractor pull."

A young, uniformed Gannon cop was brought before Danny by a Gannon detective, the kid looking scared: a prisoner of war.

"You had the Watch?" Danny started in, absently taking a swipe at the blood tickling his leg.

"Yeah. Yes."

"Yes? So where the fuck were you?"

Lorenzo listened in for the moment, letting Danny's special status and wrath on this one do some work for him.

"I was right there." The kid pointed back through the trees of the park to Gannon.

"No. You went to Mickey D's, right?"

"No, I swear. I was right there." The kid's crew cut made his eyes seem as big as poker chips. "I swear."

"And you didn't *see* nothing, you didn't *hear* nothing."

"Nothing. I swear."

"You were doing the word jumble, right?"

"No . . . What word jumble?"

"Were you in the front of the mall? Or in the back."

"In the front. Hey, I'm a month on the job. I'm not *good* enough to fuck off yet." The kid was dead serious. Bump had to look away to smother his smile.

Danny turned to his sister again. "Why didn't you go to him?"

"Brenda!" The voice whipped her around. A heavyset young black woman was calling out her name, pushing through some halfhearted police resistance, the scene getting too diffuse and chaotic to patrol. The woman's arms were out, although she was still ten paces away. Brenda extricated herself from Lorenzo and ran to the offered embrace, stopping a few steps short, as if having second thoughts about being touched.

Lorenzo exchanged glances with the woman, Felicia Mitchell— another forever kid, born and bred in Armstrong, now running all the pre-teen programs for the Urban Corps; she would be Brenda's boss if Brenda was working in the Study Club as she had said.

"So who do you think?" Bump asked Lorenzo, without much conviction. "Hootie?"

"I think he might even still be in County," Lorenzo said, scanning the crowd that was starting to come down off the refrigerator crates, get closer to the party. Almost half the teenagers infiltrating Hurley now were wearing *Top Cop* gimme caps, the show having spent the past week trailing a narco unit working greater D-Town—Armstrong and JFK Boulevard.

"Salim." Lorenzo beckoned to one of the kids who was talking to someone standing in shadow. The kid hopped to his name, coming over.

"Hootie in or out?" he asked, eyeing Felicia and Brenda and, behind them, attempting to skirt the light, Jesse Haus, the Dempsy runner. Annoyed, he moved to eighty-six her. In response, Jesse made a hands-up gesture of surrender but retreated only a few steps. Lorenzo was too stretched to pursue her.

"Hootie?" Salim turned him back around. "In. No, out, out. He just got out."

"If that child was black, none of you all would even *be* here," a blaze-eyed woman in a housedress yelled from the sidelines. "This place here would be deserted!" She raised a chorus of approval from those around her.

"Oh *please.*" Bump nearly dropped to his knees. "Not now, OK?"

Mindlessly absorbing the bedlam of Hurley Street, Lorenzo wound up keying in on Jesse Haus, who was still eavesdropping on Brenda and Felicia. This time when he caught her eye, she pressed her palms together prayerfully, then slipped out of sight. Now it would take a real physical commitment on his part to get her out of here, so Lorenzo decided to let it be, a part of him still feeling he owed her something for the article that landed him on Rolanda Watts. He resented it, though, thinking, Nothing more expensive than a free gift.

The Armstrong Bowl abruptly burst into light—that sun gun again— the people on the crates shielding their eyes. Lorenzo spotted at least one more reporter up there, sharing a crate with Herbert Cartwright, seemingly writing down everything he was saying. Herbert sat erect as a pharaoh, his hands palms-down on his thighs. Lorenzo wondered if the reporter knew that Herbert was retarded. He never worried as much about the first wave of reporters, those who hit a crime scene like it was D day, as he did about the reporters who would come later—those who knew to be patient, to lay back for a few hours until the cops withdrew; the ones who knew how to time their entrance, then get in deep.

Without ever actually having touched, Brenda and Felicia seemed to have broken their embrace. Brenda was stepping back now, and Lorenzo attempted to reclaim her.

"Lorenzo!"

Another heavyset woman was windmilling her way through the crowd, eyes bulging.

"My mother's having an angina attack and they ain't letting nobody out the houses!" Her fleshy collarbone shimmered with sweat. "Now, I'm gonna get her to the hospital if I have to run people down to do it."

"Hang on," Lorenzo sputtered. He spun around, eyed Leo Sullivan, moved to confront him, to confront *any*body, losing track now of what he was doing here, what came first here, realizing how much time he had wasted coming back, what a bad move it had turned out to be, how helpless he was to protect anybody in a situation like this. Once again he surrendered to the likelihood that this carjack job was his for only a day, before the prosecutor's office would grab it.

"Who's Hootie?" Danny came up on him again. "I'm hearing Hootie now."

"I don't think so."

"Why not."

"He's into lawn furniture."

"Lawn furniture," Danny repeated. "You're talking about Buster?" Hootie had a different tag in each city. "Buster does cars too?"

"I don't think—"

"Did you find him at least?" Danny didn't wait for an answer, just marched off looking for Hootie, for Buster.

"Carmen." Lorenzo laid a hand on the bug-eyed woman's arm. "Can you get your mother to the medics over there?" Lorenzo followed his own finger and was surprised to see that a line had formed at the back of the ambulance, as if it were an ice cream truck. People were most likely gravitating to it with everything from heart trouble to amorphous depression.

Brenda started to wander off again, and Lorenzo gently corralled her with outspread arms. She was walking with small, tripping steps, occasionally dragging the toe of a shoe, and he wondered how many of those codeine tablets she had scarfed down on the ride over here, any number over one being too many.

It was now a quarter past midnight—time, if possible, to justify this disastrous visit. Steering Brenda toward the neon-orange tape that ran across the closed end of Hurley Street, he braced himself for a walk in the park.

4

Between the second- and third-floor landings in one of Four Building's stairways, two Kevlar-vested Dempsy narcotics cops—one bearded, one bald—had a young but wizened-looking customer chest-wedged against the wall, the bearded cop digging into the guy's front pants pockets, the bald one holding some paper in his fist, pressing it against the cinder block over the poor bastard's head. From her perch one flight up on the third-floor landing, Jesse assumed it was some kind of two-bit warrant, possession or shoplifting. Keeping herself quiet and out of sight, she held her nose against the smell: Lion Piss, the odor having grown denser and more potent since she first smelled it as a kid in the Powell Houses, way back in the sixties.

"Oh shit." The bearded cop extracted two amber vials, one from each pocket, held them up for perusal. "Oh, shit."

"Fuckin' Rudy." The bald cop shook his head with theatrical disappointment. "Rudy Kazootie."

With the warrant over his head, the cinder block at his back, the hot-looking police in his face, and the jail-time bottles under his nose, Rudy's eyelids began to flutter.

"Naw, naw, naw, man." Rudy pointed to the vials. "That's *beat.*"

"It's County."

"Naw, naw, naw, it's beat, it's salt, it's pete. You you you want to lock me up, you lock me up for impersonating a drug addict, man, 'cause—"

"Who's this." The bearded cop produced a fax-papered mug shot, held it six inches from Rudy's face. "Quick. Who's this."

Rudy squinted, the picture too close. "That's Luther's brother, right?"

"You're on the money. What's his name."

"What's that . . . Hootie, yeah, Hootie. Hootie."

"Right again," the other cop chimed in.

Hootie. Jesse loved moments like this—coming into a land unformed, the story, the information just hanging there, unplucked.

"Now, like your life depends on it, *right* now, where can we find him."

"Now? Oh wow, yeah, OK. OK. You can find him maybe at Sly's house."

"Sly?"

"Yeah, that's like his partner in crime."

"Sly in Two Building?"

"Yeah, uh-huh." Rudy was still trying to control his fluttering lids.

"We need him bad, Rudy, and if he ain't there you just made the A-list."

"Yo, if he ain't there you come back here and tell me. I *want* you to come back and tell me, because I will *find* him for you. I swear on my *moms*, loc, you will get results to*night*."

The cops gave him a long stare before pulling back, the bearded one dropping the vials on the cement floor and crushing them under a work-booted heel.

"Yo, thank you, man. You just saving me from my*self*."

The cops went south, Rudy north, muttering as he lunged up the stairs. On the landing he almost plowed into Jesse. Her abrupt presence made him clutch his chest and stagger backwards into the wall.

"Easy, easy." Jesse put out a hand.

"Damn!" Rudy drawled, calming down, eyeing her now. "You a cop?"

"What do you think?"

"Naw, naw." Rudy brushed past her, continuing up the stairs. "I'm done thinking for today."

"Hootie did this?" she called out after him.

"Hootie? Who the fuck is Hootie," the words trailing down to her, disembodied, Rudy gone round the bend.

On frantic nights like this, on stories like this, Jesse always counted on people's second-guessing themselves—giving her the once-over and concluding that nobody, on the face of it, could be as vulnerable as she seemed, pegging her as either a nut job or an undercover and letting her go about her business unchallenged.

As Jesse exited Four Building, which, flanked by Three and Five, centered the high-rises that faced Hurley Street, she scanned the scene before her, a real backyard do: cops, restless tenants, the beginnings of a roaming media presence, all caught in the crossfire of headlights, the effect somewhere between a discotheque and a nighttime artillery barrage.

She picked out at least four other reporters sneaking around, including one slipping in as she watched, a lanky skinhead from across the river whom she had seen at other stories. The guy glommed on to Bobby McDonald as he came through the Hurley Street blockade, keeping pace with him but walking backwards, miming a conversation for the benefit of the border patrol until he was inside the club. McDonald looked a little unsteady on his feet, oblivious to the fact that he had just given someone a free ride.

Earlier, Jesse had simply walked in—no notebook, no cell phone, wearing a hooded sweatshirt despite the heat and putting on her no-face face. She strolled in like she lived there, which was almost true: the Powell Houses were just five blocks away.

Lion Piss. She wondered if her parents even smelled it anymore. She guessed they were more or less safe; no one really cared now if they were Commies or Socialists or Trotskyites or anything. They had survived the worst of the crack-induced chaos of the last few years, but they were still old, still white, so who could really say? Her father still talked to anyone who would listen or who had the misfortune to get stuck in the elevator or the laundry room with him, yammering on about imperialism, racism, capitalism, the CIA. Most people these days just nodded their heads, walleyed with boredom, saying stuff like, "Uh-huh, awright, I hear you, that's right, OK now, OK then," trying to avoid looking at his thin, desiccated lips, his filmy, eager eyes. Nobody really gave a shit anymore.

Laying back in the breezeway of Four Building, Jesse calmly continued to survey the players until she struck gold, locking in on the carjack victim, the mother of the child, Brenda Martin herself. The woman was engaged in some kind of anguished exchange with a large black lady of about the same age. Wondering what on earth could have motivated Lorenzo Council or any other non-brain-dead detective into dragging what had to be a fairly traumatized victim back to a zoo of a crime scene like this, Jesse made her move, easing to within earshot of the conversation, setting herself up comfortably in the big woman's shadow, then blowing it by accidentally making eye contact with the man himself.

Lorenzo threw her a tight-lipped glare, silently demanding that she evict herself from the scene since he was a good fifty feet away and had his hands full with the victim's brother. Jesse made a half-assed gesture of surrender, retreated a few steps, until she bumped into a tenant's rust-eaten sedan, and proceeded to ignore Lorenzo.

"All my life," Brenda sobbed to the big woman. "All my life. I would never—you *know* me. I would never do this to you."

"To me?" The woman reared back from Brenda's words, Jesse catching herself miming the body English.

From where she was standing, it seemed to Jesse that Brenda Martin's teeth were chattering, clacking like castanets.

"I had no idea." The words came out swoony.

"That's OK," the woman said, sounding kindly yet desperate, her head on a swivel as she looked around desperately for help.

"I loved him so much."

"I know you do."

"I'm so sorry."

"Nobody's blaming you."

"I had no i*dea.*"

"They'll get him."

"I just want to die."

"Don't say that."

Overhead, on the far side of Hurley, a Conrail train powered past Armstrong, the racket and rush turning the heads of all who were there but the tenants. Jesse embraced the noise, regarding it as another kind of cover, her concentration undeterred. Momentarily the two women before her were reduced to gesture and mask, until Brenda Martin blurted out loud enough to be heard over the tail end of the retreating roar, "I wish I could be born again. I wish, I wish—I want to still work here." She looked up, wild-eyed, into the other woman's face. "I want to work *harder.*"

Uncomprehending, tantalized, Jesse took a few steps closer.

"Brenda . . ." the big woman began helplessly.

"I have so much love in me." Her voice was now fervent and husky. "You just don't know. You just don't know . . ."

"I know you do." The response was singsong with misery, useless.

Two young boys came racing through the scene, both of them

clutching a brace of wide-mouthed shell casings, holding them upright against their bellies, each red plastic hollow filled to the brim with dirt. Jesse stepped into their path, then dropped into a squat, spooking them.

"Who's that lady there," she asked, gesturing with her head toward Brenda and the black woman.

"The white lady?" one kid said.

"The other."

"That's Felicia."

"Felicia who."

"Felicia," the second kid said, shrugging.

"You know the white lady too?"

"Salim!" Lorenzo called out to one of the kids, who dropped the casings and ran to his name.

"Brenda." The woman named Felicia leaned back in order to make eye contact. "You keep with Lorenzo, he's gonna find him."

"He is?" Brenda sounded both hopeful and hopeless, stoned.

"And I'm telling you. No one here's gonna stand for this either. They're gonna turn him out."

"Who."

"Who ever *took* him."

Jesse saw the squat white cop, the one the kids called Bump, eject two reporters from Hurley Street. Good, she thought, but then Lorenzo caught her eye again, posting another eviction notice. This time Jesse threw him a pressed-palms kowtow: Leave me be.

"Listen to me, awright?" Felicia said, trying to extricate herself from Brenda's agony now. "You go to him. You go to Lorenzo right now and he's gonna get you straight."

Seeming dazed and malleable, possibly high, Brenda staggered away backwards, nodding in obedience. Jesse saw Lorenzo move to take her in, but before he could get to her he was abruptly turned around by some hysterical fat lady howling something about her mother being sick, and then Lorenzo just lost it, going all sputter-mouthed, spinning like a top.

With Lorenzo momentarily experiencing a breakdown and Felicia cutting out altogether, Brenda began to wander Hurley Street, up for grabs. Jesse's first impulse was to snatch her but she reined it in, knowing that what she could expect here was an encounter that would last no more than a minute or two and that, if she did make true contact with the star of the show, she would no doubt get tossed from the scene. So she let the prize go, opting for Felicia, pacing her as she weaved through the jumble of tenant-owned junkers and police cars, heading for the breezeway of Three Building.

"Felicia!" Jesse called out. "Brenda—is she OK?" she asked, sounding like they were all in the same women's group. Felicia turned, squinting, unable to see the face that came with the voice, Jesse having positioned herself so that the anti-crime floods over Three Building's breezeway served as a backlight, reducing her, in Felicia's eyes, to a silhouette. "I can't believe it! What the hell happened?"

Felicia walked in a slow, purposeful arc until Jesse came into the light.

"You a reporter?"

"Yeah, but I was sitting at home and I heard . . . Does she work here?"

"I don't know," Felicia said, more uncomfortable than hostile.

"You don't know?"

"Maybe you should talk to the police."

"They said to talk to you."

"Me? No." Felicia smiled a little at that. "Who did."

"You know Lorenzo Council?"

Felicia waited.

"You remember that story on him the *Register* ran a few months ago?"

"Yeah."

"I wrote that." Jesse felt like a pud saying it like that, but blunt was good when time was tight.

"Oh yeah?" Felicia was smiling again. "OK, OK."

"That was me."

"All right, all right." Felicia was coming off mild now, almost warm. "OK, that's good, because then he'll probably talk to you."

"No, he can't. He's all jammed up. Look, I just want to help. I . . . She works here, Brenda?"

Felicia hesitated, looking off, left, right, left.

"She works here, right?" Jesse pushed gently.

Felicia shrugged, giving in. "Yeah. In the Study Club."

"The Study . . . What's that, after school?"

"Yeah, uh-huh."

"A teacher?"

"An aide."

"Works under you? With you?"

"Both." Felicia scratched her nose, stepped in place.

"You know her son?"

"Cody?"

Cody: Jesse saw it in print.

"Yeah, he'd come in but like, he was just a mascot or something because he's like, only four. The other kids—" Felicia's voice abruptly turned hoarse and she stalled. "The other kids," she started up again, her mouth trembling, "the other kids are like six, seven, eight. I hope they *get* that motherfucker, I swear to God."

Delicately she scooped a tear from under one eye with a crescent-shaped, inch-long artificial nail, and Jesse, staring at the cast of Felicia's face as the woman struggled to compose herself, involuntarily absorbed a history of bone-deep unhappiness—none of which, most likely, had to do with the boy Cody, or with his mother.

"Excuse my language," Felicia muttered, looking away.

"Hey, no, c'mon." Jesse quickly absolved her, then lost her: something back on Hurley Street had caught her eye. Jesse tracked Felicia's gaze to Brenda Martin's brother, the Gannon detective, who was getting all chesty with some of the tenants.

"That's her brother?" Jesse tried to pull Felicia back.

"Danny," Felicia announced, as if the name weighed a ton.

"You don't like him?"

"No, well, yeah, you know, he's got his job." Her voice was weary, grudgingly diplomatic. "And, like I tell the kids, stay out of Gannon 'cause those cops, they don't play, and if you pull anything cute over there they're gonna come back in here after you. But these kids, you can't tell them nothing. It's like they were born deaf or something."

"He seemed mad at her before, yelling in her face."

"That's not right."

"Why would he be mad at her?"

"Maybe he's upset."

Jesse nodded as if enlightened: the pull-quote of the month. "What was, was she working tonight?"

"No."

"So, what was . . ."

"She . . . We're just settin' up a new Study Club here, over in Five Building, and like, she said she had left something in there after we closed up and like, she had come back and got it and tried to drive on out through the park right here, back into Gannon, and got jacked. But see, I don't . . ." Felicia faltered, then shut down.

"What . . ." Jesse prodded, thinking, Drugs, boyfriends.

"No, I don't know."

"What." Jesse pushed gently again, but grinning while she did it— just two gossipy gals here.

"No." Felicia looked off.

"She go out with anybody here?"

"That's not my business," she said pointedly, going eye to eye.

"She looks a little dazed." Jesse meant stoned, smarting as she said it, as if apologizing in advance.

"Dazed?" Felicia smiled.

"You know," Jesse said, just tossing dynamite into the water now to see what came floating to the top.

"You don't have no kids, right?" Felicia asked.

Jesse shrugged, stung. "No."

"Dazed," Felicia muttered, shaking her head.

Jesse saw Lorenzo take Brenda by the arm and walk her toward the pocket park, the crime scene, and wanted to close this talk down now, get over there.

"So what do *you* think happened?" Jesse asked quickly.

"That's like you're sayin' to me she's lying, right?" Felicia ballooned up a little.

"No, I didn't mean . . . What I'm saying is—"

"She's a good person."

"Good." Jesse nodded, knowing Jose would change "good" to "be-loved"; all victims who were neighborhood fixtures or who worked within a mile of kids were automatically granted the appellation "beloved."

"I got to go see my mother." Felicia began to turn toward Three Building.

"What do you think about Hootie on this?" Jesse asked, passing her a business card.

"Who?"

"Hootie."

"Hootie?" She jerked back, twisting her mouth in derision, and began trudging through the heat toward Three Building.

Jesse took a minute to watch Felicia walk away, waiting for her to ostentatiously flip the business card in the grass before she got to the breezeway. She found herself slightly off balance when the woman finally disappeared inside the lobby, the card still in her possession.

Lorenzo held the neon-orange tape high so that Brenda could enter Martyrs Park, and Jesse, twenty yards away, watched them with the covetous eyes of a social climber—the tape a velvet rope, the pocket park a VIP room, the posted uniforms nothing more than armed bouncers.

The tape stretched straight across the Hurley Street face of the park from a garbage can positioned flush against the Conrail retaining wall to one of the concrete columns in the breezeway of Three Building. From there it made a right angle, extending back to the low rustic stone wall that trimmed the border with Gannon.

There was no way for her to slip in under the Hurley Street tape. Anxious, Jesse tried to peer through the far trees to see if the Gannon side was guarded too. It had to be, but she couldn't swear to it, couldn't make out any uniforms from where she was standing. So maybe, just maybe, if she cut out of Armstrong altogether, walked around to the Gannon side of the park, the Jessup Avenue entrance, she might be able to slip in through the back door. If she couldn't, she'd be screwed altogether, because she doubted she could reenter Armstrong like she had done the first time, but, but, but . . . she paced the rubble, clammy with desire, with indecision.

"Hey," someone said, male, low-key. Jesse turned to see a young cop sporting a Fu Manchu, a Hawaiian shirt, and high-top sneakers—an urban action figure strolling toward her from out of the shadows, something almost contemplative in his casual yet deliberate gait. Steady-eyed, he tilted his head in a beckoning gesture, Jesse thinking, Busted.

"You're a reporter, right?" He stood before her, his hands jammed in his rear pockets. "Right?"

"Yeah, but Lorenzo Council said—"

"Local, right? The *Register*?"

"Yeah."

Jesse tried to get a read on him as he rubbed the exhaustion from his eyes, both hands sweeping out along his cheekbones.

"It's like the invasion of the body snatchers," he said, waving a limp hand to take in the world. "You got half the Gannon job here, the New York press. It's like Ringling Brothers, Barnum and Bailey."

Jesse found herself easing into an alert openness. This guy wasn't about evicting her: he wanted something.

"I wish they'd put a fucking plug in the Holland Tunnel, you know what I mean?"

"I hear you," Jesse said, catching a glimpse of Lorenzo and Brenda Martin through the trees. "So you're Dempsy?" she asked lightly, as if they were at a bar.

"Same as you." He smiled at her, his eyes a cracked blue. He's hitting on me, Jesse thought, scrambling for how to play this.

"You trying to get a peek?" He nodded toward the park.

"Shit, yeah," she said, giving him a big smile.

"Well, let's face it, you can't, right?"

"You sure?" Jesse was going all coy, able to dry hump, if need be, with the best of them. The headlights of a Dempsy cruiser abruptly bleached them blind, then cut out, leaving both of them blinking away dots in the renewed darkness.

"It's nothing but a mud bowl anyhow." He shrugged. "It's . . . there's nothing to see, really. No body, no blood, no shell casings, nothing but mud and bullshit."

"OK." Jesse returned the shrug, hoping this guy felt he had to show her something, impress her. "Got any suggestions?"

"Suggestions?" he stared at her pensively. "You're Jesse Haus, right?"

"Yes, I am." Jesse stepped back, fighting off a hit of paranoia.

"I'm Mark Goldberg." He extended his hand. As she had expected, his grip firm and slightly lingering.

"So," she said, almost demandingly.

He cocked his head, as if knowing he had to produce here. "Come on."

He held out his arm to drape it around her shoulders but then started walking toward Three Building without touching her. Jesse followed at first, then walked abreast of him.

"They got me coming off a double tour. I'm so tired I couldn't bust a balloon."

"I hear you."

As they passed through the breezeway of Three, Jesse saw Felicia alone in the lobby. She was leaning against a greasy tiled wall looking lost and withdrawn, her head and shoulders framed in graffiti. Approaching the rim of the vast Bowl, Goldberg stepped aside for Jesse to go before him, as if they were walking through a door.

"Hey, Jesse?" He said her name with cautious delicacy. "I have to tell you, you wrote something about six months ago that I thought was very powerful."

"Oh yeah?" Jesse started liking him a little, liking his courtly tentativeness. But cops were so fucking nuts as a rule.

"You wrote about Efran Ortega's family, you know, after the funeral? *Very* powerful."

"Really." Jesse was wary of the compliment now, Ortega having been a grossly overweight drug dealer who died, possibly of a cocaine-abetted heart attack, while being arrested. One of the cops who had cuffed him was initially brought up on charges of using excessive force, then later cleared. The entire Latino community had taken to the streets for a week after the failure of the grand jury to indict.

Jesse hadn't really written the piece—just dumped the images and the gestures, the grief-stricken words and faces into the phone to Jose. As usual, she had been more hidden camera than writer.

"Honestly," Goldberg said, steering her through the people and the refrigerators as if the two of them were strolling through a boulder-strewn meadow. "You really gave the guy a human face."

"Thank you." Jesse wondered where they were headed.

"I mean, he was a cocaine dealer, a scumbag, had three violent priors, but whatever he had be*come,* he was not born that way, right?"

"Right."

"What's that, nature versus nurture? Heredity versus environment?" Goldberg stopped, arched his back, grimacing. From the far rise of the Bowl, Jesse gazed down to Martyrs Park and the Hurley Street block party, the scene reduced to shadowed movement and spears of light. She smelled the overpowering essence of fast-food fried chicken; below her, two young women were sharing a refrigerator crate and a bucket of takeout, the woman nearest her using a patch of dead grass as a hand towel.

"Hang on, my back is . . ." Goldberg rested his fingers lightly on her arm, and it felt good, his touch. Jesse felt jolted, abruptly reacquainted with the unnerving surge that could go through you from simple skin-to-skin contact.

"Anyways, Ortega. The guy's born a baby just like everybody else. Born into a family, born into a situation, hits the crossroads of life, he takes the path that his life, to date, has taught him. Correct?"

"Where we headed?" Jesse asked mildly.

"I mean, you cannot be what you don't know. You cannot *visualize* what you haven't ever *seen,* right?"

"Right." Jesse was watching some little kids, liberated from bed by the carjacking, taking diving rolls over the refrigerators, coming up giddy and wild-eyed.

"But whatever Ortega did in life, given the hand that was dealt him, he left behind people who honestly grieved for him. That you made very clear. I mean, the mother, the wife, the three kids . . . Like, whatever else he did in life, and whoever else he did it to, he loved and was loved in return, right?"

"OK." Jesse was restless now and vaguely alarmed that the emotional charge she had just experienced was already beginning to fade.

"I mean, what's worse? To die and throw an entire family into grief? Or to die and no one gives a shit."

From their height in the Bowl now, they were on eye level with the train tracks on the other side of Hurley Street. A satellite truck was driving along the gravel bed on the inside of the fence there, its antenna like an upthrust sword slicing the sky. Suddenly Jesse panicked. She turned to Goldberg, wondering if she could just tell him to fish or cut bait, demand to see what he had to swap, right here, right now. The news truck was making it hard for her to play games, stay flirty.

"C'mon." He winked at her, Jesse thinking, Who the fuck *winks* anymore? But as if reading her mind, he extended his hand in a promising manner, and so she continued to follow him up the Bowl toward the high end, the One Building–Two Building Gompers Street end of the houses.

"You know, the only thing I wish . . . The cop? The one they tried to indict for using that choke hold?"

"Incavaglia?"

"Yeah, Jimmy Incavaglia. You know, he was never formally charged. I mean, he was charged in the media, but departmental, Internal Affairs, grand jury totally cleared him. Except you read the paper, what did you read. You read, use of illegal choke hold. You read, six previous civilian complaints for excessive use of force."

Jesse nodded, thinking, Six.

"And like, if you continue to read, you know, like continue on page thirteen, you find out none of those complaints were substantiated. You read Ortega weighed two hundred and forty pounds, had cocaine in his system and chronic asthma, a *heart* condition, had, what I say? Three violent priors. But you turned on the TV, opened the paper, it was Incavaglia, choke hold. Choke hold, Incavaglia. Had his academy photo up there like a mug shot."

"But he was cleared, right?" Jesse said as he steered her in the direction of One Building. "I mean, you take the information as it comes in."

"No, no, no. Please." Goldberg held out his hand as if to fend her off. "Me, you, we're barely cogs in the machine, right?"

"Right." Jesse saw another news truck roll in along the train tracks. "Where we going, Mark?"

"No. Alls I'm saying is—and this is why I'm kind of glad to finally meet you—is, you did such a bang-up job on the, Ortega's family, you know, the aftermath, that just for balance it would have been very, what's the . . . informative to do a piece, just like that, no more, no less, on Incavaglia's family. What that incident did to them. You ever follow up on the Incavaglia end of things? I don't mean the—I mean, domestic."

"I would have liked to," Jesse said warily, something definitely not right here.

"No? OK. It's too late anyhow, but just for the hell of it, let me fill you in."

"OK," Jesse said, eyeing the blockade at the Gompers Street exit nearest to Gannon, people on either side of the slant-parked cruiser trying to get out, trying to get in.

"Anyways, Jimmy Incavaglia, up to the Ortega arrest, was five years AA, OK? Two days after the, the tragedy, you know—with the publicity, the demonstrations, the death threats—he's hitting the oil like making up for lost time, OK? And, like, today? He's basically a drunk. They got him on bullshit detail, you know, vouchering evidence, shit like that. And by the way, he's thirty-two years old, so we're not talking about some old geezer hanging on to the job with gin blossoms all over his nose. Thirty-*two*. So there's that."

Having completed their hike to the top of the Bowl, they entered the breezeway of One Building, usually more active than any of the breezeways at the bottom but almost deserted now, save for some cops running warrants. Jesse was desperate to blow.

"OK. His wife, Jeanette, she—they always had a rocky thing, I won't bullshit you, but now they're no more, they're not together. She couldn't take it. Jimmy and Jeanette, they're like me and you, born and bred Dempsy, still living here, so the whole family thing, they had no insulation. I mean, maybe if they lived down the shore like half the job does—you know, Toms River or somewheres—but the newspaper hits the street? They're right here, twenty-four, seven."

Jesse took a business card out of her jeans. "Do you want to talk about this tomorrow or something?"

"Come on." He took the card and began walking her along Gompers. "Just let me finish. So Jeanette, here's what else. She taught sixth grade at Thirty-one School. You know Thirty-one School? Rough, right?"

"Right."

"Anyways, half the kids, Dominican, Puerto Rican; other half, black. Now, these kids, they watch the TV, their parents read the paper. It's Mrs. Incavaglia's husband who did this. And they come into class, you know, staring at her, so she had to transfer out, which is a shame, because she liked it there and she was good. They needed her, plus, on top of that, you know, she's coming home to a drunk, going to sleep with a drunk, waking up with a drunk. And the kid, their kid—that's the worst of all. Eight, nine, goes to, *went* to Forty-four School, coming home every day bloody. The poor kid's fighting off half the fourth grade and Jimmy, what's he gonna do, go down to the schoolyard and straighten things out? He's a spic killer, right? It's in the paper—he can't. So they take the kid out, put him in Saint Mary's over in the Heights. Same shit, same shit. The kid looked like a punching bag. So now he goes to some Catholic school in Bergen County, spends two hours a day on a bus, his dad's not living at home anymore, his mom's all bent out of shape. And that's *their* follow-up profile. Scattered to the winds, each and every one of them."

They were approaching the blockade at the opposite end of Gompers, near Two Building, another slant-parked cruiser.

"I'm sorry to hear all this." Jesse was still on full alert, but she meant it, especially about the kid. Her own childhood had been marked by ostracism too.

"Well, it's nice of you to say." Goldberg came to a halt and painfully arched his back again. "You know, in all honesty, even before all this shit, Jimmy was, you know, at best a so-so cop. But given all the heartache that came out of this for him and his family? All the, the bullshit? It would have been more bearable, or more something, if he had only been indicted or if Internal Affairs had actually *found* something, but . . . It was the media. Well, shit." He took a seat on the hood of the Dempsy cruiser. "You probably hear this crap all the time."

"Hey, Mark?"

"Yeah."

"Where we going?"

"Where?" He shrugged. "We're here."

He turned to the Dempsy uniform posted by the car. "This is a closed crime scene, correct?"

The uniform stared at him for a beat, then nodded.

"You see this here?" He indicated Jesse as if she were inanimate. "This, is a fucking reporter. So do your goddamned job and kick her ass out."

He turned and left her there, just walked off, massaging his lower back while Jesse, white with rage, momentarily shook off the tentative herding touch of the young uniform and barked blood.

"*Six* civilian complaints? How many others didn't even bother to *file* . . ."

Without turning around, Goldberg flipped her a fadeaway bird, and then, unlike Felicia, he tossed her business card in the brown patchy scrub that, in Armstrong, was known as grass.

5

The tape strung across the Hurley Street face of Martyrs Park created a zone of relative peace, isolating the crime scene from the chaos by a good fifty feet, although the area surrounding the actual scene, a few yards off a paved footpath, had apparently been trampled into incoherence before the tape was in place. Lorenzo saw at least three sets of tire marks in the rain-softened earth and enough shoe prints to diagram a complicated dance routine.

The park itself wasn't much more than a ragged half acre of playground and natural scruff, the footpath separating a fenced-in grouping of swings, slides, and monkey bars from a miniwilderness of sneaker-hung, vine-throttled elm trees and a scatter of bushes.

For those who wished to shortcut their way across the city line on foot, the paved path led to a breach in a low stone wall that emptied out into Gannon, but the gap there was barely four feet wide. Those who needed to drive had to know to peel off the footpath about a third of the way in from Hurley, then slowly weave their way between the trees until they came to a second breach in the wall just wide enough for a sedan to squeeze its way through carefully. Most Gannon and Dempsy cops knew this shortcut into and out of Armstrong so well that they could exit and enter Martyrs without taking their feet from the accelerator.

Standing at the convergence of the footpath and the car trail,

Lorenzo scoured the trees, the benches, the skeletal skyline of the playground fixtures, wiping sweat from under his eyes with the heel of his hand. "OK, you be the car. You came from Five Building, right?" He flung a hand back behind him. "You drive in here from Hurley. Show me where you got off the path."

Brenda stood there blinking. "I can't tell."

Lorenzo looked directly through the park and over the low stone wall to the Gannon post across Jessup. The cop there stared back from inside his cruiser.

"I can't tell," she said again.

"OK." Lorenzo continued to eye the cruiser, which was posted beneath a fizzling streetlight in the shut-down mall. The cop was close enough for Lorenzo to see that he was drinking from a can of Mountain Dew—no way he wouldn't have seen a violent crime right here.

"OK, hold on. Can you show me where this guy came out from?"

As Brenda studied the lay of the land, Lorenzo surveyed those Lamb Pen windows in Three Building that so closely abutted the park that tenants could reach out and pluck leaves off some of the trees. Two of those windows were occupied—by Miss Dotson, leaning on her pillow-padded sill, smoking a cigarette and calmly meeting his gaze, and Mother Carver, outlined in silver blue by the TV playing behind her in the darkened room, staring blindly through her glasses out over the trees to the clapboard skyline of Gannon.

"Lorenzo, you come back and talk to me later. I got something to *tell* you," Miss Dotson said evenly, dropping her cigarette and closing her window. Directly below half the windows on that side of the building were individual mounds of cigarette butts, like half-smashed pyramids in the dusty earth.

"There," Brenda said, her voice throaty with discovery. "He came out there." She pointed out a tree. Lorenzo looked around the base of the trunk. Nothing.

"All right, and you stopped your car . . ."

"Like . . ." She took a step to the left, two steps to the right. "I don't know, I can't—"

Suddenly she darted forward, reaching for something, and Lorenzo reflexively grabbed the back of her shirt.

"My bag . . ."

"Just leave it."

It had been run over and lay there as if ironed to the ground, caked stiff with drying mud.

"OK, yeah. Now." Brenda's voice took on a trembling energy. "OK. I stopped, here."

Lorenzo pondered how to phrase what he wanted to say so as not to make her defensive. "Brenda, hold on." He waited until he had her eyes. "If I ask you a question please don't give me an answer because you think I want to hear it, OK? If I ask you something and you don't remember? Say, 'I don't remember,' OK? Don't ever be afraid to not know the answer or to tell me something other than what you *think* I want to hear, OK? Alls you got to do is say, 'I don't know. I don't remember.' " Lorenzo was overstating his point, nervous, trying to hold too many possibilities in his head at once.

She just stared at him.

"OK." Lorenzo settled himself. "You say the guy knocked you down, tore off before you could say anything, right?"

She continued to stare.

"OK, good. When you stepped out of the car, were you holding your bag?"

She hesitated, trying to read his eyes, then said, "No."

"No. OK. No. Now, where do you keep your bag when you're driving."

"I don't know. Next to me."

"On the passenger seat? On the floor?"

"On the passenger seat."

"OK. Let me ask you something else. It's hot tonight, right? Did you have your air conditioner on?"

"I don't know. Yes. I guess."

"That means your windows were probably up too, right?"

She didn't answer.

"OK. So you get out the car, the guy *pulls* you out, knocks you down, jumps in, tears out of here. Is that what you told me?"

She took a quick sip of air, held it, then cautiously nodded.

"Then how did your purse get out on the ground? The guy had to *see* the purse. If he saw the purse, no way he's just gonna flip it out the door. He's gonna look through it for money, credit cards, a wallet, and he's doing this in the dark, right? Then he's got to roll down the window or open the door to toss it, right? But that all takes *time,* you see what I'm saying?"

"What are you saying," she said, frightened. "That's my bag."

"No, no, no. What I'm saying is, maybe he was here longer than you think. You could've hit the ground *hard,* you know, like, dazed, and he could've been here for a while. Or maybe you were right! Maybe he drove right off. That's why I need you to tell me what you *truly* remember and if the answer is, 'I don't know,' say, 'I . . . don't . . . know.' "

Lorenzo sensed someone coming up behind him. He wheeled and faced the brother.

"The windows are up, they're down. Who gives a fuck," Danny Martin said, waving off the entire crime scene. "Fuck the bag. What the hell are you doing here, Council? If you're gonna work the hood, work the hood. What are you doing here?"

Lorenzo told himself he was dealing with the uncle. "Danny, hear me out. Maybe the guy did just drive off. Then he turns around, sees the kid in the backseat, panics, comes back here, dumps the kid off, and tosses out the bag. See what I'm saying? The kid might still *be* here."

Danny stared at him. Then, without a word, he turned and marched over to Bobby McDonald, who stood on the paved side of the tape, hands in pockets, squinting up at the trees as if attempting to count the number of pairs of sneakers thrown up there bolo-style and left to dangle like rubberized fruit.

"Bobby," Danny began imploringly, Lorenzo watching, listening. "Don't do this to me." Blindly Danny swung an arm back and gestured to Lorenzo, who did a quick about-face. "Bobby, this is my flesh and blood. Please. I don't deserve this."

Lorenzo felt panic creep like a cream back from his forehead, across his scalp, and down to the nape of his neck. He raised his eyes to Brenda, who, miserable, was cringing in apology. "I'm so sorry," she said.

"Danny, look, I know where you're coming from," Bobby answered calmly. "But the fact of the matter is, you got it ass backwards, kid. You just caught yourself a major break here. Lorenzo's the big dog in these houses, don't you know that? For my money, you can pull out all your people and I'll pull out most of mine. Just let the man work—we're gonna have this wrapped in no time. Think about it."

Lorenzo heard everything without turning back to the voices. Danny's blatant contempt followed by Bobby's serene pitch gave him a brand-new head on this: My houses, my catch, The End.

"Brenda." He coughed, choking a little. "You see that patrol car over there?" he said, pointing out the Gannon cruiser on post. "You know about the Watch?"

"Yeah, of course."

"You didn't think to go to him?"

"Look. I hit the ground, I got up, I hit the ground again, the car peeled out, I'm in the hospital."

"The guy dropped the kid off?" Danny's voice came up again behind Lorenzo, who slowly smoothed his brow: Easy, easy.

"OK, good," Danny said with heat. "Then where is he? Who's got him? Somebody'd of brought him out by now, right? No. *Bull*shit. This bird's on the fly and he ain't comin' back. But I'm gonna tell you something. Wherever the fuck he's gone to? If it happened here, the answer's here. And we're not leaving this place until somebody gives it up. Now, you might be king of the jungle and whatnot, but what *I* want to know is, are you gonna work the hood? Or just protect it . . ."

When Lorenzo finally turned to face him, the sight over Danny's left shoulder drained him of all anger. Out of a second-floor window of Four Building, Tariq Wilkins was dangling from a thin white cord, spinning and screaming. Lorenzo was able to see it was Tariq even from the park, because the headlights isolated and illuminated him like a solo trapeze artist in a darkened big top. People were yelling up to him and rushing under as if to catch him, but when the cord finally broke, when the truth of his weight started coming at them, they retreated. Tariq landed with a flat *whap* on the asphalt and was instantly swallowed from sight as everybody rushed back in. And once again, Brenda Martin was left alone.

When Lorenzo finally bulled his way through to the clearing, he came up on Tariq lying under a tangle of extension cords with bizarrely twisted prongs, writhing like a snake and fighting off the medics who were attempting to Velcro him into a padded head brace and body board. The crowd around him had formed a perfect circle.

"He's moving pretty good," some cop said quietly.

"Lorenzo, they threw him out the window?" one of the youngest kids asked, open-mouthed.

Lorenzo scanned faces for an answer. A Gannon narco stepped up. "We had paper on him. Kid tried to pull a Monte Cristo. We never got past the front door."

"Lorenzo, they threw him out the window?" the same kid asked again.

"Didn't you hear what he said?" Lorenzo yelled, pointing up to the open window. "He fell his own self!"

A few of the kids stepped back, looking at him like Fuck You Too.

Furious, Lorenzo suddenly remembered Brenda—what the hell did he do with her? Looking around wildly, he spotted her by one of the cars, a hand over her mouth, sobbing, "I'm sorry! I'm sorry!" Bump Rosen was awkwardly patting her back and trying to spot Lorenzo. Halfway to his charge, Lorenzo saw Bobby McDonald on a cell phone and made a quick, desperate detour.

"Bobby, you get them out of here *now* or we're gonna have us a riot."

"Hey!" Bobby put a hand over the mouthpiece. "I got the prosecutor on the line as we speak. Meanwhile, you get her down to BCI and looking at some trays or I swear, Lorenzo, I'm handing this over to somebody else."

Sobered by Bobby's rarely seen anger, Lorenzo turned to retrieve Brenda as Tariq was transported to the ambulance, someone saying broken leg.

There seemed to be no sealed-off area anymore. Everyone was milling around, the kids agitated, the cops agitated, Danny Martin pacing back and forth in his flip-flops, a news van rolling up to the blockade, Brenda chanting, "I'm sorry, I'm sorry," making eye contact with anyone who would have her. Lorenzo reached around to get at the tickling stream of sweat rolling down his spine. Yes, it was time to go.

As Lorenzo moved to Brenda, one of the teenagers in a *Top Cop* cap—a kid whose tag was Teacher, a kid who Lorenzo knew had seen Danny Martin in these houses week after week over the years, a kid who most likely had had dozens of slapstick exchanges with Danny when Danny was around looking for people—called out to him now in that same smart-mouthed bantering style: "Yo, Danny, that guy you looking for? With all you Gannon niggers over here? He's probably over *there,* tearin' hisself off some Gannon pussy." The kid was relaxed, beaming, his friends sniggering and hissing, the older residents giving the kid dirty looks, but nobody, including Lorenzo, expecting what happened next. Danny pivoted smoothly and caught Teacher with an uppercut that made a tooth arc out between split lips, high and graceful, like a dolphin. The kid hit the ground in shock but instantly sat up, feeling the grass around him for his *Top Cop* cap, which had somehow managed to stay on his head.

A silence came over the scene, Danny looking as stunned as everybody else. He opened his mouth to say something, but Lorenzo knew he wouldn't say shit, prayed he wouldn't say shit, because apologies only doubled the damage, gave people license to rage. Danny just ground his palms together, took a deep breath, and briskly walked away—the best thing. Lorenzo hoped that, when the blood connection between him and the missing child became common knowledge, people would cut him some slack around here, not for Danny Martin's sake but for their own. Lorenzo watched Danny stride out past the blocked entrance, get into a Gannon sedan, and drive away.

Leo Sullivan, the older Gannon detective, caught Lorenzo's eye and gave him a quick, tight-lipped shrug of apology. Lorenzo ignored the communication, taking Brenda from Bump. As he escorted her to his car, he quietly hooked up with some of his informants, contact coming through tilted chins, quickly dropped eyes, flappy hand jive down low at the pockets. Lorenzo set up three, maybe four meets this way: in apartments, on roofs, behind the 7-Eleven, and maybe at a craps house. He roughed out the rest of his night, straight through to breakfast, at which point he would know more or less how everybody took their coffee, what brand of cigarette they smoked, whom to play the us-versus-them card with, whom to Praise Jesus with. Gannon would be getting *none* of it, Lorenzo muttered to himself as he fumbled with the keys to the Crown Victoria—jokers coming in here doing the rockabilly shuffle like this, playing hard ball when there was no reason to, turning all his carefully cultivated goodwill to trash, fucking with the fine-tuned information palace he had created out of these houses.

"I wish, I wish I could be *born* again," Brenda, white-mouthed and dewy-eyed, whispered again with ardor, scooped over herself in the passenger seat as the car climbed onto the New Jersey Turnpike.

"You what?" Lorenzo responded, reaching for the hand radio. "South Investigator 15 to base. Leaving Hurley Street, Dempsy, with victim, heading to BCI. Mileage at 32001." Lorenzo documented every second alone with her, doing it by the book.

"Base to South 15. The time is 00:45."

"You wish what?" he repeated, eyeing two more satellite trucks heading for the projects.

"I wish I could be born again."

"You religious?"

"No, no, I just want—I feel like I know something now." Her eyes were shut lightly, her voice still holding that passionate note of conviction. "I understand something now, and I wish I could just start over."

"What do you understand?" Lorenzo turned off after one exit, seeing that tooth arc out between split lips again.

"I just feel . . . I just want . . . I just wish I could have one more chance. Just . . ."

Lorenzo could see her eyes moving beneath the fragile membrane of her lids. He tossed thirty-five cents into the toll bucket, thinking he'd give a week's paycheck to see the movie that was now playing behind those pink, papery screens.

"Tell me about the guy again. Maybe you'll remember something else."

Brenda wiped a slick of tears trickling down the side of her nose with a trembling finger, produced her packet of codeine tablets from the back pocket of her jeans, and attempted to shake one into her mouth.

Without taking his eyes from the road, Lorenzo reached across and liberated the envelope from her padded hands. Brenda gave it up without a struggle.

"Tell me about the guy," Lorenzo asked again. He could hear a tablet rolling up against her teeth.

"I'm so tired," she finally said in a defeated whisper.

Lorenzo fretted about trying to read her with drugs thrown into the mix. Then he wandered off, back to Danny Martin whacking Teacher. Teacher's mother, Frieda, was a bigmouth on the tenants council, and Lorenzo envisioned all kinds of half-assed demonstrations and lawsuits coming down the pike.

"Brenda, how many of those painkillers you take tonight?"

"What's the difference," she said, looking out the window.

"Base to South 15."

Lorenzo picked up the radio.

"Fifteen. Go."

"Pick up 13 on 6."

He switched to Channel 6.

"Bump?"

"We might got a sighting there, Lorenzo."

Lorenzo tensed, not wanting her to hear that, to get her hopes up if it didn't pan out.

"Where at?"

"Sea Girt."

"Long way."

"Not if you're jettin'."

"Sketch artist coming in?"

"He'll meet you there."

"Who."

"Pierre Farrel."

"Bang me at BCI, OK?"

" 'Kay, boss."

Lorenzo glanced over at Brenda, forming a disclaimer in his mind in case the sighting was bogus, but she was off in her thoughts and hadn't heard a word of the conversation.

As they approached the Bureau of Criminal Identification, housed below a municipal garage, Lorenzo scanned the block for press. The quiet side street was soaked in the inky shadows of ancient oak trees.

"SI 15 to base."

"Base. Go."

"South 15 off at BCI with female vic. Mileage at 32008."

"OK, there, South 15, time is 01:00."

"My brother said to me last year, 'You work in those houses long enough something bad is going to happen. And when it does it's going to be your own goddamn fault, because you know what I'm saying is true.' "

Lorenzo stepped out of the car, walked around, and opened her door. She sat there blindly, chewing over what her brother had said, then abruptly looked up at Lorenzo.

"He's so angry, Danny. Even when we were little."

"Hey, Brenda!" As soon as she cleared the car, the voice—inviting, full of good news—turned her toward the shadowed pavement, but it was a verbal sucker punch and she found herself abruptly peppered with camera flashes. Instinctively raising her padded hands to hide her face, she sank into a protective crouch, looking like a boxer weathering an offensive on the ropes. Lorenzo came around the car and lumbered toward the shooter. The guy stood his ground, documenting Lorenzo's sullen approach with pop and flash, until Lorenzo realized it was a no-win situation and reluctantly turned away.

Guiding Brenda through the municipal garage, a silent confusion of police cruisers, parks department vans, and sanitation trucks, Lorenzo led her to the worn wood stairs that descended to BCI. It was an arraignment center and criminal-records repository so untouched by time and science that it had been used as a set for a movie about 1920s bootleggers. The tired joke ever since was, "Yeah, the director said BCI was perfect; all he had to do was get his designer to upgrade the office equipment and he'd be ready to roll."

At the foot of the stairs they entered the reception area, flanked on one side by a heavy wooden bench and the other by a holding cell. In front of them was a waist-high wainscoted barrier, behind lay a vast and gloomy room of old wooden desks and metal file cabinets. An expressionless young black woman sat on the paint-thick bench waiting for someone or something and absently bouncing an infant on her crossed knee. Brenda smiled crookedly at the baby. Lost in her own troubles, the mother ignored her.

"Yo, Big Daddy," a middle-aged man in a blood-splattered Pepsi-Cola delivery jacket called out from behind the bars of the holding cell. "That's that lady, right?"

Lorenzo smiled reproachfully. "There you go again," he said.

"Yo, Miss," the prisoner called out. "You in good hands with the brother here."

Lorenzo steered her into a side room and sat her down at a Formica table topped with a coffin-shaped bank of battered army-green file cabinets. Other than a massive brass scale that had been weighing prisoners since the nineteenth century, the only things of interest in the low-ceilinged room were framed headlines and news photos of notable police actions. The clippings ranged from the Standard Oil strike of 1913 to the busting of a Black Panther arms cache in 1969. A full third of the present police force in Dempsy were descendants of the men on the wall.

"Now, Brenda." Lorenzo rested a possessive hand on top of the files. "What we got in here is all the bad guys, everybody who ever crossed the line in the last twenty-five years."

"Everybody who got caught," she murmured, slumping.

"Well, I'm telling you, there's a damn good chance that your guy is right in this box somewheres, OK?"

"I just want to lay down," she said softly, listing to the left.

"I hear you," he said, furtively tossing the confiscated painkillers behind him, into a wastebasket by the scale.

"I feel sick."

"I know."

"I don't think he's in there."

"Well, even money says he is. You want some coffee?"

She shook her head no, rested her forehead on the steel-trimmed edge of the table.

"How tall was he?" Lorenzo asked, knowing what she had said but wanting to hear if she would stick to her original estimation.

"I don't know. Six feet? I don't know."

Lorenzo extracted a long thin drawer from the cabinet, the 5'10" black tray, height being the only criterion for sorting the actors other than race. He placed the file in front of her, but she wouldn't raise her head from the table. After a full half minute, he picked up the tray and returned it to its slot.

"Brenda." He spoke to the back of her head. "You know, some people, they say the rap on me is that I'm lazy, you know, like, I only put out on something if it kind of tickles my fancy or there's, like, something that hits me where I live. Now, I don't think that's true of myself, but I'll tell you something about me that people might, misinterpret as, as laziness on my part. I know that I'm only as good as the people I'm working for. The, the injured parties, the survivors, you know what I'm saying? It's like, if they kind of start going south on me? You know, like, losing interest?"

"Losing interest?" Brenda said, rising up on that like Lorenzo had hoped.

Lorenzo leaned down close and splayed a massive hand against his own chest.

"Brenda," he said softly. "He ain't my child. You *want* me white-hot on this?" He reached for the 5'10" photo tray again, jerked it out, and dropped it before her with a bang. "You *get* me white-hot on this."

The photos were secured through their bases by a rod that ran the length of the metal box. They lay face down, staggered like straight-fanned playing cards, and Brenda started flipping them up one by one. Lorenzo sat on an empty desk behind her, tracking her pace to see if she was really working the faces or just going through the motions.

He was also primed for her reaction to a hit—the truth of it would come from her body. In his experience, when a woman found the actor, she would invariably gasp and jerk back in her chair as if yanked from behind. A man, on the other hand, tended to shoot to his feet, bang the desk with the side of his fist, and point at the guy staring up at him from the tray. There was no science to this gender distinction: it just was what it was.

If anything, Brenda was going too slowly, poring over each face as if studying a map. When she finally finished the tray, he pulled out four more for her, from 5'11" to 6'2". A wall phone that hung by the door rang with a subdued trill.

"Yeah, what's up."

"Sea Girt was a bust," Bump said.

"Yeah, I thought it was too good to be true. What's going on?"

"It's still kind of agitated, but we're leveling out a little. We got something like six news trucks setting up over by the tracks. The prosecutor's gonna do a press conference. How she holding up?"

"He's dead," Brenda suddenly said, and Lorenzo put the phone to his chest, staring at her.

She held a mug shot upright in the tray. "Cornell McCarthy. He died last week. His son is in the Study Club over in Jefferson."

Lorenzo slowly raised the receiver to his face again. "What else."

"What else?" Bump said. "I got a call from my brother-in-law over in New York? He manages the Avis outlet up the block from the *Daily News,* right? He said they just rented out everything in the barn."

"Whoa."

"Yeah, whoa, exactly. So I think we should stick to the phones, keep off the radio, 'cause God knows who's gonna be listening in."

"I hear you. How's Bobby doing?"

"He's a little goofy but he's handling it."

"He ain't checked in with me once on this."

"Yeah, well, basically—I just talked to him—all he wants to know right now is if you're getting along with her."

Lorenzo thought about that, what it meant. "Yeah, we're doing fine." He concluded that Bobby wasn't sold on this as an Armstrong crime either.

"Bobby says bang him if you need him."

"Sounds good." Lorenzo eyed Brenda, wondering what she was thinking right now as she hunched over the trays, whom she was looking for.

There was a light knock at the door, and Lorenzo opened it a crack, expecting a reporter. "Bump, I got to go." He hung up and opened the door just wide enough for the sketch artist, Pierre Farrel, to slip in.

"There he is." Lorenzo smiled at the artist, speaking in a whisper so as not to distract Brenda. He was a slender, bearded black man, a retired New York detective in his early forties. Carrying his sketch box in a black gloved hand, he came across somewhere between a roughneck and a bohemian—khaki shorts, construction boots, a large gold hoop earring in his left ear, long-sleeved flannel shirt over a T-shirt emblazoned with the United Way logo. Lorenzo appreciated the T-shirt, a nice touch to relax the victim, reassure her that the black man working the sketch was a bona fide human being.

"How you been, boss?"

"Good," Pierre murmured, studying Brenda's curved back. "I got into this art school over in New York? I start going nights next month."

"There you go." Lorenzo smiled automatically, as he always did at the mention of education.

"What's it like out there?"

"Stay in here," Pierre said. "That's what it's like out there."

Brenda was flipping the faces at a faster pace now, starting to show signs of burning out, having looked at over a hundred mug shots. Seventy-five faces was usually the limit for crisp study.

Pierre and Lorenzo sat in patient silence on the desk behind Brenda until she flipped the last photo in the 6′2″ tray and abruptly dropped her head between her knees, her hands aloft in a gesture of surrender.

"Brenda." Lorenzo spoke her name softly. She raised her head slowly and turned to them, her eyes focusing on the black leather glove that rested atop the sketch case in Pierre's lap. "Brenda, this here is Pierre Farrel."

"Hey, Brenda," Pierre said gently, his own eyes unconsciously following hers to the glove.

"Pierre's gonna make us a sketch, OK? How you doing, you OK?"

Brenda dropped her head again and reached back over her shoulders to knead the back of her neck but couldn't because of her bandages. Lorenzo had to resist the impulse to do it for her.

Pierre took a chair and sat about five feet away from her. "Before we start, all right? I just want to tell you I'm gonna do the best job I can, all right?" His voice was soothing and confident. "I got three kids of my own and I kind of feel like any kid out there could be mine, you understand what I'm saying?"

Brenda looked off, her face gathering into a frown. Lorenzo felt her start to go down again.

"Now." Pierre popped open the case with his ungloved hand, took out a tray of more mug shots, a visual catalog of facial features for her to choose from. "This here is going to take a few hours. We're gonna do this together, and we're gonna do this right."

Brenda took in the glove again.

"Now, when we get down to it? When I start drawing? I'm gonna want you over my shoulder, backseat driving me every step of the way, OK? I'm gonna want you to be the world's toughest art critic, all right? You don't like what I'm drawing? You don't think I'm interpreting your,

your words right? I want you to let me *have* it, I want you to give me *hell*."

Brenda started rocking on the edge of her chair. Pierre turned and exchanged a quick look with Lorenzo, who was still seated behind her—Lorenzo thinking, Here it comes.

"You're the brain, Brenda," Pierre said, grinning. "I'm just the hand." He rapped his black leather glove on the side of the table, the room filling with the hollow tock of wood on wood. Brenda sat up in surprise.

"And what a hand it is." Pierre was beaming at her now, holding up his prosthetic limb in triumph. "Funny thing is, when I had my real hand? I couldn't draw worth a damn." Brenda held up her own bandaged mitts and attempted a weak smile, a slight emotional rebound in the gesture. Pierre laughed like it was a damn fine sight gag, the two of them here together, Lorenzo down and out loving this man now.

"Tell me something about the bad guy, just talking now." Pierre began laying out his supplies on the desk, including his own fluorescent work light.

"He, he came on friendly, not stupid." Her voice was cracked and dry, as if from disuse.

"Good. All right. What else."

"He sounded, educated. No . . . More like, intelligent. *Kind.*"

"Good. How much time did you spend with the guy?"

"A lifetime."

"I hear you. How was the lighting?"

"Dark."

"OK, now. If I were to ask you to describe him to me, right off the top of your head what would—"

"His eyes," she said, cutting him off.

Lorenzo liked that, her going for a small feature first rather than a big descriptive overview. Through the years, he had found that most vics experienced the violence done to them as a visually fragmented event. In sit-downs of this nature, the actor's eyes usually emerged first from the nightmare haze of memory.

"His eyes. Good. What about them?"

Lorenzo hung in, waiting for just one more honest reaction.

She worked her mouth a bit before answering.

"They were scared."

And there it was. Lorenzo liked that, too, her description in the realm of emotion as opposed to the more detached and objective adjectives of color or shape. Cautiously he rose to his feet, like a parent trying to duck out of the bedroom of a half-asleep child. "Brenda." Lorenzo dropped to a bobbing squat before her, speaking up into her eyes much as the two uniforms back in the hospital had done. "Do you think I could leave you here with Pierre? I feel I can do us more good back at Armstrong right now."

"Yeah?" Pierre nodded encouragingly at her.

Brenda slowly raised a bandaged hand to the side of her head but said nothing.

"We're gonna be *great,* man." Pierre nodded to Lorenzo, waving him out, then jamming a pencil between the thumb and index finger of his gloved hand. "We're gonna do it righteous."

6

As her brother swerved into the turnpike exit for Armstrong, Jesse could see the electronic campfire a quarter of a mile away, an Islamic skyline of hot-lit discs and spires. The sight filled her with a clamorous sense of desperation.

Since she had gotten the boot from the houses earlier in the evening, there had been a fire in Gannon, a drug bust in Rydell, and an arrest in that double shooting right here in D-Town. The catching detective, Cippolino, had had to page her twice before she got around to taking down the tale over the phone: Tiger's real name was Reginald Williams. He was neither the baby's father nor the old lady's son. Both of the victims would survive.

Jesse wanted Armstrong. She wanted Brenda Martin.

The press, kept out of the Hurley Street cul-de-sac by the blockade, had set up their visual base camp in the wide gravel bed between the train tracks and thr razor-topped fence. From there they looked down on the crime scene and had a panoramic backdrop of urban misery for their on-site reports.

Ben rolled up close enough to the media village for Jesse to see that the first press conference was under way, with Peter Capra, the Dempsy County prosecutor, searingly lit as he addressed a dense wedge of photographers and reporters.

Having no interest in the straight show, Jesse had her brother drop her off two blocks from Armstrong. But as she approached the Hurley Street blockade again, hood up, an older Gannon detective, leaning against the trunk of a dope car, seemingly engrossed in eating sunflower seeds, murmured, "Don't even think it." His eyes never rose from his bag, and bristling with agitation, Jesse wound up walking back to the presser to watch the prosecutor. Flanked by various police reps, he was digging holes in the gravel bed with the toe of his loafers as he fielded the half-hostile, half-timid questions lobbed at him from within the wedge.

"Could you comment on a report that a suspect has been thrown from a fourth-floor—"

"Absolutely untrue." Capra cut off the reporter, who straight-armed her microphone and stared at him with rigid intensity. "It's my under-standing," he went on, "that an individual earlier in the evening was injured climbing out of an apartment window for whatever reason, but there were no police present *in* that individual's apartment at that time, nor did that individual have any contact with the police at any other time in the evening, and I would like to think that all you assembled here could appreciate the inflammatory potential in rumors of this nature. Next question."

Jesse, wanting in, tuned out. Looking toward the houses, she saw that the fence that separated the press conference from Armstrong was hung with cable cords, camera bags, and battery packs. The shooters kept one eye on Capra and one on the projects kids who were beginning to climb the retaining wall on the other side of the fence to get a better view of the action.

As the first wave of kids reached the fence, a few of the reporters, dissatisfied with the official information and the numbness of their own questions, started airmailing their business cards through the mesh. Jesse recognized in their energy-intoxicated faces the manic yet focused effort to sort out bit players from stars in this spontaneous production, which might run anywhere from a few hours to a number of weeks.

The Armstrong kids, giddy with the disorientation of seeing night lit like day, of seeing well-known TV faces come in for a landing in their own backyard, began bellowing in all directions, some through the fence toward the press conference, others toward the houses, calling out to friends up in their apartment windows or still leapfrogging refrigerators back in the Bowl. The more agitated ones chugged tirelessly up and down the sloped wall, time after time, to haul new people to the growing mob. The kids waved, tossed up peace signs and gang signs, the latter most likely learned from music videos, raised unity fists, and in general created such tumult that some of the assembled press started yelling back at them to chill the fuck out.

Jesse noticed that some of the quieter kids were doing something else, stealthily snaking fingers and hands through the mesh to touch the electronic accessories hanging there—not to boost them, she intuited, but to achieve some kind of physical contact with the Power.

One of the restless reporters, the thin, stubble-headed prowler she had witnessed earlier, scamming his way in through the blockade, now paced the fence, flipping business cards to the kids like a magician working a crowd. "Who's the big dog around here, who's gonna be my pipeline," the guy growled in a thick, vaguely European accent.

"Yo! You want the inside story?" a chubby twelve-year-old called through the fence. "I got mouths to feed. How much you paying?"

"How much you know?" the reporter shot back. "Who wants to be famous. Who wants the girls," he added, making all the boys bark and the girls emit high-pitched sizzling noises behind their hands.

Jesse had seen this phenomenon before, thought of it as stage 1— the locals high on the novelty and the drama. But she also knew about stage 2, due in about thirty-six hours, when the residents would become irritated by the distortions and misrepresentations coming into their living rooms off the TV, would grow jealous of the airtime given to their bigmouthed neighbors, and feel both bored and betrayed by the suddenly unwanted visitors. That is, unless somebody started making it worth their while in a more private and remunerative way.

Unlike the source-starved reporters, the shooters were less than happy to see all the kids clinging to the fence. One video fullback, having panned the assembled rug rats for a few seconds of B-roll, went so far as to poke a finger through the mesh and point at the biggest of the kids, saying, "I see you even *think* about touching this bag? I'll make you an orphan."

Gradually, some of the Dempsy cops began crawling up the retaining wall from Hurley Street, appearing behind the kids and attempting to bring them back down to the houses. No one wanted to leave, a few clinging to the mesh until their fingers were gingerly pried away. The cops tried to maintain a light mood, not wanting to attract the cameras. As Jesse witnessed some of the childish struggles to stay and watch the show, for a queasy moment she saw the fence not as part of Conrail's safety system but as the outer perimeter of a zoo, a refugee center, some kind of secured containment zone, and the vision gave her pause. It pulled her out of herself, provoked in her the impulse to actually write something in her own words, but then the moment passed, replaced with a renewed sense of panic: she had to get something going here, had to figure out some kind of end run that would separate her from the mob.

She played briefly with the idea of working the kid who had fallen from the window, but it was too much of a sidebar. So she scanned the scene for back-door players. Facing the cameras along with the prosecutor were Ernie Hohner, the Dempsy chief of police—nothing there— Bobby McDonald, another cigar-store Indian; and the Gannon chief, John Mahler, whom she just didn't know.

The only one projecting any kind of left-field accessibility was Chuck Rosen—Bump—burly, bespectacled, completely out of visual sync with the lawyers and the chiefs; Bump, in his baggy jeans and Knicks cap, restlessly shuffling in place as if desperate to get back down in the trenches. Jesse watched him, thinking, Same here, boss. His frustrated two-step came to an end only when Mahler, the Gannon chief, whispered a few words in his ear, then offered his hand. Both men broke out into big grins.

Jesse was thrown by the warmth of the exchange, the inappropriate air of congratulation, but as soon as Mahler returned his attention to the press, Bump was back doing the Squirm. They had never really met, Jesse and Bump, but she assumed that he knew of her in much the way that she knew of him; both their names were part of the urban back-buzz, minor lights in the crime-and-punishment Milky Way. And then there was her world-famous profile of his partner. Jesse wondered if this guy could be enticed by a companion piece on himself or maybe by something on Bump and Lorenzo together: Mutt and Jeff, Ebony and Ivory. Lorenzo had called him the second-best public-housing-based cop in the city, Jesse knowing a little bit of his story, although she couldn't be sure what was apocrypha and what was gospel.

The way it was told, eight or nine years earlier, Bump, at that time a city detective on loan to the Dempsy County gambling squad, had shot and killed an Armstrong teenager who had drawn down on him with an old Daisy air rifle in a darkened hallway of Four Building. Although cleared of wrongful-death charges by both the police department and the prosecutor's office, he had taken a six-month leave of absence, then returned to the job, cashing in some favors to be reassigned to Housing and specifically requesting a posting in Armstrong. Ever since, he had been putting in sixty hours a week busting jugglers, breaking up domestics, organizing midnight basketball tournaments, track meets, self-esteem workshops, and basically refusing to leave the scene of the crime.

As Jesse watched him spin out in the gravel behind the prosecutor, she could taste how bad he wanted to get back down in the houses, work the hallways, knock on doors. But then it happened again. This time Hohner, the Dempsy chief, grabbed him by the bicep, pulling him close to whisper in his ear, the murmured words producing huge grins and a warm handshake. Jesse started going nuts, feeling like she knew what it was all about, *should* know, but was unable to achieve the mental stillness required to pull the information up out of the files right now.

"Is the mother a suspect?"

"No." Capra seemed angry at the question.

"You mean not at this time?"

"I mean, *no.*"

And again: this time Bobby McDonald was shaking Bump's hand, patting his back, and Bump was beaming, bobbing his head in gracious acknowledgment. Finally it came to her, what this handshake business was all about. Jesse felt hope like a thump in her chest, and withdrawing from both the speakers and the mob, she began to work out her play.

"**Congratulations,**" Jesse called to Bump twenty minutes later, catching him on the tracks as he walked away from a quick postpresser summit meeting with McDonald and Hohner.

"Thank you," he said tentatively, squinting, sizing her up.

"You must be very proud." Jesse kept her distance, struggling to purge the desperation from her voice.

"Ho." Bump tilted his chin to the stars. "You don't know." He was shorter than she was, but his chest seemed a yard deep and his forearms had the thickness of softball bats.

"Do you know who I am?" Jesse wanted to get that out sooner rather than later.

"Yeah." He shrugged, starting to walk away. "You're a reporter." The tracks were littered with reporters, some chasing the prosecutor and the chiefs, some trying to interview what few kids remained by the fence.

"I wrote that piece on Lorenzo Council for the *Register,*" she said, hoping to slow him down.

"Yeah, I know who you are." Bump kept walking as Jesse paced him on the other side of the tracks.

"I want to do a piece on your son." *That* slowed him down. Suddenly

Jesse was terrified that some of the mob would come over, try to make it a group thing, or change the subject, or do something that would drive him away.

"You mean you came here tonight to tell me you want to do a piece on my son?"

"Of course not. I'm just saying. You know, hey, local kid, national TV show. You know, c'mon. This city's not exactly a hotbed of talent. It's news. It's something good for a change, don't you think?" Jesse said all this knowing a piece on the boy was already in the hopper, the arts editor, lord and master of exactly one page, was supposed to have reached out to interview the kid already, but Jesse was betting that the lazy, fat-assed bastard hadn't bothered to set things in motion as yet.

"You really want to do a piece on him, or you just want me all soft-ened up for a connect." A reporter approached, but before he could open his mouth, Bump, without taking his eyes from Jesse's face, held up a hand and said, "No comment." Jesse's knees trembled with joy.

"I want both," she said.

Bump nodded, exhaled in a huff, vigorously scratched his neck. "'Cause I tell you. Terry, my boy . . . You don't know. His story is *ten* times more than whatever you can imagine."

"Yeah?" Jesse forced herself to relax, bracing for the possibility of a long, clock-eating narrative, telling herself it would be worth it, telling herself again.

"You see *Law and Order* tonight?"

"I'm working." She shrugged regretfully.

"I'll get you a tape."

Jesse felt joyous over this comment too.

"Because Terry . . ." Bump looked off, eyes shining. "You know about Tourette's?"

"The—That's when you curse? Can't help cursing?"

"Well, yeah, but that's, like, only one possibility. That's, like, the high end of the scale. You can have that or other, you know, verbalities. You can have physicalities. You know—head twitches, body twists, fa-cial. Well, Terry . . ." Bump looked off again. "He's got, he's got both, physical, verbal. He's twelve now and he developed it when he was in, what, first grade? Started out like a neck jerk, didn't go away, went away, came back, went away again. Then, like, all of a sudden he started stick-ing his tongue out, maybe three, four times a minute. Took him to a neurologist, said it could be Tourette's, wouldn't swear to it, but we knew, and you know, with kids, a lot of them grow out of it, so we're kind of hoping maybe when he's, like, sixteen, seventeen, we're *praying*, but—" Bump stopped, collected himself. Jesse dreaded the rest of this story, assuring herself that it had a happy ending. The activity on the tracks around her was fading a little. "And like, when he was in fourth grade? The verbal thing started happening. Not cursing—he'd just make noises, barks, squawks, whatever, and you know how kids are."

"Yes, I do." Jesse said soberly, thinking this guy was going to owe her big time after submitting her to this.

"And the thing, the bitch of it, is that it travels. It's in your neck, it's in your jaw, it's in your shoulder. It just kind of visits a spot, then moves on. But I'll tell you, the worst, the tic that . . . Last year? In fifth grade? He got this thing where he had to drop to his knees every minute or so. He'd cross a room and drop to his knees two, three times before he got to the other side. I had him wearing knee pads for a while, but he told us if he had padding down there he couldn't feel the contact. He needed to feel the contact, so . . . Anyways, thank God that passed. And we tried different medications, had him on, like, a blood-pressure pill, a pill that lowers blood pressure? And it helped for a while, but he kind of grew out of it. We try different things. Some help, some, you know . . . And we network with other families, so—"

Jesse made an involuntary noise, a loud sigh. Bump hesitated, as if not sure whether it was a signal of impatience or empathy. Jesse had to say "Please," egging him on.

"So," he continued. "But the worst moment for us? In fourth grade after he developed the verbal thing? They came to us, said, 'He can't be in the school anymore. We know he can't help it, but it's just too disruptive to the class.' They said—" Bump clenched his teeth, blinked away rage. Another reporter approached, read his face, and stepped off without a word. "They said, 'It's not *fair* to the other students.' " He made a raw, throat-clearing noise, an alternative, Jesse knew, to other, more embarrassing articulations.

"But let me tell you something about this kid. He's like a car that sputters and rattles and jerks all over the fucking road until it hits a highway and, you know, you get it up to seventy-five, eighty miles an hour? And all of a sudden it's riding smooth as glass, riding like a Rolls. That's Terry. With all the honks, squeaks, jerks, this kid . . ." Bump started counting off: "He's a brown belt in karate, he's an all-star Little Leaguer, he's in the goddamn *glee* club of all things. And now this. Tonight. National TV. The kid gives a performance makes me and my wife so fucking proud we won't sleep for a week."

Jesse smiled, said to herself, Brenda Martin.

"Sweetest kid in the world, Terry, but on this show he plays some sick, vicious son of a bitch? I swear to you, we saw that? We didn't want to let him back in the house. He is *very, very* good."

"Yeah," Jesse said mindlessly.

"Well, I'll tell you." Bump folded his arms across his chest. "I know we got to talk turkey on this thing here, but let me just . . . let me tell you what kind of kid he is. He's in sixth grade this year, right? Now, we had to take him out of that other fucking school. We shopped around, put him in one, that wasn't so hot either. Now we got him some place down by us. It's pretty good, teachers, kids . . . Anyways, earlier this year, *Dateline NBC* did a segment on Tourette's. It was pretty damn good, like demystified it, explained how, like, there's a short in the chemical relay system from the brain to the body, and, you know, wherever the pressure builds up, there's your twitch, jerk, whatever. So we liked it and we got a copy of the show through our Tourette's association. Anyways, last October? We get a call from Terry's teacher. I'm thinking, Oh shit, here we go. She says to me, 'I'm just calling to see if it's OK with you if Terry shows us the tape,' and I'm like, *what* tape? The kid took it on himself to bring in the segment, wanted to show it to his classmates and have like a little talk with them about these things they're gonna see him do all year.

"I'm like, 'Yeah, I guess.' And I get off the phone, go into his room. I say, 'You sure you want to do this?' He says, 'I *have* to do this.' I say, 'Do you want me or Mommy to be there?' He says, 'I can handle it.' I'm standing there thinking about it. I say, 'What if I *want* to come in. Not for nothing—I have no doubt you can do it yourself—but what if, as your *dad*, could I just *see* you do it?' "

"Of course you can," Jesse said, speaking as the son, then catching herself and flushing with embarrassment.

"So I go into the school. He shows the tape and they have some pretty raw stuff, hard stuff on it, and the kids are, like, nervous. Some are laughing, but nothing mean, and after the lights go up, there's my son." Bump wiped the bottoms of his eyes. "He's right up there, says, 'So if you hear me in class this year making noises, yelling out words, or dropping to my knees or twisting my head or whatever else I might do, I just want you to know that I don't *mean* anything by it, I can't *help* it, and what you just saw on the video is the reason why.' And I'm back there, I swear I'm so, so . . . I'm gonna explode, and then he does it one better. He says, 'Sometimes? When I'm in bed at night? I think, Why me? Why did God give *me* this problem? And the thing is, I don't *know* why. He just did and I have to accept it. Thank you for listening to me.'" Bump quoted his son with a hoarse flutiness.

Jesse opened her mouth to say something—it was time to say something—and just began to sob. She stood there on the tracks, her body folding over itself as if put together with a series of hinges, and yielded to an alarmingly helpless bleating.

Bump, at first taken aback, awkwardly patted her shoulder, then became somewhat cool.

"You're killing me here," she managed to get out.

"You know, Terry's story, it's kind of like dope," he said. "It makes you feel a certain way in the moment, gives you like, a certain sense of commitment, but the next morning, you can wake up like, What the hell was *that* all about?"

He had it all wrong, but she was unable to set him straight. She had either gotten inside the boy or the boy had gotten inside her—when these things happened, she never knew which way it went, but she was always grateful, in a pained way, for the communion. And no, it wouldn't last until morning; that was part of what the tears were about too. On the other hand, her tears had always been treacherously anarchic; no footage of the Holocaust or the Middle East or Africa never brought them out, yet she was unable to sit through the most bathetic comedy or melodrama without having to wipe her eyes before the lights came up.

"Well, here's the deal," Bump murmured. "I want his story known. I want the goddamn world to know who my boy is. Now, I'll try to help you out on this thing we got right here, but if you say to me you're gonna write about Terry and you're gonna do it by a certain time and you don't deliver?"

"I'm fucked," Jesse muttered, sounding like she had a cold, breathing through her mouth. She avoided the faintly curious stares of the other reporters.

"Nah, you're not fucked." He shrugged, then leaned in close. "I'm not gonna do anything, I'm not gonna *say* anything. I'm just gonna know that you used my son to get over on me. And *you're* gonna know that I know that about you."

"Fair enough." Another glottal mutter. Her eyes were almost swollen shut.

"All right, all right," Bump said testily, as if fed up with the excessiveness of her reaction. "What do you need."

"What don't I know?" She blew her nose, still having to breathe through her mouth.

"It's pretty much what you heard."

"She a suspect?"

One of the fence kids lobbed a water balloon onto the tracks, and it landed without breaking.

"Let's put it this way." Bump grunted as he stooped for the balloon, then bobbled it in his hand. "Sixty-five percent of all children reported missing have been abducted, or done away with, by the adult who came in to report the kid missing in the first place."

"So."

"So sixty-five percent."

She realized that he didn't really know shit about what happened out here tonight.

"Where's she now, BCI?"

"Probably."

"With Lorenzo?"

"Probably."

"Where they going after that?"

"I don't know." He lobbed the water balloon at the fence, dousing the kid who had thrown it over. "Home, jail, Grandma's house—you know how these things go."

"You're gonna be humping on this all night?" Jesse stole a peek at his wristwatch: one-thirty.

"Most likely." He yawned.

"You're gonna be in touch with Lorenzo?"

"Sure, that's how we do." Bump caught another water balloon, whipped it back into the fence discus-style. The kids stood their ground, wanting to get soaked.

Jesse slipped him one of her business cards.

"I would just like, I would just like to be somewhere before she gets there."

"Done deal." Bump pocketed the card and began walking down the tracks, abruptly mock charging a section of the fence that was thick with fingers. The kids on the other side called out to him, laughing. Jesse wondered what it would be like to have a kid, lose a kid.

7

After leaving Brenda with Pierre at BCI, Lorenzo returned to Armstrong, heading for Martyrs Park, hoping to catch Miss Dotson again in her window. Almost there, he caught sight of Leo Sullivan talking to Roosevelt Tyler in the breezeway of Three Building. Tyler was one of Lorenzo's least favorite jugglers, a kid who made decent money out here running his little crew yet still found time for the odd mugging—mainly, Lorenzo guessed, because he liked it.

Leo had his hand on the wall over Tyler's shoulder and he was leaning in close, Tyler turning his head this way and that, a pained smile on his face, as if Leo had bad breath. Lorenzo strolled up to take in the show.

"This one's flesh and blood, Tyler, you hear me?" Leo said. "Now, until we get this guy? Nobody's making dime *one* out here, you understand? We're here to stay. We're setting up walking posts, doing stairwell runs, the whole nine yards. *But.* You ever play Monopoly? You know that get-out-of-jail card? Somebody gives me a good name, we're talking a lifetime pass here."

Tyler stopped fidgeting. "For real?" he drawled.

"Lifetime." Leo bowed his head in affirmation.

Lorenzo resented Leo's just coming in from Gannon and offering deals like that to Tyler or anybody else in these houses, but he felt the trade-off would be worth it. Besides, a guy like Tyler would manage to screw up in such a way that Leo wouldn't be able to come through with that free ride no matter what he promised in the here and now.

"You hear what he said?" Tyler asked Lorenzo.

"I heard it. I don't like it, but I heard it."

"Huh." Tyler pushed off from the wall, looked from Lorenzo to Leo, back to Lorenzo, then headed into the building.

"So what's happening?" Lorenzo eyed the media glow up on the tracks.

"What's happening?" Leo took out a comb and carefully swept back his thinning hair. "What's happening is we're acting like the biggest bunch of pricks you ever seen. People are gonna be fuckin' desperate to get us out of here."

"Just don't let your Klan sheet show." Lorenzo was three-quarters kidding; Sullivan a decent-enough individual.

"I always tuck mine in. You know that."

"You guys keepin' your hands to yourselves too?"

"Hey." Leo stepped back, hands up. "Danny was out of line and he's gone. He knows he was out of line too. So how'd she do?"

"Nothing so far. You got nothing out here?"

"Zip. The three monkeys. You think you'll get some prints off the handbag?"

Lorenzo hissed in defeat. "That thing was patty-caked flat. But listen." He scanned the blockades. "I need an exit corridor. I got to talk to some of my people and I got to do it off the site."

"Sure." Leo joined Lorenzo in surveying the turf. "How 'bout Gompers on the Two Building side? I'll tell my guy. Just have your people say they're with you."

"Awright." Lorenzo turned to go.

"Hey, Council," Sullivan called after him. "I don't like us being here any more than you do."

Entering Martyrs Park, Lorenzo paced the perimeter of the crime scene in delicate, anxious circles. Brenda Martin's handbag was no longer there, and he assumed—he hoped—that it had been removed by the right people. A few yards away, his eye caught a dull glint reflected off a bronze dedication tablet bolted to a thick tree trunk at eye level and featuring the solemn profiles of Martin, Malcolm, and Medgar. Martyrs was a shithole but that plaque, stolen twice, returned twice, had remained pristine since 1969, and there was always some kind of flower arrangement at the base of the tree.

Working his way to the edge of the park that lay directly beneath the

Lamb Pen windows of Three Building, Lorenzo squinted up at Miss Dotson's apartment, trying to assess the nature of the illumination in there, whether she was still awake or just using the TV as a night light. The hour was starting to tell on him, and he began to sway with the slight breeze that soughed through the sneaker trees at his back. He was lost in his thoughts when a disembodied "I'm right here" shattered the ambient rustle. Miss Dotson's voice, low and concrete, spooked him into a laugh.

The elevators in Three Building were sort of working, but Lorenzo, as always when headed for any of the first five floors, opted for the stairs. On the second-floor landing, he passed a kid whispering rhymes into a minicassette, humping his shoulders to his beat. He grinned with embarrassment as Lorenzo stumbled past him, already gasping for air.

The door had been left open for him, and the first thing he saw as he came into the apartment was a body sprawled on the kitchen floor: Curious George Howard. He was one of Miss Dotson's grown grandkids, most likely kicked out of his mom's apartment and using this one as a flop until he could get back in her good graces. George was twenty-one going on twelve, lying there dead asleep in the greasy stifle, a nubby couch pillow under his head. From the back shadows of the one-bedroom layout, Lorenzo could hear the snoring of two younger grandkids, the twin boys of another daughter, both of them evidently sharing the bed with Miss Dotson until their mother got back on her feet.

Lorenzo came into the small living room and sat on a plastic-sheathed sofa beneath a wall-to-wall photo gallery of family members—daughters, sons, grandchildren, great-grandchildren—one third of them dead. Miss Dotson sat opposite in a corduroy recliner, watching a be-your-own-boss infomercial and smoking a cigarette.

"How you doin', darlin'?" Lorenzo was eager to get to it, but he knew the pace of these things.

"How'm I doin'?" Miss Dotson kept her eyes on the TV, her voice a monotone mutter. "I ain't lettin' them get in my kitchen. Says they want to take out the 'frigerator, cabinets. Says they's lead in the paint." She waved a bony hand in dismissal; Lorenzo eyed the impossible burnished knobs, sculpted by arthritis. "Says they put it in, in nineteen hundred and fifty-five. I says, if I ain't dead of lead paint in here by now, I ain't going *out* that way."

She took a drag, fanned away the smoke, still not looking at him. "I *want* you to tell them I don't *want* no new 'frigerator, cabinets, all of that. Just let me be."

The interviews always went like this, everyone having a hidden agenda. Lorenzo had learned the hard way to withhold any promises until he had gotten what he came for.

"Miss Dotson. You know something about what happened down there?" he asked mildly, as if he had all night to kill.

"Yeah, I seen something," she told the huckster on the TV.

"Did you *see* something?" Lorenzo pointed both index fingers to the floor. "Or you *saw* something?" He touched his temples.

Miss Dotson was widely respected for her visions, which had been coming to her, as it was told, since Good Friday of 1933. Standing in a bakery that day holding her father's hand, she had seen in the display case not pastries but a riot of black roses. She knew right then her father would be dead within the year.

"Which." Lorenzo smiled, waiting.

"Well, I don't trust my *eyes* no more, so you know it's better if it comes to me from on the *in*side."

"OK." Lorenzo pushed his glasses up his nose, willing himself to be open-minded. "What you see?"

"How 'bout my kitchen." she murmured, still not looking at him. People said Miss Dotson never looked anybody in the eye, because she was afraid of what she would see for them, for their future.

"Hey." Lorenzo laughed. "You know how I do for you, right?"

There was a snuffling, shifting commotion coming from the kitchen, and suddenly Curious George appeared, sleepwalking his way to the bathroom, hands up inside the belly of his T-shirt.

"What you see, darlin' . . ." Lorenzo asked again as the bathroom door closed.

"He's with the father." Miss Dotson stubbed out her cigarette and nodded to herself.

Lorenzo jerked to the edge of the couch. In all that time with Brenda, he had never gotten a solid location or any hard information on the guy. Berating himself, he reached for Miss Dotson's phone. "You know where the father's at?" he asked quickly, not so much because he believed in the supernatural but because it was such an obvious possibility. He started punching in Bump's cell phone, not wanting to do this one over the radio.

Miss Dotson gave a gravelly laugh, then answered him in a gentle chiding tone. "You never been to Sunday school? Lorenzo. Where's the father at?"

Lorenzo hung up the phone middial, feeling a mixture of relief and irritation. "You mean *the* Father," he said, chucking a thumb toward her ceiling.

Miss Dotson briefly flicked a glance at her wall of tragedy. "That's how I see it."

The toilet flushed, and George came shuffling into the living room stopping to stand in front of his grandmother's TV and adjust the drawstring of his sweatpants.

"Big Daddy, can I tap you for five?" Lorenzo looked at him with irritation. Curious George was tall, light-skinned, and sloe-eyed, in and out of trouble since he was a little kid and Lorenzo had first come to work.

"What about that job interview you was supposed to go on last week?"

"I went."

"And?"

"They was like two hundred guys there. I stood in line for two hours, man."

"Yeah? And how about Action Park?"

"Action Park?"

"Action Park. I got that all set up for you, and don't tell me no stories either."

"Now, *that's* a long story. C'mon, Lorenzo, you know I'm good for it."

Lorenzo had a soft spot for George, believing that his problem was mostly arrested maturity.

"Don't you give him nothin'," Miss Dotson muttered and, wielding the remote, changed the channel.

Downstairs, Lorenzo went hunting for the Convoy brothers but was sidetracked once again, this time by Millrose Carter, the Man Who Never Sleeps. Millrose was squatting on his hams in the breezeway of Four Building, elbows on knees, ignoring all the chaos around him. Catching Lorenzo's eye, he pointed skyward.

Lorenzo took the elevator up first, knowing that Millrose would give it a few minutes before following. The guy wasn't supposed to be on the dance card tonight, but Millrose, who lived off a VA disability pension, was in the street all day, all night, one of those presences that the people of a neighborhood tended to christen the Mayor, and his beckoning gestures in a situation like this were to be heeded.

Taking the stairs from the top floor to the roof, Lorenzo passed

Eight-Ball Iovakas and one of the Gannon cops walking Roosevelt Tyler, hands cuffed behind his back, down to the elevator. The two cops were holding him steady by the elbows, the warrant between Eight-Ball's teeth.

"Lorenzo!" Tyler barked with desperation. "You said I got a get-out-of-jail card, man."

"Yeah. If you produce."

"How can I produce if you motherfuckers got me in *cuffs*."

Eight-Ball took the warrant out of his mouth. "You got something? Now's the time, my man. Today's that rainy day." Tyler worked his lips, trying to make something from nothing, but all he could produce was a dejected sputter, like a dying outboard motor. "Yeah, see, that's not good enough, Tyler."

The three of them continued their downward journey, and Lorenzo climbed on, not liking Tyler enough to get all agitated by his dilemma.

From the roof of Four Building, Lorenzo watched a Conrail train chug past the media camp, the engineer waving, blaring his horn, drowning out half a dozen TV reporters who were standing with their backs to the houses, trying to deliver reports to the cameras. He saw at least one exasperated newscaster drop his mike and wing some gravel at a boxcar.

The roof door banged open, and Millrose stalked out onto the tar looking agitated, bouncing on the balls of his feet and pacing like a panther. His given name was Edwin, but he had been tagged Millrose, after the track-and-field games, because he gave off the vibration of a man perpetually poised to bust out of the blocks.

And as far as anyone knew, Millrose did not sleep. At all. Lorenzo had taken him to the medical center years back, when he had developed pleurisy one winter, and he had created a minor sensation by staying wide-awake for all four days of his hospitalization. The doctors had begged him to enter into a sleep-deprivation study, but he balked when they were unable to pay him for his time. The lack of sleep never seemed to affect his energy or the clearness of his eye. The only visible problem was that, although he was only thirty-seven, most people took him for an athletic sixty-year-old.

"Yeah, OK, here we go." Millrose was taking off. "I got a goodie for you. A real goodie. Loud, common, stupid-ass, ignorant people, I'm gonna give you a whole neat package right next door to me. Set up shop, right in the *house*. Right on the other side of my goddamn living room wall. Comin' over knocking on *my* door, ask me if I want to juggle for them. *Me."*

Lorenzo eyed his watch: two-forty. Brenda would be at the end of Pierre's first rough sketch by now.

"Ask *me* to juggle? I been clean for six goddamn years, so wrong question, wrong question. See now, the best time to hit them is when the lounge closes, you know, the Camelot? Because they working out of there till two, three in the morning, but then they come back, sell right out the house, you know, till whenever."

"Can I buy out of the house?" Lorenzo asked, the old narco man coming out in him despite everything.

"Yes! Yes! Yes!" Millrose was almost hopping up and down. "See, I would cop for you, but I'm scared of it. I ain't scared of *them*. I'm scared of *it."* He charged to the edge of the roof so abruptly that Lorenzo's heart lurched, but Millrose was chugging back the other way before he could grab him.

"See, I ain't goin' *near* that shit no more. I'm tryin' to build me a life, you know what I'm saying? So no, no, no, fuck that shit. I'm gonna give 'em to you on a silver platter. Give you that whole skeleton crew."

"How much weight can I buy?" Lorenzo decided to keep his eyes off Millrose until Millrose started giving it up about the carjacking.

"A lot."

"You got any names?" Lorenzo looked back out over the projects. A few of the TV crews were erecting dioramic scaffolds, like puppet theaters; some kids, despite the hour, were still at the fence, bullshitting with whoever would talk to them.

"Damn, that boy's name just passed through my head. I'm looking right at his face right now in my mind. *Damn.* Well, I know one—Stanley Johnson. Now he's gettin' ready to do eighteen months so you *know* he don't give a fuck. Skinny-ass, braid-headed, light-skinned mother-fucker—"

Enough. "Millrose. I need help with this thing down here." Lorenzo pointed to the pocket park.

"Carl . . . Peters. That's the name. He goes across the river, he gets himself no less than a hundred bundles, maybe a quarter ki's worth a rock at a time. I'll give you that whole skeleton crew. Asking *me* to juggle? Homey ain't stupid. Homey lookin' out for the home team. I don't want that next to my house. They squatters too."

"You call the board of health?" Lorenzo was getting sucked in again, remembering how much he loved straight-up buy-and-bust narcotics, wishing he were working it right now.

"See, that ain't gonna do shit, because *Eric* Peters? You know, Carl's brother? He *works* for the board of health. See, on one hand I don't give a fuck, 'cause I'm getting ready to live with my sister in South Carolina. In fact, come the first of next month, you ain't never gonna see me again, because you can work down there, if you ain't allergic to the concept, but these next-door bastards, they got to *go* south before I *travel* south, and that's all there is to it."

Millrose abruptly stopped chugging and charging, shifting so suddenly into a serene and distant mode, standing there now almost languidly, gazing out over the projects, that it seemed to Lorenzo that someone had turned off the guy's switch. He stared at Millrose for a long moment, waiting.

"That's all there is to it?"

"Yes." Millrose bobbed his head once, blindly reached into his jacket, pulled out a cigarette, and lit it.

Lorenzo laughed, incredulous and angry. "You pulled me all the way up here for *that?*"

"Yes." Millrose tossed a match off the roof, smoke streaming out his nostrils.

"And you ain't got nothing for me up here about *this?*" Lorenzo stabbed a finger toward ground zero.

Millrose sighed and turned to him. "Listen up. I'm gonna work on that because I hear you under the gun with it, but let me ask you something. What's more important—this shit I'm telling you about right here? Or that white kid down there, you know what I'm saying? I ain't a heartless individual, but what's that song? 'One Monkey Don't Stop No Show.' You ought to do yourself a body count, my brother. But I *will* work on it because I love you and I know you got to deliver . . . Peace."

Lorenzo charged out of the building, livid and panicked—oh for two and almost 3:00 A.M. He hated when anyone pulled that brother-man shit on him, telling him to get his priorities straight. One monkey don't stop no show. If Millrose was so goddamn smart, how come he couldn't figure out how to get a good night's sleep?

Fucking snitches. Lorenzo resented how they always tried to use him, like some kind of all-purpose Frankenstein—the hours killed just bobbing his head, listening to their long-winded bullshit until they finally got around to coming across with the goods. A snitch always prefaced the information you needed by announcing his travel plans, telling you how he didn't give a fuck about these people he was about to burn, because he was leaving town at the end of the week, the end of the month, before the holiday. Going to live with his brother, his sister, his uncle, his cousin, and going south, always going south.

As he headed for the exit corridor he and Leo Sullivan had agreed on, Lorenzo passed a group of women and kids clustered around a Watchman TV, their heads clumped tight like a brace of balloons. He stood behind them as a woman from the Jefferson Houses, Rose Wilson, one of his long-ago girlfriends, spoke into a microphone on the rolling, flapping black-and-white screen.

"She was always there for our kids, you know what I'm saying? And she would bring that little boy to work here sometimes too. I mean, it's a damn shame. I hope they catch that guy, I truly do."

Lorenzo walked on, thinking this time tomorrow Brenda would be up for sainthood, thinking, One monkey don't stop no show. Well, sometimes it did. Depended on the monkey, the shade of its fur.

The pressure was coming from everywhere—the bosses, the media, the other cops, even, at this point, from the tenants themselves—and, yes, there was a racial double standard at work here and, no, a white victim's life was not more precious than that of a black victim. No one would ever say that, admit to that, anymore than they'd admit to calling this part of the city Darktown, but the pressure was like a sand storm, both overwhelming and subtle, the driven grains everywhere, sweeping people off their feet and inhabiting the finest cracks and crevices. Any impulse Lorenzo had to respond with surliness or truculence—any act or gesture he might have in mind to protest or resist the Red-Ball status of the Cody Martin abduction on the grounds of racist prioritizing—were as useless as attempting to reverse the direction of this storm with the wind power of his own asthmatic lungs.

As Lorenzo approached the Gompers Street exit and attempted to slide by the front bumper of the Gannon cruiser parked there, a young uniformed cop, someone he had never seen before, stepped into his path.

"Where you goin', Yo?" The kid was big, his jawline wider than his temples.

"I'm going out." Lorenzo flared up.

"Goin' out? Nobody's goin' out. Who do you think you are?"

"Last time I looked I was Detective Lorenzo Council. Who the fuck are *you?*"

The kid, blushing furiously, instantly stepped off.

"Jesus, I'm sorry." He shifted sideways to let Lorenzo pass, but Lorenzo just stood there glaring.

"Ain't you even gonna ask for some ID?"

"What?"

"How the fuck do you know I am who I *said* I am." Lorenzo gave it one more withering beat before walking through, offering no identification and bumping the kid on the way.

Lorenzo stood with Eric Convoy in the rear of the 7-Eleven parking lot, two blocks from Armstrong. Eric was finishing an orange soda and dabbing the corners of his mouth with the heel of his palm.

"That motherfucker Eight-Ball? He confiscated my car, come up to me an' says I got five hunnert dollars in tickets, gonna hold my car for ransom unless I find Hootie for him. But fuck it, 'cause that car ain't nothin' but a two-hundred-dollar shitbox. Holding it for half a G . . . *Take* the motherfucker. I ain't tellin' them Gannon crackers shit and *I* know who shot JFK too, so you know *I'm* pissed." He tossed the soda cup toward a full-up trash can.

"What'd you see, Eric. I ain't got all night here." It was three-twenty, almost time to get Brenda from BCI.

"Yeah, I seen her come up all bloody an' shit, you know, from the bottom end of the Bowl? But Lorenzo, can I ask you something? Reverend Longway, he's trying to evict my moms, sayin' I'm out there jugglin'. But, like, number one, when I was doin' that? It was downgraded to possession. Plus, I ain't doin' that no more. And number two? I ain't living with my moms, I'm living with my grandmother, so you should talk to the rev, tell him what the story is, 'cause my moms is real sick right now."

"What else you see down there?"

"Down where?"

Lorenzo didn't answer, giving Eric's brain a chance to catch up with his mouth.

"See down there, like what?" Eric asked.

"Like anything. Noises. Cars. Voices."

"Nah, man. Just her coming up."

"How 'bout your brother? Where was he?"

"He's with me. He saw what I saw, didn't see what I didn't see. Listen, Lorenzo, could you give me a ride to the medical center? I want to check up on Tariq."

"You think *he* saw anything?"

"Tariq? He might've but I doubt it. Maybe you should give me that ride and we can find out."

Danny Martin pulled into the parking lot, rolled up alongside them, but stayed in the car, just sitting there glaring and helpless, his left arm hanging down from the window, fingers restlessly drumming on the outside of his door. Lorenzo got the feeling that he'd been aimlessly cruising D-Town since he popped Teacher.

"Anything?" Danny asked tightly.

"Not yet," Lorenzo said gently, experiencing an unexpected wave of pity for him.

"Who's this." Danny lifted his chin, squinting. "Convoy?" Eric turned his head and looked off. "You hold back on this man, you best pray I don't hear about it."

Eric continued to give him the back of his head, and after a strained silence Danny finally pulled out.

"That motherfucker broke Teacher's jaw," Eric muttered.

"Nah, he didn't."

"Well, he shoulda kept his hands to hisself."

"Yeah, well, Teacher shoulda kept his big mouth shut."

"Yeah, well, there's that," Eric conceded, jamming his hands in his pockets and starting to walk away in the opposite direction from Armstrong.

"Where you goin'?" Lorenzo called out.

"My girlfriend's house." Eric turned to him, walking backwards now. "I ain't goin' back there," he said, waving Armstrong off. "They got us penned in, you know what I'm saying? I feel like they roundin' us up for something and I don't like it. Yo, don't forget to talk to the rev for my moms, all right?"

Oh for three.

Heading back to BCI, Lorenzo drove by a woman in the shadows of the Conrail underpass right outside Armstrong, a dangerous place to hang.

Bent over almost double, taking small, waddling steps, she was scowling at the cobblestones, searching for something, aided only by the puny illumination of a disposable lighter. At first glance, Lorenzo wrote her off as a pipe head or a junkie hunting for the Baggie or vial she had just tossed because a cruiser had unexpectedly rolled by. But she was white, another white woman seemingly in the wrong place at the wrong time. Being a great believer in hunches, long shots, and luck, he pulled his car alongside her and threw it into park.

"You looking for something?" Lorenzo asked through the passenger-side window.

"I lost my heart," she answered, not bothering to look up.

Lorenzo took a flashlight out of the glove compartment and left the car. He stood in front of her now, lighting the ground with his beam. She searched where the flashlight traveled, although she continued to keep her disposable aloft.

"What do you mean you lost your heart . . ."

"It was on my neck. It just broke." She still hadn't looked up at him. Three-thirty in the morning.

"You were at the projects there?" Lorenzo moved his light, looking himself now, not for a heart but for dope—something to squeeze her with.

"Yeah. I was seeing a friend." She followed Lorenzo's beam like a bloodhound.

"Your friend Tyler?" He took a shot.

"What do *you* think?" she shot back, unintimidated.

"You there about ten o'clock tonight?"

"When that lady got jacked?"

Lorenzo waited. After searching for another minute or so, she added, "If I seen that I woulda run right to Danny Martin, cash me in a lifetime of chips."

"You know Danny?"

"And he knows me."

"You know his sister?"

"Can't says I do."

Lorenzo stepped back—time to pack it in—when suddenly she dashed forward, yelled "Hah!" and picked up a small gold locket. Lorenzo held the beam on her, the light giving the tiny heart that she held between her fingers a rich, molten glow. She was young, but her face had that caved-in, pugilistic profile of a long-time heroin addict.

"And you thought I was looking for dope, didn't you."

At 4:00 A.M. there were half a dozen shooters hanging around outside BCI. Word had obviously gone out where Brenda could be found, and Lorenzo hustled himself in through the garage before anybody could identify him. Pierre was sitting alone in the small room where Lorenzo had left them two and a half hours ago. He was studying a charcoal sketch of the jacker that he had taped to the front of the mug-shot file cabinet.

"Hey." Lorenzo stepped in, looking around. "Where she at?"

Pierre tilted back in his chair and nodded in the direction of a defunct men's room. Lorenzo knocked on the door and, when he didn't get an answer, walked in. She was pacing from the cracked porcelain sinks to the bone-dry urinals, her face blocked by a curtain of hair. She moved with an anxious skip to her turns and she was flapping her hands.

"Brenda," he said quietly, not wanting to spook her. She wheeled around with almost violent abruptness, hitting him with those gray, panicked eyes.

"What did you find," she asked, seeming terrified of her own question. When all he could answer was "Everybody's out there looking," she wailed, "My hands are burning so *much*," continuing to flap them as if trying to extinguish flaming match heads.

"C'mon," he said almost in a whisper. He held out his hand. "Let's go see Pierre."

The drawing was of a delicately featured, almond-eyed male with the high forehead, thin nostrils, and small lips of an Ethiopian—the only bald black man under fifty years of age that Lorenzo had ever seen without a moustache or a beard. That aside, the face seemed tauntingly familiar to him, someone just outside his reach.

The three of them stood there leaning against the far wall, staring at the jacker portrait in silence, as if waiting for it to burst into song.

Pierre finally broke the spell. "Brenda. On a scale of one to ten," he said. "How'd I do . . ."

"Seven," she answered hoarsely. Lorenzo was happy with that: nines and tens were unrealistic, ratings given in order to get the hell out of there.

"You sure he didn't have a moustache?" Pierre asked, playing with his own.

"I don't remember. Maybe." She turned away.

"Maybe." Pierre folded his arms across his chest, made a figure four with a crossed leg, squinting at his handiwork. "Is there anything else we can do to make it more like him?"

She didn't answer.

"Crow's-feet, moles, dimples, pouches, any kind of blemish—"

"Please," she begged, "I'm losing my *mind*."

Lorenzo and Pierre stepped outside the room, leaving Brenda behind. Pierre held the drawing by the edges. "What you think?" Lorenzo asked, staring at the face. He swore to himself he had seen this guy before.

"I think something bad happened out there," Pierre said. "It was like pulling teeth tonight. I don't think I ever really got her good and centered in."

"You think it's a good picture?" Lorenzo asked.

"Check this out," Pierre murmured, holding the sketch up alongside his own face. It was a damn good self-portrait. "This is the eighth felony I pulled this month, you know what I'm saying?"

Lorenzo drove Brenda away from BCI in a parks department van to foil the shooters, switching to his own car, which had been driven out for him by Pierre, three blocks away.

"South 15 to base. Leaving BCI with female vic responding to 16 Van Loon Street, Gannon. Mileage at 32009."

"Base to South 15. Time is 04:30."

"How you holding up, Brenda?"

"I wish I could close my eyes and wake up," she said, gently pressing her bandages to her eyes.

"I take you home, is there anybody you can get to stay with you?"

"I don't want to go home. I can't go home."

"Where you want to go?"

"To hell," she said quietly.

"Ulysses? That's the father's name?"

"Yeah."

"Ulysses . . ."

"Maldonado," she said, to her lap.

"Give me his address."

"I don't have a clue."

"Is there anyone out there you have problems with?" She didn't answer. "Anybody at Armstrong? Any of the kids? The parents?"

"I wasn't there long enough to make enemies. Can I have my pills back?"

"You don't want any more right now." She leaned the side of her face against the coolness of the window. "Brenda, I can't stay with you once I get you upstairs. You want to call somebody?"

"No."

"No family?" She held her silence. "Friends?"

"I want to be alone."

"How 'bout Felicia? You tight with Felicia? I'll bet she'd come right over if you want."

"No."

"South 15 to base."

"Base. Go."

"Leaving city limit, mileage at 32013."

"Time is 04:40."

Lorenzo's cell phone rang.

"Yo." It was Bump.

"What's up."

"Banging on doors. Where you at?"

"Just left BCI."

"Where you headed?"

"Taking her home."

"To her house?"

Lorenzo sensed something slightly off in the question—in Bump's tone of voice. "Looks like it."

"You coming back here?"

"Hell, yeah."

Gannon was a three-mile-long finger pointing out to sea from Gannon Bay. Whenever he crossed the line, Lorenzo was struck by the abrupt change of scenery, a single stoplight taking him instantly from abandoned storefronts and end-of-the-road public housing into a land of aluminum siding and block after block of functional shopping. One of the features that always got to Lorenzo about Gannon was the travel agencies—at least two to a block, none bigger than a barbershop, and all advertising the usual discount air fares to Florida, Italy, and various pleasure spots in the Caribbean. In contrast, the few travel agencies around Armstrong, around D-Town, tended to feature flights to the Dominican Republic, Puerto Rico, Jamaica, and Guyana. And Lorenzo saw this difference in destinations as a basic difference in communities—when

Gannon took to the air, it was mostly going on vacation; when D-Town flew, it was flying home.

The official motto of Gannon was Same As It Ever Was, and that was no lie, Dempsy's neighbor a city of predominantly blue-collar white Catholic families had been living there since the end of the Civil War. There were no mansions and no slums, just modest homes and modest businesses. The only buildings over three stories tall, not counting church steeples, were the old-age home, the public high school, and the Municipal Building, which housed everything governmental—the police department, the mayor's office, the board of education, the motor vehicles bureau. The church spires numbered eight—two Lutheran, three Roman Catholic, one white Baptist, one black Baptist, and one Russian Orthodox. There was a conservative synagogue, a Christian Science reading room, a VFW hall, two public libraries, three parochial schools. There were two parks and an historical marker outside a soda wholesaler that celebrated the fact that in a Revolutionary-era tavern that had once stood there, George Washington had mapped out the battle of Staten Island.

As they rolled down Jessup Avenue, the spine of the city, Lorenzo and Brenda were enveloped by an overall stillness, a profound quiet that threw whatever was in motion out there—a cat, a drunk, a tumbleweed of newspaper—into exaggerated clarity. Even the two or three dope corners were dead, which was to say that Gannon, unlike D-Town, actually went to sleep.

Brenda lived in one of the transitional neighborhoods in Gannon, a strip still inhabited by some of its original Ukrainian and Polish residents, now stranded by the constraints of fixed incomes and increasingly hemmed in by undocumented Mexicans and Ecuadorians who had slipped into town to work in the green-card factories. The small manufacturing plants that existed in the marshy areas of Gannon produced sugar substitutes, bubble wrap, fabric trimmings, and ant traps.

Lorenzo turned onto Van Loon, a street of liquor stores, lottery ticket vendors, and Laundromats, the only housing structure a two-story, thirty-two-unit apartment complex that looked more like a cheap, rambling chain motel than a dwelling requiring multiyear leases. Brenda lived in a corner apartment on the second floor, and as Lorenzo cautiously entered the parking lot he scanned the turf for shooters. Reasonably sure there were none, he got out of the car, came around, and helped Brenda to her feet.

"Lorenzo."

On hearing the voice behind him, he had to smile, finally able to put a finger on Bump's one-question-too-many phone chat: his partner had been pumping him to set up some kind of swap for himself. He wondered what Jesse Haus could have possibly offered Bump to make him go behind his partner's back like this.

"Lorenzo, what's up?"

He turned to her as she furtively gave Brenda the once-over. "I'm gonna have to talk to you later, OK?" he said, taking in her eyeliner—looking, as usual, as if it had been applied by a drunk. She had a cell phone in one hand but, surprisingly, no cigarette in the other. Over her shoulder, he searched the parking lot for Ben, spotting him in his big-ass Chrysler, shadowing his sister, as always, and sipping his ever-present container of coffee.

Brenda, oblivious to the new presence, patted her jeans pockets, then, increasingly distraught, tried to extract her house keys with her swaddled hands. Lorenzo turned to her, feeling jammed, not knowing how to help out. Slightly frazzled, he turned back to Jesse, put out a dismissing hand.

"Not now. Call me later, all right?"

"Brenda? Are you OK?" Jesse asked, ignoring Lorenzo.

Brenda raised her eyes to the voice, and before Lorenzo could stop her, Jesse did something that no one had done all night—what Lorenzo couldn't do. She touched her. She stepped in close, reached out, and briefly touched the side of Brenda's face; gently, proprietarily, she flicked back a fringe of hair from Brenda's eyes, and that was all it took. Brenda crumpled as if Jesse had teased out the knot in the string of her musculature. Lorenzo actually had to catch her by the elbows so that she wouldn't hit the pavement.

"You're Danny Martin's sister, right?" Jesse asked. "I went to school with him."

Lorenzo glared at her, thinking, Fucking Bump. "I said *later*, all right?"

"No problem." Jesse shrugged, stepping off. "Get some sleep, Brenda. You're in good hands."

Lorenzo walked Brenda to the door, then turned back to Jesse. "Come over here for a minute." Jesse, open-faced, did as she was told. "Can you get that key out of her pocket for her?" Lorenzo requested grudgingly, as if the words were costing him cash money.

The stairway walls were cheap and smudged; a faint odor of Brussels sprouts or cabbage lingered in the hall. As soon as Lorenzo opened the apartment door for her, she bolted past him, racing for the bathroom. Fearful that she was on her way to clean something up, he got there first, saying, "Hang on," hitting the switch, and throwing an arm across the doorway to block her from entering. The porcelain surfaces—tub, sink, bowl—were unstained, and nothing worse than women's underwear and a sweater hung from the shower curtain bar. Brenda pushed his arm away and dove for the toilet, dropping to her knees, banging up the lid, and vomiting bubbling islands of brown and orange, not much else, most likely the Coke and the codeine tablets.

The bathroom was tiny, made even smaller by the matching royal blue of the curtain, the rug, the towels, the toilet and tank covers. There were two toothbrushes, one with Fred Flintstone on the grip. A spoor of striped toothpaste lay clotted on the edge of the sink, a scatter of plastic Transformer creatures lined the tub—no blood, no chaos.

"Please," Brenda yawped in a voice scraped raw, waving him away as she embraced the curve of the bowl.

Closing the bathroom door, he quickly hit the lamps, lighting up a small, glum living room of secondhand furniture and spotted gray wall-to-wall carpet. Lorenzo squatted, fingering the stains, which were dry, old, the wrong color. He looked around the room—nothing overturned, spilled, ajar; no sign of a struggle or a hasty exit; no burned-down cigarettes with long ashes, no dishes on the dining table, no puddled liquid.

Over a small round dining table, a movie poster for *101 Dalmations* was pushpinned to the wall. Above the television, a T-shirt emblazoned with a computer-generated photo of Brenda and her son hung splayed and pinned like a butterfly. There were other photos around—of Brenda and Cody together at the Liberty Science Center, at Action Park, at the Jefferson Houses with the Study Club and of Cody alone or with other adults, shaking hands with the Hamburglar at McDonald's, sitting with an older woman whom Lorenzo took to be his grandmother, feeding a black-nippled bottle of milk to a goat at some petting zoo. There were no photos of Brenda by herself or with anyone but her son.

There were old plastic child guards on the corners of the coffee table, which sat in front of a ratty-looking sofa. In the small kitchen, separated from the living room by a serve-through cutout in the wall, the dishes were unwashed but neatly stacked in the sink—no bloody cutlery, no broken glass. There were both ant traps and roach motels in all corners of the floor. The imitation wood-grain cabinets held a sugarland of kiddie cereals, a few cans of soup on a spin-tray and a few plastic-sealed six-packs of soy milk. The refrigerator held a slab of raw chuck steak in its Styrofoam wrapper, a hardened wedge of white rice uncovered on a plate but still molded in the shape of its take-out container, and a half dozen silver-foiled Hershey's Kisses, nesting in the egg tray inside the refrigerator door. So far, the apartment struck him as more sad-ass than sinister.

She seemed to have stopped throwing up. Lorenzo heard running water now from behind the bathroom door, and he was torn between getting her in sight and continuing to examine her world unhindered. Crossing the living room again on his way to check out the lone bedroom, he noticed a five-and-dime composition book on top of the television. Opening it, he saw the name CODY scripted in an unwavering adult hand, maybe five, six hundred times—seven continuous pages of CODY, like a written chant. Lorenzo was caught up short, trailing his fingertips down page after page, as if he could decipher meaning through his sense of touch. There was nothing else written on any other page.

She came out of the bathroom finally, staggering to the couch and dropping, her head almost touching her knees. He wanted to ask her about the composition book, but he was thrown by her sudden appearance. There was something different about her now.

"How you feeling?"

She didn't answer.

The bathroom smelled of synthetic fruit from the room spray she had used, and when he reached in to close the door and cut off that canned scent he saw that the sink was filled with clumps of hair. He looked at her again, finally registering the hacked, uneven coif that now barely framed her face. She had the dazed, hounded look of a collaborator who had been seized by partisans.

"What the hell did you do?" Before she could answer, his pager went off. Bobby McDonald most likely, wanting an update. Lorenzo realized that he had forgotten to log in with the dispatcher, cover his ass about coming up here alone with the victim. Her answer about the haircut was lost to the static in his head. "What?" he asked.

"I *said* because my head is *killing* me." There were tears in her voice again, and she started rocking.

Looking out the lone living room window, Lorenzo saw a dark blue van with New York plates slowly trolling her street. He also saw Big Ben, still sitting in his Chrysler, Jesse in the passenger seat talking on her cell phone. The woman didn't quit.

"Is that the boy's room or yours?" he asked, taking a step toward the bedroom.

"His."

"Can you show me?"

"You can go in." She waved him on, holding her head, making no effort to rise. The room held a bunk bed, both beds made, a chest of drawers with yellowed decals that must have been applied decades ago, and a small Formica-topped school desk. The walls were covered with centerfolds of steroid-ripped wrestlers, and plastic wrestler dolls were scattered about the floor. Lorenzo returned to the living room.

"You have another child?"

"No. The bunk bed was free, so we have a bunk bed."

"Can I ask you something? I saw that notebook there, you know, laying open?" He lied. "Did you write that in there, you know your son's—"

"It helps me sleep writing something over and over. It's like counting sheep."

"Huh. When did you write that?"

"I don't know. Yesterday, day before."

"You do it a lot?"

"Sometimes."

"You always write his name?"

"No."

Lorenzo tried to couch his next question as lightly as he could. "Can I see some of the other things you wrote? You know, names?"

"Why?" His beeper went off again. "I don't keep them or anything," she added. "What do you want to know?"

"Just . . ." He trailed off, telling himself it would keep. He had to go. "I need to get somebody up here with you."

"No. I want to be alone."

"Let me call Felicia."

"I said *no*." Her voice was sharp yet pleading.

The phone rang. She stared at him. He made a move for it but then balked, not wanting to scare off the caller. He gestured for her to pick it up.

"Hello?" Her voice was floating away. Gently Lorenzo pried the receiver a few inches off her face so that he could listen in.

"Who's dis, Mommy?" The voice was white, male, adult. "Mommy, come get me!" The caller broke into sniggers, and Lorenzo could hear at least two others laughing in the background. "Mommy, I'm fuckin' *out* here. Where the hell *are* you, you fuckin' bitch." More sniggers, somebody in the background gurgling, "Hang up, asshole." The caller said, "Here, you talk to her," then hung up.

Lorenzo took the phone from Brenda and set it down. "You have Caller ID?" he asked, knowing she didn't. His gut reaction was that the caller and his buddies were nothing but stoned or drunk morons getting high with the TV news on—having some fun.

She pinched the phone wire between her fingers and freed it from its jack. "I guess I don't want to be alone."

"Good," Lorenzo said, stooping to retrieve the phone wire. "Let me call Felicia."

"No."

"How about your neighbors? You close to any neighbors?"

"Who's that downstairs." She had hardly moved since he had taken the receiver from her hand.

"Downstairs?"

"That woman down there."

"She's a reporter."

"She knows my brother?"

"She says she does, but—"

"Can she come up?"

"Brenda, she's a reporter." Brenda shrugged, nervously running a hand through her butchered hair. "Brenda," Lorenzo began again. Then he just gave up. Fucking Bump.

Lorenzo went downstairs and hung inside the vestibule. When the dark blue van completed yet another pass of the house, he stuck his head out and gestured to the Chrysler. Jesse came out the passenger door and strolled over, casting casual glances around the sleeping parking lot, as if she were about to commit a crime.

"Here's the deal," Lorenzo said, towering over her in the overripe hallway.

"Go ahead." Jesse's cell phone, wrapped in a folded fax of Pierre's jacker sketch, peeked out of a front pocket of her jeans, and she held an unlit cigarette like a pool cue between the braided fingers of her left hand.

"Now I can scotch this if I have to, all right?"

"Scotch what?" Jesse lit her cigarette and eyed the stairs behind his back.

"She just wants company, you hear what I'm saying?"

"OK." Jesse shrugged. Her lack of reaction worried Lorenzo; she was trying too hard to be cool.

"Listen to me. There's that little kid out there, right? So whatever she says to you, I want you to run it by me before you use it, OK? I let you up there, you're in the catbird seat—we both know that but we got to have a contract on this. I read *one* thing I didn't know before I read it? You and me . . . I'm gonna cut you off at the knees."

"Lorenzo." She turned her head to blow out a stream of smoke. "Tell me one time I didn't play by the rules."

"That's *my* line. Do we have a contract?"

"You have my number?" she offered, touching the phone bulging from her pocket. She wore her T-shirt untucked to try to hide it the way a plainclothes cop would hide his gun.

"No, I don't," he said sullenly. He studied her as she removed the jacker sketch from around her phone and using her thigh as a desk, scribbled down the information.

"So what you promise Bump," he asked.

"Bump?" She rewrote her number more legibly. "I don't know what you're talking about."

Lorenzo left the building trying to convince himself that Jesse's being up there was a good idea—that she could ask Brenda things that he couldn't, could size her up, put in the man-hours needed to read this woman accurately, maybe even feed her lines supplied by him if it started to go that way. He also told himself that if Jesse burned Brenda, and by extension burned him, she would quickly find out that it's a long, long life in a small, small city.

He walked across the lot to Jesse's brother's Chrysler. Ben was huge—square-headed, straight-faced, and polite. He looked to be in his early thirties. No one Lorenzo knew could figure out what Ben's story was. He had owned a bar, been a talent scout, bitten someone's finger off, done fund-raising for Jerry's Kids, did some time, served subpoenas, repoed cars. He was ex-CIA, he was dying, he was a police informant, a genius, a black belt, a pusher. He'd gone to dental school. The only thing known for sure was that he was almost always at his sister's side, a bodyguard, chauffeur, gofer.

"Nice to see you," he said, shaking Lorenzo's hand through the driver's window and looking up at him with wide, unblinking eyes.

"Yeah, Ben. Your sister's gonna be up there for a while, I think."

"Good." Ben nodded. "Anything I can do for you?"

Lorenzo always found his implacable willingness to help out a little unsettling. "Yeah, you see that door? I want that lady to get some sleep."

"You got it." Ben bobbed his head.

"Anybody coming over here—you know, reporters, you know who I'm saying—keep 'em out."

"Absolutely." Ben extended his paw through the window again, shook Lorenzo's hand. "You have my number?"

Lorenzo backed away. "That's OK, Ben. Thank you."

"Thank *you*," Ben shot back, and started to roll the Chrysler closer to the building.

Before returning to Armstrong, Lorenzo looked up to the apartment and saw Brenda pacing from window to window, her hands on top of her head like a prisoner of war. Pulling out of the lot, he had to swerve sharply and stomp on his brakes to avoid that dark blue van swinging in, the driver bawling out his window, "Yo, sorry, sorry," a photographer jumping out the passenger side and coming up to Lorenzo's window. "Brenda Martin. You know what apartment?"

"Not here," Lorenzo told him, noting in his rearview that Ben was trotting up to cut them off at the pass. Pulling out on Van Loon, Lorenzo was afraid to look back at that open window, afraid they'd be tracking his gaze, Lorenzo vibing out to Jesse, his officially sanctioned fox in the henhouse: At least pull down the goddamn shades.

8

Waiting until she was reasonably sure that both the blue van and Lorenzo had gone, Jesse phoned her brother from inside the vestibule, requesting a quick run for cigarettes, vitamins, and her makeup, then began climbing the stairs in a state of euphoric alertness, the sensory universe of the hallway, the various textures, the quality of light, the mingled aromas of food, sleep, and garbage all striking her so keenly as to feel more like memory than new information.

Halfway to the second floor, she stopped and attempted to punch in Jose, but the squeal of a door from above made her stuff the phone back in her pocket. Looking up, she saw Brenda floating in the gloom at the top of the stairs, her eyes lost to the shadows, but the hair—even through the spectral murk Jesse could make out the chopped, stiff splash that now crowned the gaunt planes of Brenda's face like a halo of spikes.

"I'm so sorry," Brenda said, almost cringing, stepping back as Jesse reached the landing.

"C'mon, no," Jesse said soothingly, trying to touch her as she did out in the parking lot. "I know how you feel."

"What do you mean?" Brenda asked, demanded, ignoring the laying on of hands this time. Jesse was thrown by her voracious eyes: there'd be very little small talk here.

"You know, to have a child, to be . . ." Jesse faltered, feeling like she had just stepped through a rotten board.

"Boy or a girl." Another demand.

"What?" Jesse's eyes strayed to the open door of Brenda's apartment. "What do you have."

Jesse opened her mouth to set the record straight, but, panicking at the possibility of being ejected, she heard herself answer, "Boy," this woman bulling her into a lie from the jump, Jesse having no child, no husband, no lover, no constant friends, just a brother and a job.

"How old is he," Brenda asked.

Jesse hesitated, seeing one last chance to tell it true. But she folded, afraid her hesitation would expose the lie in too clumsy and humiliating a way.

"Three years. Three." Then, "Mikey," she volunteered, "Michael."

"Michael," Brenda repeated.

Jesse nodded, experiencing a queasy mixture of revulsion and determination, so that when Brenda, without another word, turned and reentered her apartment, she remained in the hallway for a moment. If Brenda wanted, she could shut her out. But the door stayed ajar, and any lingering impulse toward self-examination that Jesse might have had was obliterated the moment she crossed the threshold—obliterated by an intoxicating rush of victory.

She was immediately struck by the air of impermanence about the place, a self-conscious striving for some kind of homeyness that just didn't make it—the haphazard furniture, the posters and photos hung with pushpins, tidiness passing for cleanliness. Even the walls, a smudge-mottled light gray, gave off a transient quality.

Brenda stood by the window, at the other end of the room, her body jerking with a promise of movement though she remained rooted to the spot. "I'm sorry," she said again.

"Please, Brenda," Jesse said automatically as her eyes roamed the room, looking for reproducible photos. She liked a mother-and-son photo printed on a T-shirt, but it would never reproduce, and she rejected the one of the kid with the Hamburgler and the one with Brenda at what she assumed was the Liberty Science Center—too much shadow. But the group photo with the black kids—probably from the Study Club—that one was on the money because the cops were hitting Strongarm so hard. Brenda's own brother had broken some kid's jaw, or so she had heard.

Having made her choice, she focused again on Brenda, who was rocking from side to side. Jesse took her by the elbow and steered her to the couch, going knee to knee, a hand lightly resting on Brenda's arm like the homicide cops had taught her. "I'm Jesse Haus," she said, ducking her head to get into those gray-starred eyes. "I'm with the *Register.* You *know* that, right?"

She waited for an acknowledgment. Brenda finally nodded, looking off.

"Is there anything I can do for you right now?"

"Can you bring him back?" she answered lifelessly.

Jesse gave it a minute, then said, "What's his name?" She knew, but wanted to hear it in the mother's mouth, read how she would say it.

"Cody." It came out soft, crushed.

"Cody. OK. Now, all right, now, this is what I want *you* to do. I want you to give me a photo of him. Let me pass it on to my paper, OK? You give me something good, something with heart, something—" Brenda startled her by abruptly rising to her feet and looking around, a little wild-eyed, until she spied some videos on top of the television. Giving Jesse her back, she walked over and began sorting them out, slipping them into their cloudy plastic rental cases—having a hard time of it because of the bandages.

Jesse plowed on, slightly off balance. "You give me something with some kind of essence, and I swear to you, we're going to have thousands of people looking for him by lunchtime. That's how it works."

Brenda kept at her sorting—*Splash, Pocahontas, Rumble in the Bronx,* Jesse reading a Fuck Off in the activity, knowing that she was coming on all wrong right now, writing in her head: "Helpless, trapped in a whirlpool of despair, the mother resorted to the most timeless of women's tasks," deciding in that moment that sorting out cassettes would fall into the category of domestic arts, telling herself, Get the photo, then calm down.

She rose from the couch and picked up the Study Club shot. "This would be perfect. Can we use this? And if you have one of just you and him. I can't tell you how important this is."

Brenda stacked the videos as if she were going right out to return them, save that extra-day charge. Jesse watched her, surfed another wave of self-disgust, then spied a photo of Cody feeding a goat at some petting zoo. She picked that one up too. "Look, I'm sorry I'm coming across all business, but I'm telling you, speed—"

"What do you think is going to happen?" Brenda cut her off again, standing there holding the videos.

"I think we're going to get him back. I think if you listen to me you're going to have the best of both worlds working on this." As Brenda put down the videos and moved to the bathroom, Jesse slipped the photos out of their frames, taking Brenda's silence on the subject as permission to print. Through the open bathroom door, she watched Brenda pry open the medicine cabinet and clumsily try to extract a prescription bottle, accidentally batting it into the sink. Jesse stepped in to help, taking one of the caplets out of the amber plastic vial nesting in all that cut hair: Tylenol with codeine, prescribed almost two years ago. Jesse hoped that they were too old and that Brenda wouldn't conk out.

Brenda couldn't take the pill in her swaddled hands, and after an awkward, fumbling moment, Jesse had to place it on her tongue, looking away as she did it, scanning the open medicine cabinet—no Prozac, no Valium, no diaphragm, no Dutch cap, nothing of interest that she could see. There was a bottle of pink Amoxicillen for the kid, and she debated whether to tell Brenda that it should be refrigerated. The absurdity of the precaution, given the circumstances, eluded her at first, her nerves getting in the way of her sense of irony.

As Brenda gulped water from the faucet, Jesse took in the rest of the room—the blue-on-blue coordinated curtains, towels, and toilet covers, the Transformer toys. There were three Yahrzeit candles, short and fat, resting in their glasses on top of black cocktail napkins, one on the side of the sink and two on either side of the bathtub faucet. Jesse saw them as an effort to create an exotic, intimate mood; she was fairly sure that Brenda had no idea they were candles used by Jews to memorialize the dead. They would make a good detail for Jose, but Jesse was just superstitious enough to avoid committing to print anything that could jinx the hunt, be taken as a portent.

"You just cut your hair?" she asked, not knowing how else to phrase the question, thinking, "In a gesture as timeless as Greek tragedy . . ." Brenda didn't respond.

"Brenda, can I see his room?" Brenda escorted her as far as the threshold, then turned and walked away without looking in. Jesse remained in the doorway, absorbing the bunk beds, the wrestlers on the walls, picking up a talcy smell, a comfortable messiness. The room felt more real, less provisional than the others.

Suddenly Brenda reappeared at Jesse's back. Without saying anything and without actually setting foot inside the room, she reached over Jesse's shoulder, snaked a hand around the door frame, and turned facedown a photo standing on the kid's chest of drawers. She walked away again.

Jesse gave it a minute or so before asking, "Where do *you* sleep?"

"On the couch," Brenda answered from the kitchen.

"Can I ask where the father is?"

"Out of the country."

"Really." Jesse heard the tick and whoosh of an ignited burner. "What's he doing?" Brenda didn't answer. "Huh." Jesse finally stepped inside the room and casually lifted the downed photo. It was a generic yearbook portrait of Brenda—eyes glazed, smile lifeless, head cocked at that typical and unnatural yearbook angle. Jesse became the kid now, looking at that picture: My Pretty Mommy. Then she was Brenda, experiencing the slap down as an act of self-banishment; she tried to imagine the sense of failure that Brenda must be feeling.

Jesse walked over to the bedroom window. At five-fifteen, dawn was starting to break, dead white, more the absence of darkness than the presence of light. Ben was already back. He stood guard down below, under his arm a Finast grocery bag, Jesse's preferred brand of luggage. She also saw two more reporters, looking pissed, striding toward a Taurus with rental plates. Jesse loved her brother at that moment, his bulldog devotion, but also felt gripped by a sadness for Ben, the pain of his love for her, the absence of other people in his life. The feeling began to expand into a sadness for herself, a frightening, stoned loneliness that was married to this unreal hour, this grievous place, the mad woman in the kitchen. Jesse shook it off, opening the window an inch, tapping the glass with a fingernail, the sound distinct enough in the zero-hour stillness to get him to look up. She slid both photos through the crack, watching them swoop to the parking lot. Benny knew what to do, raising the grocery bag and pointing to the vestibule before chasing after the pictures.

"Brenda?" Jesse joined her in the kitchen, where both of them watched water boil. "Brenda," she said again, but the woman seemed transfixed by the roiling water. She wanted to ask if it was OK to call in to her editor but feared that Brenda might say no, or say yes and shut down even tighter on her, so she simply backed out of the kitchen and headed for the bathroom.

In her anxiety to make the call, Jesse closed the bathroom door before locating the light switch. She found herself in darkness punctuated by fluorescent letters that were stuck haphazardly on the walls, on the side of the sink, the mirror. Childish alphabet stickers glowed a pale green, the handiwork of the boy, his surprise presence scaring her for a moment. Without turning on the light, she opened her cell phone. The green of the illuminated numbers almost matched the green of the scattered letters. "Give me Jose." Jesse waited, turning on the water in the sink to drown out the conversation.

"Yo."

"Hey. I'm in the house."

"Whose."

"The woman. Brenda Martin."

"Jesus." Then, to someone in his office, "Jesse's in the house." Then, back to her, he said, "Jesse's in the *house*," giving it a homeboy spin. Her editor was happy. "Get us a picture."

"My brother's running it over right now."

"Lurch?"

"Fuck you."

She dipped her fingers in the running water. The sink was clogged, slow to drain, and the feel of the cut hair swirling around her hand made her stomach jump.

"All right, listen, just stay there, OK?" Jose said. "Don't let anybody else . . . How the hell did you get in?"

"Whatever, I'm in."

"Hang on." Jose addressed whoever was in his office again. After a two-second skull session, he said, "Jess? I want you to call back, start dumping in an hour, OK?"

"Whoa, whoa, give me a little elbow room here. I'll dump when I can dump, all right? And don't call *me* or you'll fuck everything up OK? We're all alone here, so—"

"She talking?"

"I'll call you later." Jesse put her phone back in her jeans pocket, turned off the water, and flushed the toilet for coverage, realizing after she had done it that she really did have to go to the bathroom. Too late. She opened the door. Brenda was standing right outside. Jesse jumped, wondering if she'd been listening in.

"Hey," Jesse said tentatively, bracing herself.

Brenda looked off, then tonelessly inquired, "What kind of music do you like?"

"96 Tears" blasted the walls from a boom box on the dining table as Brenda paced loopily in front of the drawn windowshade, which was doing a poor job of shutting out the morning's early light. Brenda was staggering more than marching, periodically casting a glance down at the growing mob outside: media vans, but also a few of the old Ukrainian ladies, already up and about, and one or two red-eyed brown baggers swaying in place and staring back up at her for a little spontaneous entertainment.

"This song." Brenda stopped moving for a second, speaking to Jesse, who was watching her from the couch. "Did you ever get nostalgic for a song you've never heard before? '96 Tears'—it's like from before I was born. I don't know what it is."

"I guess good music is timeless," Jesse said emptily, trying to keep it together. From the moment she had come out of the bathroom nearly an hour ago, it was as if she and Brenda had reversed roles. Brenda had taken over, spinning out an anguished line of chatter punctuated by musical commentary and the scrabbled gestures of someone facing a no-coke-left sunrise. Jesse had fallen into mute witness, struggling to absorb, to retain and compose the essence of this vigil without benefit of phone or notepad.

The buzzer rang and Brenda jerked, looking to Jesse. "If it's the cops they'd just come up," Jesse said.

Ben was still down there playing doorman. Periodically his sister peeked out and watched him straight-arm the competition, most likely telling people he was family. Occasionally the buzzer would ring anyway, some reporter, climbing in through a basement window and coming upstairs via the laundry room, or maybe doing a little roof hopping, attempting to crawl down to the apartment like Spiderman.

"Mommy! Mommy!" a voice called from the street. Brenda clutched her temples with padded hands as the singer continued to lament over a reedy organ: "Too many teardrops, for one heart, to carry on." Jesse jumped up and put an arm around Brenda's shoulders, battening down the shade with her free hand.

"Brenda, I want you to try to settle down, OK? I want you to start thinking about getting a little sleep."

The music shifted to "Tramp," Otis and Carla breaking each other's chops. Brenda just stood there, leaning into Jesse's side, the two of them facing the couch as if posing for a picture.

"*This* song? That's my other thing. Boy-girl records, you know, where they sing to each other? Otis and Carla, Rufus and Carla, Marvin and Tammi, Billy Vera and Judy Clay, Dick and Dee Dee—did you ever hear Dick and Dee Dee? Even Ike and Tina. You ever hear that song they did, 'It's Gonna Work Out Fine'?"

"I think so," Jesse said, taking a furtive look at the time. It was six-fifteen and she was desperate to call in, knowing Jose was going batshit by now waiting for the phone to ring. She eyed Brenda's boom box, stacked with CDs and cassettes, their plastic cases scattered on the floor. The discs were store-bought, but the tapes apparently homemade, the back of each case neatly printed with a list of its contents.

"I hear these songs, right? And I think, These people, they love each other. And listen! They're having *fun* in this song. This is great. And it's not like I don't know better, like I'm some kind of moron, but I *go* with it. Sometimes you just have to *go* with it."

Jesse surprised herself by steering Brenda into an embrace—to comfort her, to shut her up—and Brenda yielded easily, her breath hot against Jesse's collarbone. Jesse felt the leaden exhaustion in her, but also the bubbling anxiety, a steady, tremulous ripple, as if the woman were standing on a nerve. She led Brenda to the couch, helped her down, and stood behind her, trying to break down knots big as cloves lumped between her shoulder blades. Brenda went with it again, allowing her upper body to roll with the pressure of Jesse's thumbs, Jesse wanting this woman down and out.

"Your brother downstairs? Do you think he could buy me a couple of CDs? I'll give him the money. I left most of my music in Jefferson and I could really, really use hearing them right now."

"Sure," Jesse said, the music shifting to "Steal Away," a long nasal wail of enticement, the singer begging for it; Jesse thinking, This thing is writing itself.

"Can I just tell you names?" Brenda twisted around.

"Sure." Jesse was grateful for the opportunity to break out the notebook. "Go."

"Solomon Burke, Don Covay, Arthur Alexander, O. V. Wright, Ruby Johnson, Clarence Carter, Mabel John—any of them, any tape, CD, anything." Jesse was writing, not recognizing a single name, also writing: " '96 Tears,' Dawn, Hair in Sink."

"Any of them. It would be so great."

"Brenda, is this thing a convertible?" Jesse patted the couch.

"What? Yeah," she answered, squinting at the far wall, working something out.

"Why don't you let me pull it out for you. Where do you keep the pillows and stuff?"

"Once last month? I was talking to my son, I said to him, 'Cody, do you love me?' I don't know why I said that. It's a pathetic . . ." Brenda shrugged. "But, anyways, you know what he said? He's *four*, right? He says, 'Of course I love you, Mommy. Why would you even ask me that?' " She put a slow, exaggeratedly dignified spin on her son's words, something Jesse's grandmother used to do when quoting one of her precocious grandchildren to company. "He was a little man," she whispered.

"What's Your Name" filled the room, sweet and husky in Jesse's ear.

"He was my little man . . ."

The buzzer rang again. Brenda didn't jump this time, sunk in her thoughts.

"He had other parents, imaginary parents, Saul and Claire Osterbeck. He told me they lived with the good werewolf at the end of the rainbow. Who's to say, right?" She tried to laugh but it came out a nervous chirp. "I was a bad mother."

"No. What do you mean? You sound like a great mother," Jesse said, standing in front of her now, writing again: "Knots, Little Man, Photo Slam Down." She was easing the presence of the open notepad into Brenda's visual range.

"No, I was too anxious for him to like me, so I never disciplined him. I never, I never *taught* him anything. It was like I was running for office and he was a voter, you know? That's not good."

"Well, you loved him." Jesse surprised herself by using the past tense, as Brenda was doing.

"You want to hear how fucked up I was? We used to sleep together on the convertible, right? He'd start out in his room, but by midnight he'd be in here with me. But like about six months ago? He started making it through the night on his own. That's *good*, right? He's growing, learning to feel safe, confident in himself, OK. So what do I do? I miss him coming into bed with me, so I go out and I rent *Frankenstein*, the original one, and we watch it. I mean I didn't get, like, *Halloween Three* or *Candyman*—nothing bloody—but I just wanted him to sleep with me a few more times, get him a little scared, not . . . We were watching it, and he starts crying. I said, 'Cody? Are you scared?' He says, 'No, Mommy. I'm not scared but I hate this movie. Everybody's acting so mean to him.' I say, 'To who?' 'To the monster. He can't *help* it, don't they know that? I *hate* this movie.' That was his heart." Brenda's voice was falling apart now, shivering with exhaustion. "That was my boy's heart."

"Sounds like he had a beautiful soul," Jesse said, immediately cringing at her own blather, but Brenda was off somewhere, in no shape to be a critic.

"You know how he got back at me? He wouldn't let me turn off the movie. I mean, we were only a half hour into it when he started crying, and now I just want to turn it off, but he wouldn't let me. He insisted we watch the whole thing, tears and all. So I have to sit there, and I'm dying because I *know* how much worse it's going to get for the monster, right? And I know Cody is just gonna get more and more upset, but he wouldn't let me turn it off. So I had to sit there and watch him suffer."

"Did he sleep with you at least?" Jesse asked, scribbling down "Frankenstein."

"No. He was too mad at me. He could see right through me."

"Rainy Night in Georgia" filled the air. Brenda, nodding to the words, dipped her head below her knees.

"Brenda, who made this tape?"

"I did," she said, straightening up. "I make tapes all the time. If I like somebody, I make them a tape of songs that remind me of them or, you know, songs I think they'd like. I'll make you a tape if you want."

"Thank you," Jesse said, slightly moved by the offer, keeping herself on a steady course by writing down "Make Me A Tape."

"Did you ever make one for Cody?"

"Frankenstein," Brenda responded, and Jesse wasn't sure if she was ignoring the last question or just didn't hear it. The buzzer rang again, making Jesse jump this time.

"Do you know how hard it is to get a kid to sit through a black-and-white movie?" Brenda asked. "Well, you should know."

"Me?" Jesse was thrown, then remembered her cover story—another surge of adrenaline.

"What movies does Michael like?"

"*Rocky,*" Jesse said. "*Four. Rocky Four.*"

"How old is he?"

"How old?" Jesse scrambled, unable to remember what she had said before. "You know, same as yours."

"You know what I bet he'd like?" Brenda was growing desperately animated again. "*Big.* What else . . . *A League of Their Own, Fried Green Tomatoes, The Secret Garden, Harvey.* You ever see that? With the six-foot rabbit? What else . . . *Captains Courageous.* Actually, that was too sad, plus it's black-and-white."

"That's a lot of movies," Jesse said, wanting to move out of this dogleg in the conversation.

"Oh, Jesus, we'd watch one every night, seven nights a week. The guy at this little shitty video store down the block? He gave Cody his own membership card. It was our favorite thing to do. Every night, every night."

"Sounds great to me," Jesse said, and she meant it.

"We'd do everything together. He used to come in to work with me? I have to show you." She got up from the couch and walked toward the window. Jesse realized she was going to retrieve the group picture of the Study Club, the one that was now at the *Register,* and wondered how to play this. But Brenda just seemed to shrug off its absence.

"Anyways, I'd bring him into Jefferson with me? He'd just get down with the other kids, wouldn't even bat an eye, the only white kid there. But that's good, you know, to see how it feels to be the other."

"I hear you." Jesse came around and took it on herself to pull out the convertible, hoping the visual aid would help Brenda fall out.

"I mean he was too young to get it, you know, the black-white thing. Most kids, they start to get it about eight, nine years old. That's when they usually separate out." She peeked around a crimp in the drawn shade. "It's raining. He's out in the rain."

"Brenda, where do you keep the pillows and stuff? I want you to rest." Brenda turned from the window, her eyes shining like wet steel.

"You know," she began, her voice feathery, tentative, "I'm still pretty young." She looked across the room at Jesse as if she couldn't believe she had just said that. Jesse stared back at her with a cockeyed, spastic grin, telling herself that she would take this moment with her to the end of her days.

"I really need to sleep now," Brenda said carefully, shaken sober, her voice deeper now.

"Good," Jesse said.

"Not out here. It's too bright. I'll go in Cody's bed if you can help me with the shade in there."

"Absolutely."

Jesse had to climb onto the windowsill to reach the tightly furled opaque shade in Cody's bedroom. It had been raining for a few minutes, nothing more than an early morning sun shower, and she watched the bulk of the crowd down below reluctantly retreat to the shelter of a red-and-yellow bodega awning across the street. A few sodden individuals, including one or two whom Jesse recognized from other papers, were still arguing futilely with Ben—Ben of Gibraltar. The rain was matting his hair down into a monk's tonsure: Jesse had never realized that he had a bald spot.

With the shade drawn, the room became dark enough for Jesse to see more fluorescent stickers glowing on the walls, the desk, and the frame of the bunk bed—numbers, letters, dinosaurs, comets—pale green, floating.

Jesse unbuttoned Brenda's jeans for her, helped her step out of them, and waited in the bedroom while she used the toilet.

"Are you going to stay here?" Brenda asked, coming back in and sitting on the lower bunk.

"I would like to, yeah."

"OK," Brenda said, still hunched over the edge of the bed, her head in her hands.

"Do you want me to get you a fresh T-shirt or something?"

"No. And your brother can get me those records? I keep my money in the microwave in the kitchen."

"Sure."

"They'd come here if they found something, right?"

Jesse hesitated, confused, the word "something" throwing her for a moment.

"They'd be here in a flash."

"Jesus." Brenda closed her eyes, her entire face pulling into a pucker in her effort not to cry. "You know, it's, like, if I keep talking, keep talking, keep talking, I for*get* for a few minutes, but now I'm really, really tired." Jesse sat next to her on the bed and gently kneaded her upper back.

"I used to be afraid of dying," Brenda said. "Not afraid. More like, it was unthinkable, becoming, you know, just *nothing*. But I don't know, I'm not, I don't feel that way now. I can die. I can see dying."

"Nobody's dying," Jesse said automatically.

"You know, the phone's unplugged, but if you need to call in a story to your paper? Just put the jack back in."

"Thanks. Thank you."

"Yeah, you don't have to hide in the bathroom. I know you're working here. It's OK."

"Why don't you lie down," Jesse said softly.

"I'm good," Brenda said, gesturing for Jesse to leave her be.

Jesse moved out to the opened convertible in the living room, punched in Jose on the cell phone, then killed the call before it could ring through. She looked at her cryptic scrawls and started to compose, something she usually left to others. She wrote: "As this tortured night melts into merciless dawn," then, "In a timeless gesture of grief as old as . . ." She lit a cigarette, put it out, wrote: " '96 Tears' reverberates off the walls of this anguished room." Her eyelids felt like singed paper. She gave it one last stab: "The bathroom sink in this shabby but proud apartment is a nest of shorn hair, the mother taking scissors to her own locks in an impulsive gesture of otherwise inexpressible anguish."

She pulled back from her own paragraph, impressed, and flipped through her notes for another trigger phrase, her eye settling on "Frankenstein" just as a low moan crept through the walls of the apartment. Jesse sat up fast, then skittered into the bedroom to see Brenda, finally on her back, lying there rigid and staring at the bottom panel of the upper bunk.

Jesse dropped to her knees. *"What,"* she said, following Brenda's gaze to that white panel, alive now with fluorescent planets, animals, lightning bolts, an entire cosmos of swarming imagery. Jesse finally saw what tore at Brenda's eyes: in a clearing ringed by giraffes and shooting stars, four letters floated in a wobbly, childish line, hovering directly over the mother's face, luminous, insistent: C O D Y.

Part Two

96 Tears

9

Lorenzo returned to the projects just as dawn was beginning to break, washing Armstrong in a flat, sourceless light. A long train of container cars sat quietly on the tracks overlooking the houses—no matter how many times those booty boxes were broken into overnight, Conrail never learned its lesson. Lorenzo himself had partaken in a raid or two in his teen years, getting away with a box of turtleneck dickeys the first time, four cartons of kitty litter the next. He would have gone back again if one of his partners in crime hadn't lost a leg to a suddenly mobile train on a night when Lorenzo had been grounded.

At this hour, the media settlement alongside the silent train had taken on the aspect of a nineteenth-century military encampment. The electronic gear hung on the fence like cartridge belts and canteens, the swirling dawn making ghosts of the few still-standing shooters, moving stiff and slow, working out night kinks. Others huddled over coffeepots hooked up to power sources in the satellite trucks. A few of the shooters had slept outdoors, were still asleep now, sprawled on folding lawn chairs, blankets to their chins. But Lorenzo spied one guy, in construction boots and tinted shades, doing jumping jacks in the gravel, and another, in bandanna and khakis, swiveling and crouching his way through early-morning tai chi.

Armstrong itself was quiet, the only action at the exit points, where cars were stacked up, waiting for permission to leave. Some of the drivers stood outside their rides, pacing, fuming, late for work, as the cops ran through everybody's papers—registration, driver's licenses, tags—looking for outstanding violations or, worse, outstanding warrants, searching trunks and crawling into backseats as if Hurley and Gompers were international borders.

The sun, coming up over New York, briefly peeked out through the filmy dawn, slashing the Bowl with light. It illuminated the refrigerators on the high end, closest to the Gompers exit, converting the field into a massive druidic sundial. Lorenzo stared at this mysterious transformation a full minute before he saw Danny Martin sitting alone on the edge of a crate in the center of the Bowl. Elbows on knees, Danny had a huge 7-Eleven coffee cup in one hand, the police sketch of the jacker dangling from the other. The cup was held limply enough for there to be a constellation of coffee spatters on one of his rubber-thonged feet, and when he slowly raised his head at Lorenzo's approach his eyes were like pale red stars.

"What you got?" he asked.

"Nothing." Lorenzo took a seat a few feet away on the same refrigerator, deciding to hold off on any discussion of Danny's punching out Teacher.

"Yup." Danny nodded. Then, without looking Lorenzo in the face, he extended his hand.

"I was way off base last night and I apologize."

Lorenzo gave it a few seconds before taking the offered hand. "Yeah, well, you were under some crazy mad stress there, boss."

"Thanks." Danny took a sip of coffee. "Thank you." He offered the container to Lorenzo. When Lorenzo passed, he tossed the contents of the cup into the dirt. "Me and you, we always got on, right?" Lorenzo refrained from answering, the truth being yes and no. "So, nothing, right?" Danny slowly rolled his head from shoulder to shoulder. "I shook every fuckin' tree in the forest."

"Same here, boss." The sun withdrew, the light turning milky again; a scent of rain was in the air. "You know the father?" Lorenzo asked.

"Some PR, made a beeline back to the island the minute the rabbit died. Don't waste your time, if that's what you're thinking."

"OK," Lorenzo said noncommittally.

"In fact, next time you see Brenda? Ask her if she remembers the guy's name. I'd be curious."

"She does, Danny," Lorenzo said, flipping his notes. "Ulysses Maldonado."

"Ulysses!" Danny barked mockingly, then recanted. "Shit." He looked away, disgusted with himself.

"You close to the boy?"

"No," he said, pausing before adding, "My son's the same age, though."

Lorenzo nodded, not knowing what to say next.

"Lorenzo . . . let me ask you." Danny hesitated. Lorenzo knew what the question would be; it was the one he wanted an answer to himself. "Lorenzo," Danny started again, then, his voice husky with strain, "What do you think about my sister."

"What are you asking?"

"You know what I'm asking."

"Hey, you know. I got to explore all possible avenues."

"Just answer me."

"I don't know, to tell you the truth." He arched his fatigued shoulders. "She's your sister. What do *you* think?"

Danny took a while before answering. "She's a fuckup, but she's got a good heart."

A figure appeared, heading up from Hurley Street at the bottom of the Bowl, marching on a diagonal. It was Hootie Charles, striding with a bouncing step, a shopping bag in each hand, the cops in plain view but seemingly of no consequence to him. Danny had to rise and call "Hey!" to even get him to look their way. Without slowing his pace, Hootie changed course, heading to their crate with unblinking, crack-stark eyes.

"Where the fuck did *you* come from?" Danny asked.

"I was in the park." Hootie put down the shopping bags and shook out his arms.

"You just come from the park? How the hell did you get in?"

"I walked."

Lorenzo and Danny scanned all the entries, fully guarded.

"How the fuck did you walk in?"

Hootie looked at Danny, confused. "Like, how you *walk*." He turned to Lorenzo. "What's he asking me?"

"Don't you see those police cars there?" Lorenzo twirled a finger over his head, taking in all points of the compass.

"You know everybody's been looking for you?" Danny said.

"For me? For what?"

"Where you been last night."

"Me?"

"You back to jackin' cars?" Danny lit a cigarette.

"Me?"

"You jacked my sister's car?"

"Me?" He turned to Lorenzo again. "What the fuck's he talking about. Who's his sister?"

"Where were you last night?" Danny asked again.

"Me? I was at a repast for my father."

"A what?"

"A repast, at the . . ." Hootie snapped his fingers rapidly. "What's the name of that . . . the *Camelot*. He died, so we had a repast. Oh!" He barked so abruptly that both cops jumped. "She got carjacked? Yeah, I heard about that. How she doin'?"

"What's this." Danny nodded to the shopping bags. "Let me see." Reluctantly Hootie opened one of the bags. Lorenzo spied a plastic-sealed gross of Hall's Mentho-Lyptus drops.

"You must got one hell of a sore throat there, boss," Lorenzo said, looking in the other bag: another sealed gross. "Conrail having a sale?"

Danny stared into his empty coffee cup, then tossed it in one of Hootie's bags.

"Naw, man. I found this."

"Yeah?"

"In the park. Look at my pants, man." Hootie jiggled his pockets, making the cuffs dance. "That's mud. That's *park* mud. I don't go near them trains."

"This is what I got." Danny flapped out the police sketch. "Who's this."

Hootie took the sketch. "Nobody *I* know," he said, giving it back. "This for the carjack? Shit, name I heard on that was Army Howard." Hootie said it out the side of his mouth, as if a murmur would somehow finesse the fact that he was dead center in the middle of the projects talking to two cops in the middle of the otherwise deserted Bowl.

"Where'd you hear that?" Danny asked listlessly, Army Howard being a whole different animal.

"At my father's repast. Somebody said it but I can't remember who. Damn, who said that . . ."

When neither cop spoke for a long moment, Hootie picked up his shopping bags to leave, but Danny grabbed his wrist. "Buster," Danny said, using Hootie's Gannon tag. "This is my flesh and blood. We're talking a lifetime pass, you understand?"

"Well, shit, then." Hootie put the shopping bags down. "In that case you can call me Tonto, 'cause I'm headin' into town and getting the information."

Hootie took up his bags again and marched off. The cops sat, broodingly silent. Lorenzo could feel the tendons in his knees yawning for release.

A few minutes later Leo Sullivan appeared, walking in from the Gompers exit, a folded *New York Post* in one hand. When he reached the crate he crouched down before them, holding the paper by the top edges so that the front page unfurled like a proclamation.

Lorenzo stared at a half-page photo, taken last night in Armstrong. It was Brenda, hunched over as if pleading with someone, her face clenched in grief, her bandaged hands raised in supplication. In the background, a dozen project tenants looked at her or at the camera with flashlit eyes, and there was Danny, partly cropped out of the frame, the camera freezing him in the act of waving her off. The headline, in Pearl Harbor–sized type, read:

FROM THE DEATH OF MY HEART

The first heavy drops of a brief but intense shower rattled the newspaper and starred the ashy dust of the Armstrong Bowl. Leo Sullivan took off for the nearest breezeway, but neither Danny nor Lorenzo made the slightest move to get out of the rain.

Seven in the morning was not the greatest hour to cruise JFK for snitches, but Lorenzo agreed to give it a whack with Danny riding shotgun, mainly to cement the new truce. "My men's group," Danny muttered, indicating a half dozen noddies clumped on the steps of a synagogue turned Pentecostal church.

Lorenzo smiled meaninglessly and rolled on. He always liked the boulevard early in the morning. The soft light and silence graced the harshly painted storefronts and abandoned buildings with a stately, melancholy air that to Lorenzo revealed a deeper truth about this street than did all the restless activity evident at any other time of the day or night. Most of the people up and about on the verges of JFK were already on the case. Cops and civilian volunteers, roughly one to a block, taped flyers of the jacker to lampposts and boarded-up store windows, to paint-flaked shingles and rolled-down riot gates.

At the beginning of the boulevard, deepest into Dempsy, all the se-

cret hand jive and short pull-over conversations were directed at Lorenzo, mournfully sincere smoke for the most part. As the car crawled
toward the city line with Gannon, Danny started getting some customers
too—off-duty Gannon cops who had volunteered to help with the posting and some Dempsy street people with whom he shared both a history
and an understanding.

To Lorenzo's ear, Danny's side of the conversations seemed halfhearted. He sensed that Danny was just going through the motions,
fending off some hard-to-absorb speculations about his sister.

"Pull over," Danny said, nodding toward a seven-foot ghost who was
furtively trying to flag them down. One hand fluttering at knee level, the
guy was looking everywhere but at the two cops in the unmarked car.

"Luther," Lorenzo drawled as he turned off the drive and parked
halfway down a side street. He and Danny sat in silence for a few minutes, waiting for the guy to make it to the car from the long way around
the block. Lorenzo was sullen: of all the jugglers, Luther Ingram was the
one he most hated to see out here. Fifteen years ago, Luther had been
an all-county center at Saint Mary's high school. A year after that, he got
arrested in a police sweep of Las Vegas crack houses. It was during his
first term at some junior-college basketball factory, and his life had been
a greased pole ever since.

"What's up, brother?" Danny squinted blearily at the guy, who had
to bend so low to rest his elbows on the window frame that his spine
wound up arching a foot higher than the nape of his neck. "What do you
know, what do you say."

"Yeah, I just want to thank you for that thing you did for me with my
son, Danny," Luther said.

Lorenzo looked out the driver's window, giving Luther the back of
his head. Up the boulevard, he saw Rafik Aziz, doctor of Islamic nutri-
tion, opening up his Child of God Cafeteria and Black History Museum.
Rafik's precise jawline beard and brocade *kufi* made him look like a sor-
cerer. He was a jailhouse Muslim, a proselytizing, self-educated Afro-
centrist whose stated mission was to wean the inner-city black man from
his suicidal palate. He was also one of the angriest men Lorenzo had
ever met.

"How you doin', Big Daddy?" Luther suddenly asked loudly, goofing
on Lorenzo's cold shoulder.

"I'm good," Lorenzo said slowly, throwing him a tight, humorless
smile. "How about you?" Luther shrugged. The first few times Lorenzo
had had to arrest Luther for juggling rock, they had talked about his

getting back into shape, maybe taking a crack at semipro ball or going back to school and getting into coaching. Lorenzo went so far as to arrange a tryout with the New Jersey Ruffnecks of the North American Basketball League, but Luther had been a no-show in the gymnasium that day, and, in thirteen subsequent arrests, there was no more real talk of sports or education.

"So Dion, he's back in school?" Danny asked, popping his thumbs.

"Yeah, it was nothing but a experiment in 'Who I am,' and I believe, I *hope,* the experiment was a failure, so—"

"I gave him a little one-on-one tour of County, he tell you that?"

"We don't talk individually. I had just heard he had been fuckin' up from his mother, so . . ." Luther stood straight, rolled his head a few times, then stooped to the window again.

"Lorenzo, you know Luther's kid, Dion?" Danny asked, stifling a yawn.

"Oh yeah," Lorenzo grunted, looking Luther over. The guy looked dope-sick—swollen hands, cloudy-eyed, on his way out.

"A little wanna-be gangster man, right, Luth?" Danny went on. "He was out there rollin' deep on Willow and Parkway, it's like 2:00 A.M. Luther comes up to me, 'Yo, Danny, *do* something,' so I get out, pull him away from his crew, pat him down. He starts gettin' all chesty on me. You know: 'I got my *rights*'—"

"So here's a left to go with your rights," Lorenzo mumbled, looking away again. He spotted Eight-Ball walking the boulevard, taping up flyers.

"Exactly. Kid's on his ass. 'Yo, what you hit me for? I'm only thirteen.' I say, 'Oh yeah? You was a full-blown *man* two minutes ago.'"

Lorenzo could hear the forced bravura in Danny's retelling of the tale, the guy trying to inflate his own listless, troubled spirit with a little war story.

"'I got my rights,'" Luther said, chuckling. "That's Dion." He dropped his forehead to his wrists but came up, still smiling, a few seconds later. There wasn't a cop in Dempsy County who hadn't cut Luther a break at one time or another. No one really wanted to lock him up, given the broken promise of his talent and his gentle melancholy demeanor.

Luther extended a hand into the car. "Yeah, so I just want to thank you about that, 'cause you know I was afraid he was goin' *my* way, like, wantin' a piece of the *rock,* you know what I'm sayin'? And that would be, like, a tragedy, because my son, he's got a lot of potential, he is not unintelligent. However . . . he is what I call *under*intelligent. He is not in full command of the intelligence God has given him, you know what I'm saying?"

"How 'bout you, Luth? What are you?" Lorenzo couldn't help it— the guy just pissed him off.

"Me?" Luther sucked what teeth he had left, looked off down the street, opened his mouth to answer, then thought better of it, addressing himself to Danny. "Anyways, I do believe he got the message, so I thank you." Danny took the offered hand and held on past the moment.

"Luther." Danny held out the police sketch. "Who's this." Luther made a noise like escaping steam. "What do you hear."

"What do I hear? I hear Army Howard, but you didn't hear it from me."

Danny turned to Lorenzo. Lorenzo nodded—I got it covered—auto-matically reciting Army's beeper number to himself. Softly thumping the roof of the car in farewell, Luther walked off. Lorenzo was surprised he hadn't hit them up for a few dollars.

Back up on the boulevard, Eight-Ball was working his way toward the Child of God, taping the jacker to telephone poles and store windows. Rafik was still out there, too, sweeping clean his three squares of storefront pavement. Lorenzo saw Rafik finally notice Eight-Ball, take in what he was doing, grip his broom tight as the posters crept closer and closer to his place of business. Lorenzo, transfixed, felt like he was watching a slow-motion collision.

By the time he and Danny pulled up to the Child of God, Eight-Ball and Rafik had already locked horns. Eight-Ball was cherry-faced, waving a fistful of flyers; Rafik stood spread-legged, like a genie, his arms folded across his chest.

Lorenzo eased out of the car and strolled up to the face-off as if he were just coming around to shoot the breeze. Danny stayed put, staring into the middle distance, his eyelids drooping and his head jerking.

"I don't understand you." Eight-Ball tapped his temples with the fly-ers. "What, you *want* this guy out here? I thought you were this big community man."

"What guy." Rafik's eyes gleamed like ball bearings.

"This guy." Eight-Ball whapped a flyer with the back of his knuckles. "Who *is* he."

"I don't know," Eight-Ball barked. "That's why we're *do*ing this."

"*Ex*actly," Rafik barked back. The conversation was taking on a bru-

tal seesaw rhythm of mutual loathing, and Lorenzo inched forward, looking for an opening to slide himself in.

"Exactly," Eight-Ball repeated with disgust. "I don't understand you."

"I know you don't." A few early risers started to gravitate to the
scene, curious, frowny.

"Let me ask you something," Eight-Ball said more intimately, turning sideways, lowering a shoulder, and taking a step closer to Rafik. "If
this motherfucker was a white man you'd let me tape this up in a heartbeat, wouldn't you?"

"Yo, Nick." Lorenzo forced a laugh, addressing Eight-Ball by his real
name, and finally wedging himself between them. Both men stepped to
the left to keep each other in their sight lines.

"Hold on." Rafik cocked his head, studying Eight-Ball. "You that
Deputy Dawg cracker that took out the Hispanic brother last year, right?
What's your name? *One*-Ball, right?" Some kids in the know cracked up,
repeating, "One-Ball," Lorenzo thinking. Time to go.

"You mean the Hispanic brother who shot the two *black* brothers?
Yeah, that was me. What the fuck were *you* doin' that day, my brothuh."

Lorenzo looked back to the car; Danny was dead asleep.

"Man, you a redneck racist from the door."

"*I'm* the racist? Why don't you bring out some of them Jew pam-
phlets you got back there in the hate museum."

"You a got-damn hillbilly-ass pine-top motherfucker, and everybody
knows it. How many civilian complaints you got filed against you, huh?
How many."

"You know what I do all day?" Eight-Ball spoke through his teeth.
"I'm in that fuckin' project every day. You know what I do? I lock up drug
dealers, I lock up shooters, I lock up wife beaters. What the fuck do *you*
do. Who the fuck are you?" He cast a contemptuous glance at the hand-
lettered Child of God Cafeteria sign. "Allah's dietician?"

Rafik went ear to shoulder, his head cocked at that D-Town matador
angle. "You lock up brothers for walking too fast, you lock up brothers for
not kissing your ass, you lock up brothers for hanging around in front of
their own homes 'cause they got *no* jobs, *no* money, *no* recreation, *no*
place to go."

"Tell it!" someone yelled from the crowd.

"Fuck you, motherfucker," Eight-Ball said, inching ever closer. "You
want to lock assholes with me? Bust a move, you mope. *Please,* by all
means, bust a fuckin' move."

Lorenzo saw two police cruisers and a news van about four blocks away, everybody smelling blood now. "Nick." Lorenzo put a hand on Eight-Ball's shoulder, felt his bunched rage like a buffalo hump under his shirt. "Nick."

"Please," Eight-Ball whispered to Rafik, wanting this fight so bad that Lorenzo saw his eyes tear up with desire. "C'mon, you bogus bull-shit motherfucker. Bust a move."

"All's you got to do is take off that shield."

"Don't let that stop you."

"Take off that shield."

"Don't let that stop you." Both men were trembling, spraying each other, the only thing holding them back an innate awareness of postfight consequences.

Finally Lorenzo compressed his own shoulders in order to put a palm on each chest, parting them in a breaststroke, pushing Rafik into the shadows of his store and Eight-Ball out to the curb. "C'mon, c'mon, take five," he told Eight-Ball, bumping him away from the store with studied clumsiness.

"Don't you fuckin' 'Take five' *me*. This your idea of *back*up?"

"You're goin' off, Nick."

"Bullshit."

Rafik disappeared inside and emerged a moment later holding an eighteen-inch-long lead bat. Eight-Ball eyed the weapon with contempt, then turned to Lorenzo. "How dare you take his side . . ."

"Hey, lookit." Lorenzo gestured toward the news van, just now double-parking. "You want to be Pig of the Month? It's *your* ass I'm saving, not his."

Eight-Ball paced in a tight circle, working it out. Turning, Lorenzo pointed to the fish priest in Rafik's hand. "And you best make that disappear."

"Yeah, that's right, Uncle Cecil," Rafik spat, "save Lil' Abner's ass."

"Hey," Lorenzo said, stepping forward. "I guess you don't know me after all, 'cause if you did you'd keep your mouth shut."

Rafik dismissed him with a flick of the hand and sauntered back inside.

Furious, Lorenzo stood there glaring into the doorway for a few seconds before he could recover himself and return his attention to Eight-Ball.

"C'mon, take a ride," he muttered, feeling like bashing both their skulls together.

"Hold on." Eight-Ball spun around Lorenzo's body block and faced the storefront again. "Hey! You don't want to hang this baboon?" Eight-Ball squawked. "No problem." Before anybody could stop him, he flipped his whole load of flyers through the doorway; hundreds of jackers rained down on the tables and counters. "I'll just leave a few in case you change your mind, ah'ite?" He brushed past Lorenzo and stormed off down the boulevard, toward the center of Dempsy. A half block away he turned and, walking backwards now, bellowed, "Pick a color, Council. Black or blue."

Enraged, but neutralized by the crowd, by the eyes, Lorenzo returned to the car. Danny Martin was gone too. Lorenzo straightened up and spotted him walking in the opposite direction from Eight-Ball, marching stiff-legged, hands to his temples, elbows out, heading for the Gannon city line.

After cruising the boulevard by himself for another useless hour, the infuriating, obsessive playback in his head making him blind to the outside world, Lorenzo returned to Armstrong, planning on sneaking up to his mother's apartment to catch a few hours' sleep.

Although it wasn't quite 10:00 A.M. when he stepped from the air-conditioned shell of his car onto the fissured asphalt of Hurley Street, he could see the thick air shimmy up from the pavement as if from a barbecue pit. Up on the tracks behind the media camp, a string of Tropicana container cars crawled toward Newark, their filthy bright orange sidings seeming to underscore the choking, no-exit oppressiveness of a humid summer's day in the projects. Most of the kids running up and down the sloped retaining wall, both boys and girls, were now stripped to their tailbones, and many of the shooters on the hill had taken to wearing wet hand towels under their baseball caps. But to Lorenzo's eyes, the only significant change of scenery from the night before was the presence of more black cops; someone upstairs had had the political savvy to make that move with the 7:00 A.M. shift in tours.

Ducking into the lobby of Five Building, Lorenzo decided he was too tired to take the stairs and wound up waiting a full ten minutes for the elevator. He almost nodded out in the car as it clanked and shuddered its way to the fourth floor. Coming out into the sepia gloom of the long, narrow hallway, he saw Felicia Mitchell down at the other end, leaning into the door of his mother's apartment, apparently waiting for him.

"Hey." Lorenzo slowed down as he approached her, trying to intuit the problem. "I was gonna call you today."

She looked disheveled, her blouse partly out of her jeans and her short hair shooting off from her head in a half dozen directions. "They find her boy yet?" she asked, a little mechanically.

"Not yet," he said slowly.

"Lorenzo, I got to talk to you." Her voice took focus. "You know Billy?"

"Billy . . ."

"My boyfriend."

"No, I never met him."

"He started hitting me, Lorenzo."

One of the apartment doors opened a few inches, and Lorenzo wiggled his fingers at the old lady who peeked out, a combination "Good morning" and "Mind your own business" gesture. The door closed.

"He hit me, like, yesterday and today."

"What do you mean?" Lorenzo asked, distracted by another infinitesimal door opening, another eye peering out.

"I mean this." Felicia tapped her cheekbone, but the light was too sickly for Lorenzo to see any damage. "Lorenzo, we been living together for like three years, he never . . . and Lorenzo, you got to come up to my house, give him a *talk*."

"I can't do that right now, Felicia."

"Then you come tonight."

"I'll try." He fingered his key ring blindly, feeling for his mother's key in the deep-fried murk of the hallway. "You know I got a full dance card right now."

"I know."

"You got anything for me on this?"

"Brenda?" Lorenzo waited, refraining from opening the apartment door. "I don't know." She looked off. "She's a nice person."

"Yeah? She got a boyfriend?"

"I don't know. She's just a nice person, you know? I don't know."

"You gonna be at Jefferson later?"

"Yeah." Felicia touched her cheekbone. "If he don't kill me first."

"I'll come by, see you there, OK? I want to ask you some stuff."

"Awright." She sighed, then grabbed his key hand. "Lorenzo, you got to come to my house tonight and talk to him. Otherwise, I swear to God, I'm just gonna go to the police."

He let himself into the apartment. The game plan was to grab an hour's sleep, run some conversations, then pick up Brenda around noon, take her back to the scene of the crime, see how things looked to her after a few hours' reflection.

His mother was in Atlantic City on a three-day gambling junket with her two sisters, so Lorenzo had the apartment to himself. Stripping down to his boxers and standing before the open refrigerator to catch a little coolness, he chugged down an entire quart of orange juice while running back Eight-Ball's "black or blue" comment, belatedly retorting, "There ain't no black or blue, just right or wrong." This was the answer he usually gave when he was black or blued by the brothers, although the riff from that camp was a little more poetic: "Either you're blue or you're black, and if you turn your back, you might wind up both."

He inhaled two pints of yogurt and three Eggo waffles, the last untoasted, and succeeded in evicting Eight-Ball from his consciousness. He tried doing the same with Rafik, but that flip Uncle Tom put-down was like an ingrown eyelash. He was used to white cops occasionally accusing him, mostly indirectly, of being black first—that was no big deal. But nothing pissed him off more than having his sense of self challenged by someone in the black community, no matter how off the wall or what segment of the political spectrum the charge came from.

Uncle Tom . . .

He took a shower, put on clean shorts, and moved into his old bedroom. The posters of Gil Scott-Heron and the Last Poets overlooking his bed had been taped to the walls since 1972. The picture of the Dempsy High School gymnastics team on his desk, featuring the 145-pound vaulter Lorenzo Council, had been nesting in its scratched, foggy plastic Woolworth's frame since 1969.

At the age of forty-seven, Lorenzo was a grandfather three times over. There were two girls by his son Reggie, a math teacher, and a two-year-old boy by his other son, Jason, who was currently—Lorenzo once again reminded himself, lacerated himself—doing three to five in the state annex of Dempsy County Correctional. So at this point in his life, the act of slipping into the narrow twin bed of his childhood always triggered an attack of dread, a vertigolike sensation of both intense isolation and impending death. As he lay there now, on top of the thin floral-patterned blanket, staring at the ceiling and riding it out, he wondered how long this most recent stay with his moms would last.

Lorenzo and his wife, Frankie, had been together since high school, their history of separations and reconciliations tracking over the last twenty-seven years like an endless series of figure eights. Most of the splits had been provoked by his drinking and drugging, but after he had sobered up, the fights had taken on a more disquieting character, involving, as they did, cold, clear assessments of each other, without the external drama of addiction to jazz up the picture.

Lorenzo was convinced that Frankie had liked him better when he was high. She was used to, and comfortable with, being the responsible one. She seemed angrier at him now than at any time in his juicehead, pothead life, accusing him of being unappreciative, disrespectful, insufferable; she seemed to be enraged at him for assuming that with sobriety came the resumption of control over the family's destiny—as if all she had been doing over the years was keeping his throne warm, and now that he was straightened out she was supposed to step off for the Natural-Born Man. He refused to consider the possibility that she was right, refused to consider the possibility that he was doing a number on her yet again, this time the clean and sober way. He refused to consider any and all of this, because although he didn't have a particularly hard time admitting to most people when he was wrong, somehow he knew that if he apologized to Frankie for anything, no matter how small, the dam would break and he'd wind up apologizing to her nonstop for the rest of their lives together, each apology for a transgression greater than the one preceding it, all apologies leading to the big one: Jason in jail.

But she *did* like him better all fucked up—he'd swear to it. Lorenzo set his alarm, thinking, We'll work it out. He rang up Army Howard's beeper, punching in his phone number and the suffix 666, thinking, We always sort of do.

Army called him back in five minutes.

"Big Daddy, what's up."

"I need to see you."

"When."

"Right now. In an hour."

"An hour?"

"That's sixty minutes."

"Awright."

"That's sixty minutes from now."

"I'll be in front of the jail," Army said.

"Old jail or new."

"Old."

"Sixty, Army."

"I'll be there."

"How's your granddaughter?"

"We had to leave her in the hospital."

"She gonna be OK?"

"I don't know. I hope so."

"Awright. Sixty minutes."

Lorenzo hung up and closed his eyes. Rafik calling him an Uncle Tom . . . Lorenzo opened his eyes. He hadn't said Uncle Tom, he'd said Uncle Cecil. Lorenzo sat up: What the hell was an Uncle Cecil?

10

On this first day of July, Jesse woke up to a gentle clattering. Shooting upright in the easy chair, disoriented, she saw Ben in the kitchen, Brenda facedown on the pulled-out convertible. Panic-stricken about the time, she looked to her brother, who whispered, "Nine-thirty," without her asking. Jesse needed a minute to lay out the timetable: call now, say good morning, hang up, call back at one with a heads up for the afternoon meeting—just a taste to keep them happy, don't make anybody crazy. Since the *Register* was an evening paper, she would have until five-thirty or six to dump. Everything was under control, Jesse intending to keep her editor at arm's length with one hand and hold Brenda close with the other, tucking her in like a Siamese twin through the day or days to come—holding her hand at the funeral or the reunion. Thinking about it, Jesse put her money on a funeral, possibly an arraignment.

Gouging the sleep from her eyes, she watched Ben scour the kitchen counter with a small scrub sponge, the fastidious and dainty proprietariness of the act magnifying his bulk. "What are you doing up here," Jesse whispered, firing up a cigarette.

"I got the downstairs neighbor to watch the door for me." Ben held up half of a torn twenty-dollar bill. "Very nice guy."

"How'd you get in here?"

Ben placed two glasses of orange juice on the dining table. A full grocery bag sat by the sink. "Try locking the door next time."

Brenda awoke with a sob, levitating to a sitting position on the couch, the skin around her eyes looking pink and flayed. She put her hands to her head, looked around wildly. "What happened?"

Jesse didn't know if she wanted a complete recap of the nightmare or an update on the last two hours. "No news, Brenda."

"They didn't find him?" Her voice was a metallic croak.

"No."

Brenda stared at Ben. "Good morning," he said, sliding a juice glass a few inches in her direction.

"Where's the detective?" Her fingers snagged in her hair.

"He's probably letting you sleep."

"He took my painkillers. Oh!" She lowered her face into her padded palms. "Oh God, Cody. I had this dream." Jesse reached for her notepad without taking her eyes from Brenda. "I had this dream." Brenda's face came away from her hands wet and raw. "There were nine Codys, I had nine Codys. Each one was like a half a year younger than the next one— like, two years old, two and a half, three. I mean, you know, at this age you turn around, you go away for a weekend or something, you come back and they're like an entirely different person, but this was, like, they must've popped *out* of each other and become separate people, you know, from a baby to a four-and-a-half-year-old. And all of them were doing different things, you know, for their age, and they weren't playing with each other. There were nine of them, and it was like each one was all alone, and I couldn't *help* them, I couldn't bring them together. I just wanted them to be friends and not be lonely, but they were, like, orbiting around my bed. It was so sad, I just wanted them to protect each other, you know, to *love* each other, because . . ." She faded, pummeled by her own visions.

"It was a dream, Brenda," Jesse said, scrawling blindly.

"I can still smell the baby's scalp." She wiped tears with the corner of the blanket. "Jesse, is there any smell in the world like the smell of your baby's scalp?"

"None," Jesse said carefully. She didn't think Brenda would have remembered her name and she found the sound of it in Brenda's mouth unnerving.

Ben poured two cups of coffee. In addition to Jesse's smokes, vitamins, and makeup, he had brought up a fresh T-shirt, jeans, and a change of underwear, all of it folded neatly on the floor next to her chair, a toothbrush and a comb crisscrossed on top. Sometimes Ben gave her the creeps.

Brenda sat up on the couch, trying to gather focus.

Ben took a red plastic bag from the kitchen, came around the cutout, and carefully fanned out a dozen CDs on the foot of the convertible. "I got Solomon Burke and Don Covay. I couldn't get ahold of the others, but I called some people and the general consensus was that if you liked that kind of stuff you'd probably go for these here too." He gestured to the discs: Linda Jones, Joe Tex, Johnny Taylor, Z. Z. Hill, Chuck Jackson, Doris Troy.

" 'Just One Look,' " Brenda said, mostly to herself.

"One guy I asked used to live in Memphis and he said these here should be right up your alley."

Brenda stared at the CDs, blinking, then looked up at Ben. "Thank you."

"My pleasure. Anything else I can do for you?" Brenda weakly tossed off her blanket and made it to her feet. Three steps from the bed, her legs gave out, but Ben caught her before she could hit the floor. "I got you," he said, in a light, encouraging voice, holding her by the elbows, his face suddenly blanched with exhaustion. Still holding her, he turned to his sister and gave her what Jesse assumed was supposed to be a reassuring wink but which, in his present state of fatigue, came off more like a facial spasm.

Unsteadily, Brenda twisted out of his grip and made it to the bathroom on her own, closing the door behind her.

Ben dug in his pocket and handed his sister two phone numbers printed on Post-its. "This one's the downstairs neighbor's, the Cromarties—they don't really know her—and this is her mother. I don't know how you want to play that one."

"You OK?" Jesse considered asking Ben how he had gotten ahold of the music so fast, same for the mother's number, but knew he would take great pleasure in going all cryptic on her.

"I'm good," Ben said, passing a hand across his sweat-fringed forehead. "It's hot today."

"Drink my juice."

"I'm good."

"Can you still handle downstairs?"

"Absolutely."

"I don't like neighbors."

"I got you." He moved toward the door.

"Ben, where'd you get the CDs?"

He shrugged. "The favor bank," he said, trying not to smile, proud of himself. He opened the apartment door, ducked his head out, came back in. "Hey, Jess?" His voice was lower now. "Twenty bills says she knows more than she's saying." As he closed the door behind him, Jesse considered dialing Jose on the cellular but thought better of it, fearing Jose's ability to coax a story out of her before she was ready to give it up. She knew all too well how easily 9:00 A.M. gospel could turn into 6:00 P.M. horseshit.

Brenda came out of the bathroom, face and fingers dripping. Jesse attempted to give her a hard read but Brenda seemed to pick up on it, meeting Jesse's eyes with an assessing gaze of her own. Jesse turned away as if shy or embarrassed, telling herself it would keep.

An hour later, sitting on the toilet in Brenda's apartment, Jesse heard voices directly over her head.

"Anybody talk to the brother?"

"Don't know."

"How about the father?"

"He's in the wind somewheres. Costa Rica?"

"How 'bout Grandma?"

"We're working on it."

"Who's in there with her?"

"Some runner from the local rag."

"Shit. Where's the apartment?"

"I think it's right under us."

Jesse looked up. The voices were coming from the roof, traveling down to her through the overhead exhaust vent.

Runner, Jesse bristled, thinking, Least I got through the door, roof boy.

Returning to the sealed and roasting living room, she saw Brenda peering around the drawn shade. Coming up behind her, Jesse looked down on the loose collection of shooters and neighbors on the street below. A few of them were calling up, as if they wanted Brenda to come out and play, and Jesse turned up the volume on the CD player to drown them out.

"Come away." She put a hand around Brenda's waist and steered her back to the bed.

"What do they think of me?" Brenda asked.

"They think you're going through hell. What else could they think?" The question was purposeful, but Brenda didn't take the bait, just sat on the edge of the convertible and sang along in a whisper—something about the greatest love, the greatest hurt.

"When's the detective coming for me?" Brenda rolled into the question as if it were a discordant line in the song, making it sound like Lorenzo was an executioner.

"He's just letting you rest. He'll be here, believe me." Jesse could have raised him on his beeper but was seized with a powerful anxiety herself. The new day terrorized her as much as it did Brenda: Lorenzo's arrival would signal the end of her monopoly. In a rush of panic she felt the urge simply to ask Brenda if she knew where her son was, yes or no. "You know, I have to tell you. When Lorenzo *does* get here? He's the best, but you should prepare yourself, because if they haven't found your son yet he's probably gonna ask you some difficult questions." Jesse left it hanging, watching her.

Downstairs, some smart-ass sang out, "War-ri-ors, come out and play-ee-yay." Another voice: "Brenda! Come down! We'll get you on TV! You can talk to the guy direct!"

Brenda put on a new CD, and the room exploded with the opening refrains of "Higher and Higher." She closed her eyes, going slightly up on tiptoe, as if the soaring ecstasy of Jackie Wilson's voice was enough to float her out of here, this room, this pain.

Once, I was broken-hearted . . .

She moved her lips to the words.

Disappointment
Was my closest friend.
But then you came,
And he soon de-parted

She swayed to the tune, in a rapture of avoidance.

And he never
showed his face again.
Because your love . . .

"Your love keeps lifting me," Brenda crooned in a high whisper.

Lifting me high-er.

"Brenda!" Another shout from outside. "Help us help you! Do it for Cody!"

High-er . . .

Brenda abruptly lurched for the window, shouldering Jesse to the side, then snapping up the shade, her sudden presence provoking a whirlpool of activity down there.

"Brenda, whoa." Jesse gently swung her around by the waist again, a square-dance move.

"I want to talk to them."

"You think you do, but you don't," Jesse said, trying to sound flip and reasonable as she gently pulled Brenda back across the room to the boom box and turned down the volume. "Trust me. You have something to say, down there's *not* where you want to say it, and those people out there are *not* who you want to say it to."

Brenda stopped and stared at her, not stupid, and Jesse told herself to tread lightly.

"Come here." She walked Brenda back to the drawn shade and made her take another peek. "Right now, those people are in a feeding frenzy, OK?"

Three shooters were sitting in their collapsible chairs reading paperbacks, but others were pacing, still worked up by Brenda's surprise appearance.

"Those guys down there? They have deadlines, they're under the gun, it's *hot,* they're bumping into each other, jacking each other up, and as a result—"

"I just want to say how much I miss him."

"They'll even fuck *that* up. You go down there, I don't care *what* you want to say . . . Wait. Hang on." Jesse grabbed Brenda by the hips and maneuvered her until she was positioned dead-center in front of the window. "Just don't move. Just . . ."

Jesse stepped to the wall and hit the pull cord, the shade flying up with a sharp zip, and she watched Brenda absorb the reaction downstairs, the abrupt transformation from contained restlessness to jostling bedlam. Counting to five, then pulling down the shade, Jesse provoked a round of exasperated entreaties. Brenda looked spooked now.

"What I'm saying is, that those guys? They don't have the time or the inclination to truly listen to you, do you know what I mean? You go out, open your mouth, they'll cut you down to three, four sound bites, paint you black or white, and when you read what they write about you? When you hear what they *say* about you? Given what, you know, you said to them? God as my witness, you'll be pulling out your hair by the fistful, you'll be screaming into some black hole. And you know what? People are gonna read that shit, see that shit, and they're gonna think they *know* you, they're gonna think they have your number."

Seeing Brenda's attention fading, Jesse forced herself to come to the end of her pitch. "You go down there, open up, it's gonna come back to haunt you, that's all I'm trying to say."

Brenda sat down, stood up, switched CDs.

"God as my witness, Brenda."

A wrenching female version of "For Your Precious Love" filled the room. Brenda was back down on the edge of the opened couch, her face close to her knees.

"Now, given all that"—Jesse took a breath, gearing up for the closer—"given all that, you still want to say something? There's a way to avoid that whole shark pit down there—by telling *me*. Why, because I'm not like them? Because I'm the pick of the litter? No. No. If I was down there, I'd be biting anything that moved, just like everybody else. But I'm not down there. I'm up here, and you and I, we have put in *hours* together. I heard your dreams, I listen to your music, you're a *person* to me."

Jesse reached over and touched one of Brenda's trembling knees. "Look, you say to me whatever you want, I'll get it right. You'll help me get it right. Believe me, when I get it down? When *we* get it down? The way we want? That's the way it's going out, and they'll all pick it up. But we have to control this at the source, OK? Otherwise . . ."

Jesse faltered, experiencing a swoon of exhaustion, an amorphous rush of love—for her job, this woman, this situation—and, knowing it could leave her as fast as it came, she threw everything she had into the punch line. "Brenda, I just want to be with you all the way." She was surprised to feel the words catch in her throat, surprised to hear the ardent, if selective, honesty of her declaration.

Brenda looked off, muttered, "Nobody could be with me all the way."

"I don't understand. Why not?" The set of Brenda's mouth told Jesse that she was pushing too hard again, talking too fast, and she forced herself to sit upright, give this woman some air.

Brenda turned to the CD player, slipped on a fresh disc, jacked up the volume, and retreated to the bathroom. Jesse lighted another cigarette, telling herself to back off or at least find some way of advancing that would look like a retreat. Brenda came out again, her face brightened by water.

"Where did you give birth?"

"You mean what hospital?" Jesse responded, on her toes. Brenda stood there waiting.

"In Florida," she murmured.

"You know where *I* gave birth? In a bathtub."

"What, that underwater-delivery thing?"

"I was living by myself in New York, one of those old walk-up tenements on the Lower East Side? It had this half tub in the kitchen. I was alone and I could tell he was coming. It was . . . There wasn't any time. I climbed in and I just, like, squatted. I just did it. Me and him, *we* did it."

"Jesus, Brenda." Jesse was momentarily awed, trying to slip under the skin of pain like that.

"Listen." Brenda cocked her head, raised a finger.

> *Love is a stranger*
> *And hearts are in danger*
> *On a smooth street paved with gold,*
> *True love*
> *Travels on a gravel road . . .*

Jesse scribbled down the lyrics, her notebook filling with snatches of songs.

"Percy Sledge," Brenda announced, helping out.

"Bathtub," Jesse unconsciously mumbled, thinking about isolation, vast isolation giving way to a most profound and delicate intimacy. The umbilical cord—how did she cut the umbilical cord?

"You say the word *mother* and people are supposed to weep or something," Brenda said, bowing her head and running her fingers through her tangled crop. "The mother, the mother . . . I never felt that way about mine, that sentimental way. You know, you do word association, someone says 'mother,' you're supposed to say 'Love. Warm. Comfort.' You know what *I* say? 'Dog biscuit.' "

Jesse drifted off, thinking about her own parents, the way political dementia led to years of second- and third-party child abuse.

"You get mad at Michael, what do you do?" Brenda asked abruptly.

"What?"

"You ever give him the silent treatment?"

"No." Jesse ran a finger across her brow. "Of course not."

"The silent treatment. I would have rather"—Brenda paused—"I would have rather my mother beat me with a fucking club. I would do something, right? Steal, mess up, anything, and she'd start in, 'Why do you torture me like this, why—the person who loves you more than anybody. Why do you hate me so much, because you *know* how it kills me when you do this, things like this. I know you know this is stabbing me in the heart, these things you do. Why, Brenda, *why*. What have I done to be punished like this. Why is God punishing me for loving you. *Why*.' "

Jesse watched, fascinated as patches began to bloom on Brenda's throat and cheeks.

"And, you know, she'd start in on me like that and five minutes into it I'd be belly-down on the floor, you know, *writhing*, and this one time I just said to her, 'Mommy, maybe you shouldn't love me so much.' I was like eight, nine, and she stopped for a minute, you know, beating her breast, and she looks at me, like . . ." Brenda narrowed her eyes and cocked her head to one side in an attitude of sinister assessment. "And she says, 'You don't want me to love you so much? OK.' " Still playing her mother, Brenda nodded to herself as if making some internal decision. " 'OK'—and I swear, that woman did not talk to me for three days. Three *days*, until I was pulling on her, begging her, 'Mommy, Mommy.' And then she looks at me, gives me one of those *smiles*, says, 'All right. Just remember this the next time you think I shouldn't love you so much.' "

Brenda looked at Jesse and barked out a laugh. "Whoo!"

"Jesus," Jesse whispered, assigning that one to a back burner, only to be used if Brenda went to jail.

"You know what growing up was all about for me? It was the journey from I would die without her to wishing she were dead—to not giving a shit one way or the other as long as she keeps her distance."

"My mother was a Communist," Jesse volunteered, unsure if her words were audible.

"What you give your children is who you are. You make them suffer in any way that involves a choice of action on your part, you make them suffer from any behavior of yours that you could have, *mastered*, then you're an obscenity. You're shit in God's mouth." Brenda's voice was as raw as her words, full of self-loathing.

"I hear you," Jesse said mindlessly, scribbling furiously, writing down

"Silent Treatment," writing "Power," writing "Control," the pencil slipping out of her fingers as she succumbed to a wave of fatigue.

As she stooped to pluck the pencil from the rug, she became aware of a distinct silence from the street below—a roaring, implosive silence that was familiar to her, the nonsound of an abrupt funneling of energy from a vast, vague field to a focal point—and she anticipated the clicks and whirrs seconds before she actually heard them.

Racing to the window, she saw Ben on his knees, Danny Martin standing behind him, struggling to snap cuffs on his oversized wrists, every image-starved shooter down there working in a purposeful arc. A low, tense murmur now rose as the shooters began to ask one another what exactly they were documenting here. Jesse imagined the scene five minutes before—Ben, claiming he was family, trying to stop Brenda's brother from entering. She was frightened now, knowing she had only a few minutes left before she got tossed out the window, unless she could come up with a way to neutralize this bastard at the door, find some way to seize the reins. If she couldn't, if she was on her way out no matter what, then she had the same few minutes to hit Brenda with some last-ditch, nothing-to-lose questions: "What do you know that you're not telling me. Where is your son" all the way to "Did you kill him," the questions leaving nothing behind, scorched earth bombers. Jesse was frantic, trying to decide: play it cool and get bounced; play it cool and make it through this; throw a match in the ammo box, step back, and watch the fireworks.

Brenda stood over the boom box by the far wall. "What," she said, trying to read what was going on downstairs in Jesse's eyes.

"Your brother's coming up." Brenda opened her mouth but nothing came out. She raised a hand like a stop sign. "He's going to try to throw me out. If you want me gone, that's how it's going to happen. If you want me to stay, you got to remember this is *your* house," Jesse said, hearing Danny on the stairs, bracing herself, rehearsing: "Danny, I was taking care of her all night." "Brenda, where's Cody?" "Danny, I was put here by Lorenzo." "Brenda, you killed your son, didn't you . . ."

The door was unlocked and Danny just walked in without breaking stride, Jesse smelling his all-night breath from across the room. Brenda worked her mouth soundlessly while Danny stared at Jesse with half recognition, having seen her at various crime scenes over the years. Jesse knew he'd put it together in seconds.

"Who's this," he asked his sister, his eyes still on Jesse.

"She's a reporter," Brenda said, then sucked air. Jesse sensed that she hadn't meant to say that but . . .

Danny took a step toward Jesse. "Out," he said, gesturing toward the door. Jesse stepped back and shot Brenda a desperate look.

"She's been helping me," Brenda offered.

"Yeah, I'll bet." Danny shocked Jesse by grabbing her wrist. She didn't think he'd get physical, and her reaction was to lean back from his grip as if she were water-skiing, digging her heels into the carpet.

"This is *my* house," Brenda said, trying to put some heft in it.

"This is what?" Danny let go of Jesse's wrist, wheeled to face his sister. "Meaning *what*. What the fuck is wrong with you. After what you put us through, you buddy up with a *reporter?*"

"She's helping me." Brenda kept bobbing forward and then rearing back; Jesse feeling for her, So hard to be brave.

"What, you don't have *one* friend? You have to go out and . . . Are you *sick* or something?"

Jesse saw Brenda begin to tremble, and against her better judgment, she opened her mouth. "Look, I've been in this house since four in the morning. Lorenzo Council put me here. I'm not gonna screw anybody. My brother's down there keeping people away for the last five hours. I haven't done nothing but watch your sister's back, from the jump."

"Lorenzo." Danny nodded, a bad sign. Jesse found herself backing up, as if to hold on to something. He stared at her for a long moment, then snapped his fingers and pointed at her. "Yeah, OK, sure, you're the one that got him on the Rolonda Watts show." He tapped his head. "Duh. Now *he* puts *you* in the cockpit on this," he said, tapping his head again, turning to Brenda.

"She's gonna write a fuckin' *book* on this, Brenda."

"On *what*," Jesse snapped.

"You're fucking pathetic," Danny said to his sister in a near-whisper, eyes half closed with passion. Brenda responded by cocking her head, birdlike, staring at her brother until she had his full attention, then swiveling on one hip like a discus thrower, swinging her left arm in a full backhand arc across the front of her body, and slamming that injured hand into the metal door frame of her son's bedroom.

Both Danny and Jesse went up on tiptoes at the sound of the impact, Danny seizing his head and hissing "Jesus!" Brenda, impassive, held his eyes, then did it again—swivel, swing, and crack, the second collision making Jesse nauseated. Jesse forced herself to stay put—let the brother stop her; it would be good for him. But Danny stood rooted through a third smash, when the pain caught up with Brenda and she slowly sank to her knees, quiet and stunned. Danny followed her down.

"Brenda, Brenda." His voice was calmer now, the violence having done its work. Brenda cradled her reinjured hand and gazed off as if no longer interested in pleading her case. "Brenda." On one knee, Danny reached out with both arms as if to embrace her but never made contact. He turned to Jesse and jerked his head toward the front door—Get lost—but Jesse turned away and busied herself looking out the window, hoping he was incapable of rising to his feet right now and ejecting her himself.

Downstairs, Danny's car was being mobbed by shooters. Jesse envisioned Ben cuffed in the backseat, staring at his knees, patient, immobile. She turned to the sound of a closing door, turned to a now-empty room, and for a moment she panicked, thinking that Danny had taken his sister out. Then she heard their voices from the kid's bedroom.

"Tell me what happened."

"I *said* it ten times."

"Say it *again.*"

Jesse turned down the music and stepped closer to the closed door, since Danny's voice was coming through softer now, pleading.

"Brenda, we're chasing ghosts out there. Where's the kid, where's the car, we can't even find . . . Are you doing dope again?" Danny's question sounded almost tender.

"No."

"Please, I won't yell."

"No."

"No, you're not doing dope? Or no, I won't tell you," he said. Jesse could hear him begin to steam up again.

"No!"

"Brenda, I'm your brother. I love you. Just tell me what happened."

"No!" Brenda's voice was taking on timbre.

"I fucked up with you, didn't I."

"Please." Brenda was doing the pleading now, as if Danny's self-castigation were more hurtful than his anger.

"I always fuck up with you, I'm so hard on you. I should know better. I should be more understanding. I don't know why I can't—"

Jesse jumped back as the bedroom door banged open. Brenda stood there wild-eyed, desperate to escape, racing to the CD player, putting something on and jacking up the volume, calling on the power of Soul to blast her brother out of the house.

11

The Dempsy County jail stood half demolished, and the only surviving section of exterior wall, the southwest corner, was a grotesquely defiant crumble of plaster and brick, a raised fist thrust into the flawless blue of a hot summer morning. The prison bars, running the entire length of the building but hidden from view for ninety years by a sooty gray facade, had now, in these final days, revealed the building for what it truly had been: a seven-story cage. Those bars were naked to the sun, intersecting in a grid pattern, with seven layers of sheared prison cells hanging open and raw. A century's worth of graffiti, startlingly legible to anyone walking by, marked the plaster backwalls, a titanic bulletin board shot up from hell.

When Lorenzo pulled up to the main jailhouse steps, which now led to nothing but their own height, he saw Army Howard out front sitting on the open tailgate of an old pickup truck, still wearing his Perry Ellis America warm-up suit from the night before. As Lorenzo approached, treading his way through small chunks of jail, Army flicked his cigarette into the debris. "Hey, boss," Lorenzo said, clasping Army's hand upright, as if they were going to arm wrestle.

" 'S up." Army yawned into his fist and leaned back against the edge of a coffee-table-sized object in the truck bed. It was covered with a filthy children's blanket printed with dinosaurs.

"What you got there?" Lorenzo tilted his chin toward the mystery.

Army looked right, left, right again, then lifted the blanket, revealing a jagged chunk of the 1909 cornerstone, the letters NTY JAIL carved deep into the granite face.

"Get outta here." Lorenzo's voice went high, trailing off with surprise.

Army replaced the blanket, lit another cigarette. "My brother-in-law's on the demolition crew. I got this here sold to two cops and a prison guard."

"Together?"

"Separate. Paid me three hundred each up front."

Lorenzo laughed, a guttering sound. "Sounds like a Army special . . ."

Army nodded. "Yeah, I'm gonna tell 'em somebody else got it first but I can buy it from them, but you know three hundred ain't enough, so how high can you go? Give it to the winner." Army smiled distantly and patted the stone under the blanket. "Yeah, it does sound like a Army special, don't it? Sounds like a Army classic."

"Yeah." Lorenzo stared down at his shoes, pacing himself. A water bug crawled over the rubble, a last tenant.

"Shit, man," Army drawled, "been in this joint so many damn times? I feel like selling this thing to my *own* self, you know, like a, a keepsake or something. Like the last laugh, you know what I'm saying?"

Lorenzo idly kicked what looked like a tooth. "How you doin' otherwise?"

"How'm I doin'?" Army shook his head. "Not too good, not too good. I got me bills longer'n train smoke. You know Sheryl? The one I got on Boulware Street? She thinks I'm fuckin' around on her, so she goes into Western District, tells Valentine I robbed her at gunpoint, and now this time I can't fuck around. I had to go get me Rosenfeld. I ain't takin' no chances with Legal Aid, 'cause you know Valentine. He's been lookin' to put me away from back in the *day*, you know what I'm sayin'? And Rosenfeld, he gets his money up front. So there's that, awright?"

Lorenzo nodded sympathetically.

"Yeah, and then my wife, Pauline? She wants to have another goddamn baby, can you believe that? The woman is forty-two years old, doctor says she can't *have* no baby. I tell her we got one grandchild livin' with us already, what you want with another kid now for?" Army hissed in disgust. "So, you know, next thing I know I'm out somewhere in Bayonne, go to this clinic where they get you pregnant? You know, they take some eggs, take your sperm. Hey." Army waved it off. "I don't even want to talk about it. Woman's forty-two years old, she's a goddamn grandmother, but you know, that's what she wants, so . . . We did it three times, right? You know, three implantations? That's three times fourteen thousand dollars. Fourteen thousand dollars times *three*. And it ain't even worked, but they're, like, 'Pay up,' and I'm, like, 'Yeah, I'll give you your money. Come to the baby's first birthday party, I'll have a check for you,' you know what I'm sayin'? I mean, you go into a restaurant, do you pay *before* or *after* the food comes, right? And, like, I don't even hear no pots bangin' in the kitchen yet, so . . ."

"I hear you." Lorenzo smiled at his own shoes.

"Yeah, an' so now I got this motherfuckin' collection agency on my back, and, damn, you ever deal with those people? So, like, I got *that*—Sheryl, Valentine, Rosenfeld, my wife, my granddaughter's sick 'n' shit. Too much, too much. An' alls I got right now is a nickel and a nail, and the nail don't spend, so you know I had to close up the motherfuckin' store. Can't pay the delivery bills, can't pay the rent, had to shut it down before the landlord kicked me to the curb, you know what I'm sayin'? An' so now, like, where am I gonna run this shit here?" Army took a pair of red translucent dice from his pocket, rattled them loosely in his fist. "This the cash machine, right? And, like, I ain't even got a setup for this now, no backroom, *nothin'*."

"You know what my moms used to say?" Lorenzo knuckled down a yawn. " 'The world don't owe you nothing but hard times and bubble gum—' "

" 'And it's fresh out of bubble gum,' " Army said, finishing it up for him.

"Yeah, you got your problems." Lorenzo read some graffiti off the exposed back wall of a third-floor prison cell: EL HA RECUSITATO.

Lorenzo grunted one last time and then got into it. "So, you hear anything?"

"About what, last night?" Lorenzo settled in with a heavy-lidded nod. "Yeah, you know what I heard? I heard *I* did it."

"I heard that too."

"Yeah, I didn't think you were calling me just to listen to my problems. No, I didn't do it. Sorry."

"How come people say you did?"

"You know what I think? I think my goddamn nephew's been talking that shit about me again."

"Curtis?"

"Naw, the other, Rudy, my sister's kid. That boy gets two beers in him, he's got me robbing Fort Knox. Tells people all kinds of shit 'cause he, like, idolizes me all the time, you know? I tell him, 'Don't idolize me, idolize your teachers, 'cause if you want to make it in this world you got to know how to *speak* it, *spell* it, and *read* it.' "

Lorenzo dug a toe into some sky-blue plaster, watching a chunk of brick molt off the southwest corner, skip its way down the jagged edge of the facade, picking up speed with every hit, and finally dive twenty feet out from its last bump, landing in a mound of wet Masonite.

"I tell him, 'You want to see the light at the end of the tunnel? You got to keep your nose to the grindstone.' " Army lit a third cigarette. "It's got to be Rudy."

Lorenzo unfolded a copy of the flyer and passed it over. Army glanced at it. "Yeah, I saw this. Huh. You know who this looks like? Looks like my cousin George. Don't that look like George Howard?"

Lorenzo took back the flyer, carefully folding it in quarters. He had seen Curious George dead asleep on his grandmother's linoleum last night. "So you didn't hear—"

"Nothin'."

"How about Rudy? Where was he at last night?"

"Rudy? He's in a wheelchair, Lorenzo." Army laughed.

Lorenzo snapped his fingers, chagrined. "I'm mixing him up. Awright, so nothin'?"

"You know who I'd tell." Army slid off the tailgate and slammed it shut.

"I had an uncle was in demolition," Lorenzo said, eyeing the blanket-draped cornerstone. "You know what he called it? Making sky."

Army walked around to the cab. "Put a positive spin on it, huh?" He slipped into the driver's seat, stuck his head out the window. "Yo, Big Daddy." Lorenzo turned to him from his car. "*You* want to buy this? I'll give it to you right here and now, five hundred dollars."

Lorenzo considered it for a second, then passed. "Naw, man, it would be too much like taking my work home with me, you know what I'm saying?"

Army laughed, a lazy bark, then pulled out.

Bobby McDonald's office was hung with a bizarre combination of sunset paintings, crime scene photos, and action shots of his son banging under the boards for Our Lady of Solace high school. Dressed in a cheap wheat-colored sport jacket and chinos, Bobby sat on the windowsill. The prosecutor, Peter Capra, sporting a steel-gray three-piece suit, sat, knees crossed, on a nubby brown-and-yellow couch.

Coming into the room less than an hour after meeting with Army, Lorenzo felt awkwardly underdressed in jeans and a black T-shirt that read PRESS ON. He had no idea where to position himself and finally settled for leaning against the wall nearest to the door, his arms folded across his chest.

"How she holding up?" Capra asked, stubbing out a cigarette.

"Bad." Lorenzo tightened his mouth for emphasis.

"Bad, like tragedy bad?" It was Capra again; Lorenzo was pretty sure that Bobby would say next to nothing.

"Bad, like banged up—you know, emotional." Lorenzo inadvertently hit the wall switch behind his back, blinding everybody with fluorescence.

"Sorry," he said, flicking it off, telling himself to relax.

"She talking to you?" Capra again.

"Oh yeah."

"Anything worth hearing?"

"Not, you know . . ." Lorenzo moved to the edge of Bobby's desk, perched there for a while.

"Is she a piece of shit?"

"How do you mean?" he said. Then, reflecting for a second, "Not, no. I don't think so."

"So, like, you don't see her hanging tough on this story."

Capra's cell phone rang inside his jacket. He slipped a hand in and killed the call, waiting on Lorenzo.

"Well, not, you know—once again—if it *is* a story. But no, I can't see her holding out for too long, no."

Bobby squinted out his window. Lorenzo knew how much he hated surrendering his office like this.

"Can you see her giving it up to you?"

"Hey." Lorenzo laughed nervously. "We just met."

"You like her?"

"What do you mean?"

Capra lit another cigarette. "You *feel* for her."

"Yeah." Lorenzo fanned away the first waft of smoke. "I do."

"Good." Capra nodded. "So, OK. Why don't we set up a kind of two-pronged offensive here. You let us worry about the jacker, the car, the witnesses, and you stick with her. You know, keep her talking."

Lorenzo hesitated for a moment, not sure if this signaled a promotion or a demotion. Capra looked to Bobby on the windowsill. "Yeah?" Bobby nodded. It had clearly been a done deal between them before Lorenzo ever walked in the door.

"What if she's telling the truth?" Lorenzo asked, folding his arms across his chest again.

"That's why we're doing a two-pronged offensive. Cover our bets."

"Would you rather be working the jacker end?" Bobby said, speaking up. "You want to pass her off?"

Lorenzo thought about it, decided that he wanted to be where the action was on this one. "No, I'm good. I can, I'm good."

"Do you want any help with her?" Capra offered.

"No," Lorenzo said, thinking, Too many cooks. "No. I mean, maybe, but not yet."

"Because as you can well imagine . . ." Capra stubbed out his second cigarette. "We have people waiting in the wings. I mean, they're camping out on *line* for this one."

"What, FBI?" Lorenzo said, the final drift of cigarette smoke making his lungs flare.

Capra nodded. "So what do you think?"

Lorenzo experienced a surge of possessiveness—she knew more than she'd been saying, and he would definitely have it out of her.

"The FBI, can you keep them away?" He looked to Bobby for backup or approval, but his boss's gaze was directed out the window again.

"You think we should?" Capra asked mildly.

Bobby finally turned back to the room and tersely nodded to Lorenzo. It was a craved-for gesture of support that somehow boomeranged. Lorenzo panicked momentarily, much as he had the night before in the hospital when he first realized the enormity of the potential fallout from this situation.

"How about can you give me just today?" he said.

Bobby and Capra looked at each other. "OK." Capra shrugged. "We can play it by ear."

"And can you do something else for me?" Lorenzo said, feeling stronger now. "Can you get all them cops out of Armstrong?"

Capra took a deep breath. "Lorenzo, you remember five years ago in the Powell Houses they shot the principal of Twenty-eight School?"

"I was right there," Lorenzo said. He had hoped Capra wouldn't compare that situation to this one.

"Guy was just walking." Capra proceeded to lay out the tale, ignoring Lorenzo's claim to having been on the scene. "Bang, out of the blue. Nine million windows—could have come from anywhere, right?"

"I was there."

"We closed off the houses, and what happened. Three hours, that's all it took. The jugglers brought us that knucklehead on a silver platter. Three hours."

"Yeah, well, number one . . ." Lorenzo eased off the edge of the desk, checked his watch. "It's been fourteen hours, OK? And number two, there very well might not be any knucklehead to *bring* this time."

"Well, what if there is?" Capra countered lightly.

"No." Lorenzo smiled through his anger. "I don't see nothing good coming out of this blockade you got goin' on over there."

"No, I hear what you're saying," Capra said mildly, Lorenzo reading it as Tough shit.

Bobby stared at his shoes, outgunned.

"Well, can you at least get Gannon out?" Lorenzo said.

"I tell you what." Capra sucked his teeth. "Get her to talk to you."

A few minutes later, still smiling, still angry, Lorenzo left Bobby Mc-Donald's office, feeling like the prosecutor was doing to him what the cops were doing to the Armstrong Houses.

Lorenzo rolled up to Brenda's apartment house a little before noon and had to wade through the shooters, head down, hands up, nothing to say. Ben came out of the vestibule and helped clear a path to the door. Inside the building, Lorenzo gave him the once-over: gray marble forehead, mouth slightly ajar, a flutter in the hands. He saw the angry cuff marks on the wrists. Ben put his hands behind his back, embarrassed.

"What happened?" Lorenzo said.

"Nothing."

"The brother?"

"I'm good."

Lorenzo decided not to pursue it; they were in Danny's town now. "You here all morning?"

"No big deal," Ben answered with fatigued chirpiness.

"I'm gonna get her out of here for a while, so you go call it a day, all right?"

"You taking her?" Ben said quickly. "How about Jesse?"

Lorenzo shrugged, thinking, No way. "We'll play it by ear," he said, not wanting to give Ben a negative answer. He started to climb the stairs, then couldn't resist. "It was the brother, right? Danny?" He ducked down so Ben could see him halfway up the stairs.

Ben blushed, turned away. "I'm good."

When Lorenzo entered the apartment, Brenda was sitting on the edge of the convertible, tense and expectant, hands in her lap, waiting for him. She had on fresh clothes, even a touch of makeup, but looked baggy and rumpled. Jesse did too—clean clothes, a little mascara, but somehow disheveled. Lorenzo needed only one look at her to know that, much like himself, she didn't have shit; otherwise she wouldn't be standing there like a human corkscrew, hugging herself, glaring at the floor, most likely racking her brains for a pitch that would allow her to hold Brenda's hand through the coming day.

"What's going on?" Jesse asked, looking off, not sufficiently armed to make eye contact with him yet.

"We're out there humpin'," he said, feeling sorry for her, then turning to Brenda. "Did you get any rest?" He was just asking to be polite.

"Cody," Brenda whispered.

He caught a glimpse of himself in a mirror and saw that he didn't look so hot either, the three of them turning this room into a 4 A.M. Greyhound terminal. "Brenda? What I'd like to do is take you back to the houses, take a look at the scene in the daytime. Maybe we can talk a little more, go over some details."

Brenda nodded, then slowly, carefully hung headphones around her neck, the padded earpieces coming to rest on her collarbone. She took up a Discman and a zippered CD case, rose to her feet, but lost her balance, flopping back to a sitting position. On the second attempt she finally made it up. Lorenzo watched her, thinking she should be going berserk right now, assaulting him with questions, on her knees praying, *anything* other than this moving around as if she were made of fractured glass, Lorenzo thinking, It's here, right here.

"Can I speak to you?" Jesse asked, walking into the kitchen area and waiting there as he gestured for Brenda to hang tight.

"So what's shaking out there . . ." Jesse asked tonelessly, playing with a spatula.

"Brick wall," Lorenzo said. "What happened to your brother?"

"Tried to play doorman with Danny Martin."

"Whoa." Lorenzo yawned. "Excuse me."

"Yeah, Danny came up here, got into a shout-out with his sister, went back down, and I guess he just changed his mind, cut Ben loose, and took off."

"Other fish to fry," Lorenzo said. "Anything I should know about that shout-out?"

Jesse shrugged. "Guy's all buffaloed."

"Buffaloed," Lorenzo repeated.

"Yeah, it's been pretty wild around here," she said tensely, flipping the spatula into the sink.

"Yeah, huh?"

"I'm not blowing my own horn or anything, but I have to say, if I wasn't on my toes, like, nonstop? You'd probably be needing a body bag this morning." She finally raised her face to him. "I can keep her functional."

"I can't do it, Jesse. You know that." He smiled to soften the cutoff, seeing in the pouches and crevices of her exhaustion a glimpse of the old woman to come.

"Are you bringing her back here?"

"I can't say."

"You can't say, because . . ."

"I can't say." His smile shrunk a little.

"Yeah, well, she said some interesting stuff last night." Jesse picked up a box of Lucky Charms.

"Like?" Lorenzo was too tired for this.

"I can't say." Jesse looked him in the eye again.

"No. You cannot *play* me like that." He leaned into her, making her arch backwards, her spine pressed into the sink. In her retreat from his anger, he saw again that she really didn't have shit.

Outside, the shooters came at them in a rush, Lorenzo trying to shield Brenda, Jesse hanging on to his coattails, the barking of the mob divided between calling out for Brenda to watch the birdie, to say something, and yelling at Jesse to get the fuck out of the picture. Brenda reacted to this gauntlet by cowering, shell-shocked, then abruptly turning to the cameras with an open-faced eagerness, a wide-eyed, guileless hunger for reassurance. Lorenzo got the impression that it was not the cameras she was facing—those she ignored. Rather, she was facing the shooters, the individuals. She turned to them because they were *there*, personally engaged with her plight and therefore capable of granting her some kind of boon.

As they headed for Lorenzo's sedan, they passed two reporters rooting through the garbage cans, bringing up Red Dog, Pizza Hut, a prescription bottle, one guy squinting as he read the label. Brenda turned to them, said, "That's not my garbage," with the same undisguised hunger for connection she had shown the shooters.

"Let me ride with you." Jesse was almost begging.

"Jess," he said, once and for all time. Ben pulled up behind Lorenzo's car, leaned over, and pushed open the passenger door for his sister.

Pulling out, Lorenzo saw Jesse in his rearview. The expression of anguish on her face was, to his thinking, way out of proportion to her loss.

Once they had rolled clear of the video mob, some of whom had jogged after the car for the first few blocks like rice throwers at a wedding, Lorenzo calmed down enough to eye Brenda's discs: Al Green, Ann Peebles, Curtis Mayfield. She was listening to something now, staring straight ahead and moving her lips to the lyrics; Lorenzo could hear "Feel Like Breaking Up Somebody's Home" coming through her phones, minute and metallic. He didn't hold the music against her, figuring that the phones were there to keep her brains from leaking out her ears. The only alternative was to conclude that she was both cold-hearted and stupid. Nonetheless, he recommitted himself to breaking her down, to maintaining a one-prong mind-set on this.

Brenda sang along with her disc in the hoarse, loopy, half-whispered croon of someone who doesn't realize that she can be heard. Lorenzo touched her arm. She slipped off the headphones.

"Anything come to you last night?"

"Nightmares."

He took out the folded police sketch, passed it to her.

"How does he look today?"

"Did you arrest anyone?"

"Not yet."

She nodded, pressed her bandages to her eyes. Again Lorenzo thought, She should be all over me, chewing my ass. He could swear that what he sensed coming off her at this news of no news was relief. "How you feeling?" he asked, looking at her bandages, seeing that the gauze on the back of her left hand was blotted the dark brown of dried blood.

"They want me to go on TV," she said.

"Yeah?" Lorenzo didn't tell her that she had been on already, that this morning's gauntlet would put her back on tonight.

"I won't do it."

"OK."

"They . . . I won't. I just want to be left alone."

Lorenzo nodded.

"I feel like I'm being crushed." She stared straight ahead, knees running.

"I hear you," Lorenzo said, laying back.

"I just want to be alone. I know I can't, I know I can't be *allowed* to now," she said, her voice climbing to a penitential singsong, Lorenzo thinking, Allowed.

"But I just won't do it. No television."

"What if it helps find your son?"

"No," she responded bluntly. She slipped on her headphones again and Lorenzo let it be, losing himself in running down the game plan for the next few hours, hoping that Bump had set the scene as requested.

Brenda bobbed gently in her seat, as if in prayer, her sing-along reduced to a high, toneless keen from the back of her throat. She remained in that state until they came abreast of the Mumford Houses, a mock-Federal-style low-rise project that covered two square blocks of the city. She looked up at the blue-and-orange billboard announcing the name, turned to stare at the buildings as the car passed them, then took off her headphones.

"Did you work the Kenya Taylor murder?" she asked.

"No, that wasn't mine," Lorenzo said, wondering where she was going with this. Brenda was referring to the stabbing death of a thirteen-year-old girl in those houses, the actor the jilted boyfriend of Kenya's mother. The actor had waited for his ex-girlfriend to drive her new lover to work that morning, then come into the apartment and taken his revenge out on the woman's daughter, afterwards writing with lipstick on the living room wall, YOU ROCK MY WORLD I ROCK YOURS. James White— Lorenzo saw his face now—James White.

"The guy, he's still out there, right?" Brenda asked.

"Yup. Got married last month too." Lorenzo left out that he had shown up at the killer's wedding just to fuck with the guy's big day. White didn't have the guts to kick him out. Fucked up Lorenzo's day too. "Did you know her, Brenda?"

"Yeah," she said, looking at her hands. "I was a teacher's aide at

Forty-six School when that happened. That day, I swear to God, the kids, when they heard what happened to Kenya? The whole school fell apart. All these thirteen-year-old hard cases, hard boys, everybody, they were all crying like babies."

"Yeah, I heard about that."

"Nobody could teach. They had to send in this trauma team from Trenton. It was like a disaster area, that school. They had to set up, like, for a hurricane or a flood. They had this one born-again teacher, Mr. Conklin? He turned his classroom into a praying room, and they put a bunch of the trauma team people in the library, made that the time-out room for anybody wanting to come in, have a cry, talk about it. And the rest of the trauma people, they just roamed the halls to spot kids looking like they needed some help. And thank God they were there, because the teachers, they, we weren't in much better shape than the kids."

"Huh." Lorenzo knew all this.

"I remember they put some movie on in the auditorium, just played it all day, anybody wanted to watch it, and they opened up the gym, threw all the balls out on the floor, anybody could play, let off steam. And on the fourth floor, they had this double-sized classroom. They made that the game room, and I was in charge of that, if anybody wanted to come up, play Monopoly or whatever, and, I remember everybody in my room, we had this enormous, like, life-sized jigsaw puzzle of America, all the pieces different states. I mean, I swear, this thing was maybe thirty feet across, and I just remember watching maybe a dozen freaked-out kids, each with a different state in his hands trying to put the country together. And this one boy, Reginald Hackett, very tough kid from Mumford, real hard-core, I remember him standing in the middle of the country holding, like, Kansas or Nebraska or wherever, and he couldn't figure out where it belonged, and he just bust out started to cry . . ." Brenda faltered, crying herself now.

"These kids . . ." She tamped her tears by pressing her face into her shoulder. "These kids, they couldn't handle it, you know, because Kenya, she was from Mumford, and, like, Mumford's the big feeder for Forty-six School, everybody goes to Forty-six, and the projects, you know what they're like. It's just one big cousins club, so it was like losing a relative or something, but . . ." She wiped her face and started in again, her voice fluttering through her tears. "But I often wonder *why* everybody fell apart like that over her. I mean, they had other kids, over the years, you know, die, but, I don't know, maybe it was because she didn't do anything to, I know this sounds horrible, but she didn't do anything to *deserve* it. I mean, she wasn't hanging out on the street corner, she wasn't riding around in some dopemobile, she wasn't playing hookie. She was *home*. It was early in the morning, she was getting dressed for school, she didn't *do* anything." Brenda stared at Lorenzo as if pleading Kenya's case, her face flushed and distraught, demanding.

Lorenzo grunted, shook his head in sympathy, waiting.

"I mean, things happen like that, it's lot easier to accept it if you can find some kind of, of lesson in it, but, you know, nothing. It was like the world had lost its mind. I mean, *nothing.*" Brenda licked her chipped and peeling lips. "And, like, Kenya . . . See, I think the school freaking out like that, I think it had a lot to do with Kenya herself, like, how she came across. Because on one hand, I'll tell you, she was no angel. No way. But she had, like, this, this charisma. She was a big girl, big, big-boned, tall. And she was a fighter, all the time, all the time. And she wasn't afraid of anybody. Like, even the boys kept their distance, because she was too independent for them and they probably knew she wouldn't put up with any of their shit, you know, everybody calling their girlfriends 'my shorty' and all that. But she had this great smile. And something else. She loved little kids and, you know, that school goes from kindergarten on up, and I remember seeing her around the little kids? She was the most sweet-tempered, gentle teenager I'd ever seen. I mean, if you were on eye level with her you had hell on your hands, but with the first graders? The second graders? She never raised her voice. And, you know, the thing with a lot of projects people, it's like they're always yelling, yelling at their kids. I mean they might not even be angry, but it's bark, yell, shout." Brenda winced and pressed her hands to her temples.

Lorenzo saw the towers of Armstrong in the distance and felt fatigue like a fine drift of grit under the skin around his eyes, in his joints.

"I don't know, maybe people think that unless they can *see* a reaction from a kid, you know, tears or something, maybe they don't think they're getting anything across. Like, people don't know that there's this world *inside* a child, and maybe the more you yell, bellow, smack, the quieter the kid's gonna get, the more that kid's gonna hide from you. I mean this city . . . Most people don't think like that, but Kenya, she was, she had a gift for being with kids. She had a gift . . ." Brenda trailed off, wiped her eyes, sniffing wet and raw. "Jesus."

Lorenzo nodded, not telling her that Kenya was one of his many godchildren, that the killer, James White, had about six more months of legitimate police investigation coming at him—the exercise of perhaps a half dozen more angles of pressure on various buddies, ex-girlfriends, relatives, anybody who could place him in the apartment at the time— and that, if all of those avenues turned into dead ends, one night there might be this terrible accident . . .

"But anyways, Kenya. The day that happened I come home and Cody, he can see I'm upset and he asks me what's wrong. I tell him a bad thing happened to this—I don't know how I described her—this *big* girl in school, I think, and I leave out the details, but I tell him why I liked her, how she was a handful with kids her own age, how everybody was a little scared of her, but I also tell him how sweet she was to the little kids, how they all loved her, and Cody, I see in his eyes how he's absorbing her, and he looks at me . . . He looks . . ." She paused, got a grip. "He looks at me and he says, 'Mommy? Would she have liked *me?'* And . . ." Brenda took a breath. "And I said, 'She would have *loved* you.' And he nods, my son, this little nod, and he says 'Good.' I'll never forget that. 'Good.'"

"Brenda." Lorenzo parked the car two blocks from the Hurley Street blockade, alongside a surveillance van with heavily tinted windows. "Why are you telling me all this about Kenya?"

"About . . ." She hesitated, then said, "No, no, no," touching his arm. "I'm telling you about my son."

Slipping on her headphones again, she slunk down in her seat and pushed Play.

Bump hopped out of the surveillance van, and he and Lorenzo quickly swapped vehicles. Someone had left a copy of the *New York Post* faceup on the dashboard, the tinted windshield creating a mirror image of Brenda in her crouching anguish of the night before. Lorenzo snatched the paper away before she could see it and passed it out the driver's window to Bump, who was on the street.

"How's she doing?" Bump asked, rolling the paper into a baton. In the passenger seat, Brenda, phones to her ears, started to sway. Bump stared at her, then shot Lorenzo a look.

Lorenzo shrugged: Let it be.

Squinting through the heat toward the houses, Bump whapped the paper baton into an open palm. "We had us a big fuckin' roll-around already this morning."

"Who."

"Jamal Bankhead."

"And . . ."

"Me. Fuckin' bonehead's out there on the edge of the sprinklers hangin' with his crew, throwing back forties."

"He ain't allowed to drink there."

"No shit. I say, 'Yo, Jamal, you got the DMZ we gave you guys under the overpass for that. Do your drinkin' there.' He says, 'They's *bees* over there.' I say, 'You can't drink here. There's all these kids barefoot in the sprinklers. You drop one of them forties, it's a disaster. You don't like the DMZ? Then go the fuck upstairs, do your drinkin' there.' He says to me, 'If I was drinking glass-bottle Pepsis, you wouldn't be saying shit, so later for *that*.'"

"What the fuck is wrong with him . . ." Lorenzo said, finding himself craving a beer for the first time in years, an unnerving sensation.

"I say, 'Just get the fuck up there.' I turn my back—ba-*doom*—I get it right between the shoulder blades. Some little kid sat on a sprinkler head, and the water, as they say, got misdirected. I turn around, there's Jamal, like, 'Haw, haw.' I couldn't help myself: drunk and disorderly." Bump started counting off. "Resisting arrest, assault on an officer. Clipped me a good one too." He waggled his jaw.

"His grandmother just died last night," Lorenzo said with disgust, but still thinking about that beer.

"Yeah, well, he might just have to miss that funeral as it stands now."

"How about the other. They behaving themselves down there?"

"Who, Gannon?" Bump shrugged. "I think they're getting homesick." He scowled into the sun. "To tell you the truth, we're all startin' to come apart around here. Supposed to be like ninety-eight today? Heads up."

"I hear you."

"No bullshit, Lorenzo. We got to wrap this up. This place is ticking like a time bomb."

"Awright. You got me set up down there?"

"They're all in Three Building, the stinkhole stairs." Bump passed him a tagged apartment key. "I even got fuckin' Tyler out on loan from County for this. That's one kid gonna owe me big-time."

As Lorenzo began to roll off, Bump shouted, waving for him to stop as he jogged up to the van. He passed a videocassette through the driver's window.

"I almost forgot."

It took Lorenzo a moment to realize that what he had in his hands was a tape of last night's *Law and Order*.

"Wait till you see that thing." Bump grinned.

"Yeah, I forgot something too." Lorenzo gave him a half-mast stare. "How do you like my girlfriend?"

"Who." Bump squinted.

"Jesse Haus."

"*Who?*" He was playing it all bewildered.

Lorenzo lowered his lids so his eyes were slits. "Yeah, OK." He began to roll again. "And my name is Patsy Fool," he said, dropping it, not having the head for this right now except to note that the next withdrawal from the favor bank was his.

Driving through the blockade without incident, Lorenzo backed the van up to the breezeway of Three Building, then hustled Brenda inside without anyone's making a commotion. Avoiding the elevator banks, he turned her directly into one of the stairways, the superheated stench like a solid wall, the humidity giving the cinder blocks a waxy sheen and turning the graffiti into a fire-blackened smudge.

A few steps up from the ground floor, Brenda hesitated as she made out the four teenagers lounging along the stairs, another two on the second-floor landing. They had been placed there by Bump to eyeball her, see if she was any kind of customer—sort of a reverse lineup. Lorenzo didn't care for the stiff, unnatural poses, the jugglers all stone-faced, nobody even talking, each of them taking the task seriously, desperate to get the police out of there so they could start making some kind of money again.

Lorenzo led her past this crew, not one of them acknowledging her passage, and saw that three more jugglers were planted on the third-floor stairs like homeboy wall sconces. There was an uninvited presence, too, a stubble-headed reporter leaning against the glistening cinder block between knuckleheads one and two, smiling almost apologetically. When Lorenzo and Brenda came abreast of him, he slipped Lorenzo his card, said, "How's it going?" and made as if to join them in their ascent. Lorenzo had to turn and gently shove him off. "You ain't even supposed to be in here."

"No, I just—"

Lorenzo continued to climb, quickly taking Brenda out on the third-floor landing. "What's up there?" the reporter called after them.

Despite the disruption, Lorenzo was left with the sense that Brenda had just cleared local customs: none of the jugglers on the stairs had given any indication of having ever seen her before. As he unlocked the door to 3P, Brenda slipped off her headphones and ran her forearm across her brow. "So did I pass inspection?"

The apartment was vacant, freshly painted, and explosively hot. Lorenzo was instantly nauseated by the fumes; his shirt matted to the small of his back before he could cross the living room to crack a window. The view was directly over the pocket park, one floor up from Miss Dotson's, and he gestured for Brenda to come over and take in this aerial of the crime scene, holding her back slightly, not wanting her to stick her head out and cause some kind of stampede from the train tracks.

Bump had suggested 3P, arguing that it was the ideal setting, allowing Lorenzo to take her out of her element and go one on one without making her defensive, the view of Martyrs Park justifying both the journey and the isolation. It was good thinking on Bump's part, although Lorenzo wouldn't have objected if his partner had bothered to crack open a window or two beforehand.

"What do you think?"

Brenda stared down at the scene drunkenly, the ferocious glare combined with sleep deprivation turning her eyes into sun-snuffed blisters.

"It looks so easy."

"What does?"

"Driving through the park."

She was silent for a while, studying the canopy of trees. Lorenzo watched her, thinking any second she'd conk out, but then he saw the tears again. Her hair was shot with gray, something he hadn't noticed the night before, perhaps, he thought, because the gray of her eyes was so overpowering that it absorbed all similar shades about her. Her clothes, an indifferent pair of jeans and an old Pearl Jam T-shirt, fit her as if she had lost a great deal of weight since she bought them. He intuited that she had no idea how to dress herself in any but the most shapeless and shambly manner, that clothing in general both baffled and bored her.

"Brenda," he began quietly, looking out over the humble turrets and spires of Gannon. "What are you thinking?"

"I was remembering something," she said distantly, her eyes roaming the room.

"Yeah?"

"Reliving something."

"What's that . . ." He leaned against the wall, felt the tackiness of the fresh paint.

"I can't get rid of it."

"What."

"I can't get it out of my mind." She started walking the perimeter, her movements clunky and stiff.

"What."

"It's complicated."

"Is it about last night?" He found himself ducking and weaving as he tried to catch her eye. She wouldn't answer. "Because that's what we're here for." She shuffled around the blank room, her right shoulder sliding along the walls.

"Is it about your son?"

"You have two parts to your life," she announced abruptly, continuing her tilted march. "Before children and after."

"I hear you," he said, allowing her another circuit around the room. "Just say what's on your mind."

"It's not going to help anything."

"You never know."

"It's complicated."

"I got time," Lorenzo said mildly, reminding himself that right now there was no more critical place to be than this vacant apartment, right here. "Hang on." He left the room and searched the apartment for something for her to sit on, finding in one of the closets a metal folding chair spotted with what appeared to be dried red nail polish. Bringing it into the living room, he wrestled it open for her.

"Take a rest."

She sat, got up, moved the chair into a shaded corner, then sat again. Lorenzo perched himself on the edge of a windowsill. The sun was hitting his shoulder as if through a magnifying glass, but there was nowhere else for him to sit without ruining his clothes.

"About, like, ten years ago?" Brenda began slowly, addressing the floor between her feet. "When I was about twenty-one? I moved over to New York to, like, get out from under the bell jar."

"The what?" Lorenzo said, moving to the paint-tacky wall, the sun just too much.

"To get away from home. And, I got a job at the Hayden Planetarium and I started seeing this guy there, and he was in this group where everybody in it was in the same kind of therapy. They were all organized, with all these shrinks seeing all these patients. Maybe, like, a hundred and fifty people all knew each other. They lived in group apartments, five, six people sharing a loft or a giant apartment or whatever, everybody seeing the same dozen or so shrinks, the shrinks seeing each other, everybody kind of hanging out with each other. It was like this secret society right the middle of the city."

"Get out of here," he said faintly, neutrally, marginally musing on the fact that most of the people he knew who were in psychotherapy were there under court order.

"Anyways," she continued in a tired murmur, "this guy, he brought me to this party—they had these huge parties—and there's no boyfriend-girlfriend match ups, everybody's having a good time, drinking dancing getting high, making out, and, I was kind of lost at that point in my life, you know, so I'm, like, Where do I sign up? And before I know it, I'm in therapy with this shrink, he's charging me next to nothing, and I'm living with a half dozen other women in this huge loft in Tribeca, I have all these new girlfriends, I'm seeing all these men, everybody's on the same wavelength, and at first it was a lot of fun, you know? But there was this basic, I don't know, *worldview* they had that was, like, there's two types of people around: us, the group, and everybody else, the rest of the world, which was basically a bunch of psychopaths . . . And that, that *family* you came from? That was nothing more than a psychopathic unit. Like, your parents' basic mission in this life was to destroy you. And if you came to the group married? Well, your marriage was nothing but a psychopathic partnership, so break it off, and, and *you* . . ." She raised her eyes, pointed an accusing finger at him. "If *you* reject this worldview of theirs? You're probably a two-bit psychopath yourself." Her gaze dropped again, her head almost between her spread knees. "It was, like, as a person you're either growing or deteriorating, and the message was, If you reject us, our values, our wisdom, you're obviously deteriorating, or worse, you're *choosing* to deteriorate."

Lorenzo, thinking, Jonestown, Moonies, sank into a squat before her. "Did these people . . . You don't need to be afraid of nobody. Did these people have something to do with your son last night?"

Brenda waved him off. "I mean, as I'm saying this, it sounds obvious and, you know, creepy, but they get to you, they *get* to you. You get so wrapped up in this, this giant community, this friendship thing, this living-together thing that, and, you know, anybody who's deciding to see a shrink, I mean, obviously you're kind of miserable in your life to begin with, so they already got a leg up on you the minute you walk through the door, you know, offering you such a *sweeping* change that . . . So anyways, I wound up cutting off my family, living with a bunch of women, and fucking a lot of men. Everybody did. I mean, you know, I come from a police family, so it was kind of easy to take them apart with a shrink. But anyways, I was in this group, and it was OK for a while, but then we would have these weekly house meetings that were, like, half house business, half amateur therapy. Like, a roommate would say, 'I'm mad at Brenda?' You know, every sentence would go up at the end. So anyways, it would be, like, 'I'm mad at *Bren*da? She didn't lock the front *door* last night? And I think that was very *an*gry?' or, 'I'm mad at *Bren*da? She didn't feed the *cock*atiel? And I think that was very *an*gry?' And then everybody would be, like, 'Yeah, me too. What's going on with you, Brenda?' And I'd say something like, 'I guess I'm *an*gry? Because I've been doing my family *his*tory? With *Ted*? And I guess I'm starting to get in touch with, like, how much my mother was an angry *per*son? And it really makes me *an*gry? But I think it like also really *scares* me? To think about growing up around that much *rage*?' And then I'd start crying and everybody would give me a hug and *they* would start crying, and then I would feel really great and loved, and for the next few days I'd make sure the front door was triple-locked and I'd overfeed the cockatiel. It was like being a battered wife or something. You know, slap, caress, slap, caress."

Lorenzo stood up and backed himself to the nearest wall. He was losing a lot of what she was talking about now, her comment about fucking a lot of men still ringing in his head—not the act, but the language. Lorenzo had an oddly prim sensibility, given his line of work: he did not like profanity in the mouths of women.

"But anyways." Brenda exhaled with a huff. "After a few months, I'm hanging in, I like some of my roommates, I'm definitely not lonely, and then this one Saturday, I come downstairs and there's my brother, there's Danny in a parked car, like, staking me out. And I'm scared shit because I just cut my family off, like, wrote them a note or something. So I go back upstairs, I tell my roommates he's down there, they're, like, 'Oh my God, the *cop*?' They asked me how could he find me? I said, 'Well, I think I might have talked to my mother last week just so she would know I wasn't dead and I might've mentioned where . . . You know, that I was living in the neighborhood that I was living in, but I definitely didn't give her the address.' So they go nuts, everybody's ringing up their shrinks. We have this emergency house meeting where it was, like, de*creed* that I was a psychopathic bitch, viciously and willfully exposing my roommates to an armed and possibly homicidally enraged cop, that I had put the entire therapeutic community in danger. And they gave me two hours to leave, kicked me to the curb."

"Get out a here," Lorenzo said again, in that high, trailing tone of disbelief, desperate for the punch line.

"Well, I didn't need two hours. I was out the door in five minutes. Left everything there. I mean, those spineless . . . I mean, it was hard work for me living like I was living. But I was really trying. I was doing the therapy, doing the house meetings. It was *hard*, but I thought they kind of liked me and I kind of liked them, but in five minutes it was over. I was a nonperson because my asshole brother shows up, I mean . . ." She rubbed her face, taking a breather.

Lorenzo grunted in sympathy, eyed the time: twelve-fifty.

"So I go downstairs, I go right up to Danny in the car. He says, 'You're breaking Mommy's heart.' I say, 'She doesn't *have* a heart,' and off we go back through the tunnel. And you know, when I left that apartment I'm sure they were back on the phones to the shrinks, you know, 'She's gone, Tom, Tod, Sheila, Lorraine.' And then they all probably asked for emergency sessions where they were all told that Brenda's therapy was probably freaking her out, making her get too close to the truth of her family's anger, that her therapy was way too terrifying for her, so in her hateful rage at her shrink and at her peers, who were perpetually challenging her to grow, she tried to sabotage the whole show for everybody, all the people who were trying to help her." She was swaying to the rhythm of her rant, gesturing like a conductor, her voice a mocking singsong. "They were probably told that my psychopathy was too formidable and—" She came to a full stop, began to cry, a bitter, quivering wail that she attempted to master by compressing her lips, squeezing her eyes shut, and pressing a bandaged fist to her forehead.

Lorenzo was still a little lost, but he felt for her.

"And, like, for *years* after that, that's how I felt about myself, like a real piece of shit and, and everytime I fucked up after that, when I did drugs, when I—when I lost a job, lost an apartment, when I had to move back home because I didn't have the money—every little fuckup in my life, they were like this audience in my head, you know, watching me screw up just like they predicted . . . But do you know when all that stopped? When I had my son, when I had Cody. As soon, as soon as I had him in my arms, I became *more*. I became . . . fuck, *you*. Fuck, *all* y'all. You cannot *touch* this. You cannot *be* this, this baby's mother. Me. *I* am that . . . And then, I would still see them in my head, like, watching me? But it was like, it was like, they were blown away. That's how I imagined it. It was like, I would see them, I don't know, gasping or, I don't know, humbled, ashamed, but—" She stopped again, leaned back in the metal chair, her chin aimed at the ceiling. Lorenzo watched grayish rivulets of sweat meander around her throat.

"They're still in my head, you know? They're still—" She swallowed audibly, her voice fluttering with defeat. "And so what are they thinking now, huh? It's all in the papers, on TV . . . This must be like a fucking home run for them. Talk about 'I told you so.' " She rose from the chair, moved to another corner of the room, and sat on the floor.

"OK," Lorenzo said, to acknowledge what he hoped was the end of the tale. "OK," he repeated, taking a beat to gear up, many forces at work in him now. Having finally absorbed the brunt of her tale, he was torn between feeling angry at her and angry for her. Fighting down panic in the face of the relentless pressure of time, he felt pity, frustration, but underneath it all, independent of this crime, this woman, he experienced a powerful afterburn of indignation. He had to restrain himself from saying how flippant and self-indulgent he had found the group's attitude toward family. Sometimes it seemed to him that he spent most of his waking hours trying to hold families together. Lorenzo regarded a mother and a father together under one roof as a blessing, regarded a mother or a father's swat to the backside or even to the side of a teenager's head as commitment, as concern. Parents, no matter how angry, how strict or repressive, as long as they provided three squares, a cot, and consistent rules to live by, were to be respected, were to be honored, were to be treasured because, without a family in place, without at least some facsimile of a family in place, no kid stood a chance, at least not in Lorenzo's neck of the woods.

"OK," he said yet again, still marking time, then deciding to work this thing through the biggest hammer of all.

"Brenda," he finally addressed her. "Do you believe in God?"

"God?" She slowly raised her face to him. "I don't know how to answer that in an unclever way." Her words left a slight tang in the air.

"Try yes or no," he said patiently. There was some kind of shouting match going on down in Martyrs Park. Brenda didn't answer. "See, I don't know if I believe all that much in psychiatry and roommates and giving people negative labels and whatnot. But I *do* believe in God, and I believe that whatever happens to us on Earth, good things, bad things, they happen because God wills it," he semi-lied, actually believing more in the act of believing than in God himself.

He took possession of the folding chair, dragging it over to her corner, so that when he sat he was basically hovering above her.

"See, like now, with your son, looking for your son." Lorenzo hunched forward, his hands clasped in front of her face. "I know," he said, his voice dropping to a gentle, hoarse whisper. "I know that in the back of your mind is the great *fear* of it coming out, you know, unhappily."

Brenda turned her head until it was a profile against the wall.

"Me too. Me too . . . But you got to draw strength from God. You have got to believe that if something, you know, *hap*pened . . . that, if that's the case, then that's because God *wanted* that boy like he's gonna want all of us one day or another, and at least on one level it was nobody's fault—that, that there was nothing anybody could do about it." He paused, smiling down at her through half-mast eyes, his hands in that cross-gripped clasp.

"See, you can think of people as good, bad, guilty, innocent, but whatever *we* do, whatever mistakes *we* make in life, *He* don't make mistakes, and me, you, everybody out there, we're nothing more than His agents. You see what I'm saying?" Lorenzo beamed at her, trying to get inside. Brenda was still looking away. "And if He calls for someone? They got to go. They just, got, to go."

Brenda stared at her hands, her face all reddened triangles. "Understand me," Lorenzo said, hunching over even more, as close to her as breath. "I will not rest until I find your son *and* the person he was, last with. But what I'm trying to say to you is that sometimes the more you try to know, the more mysterious life will get."

The ruckus downstairs was growing louder, and Lorenzo could identify voices now—a Dempsy cop named Beausoleil and a projects kid, Corey Miller.

"Like, why Kenya Taylor. Why'd she have to die. Why, why, why. We don't know why. But *He* does. *He* does . . . It's just sometimes his reasons are too deep for us, and the more we try to, to, compr*ehend,* the more lost we're gonna get, and so sometimes, the best thing for us to do, the *on*ly thing for us to do, is to surrender—surrender to Him, surrender to our own *weak*ness, our own *ig*norance, our own *hu*manness. Because if you do that . . . If you, do, *that* . . . You will have more peace in your life than you can get with a whole army of therapists, psychiatrists, witch doctors, gurus, and what have you . . ."

Lorenzo waited, elbows on knees, slowly rubbing his hands, bobbing and weaving again to find her eyes. She turned her face completely to the wall and Lorenzo could see a knot in her chopped hair the size of a marble, could see the knobs of her spine, like braided rope.

"Of course you try to do the right things in life, but when things go wrong you got to know that we aren't the ones calling the shots, and sometimes there's nothing else to do but let go, let go, just let go and surrender . . ."

Lorenzo nodded, smiling softly, trying to remember how many times he'd given this speech in the last fifteen years. He always expected the perps to laugh in his face, to call him out on his transparent shit, but it never happened. They were often so desperate to latch on to anything, any kind of reasoning that would help them find a way to continue living with themselves. That did not mean, however, that they would hear his "Let go, surrender" rap and then surrender. At first, most of them simply wanted to find a way to get just one more good night's sleep.

Brenda was quiet, breathing evenly—digesting his words, Lorenzo hoped. He had said all that could be said on the subject without beginning to preach in circles. He rose from the chair and leaned out the window, taking in the sizzling sky, then glancing down at the beef on the street. Beausoleil and Corey Miller were starting to chest bump each other in front of Martyrs Park, both of them silent now, giving each other big "Fuck with me" stares—the fight itself coming up in about two minutes.

He turned back to Brenda, who was still down on the floor.

"Yeah, and if you ever see that therapy group again? You can tell them there haven't been any psychopaths around since 1930. It's called antisocial personality disorder these days." Brenda made a chuffing sound approximating laughter. "Come on up here." Lorenzo beckoned to her. "Get some air."

Slowly she got to her feet and joined him at the window, just as Beausoleil and Miller started shoving. "Look at that there." He clucked his tongue as three of Corey's friends and a bunch of cops converged on the confrontation, which, as Lorenzo and Brenda watched, became a wild exchange of headlocks and haymakers. The cops flipped Corey, belly to the mat; Beausoleil, sporting a bloody mouth, pressed the kid's face into the steaming asphalt, while another cop cuffed his hands behind his back. Corey's boys circled the action, cursing out the police so ardently that Lorenzo could see their neck cords standing out like pipes.

"You hear what Bump said before we came up here today?" Brenda didn't answer, just leaned into his shoulder, exhausted, the unexpected physical contact producing in him a confusing wave of tenderness. "He said these houses are ticking like a time bomb. Well, you know what this place is like. You ain't no tourist."

"I'm so tired." It was a whisper.

"Brenda, I pray to God I can find your boy. That's number one, you know what I'm saying? But I also pray to him that I do it before somebody around here gets *really* hurt." Lorenzo grunted at the action below. "Look at this shit."

Two of Corey's crew had joined him on the asphalt, a knee in each of their backs. Others were rushing over now—kids, the elderly, more cops, and more cops after them—everybody looking hot, half crazy.

"I don't know, Brenda, we're banging our heads against the wall here on this. We're doing everything we can . . . If there's *any*thing else you can tell us about what happened, any *way* you can help bring all this to an end. Now's the time . . . Now's the time."

Brenda stepped back from the window and sat unsteadily in the chair. She dropped her head between her knees and held it there, motionless. Frantically Lorenzo debated with himself whether he should quickly reach out and chin-lift her face to him before she could collect herself or whether the best thing would be to let her come around on her own.

He took a gamble on restraining himself—no physical contact, no talk to break her train of thought—and when she finally sat up it was as if she were emerging from a lung-bursting dive, mouth open, shoulders lifting to her ears before settling back into her frame.

"I'm trying, I'm trying," she pleaded, face twisted in misery. "It's so *hard,* you don't *know.*"

12

Ignoring the cop-hoodie roll-around and mass arrest taking place in front of Martyrs Park, Jesse, tense as a dog tethered outside a butcher shop, continued to stare at the empty surveillance van that had transported Brenda to Three Building almost an hour earlier.

From her vantage point inside Ben's Chrysler, which was parked outside the Hurley Street blockade, she also had a clear view of the media camp up behind the train fence. Another press conference was under way, but she just wasn't interested. After last night's intimacy, the idea of being just another dog in the pack under this white-hot sky was unbearable. Brenda was hers, and she would not see her shared.

Stepping out of the car for a cleaner view of Three Building, she unknowingly put herself in the path of Lorenzo's Crown Victoria, Bump Rosen having to swerve wildly and stop to avoid mowing her down. Without missing a beat, Jesse draped herself over the open driver's window. "Hey . . ."

"Hey," Bump responded faintly, flushed and breathless from the near disaster.

"Can you get me inside?" Jesse nodded toward Armstrong, anxiety purging her voice of all charm and play.

Bump stared at her hands, which, dangling over his lap, were loosely clasped in mock supplication. Reaching into Jesse's bag, he took out her notepad, opened it to a blank page, and scrawled down a number.

"Here." He handed back the pad. "This is my home phone. My son is there as we speak."

"What?" Jesse said weakly, the paper drooping between her fingers.

"Hey, I did *my* part. You want to keep going on this? Tit for tat. You have your interview with Terry, then it's my turn again. Watch your hands," he said, giving her a two-second warning before peeling out.

Wheeling almost drunkenly, Jesse came down on her ankle and, spinning completely around on her way to the ground, inadvertently flung her cell phone like a discus, the plastic housing separating into three skittering pieces on the asphalt. There had been moments last night at Brenda's apartment when Jesse loved her job, her life so much that she could have cried. Now, a few hours later, she wanted to cut her throat; this twelve-hour journey from soar to crash was all too familiar. She felt her brother's hands slipping in under her arms, felt herself being floated back to the car.

"Don't you think you should call Jose?" Ben asked her. Jesse was sitting glassy-eyed in the passenger seat again, her brother's cell phone in her lap. "Jess?"

"Not yet."

"He's waiting." She didn't answer. "How about the mother?" he offered.

"The mother?" Jesse turned to him, blankly.

"Brenda's mother."

"*Shit.*" Jesse came to life. "I left the number."

"Here you go." Ben slipped the forgotten Post-it from behind his sun visor. "Better than nothing, right?"

Elaine Martin, Brenda's mother, lived on Farraly Place in Gannon, a densely packed land of smallish turn-of-the-century clapboard homes, some onion-domed, some with miniature turrets. The houses were painted pea green, mud yellow, or battleship gray, each structure fronted with a square plug of grass, the overall gloominess tempered by the nylon banners with simple summery images—dolphins, shamrocks, rainbows—that hung, thrusting out into the street, from almost every small porch.

The house at 144 Farraly seemed to be guarded by a benumbed-looking old man wearing a crushed Dobbs hat, a white shirt, and brown slacks cinched a few inches below his chest. The guy scowled at Ben's car as it pulled up, Jesse, thinking, Street mayor. She gave him a short wave from the passenger seat. "Hi there."

"OK, then," Ben said to her, yawning.

"Are you going to wait for me?" Jesse began collecting herself for work.

"No, I got to see some people, make some calls."

"For what."

"For something."

"For *what.*"

He shrugged, and she knew it was for her, something for her, believing it like a child believes in Christmas. "You're going to be OK here?" he asked.

"Yes," she said slowly, sarcastically, as she got out of the car.

"Here." He passed her his cell phone through the side window. "I'll call you."

As Jesse turned from the car to the gate, she was surprised to see Elaine Martin standing in the shadow of her open doorway. Brenda's mother was young—early sixties maybe—trim, almost petite, wearing slacks and a top that seemed to be made of the same material as the dove pennant hanging over her porch. She had a feathery nest of gray hair, a fine tracery of capillaries bracketing her nose, and eyes that were swollen from crying, the underrims shining as if smeared with gel.

"Mrs. Martin?"

"It's OK, Angelo," Elaine Martin addressed the old guy who was still standing outside her gate. "My bodyguard," she muttered, and walked back into the house, leaving the door ajar.

The spotless living room was small, made to seem even smaller by the thick, dark furniture, the dense wall-to-wall carpeting, and the ornate frames for the photos and solemn certificates that hung on every wall. Jesse felt like she was in a home where the predominant soundtrack was a deep hush punctuated by the soft, steady ticking of a clock. Brenda's mother sat on a brown velour couch, Jesse at right angles to her on a matching velour easy chair. The woman was wearing sparkling new low-cut Nikes, suggesting to Jesse that the immaculateness of the surroundings was the handiwork of a youngish widow with too much time on her hands.

"How are you holding up?" Jesse asked quietly, as she dug out her notebook.

"My son comes in this morning, he looks like hell, he says, 'Mom,' sets me down, says, 'Better you hear it from me than the television,' says, 'Brenda got beat up in Dempsy. The guy stole her car with the baby sleeping in the backseat' . . ." She trailed off, nodding at the far wall. "So how am I holding up? I'm sitting here three hours waiting for that phone to ring."

Jesse nodded, thinking, Ring from Brenda? Why the hell don't you call her? But she kept her mouth shut, having found over the years that there was nothing so effective as attentive silence for keeping people talking.

"Every family has its own crazy bylaws," Brenda's mother finally added, as if reading Jesse's mind. Jesse stared at her like an alert, well-trained dog. "With Brenda I learned the hard way. Let her come to you."

Jesse nodded, thinking, Pick up the phone, Mom.

Elaine Martin plucked a tissue from a box that sat on an end table and swiped at the sheen under her red eyes. "So how is she," she asked dully.

"Not great."

"Yeah." Elaine Martin shook her head. "I wouldn't think so. Danny said she was injured?"

"A sprained wrist, I think." Jesse flipped her pad to a blank page.

"You think I should call her?"

"That's, you know, up to you," Jesse said, inching forward on the sofa.

"Wouldn't *that* be a coup," she said mildly, distantly, as if thinking out loud. Jesse was thrown, not sure if the mother was reading her mind again, putting her in her place. "You said on the phone that it was important that you talk to me." Elaine Martin looked at her, waiting.

"It's like, I'm trying to write something here," Jesse began. "I want to help. I want people to *know* Brenda. I want . . ." She stopped, as if flustered, as if overwhelmed with her desire to do the right thing, but Elaine Martin stared at her in such a way that Jesse knew to cut the act—there were two generations of cop world in this house.

"You just want background, right? You want me to ask you to sit right here, next to me . . ." She patted the couch. "Then whip out some old photo album and walk you through baby pictures, confirmation pictures, wedding pictures, right? There's nothing important about that. She's the victim. Do you study the background of the victim to catch the actor of a random street crime? If you do, then that angle of approach has eluded both my husband and my son, I have to say."

"Would you like me to go?" Jesse offered calmly, knowing storms like these blew themselves out fairly quickly.

"You want some background on Brenda?" The mother rode over Jesse's offer. "Which do you want—the Pollyanna version or down and dirty."

"Whatever you think would be helpful," Jesse said evenly.

"Whatever I think is helpful? OK, let me tell you a thing or two about my daughter, and you tell *me* if you think this is *helpful,* OK?" Her voice was beginning to buckle, despite her icy words. "She's a bright kid who dropped out of college after *one* term, an attractive girl who brought nothing but black and Puerto Rican boyfriends into this house, then went off to New York, got into some kind of cult therapy, cut off her family for more than a year, got herself a nice little drug habit, got pregnant—nobody has a clue who's the father. Anything helpful yet?" Jesse stared at her, not daring to scrawl any of this down. "No," Elaine Martin said, bobbing her head, "I didn't think so. And you know why? Because, unless she's the criminal here, none of this is yours or anybody else's business. Would you agree?"

Jesse resisted repeating, "Unless she's the criminal," and said instead, "Would you like me to go?" She felt fairly confident that she would ignore this second offer too. In fact, as Elaine Martin seemed suddenly to withdraw, eyes taking on a reflective cast, fingers worrying the fabric of her slacks, Jesse sensed that, in all likelihood, this woman was just getting started.

"I tell you," Elaine Martin said, coming around. "You want something for the record?" Her voice was softer now, taking on a burdened timbre. Jesse waited. "Brenda? When she was little, kindergarten age, her father and I one time had a fight. Pete, he used to like his cocktails back then, and it was real bad. He was never a mean drunk, never raised a hand, but it was hell, and I told him that I was taking the kids and leaving—I had had it—and, he started crying, telling me he'll straighten out. He's crying, I'm crying. We're both in the kitchen, and Brenda comes in. She comes in, sees us, and gets this stricken look on her face. And we had a radio in there back then. And the song that was playing was 'September Song,' being sung by, if you can believe it, Jimmy Durante. Brenda, she looks at us crying, and I say, 'Sweetie, isn't that a sad song? Me and Daddy are crying because that song is so beautiful and sad.' So of course *she* starts crying too, so I go and I pick her up and it kind of broke my train of thought there with Pete, so I don't go through with it. I don't walk out on him so—which was good—but, Jesus, Jimmy Durante. You know, I have *never* heard him singing that song on the radio ever again. Not before, not after, OK?"

Jesse grunted softly, notepad blank.

"A few years ago, Pete passed on. Brenda came to the house. She takes me into the kitchen, says, 'Mom, I have something for you,' and she gives me a tape she made. She likes to make music tapes for people. She gives me a tape, it's Jimmy Durante singing 'September Song.' I have no idea how she remembered, or where she found it, or, better yet, how she even knew who the singer had been. She was *five years old*. She gives me the tape, says, 'Mom, if you're ever missing Daddy too much maybe you could play this for yourself.' See, all those years she believed me, that we were crying because . . ."

Elaine Martin looked off again, blinking furiously. Then it came to Jesse why she was really here—because this house had known Brenda, this woman had known Brenda, and, like a drunk upending an empty liquor bottle onto her tongue, if Jesse couldn't have Brenda in the flesh anymore, then she would settle, would have to settle for her haunts, former haunts, the people and places that had known her. As Jesse came to this realization, it was all she could do not to ask to be shown Brenda's childhood bedroom.

"Cody." Elaine Martin almost choked on her grandson's name. "I have seen that child—I have been *allowed* to see that child—four times in four years."

She glared at Jesse, waiting, demanding.

"Why is that?" Jesse finally asked.

"Brenda, she goes and gets pregnant. I say, 'You're not married? What can I do. You're over twenty-one, you make your own bed. But just answer me this . . . Do you know who the father is?' She says to me, '*Fuck* you.' " Elaine half whispered the profanity. " 'How dare you insult me like that. You'll never see this baby, I swear before God.' Bang, she's gone. So . . ."

"Huh." Jesse threw her another grunt, knowing exactly where they were going now.

"Well, look." Elaine Martin stared at a blown-up photo of Danny and Brenda as children that hung over a television console. "Brenda always had a problem with me. The father—well, kids always go for the father. Pete was on the job twenty-nine years, but in this house *I* was the cop, because Pete—he'd come home half loaded, say to them, 'Hey, whatever you did, I'm too tired, so go up to your room and spank yourselves.' " She shrugged, smiled tightly. "So where does that leave me, do you understand?"

"Absolutely," Jesse said automatically. This was drifting further and further from the news and she began to preview possible exit lines.

"What I don't understand is . . ." Elaine Martin began twisting her hands, slid to the edge of the couch. "She hates me, she's afraid of me, she thinks I'm all over her, but it's like she can't get enough of me. She keeps testing me or testing things *out* on me. Like with the boyfriends. This one's black, that one's Puerto Rican, and it was all, you know, to get a rise out of me, because, you know, I'm from a different generation and the first time she pulled that I fell for it, hook, line, and sinker. She brings in this black kid to meet me—who, incidentally, looked totally miserable and uncomfortable, so what she was doing for him I don't know—she brings in this kid, and I got, I go crazy."

Jesse withdrew, thinking briefly about Charles, her tenth-grade Jamaican boyfriend, both of them expending all their energy watching people watch them.

"I made her break it off as soon as he left the house. And by the way, you know she made damn sure that she showed up with that poor kid when she knew her father wasn't around, see what I'm saying? So I go nuts, say, 'Break it off, break it off *now*,' and she acts outraged, but I could see . . ." She narrowed her eyes, peered into the distance. "I could see that, beyond all the, the storm and thunder, she couldn't have been more happy with my reaction than if I'd crowned her Queen for a Day, so I said to myself, OK, I get it. I'm never falling for *that* again. She could go out with Malcolm X for all I give a damn, because I have found out, as a parent, that the best way to, to curtail a child's negative behavior, a child's *ac*tion, is to withhold the *re*action. But Brenda, she's tough, she's stubborn, she's like her brother. You know her brother, Danny? You're a reporter. You had to have met Danny."

"We met."

"Or, like—I'm going back ten, twelve years—she leaves home, goes to New York, like *this* . . ." She snapped her fingers. "She's in some kind of cult therapy, they tell her 'Your family is poison,' so she writes us some note, 'Please don't contact me,' cuts us off. But let me ask you something. You cut off your mother like that, do you wind up thinking about her *more* or *less* than if you saw her on a natural basis? And let me tell you, cult, no cult, she'd call here once a week maybe, call to fight with me, with *me*, because she knew, once again, she knew when her father was out and when I was home."

"OK."

"She sets me up as this monster," she went on, pressing a clotted tissue to her eyes. "But—Well, I'll tell you. In all the time we had together?"

Jesse was thrown by the past tense, the woman saying it like Brenda was dead.

"In all the time, to be perfectly honest, there's one thing I did which I would cut off my arm to undo. She must have been close to eighteen, living at home, and I think this might have been what tipped her over to the therapy in New York. I was talking to my sister on the telephone in the kitchen, and I was feeling kind of down that day and I said to her, 'Jean, I have to tell you, compared to your kids? I'm kind of disappointed in how mine turned out.' I just said it, and I get this feeling, and I turn around, and there's Brenda standing in the doorway, looking like—" She cut herself off again, a tissued fist to her mouth. "And there was nothing I could say. I knew anything I said would only make it worse."

"Oh, no . . ." Jesse said softly, a puff of pain. As if in recognition of Jesse's one true response of the day. Elaine Martin abruptly reached across the coffee table and seized her wrist.

"You asked me a lot of questions, you know?" she said brokenly, Jesse thinking, No, I didn't.

Brenda's mother took a deep breath, then just caved in, her voice a wet stutter. "Now I have one for you." Jesse waited, this woman's touch hard to bear. "My grandson—do you think he's going to be OK?"

The cell phone rang, spooking both of them. Reluctantly Elaine Martin released Jesse's hand.

"Excuse me," Jesse said, then twisted around and talked into the phone. "Yeah."

"May I speak?" Ben asked delicately.

"What."

"Nothing's for sure, but I had a long conversation with some people, and I think there's a decent chance I can get you back with Brenda later today."

"No!" Jesse whispered, sizzling with joy, keeping her eyes down, aware of Elaine Martin sitting on the edge of the couch, Jesse beating out the mother to her own daughter.

"Where'll you be later?" Ben asked.

"Home."

"I'll call you. Everything else OK?"

"Yeah."

"Good," Ben said lightly, then hung up.

"Sorry," Jesse murmured. Then, realizing that the woman was still waiting to be fed, she added almost as an afterthought, "Do I think he's going to be OK? Yes. I do. You have to think positive, be positive."

"Yeah?" Elaine Martin responded, oblivious to how distracted and lazy Jesse's response had been. "I don't know." She shrugged, clutching her knees. "You know, with drugs, AIDS, crime—You ask Danny— These days, there's so much hate, you can't even *look* at anybody, everything's a weapon. I mean what kind of world is this to live in?"

Buzzed with anticipation, Jesse tried to respect the mood of the room, but her body took over and she began to make wrap-up gestures, closing her notebook, demonstratively dropping her hands on her thighs. Elaine Martin took in the pantomime with bitter comprehension.

"Look, the detective who caught the case?" Jesse said. "He's the best. Ask your son." Then, sensing that her parting gift was sorely inadequate, she reopened her notebook, tore off a sheet, and wrote down her pager number. "I just had a work emergency come up, but here—Whatever I can do for you, anything, just call me." Jesse slid the sheet across the table, realizing as she did that Bump had written his home number on the other side.

Elaine Martin regarded this final offering with a knowing eye. "Our one millionth customer, huh?"

Jesse, swallowing a hit of shame, simply shrugged in apology, thinking, Lady, if you only knew.

Jesse left the mother's house to face that same dumbstruck, bristle-chinned sentry leaning against the Martin gate. He stared at her with an open-mouthed scowl, as if possessed by an anger whose source had been lost in time. As she headed for the nearest PATH station, the afterburn of her graceless exit set up house in her—there had been no real need to beat it out of there like that. As long as she had the phone, Ben could reach her anywhere. It was the job, she decided, a reflexive world of brusque gestures, brusque prioritizing, everyone conditioned to race the clock, race the information.

The problem with convincing people who were in the clutch of some personal catastrophe to open up to you was that they opened up, and the trick, always, after you had gotten the information you came for, was the getaway. Once you got them going, they never seemed to be able to stop talking, they never wanted you to leave the house, hang up the phone. Instead, they nailed you with their silent response to your "OK, then," your "Hey, I'll call you in a few days, OK?" Any kind of closer you could think of met with a mute plea to stay on the line, stay in the kitchen—the wife wasn't finished convincing you and herself that it was OK that her husband was killed, the grandmother wasn't finished babbling on about how her grandson, her granddaughter won't ever have to deal with AIDS, drugs, prostitution, how they're "safe," now that they're dead. All of them going on and on, and all you can think of is, How do I get off the phone. How do I get out that door. This story's got a forty-eight-hour shelf life, maybe less, and I gots to go, I gots to go. Jesse was telling herself, It's the job; asking herself, What else is there?

A rank and clammy riverborne current of air rose to meet her as she tripped down the stairs of the Allerton Avenue PATH station. The Allerton stop was one of two stations in Gannon, and Jesse was planning to take the train to Burke Avenue in Dempsy, three blocks from her apartment.

On the dingy mezzanine level of the station she caught a glimpse of that day's *New York Daily News*, with two pictures side by side—the police sketch of the jacker and the photo of Cody feeding the goat from a baby bottle—and above that, the header, in blaring type: HAVE YOU SEEN THEM? Jesse continued downward to the trains. It was a dead hour, and, save for a scatter of commuters, the station was deserted. In the middle of the long Dempsy-bound platform, there was a pole-mounted pay phone beneath a suspended, blue-screened video monitor that flashed the time: 2:45 P.M. The readout and the lonely phone made her almost crazy. She had roughly two hours to put something together for Jose. So far, all she had was texture and anecdote, miles of texture and anecdote, no hard information. That was probably OK with the paper, given the nature of the assignment, but it drove her wild to have been so close to the principals and have nothing to show for it.

As she waited for the train, compulsively leaning over the edge of the platform and peering into the depthless tunnel, her ear cocked for that telltale rumble, she began to work out the right tone for her experience so far, something sympathetic to Brenda's ordeal but devoid of any emotionality that would set her up as a horse's ass if it turned out that Brenda was a bad player. Elaine Martin's tale was tricky too. Jesse was more or less unable to use the history-of-interracial-boyfriends angle, the withholding of Grandma's visitation rights, the cult-therapy angles, unless it came to pass that Brenda had done the deed. With her eye straying to the time again, Jesse returned to assessing what she could run with right now regarding Elaine Martin—cop widow, cop mom, the lonely vigil—then surprised herself with the realization that she was actually thinking in terms of shaping, of writing, rather than just dumping to Jose.

Feeling both pleased and shaky, she became so absorbed in the possibilities that she didn't see trouble until it was almost upon her—three white teenagers, Gannon homeboys, dressed in black-boy droop, baggy-assed shin-length denim shorts and oversized hockey jerseys. It was big-time trouble, the three of them lumbering purposefully down the near-deserted platform, their averted eyes giving them away, looking everywhere but at her, furtively scoping out the sidelines, the hulkiest kid on point, eyes downcast, mouth tight, his chest heaving with excitement. Jesse recognized the group body language from a dozen urban shit storms, having once had her nose broken covering a Save the Children concert turned riot in the Dempsy Arena. She felt powerless but calm, her thoughts, her history, involuntarily coming at her in isolated images, slightly fuzzed and trembling like fixed video shots on the control panel of a surveillance system—her desk, her doll, the beach, her parents . . .

With her mind momentarily purified by fear, she looked at the Gannon boys bearing down and she had the odd sensation of knowing, absolutely knowing, that at least one of them was named Mike—which one, she had no idea—and when they were close enough to touch, Jesse barked, "Mike!" Not one of them reacted to the name.

Leaving her body behind, Jesse numbly waited for what was to be, but as they came up on her, they simply parted and regrouped behind her, heading for the end of the platform, for the black kid standing thirty or so feet to her rear, and she experienced a wave of embarrassed relief.

The black kid looked to be in his early twenties, wearing jeans and a button-down shirt. He held a stack of manila folders under his arm—some kind of messenger or student—and he stared at the three-man convoy with the same perfect, helpless comprehension that Jesse imagined had been on her face a few seconds before. They came to a halt in a rough triangle, one behind him, the other two flanking his front, all of them big-eyed, everybody waiting, four hammering hearts, the black kid just standing there flat-footed, breathless, waiting along with the rest.

The punch came from behind, from the biggest kid—snowy blond crew cut and Pittsburgh Penguins jersey—clocking him on the side of the head with an impossibly fast roundhouse, then hopping backwards, bobbing up and down as if sent to a neutral corner. The black kid said, "Ow," lucid and chatty, his ear instantly ballooning, his kneecaps running as he struggled to hold on to his manila baggage. One folder spilled to the platform.

And then they all waited again, standing there under the lingering resonance of that shell-shocked "Ow," the four of them seemingly in the grip of a strange hyped-up shyness. The kid made no move to escape. Trembling, frowning, he busied himself realigning the remaining folders under his arm. Jesse was scared but finally shouted, *"Hey,"* following it up with an angry *"Fuck,"* for no reason that she could explain. She raised her brother's cell phone, as if threatening to make a call.

Finally, one of the other two swung out with a half-assed karate kick aimed at the ribs, the point of the blow absorbed by the folders but the momentum shoving the kid sideways into a support girder. His right temple slapped up against a paint-chipped rivet with an audible vibration. Still clutching his folders, he finally dropped to his knees, as Jesse yelled, "Stop it!" then "Police!" No one paid her any attention. She was too scared to do anything but harangue them and fearful that, if she left the platform to get help, the kid would be killed.

The third hitter took his shot, a sneakered dropkick to the chest. The kneeling vic arched backwards, over his own calves, bursting out with a teary "God!" that sounded more exasperated than frightened but that propelled Jesse to physical commitment. She found herself kneeling next to him, shoulder to shoulder, not knowing what her point here was, some kind of "We Shall Overcome" reflex from her childhood perhaps, better late than never.

The three hitters exchanged looks and began to walk off, the biggest one first dropping to one knee on the other side of the dazed kid and, almost gently, prying the manila folders from under his rigid elbow. Casually he flung the folders onto the Dempsy-bound tracks. "That's for Cody Martin, all right?" he said in a conversational, almost solicitous tone, completely devoid of rancor, as if he were relieved to be finished with the deed and was now offering a detached explanation for his actions. Using the black kid's shoulder as a support, he rose to his feet. "Spread the word, my man," he declared, walking away backwards, until he caught up with the other two heading for the turnstiles. The karate kid spun to face them now, bellowing, "This ain't D-Town, Yo. This is *Marl*boro Country!" The three of them hopped the turnstiles and, clambering back up the stairs, disappeared unmolested onto the street.

The police came on the scene in less than ten minutes, but for all they did when they got there, Jesse decided, they could just as easily have shown up the following day.

Leaning tiredly against a support girder, growing nauseated from the dank, tidal stench of the PATH tunnels, Jesse noticed that the two responding cops had the same last name. One looked twice the age of the other, and she had to wonder if they were father and son. Gannon was supposed to have something like eight multigenerational families actively on the job, one family, to her knowledge, bragging three brothers, two sisters, and both parents. Another family, the Longos, had a grandfather who was the assistant chief of police, with two detective sons and three granddaughters, one in narcotics, the other two in patrol cars.

Related or not, the two Officer Mullanes were on opposite ends of the stick on this one, the younger willing to take this thing all the way, the older doing everything he could to keep the beating of the black kid a ghost incident.

"So where is he?" Mullane Senior asked, hands on hips, grimacing as if he had cramps. "Where's the victim? We don't have a victim, what do you want me to do?"

Jesse had expected this reaction. Freaked, the battered kid had taken off as soon as she dialed 911. Nonetheless, she had gone ahead and called in, if only to give the incident an official, documentable existence, to start a paper trail in case she wanted to write about it—first-person, something with a real voice.

"Those are his envelopes." Jesse pointed to the large manila folders scattered on the tracks. "I can see a return address from here. It shouldn't be that hard to track him down."

"Awright." Mullane Senior shrugged. "I got to call it in to the PATH, get them to shut off the juice." Jesse stared at him fixedly, made an ostentatious show of writing down his name and shield number.

"Nah, Jimmy," the younger cop said, gauging the drop from the platform to the tracks. "I'll just jump down."

The elder Mullane grabbed him by his elbow. "No, no, no. This tunnel, you can't tell if the train's two stations away or two yards. Forget it. This lady wants us to shut down the line? That's what we got to do."

Jesse looked at the time on the blue screen: 3:15. Fuck. "This is such bullshit," she said.

The senior officer cocked his head, staring at her. "Nah, this isn't bullshit. You know what's bullshit? You trying to fan the flames around here just to grab some ink. *That's* bullshit."

Jesse flushed. "It *happened*."

"Yeah? I promise you, you run with this? Make us go through with some kind of investigation? A lot more is gonna happen too. Shit like this tends to have babies. You want to write it up? Hey, it's a free country. Just remember, if you do? The next cracked head is because of you."

The younger cop seemed embarrassed. He busied himself with studying the envelopes on the tracks until a Dempsy-bound train abruptly appeared out of the blackness and the envelopes were no more. The older cop leaned into Jesse and tapped his shield. "Mullane 45382."

"Let me ask you." Jesse opted to be less confrontational. "You get any other incidents like this today? Is this going around?" He gave her another of those lead-lined stares. "C'mon, Mullane, I'm a working girl."

Shaking his head, he hooked his partner by the arm, flashed her a V, said "Peace," and walked away.

As Jesse entered the lobby of her apartment house, the smell of canned air made her feel like she was in the first-class lounge of a regional airline. Rhythmic clanking could be heard from the ground-floor health club, someone in there roaring through clenched teeth like a constipated lion.

"Yes?" The maroon-uniformed doorman tilted forward over his desk, his knuckles resting on the photo of Cody Martin feeding the goat in that day's *Jersey Journal*.

"I live here," Jesse mumbled, dangling her key and heading for the elevator.

The apartment was suffocating, sealed tight with the air-conditioner off, the contained heat dense enough to peel steel. Through the half-open door of her roommate's bedroom, the real bedroom, she spied a bald, naked man, belly-down asleep on the unkempt bed. Jesse stared at his body, trim but hairy, thinking, A jogger. She moved to her own, make-do room—mattress on the floor, laundry piled high enough to be considered furniture, her poster photo of the New York skyline pushpinned into the wall next to her view of the real thing.

The heat had caused the window frame to expand, and, sweat running in rivulets under her clothes, she strained unsuccessfully to get the window open. She didn't want to call in to Jose. She had to call in to

Jose. Leaving the room, she went into the kitchenette, the smell of the flavored coffees making her sick, and studied the naked man through the bedroom door. She took a shower with the bathroom door open, willing her mind to go blank.

Jose.

Wearing a towel, she came out into the living room—the small space left over from the creation of her bedroom—turned on the TV, hit the mute button, caught footage of Brenda standing in her window this morning, and saw her own arm snake out and pull down the shade. She always watched the news with the sound turned off; data compiled by others made her too crazy. In a last spasm of delay, she switched channels and resumed the volume, staring blindly for a few anxious minutes at a fat chef dicing something up. She levitated clean off the carpet when the naked man violently slammed shut the bedroom door.

"Jose . . ."

"Fuck! Where the hell you been?"

"I was busy." Sitting nude on her unmade mattress, Jesse spoke with the phone locked between her jaw and her shoulder, her hands free to check her notes.

"I heard you lost her," he said.

"Where'd you hear that?"

"Your brother called in. Said you interviewed her mother?"

"I did."

"We already got the mother."

"Who."

"Jeff."

"Thanks for telling me."

"Call in now and then and you'd know. So tell me about Brenda. She do it?"

"Can't say."

"But did she *do* it."

"I don't know." Jesse stood up; the mattress was too inviting.

"Are you in love?" he asked.

"I don't think so. She's hurting for real. I mean, you know, for what it's worth."

"Oh, yeah?" Jose cleared his throat, ready. "How so?"

"She's alone."

"Right."

"I mean *alone*. No family, no friends. I mean, she's like, hunkered in the bunker. Well, the brother came by."

"The cop? What was he like?"

"A bottle rocket. He almost threw me out the window. He thinks I'm writing a book."

"How was he with her?"

"Not too good, I thought he was gonna punch her out."

"He thinks she did it?"

"I don't know, maybe, but tread lightly with that, OK? I'd say, he was 'distraught yet determined to help.' "

"To help," Jose repeated.

"I tell you, Jose, this lady's got nobody in her corner."

"OK."

"The mother's got no use for her, the brother."

"OK."

"That phone never rang."

"OK."

"Neighbors, girlfriends, boyfriends, family, *nobody*."

"OK."

"She couldn't stay in the kid's room, just couldn't do it."

"OK."

"She slept on the couch, maybe like an hour, two hours."

"OK."

"Woke up, had a nightmare."

"About."

"Something with the kid splitting up into nine people. Just say she woke up from a nightmare about the boy. How she couldn't help him, save him."

"OK."

"Her hands are . . . swaddled. They look like the cloth wrappings at the end of a torch. You know, like the villagers use when they finally go after the Frankenstein monster?"

"OK."

"She's in pain, physical pain—the hands."

"OK."

"So sleepless except for a nightmare, in pain, and isolated, utterly fucking alone. Said the kid was her whole life."

"OK. Good. The apartment?"

"Shabby. Say, 'Poor but house-proud.' "

"OK."

"Kid has the only bedroom. Mom sleeps on the couch."

"Great. OK."

"Pictures of the kid all over the place."

"OK."

"She cut her hair."

"What?"

"She cut her hair off. You know, like she flipped and just . . . Hold on." Jesse riffled through her notepad, looking for her dawn-time writings. "Yeah, here we go: 'The bathroom sink in this shabby but proud apartment is a nest of shorn hair, the mother taking scissors to her own locks in an impulsive gesture of otherwise inexpressible anguish.'" Jesse felt jarred by her own dictation, by how florid it now seemed, how committed in its sympathy, how dangerous.

"Jesus, she really did that?"

"You want me to repeat it?"

"I got the essence. What else."

Jesse hesitated, feeling both relieved and slightly wounded. "She listens to soul music nonstop."

"OK."

"She burrows in with it. Headphones. Sings along. The whole nine yards, but it's not, *flipp*ant. It's, it's understandable. Say, it's like, it's a lifeline. It keeps her from going totally around the bend."

"OK, good. Any favorite songs?"

"'96 Tears'?"

"OK, great. What else."

"She likes . . ." Jesse checked her notes. "Judy Clay? Ann Peebles?"

"Who?"

"It's an education up here, I tell you. How about Jackie Wilson?"

"Why can't she listen to Whitney Houston like everybody else?"

"You listen to Whitney Houston?"

"Don't you?"

"OK, now, the mom, Grandma, she told me that Brenda's got a history of black boyfriends, Puerto Ricans. I mean, I wouldn't say as much, but, you know, between the music, the boyfriends, working in Strongarm, she's just about an honorary sister. So I *would* say that she's kind of culturally, spiritually *dedicated*. I mean, there's a certain irony here."

"I'll work with it. Got any quotes?"

"Yeah, hang on . . . 'I want him back so bad. I just want to be with him.'"

"Give me a break."

"Hang on . . . 'He's my whole life.' "

"You're killing me, Jesse."

"She called her mom a dog biscuit. You like that one?"

"Stop."

"You want a quote? How's this . . . 'You know, I'm still pretty young.' "

"What?" Jose came to a full stop. "Meaning what."

"Guess."

"Jesus."

"Look, Jose, I am sitting on some shit here, but . . . Look, if she turns out to be the actor, I'll unload, but for now I don't want to burn her unduly, you know?"

"You're in love."

"But I also don't want to get burned here myself, so I would like it if we could keep it on the somewhat sober side, all right?"

"You know the definition of a sociopath?"

"Yeah, someone who fools a reporter."

"What else."

"Not much."

"Boyfriends?"

"Not that I know of."

"You believe her?"

"Well, if he's out there he's laying low. I didn't see any pictures, any letters, birth control, nothing."

"I don't know, Jess—young girl, single and free. What do you think?"

"Well, first of all she's not single and free, she's strapped with the kid."

"My point exactly."

"Well, fuck it, Jose. All I can tell you is she didn't confess, she's utterly strung out, I can't really see her running off to Atlantic City with the milkman anytime soon, and, like, hey, tune in tomorrow."

"You sound hot, Jess."

"Fuck off."

"I think you're in love."

"Fuck off."

"Where she at now."

"Out and about. With the detective, I guess."

"Any chance you hooking up with her again?"

"Actually, there is."

Jesse dropped to the mattress, her legs giving out.

"Yeah? How so?"

"People," she said, keeping Ben's name out of it. "But Jose? If I do?" Her words were coming a little faster than her thoughts. "I'm not dumping this anymore."

"Excuse me?"

"I want to write it up."

"Yeah?"

"Yeah."

Jose hesitated. "What do you mean, like a diary?"

"A diary?" Jesse began blinking, her stomach going to hell. "What do *you* mean?"

"A diary, like, 'My day with Mom. The vigil continues.' I could live with that. Shit, you get back in with her? I could definitely live with that."

"Cool," Jesse said faintly, needing another shower, thinking, HAVE YOU SEEN THEM? There was no word yet from Ben. Suddenly the world seemed supported by the bird legs of "If," of "Maybe," of "I may," "I might."

"Jose, I got to go." She felt sick.

"Keep me posted."

"Sure."

"When will you know?"

"Soon."

"And, Jess, if you do?"

"Do what," she said, blank with anxiety.

"Hook up with her."

"Yeah?"

"Be careful."

"Of?"

"Everything." Then, in a lighter tone, "Think boyfriend."

13

Brenda had hung tough in the empty apartment, but as they silently exited into the swelter of the hallway, Lorenzo sensed an air of great disappointment about her, which intensified his own mood of failure. She had wanted him to make her open up, had needed him to make her open up, he'd swear to it, and this uncomfortable realization made him feel that he had failed both of them in a way that transcended the job, justice, or any other legalistic aspect of the situation.

A few minutes later, coming out of the shadows of Three Building, Lorenzo went instantly blind, the midday light a searing white sizzle scourged of all color, the disparate voices of Armstrong coming to him in this hallucinatory heat as if he were half asleep on a beach. Brenda had something of the same physical reaction, stepping into the daylight, abruptly stopping, then staggering backwards into the shade of the breezeway, holding on to a concrete pillar for balance.

Across Hurley Street, from the elevation of the retaining wall, the video and camera shooters suddenly became aware of Brenda's presence, their instantaneous response making the chain links of the train fence clash and sing, a mad chorus baying out her name, imploring her to step free of the breezeway.

Someone had moved the van; Lorenzo spotted it parked in front of Five Building now. Turning back to Brenda, Lorenzo saw that she stood flanked by posted printouts of the jacker sketch, one taped to the column she was leaning against, the other mounted on a square of graffiti-covered plywood nailed over a shattered ground-floor window. They had to have been put up in the last hour, yet one was already defaced, the image crossed out with a fat spray-painted X.

A quiet crowd of tenants started to gather in a loose semicircle around Brenda, teenagers and children mostly, the younger ones gawking with open-mouthed curiosity but the adolescents and mothers straight-up glaring. People ahead of schedule, Lorenzo thought, everybody around here sick of this shit not even twenty-four hours into the drama.

Attracted by the splashy squawks and squeals of giddy children, Lorenzo turned to the Armstrong Beach Club, a shallow oval bowl between Three and Four Buildings designed for water play. Mercifully, the sprinklers were working, four arches of drizzle converging atop a bony crew of kids, some in bathing suits, some in underpants. Lorenzo took imaginary relief in the sight, remembering stutter stepping across that very same wet cement, feeling that benign scraping sensation on the soles of his feet.

He turned back to check on Brenda in the breezeway, then turned again to the sprinklers. Through the rainbow-dappled crossfire he saw another major beef shaping up at the Hurley Street exit, where the Reverend Henry Longway, on-site manager of the Armstrong Houses, was chewing out the two Dempsy cops, both black, who were blocking his path.

Longway was about sixty, a bespectacled, chesty bantamweight sporting a snowy goatee, a Kangol cap, and orthopedic shoes. About a dozen people stood behind him. Lorenzo recognized them as relatives and friends of old Miss Bankhead. The youngish men, despite the heat, all wore long-sleeved white shirts and ties; the women, mostly older, were decked out in churchgoing dresses and hats.

Lorenzo thought the reverend was supposed to be in the medical center recovering from some kind of heart trouble and imagined the old guy flinging off his blanket and marching out of the hospital barefoot, not wanting to miss this scene even if it killed him.

Without hearing the words, Lorenzo knew exactly what was going down. The reverend was attempting to take these people to a memorial service for Miss Bankhead outside of Armstrong, willfully ignoring the blockade, using the woman's death as a battering ram against the indignities of the last sixteen hours. He also knew both the uniforms, kids with less than a year on the job, too unseasoned to be assigned to such a sensitive post but deployed, he was sure, as a matter of racial cosmetics. The downside of the gamble was evident in their faces as the rev, an old political street fighter, went about whittling them back down to little boys. Signaling to one of the young cops to come back and hang in with Brenda, Lorenzo made his way to the checkpoint.

"Rev, I know it's a memorial service and I respect that," pleaded the other young cop, Anthony Cooley, whose own father, Lorenzo knew, was a pastor too. "I just got to run through some ID." Cooley sounded hollow, scared, his mouth hanging open well after the words were out.

"You ain't running these people through nothin'," the rev said dismissively. The group behind Lorenzo was silently grim, their loss, Lorenzo sensed, outweighing their indignation.

"Look," Cooley tried again.

"Naw, *you* look." Longway thrust a finger in the cop's face, his eyeglasses magnifying his anger. "There was twenty-seven homicides in the last twelve months in this precinct, *six* alone in these houses and there ain't never been a police presence, a police action, like you got over this *one* missing white child."

Cooley looked helplessly to Lorenzo.

"How come nobody did all this when Darryl Talley got shot over in Three Building last month, huh? Or, or when Hakim Watrous got killed right here on Hurley, huh?"

"C'mon, Rev," Lorenzo said, laughing his respectful, humoring laugh. "There's a child involved."

"A child? There was a fourteen-year-old *black* child shot dead two blocks from here six weeks ago. Tyrell Walker. I didn't see no police strip-searching people for Tyrell Walker."

"Hey," Lorenzo said, "nobody's strip—"

"I didn't see no police checking IDs on people for Tyrell Walker," Longway plowed on, running over Lorenzo, getting louder.

"You're not wrong," Lorenzo said quietly. "But that's the way it is."

"I didn't see no cops do nothing for Tyrell Walker, and I *know*," the reverend said, almost shouting. "I didn't see any of *them*"—he pointed flamboyantly at the reporters and photographers, a real "Land ho!" gesture—"coming round, for Tyrell *Walker*." Longway was trying to catch their eyes, their ears; he wasn't really talking to Lorenzo anymore, just trying to attract media flies with the honey of visual outrage. It was an attempt to set up a swap, the only way to get concessions in this part of town, leveraging every newsworthy incident for a trade-off. Get the cameras in on it, back the city into a corner, then swap moral exoneration for whatever crumbs were to be had—more black jobs, black cops, social services, playground equipment, anything, anything. Lorenzo let him vent. Most of the shooters were still fixated on Brenda in the breezeway, but a few were heeding the call, jogging the length of the fence to catch the drama at the checkpoint.

Lorenzo looked over to Brenda, who was resting her forehead against the concrete pillar, the other young cop standing by her side. Lorenzo attempted to signal him to get Brenda back into the building but was unable to get his his attention.

"I didn't see no, no television crews for Tyrell Walker. I didn't see no newspaper reporters." Lorenzo was just about ready to let the rev have his way, walk on out of here with his mourners, when the man stepped over the line.

"And hell, Lorenzo." Longway lowered his voice. "While we're on the subject, I don't even remember seeing *you* here for Tyrell Walker."

Lorenzo took him by the elbow, the pressure of the grip showing in the rev's eyes. "Hey." Lorenzo's voice was small, for one set of ears only. "Don't you *dare* lump me in with nobody else. You *know* what I'm about, and ain't nothing changed about *that*."

Lorenzo's main memory of the night that Tyrell Walker was killed was of being in bed with his wife for only the third time in the last six months—not the rev's, or anyone else's, goddamn business. And as far as the murder itself, he had helped broker the surrender of the actor to the prosecutor's office the night after the shooting, all that could be done short of bringing Tyrell back to life.

"Yeah, well, to tell you truth, I don't know shit no more," the rev said, calmer now, one on one.

"Then I suggest you look around you," Lorenzo murmured, eyeing the perimeter with its Gannon cops, their Dempsy brothers, the combat-ready press. "Look around you before you get in my face, 'cause right now I'm about all you got."

The rev took five, his voice both intimate and wounded. "I heard the mayor went and visited that woman. She don't even live in Dempsy."

"Yeah, well, that's incorrect information."

"He didn't come see Hakim Watrous's mother." The rev started pumping it up again. "He didn't come see Tyrell Walker's mother. He didn't come—"

"Let me ask *you* something, Rev," Lorenzo said, cutting him off. "Where you having this service . . ."

"Mumford."

"Mumford." Lorenzo nodded. "She lived right here in Armstrong. Why you havin' it there?"

"She had family there too."

"Nah." Lorenzo scanned the land, grinning angrily. "You just want to test this thing here."

"This whole thing is racist, double-standard bullshit, and you know it."

Lorenzo shrugged. It was. No doubt. But you got to function. Daily.

"How's your heart?" he asked under his breath. "You come out OK on that?"

"Hey, when it's your time, it's your time."

"I hear you," Lorenzo said mildly.

"Meanwhile I got to play the cards I got left."

"I hear that too."

Lorenzo regarded the quiet, slightly dazed-looking mourners. "Awright." He gestured to the young cop. "Just let 'em through."

Cooley exhaled in relief. The rev hesitated, not really wanting to go—the battle right here, not in Mumford.

"You know, Rev." Lorenzo gave him one last little, not unfriendly elbow grab. "Sometimes people just want to grieve, you know what I'm saying?"

"Shit, Lorenzo, we grieve every day."

"Yeah, OK." Lorenzo turned away: Enough.

Looking to Brenda, he saw that the cop assigned to watch her was nowhere to be seen and that Brenda was standing alone, slashed by shadow as she faced that ragged semicircle of the curious and the hostile. Before Lorenzo could move to her, one of the Armstrong teenagers, a squat, powerfully built kid wearing a Knicks jersey that highlighted his almost cartoon-huge deltoids, broke off from the crowd and, locking eyes with Brenda, strode forward, brisk, lumbering, centered, his hands down low, knotted into fists. Brenda held his eye with an almost voracious openness—with that same innocent and eager expression that she had offered the shooters as she came out of her house earlier that morning. Before Lorenzo could even call out the kid's name, he was up in her face, Brenda waiting, not even blinking. He slid left at the last possible moment before collision, then reached out and tore down the police sketch taped to the plywood, crumpling it and flinging it away before disappearing inside the shadowed stairway.

Brenda looked out at the others still facing her, as if she were staring into the sun, then slipped on her headphones and closed her eyes.

When Lorenzo reached her, he could hear the Impressions like a whispered wreath around her stark and chopped hair, Curtis Mayfield singing in a soothing croon, sayin' "It's all right."

Escorting Brenda to Bump's van, Lorenzo was distracted by an abrupt stream of people racing up the incline behind Four Building. Stepping back through the breezeway, he saw that someone had set fire to one of the crated refrigerators in the Bowl, and he knew instantly—by the animated faces around the pyre, by the bellowing to friends, by the dashing to and fro—that unless some cops were posted to guard the Bowl right now, this entire crate-planted arena would be a blazing grid by midnight. Good news for the video shooters, bad for everybody else, people so pissed off, *sealed* off that, like convicts flooding their toilets and burning their mattresses, they would readily trash their own property to send out a message. And that would be just the start of it.

Walking backwards to Brenda while radioing in the fire to the central dispatcher, Lorenzo accidentally bumped her into the side of the van, forcing her to thrust out her left hand to catch herself against the door panel. The relatively light pressure of her body leaning into that wrist made her scream so loud that the kids in the concrete sprinkler pond froze midplay, the steady chatter of splashing water suddenly a distinct and unchallenged sound.

A moment later, with Brenda crumpled into a corner of the passenger seat, Lorenzo, feeling both embarrassed and unnerved by the alert yet expressionless faces of the tenants, flew past the Hurley Street checkpoint so heedlessly that the young cop Cooley had to broadjump backwards onto the grass to avoid getting plowed under.

And a few minutes after that, topping a rise overlooking the medical center, Lorenzo phoned Dr. Chatterjee to give him a heads up. Unable to assess the seriousness of Brenda's possible reinjury and fearful of the legal ramifications of withheld medical attention, Lorenzo had no choice but to take her back where it all began. The trick would be getting her inside the hospital without the word going out.

Chatterjee suggested that Lorenzo bring her to the ninth-floor obstetrics ward, where he would be waiting for them, hopefully away from all prying eyes. But there still remained the problem of getting her into the building.

From his vantage point above the complex, Lorenzo took a moment to ponder his back-door options. Then it came to him: the morgue. It might be the worst judgment call he would ever make in his life, Lorenzo was thinking, or, less likely, just the thing to shake her tree. Still, he balked at the cruelty of it, and to egg himself on, he conjured up a vision of the Armstrong Houses encircled by fire, expanding the circumference of the Bowl in his imagination until it encompassed the six high-rises that stood outside its perimeter. As he began the descent with Brenda to the meat-wagon ramp, he wondered if there was anything—Freon, some kind of motor oil—that would make a refrigerator explode once it had become engulfed by flames.

Standing by the roll-down gate that fronted the morgue's vehicle bay, Lorenzo and Brenda found themselves alongside an open Dumpster. It was parked beneath a handwritten sign—DISCARD ALL BLOOD-TAINTED SHEETS AND OTHER MATERIAL BEFORE ENTERING—and decorated with crudely drawn bright yellow happy faces.

"Is my son here?" Brenda asked in a high, frightened burst, her eyes transfixed by the rippling corrugated gate as it slowly began to rise.

"No, no, no. This is just the quickest way to get inside to the doctor, you know, as far as getting in private, OK? I swear to you, OK?" As the gate continued its rattling ascent, refrigerated air mingled with the heat of the day, immersing them in alternating waves of stifling humidity and a damp iciness. Lorenzo put a herding hand to the small of her back. "We're gonna go fast, OK? I want you to keep your eyes on your shoes. We'll be out and through in a minute, all right?"

There was a body on a gurney under the digital scale in the receiving area, a tall black teenager wearing matching plaid shorts and shirt, one foot bare, the other sporting a white high-top. His eyes were shut lightly, eyebrows arched, mouth agape as if whatever caused his death came to him as a big surprise. The lone morgue attendant, Humpy, a walleyed chronic mutterer, stood hunched over the gurney, absorbed in measuring the body, one end of an old-fashioned yellow cloth seamstress's tape inserted between the rigid toes of the naked foot, the other held to the back of the head.

"Yeah, look at you, you big-foot motherfucker. What they tell you about that shit, huh? You don't listen to nobody, do you. Yeah, well, who's sorry now, huh? Who's sorry now."

Lorenzo put his arm around Brenda's shoulders, his extended hand shading her brow so as to block her view as Humpy leaned over the body to enter his measurements on a clipboard that rested on the dead kid's chest.

"Humpy," Lorenzo said softly. The morgue man turned to his name. "I got to go through."

Humpy stared at Brenda for a long moment before recognizing her. "He ain't here."

"Nah, nah, nah, we just want to shortcut through to the hospital."

Humpy took a down-filled nylon baseball jacket from a wall peg—"Dempsy County Morgue" scripted in a sporty chamois across the back—shrugged it over his shoulders, and led them to what appeared to be the stainless-steel door of a restaurant-sized refrigerator.

"Just keep your eyes down," Lorenzo murmured to Brenda, hoping she would, hoping she wouldn't, and through this simple portal they entered a vast and frigid necropolis with the interior dimensions of a church. They beheld what seemed at first an inconceivable number of corpses in open storage, some fresh, some unclaimed, others backlogged for autopsy. More than half, Lorenzo knew, were guests from neighboring Essex County, where the Newark-based morgue had suffered a cooling-system blowout. The bodies were laid out on deep steel shelves, seven high, four across, on either side of a center aisle. Their varying postures and conditions were like an inventory of final exits, the dead lying there on their backs, their bellies, curled on their sides as if cold or frightened, lying there in attitudes of agony, of repose, of resistance, of surrender. Lorenzo walked Brenda down the aisle as if he were giving away the bride, walking her past the headless, the limbless; past bodies purple and bloated, skeletal, pristine, fire-blackened; past bodies nude, clothed, hospital-gowned, all races, all ages. Lorenzo felt overwhelmed, as always when circumstances brought him here, not so much by death itself, which, despite his line of work, had always seemed a little abstract to him, but by the stillness, the unwavering, unvarying, absolute stillness of death, of dozens of assembled deaths. No matter how many times he walked through that steel door, no matter how many times the morgue's perpetually changing guest list confirmed and reconfirmed that awesome stillness, he forever found himself braced to see the *one* body that would move, to hear the *one* voice that would cough, moan, or cry out for a blanket.

Halfway down the center aisle, their path was blocked by an old woman in an open-backed hospital gown lying on a plastic pallet that itself rested on the front prongs of a parked forklift. They had to back up into one of the storage lanes as Humpy maneuvered her out of their way.

Standing in silence between a charred adult male, arms bent in pugilistic contraction, and an infant who was wrapped, for some reason, in a shower curtain, Lorenzo could feel the physical pop and ripple of Brenda's distress through the arm that still lay protectively across her shoulders. He tried to recall the line of reasoning that had made him think that bringing her through here would speed things to a conclusion. Something about burning refrigerators—the rest just wouldn't come.

"You OK?" he asked in a whisper, as if the presence of the dead had really turned this room into a chapel.

"How *dare* you," she answered in a teary strangle, her shoulders trembling. *"Fuck* you."

"Brenda, if we had gone in the front door—"

"Fuck you."

He made no effort to finish his explanation. Eyes to the ground, avoiding looking at the shelved bodies that lay on either side of them, they just stood there in silence—listening to the grinding whine of the forklift, Humpy's never-ending basso mutter—until Lorenzo coughed, cleared his throat.

"I'm sorry, Brenda."

They rode a service elevator from the morgue to the obstetrics ward, from omega to alpha, and the moment they exited onto a floor full of jazzed parents and squalling newborns, Lorenzo realized that, although Brenda didn't say anything, this scene up here had to be even more punishing to her than the frozen netherworld they had left behind. And almost as an act of penance, he found himself brooding about Jason, his son in jail, and about his own blown history of failed parenthood.

Chatterjee was waiting for them in a remote examination room, sitting on a caster-legged stool, his hands clasped around a crossed knee. It must have been early in his shift, because his threads were still immaculate, folds of pink, gold, and chocolate brown flowing softly beneath a blinding white lab coat.

"Baby Doc," Lorenzo said.

Chatterjee stood up and gestured for Brenda to hop onto the examination table. When Lorenzo offered to help her up, she ignored him, although she was unable to boost herself with either hand. Chatterjee solved the impasse by lowering the table with a foot pedal. Gently stripping off the Ace bandage on her reinjured hand, the doctor studied her face.

"When was the last time you urinated?" Lorenzo automatically turned his back at the question but didn't leave the room.

"What?"

"Just what I said."

Brenda stared at a tray of scissors. "This morning?"

"Are you sure?"

"I guess."

"Do you need to go now?"

"No."

Chatterjee removed the last of the Ace bandage and began unwrapping the Curlex. "Open your mouth."

Brenda did as she was told, and Chatterjee cast a cursory glance at her chalky tongue. "Are they still looking for your son?" he asked in a businesslike tone.

"Yes."

He slipped his palm under her armpit, then probed the soft nodules above her collarbone. "You're dehydrated, did you know that?"

"No."

"It's ninety-nine degrees out there. Look at this man," Chatterjee said, gesturing to Lorenzo. "He's soaked right through his shirt. You're dry as a bone."

Brenda shrugged as if he were criticizing her.

"We have to get some fluids into you, OK?"

Brenda shrugged again, indifferent to her condition.

"Ninety-nine degrees." Chatterjee grunted. "Let me ask you something. With this weather, the trauma room, you'd think we'd be pretty busy right now, yes?"

"What?"

"Assaults, knifings, shootings—you'd think this is the weather to bring that out, correct?" She stared at him uncomprehendly. Lorenzo, on the other hand, had heard this speech before. "Well, let me tell you. It's as quiet as a church in there right now, would you believe it?" He took off the last of the Curlex. The back of Brenda's left hand was soft, swollen, and blue. "It's ninety-nine degrees outside, but I could sit in there and read the five Books of Moses from beginning to end without being disturbed. Do you know why?"

Brenda shrank back in distress. "What are you *talking* about?" she said, her voice breaking.

"It's too hot!" the doctor crowed in triumph. "There's no energy out there. Maiming takes energy. Rage takes energy. But I promise you, three days from now, when this heat wave passes? We'll be up to our chins in blood. The first cool night after a heat wave is the deadliest night of the year. Ask the detective here." Chatterjee nodded to Lorenzo, who nodded back halfheartedly.

"What happened to the back of your hand. You didn't have this injury last night."

"I hit a door frame," she whispered. Lorenzo perked up, curious.

"I want some X rays," he said, as he began stripping the Ace bandage from the right hand. "History responds to weather, too, did you know that?"

Brenda took a deep, dejected breath. "I need something for the pain."

"If you replace the word *humidity* with the word *oppression* . . . Let me put it to you like this. Without opening a history book, when do you think people are most likely to rise up against an oppressive regime? When the abuse becomes the most unbearable, right? Wrong. The people are too weak then, they're demoralized, terrified, depressed. No. Revolution comes about when the liberals come to power, the accommodationists, the reformers. As soon as the underdogs start to feel a little breeze between their necks and the yoke? Get some snap back into their spines? *That* is when heads begin to roll. Russia, France, Africa, Asia. What do they say here? It's not the heat, it's the humidity."

Lorenzo always felt thrown by Chatterjee's little theories and history lessons, not because they didn't make sense but because he could never figure out which side the doctor was on.

"OK." He held both her hands palms-up, last night's punctures and abrasions dyed tobacco brown. "I want to get some X rays, then I want to put you to bed. I'm going to get some fluids into you with an IV drip, shoot you up with a little Valium, and pull down the shades. Yes?"

Brenda stared at him for a moment, then looked off without responding. Chatterjee turned to Lorenzo. "Yes?"

Worried about Brenda's getting a second wind, Lorenzo hesitated but then thought of all the people he would be free to hit on while she slept.

"How long would she be out?"

"Four, five hours, maybe more," Chatterjee answered, then took another shot at Brenda. "Doesn't that sound good?"

"I just want my son back," she said, exhausted.

"If there's any news we'll wake you," Chatterjee said. "Right?" He looked to Lorenzo, who nodded.

"I like you." Chatterjee finally smiled at her, gently taking her hands again. "I think you're an agent of history."

Returning to the van, which was parked outside the morgue, Lorenzo was surprised and somewhat annoyed to see Ben leaning against the driver's door, reading the *Village Voice.*

"Whoa." Lorenzo forced himself to laugh. "Man, you should be with the CIA."

"Hey!" Ben grinned, folding the paper. "How are you?"

"You follow me?"

"Nah, I was just driving by, saw the van. I thought I'd see if you needed anything. How's it going?"

"Just driving by the morgue." Lorenzo smiled, a gimlet-eyed grin, waiting.

"Listen." Ben grimaced as he rubbed the hollows under his eyes. "I made some calls and I think I found somebody can speed things up for you."

"Speed things up . . ."

"You know, help Brenda out. Make her remember details and such. This individual I know . . ."

Lorenzo waited for more. "Lorenzo," Ben said, touching his arm. "You know me a little bit. I'd never waste your time at a time like this."

"What, a hypnotist?" Ben jerked back in disdain. "One of your PI buddies?"

"Please." Ben waved him off.

"Well, what we gonna do, play Twenty Questions? I thought you said you wouldn't waste my time."

"I wouldn't."

Lorenzo stared at him for a long moment, then burst out laughing at the balls on this guy. "What, you want me to put Jesse back in the cat-bird seat, right?"

"I thought they got on very well."

"Yeah, I'm glad to hear that." Lorenzo shook his head in amazement and moved around Ben to unlock the door.

"Lorenzo, my friend gets involved, it's gonna be all over in twenty-four hours."

Lorenzo straightened up despite himself. "Your friend knows Brenda?"

"Not yet," Ben said brightly.

Irritated, Lorenzo found himself going into a stare down, but he really didn't have the time. Besides, Ben's unflappably pleasant resolve was, in its own way, worse than any jailhouse glare. Tempted, Lorenzo opened his mouth, then checked himself and got into his car.

"I tell you what," Ben said, scrawling a number on the back of a business card. "I totally understand, but if you change your mind?" He handed the card, embossed on the front with the particulars of a place called Phatso's Lounge, to Lorenzo, who flipped it over to check Ben's chicken scratch on the back. "If you change your mind, I'll be at the Quality Inn by the Holland Tunnel, Room 303. I'm doing a favor for an associate. Just call. I'll be there for like the next three hours. After that . . ." He shrugged, the sales-pitch coming to an end.

"Base to SI 15 on 2."

Driving back to Armstrong, Lorenzo reached for the handset. "SI 15 to base."

"Call Investigator 13 forthwith."

Lorenzo pulled over to a pay phone on JFK. From one end of the block to the other, he could see over a dozen storefronts, all derelict except for a congressman's office.

"Bump, what's up?" Lorenzo waved to two elderly women passing by, one, he had heard, an old girlfriend of his father's.

"You headin' back to Armstrong?"

"Yup."

"I just wanted to give you a heads up. We got a function at the junction over here. Longway is getting ready to do a presser by the Conrail tracks. I think he's gonna blow the house down, so you might or might not want to make the scene here."

"What the hell you talking about? I just saw him go out of there couldn't be two hours ago."

"That was two hours ago," Bump said.

"How the fuck he get it together so fast?" Lorenzo said, hearing the unsorted anger growing in his voice.

"Hey, the people are primed. Each one phone one. The cameras are right there anyhow, right? Alls you gots to do is step on up."

Lorenzo watched an orange-and-black butterfly spasming by.

"Who's he got with him . . ." He asked it grudgingly.

"Like, everybody—Jesus, Allah, half the city council, the Mommy Squad, you name it. It's goin' down, Big Daddy, and frankly I think it's about fuckin' time."

Ten minutes later, Lorenzo pulled up across the tracks from Longway and the press camp, about a dozen yards from the action, and, windows down, AC blasting, watched from inside the van as the reverend paced back and forth in the gravel, short, brisk ten-step loops, hands on hips, collecting himself before addressing the media people, who were assembled before him in a compressed wedge of microphones and Betacams. Standing behind Longway were many of the major minority players in town—five ministers, four black, one Latino; two Islamic leaders; two city council members; three tenant representatives to the city Public Housing Authority; the head of the YMCA; the formerly airborne Tariq Wilkins, sporting a plaster cast on his broken leg; Tariq's grandmother Yvonne; Teacher Timmons, minus one tooth; and Teacher's mom, Frieda, head of the Armstrong tenants council. On the projects side of the train fence, the tenants were packed three-deep to the mesh, the chain link sprouting fingers and knuckles by the hundreds.

Lorenzo was furious. He considered himself one of the principals of the racial power collective in this town, and to not have been notified in advance by any of the people facing the press right now was a slap in the face. Even if they had refrained from getting him involved out of consideration for his status as catching detective, someone other than Bump Rosen, a white cop, should have called him with that heads up.

Longway did three final ten-foot circuits, then stepped up to the mike. "Let me keep this, *short,*" he said, glaring at the cameras, "and *sweet.*"

A chorus of "Yes's" and "Awright's" erupted from the fence, but the power players behind the rev were holding back for now. Only one of the ministers was nodding and clapping, the others just bobbing their heads, taking in the lay of the land.

"Of course, the primary, the instinctual, the natural desire of any decent, God-fearing member of this community, this city is to see the child, Cody Martin, safe, back in the arms of his *mother.*"

There was another spatter of yeses from the fence, the power players nodding behind him.

Longway pushed his glasses up his nose. "But to quarantine, to, to seal off . . . to, to ghettoize—no! To *double* ghettoize the seven hundred

families of the Henry Armstrong Houses"—the fence began to erupt in
"Tell it"s, the players now clapping loudly but still nonverbal—"on the
assumption! The assumption that the basic mentality, the basic impulse
of these seven hundred families would be to harbor a criminal of this,
this *ilk* . . . is nothing less than state-sanctioned racism of the most per-
nicious, the most massive, the most monstrous *nature*."

The fence started to rattle as if a train were coming, many of the
shooters forsaking Longway to focus on the crowd.

"And I am here, to*day*. We!" He swung an arm behind him. "We! Are
here, to*day*. To serve *not*ice, on the police department of the city of
Dempsy. To serve *not*ice, on the police department of the city of Gannon. To inform them before the eyes of this community, this state, this
country, before the eyes of the *world!*" Longway thrust a finger at the
Betacams, "That, unh-uh! *We* ain't *hav*ing it!"

People began to bellow now, the fence undulating with the force of
their emotion. Lorenzo, still sitting inside his ride, felt the rightness, the
righteousness of Longway's words yet held himself in check, continuing
to suffer the sting of exclusion.

Whatever other cops were around also kept their distance, standing
mostly on the tracks, looking impassive yet alert, their arms folded
across their chests. Bobby McDonald, hands in his pockets, scowled at
the gravel beneath his feet.

"I wish, I wish y'all could *see* yourselves right now," Longway said,
speaking directly to the fence, his voice now an almost sensuous hiss.
"Y'all look like a, a, magazine photo of some African, *refugee* camp . . .
Y'all look like some magazine photo of some, some, African, *internment*
camp."

The tenants exploded in "Yes's" and "No's," their cries interspersed
with a nonstop bellowing of names, people calling to their families and
friends still back by the buildings, an endless agitated beckoning. The
Betacams abandoned Longway almost completely now for creeping
sweeps of the fence.

Lorenzo, anxiously looking toward the seething crowd, saw a dazzle
coming at him from over the tenants' heads, a multiplicity of dazzles in
fact, and he panicked. Every refrigerator that he could see back up in the
Bowl seemed to be on fire, each crate sporting its own meticulously
precise, diamondlike flame. He shot out of his van and, staring over its
sizzling roof, was relieved to see that the grand-scale arson was simply
the afternoon sun winking at him as it bounced off whatever white
enamel or chrome it could catch peeking out through the wooden slats.

Slumping back into the driver's seat, he palmed the sweat from his dome and stared at the reverend, thinking, You said short and sweet.

"Y'all look, de-*tained*, y'all look, im*prisoned* . . . But for *what*. *I'll* tell you for what." Longway counted off on his fingers: "For being black. For being poor . . . And for livin' where you live."

Lorenzo noticed that the people closest to the fence were beginning to be mashed into the chain link, their faces showing distress, and he experienced a cool fluttering in his gut.

"This blockade, this *siege*, this criminalistic wholesale denial of the basic freedoms guaranteed to us in the Constitution of the United States of America is nothing less than a class-action insult to the hard-working, the struggling, the upright . . ."

"The crack-smoking," Lorenzo heard from behind him. Looking in his rearview mirror, he saw nothing but poker-faced cops.

". . . the God-fearing families not only of these houses, but of *all* public housing communities in this city, in this *coun*try. And I am here, to*day*—*we* are here, to*day*—to say, to you . . . that, Unh-uh, we ain't *hav*ing it!"

The players were all clapping now. One minister came up behind Longway like an ecstatic deacon and joyously patted him on the back, Longway mopping his furious face, tightly pacing again, that fence now holding back people six deep, and more coming on the run from the high end of the projects. Lorenzo was about to step out of his van again to deploy some uniforms to loosen up the mob, but Bobby McDonald beat him to it, sending a half dozen cops to the Hurley Street entrance to go into the projects and come up on that side of the fence.

"To descend on these houses under the cover of night, to, to *brutal-ize* and *maim* the young men of this community." Longway flung an arm back to Teacher and Tariq, both of them looking somewhat embarrassed.

"To, to, to strike *ter*ror, into the hearts of their mothers, their *grand*mothers . . ." Another flung back arm, Tariq's grandmother in tears, but Teacher's mom's face a rage-chiseled rock. ". . . Kicking in doors like a bunch of *got*-damn South African *storm* troopers, like a bunch of . . ."

Longway abruptly cut himself off, and waved in disgust at the microphone, as if his indignation were throttling him. The ministers and parents were shouting and clapping, egging him on, the fence ballooning crazily, Lorenzo silently praying, End It. Longway finally stepped back up, his voice now as hoarse and raw as if he had been screaming all day.

"Well, *I* am here, to*day*. *We* are here, to*day*, to say to you that this, po*lice* action . . . this, Jo*han*nesburg-izing, this, So*we*to-izing of the

Henry Armstrong Houses has just come to an *end,* because, unh-*uh . . . we,* ain't, *havin'* it!"

The roaring behind the fence turned the world into a waterfall. Sober-faced, Longway quickly turned and, raising his arms like a conductor, silently directed the assemblage behind him into two more or less straight lines.

And with the rev counting cadence, they finally stepped off, arm in arm, some people behind the mesh joining in on the chant:

> *Hey, Dempsy,*
> *Have you heard,*
> *Armstrong ain't*
> *Johannesburg*

The players shouted with varying degrees of passion, the women and ministers full-throat, the two council members more circumspectly. Teacher Timmons and the crutch-swinging Tariq Wilkins were down almost to a lip sync, both boys still looking more embarrassed than enraged.

As soon as Longway and his contingent began to march, they were flanked by reporters, the shooters racing ahead, then furiously backpedaling to document them coming forward, the total media glom-on tripling the population of the protesters.

Lorenzo was relieved to see that the tenants were pacing the marchers on the other side of the train fence, the fanning out of the crowd pretty much eliminating the danger of someone's getting crushed against the mesh.

> *Hey, Dempsy,*
> *Have you heard,*
> *Armstrong ain't*
> *Johannesburg*

He figured they were heading for the Hurley Street checkpoint, the plan to just march on in, violate the ID checks, and blow off the blockade. Lorenzo was finally, grudgingly, transcending his own bruised ego, giving it up, thinking Bump said it right: About fuckin' time. Rising from the van, he saw Bobby McDonald horse whistle, knuckles to teeth, a piercing blast, catching the eye of the two Dempsy cops manning that exit. McDonald waved to them, a short, chopping "Let 'em through" gesture. Both cops nodded, stepping back, and the siege of Armstrong was officially over. The reporters raced past the marchers into the houses to interview the interned tenants, and the tenants raced out of the exits, simply because they could.

Coming away from the train fence, Lorenzo backed up to Bobby McDonald, standing between the rails.

"Glad that's over," Lorenzo said, half under his breath.

"Nothing's over," McDonald said. Then, looking up at him, "What are you doing here?"

Lorenzo pointed to the abandoned checkpoints, speechless, wanting to say, What the fuck you *think* I'm doing here, but finally muttering, as if embarrassed, "They got her doped up over at the medical center."

"Yeah? So?" McDonald continued to squint up at him.

"I'm on it," Lorenzo said.

"You said give you today, right?"

"I know." Lorenzo, flustered, didn't know where to rest his eyes.

McDonald made a big show of studying his wristwatch, gave him one more long look, then walked away, leaving Lorenzo standing there feeling blank and talentless.

The motel operator put Lorenzo through to Room 303 at the Quality Inn.

"Cesar?" Ben came on in a semiwhisper. "The guy never showed."

"Ben?" Lorenzo reared back, thinking, Cesar. "This is Lorenzo Council."

"Hey!" Ben's voice became brighter. "How are you?"

"You know I can't really show preference to one member of the media community over the others," he began, hearing the self-conscious formality in his choice of words.

"I understand," Ben said respectfully.

Lorenzo hesitated. "Give me a number for your sister."

Ben rattled off a cell phone number, and Lorenzo carved it into the cover of his notepad with a dried-out pen.

"You tell her I'm gonna call."

"You got it."

"You tell her to wait for my call."

"You know she will."

"And you tell her our contract still stands."

"Absolutely," Ben said, another fervent acquiescence. "May I ask where they'll be hooking up?"

"No, you may not."

"Could you tell me about *when* this hookup will take place?"

Lorenzo hesitated again, then said, "A few hours."

"Excellent. And can I offer my services to them as a driver?"

Lorenzo thought about it. Jesse and Brenda without wheels would be a mess.

"Can I trust you to honor your sister's arrangement with me?"

"Lorenzo, please." He could envision Ben on the other end of the line, eyes shut, hand on heart.

"All right then," Lorenzo said.

"Thank you," Ben said solemnly.

"Now . . ." Lorenzo lowered his head, saw stars behind his eyelids. "This best be good on your end."

14

An hour after calling Jose, Jesse wandered the confines of her room, her anxiety such that, when the apartment's phone rang, its shrill signal sounded to her as abrupt and jolting as a car alarm.

"Ben?"

There was an off-balance silence on the other end of the line, followed by an off-balance voice saying, "Is this Jesse Haus?" Adult, male, most likely white.

"Who's this," Jesse said, impatient, thwarted.

"I could tell you more than you know."

"About . . ."

"You know."

"Just say it."

"Brenda Martin."

"Who are you." She hauled on a fresh pair of jeans.

"I have a history with her."

"Yeah?" Jesse jumped a few inches off the ground in order to jerk the zipper up to the top snap. "Is this Ulysses?" she said, taking a stab.

"Who?" The voice sounded genuinely thrown.

"How come you're calling me?"

"I saw you with her in front of the house this morning."

"Yeah?" She began brushing her hair with her fingers. "Do you know what happened to the kid?"

"Do *I?*"

"You. Do you know."

"I have no idea. But I know Brenda."

"You're not going to give me your name, right?" Jesse reached for a cigarette.

"There's a bar in Dempsy, McCoy's?" The voice became a little steadier.

"Uh-huh."

"Can I meet you there in an hour?"

"At McCoy's?"

"Yeah."

"I hear that's where all the news crews are hanging out." Jesse scanned the room for matches, for socks. "The reporters and all. You sound like you kind of want to lay low."

"It's not like I'm famous," he said.

"Just giving you a heads up," Jesse said evenly, thinking maybe she'd show, maybe she wouldn't. "Where do you know Brenda from again?"

Ben's cell phone rang, a discreet flutelike trill, somewhere from within the swirl of sheets on her unmade bed.

"OK, McCoy's," she said quickly, then hung up, diving for the other phone.

"Ben." The command was this time obeyed.

"Well, I got some good news." He sounded as if he was about to take some goodies out of a bag, one by one. "I talked to Lorenzo."

"And . . ."

"And I got her back for you."

"*Yes!*" Jesse spun herself around, feeling recharged, fresh.

"He'll call you in a bit. I gave him the cell phone number in case you want to go out."

"When do I get her."

"A few hours."

"Where."

"I'll come get you," he said with studied casualness.

"Just say." Jesse suddenly became wary. That tone of Ben's was the one he used when he had to string people along.

"It's—I'll come get you."

"Why can't you just say." Jesse was on full alert now.

"I'd rather not."

"Well, that's fucked. What's the deal?"

"Let me just come get you."

"Well, I'll be out," she said childishly.

"No problem. Just take the phone."

She hung up, angry, then remembered the punch line—Brenda. Jesse felt herself brimming with joy, with life.

McCoy's was an obscure and surly bar situated in a ground-floor corner of a mansard-roofed, purple-gray Victorian that straddled the Dempsy-Gannon line, two blocks north of the Armstrong Houses, and was surrounded by history. Directly across the street, on the Dempsy side of the border, standing alone and surreal in a junk-strewn field, was a fifty-yard-long, ten-foot-high time-pocked cement wall, all that remained of a POW camp built during the First World War. Three hundred yards in the opposite direction, on the Gannon side of the bar, sprawled an abandoned abattoir, the setting of a notorious labor strike early in the century, during which Ukrainian and Slovak meatpackers toting rocks, pistols, and homemade bombs had taken on a small army of local cops and imported Pinkertons in five days of spasmodic street fighting that had yielded a death toll of eleven.

The saloon itself, known as Koerner's in those days, served as headquarters for the Pinkertons, who tossed Koerner out of his own establishment after he refused to serve them. When Jesse finally got it up to enter the damp, beery room, she looked for the last memento of that bloody week, five bullet holes preserved behind a Plexiglas shield between the dartboard and the pay phone. The damage had been done when a handful of armed meatpackers, led by the proprietor himself, had attempted to liberate the bar from the goons. The assault left three dead, including Koerner, who was accidentally shot from behind by one of his own raiding party.

Jesse had heard that the press had basically commandeered McCoy's for the duration of this story, but she didn't believe it until she saw the inordinate number of rental cars parked on the POW side of the street. Whenever a story broke nationwide, in no matter what state, city, or town, the media people drawn to the scene would instinctively home in on one particular bar-restaurant not too far from the visual base camp and could reliably be found there in force each night after sending off their copy or stowing their gear.

But McCoy's . . . The air conditioning gave off Legionnaires' disease, and although there was some kind of grudging, nominal menu, the geriatric cook had TB and it took twenty minutes for him to dismount from his bar stool, the resulting hamburger on white bread, with a side of potato chips, finally showing up something like six drinks after it had been ordered.

Scanning the room from the bar, Jesse found it easy to separate the media people from the regulars. Relaxed and chatty, almost schizo-phrenically so, compared to their daytime personas, the reporters and shooters were, for the most part, younger, thinner, and possessed of a more expansive, easy air than the McCoy's regulars, who either talked to each other tonight with one eye on the invaders or sat alone, smoking and glaring at their drinks. With one elbow kissing the edge of a small, sweetish-smelling puddle on the bar top, Jesse watched a New York tab-loid columnist shoot minipool with a gaunt, bearded photographer wear-ing a *USA Today* T-shirt.

Over by the pay phones, a newscaster from *Hot Copy* was putting the moves on a heavyset, chain-smoking woman who Jesse thought might be with the *Washington Post*. Directly across the room from her, all three of the torn vinyl, smoke-wreathed banquettes were elbow to elbow with visiting press scarfing down burgers and throwing back drinks, the volume of chatter like the magnified thrum of bees. It seemed to Jesse—as it always did when she was given the opportunity to go after an out-of-town story and found herself entering one of the countless crime-scene-convenient, courthouse-convenient, disaster-area-convenient McCoy's of America—that she was surrounded by a group of people who had known one another for years, that what she had walked into, yet again, was some kind of spontaneous cousins club. In fact, as she well knew, the overwhelming majority of those assembled here now had never even set eyes on one another before last night, be-fore Brenda walked into that emergency room bearing two palmfuls of grief.

Usually, when encountering a roomful of her down-time peers like this, Jesse felt defensively contemptuous and intensely alone. This eve-ning, though, with the double prospect of both an inside connect and a rendezvous with the birthday girl herself, she felt more plummy than scornful, more awkward than isolated.

As for her phone caller, she saw two possibles, both looking to be in their thirties, each sitting by himself. One was as big as a bear, puffy-faced, wearing a too-warm sport jacket, his pouchy, burdened eyes con-stantly flicking from Jesse at the bar to the untouched drink between his motionless hands. The other was deeply tanned and neatly dressed, a squared-away-looking gentleman whose short black hair and trimmed goatee were laced with streaks of gray.

At the moment, this second guy seemed to be completely absorbed in sculpting the fragile ash barrel of his cigarette against the curve of his glass, but there was an air of self-consciousness about him, an almost theatrical determination to focus his attention on the task at hand, that made her continuously glance his way, waiting for his eyes to lift and confirm her hunch. In any event, there was nothing for her to do now but wait.

Two stools down from her, one of the few McCoy's regulars willing to breach the gap, a red-faced, white-haired old-timer, sat jawing with a woman Jesse's age, who wore a *Deadline U.S.A.* T-shirt and nursed a scotch on the rocks.

"You see crime now? Bad, right? You know what I blame? Increased communications."

"Oh yeah?" The woman from *Deadline* stabbed out a cigarette, lit another.

"Videotape, radios. Something happens, they get you on tape, you're dead. Like Rodney King, OK? But also this. A cop has a situation these days, what does he do. He radios for backup. Call goes out, five minutes later you got yourself a block party—the neighbors, the family, other cops, reporters—and you got to watch it. Watch what you do, watch what you say. It's like, your hands are tied, and you have to be careful, OK? Very careful. But in *my* day—now, I'm going back thirty, thirty-five years—you had a situation, you're all alone, you did what you had to do. No videotape, no radio transmissions, no news at eleven. You did what you had to do to address the situation at hand. And the individuals you dealt with? They knew the score, they knew what was coming to them, and they respected that. See? Increased communications. They put the handcuffs on the wrong people."

Surveying the room in the bar mirror, Jesse saw that her two possibles were hanging in, the cigarette sculptor briefly meeting her reflected gaze now, his face tense and melancholy. Jesse threw him a small nod but he coughed into his fist, and she wasn't sure if he had caught it.

The bartender, thirtyish, with Moe Howard bangs, a brush moustache, glasses, and tattoos on both arms, put a second screwdriver in front of her without her asking.

"On me." He rapped wood.

Although poker-faced, he seemed excited by the new crowd.

"You got anything green?" A TV reporter from New York, one of the networks, Jane something, bellied up to the bar. Jesse recognized her more from her voice than from her appearance.

"Green?" The bartender lazily stiff-armed the counter, leaning into his palms.

"Green. Vegetables. Salad. I need something green."

"How about carrots?" he said slowly, having a ball. "I think we got some carrots in the kitchen. But they're not green."

"No problem. Give me carrots," she said in an exasperated tone, putting it on a little. She turned to Jesse. "New Jersey's the Garden State, right? You'd think they have to haul this shit up from New Zealand."

Before Jesse could respond, Jane turned to the old-timer. "Are you telling her that crap about how videotape causes crime?"

"I think he's got something," the woman from *Deadline U.S.A.* said.

The old guy, eyebrows dancing, watched them with open-mouthed pleasure.

"So the mommy, what's she thinking?" Deadline asked Jane, signaling for another, gesturing for the bartender to pour one for the old guy too.

"Right now?" Jane shrugged. "I'd say she's thinking, Hold it together. Hold it together. It's almost over."

"Yeah?" Deadline tapped ash. "I don't know. I think she's the goods."

"She's an ice-cold, lying-ass sack of shit." Jane lit a cigarette too. Jesse felt her guts shift, as if she were overhearing vile slander about herself or a relative. She eyed her two possibles again: Let's go, let's go, let's go.

"To your health." The old guy raised his free drink to Deadline.

"Next year in Jerusalem," Deadline said, returning the toast, then dismissed him from her world with a twist of the shoulders. "You remember that lady out in Oklahoma gassed all three of her kids?" she asked Jane. "What she say?"

" 'I guess I was having a real bad low-self-esteem day,' " Jane recited, as Jesse ran the same quote through her mind verbatim. The old-timer, realizing his moment here had passed, slid off the bar stool, his face congested with anger and disappointment.

"Low self . . . OK." Deadline fired up another cigarette. "OK. Say she did it. Was it an accident or did she have some plan?"

"I think . . ." Jane eyed a plate of carrots coming to her like a stack of

Lincoln Logs. "I think it hit her maybe an hour before she did it. She chewed it over for an hour. So, it was like, semispontaneous."

"And *why*."

"Why'd she do it?"

In the mirror, both possibles were looking directly at her now. Jesse slid over one stool, making a space.

"Check it out." A young bow-tied reporter, impeccably dressed in a crisp white shirt and razor-creased khakis, took up the just-vacated seat, almost sitting on Jesse's hand. "You see that fat guy by the dartboard? He says he went out with her last year."

"Is he talking?" Deadline took a carrot from the plate.

"He says he'll shoot pool with you for twenty bucks a rack."

Jesse leaned back on her stool and scoped out the fat man. It was Tony Kowalski, an ex–volunteer fireman, just out after spending three years in jail for setting fires all over Dempsy County. She had covered both the fires and the arrest.

She caught the cigarette artist staring at her again in the mirror. She threw him another tacit nod, this one definitely received, but all he did was look away.

Another reporter, a black kid in his twenties, wearing gold wire-rim glasses and a polo shirt, leaned into the rail, ordered himself a beer.

"We're going over to Armstrong tonight," bow-tie boy announced. "Check out the scene."

"When."

"What time was the . . . Same time she said it happened. Get the lay of the land, see who's around. Talk to people."

"You're going with that bow tie?"

"No, no, no, I'll go back to the room. I got this, like, Eddie Bauer duck-hunting outfit. It's really casual. The brothers are gonna love it. Besides"—he draped his arm across the shoulders of the young black reporter—"I got Shaka Zulu here on point."

Jesse suddenly got the bow tie, a tongue-in-cheek nod to Jimmy Olsen. She liked that.

Checking out her two possibles again, Jesse keyed in on number one, the guy in the winter-weight sport jacket, whose heavy, haggard face made him appear simultaneously bloated and gaunt. She noticed that he wore an earring, an affectation completely out of sync with his otherwise bookish aura. And although he looked stressed enough to have some personal stake in this ongoing ordeal, he had ceased returning her pointed glances in the mirror. She still liked number two.

"I was talking to some of the brothers in Armstrong?" the black reporter said, sipping his beer. "They're telling me that over in Gannon they got this cell they throw you in—no door, no window, no food, no toilet, no phone call."

"Then how do they throw you in?" Jane asked.

"They told me they put you in there for like a *week* before you can call your lawyer or something, right? So I run that by this Gannon cop. He's laughing, says, 'Yeah, I heard that's what they think, and we don't want to do anything to *relieve* them of their misperceptions.'"

"Nice."

"We shall undercome."

Jesse knew that room, the holding cell right out front, first thing you saw walking over to the sergeant's desk. The only thing unusual or disturbing about it was that it was Plexiglas—four see-through walls, no bars.

Bow-tie boy's cell phone rang, and he gave everybody his back as he hunched down, speaking into the phone with a finger in one ear. The three others were suddenly silent, casually alert, trying to suss out whom he was talking to.

In the mirror, Jesse saw bachelor number two get up from his table and head for the bathroom area, around the bend from the bullet holes. She eased herself off the bar stool and began to follow, but a few steps from the bar her own cell phone began to ring. She returned to her seat with her back to the others.

"Yeah?"

"Yeah, Brenda," Lorenzo said, then corrected himself. "Jesse." He sounded flustered by the mistake. "This is Lorenzo Council."

"Hey," she said softly, thinking, First name, last name—the guy is hanging by a thread.

"Did your brother tell you what's happening?"

"Nope."

"He's gonna take you to her."

"OK."

"I got some people I need to see."

"OK."

"I got some people I got to talk to."

"OK."

"So I want you to stay with her."

"OK."

"I want you to take her home and I want you to stay with her."

"Right."

"Do not go *anywhere.*"

"No problem."

"You be where I can find you."

"No problem. Where's she at now?"

There was a long silence on Lorenzo's end. Jesse held her breath, praying he wasn't changing his mind.

"Over at the medical center on the obstetrics ward, Room 907," he said as if giving away his life's savings.

"Yes," Jesse said, bobbing her head.

"You pick her up and you take her right back to her house."

"Absolutely."

"Anything she says to you? You keep it to yourself. Something comes up? You page me on the spot."

"Absolutely."

"Now, I already spoke to your brother about all this, and he's gonna take you to her."

"OK," Jesse said, refraining from making a comment about his repeating himself.

There was another silence, this one Jesse read as sheer anxiety, as Lorenzo searching his mind for something else, some other bottom-line mandate that he could lay on her. "Lorenzo, you OK?" Jesse said, just to break the silence.

"I'll be better when this is done with."

"You getting anywhere?"

Lorenzo hung up. Jesse was buzzed again, going out of focus, hearing things as if through ear plugs.

"I talked to the guy in the video store?" Deadline yawned into her fist. "You know, around the corner from the house? Every night they took out two, three cassettes."

"Did they have a record of the movies they rented?"

"Yeah, the usual." Deadline fired up a fourth cigarette. "You know— *Serial Mom, Henry: Portrait of a Serial Killer, The Bad Seed—*"

"*Children of the Damned—*"

"*Child's Play.*"

"*Mommie Dearest.*"

Jesse drifted off, wondering why on earth a catching detective would hand over someone like Brenda, *return* someone like Brenda to a reporter for baby-sitting, instead of to another cop. She wondered what the hell Ben could have said to Lorenzo, offered Lorenzo, in exchange.

There would be a price to pay, she knew that for sure, but she didn't have any idea of its nature.

"The kid even had his own membership card," Deadline said. "See, I really don't think she did it myself. They sound like they were pretty tight."

"Till the boyfriend popped up," Jane said.

"What boyfriend?" bow-tie boy asked.

"There's always a boyfriend. That's how they do," Jane said. "Mommy and the kid, they're tighter'n a crab's ass. Then Mommy goes and gets her a boyfriend." Jesse's chief possible returned from his trip to the bathroom, throwing her a quick glance. The call from Lorenzo had made her forget him. Shit. "What did that guy in Louisiana say to that lady before she poisoned her daughter last month?"

" 'I would ask you to move in with me and my mom 'cept for that nigger kid of yours,' " bow-tie boy piped up.

"No. ' 'Cept for that *half*-nigger kid of yours,' " the black reporter said, correcting him. "Half-nigger."

Pushing off from the bar, Jesse headed for the bathrooms behind the bullet holes, trying to draw number two up from his table again.

Standing in the dank, yeasty vestibule between the two restrooms, Jesse eavesdropped on two reporters as, one after the other, they argued with their editors over the pay phone. Each of them hinted at explosive revelations to come—new, almost-confirmed information that would yield a chain reaction of headlines—and, in general, blew all kinds of smoke in an effort to secure for themselves a few more inches in tomorrow's edition.

After ten minutes of leaning into the shadows, her eyes beginning to sting from the endless waves of bathroom air fanned her way with each exit and entrance, she started to return to the bar and promptly collided with prospect number one, the bearish man with the hangdog eyes. The light bump backed her up to the wall again.

"Can we go somewhere?" he asked under his breath, towering over her one moment, then pulling back the next, the body language of someone who saw himself as too big. Her brother did the same thing.

"Go somewhere . . ." She let it hang.

"To talk"—he pressed his palms together—"about Brenda."

Walking through the the small kitchen they slipped outside via the delivery door. The slanting rays of the dying sun, that peculiar angle of light, made Jesse reassess this guy's age as closer to midforties than any-where in his thirties. Stepping away from a cluster of garbage cans, they took seats on the front steps of a run-down brownstone. A wooden plaque under the doorbell identified it as a halfway house run by the local diocese for recovering drug addicts.

"Can you give me your name now?" Jesse asked, watching the guy wrestle his way out of his sport jacket.

"I'd rather not."

"OK."

"I'm from Philadelphia."

"OK."

"I'm a writer."

"Fuck off." Jesse was up and two strides down the block before he could lunge after her and grab her elbow.

"No, no, please, I write self-help books. I'm not here for that. I write self-help. I used to go out with her, I swear. I just need to tell somebody. Please."

"Books." Jesse turned to him. "Give me two titles."

"I won't do that. I need to be disconnected from this. Look, I'm not going to *ask* you anything. This here is not my thing, OK? Please."

His face was bearded with sweat, the downward trajectory of the rivulets accentuating the droop of his eyes.

Jesse returned to her perch on the steps. "Go ahead."

"About three years ago? I had this book coming out and my publish-ers had me doing a little tour—just East Coast. Sit in a bookstore for a few hours, come meet the author."

"What do you self-help people with?"

"Happiness." He gave her a shrug. "Aspects of happiness." Then, as if reading her mind, he added, "I'm happier than I look."

"So . . ."

"So I'm in New York in this big chain store in Greenwich Village, sat there two hours, signed four books. I'm wrapping it up, another wasted day, and, I see her, Brenda, just walking around. She's got the baby in that back papoose, she's not there for my book, but we look at each other, and she's got those eyes, those light gray eyes, and it's like bang, I'm goofy. And I never—this is not my style—but I say something like, 'Excuse me. Could you please tell me what I can possibly say right now that would convince you to come have a coffee with me?' It just came out of me. I'm never that loose around women, but those eyes of hers, they were like, like *anarchy*."

"So . . ." Jesse was liking this guy.

"So she says to me, 'You just said it,' and the three of us leave the bookstore together, me, her, and the baby, and we go to Washington Square Park to watch the circus. Talk, talk, talk. I like her, I like her a lot. She's smart, she's dry, and, about an hour into talking, I take her hand. That's it. I take her hand like we're thirteen years old, and she lets me. And it's like . . ."—he put a hand to his heart—"like more exciting to me than, you know, if we had rented a room somewhere." His hand came away, leaving its imprint in sweat on his shirt, purple on light blue.

"OK," Jesse said, moving him along, then noticing that she was dressed completely in black, perfect for summertime.

"We walk around, walk around, finally she says she's got to go home, she lives in New Jersey, so we go to the PATH station in the West Village. I say, 'Can I see you again?' She says, 'Sure.' And, like, in the street, we start kissing, just kissing, no grab ass, just like, arms." He shut his eyes. "And lips and oh my God. Did you ever have an encounter that makes you remember everything you forgot you knew? Kissing her was like, like, 1966. It was . . ." The big man halted, shaking his head in remembered awe.

"OK," Jesse said carefully, rolling with his words, remembering a damp forest, the scent of discount cologne. "So."

One of the residents of the halfway house, a wiry middle-aged Latino with ravaged skin, exited the front door and, slipping a Marlboro between his lips, descended to Jesse on the bottom steps. Without saying a word, he cupped Jesse's cigarette hand in both his own and, bowing his head, bummed a light. His touch felt like sandpaper.

The big man smiled down at his shoes as if embarrassed, as if this guy had cut in on a dance. He waited until the guy had disappeared around the corner before resuming.

"So it was 1966 all over again," Jesse said.

"So I go home, OK? And we talk all week on the phone. She's going to come down to me in Philadelphia the next weekend. I'm, like, jumping out of my skin. Like . . ." He held up his hands in surrender. "So she comes down, I meet her at the train station, it's like we haven't seen each other since the *war* or something—kiss, smooch, hug—and she's got the baby with her again. I kind of forgot about the kid. I mean, he was sleeping in that backpack most of the time the week before, but whatever." He shrugged. "It's just a kid, her kid—I don't have a problem with kids. Don't *have* any, but . . . So we go back to my place. It's a one bedroom, we go in, the kid's sleeping, and she knows that we're heading for the bedroom, so she gently, like, lays the kid down on my couch, puts some chairs up against the pillows so the kid won't fall off."

"You have to do that," Jesse said, surprising herself.

"Yeah, I know." He hauled a leg up across the opposite knee with both hands. "So the kid's down. We do a backwards tango into the bedroom, kiss, grab, grind, fling off this, fling off that, the whole nine yards, get about halfway there . . . the kid wakes up, starts crying. She goes out to the living room, stays with him maybe twenty minutes, comes back in the bedroom. We're a little out of sync, but not much. We get back into it. Ten minutes, the baby starts crying again. It's, like, we got to my house at 3:05 in the afternoon, started trying to have sex at 3:09, let's say, and we were interrupted so many times by that kid that I'd have to say that we didn't, scientifically speaking, actually *do* it until maybe five hours later, at which point both of us, we were doing it, like, just to get it *done*.

"The job of sex," Jesse said quickly, not dwelling on it. "How was she with the baby?" She peeked at her brother's cell phone, making sure the power was on.

"Fine. She was totally unfrazzled about it. I mean, she was apologetic to me—I mean, hey, it's her sex life too—but the kid came first. Which is fine, I understand that, I honor and respect that. I'm not by nature a selfish individual. In fact, I never complained or got foul on her or anything, but here's the deal. It went on and on like that for three days, Friday through Sunday. I don't know if the kid was colicky or disoriented or whatever, but after a while you kind of get into this trance, like this obligation trance, like a worker bee or something. I mean it was get up, lay down, get up, lay down, walk the kid, change the kid, burp the kid, up, down up, down up, down, and I have to admit, that by Saturday afternoon? Those gray eyes had kind of lost their magic on me a little, you know? And by Sunday? Frankly speaking? I couldn't wait for her to leave."

"That's a shame," Jesse said openly, falling into the story, plucking her T-shirt free of her chest—get a little air in there. "But she was totally OK with Cody?"

"Cody?" he said falteringly. Jesse realized that he had never known or had forgotten the baby's name and that the sound of it now had thrown him off, made the squirming, crying mass in the papoose, on his couch, more of a reality.

"Yeah, she was fine with him. I mean, it was her kid. And my theory? It was like, the day we met? In New York? I can't speak for her, but for me, when we started kissing by the PATH station, I was, I was full-tilt in love. I would have married her on the spot. And all that week? I was like a gut-shot dog. I couldn't *breathe* without thinking about her. So let's say that she maybe felt a little of the same way, OK? So at first I'm thinking, here comes the big Philadelphia weekend, she gets scared of her feelings, right? Scared of losing control. So she brings the kid down with her like a buffer, to keep things from happening. Makes sense, right?" Jesse didn't answer. "I mean any idiot pop psychologist can come up with that one, right?"

"OK, yeah," she said quickly, not liking to throw off a narrative with her own opinions on things.

"And it worked, if, you know, if that's what her game plan was, but here's the thing. It's Sunday afternoon. We're at this park near my apartment. I say, 'What time's your train?' She looks at me, and I see in her eyes . . ." He peered through his upheld hands. "I see in her eyes, just for a flash, this look of, I want to say disappointment, but stronger."

"Betrayal?" Jesse volunteered.

"No, more like, *puncture.* I don't know, like dejection, deflation, just . . . I mean it only lasted for, you know, long enough for me to *see* it, then she was, 'Oh yeah, I forgot to check the schedule. How often do the trains run, every hour?' Blah, blah, blah, but it was like she really expected me to ask her to stay or move in or something, like it had been a great weekend experience. I guess, I don't know, it was so unrealistic a frame of mind. I mean, maybe it was because I never complained about the kid or something. You know, what's the saying? No good deed goes unpunished?"

"That's the one," Jesse said faintly, thinking, Alone is good, thinking, Alone makes you crazy.

"Anyways, I bring her to the train later, and it was like someone had blown out the candle. We both knew that that was it. No kisses, no—I mean, nothing hostile or angry, at least on the skin of things but . . . Anyways, so I drop her off and I go home. I'm a little depressed, but these things happen. So I'm home. I get a phone call about nine, nine-thirty that night. It's a cop, an Amtrak cop, asks me if I know a Brenda Martin. I say, 'Yeah, what's wrong?' You know, scared something happened. 'Is she OK?' The cop says, 'I guess.' I'm like, 'You *guess?*' " He took a breath. "It turns out, what happened was, the Amtrak waiting area? It's like twenty-four benches, six rows of four facing each other in a square, OK? The baby, her, Brenda's kid? Is sitting strapped into his stroller in front of the first bench on one side of the inner square. He's there alone, no one on any of the front four benches, and he starts to cry. Baby's parked there, by himself, crying. Now, there's a few dozen people seated throughout the benches but the baby's all alone. Cop comes over to the stroller, calls out, 'Whose baby is this?' Everybody's, like, 'Huh?' *More* cops come over, looking at each other, another shout-out, 'Whose baby is this?' Nothing. Cop tells me they must have called it out half a dozen times, even ran it through the PA system: 'Whose baby is this?' So now they think they have an abandoned child on their hands, OK? They're standing around, ten fifteen minutes, trying to figure out what to do, how to deal with it. This cop who called me said he gave it one last shot, announces, 'Did anyone see who left this *baby?*'

"All of a sudden, he tells me, Brenda gets up. She was like only three rows back from the stroller, apparently sitting there the whole time. She stands up and says, 'I'm right here.' Very calm. 'I'm right here.' They're looking at her. 'Did you leave this child here?' She says, 'I didn't *leave* him there. I *put* him there. I'm sitting right here.' And, in truth, she was only maybe twenty feet away the whole time. Cop says, 'Didn't you hear us ask who's the mother?' She says, 'Yeah, you just said it.' He says, 'You didn't hear us all those other times?' 'I'm kind of tired,' she says. 'I guess not.'

"And you know, they're looking at her, checking her out, and they see she's apparently sober, calm, what's that, clear of eye? Cop says, 'You didn't hear your child crying?' She says, 'Yeah, sometimes he cries. I was just waiting to see if he'd stop on his own. A lot of times he'll stop on his own. I told you. I'm really tired right now.' So," the big man said, slapping his knees, "this cop tells me they weren't sure what to do. The baby's not abandoned, the mom's right there, she's apparently, you know, mentally speaking, present and accounted for." He shrugged.

Jesse pictured it—Brenda physically distancing herself from the baby as she mulled over the lost weekend, shutting down her eyes, shutting down her ears, an experiment.

"Anyways, they take her vital statistics, get *my* number from her— you know, 'What were you doing here in Philadelphia?' et cetera—and she boards the next train for home. And the reason this cop is calling me is because it's bugging him, her not responding to those call-outs. I mean her letting the baby cry too, of course, but mainly her sitting there twenty, thirty feet away, her child surrounded by uniforms, and not re-sponding to all those call-outs. And this cop, he says to me, 'The reason I'm calling you, sir, is so that you can reassure me that everything is OK with that lady and her child and that I didn't fuck up by not calling social services to come and check out that kid.' And you know, what can I say? I'm, like, 'Hey, if anything, that woman is diligent to a *fault*.'"

"Do you have that cop's name?" Jesse asked.

"Even if I did, the thing was a non-incident. There was no report on it the way it sounded to me."

"Did you ever see her again?"

"Nope." He shrugged.

"Do you know anyone else she went out with?"

"Nope."

"So you don't know if she's got a boyfriend now."

"Hey," he said, "I live in Philadelphia."

Rising to his feet, he dusted the rear of his slacks. "One last thing," he said. "I left her at the station that day? It couldn't have been more than twenty minutes before her train was due, OK? There's a train, that same train, leaves every hour on the hour. I ask the cop when this all happened? It was *four hours* after I had dropped her off."

"So what are you trying to say?" Jesse asked, willfully fuzzy, wanting it all laid out for her.

"What am I trying to say?" He looked off, smiling uncomfortably. "I just said it." And instead of returning to McCoy's, he trundled off down the street.

Another one for the hold-back bin, for the Brenda-as-bad-player file, Jesse thought. This slowly burgeoning accumulation of anecdote and gesture, of half-remembered utterance and act told her everything, told her nothing.

Heading back inside the bar, she heard her cell phone ring again, and she wheeled around to the bathroom area.

"It's me," Ben said. "May I ask where you are?"

"McCoy's."

"The bar?"

"Yeah."

"May I come pick you up?"

"Yes, you may."

"Ten minutes?"

"Ten minutes."

"Excellent."

Back at the rail, they were still going at it—Jane, Deadline, and the two boy reporters. Jesse reclaimed her spot and ordered herself a Stoli neat in preparation for Brenda, for whatever Ben had offered Lorenzo in exchange for Brenda. When her drink came she threw it back, a fireball, and tried to envision Brenda sitting in that square of train station benches, distancing herself from the baby. But for how long? Fifteen minutes? An hour? Four hours?

She began to signal for another shot, then held herself back, not liking the sloppy edge of her current buzz.

Bachelor number two was still seated by himself out there on the floor, still throwing her quick oblique glances. Jesse was confused now, regretting the Stoli altogether.

"You know about the cop's son?" bow-tie boy asked the others.

"What cop . . ."

"Council, the catching detective. He's got a kid doing five to seven for armed robbery."

"Nice," Jane said.

"Yeah, Daddy's on Rolonda Watts telling everybody 'Just say no,' he's got a kid in the slammer for robbing drug dealers."

" 'Just say mine,' " the black reporter said.

"Yeah, turned out he was using his father's piece to pull the jobs too."

"Ho."

"The cop was on Rolonda?" Jane asked.

"Twice."

"Whoa."

"Physician, heal thyself," Deadline said.

"Yeah, well, he's also got another son teaches math in a junior high school down in Camden." They all turned to Jesse, Jesse not a hundred percent sure she had said it, but she had. They eyed her with mild curiosity, taking her for some journalistic foot soldier or other, until the black reporter made the connection.

"You were with her, right?"

"Yup," Jesse said, vibrating like a tuning fork.

"And?" Deadline said, with a hint of impatience.

"And now I'm down here." Jesse's response was a shade pugnacious, the four of them glancing at one another, Jane then pointedly looking off, rolling her eyes.

"So what do you think?" bow-tie boy asked soberly—no more banter.

"I can't tell," Jesse answered earnestly, trying to make up for her clumsy evasiveness a moment ago.

"Can you, *steer* us?" Jane asked, breaking balls.

"I'm doing what you're doing." Jesse shrugged. "I'm in the same boat."

"You from here?"

"The *Register*."

"Des Moines?"

"Dempsy."

"How'd you get in?"

"Friend of the family." She pushed away from the bar, suddenly desperate to get out of there.

"Yeah?"

"Yeah."

"You want to come with us tonight?" bow-tie boy offered quietly. "Show us around?"

"Over to Armstrong?" He didn't answer, just stared, taking her measure. "I can't." She rose to her feet, felt their eyes on her, envisioning herself as a mass of flutters and twitches.

"Do you know where she is now?" the black reporter asked.

"I wish I knew." Jesse's bar stool scraped against the floor loudly as she tried to move past herself.

"Who was that big stiff in front of the house this morning?"

"I have no idea," she said, weaving her way through the tables, aware once again of bachelor number two. He was still studying her, and, blaming it on the Stoli, she impulsively veered off course, intent on asking him about all this eyeball action. Once it became apparent to him that she was heading directly for his table, he tensed visibly, then shot up from his seat, swept up his cigarettes and lighter in one smooth move, and brushed past her for the front door.

Leaving the bar, Jesse saw Ben double-parked parallel to the POW wall. Someone was in the passenger seat, a big Italian-looking lady, square-shouldered, wearing a red satin baseball jacket. Then Jesse noticed the Chevy Blazer double-parked behind her brother's ride, full up with three more women, two wearing that same red satin jacket. Behind the wheel of the Blazer sat a black man, fortyish, sporting a thin, dapper moustache, this guy, too, wearing the red team jacket of the others.

As she began crossing the street, Ben threw her a big self-conscious grin from the car.

"Jesse, hey." He sounded like he had never uttered her name before. "This is Karen Collucci from the Friends of Kent."

He flattened himself against the headrest so the women could size each other up through the driver's window. The great Karen Collucci, Jesse thought, looking into her muddy brown eyes, Karen's return gaze both assessing and detached. Jesse began to intuit something about the price to be paid for a continuing relationship with Brenda.

"How you doing, Jesse?" Karen asked in a casual yet authoritative tone, her voice man-deep. She extended a red-nailed hand that enveloped Jesse's own, holding the grip a shade longer than necessary, as if Jesse's fingers were laden with data. Beneath an almost blue-black lacquered nest of hair, Karen's face was dark-toned and long-jawed, the set of her lipsticked mouth, the slightly off-angle tilt of her head, and the heavy-lidded steadiness of her eyes all coming together to exude an air of unflappable challenge. On the left breast of her bomber jacket was a stylized drawing of two stick figures—an adult and a child, the adult's left arm draped protectively across the child's shoulders, FRIENDS OF KENT printed beneath their feet.

Kent was Kent Rivera, a six-year-old found strangled and perfunctorily buried five years earlier in a wooded area behind the boy's school. Ben, a part-time Friends of Kenter himself, had told Jesse the story more than once: how Karen and her people—originally a loose collection of neighborhood women—assembled in her backyard for a gin game one evening and, hearing the boy's father trolling the streets in a PA-equipped van, calling out his missing son's name in a teary, panicked voice, impulsively decided to form their own search party that night. To their astonishment and horror, they actually found the boy two hours past dawn.

According to Ben's awestruck retelling, Karen herself had been the one to discover the body. Drawn by a blue plastic recycling bag near the base of an oak tree, she had tossed it aside to reveal a patch of ground littered with clay balls. Unaware that those knotty clumps were a sign of recently turned soil, she nonetheless brushed the surface with her fingers and quickly came upon five pale toes, like a brace of pearls sprouting from the churned earth.

The gospel according to Ben then continued with the Crime Scene Unit collecting enough forensic evidence at the site to arrest the school's

assistant custodian. Almost religiously galvanized by their gruesome suc-
cess, Karen and her gin game formed the Friends of Kent, destiny-
graced and unblinking, eight former housewives perched at the end of a
hot line. Although basically a low-profile ad lib organization with only a
dozen hard-core members, it was known well enough by various local
police departments to be called on now and then to organize and conduct huge volunteer search parties for missing children. On occasion, its
members acted as intermediaries between the child's family and the local cops, which sometimes meant soft-grilling the frantic parents and
other relatives in a way the police couldn't for fear of snapping the lines
of communication.

"Karen's gonna have a sit-down with Lorenzo tonight, about eight,
eight-thirty?" Ben nodded, as if agreeing with himself. "She's gonna see
if her people can be of any help here, and I *told* her she should *meet* you,
you know, because, like, you spent so much time with her, you know,
Brenda," he said, doing everything but winking at her in Morse code.
Ben was taking over here, converting her relationship with Brenda into a
three-way.

Jesse leaned into his window and caught a faint whiff of nail polish
and nicotine.

"Yeah, well, I've been with Brenda pretty much since the jump—
more than anybody else *I* know of."

Karen nodded and tossed her lipstick-imprinted cigarette butt out
the window. "Are you writing about her?" She raised her chin, aiming it
at Jesse.

"That's what I do," Jesse said, looking off.

Karen nodded. "How does she strike you?"

"What do you mean?" Karen waited. "If you're asking me if she's
hurting over this, all I can tell you is she hasn't eaten, hasn't slept, and
she's been hospitalized for dehydration," Jesse said, bodysurfing a wave
of exhaustion herself. "Now, if all of that's grief or a guilty conscience, or
both, or whatever, your guess is as good as mine."

Karen nodded again, stared straight ahead. "You think the boy is
findable?"

"God, I hope so," Jesse answered easily.

"Alive?" Karen took another cigarette and her lighter out of a vinyl
case.

"I would like to think so," Jesse started out cautiously, then shocked
herself by adding, "but no, probably not."

Karen lit her cigarette off the disposable lighter, the pungency of butane hitting Jesse between the eyes. She noticed the woman wore pressed jeans.

"OK." Karen clicked and snapped everything away. "We're gonna have a sit-down with the detective, and if he gives us the go-ahead, we're gonna meet with the mother. Your brother here would like you to be at that meeting. Now, I don't really *like* being around reporters at this stage of the game, but your brother's a living ace, he's never not there for us, and *he* says we can trust you."

"Trust me to what . . ."

"To not write anything we need for you to keep under your hat."

"Whatever." Jesse shrugged and looked away again, her anger blossoming at Ben for having gone behind her back, then having the balls to offer her up like this, yanking her out of the driver's seat and forcing her to her knees, a supplicant.

"All right." Karen turned to her with those muddy yet drilling eyes. "So all I have for you is one last question. Would you ever do anything to screw with your brother's good name?"

"I have my own good name to worry about," Jesse drawled, looking off at the POW wall, thinking, I'll kill him.

Karen Collucci left Ben's car to return to the Blazer, and as the Friends of Kent pulled out and passed them, Jesse noticed the silhouetted snout and ears of a German shepherd that was pacing restlessly in the rear of the van.

"Where the hell do you get the nerve to bring her into this?" Jesse asked Ben, hissing down low, as if Karen could overhear her.

"Na-h-h," Ben growled happily as he took off for the medical center. "Karen's the best."

"She's gonna walk all over me." Jesse felt herself flushing: Brenda slipping through her fingers.

"Na-h-h," he said, the same noise as before, his grin locked in. "Jess, you got to see her work."

Jesse lit a cigarette at the wrong end, tossed it out the window. She should have guessed from the start. Her brother and Karen went back three years, to the Gregory Towles disappearance. Ben had responded to a Friends of Kent radio call to search for the boy, whose mother claimed he had been abducted from a farmers' market in Yonkers. They never found the kid, and before his mother could be brought in by the cops for more intensive questioning, she vanished, too, along with her new state-trooper boyfriend. For nine consecutive days, Ben would come at dawn to the church parking lot that served as base camp, and he never came empty-handed. One of his poker pals, a Waldbaums manager in Jersey City, had agreed to pay off his debts with boxes of bakery goods— crullers, cinnamon twists, carrot cakes, rainbow-sprinkled doughnuts— and by day three, the entire search party had become completely fixated on Ben's arrival.

Jesse was told of other Kent searches, some unhappily successful, others destined to remain agonizing mysteries. Her favorite was the search for a teenager who, as it turned out, had simply run away from home but for which Ben, in exchange for shadowing the wife of a Queens building contractor and delivering to the guy photographic evidence of her motel shenanigans, had secured for the Friends of Kent six Portosans, including installation and daily servicing, to be placed at selected locations along a running path in Cheesequake State Park in southern New Jersey.

"Jess," Ben said, trying to placate her. "Jess, let's say I asked you for your permission before I reached out to Karen, right? You'd've said no way, but then, let me tell you, if she didn't come on board? You'd still be back in that bar right now throwing down Stoli shooters. Please. You have to know I'm thinking about you too."

Jesse sat up a bit; how the hell did he know what she had been drinking? "She's married, Ben," she said in a burst of impotent nastiness. "Didn't you see the ring on her finger?" It was a meaningless sputter of a crack, but a shadow passed over her brother's face, quick as bird flight, then gone, and Jesse knew to shut up.

Save for the mention of their destination, they drove on in silence. Jesse, chastened by her unintentional blood drawing, mutely pondered her brother's secret yearnings. The silence continued until Ben pulled up in front of the medical center.

"Here," he said curtly, passing over a bag containing sunglasses and a wig. The shades were like twin silvered eggs, futuristic; the hairpiece was shoulder-length and reddish brown.

"What the hell am I supposed to do with these?" Jesse held one item in each hand.

"They're for Brenda."

15

With Brenda laid out over at the medical center and his meeting with Karen Collucci and the Friends of Kent not until the evening, Lorenzo, with Bobby McDonald's grudging approval, decided to use his free time to hit on Felicia Mitchell, Brenda's boss at the Study Club. And so, in the late afternoon of this grueling, suffocating day, Lorenzo found himself wheezing and sweating his way to the fifth floor of the elevator-busted Crispus Attucks high-rise in the Jefferson Houses.

The Study Club, at this time of year more a knock-around day camp than any kind of tutorial center, was situated in two adjoining apartments. Housing had punched through the connecting walls to give the club six large rooms, which were lined up like boxcars, each one having a designated use—computers, free play, homework, pool table, library, and the cool-out corner, this last room bare, except for a few stiff-backed school chairs. Its walls were covered with instructional posters—Argument Rules, Classroom Rules, Homework Rules, Pool Table Rules, Cooperation Rules, Conversation Rules, Fire Drill Rules, Good Health Rules, and How to Express Frustration Rules.

Normally, on a hot summer day, Felicia and her aides would have been outside with the kids, but because of the media invasion it was decided to make the best of an indoor play day. They had only four portable fans to cover the six rooms, and even with all the windows open it seemed as if the very walls were running with sweat.

When Lorenzo entered the club, Felicia was bellowing at a nine-year-old boy who was playing Nok-Hockey too close to the pool table. Felicia stood there, arms akimbo, calling him out.

"Ex*cuse* me. Ex*cuse* me. What I say to you, hah? What I say . . ." Despite her harsh tone, Lorenzo could tell she was in a better mood than when he had come upon her earlier in the day, waiting for him outside his mother's apartment door. "I'm waitin' for a answer. What I say . . ."

The kid shrugged. "I don't know."

"What happens if a ball jumps the rail, hah? What happens . . . ?"

Before he could respond, she turned on the two players at the pool table, an eight-year-old girl who had a knife scar that ran from under her jaw to her right ear and Curious George Howard, Miss Dotson's grandson—all six foot one and twenty-one years of him.

"What happens if that cue ball jumps the rail . . . ?"

George drew a bead. "He better duck." He fired too hard and fouled up a bank shot, the three ball hiccuping over a rip in the green fabric as it rolled to a stop in the middle of nowhere.

Lorenzo surveyed the club. Most of the kids were in the Home-work Room, hunched over the tables, building stuff out of white glue and Popsicle sticks or stringing plastic beads. Above their heads hung a bulletin board, the Brag Board, covered with photos of the kids and handwritten two-paragraph compositions, each entitled "What I Like About . . ." and ending with the name of a kid the author had just fought with. This was Felicia's tried-and-true conflict resolver. Lorenzo had seen it work with his own eyes, watching the faces of yesterday's mortal enemies struggle with involuntary grins when they heard positive things about themselves emanate from the mouths of their sworn foes.

"Where you supposed to be at right now . . ." Felicia turned on the nine-year-old again. *"Where."*

"I want a snack." The kid rose to his feet, brushing dirt from his baggy-ass shorts.

"A *snack?*" Felicia's eyebrows jumped. "Last time I come in here with food you greedy little monsters ate it all before I could even get my coat off."

"You don't have no coat today." The kid smiled, making her laugh. Felicia shooed him away and looked up to see Lorenzo.

"Whoa!" She jerked back as the kids took him in, too, charging toward his legs. Lorenzo loved when this happened, counted on it happening too.

"Big Daddy," the nine-year-old boy said, yanking on his front pants pocket, "give me a dollar."

"Shamiel!" Felicia barked.

Lorenzo laughed. "You sound like my wife."

Another kid, about ten, with a weak eyelid muscle that made him look half asleep, punched Shamiel on the arm. "Yo, Big Daddy just called you his *bitch*."

"Michael!" Felicia barked.

"Oh yeah? How you like it I make you *my* bitch." Shamiel shoved Michael in the chest.

"Hey!" Felicia grabbed both of them by the arms. "Y'all sit down *right* now and write me something for the Brag Board."

"What *I* do?" Michael's one good eye bugged. "Big Daddy said it, not me."

"Now." Felicia sent them in opposite directions with a cross-armed shove.

"Haw, haw," the eight-year-old girl playing pool with Curious George crowed in triumph, "you lose."

"What you . . . *Haw, haw.* Naw, naw, *you* lose." George's face turned dark.

"You said eight ball in the corner. It went in the side, so *you* lose," the girl said.

"It don't make no difference! It don't make no difference!" George leaned over her, purple with anger.

"Too bad." The girl shrugged, brought up the eight ball. "You lose."

"Naw, naw, no way." George snatched the retrieved ball. "You don't win."

"Yes, I do."

"What the . . . Git the fuck . . ." George spluttered.

"Hey!" Felicia barked at him.

"You don't." He ignored Felicia, then turned to the room at large, the eight ball in one hand, the tipless cue stick in the other.

"Next!" he bellowed. "Next!"

"You lost . . ." The eight-year-old girl walked off.

"Next!" George bawled, flirting with a coronary.

In Lorenzo's estimation, George—despite the outburst—was one of those young men who are at their best in the unthreatening presence of little kids. He had a talent for hearing kids out, for taking them seriously, that was at total odds with the knucklehead qualities that made him game for every play on the street and had so far landed him in jail twice.

Musing on Army Howard's less than helpful observation about his cousin's likeness to the jacker sketch, Lorenzo took in George's T-shirt: black, with a spray-painted image of a tough-guy mouse smoking a stogie and clutching two moneybags, I GOT BIG PLANS scripted in an arch over the mouse's head. George had no official job here in the Study Club, but he was not unwelcome.

"You coming over to talk to Billy tonight, right?" Felicia touched Lorenzo's arm. "You promised."

"Give me a minute," Lorenzo said, approaching George, who was now playing pool by himself.

Felicia clucked in frustration, then moved off in the opposite direction.

"I thought you was supposed to be working at Action Park," Lorenzo said.

"I thought so too." George sank the cue ball. "They din't have no transportation for me."

"Didn't have . . ."

"They was supposed to pick up the Dempsy workers by charter bus—otherwise it's too hard to get there—but they only hired like three people from Dempsy, and they said that's not enough for a pickup stop."

"Where they picking up from closest to here?"

"Jersey City."

"So get your behind to Jersey City."

"Too late." George shrugged, the six ball jumping the rail, bouncing sharply on the floor.

"Then you best keep looking for a job," Lorenzo said, glaring at him.

"Yeah, OK."

"And you watch your mouth around these little kids here."

"Me!" George squawked. "Daddy, you should hear some of the shit comes out their mouths. Half the time they teaching *me.*"

At the far end of the double apartment, Felicia Mitchell yelled out, "Fruit salad!" precipitating a stampede to the Free Play Room, followed a moment later by a massive scraping of chairs. George, peering down the barrel of doorways, started to move to join the younger kids. Then, realizing that Lorenzo was watching him, he flushed with embarrassment, stutter-stepped back to the pool table, to the window, and then, without a word or glance, left the Study Club altogether.

Felicia worked her way back to Lorenzo from the Free Play Room, and he gently took her wrist. "I need for you to help me here with Brenda's boy," he said quietly. "Anything you can think of."

"I don't know, Lorenzo, it's sad." Felicia leaned against the cinder-block wall. "She loves that child, she brings him in here all the time. Look."

She led him back to the Homework Room, empty now, except for a Latino girl working on a Popsicle house. Scanning the Brag Board, she said, "Where'd that . . . here." She liberated a Polaroid of Brenda with Cody on her lap, the two of them encircled by the children of the Study Club, everyone smiling at the camera with flash-starred eyes.

From the distant Free Play Room Lorenzo heard the loud rote voice of an aide: "Why do we play fruit salad . . . ?" The children answered in a not quite monotone chorus: "To provide focus on positive attention."

"See this here?" Felicia offered him a stack of homemade cards, each one designed by a childish hand. "The kids, they all made her cards today. You know, like, get well cards. It wasn't even my idea. They just done it on their own."

Lorenzo skimmed a few. I HOPE YOUR OK; DON'T WORRY HE'S OK; DEAR BRENDA I LOVE YOU AND CODY—that one bearing a crude drawing of Brenda and Cody running toward each other from opposite ends of the paper, Cody saying, MOM! I'M BACK! in a wobbly word balloon, Brenda's balloon encircling THANK GOD!

"She's very good here, Lorenzo. She gives it her all," Felicia said.

"She have any problems with anybody?"

From the Free Play Room, a kid shouted "Tangerines!" provoking a hectic rumble and squeal, the momentary chaos of musical chairs.

"Not really. Well, yeah, once, but . . . See, there was this little girl we had coming here? Tamika Jackson—you know her?"

"Nope."

"She showed up here one day and she had all these bruises and we're, like, thinking maybe she was abused, but we didn't know, 'cause her family had just moved in from the Roosevelt Houses. So I put a call in to my supervisor, you know, June? Ask how we should deal with this. But Brenda? I'm still waiting for June to call me back, Brenda disappears. She just went right up to Tamika's apartment on eight and, like, straight out confronted her mother. I mean, *whoa*." Felicia put a palm to her chest. "You don't *do* that. Even if you're right. That lady, Miss Jackson, she threatened to sue Housing for false accusations. Now, I don't know if she did it, her boyfriend did it, or nobody did it. The girl, she just said she fell or something, but the thing is, Lorenzo, we ain't never gonna find out because that lady took her daughter right out of here and, like, even if she *was* gettin' hit? We were *here* for her, we gave her a place to go, and Brenda just threw out the baby with the bathwater. I mean, I know she did it out the goodness of her heart but you know, step back, do it right."

"Apples!" someone shouted, and the walls shook with the reaction.

Gazing out the window, Lorenzo saw Eight-Ball Iovakas down on the street, leaning against his double-parked cruiser, and saw Curious George exit the building.

Eight-Ball gestured for George to come on over, and after a moment's hesitation, George complied.

"See, Brenda . . ." Felicia touched Lorenzo's arm to get him back. "She's like a real contradiction. I mean, she's scared of doing simple things, like tell so and so's mother that they got to start making sure their child's got better grooming habits 'cause the other children are starting to make fun of them. I mean, yeah, that could be tricky, but it ain't that hard to find some nice way to say it, you know, some positive way. But Brenda, she gets so nervous in advance she can't do it without putting out all these confrontation vibes. So usually I talk to them myself, but I'll tell you, when Brenda decides to bust a move on someone? She goes all the *way*. Like with Miss Jackson. I mean, I don't want to give you the wrong impression of her. Mainly she does positive things, like she had started bringing in people to talk to the kids, you know, positive role models. She brought in this one guy worked for the Reverend Al Sharpton, sort of like his aide or something, talked to the kids about staying in school."

"You remember his name?" Lorenzo took out his notepad.

"Not on the tip of my tongue, but I'll get it for you, and then, yeah, she had this lady come in from an advertising company. She talked about making commercials, and that was fun because she brought this new bubble gum for everybody, had us taste it, and then we all had to come up with names for it, you know, a slogan for it. But I don't remember her name either. She even brought in this mailman to talk about delivering the mail, and that was fascinating to me, because I like that stuff where they tell you about things you take for granted, and *his* name was Eddie Taylor, I remember *that* because . . ." Felicia grabbed Lorenzo's wrist, leaned in close, and exaggeratedly murmured through stiff lips, "He was a *nice man*."

He laughed, wagged a finger at her, wrote "Eddie Taylor."

"And she brings the boy here?" Lorenzo asked. "What's he like?"

"He's very smart for his age, and the kids here, everybody likes him. He's kind of the mascot 'cause he's only four and the youngest kid here, you know, officially, is like six, but he's nice, he plays with everybody, you know?"

"And how is she with him?"

"Good." Felicia shrugged. "You know, like a mother. I don't think she has too many friends on the outside, so it's like, they seem very close."

"She have any boyfriends?"

"I don't know. Maybe, maybe not. I can't say. I mean, Lorenzo, she's from Gannon. She leaves work she goes home to America, you know what I'm saying? I have no idea what's going on with her outside of this place right here."

"I hear you," he said, smiling. "When was the last time you saw her before last night?"

"Before last night? Like, that day. Yesterday. And it was crazy here because we were, like, half here, half in Armstrong, you know, setting up a second Study Club there? Which is on hold now, as you can well imagine."

"How she seem to you yesterday?"

"To me? I would have to say she seemed kind of out of it, but you know, that could just be me reading into things, you know, with all this goin' on now, so—"

"Out of it, like how." Lorenzo rubbed his eyes, rolled his neck.

"Bananas!" some kid screamed, and there was another controlled eruption in the next room.

"Out of it like, OK, this is just a little thing, but we're supposed to help the kids with their homework, you know, the kids that got summer school? And she was sitting with this girl Angela. Angela has got a problem with math. And I see Brenda sitting with her, and I look, and Angela's just, like, *out* there, daydreaming. And I see that Brenda's sitting there doing Angela's math—like, *I'll* do it. Just doing it herself, not talking to Angela, not showing her nothing, just getting through it, and she, that's not like her. She's very conscientious, Brenda."

There was a brief boy-girl argument from the Free Play Room, ending in an aide barking out, "Shamiel!" and the nine-year-old boy snapping back, "Yell at *her* ugly ass."

A moment later Shamiel appeared, walking through the Library Room on his way to the Pool Table Room, hiking up his pants and muttering to himself like an old man.

"Yeah, OK," Felicia said, watching the boy until he was out of earshot. "Let me tell you what stayed in my mind about yesterday."

She stepped closer, speaking in a whisper now.

"Shamiel? That boy is like the devil sometimes, and yesterday he got himself ahold of some pushpins, right? And he put them on the teacher's chair in the Homework Room, by the phone? This girl Mary Stevens, Dottie's child? She gets me, tells me what he's done, so I come in the room and I see Brenda standing there talking on the phone and just, like, as I came in? Brenda's about to sit down and before I could say stop, *whomp,* she sat right down on those tacks, and, nothing . . . She's just sitting there talking, and at first I thought I had misheard Mary about what Shamiel had done, but I look over to him . . . Lorenzo, and the boy was *crying.* He's, like, looking at her sitting there and he's crying. He was *scared,* Lorenzo. And she's talking on the phone I don't know to who, but when she's finished? She gets up, there's all these pushpins sunk into her jeans, and that must of *hurt.*"

"You know who she was talking to?"

"No, I don't."

"You remember anything she said?"

"I wasn't really listening."

"Huh," Lorenzo nodded, thinking, Get the phone log.

Looking out the window again, Lorenzo saw Curious George and Eight-Ball, deep in conversation, both of them talking with their arms crossed over their chests. His eye was then drawn to an unmarked Gannon sedan, floating up behind Eight-Ball's Dempsy cruiser. Leo Sullivan eased himself out of the driver's seat, standing on tiptoe to stretch and yawn.

Felicia ran her hand through the crook of Lorenzo's arm. "You want to know what Brenda was mostly about in here?" She pulled him away from the window and ushered him through the double apartment until they came to the Free Play Room. Standing in the doorway, Lorenzo watched as a young girl, standing in the center of a ring of chairs grinned, worked her mouth a bit, then blurted, "Limes!" This provoked a selective scramble as she and three other kids dashed around for new seats until the droop-eyed boy, Michael, landing on Mary Stevens's lap, was pushed off. Taking center stage, Michael yelled out, "Coconut," causing another three-kid scramble for chairs. Lorenzo saw that each kid held a piece of paper that bore the name of a fruit.

"You see this game they're playing? It's called Fruit Salad. It's like musical chairs, but we were having a hard time with musical chairs because nobody wants to be out the game, so there was like, a lot of fights all the time. So Brenda, she made up Fruit Salad. Every kid's a particular fruit and one kid, like, calls out strawberry, banana, or whatever, and those kids got to jump up find a new seat, and the kid who gets squeezed out? He's the next caller. It's like a reward for losing. Then when he calls out his, you know, 'Orange,' say, he's back in the scramble. Nobody loses. She figured that out, and it stopped a lot of the fighting."

Lorenzo smiled absently as the game went on. "So you don't know who was she talking to on the phone?"

"No, I surely don't."

"Was the boy with her that day?"

"No. She said he was sick."

"Sick? She say with what?"

"Nope."

"Tell me something else."

"Like what?" He waited. "Lorenzo, you ever see her teeth?"

"Her teeth?"

"Last week we were talking about cavities, going to the dentist. And I opened my mouth so the kids could count my fillings, you know, until they started stickin' them greasy little fingers in there. Mary and some of the other girls they go over to do Brenda, count her cavities? She opens her mouth? Lorenzo, her teeth are down to nothing."

"What do you mean?"

"They're, like, *flat*. She must grind them something awful."

"Oh *shit!*" Shamiel's sharp exclamation from the Time-Out room turned Lorenzo's head. "Oh *shit!*" again. Shamiel was peering down at the street, an odd tenor to his outburst, distress mixed with excitement.

Lorenzo began to move to the window, but, once again, Felicia hauled on his arm. "You're coming to my house tonight, right?" Lorenzo wanted to beg off or at least hedge, but Felicia's voice seemed to be freighted with true anxiety now.

"I'll do my best," he said.

"He's crazy, Lorenzo. He's hittin' me. Cryin' all the time. Lorenzo, you can*not* not come."

"Lorenzo!" Shamiel cried out, his face fixed between a grimace and a grin. "They just arrested George!"

"*Who* did." Lorenzo was on the move to the window, along with whoever else had heard Shamiel's announcement. "Eight-Ball?"

"No, no," Shamiel said. "He got took off in the other, the *plain* car."

Leo Sullivan, Lorenzo thought, looking down at the street. Everyone was gone by now, a suspect was in custody—news at eleven.

Lorenzo slant parked in front of the Gannon Municipal Building and took a side entrance to a second-floor landing, exiting out into a spacious, harshly lit vestibule. It was barren, save for two pay phones and a reception window manned by a black Gannon cop, Julius Raymond, an old whist buddy. Julius acknowledged him with a nod, buzzing him through a paint-chipped metal door.

Lorenzo stepped through to the Gannon PD intake center. Four wreathed photographic portraits of martyred cops were suspended over a wall-length booking counter, staring across the room at a Plexiglas holding cell that, at this moment in time, hosted three prisoners—an Iranian steroid dealer, who Lorenzo knew by the tag Elvis; a bored-looking black kid unknown to Lorenzo, sitting sprawled on the floor, an Afro pick sticking up behind his right ear like an antenna; and an out-of-towner, a red-eyed, blond-bearded dude in jeans and a black T-shirt. Lorenzo guessed he was a long-distance trucker on his way to New York, popped for scoring some rock in the Roosevelt Houses—the last dope spot before the Lincoln Tunnel—and snatched up by Gannon narcotics as he cut back through town toward the New Jersey Turnpike.

No way would they keep George Howard out here in plain sight.

"Lorenzo." Julius Raymond, who stood behind the booking counter now, tilted his head toward yet another door, buzzing the latch. Lorenzo found himself marching down a long, shadowed corridor, the walls lined with old photos of tommy guns and Model Ts, Saturday night specials, and bell-bottoms—decade-by-decade group portraits of long-gone coppers, laminated and framed reproductions of ancient local headlines featuring labor strikes, explosions, derailments, crashes, and sinkings. Lorenzo ducked his head into door after door, chanting to himself—Stay calm, Stay respectful, Stay calm, Stay respectful—until he found what he was looking for, the detectives' squad room. Lorenzo walked in, and George Howard, encircled by six plainclothes detectives and handcuffed to a desk, his left eye a red egg, almost leaped at him, blurting out his name and dragging that heavy piece of furniture halfway across the room before he was restrained by Leo Sullivan and the others.

"What's goin' on?" Lorenzo asked, forcing himself to smile.

"Ask him," Leo said, folding his arms across his chest and perching his butt on the edge of the desk.

"Yo, Big Daddy, this is whack." George looked like he was about to cry.

Lorenzo's eyes strayed to a fax of the jacker sketch taped to the wall.

"Whoa," Lorenzo laughed. "Fellas, you got to go through *me*."

"Not for this," Leo said, shrugging.

"Not for *what*."

"Child support."

"For what?"

"George, where does Keisha live? The Mary Bethune Houses, right?" he asked. Then, to Lorenzo, "Local girl, Big Daddy."

"Lorenzo," George started to blubber, his lower lip shivering, "they tryin' to set me up."

"Set you up for what, brother?" asked a black detective, Boris Hope, a big, broad man in a three-piece suit. "You hear anybody talking about anything other than you being a suck-ass father?"

George rested his forehead on the edge of the desk, inches from Leo Sullivan's knee.

"You pick him up in Jefferson?" Lorenzo asked.

"That we did. Right, George?" A little tremor of adrenaline belied Leo's chipper tone.

"Hey, fellas," Lorenzo said. "You can't just bop on over—"

"We did it by the book, boss," Boris Hope interjected. "Went in with one of your guys, everything strictly kosher."

"One of my guys?"

"Nicky Iovakas."

Eight-Ball. Lorenzo tamped down his rage, taking in Leo and the others, all slouched around the prisoner, looking like a hard-ass Dutch masters portrait.

"But I tell you, Council," Leo said. "We came up on my man here with this two-bit warrant? Guy gives us them bug-eyes, like to jump out of his skin. Right, George?"

"No."

"No? You went all-out rabbit on me, right?"

" 'Cause you were coming for me."

"So? So fuckin' what. You didn't run all those other times, right?"

"Well, you was chasing me."

"Let me ask you." Leo Sullivan stood up, hitched his pants. "How many times I come on you with paper, huh? Do I or do I not always give you fair play. Now, all those other times, what was it? Possession, possession with intent, *assault* that one time? All that stuff a *lot* fuckin' heavier than this piece of shit, right?" He flicked the warrant with a thumb. "Right?"

"I don't know what you got writ on there," George muttered, dropping his head between his knees. "I ain't a mind reader."

"Well, you must've thought it was something pretty fuckin' bad, right? First you pull a Carl Lewis on me, then we catch up, you go *swing* on me?"

Ergo the shiner—George playing right into their hands. Lorenzo turned to the window, knowing this was all bluff and bluster, not worth getting into Gannon's face over.

"But you know what, George?" Leo continued his play. "I'm no mind reader either, so maybe you can tell me what you *thought* we were coming at you with that was *so* fuckin' bad that you rather go down swingin' than play the game, 'cause I know you know how to play the game, and I *know* you're not so stupid as to take a poke at me over child support, right? Right?"

"No."

"So what are you hidin'?"

"Lorenzo." George looked to him for help, then to Leo. "I ain't done nothing."

"Think hard," Boris said.

"Damn, man, you ask Lorenzo. I'm looking for work, got squeezed out at Action Park, had this other job, guy that was hired like two weeks before me? He din't put down on his application that he did time. The boss, he found out and he wanted to fire him, right? So they fired me, too, 'cause I come in after him and this way they could say it was a layoff, you know, it don't look like they're picking him out. You ask Lorenzo, man."

"Think hard, George."

"Aw, see, you motherfuckers, man, you think—" George cut himself off.

"We think what?" Boris Hope asked, but George dug in.

"You best do some soul searching, Bubba." Leo Sullivan stood up. "I make one phone call, you're a career offender. That means no bail, hot sun, summer in the city. You go into County right now? I hear they're like at six hundred percent over capacity. I hear they're bunking up in the gym, I hear they're bunking up in the laundry room. In the *laun*dry room. In *this* fucking heat? Oh!"

"Career offender for what?" George squawked. "For *child* support? I don't even have a motherfuckin' *job*. What's puttin' me in jail gonna do for me payin' child support. Whose child is gonna get supported with me in jail, huh?"

"Fuck the child support," Leo said, then tapped his still-red cheekbone.

"Aw, Lorenzo," George begged hopelessly. Lorenzo shrugged, turned away. "Yeah, an' like you ready to lock me up over this except if I fess up to something more worse, *much* more worse, and then what, I walk?"

"The less you jerk us, the less you get jerked in return, right."

Diverted by the skirl of bagpipes, Lorenzo looked out the window and saw a funeral procession inch down the stairs of a massive church across the street. Even given the bagpipes, there was a minimal uniformed presence; Lorenzo guessing that the body was the widow of a retired cop.

"Oh man, I don't understand the motherfuckin' system no more," George moaned.

"No?" Leo reached for a golf club that stood in the corner. "I think you understand the system very well, George." He braced himself for a putt, wiggling his hips. "In fact, I think you got a fuckin' Ph.D. in the system."

Lorenzo watched as the coffin came out of the church, the pallbearers negotiating the long, steep stairs.

"Where'd you get that T-shirt, brother?" Boris Hope said, grimacing. "Put a *mouse* on your chest? Man, you must really hate yourself."

"Yeah, see, you think I jacked that baby last night, right?"

There was a barely perceptible ripple in the room, Leo not even looking up from his invisible golf ball. "I didn't say that. I didn't even bring that up. Did you hear anybody say anything about that?"

"George," Lorenzo finally eased into this. "Brenda Martin, she know you?"

"Yeah, from the Study Club. What I'm gonna do, jack someone I *know?*"

"You mean, as opposed to jacking someone you don't know?" Boris said.

"Naw, man, you just . . . Hey *Lorenzo,*" George beseeched again. His shiner was as slick and dull as steel.

"Leo, you want to put this to rest one way or the other?" Lorenzo offered calmly, threading the diplomatic needle. "Pick up the phone, call her, ask her if it was George Howard. 'Cause *I* would like to know myself."

"Yeah, well, I'd love to do that, Council, except we can't fuckin' *find* her right now."

"Well, hey, if you had reached out to me from the jump . . ." He faltered, seeing George's good eye go white all around, the kid half rising, frightened. Before Lorenzo could turn to see what had scared him, he was bulled sideways into a file cabinet—someone barreling into the room full speed.

Despite being handcuffed to furniture, George was the only one set to receive this violent presence and, fueled by fear, he caught Danny Martin square in the face with his free hand. Danny, not even recoiling, cracked George's temple on the corner of the desk, coming down on top of him and grinding a balled copy of the jacker sketch into his bloody mug, snarling, "This is you? This is you?" The detectives hauled Danny off by the chest and throat, dragging him backwards out of the room as he bellowed, "Hey George! You know God? Fuck God. There *is* no God. *I'm* God. It's just you and me, motherfucker! Just you and me, you *hear* me?"

George, upright now, was trying to jump out the window, bringing the desk with him. Lorenzo staggered to his feet and felt the blood tickling the nape of his neck, the steel drawer-pull on the top file cabinet having caught him in the back of his hairless head. Ignoring George, who was moaning, his bowed head spattering the desk with blood, Lorenzo followed the commotion into the history-lined hallway, where Danny was being restrained by all six of his fellow detectives. Only now was he starting to calm down, the mulberry flush of his face receding in patches.

"What do you think you're doing?" Lorenzo found himself shouting it out, his hand coming away bright red from the back of his head.

"Me?" Danny started writhing against the glazed wall, knocking a photo of a fifty-year-old homicide to the floor.

"Council!" Leo Sullivan barked, his forearm pinning Danny, chest to the wall. "Take a hike!"

"Me?" Danny shouted. "I'm doing *your* job, you fuckin' deadbeat! You're supposed to be king of the jungle out there? How'd you miss *this* monkey, hah?"

"You best get out of here," Boris Hope said to Lorenzo, sounding calmer than the others, as if being black gave him more communication skills in a situation like this—Lorenzo thinking, Fuck you too, Boris.

"You ain't doin' nothin' but balling things up for everybody, your sister included," Lorenzo said evenly, the laceration starting to sting. "And if your people here got any kind of sense, they'll tell you the same."

All six of the detectives were nodding, winking, bobbing their heads at Lorenzo, each one in his own way signaling him, begging him, to get lost. Disgusted, Lorenzo turned and began to walk off, looking for a bathroom, for some cold water and a mirror.

"Hey, Lorenzo," Danny barked out. The detectives, who had cautiously eased their grip, now lurched drunkenly to restrain him again in the middle of the hallway.

"What are you doin' here, protecting your own?"

"I don't know." Lorenzo stopped, turned back. "Maybe I should ask you the same damn question."

Coming out of the men's room ten minutes later with a wet wad of toilet paper pressed to the back of his head, Lorenzo caught the tail end of the arrest procession heading toward the reception area. He fell in beside Leo Sullivan and the handcuffed, bloody-faced George Howard.

"I swear to you," Leo murmured to Lorenzo. "We didn't even tell Danny that we picked him up."

"So now you going through with the arrest anyhow, huh?" Lorenzo winced, his cut deep. Leo shrugged, not too happy about it. "This don't even make no sense, Leo," Lorenzo said, his voice low and urgent. "You lock him up on this child support thing, he lawyers up, you can't even *question* him about the other. C'mon, man, what are you doin'? Talk to Brenda. She'll settle it in a heartbeat."

Leo sucked his teeth. It had become one of those legalistic miscalculations that seem to take on lives of their own, demanding of their actors that they be played out to the end. "Hip-deep in the Big Muddy, huh?" Leo said regretfully. "Fuck it. We'll work something out."

At least Danny Martin was gone. As they entered the barren outer vestibule, they were bushwhacked by Curious George's family.

George's people were all women—his grandmother, Miss Dotson; his aunt Risa, a blaze-eyed, coal-black woman; and his older sister, Charise, pregnant, her hair up in rollers. The two younger women screamed at the sight of him, cuffed and bloody, the grandmother swooning, slowly clapping her hands in despair. Lorenzo realized he had never seen her standing, let alone outside her apartment, and as Risa and Charise screeched in rage—as the detectives, pissed and disoriented, began barking to Julius Raymond at the reception window to get these fucking people out of here, the room becoming airless and rank with anger—Lorenzo wondered how this old swollen-footed lady had made it up the stairs to the second floor.

"You beat him for *child* support?" Charise howled, fists knotted at her sides, her throat bulging. "You motherfuckers did all this to him for *child* support?"

"Lord have mercy." Miss Dotson continued clapping her hands.

"We're gonna sue your motherfuckin' asses." Risa swung at Leo, and Lorenzo grabbed her in a bear hug, talking in her ear, Leo's eyes filling with murder.

"And look at this nigger here," Charise spat at Boris, who returned her contempt with a thick pointed finger. "Yeah, what you gonna do to me, I'm *preg*nant, you black motherfucker. You gonna kick me in the belly?"

Rather than use force to evict George's family, the detectives decided it would be wiser to retreat back through the intake center, Charise kicking the swiftly shut and locked door, screaming after them, "He din't take that white bitch's kid!"

Lorenzo felt momentarily torn between staying with George's family and retreating with the Gannon squad, then decided to hang in, try to calm them down. He put a hand on the pregnant woman's shoulder. "Charise, Charise."

"What they do that for?" Charise trembled with anger, her spittle like a fine mist on his face.

"It's gonna be OK, it's gonna be OK," Lorenzo crooned, nonsense words that Charise returned with an open-handed pop in the chest.

"I don't know who the fuck you think *you* are," she said through quivering lips, pointing over his shoulder to the locked door. "But I think you best be sticking to *them*."

16

Room 907, Brenda's room on the obstetrics ward of the medical center, was empty, the bed unmade and the injection end of an IV drip lying in a puddle on the tossed blanket. To Jesse, this did not make any sense.

An hour earlier, when Brenda had been laid out here dead to the world, Jesse had stood in this doorway, watched the rising and falling of her chest and, despite a churning desire to spirit her away, did not have the heart to wake her. She had taken up post on a hardwood bench directly across from the room and, settling into the chronic pop and ripple of her own agitation, waited for Brenda to come around.

Facing the recently vacated bed, Jesse deduced the unthinkable— while waiting for Brenda to awaken, she herself must have fallen asleep, and now Brenda was gone. Shooting back into the hallway, moving left, looking right, Jesse collided with a woman, probably recovering from a cesarean, who had been inching her way along the corridor, using her drip stand as a staff. The woman staggered backwards, hooting in pain from the effort to regain her balance. Jesse cringed, whispering an apology through clenched teeth.

On the way to the nurses' station, Jesse's eye caught the color-shifting busyness of TV cartoons through the open door of the visitors' lounge and then caught Brenda, sharing a stained cranberry-colored couch with an elderly black couple. Brenda was staring pie-eyed at the screen, her bare legs fanning under her thin floral-patterned hospital gown. On seeing her, Jesse felt a hum of fulfillment not unlike love. Thinking, How do I approach thee, she tiptoed into the room and sat lightly on the blond wood arm of the couch, her stomach lurching at the sight of the blood still lazily trickling from the gummy patch of forearm where Brenda had torn out her IV.

"I can't *do* this anymore." Brenda gestured weakly to the cartoons, addressing Jesse without looking at her. "I can't *do* this anymore, I can't *do* this anymore," she wailed in a high, teary whisper, the two old people leaning away from her.

"Brenda, it's OK," Jesse murmured back, resting a hand on the nape of Brenda's neck. The damp coolness that met her touch there was a jarringly discordant sensation at the end of this blistering day.

"You don't understand," Brenda continued in that cracked, whispery wail. "He's everywhere, he's everything. I can't even close my eyes, he's inside my eyes."

Jesse dipped awkwardly from her perch on the armrest and embraced her, a sour scent of calamity rising from Brenda's skin, a surge of inarticulate information leaping the breach. Suddenly Jesse felt woozy, felt herself filled with that buzz of connection again, that buzz of Home. "Tell me how to help you," she asked quietly, honestly, as she pulled back from the clinch.

"I want my mother." This brought softer looks to the faces of the old couple.

"Do you want me to call her for you?" Jesse asked, wanting a tangible task.

"She's my mother. Why doesn't she *come* for me?" Brenda wailed, ignoring Jesse's offer, her eyes returning to the cartoons as she fingered the flimsy hem of her gown.

"She'll be here," the old lady intruded, putting a hand on Brenda's pale, freckled knee.

"What did you have, a boy or a girl?" the old guy asked, his voice furry with kindness. He was dressed in shades of pink and maroon that clashed violently with the cranberry corduroy of the tatty couch.

"It's OK," Jesse answered for Brenda.

"He loved me so much," Brenda said, rocking, looking up at Jesse for the first time.

Jesse tossed the wig bag onto an empty chair, turned her face from the sight of that bloody trickle.

"So much—"

"Brenda, stop," Jesse begged.

"Did she lose her baby?" the old woman silently mouthed to Jesse, who nodded in assent.

"Who's gonna love me now, huh? Who's gonna love me now?" Brenda began to bang slowly on her thighs with limp fists, and the old woman, as if on cue, reached inside her husband's sport jacket. She extracted a thin blue flyer, which she gently placed in Brenda's hand. Printed above an open-armed image of Christ, the words A LOVE SU-PREME were scrolled in a rainbow arc like the ornamentation on Heaven's Gate, Jesse thinking, Christ; Brenda moaning, "Jesus."

"That's right." The old lady nodded, then touched a knuckly hand to Brenda's knee. "And you listen to me, 'cause I lost *three*."

Exiting from the hospital on a steep side street, Jesse and Brenda had only to wait a few minutes before Ben floated past, Jesse envisioning her brother circling the complex since she had entered the main building more than an hour earlier. Brenda got in the rear and lay down along the length of the seat, curling into herself as if cold and staring at the seat back a few inches from her face.

"Karen said the meeting went very well," Ben said quietly, so as not to disturb Brenda.

"What meeting."

"With Lorenzo."

"Who's Karen?"

"The Friends of—c'mon." Ben grinned painfully. "Play ball here, Jess."

A half dozen blocks from the hospital, in a quiet neighborhood of federally funded prefab homes, Ben pulled up alongside Lorenzo's se-dan. Lorenzo was leaning against the hood, looking like he'd been wait-ing there for quite a while.

"Brenda, sit up," Jesse whispered, reaching back to touch her arm.

Brenda made room for Lorenzo in the rear seat, the air inside the car instantly suffused with the funk of his exhaustion, his sudden presence causing Ben to pop out of the driver's seat as if the vehicle could only hold one oversized person at a time. He wandered off a short distance to give them privacy.

"Jesse," Lorenzo said. "Can you give us a moment here?"

"Sure." Jesse reached for the passenger door.

"Can she stay?" Brenda quickly whispered, and Jesse felt that hum inside herself again, her hand returning to her lap. Lorenzo offered no protest.

"Brenda, I just met with this woman who runs a group that searches for missing children," he said in a low, steady voice. "They have an excellent reputation. They're called the Friends of Kent and they asked me if they could meet with you." Brenda pressed the heel of a padded hand to her forehead. "Now"—Lorenzo touched her knee with a fingertip—"this group, they're not looking for publicity. They're strictly volunteer, but they're very experienced. They know how to raise up a search party and they know how to find what they're looking for." Brenda slowly tilted away from him until her right temple came to rest on the window glass. Jesse watched Lorenzo absorb Brenda's withdrawn reaction to his sales pitch.

In front of the car, Ben leaned against a tree trunk: Brenda hemmed in by giants.

"Now, these people, they want to come over and meet with you at your house, OK?" Brenda closed her eyes. "Brenda, this is your call, this is entirely up to you, you know, meeting with them, but I would recommend that you do. It's like a whole army working on nothing but finding your son."

Lorenzo gave her a long moment to respond. "Can I tell these people to come up and talk to you?"

"OK," she whispered, shrugging. Jesse saw Lorenzo register that apathetic response too.

"Good," Lorenzo said softly. "Very good. Now I won't be with them, but I'd like to check in on you after they're done—see how you're feeling, give you an update on things, all right?" Brenda, her head still against the glass, appeared to be asleep. "All right, then," Lorenzo said awkwardly, opening the car door.

Jesse left the car after Lorenzo and caught up to him as he was about to reenter his own ride. "They're letting you do this?" Her voice was filled with misgiving.

"Who's *they* . . ." Lorenzo answered heavily.

"The prosecutor, McDonald, whoever."

"They got nothing to do with it. She's a taxpaying civilian. She's free to do whatever she wants."

"OK," Jesse said lightly, but she could see in his face, hear in his voice the panicky impulse to make all-or-nothing moves. And she knew, absolutely knew, that Lorenzo had consciously kept news of the Friends of Kent, of Karen Collucci, from his bosses not because it was strictly a matter between civilians but because he feared that his superiors would nix the contact. Her hunch here was that he was counting desperately on Karen and her people to pinch-hit a homer for him. Jesse watched as Lorenzo fumbled with his car keys, and she felt as if she were witnessing him fall apart before her eyes.

"You trust her?" Jesse leaned into the driver's window as Lorenzo finally keyed the ignition.

"Brenda?" he asked.

"No. Karen Collucci."

Lorenzo shifted into drive. "About as much as I trust you."

He tried to smile, couldn't manage it, then rolled off.

They entered Brenda's apartment building through the basement, that point of entry not without its gauntlet, but less so than out on Van Loon. They moved fast, Ben clearing a path. Once inside, Ben dropped back behind them to prevent any of the shooters from following, and Jesse and Brenda were up the stairs and inside the apartment before the news of their return could mobilize the great mass out in front. Brenda instantly fell out on the unmade convertible, facedown, one knee drawn up to her ribs. Despite the heat, Jesse felt the need to cover her with at least a top sheet, and as she brought it up to Brenda's shoulders, Brenda feebly grabbed her wrist, whispered, "I have to make you a tape," then fell asleep.

With Brenda down and out, Jesse began aimlessly pacing the room, reaching out and touching things—tapes, posters, tabletops, dishes— just touching as if the simple act of tactile connection transmitted to her some kind of sustenance or balm. Thinking back on her conversation earlier in the day with Jose, she recalled his asking her, challenging her with, "Are you in love?" In terms of the reporting required of her, Jesse felt in no danger of losing her focus. But she was very much in love. Again. She thought of all reporters, but especially street reporters, as junkies. And although there was a universal undercurrent of adrenaline running through each of them, the true drug of choice varied from writer to writer. There were those addicted to the information race, the desire to get there first—some of her colleagues lived crouched in the blocks round the clock, the pagers on their hips nothing more than starter's pistols.

For others, it was a compulsive craving for the truth, not in any abstract or philosophical way or in any noble or public-minded sense either. These reporters suffered from an unquenchable desire to know what the hell happened, what really fucking happened here—*why* did it happen, *when* did it happen; who said what to whom and what was said in return; how did this blood truly get here on this stoop, on this bed—the information most often serving no higher purpose than to relay the specifics with reasonable accuracy to the public and, more personally, to scratch that unappeasable itch.

There were those who got off on being around cops, around violence, around death, those who enjoyed living dangerously and getting paid for it.

And then there were those, and in this group Jesse included herself, who were addicted to something she thought of as the Infilling—the compulsive hankering to witness, to absorb, to taste human behavior in extremis; the desire to embrace, to be filled with, no matter how fleetingly, the power of human grief, human rage; to experience it over and over; to absorb the madness of others, the commitment of others, the killers, the killed, the bereaved, the stunned, the liars, the fuckers, the heroes, the clownish, and the helpless. Jesse needed these people to come inside her, to give her life, *a* life, and she loved them for it.

Like any other halfway decent professional, she had been called all the names—vampire, ghoul, bloodsucker, parasite—but it never bothered her, because she knew her love was ardent and true, like her love for Brenda, sleeping before her now in a twist of sheets, her chin thrust high, mouth agape, as if frozen midhowl, her exhalations punctuated by nightmare yips and moan fragments, her skin morgue-damp, almost blue.

The Infilling was the how and why of her love for Brenda—Brenda's anguish, mortification, and insanity filling Jesse, like water taking the shape of its vessel; Jesse's every thought, gesture, daydream, and impulse over the last twenty-four hours ringing with Brenda's name; Jesse looking into a mirror to brush her hair, wash her face, and seeing Brenda, *being* Brenda, and knowing, at least for the time being, who she was.

Roughly an hour later, just as Brenda was beginning to come around, Jesse heard the trudge of footsteps on the stairs, the low murmur of multiple voices, then a knock on the door. Bolting upright, Brenda quickly but unsteadily got to her feet and, without asking for help, shoved the bed back into the couch. Jesse waited until Brenda was both seated and somewhat composed before she opened the door to

Karen Collucci and four others, all but one wearing the red satin warm-up jacket of the Friends of Kent.

"Hi there, Jesse," Karen said briskly, looking over Jesse's left shoulder to Brenda on the convertible. "Can we come in?" Without waiting for an answer, Karen brushed past her at the door. Three other women and the black man who had been behind the wheel of the Blazer earlier in the day filed in behind her.

As the others stood quietly, almost respectfully, outside the perimeter of the living room carpet—as if to proceed further required a second invitation—Karen dropped to one knee before Brenda on the couch, took a bandaged hand in both her own, and began the search for Brenda's eyes. "Brenda?" Her voice was firm and soothing. "I'm Karen Collucci from the Friends of Kent. Did you know we were coming?"

"Yes," Brenda answered in a flat, distant tone.

Jesse, intimidated, hanging back with the others, reconfirmed that she out-and-out disliked this woman, her energetic, presumptive air, her steamroller positiveness.

"We're here to help you if you want our help. Do you know about us?"

"Yes," Brenda answered in that same monotone, fear manifesting itself as dullness. The other Kenters maintained their silence, all eyes on Brenda.

"We just came from talking with Detective Council," Karen said. "He brought us up to speed from the police point of view, but we're not here as cops, we're here as parents, we're here because we have kids, too, and what happened to your son could have happened to any of our own children, OK?"

"OK." Brenda kept her eyes on the hand still smothered in Karen's grasp. Karen looked back to the group, and the Friends of Kent took a few steps forward, Jesse moving with them.

"This is Elaine," Karen said, introducing a taut woman who, despite her gray hair, looked to be still in her early thirties, a wiry, burning presence, the only Kenter not wearing a team jacket. Her plain face was dappled with a splash of port-wine stain from her throat to her ear, and her hands were thrust deep into the pockets of her jeans as if she were cold.

"Hey." Elaine spoke in a hoarse, funereal whisper. "We're gonna do everything we can." Brenda avoided Elaine's eyes too.

"This is Marie," Karen gestured to a woman in her sixties, chunky, with charcoal-black hair and a ferocious tan that gave her eyes a bottomless depth. Marie stepped forward and kissed Brenda on the right temple. Brenda closed her eyes at the contact.

"This is Teenie, Marie's daughter." Another deeply tanned woman, with the same chunky build as Marie's, wearing a gold chain on which hung a *chai*—the Hebrew symbol for life—and a gold charm, the two stylized stick figures, adult and child, that were the logo of the organization.

"And this is Louis." The black man nodded. His clipped moustache and gleaming processed hair reminded Jesse of Billy Dee Williams, although his shoes said cop. The Friends of Kent now stood in the center of the room.

"Who's Kent," Brenda asked Karen, who was still kneeling, holding her hand.

"He's a boy we helped find about five years ago. We've been helping find kids ever since."

The front door swung open behind Jesse, Ben entering, hunched over a cardboard flat of sodas, bottled waters, and pastries. "Hey." He was pale with exhaustion, his forehead fringed with sweat again. Moving quietly, he slipped into the kitchen and began setting up a snack counter on the serve-through cutout.

"Brenda?" Karen held her bandaged hand. "Would you like our help?"

"How old are your kids," Brenda asked—a delay tactic.

"Mine? Ten, eight, and four."

"Huh."

"You see Teenie here? She's Marie's daughter. Plus she's got a four and a six of her own."

"Huh."

Elaine moved to the window, her back to the room. Brenda looked at Louis from under the canopy of her left hand, Karen following her eyes.

"Lou's got three kids."

"You two are married, right?" Brenda addressed Karen's midsection. Karen nodded. "Twelve years."

"I don't know. I could just feel it. Jesus, everybody's got a four-year-old." Brenda yawned, a nervous shudder. "Jesse too."

Jesse looked down and scowled at the carpet. Ben stopped setting up for a moment, frowning at his hands.

Karen turned to face Jesse. "Is that true?" she asked in a luxuriously significant voice, and Jesse knew that she was fucked, understood that this woman could and would blow the whistle on her the instant she considered Jesse out of line.

"Yup," Jesse said tightly, fingering the cell phone in her pocket, a new one that her brother had secured for her. I have a job to do, she told herself, feeling marrow-tired, the world turning gray.

"Brenda." Karen turned back to her, took both bandaged hands in her own again. "Do you want our help?"

Brenda sighed, an exhausted, despairing exhalation. "OK," she said, her voice floating away. Jesse knew that she just wanted these people gone, perceived them as further punishment.

Jesse raised her eyes to the room again, saw Elaine staring at her from the window, focused but expressionless. "Can we sit down?"

"OK."

Karen slid in next to Brenda on the couch, Teenie and Marie pulling up dining chairs to form a semicircle. Elaine remained by the window, and Louis held his post against the wall, self-possessed and quietly alert.

"First thing. I need to hear from you what happened."

"No. I can't do that anymore. I can't say that anymore. I told the police everything—"

"I know, I know, I know." Karen amiably drowned her out. "It's just . . . Look, like I said, they have their priorities and we have ours. Right now, they're off doing their cop thing, they have certain pressures on them, certain . . . Us and them, we have different ears, we hear different things. So Brenda, please, just one more time, I wouldn't put you through this if I didn't think it was worth it. Please."

"No." Brenda took back her hands, covered her face. "I can't. I just . . ."

It was a standoff, Karen waiting, Brenda hiding behind her bandages; Karen letting the silence run a good two minutes, Jesse wanting to warn Brenda about how she was coming across; the others hunching forward, elbows on knees, staring at Brenda or at the carpet.

"Brenda. You got to help us help you." Another two minutes passed. Jesse had to walk off; the silence was excruciating. "OK," Karen finally acceded. "I understand. We can go with the police report if you want." Brenda nodded, dropped her hands back to her lap, palms-up. "OK. This is what we do. We put together a flyer, run it out there right away. Post it, hand it out, get it in the papers. Now . . ."

Karen went into a dufflelike shoulder bag, extracting a Hagstrom grid map of Dempsy County. She unfolded it to the Gannon-Dempsy border and showed Brenda the scene of the crime, marked with a red dot. "This is what we do." She drew a three-inch square around the dot with a felt-tip marker. "We like to do a canvass ten blocks square around the crime scene."

"In Armstrong?" Brenda groaned.

"Armstrong and the streets around. Just knock on doors."

"You're probably not gonna get anything," Jesse volunteered, measuring her words carefully. "Those people are pissed. The cops just went through there like storm troopers."

Karen looked at Jesse for a few seconds before answering. "Exactly. We come around, like I said, we're parents."

"You'd be amazed what people tell us, don't tell the cops," Teenie said, pulling on her gold charms.

"Jesse, you got to see them," Ben crowed from the serve-through, grinning goofily.

Jesse wouldn't look at him.

"You ever been through those buildings?" Jesse asked—a casual warning, her last comment. Elaine was still staring at her from the windowsill.

"Honey?" Teenie's mother's voice sounded like boots trudging through gravel. "You wouldn't be*lieve* some of the places we been through."

Marie's comment made Karen and Teenie smile. Jesse noticed that Marie and Karen wore that same gold-charm logo that Teenie did— Karen's on a bracelet, Marie's on a neck chain, like her daughter's. Elaine's throat and arms were as bare of ornamentation as her face was of expression.

"So, Brenda." Karen tapped the red square on the map. "Right now, on the phone, we can put a hundred volunteers together within the hour. We have kind of a volunteer reserve corps for situations like this, but they're all from around Hoboken, Bayonne, Jersey City. They don't really know this town. Now, we already have the names of everybody on the Armstrong tenants council. We'll call them first, see if they can help out, raise some local people. But how about you? Do you have any friends, family . . ." Brenda shrugged, dropped her eyes. "No?" Karen cocked her head. "OK. How about at work, people from work."

"Just the, Felicia."

"Felicia, OK, we call Felicia."

"Felicia . . ." Teenie, pen poised, let the name hang.

"Mitchell," Brenda said.

"Good. Excellent. We call Felicia Mitchell, see if *she* can raise some bodies for us."

"You have her phone number?" Teenie asked.

"We'll get that." Karen waved off the query, then turned back to Brenda. "OK, so I understand you work in, like, what, an afterschool program, right?"

"The Study Club."

"The Study Club. The kids are, like, what . . ."

"Little mostly."

"Teenagers?"

"A few."

"Good. They've just been drafted. And they can bring *their* friends. See? It's gonna happen, OK? It's amazing how it comes together." She tapped the map again. "OK, so we do this ten-block canvass. We do it tonight. Now, if that doesn't play out?" Karen drew a larger square, superimposed over the original, doubling the area.

"We never quit. We just get angry." The women nodded in agreement, Jesse thinking, Our motto. "OK. Now this is what I need from you, and we should get this right away so we can get humping on that flyer. I need a good picture of him. I need a description of his clothes, his hair, any scars, height, weight."

Brenda protested the request with a deep, heaving sigh, then got into it yet again. "Four foot three, forty-seven pounds, hair crew cut on top, long in back, like some professional wrestler I don't *know* the name . . ." Brenda rattled off the vitals in an aggressive, high-pitched monotone meant to express her exasperation. Karen, unaffected, nodded. Teenie wrote it all down. "Got Ren and Stimpy pajamas, *big* dinosaur slippers, growl when you step on the heels; got a scar line through his right eyebrow . . . He had stitches from when this kid in the playground . . ."

Jesse had never heard about this scar before. It was a fresh recollection and she saw Brenda begin to falter, tripped up by the vision that began to materialize despite her best efforts to keep this fact-laden prattle on the level of a tantrum.

"This kid, it was an accident," Brenda said, her voice beginning to drift. "And it was, like, you know how you see stuff happen before it actually happens? He was on the top of this sliding pond, Cody, and this other kid, Brian, he was standing on the bottom, you know, to try to walk *up* the slide? And mentally I was already there, you know, like scooping one of them off before—"

"Scar line through the right eyebrow," Karen said, to bring her back.

"That's all," Brenda said, ingesting a fresh gulp of grief, her hands crossed over her face again. Jesse anticipated the gesture before it was made, the repetitiveness of this reflexive movement over the last day and night having taken on the weight of a leitmotif, a physical refrain.

"OK. We need a good picture," Karen said, her eyes roaming walls and tabletops.

"Can't you just use the picture in the paper?" Brenda pleaded from behind her hands.

Jesse was surprised, unaware that Brenda had caught sight of herself on the newsstands.

"I want to show you something," Karen said, extracting a large manila envelope from her shoulder bag, sticking a hand in there, raising a thin clatter. She pulled out a metal photo button—the envelope was bulging with them.

"Look." Karen held up a color reproduction of Cody feeding the goat, the image heat-sealed around the disk. "I got my guy to do this." Karen looked from the button to Brenda. "I made up a gross. We'll pass them out, you know, to keep up the awareness out there, but Brenda?" Karen pointedly squinted at the image. "I swear to you, I swear this—I don't really think I could recognize him in the flesh, coming off this picture, could you? It's too shadowy. And let me just ask you. How old is this picture, because you say he's crew cut up top, long in back. This kid here's got hair in kind of a bowl cut, a mushroom cut, so—"

"That was almost a year ago."

"Yeah, see?" Karen sounded sad.

Jesse found herself becoming increasingly irritated by Karen's slow, exaggerated tones, her patronizing cue-card emotions.

"If I may speak freely." Ben turned heads his way, then held up a four-picture photo booth strip that had been attached to the refrigerator with a magnet.

"That's good." Karen nodded. "Brenda?" Brenda nodded without looking.

Elaine, finally pushing off from the windowsill, took the photo strip from Ben, the written details from Teenie, and left the apartment. Jesse experienced a great wave of relief at her departure.

"Now we're gonna have two phone numbers at the bottom of the flyer," Karen told Brenda. "The police and the Friends of Kent hot line. We have a twenty-four-hour operator. I'd rather not give out your home number, if that's OK, because—"

Brenda cut her off. "OK."

Karen hesitated for a beat, studying her. "About phones. Brenda?" Her voice lifted Brenda's eyes. "Let's say the guy panicked, saw your son in the backseat, pulled over somewheres, let him out of the car." Brenda gave one of her wet herculean sighs of despair. Karen waited on the side of the road. "He let your son out. Does Cody know how to call home?"

"What?"

"Does he know his phone number?"

"Yeah. Yes." Brenda's eyes turned to the phone, then down to the disconnected jack. Karen followed her gaze. "I started getting prank calls," Brenda said, quickly, as if Karen would punish her. She struggled to her feet to reconnect the jack, but Ben beat her to it, raising a hand for her to take it easy. "I was getting prank calls," she repeated.

"Hey, I understand." Karen raised a hand in the same gesture as Ben had: Take it easy.

"Now. Do you have an answering machine?"

Brenda shook her head, and Karen, dipping into her shoulder bag again, pulled out a gray plastic model that had an 800 number painted in red on the body. "Before we leave you tonight, I'm going to have you tape a message for your son on this in case he calls when you're not here, OK?"

"Yeah," Brenda said to her hands. "And in case the guy gives him a quarter when he throws him out of the car."

Karen and the others seemed to absorb this rebellious comment nonchalantly, and Jesse sensed that Brenda was in great peril, that the forces slowly coming together against her were drawing greater and greater strength with each evasive or inappropriate response. She looked across the room to her brother, who returned her gaze with a galling wink.

"So, OK." Karen laid a light hand on Brenda's knee. "We're out there canvassing tonight. Hopefully we're getting some tips that people wouldn't give the cops, getting some leads on the actor. And now we come to the question head-on. Where is your son. Where do we look. Where do we look." Karen flattened out the Hagstrom map, touched her felt-tip pen to the crime scene. "What's your gut feeling, Brenda?"

"He took off in a *car*." Brenda sounded angry again. "How would *I* know."

Karen leaned forward on the couch. "Let's say, your son woke up sooner rather than later. Let's say, the guy realized he had a passenger in the backseat sooner rather than later. So let's keep it within a mile." She drew a nine-inch circle around the two canvassing squares, the crime scene dot now taking on the aspect of a bull's-eye. "Look at this." Karen slipped a hand behind Brenda's back, to nudge her forward. "Gut feeling. Where should we look . . ."

"I don't *know*."

"Well, what does he like to do? What is he attracted to?"

"He's in a *car*," Brenda sobbed. "It's *night*. He's *four*."

"Well, my four-year-old? He sees the word *pizza*, he starts foaming at the mouth." She turned to her husband. "Right, Lou?" Louis gave a perfunctory nod. "Now, Teenie's four-year-old, Adam? He sees a park, he drops to all fours, starts running like a dog. Right, Teenie?"

"Tell me about it," Teenie muttered.

"What's *your* four-year-old like to do, Jesse?" Karen asked, turning to her with tight-lipped, unblinking attention, giving the leash a little tug.

"You name it," Jesse shrugged, looking off.

"So what's Cody like to do?" Karen eased it back around to Brenda.

"Be with me. He likes to be with me."

"Huh." Karen gave it a moment to absorb the straight-arm, then picked it up again.

"OK, well, look. The fact is, it's been almost twenty hours, about, so the odds of him still wandering out in the street somewheres, not getting picked up by now, helped out by now, are not so good."

She tapped six blobs of mapped green within the one-mile circumference. "Now, we looked at this map earlier today and on paper we saw six possibilities where a kid could conceivably get lost or hide out for a whole day and night, not get noticed. But then we drove around and eliminated three—this is a golf course, this is a cemetery, this is a ballfield." She drew X's through the rejects. "There's no cover, no trees, no hollows, no structures, no place to hide, if that's what he's doing, which leaves us"—she circled the other greens—"the old Chase Institute, Freedomtown, and Hudson Park, OK? So, Brenda. What's your heart say . . ."

Jesse sucked it in as Brenda eased back on the couch, blinked wetly at the ceiling. "Chase."

"Chase it is." Karen gave the abandoned hospital grounds a second ring of red. "OK, so tomorrow morning Lou and a few of the guys'll make a quick walk around Chase, maybe Freedomtown or Hudson Park if we can stretch. We'll do what we can do tonight, and tomorrow we're all gonna meet in the parking lot of Saint Agnes on Turner and Blossom—

all the volunteers. We'll get organized and hit the grounds, OK? Now, tomorrow . . . How do you feel about coming out with us."

"What?" Brenda hunched forward in dismay.

"Aw, *no*," Jesse said, before she could stop herself. Karen and the others ignored her.

"If you're up for it, Brenda, I'd kind of like to have you with us."

"There's nothing like maternal radar," Marie added.

"Brenda, we've been doing this five years, and I'm telling you, I don't know if it's God, mother love, the supernatural, or what, but the mom gets out there? This sixth sense kicks in, it's like nothing else." Karen massaged Brenda's neck. "Teenie, tell her about Donna Cord."

"This boy Michael Cord, five years old, goes missing over in the Bronx—the family lives near the Bronx Zoo, right? We're out there twelve hours poking around. The mom? Donna? She was in the hospital. She finally comes out with us at the end of the day . . . Bang. She finds him in forty-five minutes. He was asleep in a culvert. I don't know how she did it."

"And we had the dog out there too," Marie added, all of them warming up to the war story.

"Well, in all fairness to the dog"—Louis finally opened his mouth, shifted his weight—"we were right outside the second-biggest zoo in the country. You know how many different scents were in the wind? The dog almost had a nervous breakdown."

"The point I'm trying to make, Brenda." Karen stroked her hair. "Be it God, love, or whatever, you come out with us, you're gonna see something, sense something that everybody else is gonna miss."

"It could just be like clothes or colors," Marie added.

"We're not gonna shape up much before nine. You can get a good night's sleep."

"Right." Brenda's voice was striving for the sarcastic.

"Will you come with us?" Marie asked.

Brenda stared blindly at the map, the room descending into another focused silence, the Friends of Kent waiting. Finally, crumpling under the weight of their stares, Brenda issued a quivering "All right."

"You OK?" Karen stroked her face, then specifically turned to Jesse. "Can you get her a glass of water?"

At first Jesse simply returned Karen's stare. But then, realizing that she was trapped between standing up to this domineering saint in training and appearing unsympathetic to Brenda, she looked to Ben in the kitchen to get the water for her. Ben, in an act of stunning betrayal, returned her look with a silently mouthed "You do it," giving her a reassuring nod, like there was nothing finer in the world than to kiss someone's ass. Jesse got the water, put it down on the map.

Karen said, "Thanks, Jesse," underlining her name, then plugged in the answering machine, setting it before Brenda on the coffee table. "I want you to leave a message for your son." Brenda looked away, crunched her eyes. "I want you to leave a message," Karen said calmly, insistently.

"Like what." Brenda refused to turn back to her.

"Like, 'Cody, if that's you, Mommy loves you. Mommy misses you. Where are you. I want to come get you right away. I'm not mad. Please tell me where you are. Can you see any people? Can you get someone to the phone?' "

"I'm not *mad?*" Brenda exploded in a guttering squawk. "Why would I be mad?"

"Ssh, Brenda. Kids in this situation, sometimes they feel like they're in trouble, that the parent could be mad that they're not home. You have to think like a four-year-old. Of course you're not mad, we're just covering all the bases, OK?"

"Ho *God,*" Brenda gasped.

Jesse eased her way into the kitchen, touched her brother's hand. "Get her to stop this," she murmured through clenched teeth.

"Watch," her brother whispered back, his eyes never leaving Karen.

"Now, can we make that message?" Brenda stared at the machine. "Maybe it would help if you wrote it down first. Do you want to write it down?"

"Please, God," Brenda continued to wail. "I just want to die. Please let me die."

"You're not in this alone." Karen stroked her hair again. "We're here for you."

Jesse heard this, thought, No, you're not. Taking a swipe at her face, she was surprised to see her fingers come away wet.

"C'mon, Brenda, leave him a message."

Brenda struggled to her feet and walked drunkenly to the bathroom, her sudden absence pulling the room into a new and disorienting equation. Jesse experienced a terrible freedom in the air. Surprisingly, no one spoke—nothing of logistics, no strategizing, no hurried assessments. Even more unnerving was that no one even made eye contact, which left Jesse feeling that what was going on here was pure sham, a play for an audience of one, all the players in such perfect communion with one another that they could just shut down for this abrupt intermission, their lines so well memorized that there was no need to do anything but rest.

The silence was such that whatever was happening in the bathroom of this small apartment should have been easily heard in the living room, but there was an equal stillness on the other side of that door—no water, no flushing, no occupying noises. After five or so minutes, Karen rose from the couch.

"Brenda? You OK?"

Receiving no answer, she simply opened the bathroom door to reveal Brenda, fully dressed, sitting on the toilet lid, her face in her hands, hiding in her own home. Karen extended a hand, lifting, then leading Brenda back to the couch. Once seated, she sat rocking before the tape recorder, Karen's arm around her back. Karen gave her a thirty-second grace period, whispered, "Time is tight," and pushed Play. Brenda continued to rock.

"Come on now," Karen said, a little sternly.

"Cody, I love you so much," Brenda abruptly declared, eyelids lightly clamped, as if she were singing a love song.

The Friends of Kent looked up, down, out, anywhere but at Brenda, out of respect for the intimacy of her words.

"Where are you, sweetheart," she said brokenly, clutching her stomach. "I want you with me so bad. I want to come get you. Please tell me how to come get you. I miss you so much. Tell me how to be with you. Tell me how I can be with you." Brenda brought a hand to her face, dismissed the answering machine with her other, ruddy furrows appearing above her brow.

Karen stopped the recording, rewound it, played it back, Brenda's rocking becoming more pronounced as she heard her teary plea. "Would your son respond to that?" Karen asked calmly. Brenda kept her face hidden. "Does that sound like you? Would he *hear* you in that?" Brenda shrugged. "I think, I think maybe we should take another shot at it, Brenda. You sound pretty upset. You could scare him off."

"No," Brenda said.

"You feel OK with this?"

"I'm not doing it again."

"No?"

"She *said* no." It just slipped out of Jesse. Karen gave her a quick up and down, a flat-faced promise of retribution.

"All right, if that's what you think he'll respond to best." Karen put a bit of singsong reproach in it. "And don't worry about the prank calls. Once they hear that, they'll just hang up."

"OK," Brenda said quickly, still looking away.

"If you want, I'll ask Detective Council to hang a wire on your phone. I'm surprised he didn't think to do that already."

"I don't care." Brenda continued to rock.

"Now one last thing. Lou? He's a dog trainer. Trains dogs for the Newark police, and we like to use tracking dogs on a search like this. These dogs, they can clear a building in five, ten minutes, go through nooks, crannies, darkness, rubble, underbrush, you name it. You know, because for them it's just scent. It's kind of like radar. They do ten times the area in a tenth of the time, and it's safer, too, because sometimes we go through some structures, you know, the floors rotted out or whatnot, and the dogs are pretty light on their feet. I mean, lighter than *me* at any rate."

Ben laughed appreciatively. Jesse was sure of it—her brother was head over heels with this bitch.

"But in order to use the dog"—Karen pulled a gallon-sized Ziploc bag out of her duffle—"we're going to need to make a scent bag."

"A what?"

"I want you to go in his room and fill this. I want his pillowcase. I want—do you have some unwashed laundry in there? Separate from yours?"

Brenda just stared, then said, "In his closet."

Karen rose, helped Brenda to her feet. "Do it for me now, OK? So we can get out of your hair." Brenda looked to Cody's room, then back at Karen. "Do you want me to come in with you?" Karen offered. Brenda looked to Jesse, Karen tracking her gaze. "Me, you, and Jesse," Karen said, taking Brenda by the elbow, turning to Jesse.

"You coming?"

Brenda stood before Cody's open closet: three pairs of jeans on hangers, a few shirts, two pair of high-top sneakers on the floor, a dozen or so battered board games stacked haphazardly, and, in an open wicker laundry basket, a tumble of T-shirts, socks, shorts, and a New Jersey Nets tank top. It might just be the power of suggestion, but Jesse still felt staggered by the overwhelming reek of boyness.

Brenda stood before the open door, making no effort to reach for the laundry. "Can you do it?" she pleaded to Karen.

"I can't. The dog knows my scent. I'll throw him off."

"I'll do it." Jesse reached for the bag, but Karen intercepted her.

"I really think Brenda needs to do it."

"Have you looked at her *hands* tonight?" Jesse's voice came out sharp and hard, fed up.

"Can I talk to you a second, Jesse?"

Karen put out her hand, as if to corral her by the shoulders, and Jesse moved for the door to avoid her touch.

Three steps outside the room, Karen came up on her like a shadow, Jesse turning, her eyes on the level of the other woman's mouth.

"I want to tell you something." Karen spoke in a whispery sizzle. "In the last five years I have found twelve missing children, four living, eight *dead*. I *find* missing children. That's what I *do* and right now I don't give a flying fuck about anybody but that little boy. I will find him and I will find out what happened to him. Now, you don't like me? Fine. If it's any comfort to you, you're not alone. But if you ever get in my face again on this, I swear to Christ I'll ruin you. You know I will, and you know how I'll do it."

Jesse felt breathless, trying to return the anger but too overwhelmed by the precision of Karen's fury.

"Now, Brenda seems to need you, so you go be with her, but you best have what I just said to you memorized for the duration of this or I'll bounce your ass from here to the river, you *got* that?"

Despite herself, Jesse nodded yes. For some reason she couldn't begin to understand, she lost all dislike for this woman, was actually consumed, at least for the moment, with a desire to gain Karen's respect. She followed her back into Cody's room, where Brenda was still standing in front of the closet, the empty Ziploc bag dangling from her right hand.

"C'mon, Brenda," Karen said, "time is tight." Dropping to her knees, Brenda began to fill the bag, working slowly because of her bandages, using her fingers like chopsticks, plucking the articles of clothing one by one, her face twisted in distress.

"You need the pillowcase too?" Jesse said to Karen, careful of her tone. "Because I don't think she'll be able to get it off the pillow by herself."

Karen said, "Don't worry about it," not even looking at Jesse, her eyes on Brenda, taking her measure. Jesse sensed that Karen considered her neutralized, not even worth eye contact, and that powerful new craving for this woman's respect or approval was replaced by the old loathing—now doubled because Karen had scrambled her heart.

Brenda put the last pair of underpants in the scent bag, but instead of handing it over to Karen she held it to her midsection and eased herself down to the floor of the closet, sitting there cross-legged, clutching the bag and staring out into the room. "You know what I'd do sometimes when I couldn't get him to do what I wanted? I'd cry. You know, say he won't eat his breakfast or won't go to bed. I'd pretend to cry, like 'Boohoo, Cody doesn't love me no more,' real head-fuck stuff, and he was so smart, he'd get so angry at me, he'd, like, *run* at me, 'Mommy! That's a pretend cry! Stop it! Stop it right now!' and I'd be laughing inside, because it *was* such a hokey bullshit cry, but I wouldn't stop it, because I knew if I kept it up long enough, whatever he knew about it, how phony it was, it would still *get* to him and eventually he'd start to cry too and, you know, do what I had asked him to do to begin with. I'd win, you see. I don't know if it's all little kids these days or just him, but I don't ever remember being that perceptive, you know, reading my parents like he could read me."

Karen stood in the closet door, hands crossed over her belt, alert, waiting for more, and Jesse suppressed the impulse to tell Brenda to shut up.

"It's kind of like ants. They say that ants can lift like a hundred times their weight and, like, you know, proportionately ants are the strongest things on earth. That was like Cody with reading people. He was so, *smart* for his age, so, so out of proportion to his size. But despite all that? I could still make him cry. He was four years old. I mean, you look at an ant and say, 'Wow, strongest creature for its size.' But it's still an ant."

"Brenda." Karen dropped into a squat to be on eye level. "What are you trying to tell me right now."

"He was just a baby." She began to weep. "How could he know?"

"Know what . . ." Karen said.

"The world," Brenda said, almost inaudibly. "You know . . ."

When they returned to the living room, both Jesse and Brenda were startled to see a German shepherd on a short leash, Louis giving the dog no more than nine inches from fist to collar.

Karen broke out into a smile. "Hey-y, Sherlock!" she said, then turned to Brenda. "Sherlock's our secret weapon. He can sniff out a daisy in a cyclone."

"I hope you don't mind I brought him up for a second." Louis patted the dog's shimmering flank, its tongue hanging out in a panting grin. "I had him in the car. I'm just worried with the heat and all."

Brenda stared at the animal as if it were a wolf. Jesse assumed it was a cadaver dog, an animal trained on buried pig fetuses and tennis balls coated with Cadaverine, a chemical solution that simulated the scent of human decomposition. She had seen them in action once or twice over the years. Nothing successful, but she had heard some amazing stories.

"Do you think I could get, like, a dish of water for him?" Louis asked.

"I'll get it," Ben said.

Karen put her arm around Brenda's shoulder and turned her away from the dog. "From now on, Brenda? We're gonna be with you all the way. We never abandon our mothers."

Or the dog might be cross-trained, Jesse thought, able to find lost or disabled people, too, the living as well as the dead, maybe even sniff out drugs or dig up buried weapons. She was almost sure of it, though—working for a group like this, whatever else he might be, Sherlock was a cadaver dog.

"Kent? That boy Kent?" Brenda said to Karen, her back to the room. "When you found him? Was he dead or alive."

"Dead," Karen said flatly.

Ben put a dish before the dog, who stared at it but made no move to drink. Jesse absently reached out to pat the animal's flawless coat and was startled when Louis roughly stayed her hand.

With Brenda for the moment turned away from him on the far side of the room, Louis quickly knelt alongside the panting, patient dog, lifted its head by the snout, whispered, "*Body,*" a flat command into the peaked ear, then quickly unclipped the leash, Jesse thinking, Nothing like an early start.

17

After agreeing to keep his distance from the Friends of Kent sit-down with Brenda Martin, Lorenzo, overwhelmed but with nothing really to do, mindlessly cruised JFK Boulevard. He felt impotent and desperate. Every facet of the investigation seemed to elude his grasp. Military occupations, civic demonstrations, wrongful arrests, civilian search parties, baby-sitting journalists, outraged families—Lorenzo felt unable to control or prevent any of it.

Of all the spinouts and misfires of the last twenty-four hours, the most painful and maddening for him was the arrest of Curious George Howard. Gannon had tossed George into the system, and that move would simply have to play itself out. Even if Gannon could be coaxed into dropping the child support charge for the time being, George had apparently broken Danny Martin's nose, and there you had it. An Armstrong youngblood swinging on Leo Sullivan, swinging on Danny Martin like that was what Lorenzo usually called "going and getting stupid on yourself." But there was nothing "usual" about the last twenty-four hours, so all street-survival lectures were suspended until further notice.

To make matters worse, as Lorenzo had anticipated, the media had been quick to announce that a suspect was in custody, and George's sisters, subbing for the star of the show, had taken to the cameras like preachers to a pulpit, bitterly complaining about racist cops, police brutality, and the persecution of the innocent. And it wasn't just the Howard sisters who were doing the talking. Despite the termination of the blockade, a lot of the Armstrong tenants had embraced the cameras by now, going on about poor housing conditions, about the city's turning its back on Armstrong and the other projects, about racial double standards, about broken campaign promises by the mayor, about municipal contempt for the underclass in general, about the absence of full-time employment, the absence of summer jobs for teenagers, the absence of recreation programs, the absence or presence of this, that, and the other, each bitter complaint taking this thing further and further away from the alleged crime that started it all.

What made Lorenzo angriest was his own mishandling of the case, first letting Jesse weasel her way into the situation, then sending Karen Collucci up to bat. At least Karen, unlike Jesse, had something to offer. Earlier in the evening, when he had first met with her and the other members of her group, he had found the mechanics of their canvass-and-search program impressively organized, possibly even helpful, although, consistent with his grabbing-at-straws approach, he saw Karen as mainly another shoulder for Brenda to cry on, a potential confessor. Somewhere in the back of his head the expression *a woman's touch* rattled about like hope incarnate.

He had been careful about what he said to Karen, not wanting her to go in there with any cop-fed predisposition that would taint her testimony in court if it came down to that. She was verbally cautious right back at him, both of them tacitly understanding the importance of threading the needle.

If Brenda was all wrong, Lorenzo was reasonably sure that Karen would pick up on it; it would just be better for all concerned if she came to that conclusion on her own. And no way was he going to inform Bobby McDonald or anyone in the prosecutor's office tonight of Karen Collucci's involvement. For the time being, Brenda was a free agent. She could see, go, do anything she wanted, but Lorenzo still feared that the higher powers, if given the opportunity, would nix this dicey move with Karen. He had long ago learned that the trick to getting permission was to not ask for it. They'd find out soon enough—the first open-to-the-public search party was scheduled to roll on out the next morning.

Cruising slow, Lorenzo drew in the usual salutes from the jugglers on every corner, some pantomiming running away, a few taking off for real. Lorenzo wore a fixed grimace of reproach on his mug, exuded a chronic low-key case of the angries, people fucking up everywhere he looked.

The boulevard, as usual, was strobed with reflector tape—on T-shirts, high-tops, shin-length baggy shorts. Lorenzo remembered driving down here with Bump two weeks earlier, Bump taking in the light show and saying, "Once a slave, always a slave." A kid had explained the reflector-tape craze to Lorenzo last week, telling him, "If all of us are wearin' it, the cops get all confused." Lorenzo had countered, "Well, if you all *don't* wear it, won't the cops be confused that way too?" To which the kid had replied, "Yeah, but if we don't wear it, then we're just us."

Another fashion fad this summer was ski goggles tinted rose or yellow and worn propped at the hairline. About one kid out of every three was going for that effect, as if they were about to hit the slopes, though very few of them had ever set foot on anything but cement or city-owned grass. These were the same damned kids who always referred to their neighborhood as Darktown, D-Town, as if the redneck appellation were a badge of honor. They were ignorant of the etymology, the history. All Lorenzo's pit-stop mini-lectures about how this section of the city, back in the nineteenth century, had been a shanty town—the only area in which blacks were allowed to live, so-called Coontown, Darktown—had come to nothing. The kids mostly shrugged off his street-corner harangues, his stairwell browbeatings, telling him, "That's old-school shit. We *own* this bitch now."

Though not crazy about the majority of individuals out here as a rule, he nonetheless knew that nine nights out of ten he would unflinchingly go the distance to save just one of them. But tonight was that tenth night, and he was just fucking pissed. The angrier he got, the slower he drove, looking for someone to take it out on, zeroing in, then checking himself, zeroing in, checking himself, understanding that his rage had nothing to do with the JFK all-night ski patrol. Sorely tempted, he went ten miles an hour, the jugglers picking up his mood, cutting down on the clowning, starting to look off, as if working out math problems in their heads, cars honking, impatiently pulling around him on the narrow two-way boulevard, the screeching of their tires like a shrill reproach. Lorenzo was unaware that someone had been chasing his car on foot for the last few blocks until the person finally came up close enough to pound on his trunk. Jumping out of the car, ready to deal, he saw that it was Felicia Mitchell, doubled over now and gasping for air.

" 'Renzo," she gulped out his name, grabbed her guts. "Luh-renzo," she said, leaning into his taillight for support.

He couldn't tell if she was injured or just winded until he saw her slowly straighten up, lapping at the air open-mouthed, one hand to her forehead, the other fanning her throat. He was double-parked, the cars behind him curved in a steady stream into the oncoming lane, no one honking, because they all knew his name.

"Lorenzo." Felicia tried again, dipped at the waist, struggled to get her breath back. "Lorenzo." She grabbed his wrist. "I saw you go by. You said you . . ." She dipped again. "Whoo . . . You said you'd come up to-night."

"For what?" he asked, and the hurt look on her flushed face sealed his obligation.

Felicia had reluctantly allowed him to hit a drive-through Hardee's before going to confront her boyfriend, and Lorenzo was wolfing down two cheeseburgers and a strawberry shake as he climbed the stairs to her fourth-floor walk-up. Situated on a side street off JFK Boulevard, her apartment had too many things in it—too many textures, too many surfaces, too many colors. Lorenzo's automatic reaction on entering was to take a hit of asthma spray. The small living room was chockablock with fancy: a rose-tinted glass coffee table fronted a black velour couch, sheathed in plastic and flanked by two smoke-tinted glass end tables that were topped with chrome gooseneck lamps. This arrangement faced a large-screen TV that anchored a floor-to-ceiling gold-plated wall unit, the glass shelves filled with sentiment and whimsy. There were dolls, figurines, photo albums, videocassettes, Nintendo gear, and framed eight-by-ten cap and gowners—Felicia graduating high school, graduating college; her brother graduating college; her son, Shawn, grad-uating elementary school. The living room floor was painted jet black and lined with knee-high vases filled with peacock feathers, ostrich feathers, and stalks of multicolored wheat.

To add to his sense of claustrophobia, the sound on the TV was too loud, George Benton singing "Masquerade," the picture on the yard-square screen both snowy and rolling, impossible to make out. The air itself was too busy for him, dense with the smell of fried meat and, under that, the odor of beer, lots of beer.

"So did he . . ." Lorenzo tenderly probed the cut on the back of his head, blinked away the meat-tinged air. "Did Billy hit you tonight?"

"Not yet," Felicia drawled. "But he's over there in the bullpen warmin' up." She gestured toward the far wall. "Wait till you see *this* shit." At first, Lorenzo was confused—they seemed to be the only people in the room. But when Felicia turned off the TV, George Benton continued to sing and Lorenzo realized that the living room wasn't as small as he had thought. What he had taken for the far wall was a partition, the music coming from behind a four-foot-high bookshelf, this one filled with books. When he left Felicia behind to circle around the shelf, he decided that "partition" wasn't the right word, that a more appropriate one would be "barricade."

Billy Williams was a young man, fleshy and tall. He sported a thin, parted moustache, which had the paradoxical effect of enhancing the babyishness of his open, round face and converted his eyes into artless magnifiers of whatever emotion churned through his brain at any given moment.

Wearing only a pair of white BVDs, he sat in a beery haze on a sheetless foam mattress behind the bookshelf. The mattress was on the floor, so his knees came up to his shoulders and his moderate gut pressed against his thighs. The music was coming from a miniature boom box, the detachable speakers positioned like earmuffs on either side of his pillow.

Billy's world behind the bookshelf ran about eight feet by ten, with a single, unshaded window. Two pressed suits hung from a curtainless rod, like misshapen drapes, imperfectly blocking out the light from the street, cutting it up into odd curves and angles so that it hit the wall like dispersed fragments of a kaleidoscope. Underneath this light show, lined up along the baseboard, were three spit-shined pairs of dress shoes, flanked by crisply folded piles of T-shirts and boxers on one side and a stack of razor-creased slacks on the other, a semicircle of balled dress socks trimming the lot like the fanciful border of a garden.

Beneath the window, at right angles to this dresserless wardrobe, sat Billy Williams's entertainment center, an orderly arrangement of paperbacks, textbooks, CDs, and four stacked six-packs of beer. The CDs were mostly jazz, the paperbacks science fiction, and the textbooks business-oriented.

Even given the almost military orderliness of the possessions arrayed before him, indicative of discernment, education, and aspiration, Lorenzo, who had never set eyes on this guy before now, felt as if he had just entered the half-cocked make-do world of the homeless.

"Hey, Billy."

Looking up to the sound of his name, Billy eyed Lorenzo with a liquored vagueness. He wasn't all the way drunk, just slow on the draw.

"What's up?" Billy said tentatively.

"I'm Lorenzo Council." He stooped to extend his hand, Billy taking it, still off balance.

Then Billy's eyes sparked, his mouth tightened into a grin, and his grip became firm. "Yeah, OK, OK. Yeah, I know you. How you doin'?" Billy's greeting had the hard joyfulness of a man starved for contact.

"I'm good. How 'bout you?" Lorenzo tossed back, wishing the guy would put his pants on.

"Hey," Billy said, raising his hands, taking in his space with a smirk. "Hangin' on, you know." He turned down the music, the sound of canned laughter rising now from the TV on the other side of the room.

"I hear you got a problem."

"Me?" Billy curled his fingers into his hairless chest. "I got lots of problems. Which one are you inquiring about?" Before Lorenzo could kick in, Billy's face suddenly transformed, his eyes and mouth going round with delayed panic, as if he had just remembered leaving the gas on somewhere. Looking back over the bookshelf, Lorenzo saw Felicia slouched sideways on the couch, eyeing the rolling, snowy TV show, her glum face smeared into a supporting fist.

"What"—the sound of Billy's voice turned Lorenzo around again—"What's wrong." His face still held that almost stricken look of anticipation.

"I understand you been doin' a little, layin' on of the *hands* there, brother."

"I what?" Billy ducked his head, mouth agape.

"She says you been hittin' her." Lorenzo found a place to sit, balancing himself on a stack of hardback books, getting closer to eye level with the man on the floor.

"*Who . . . her?*" Billy said, raising his arm and crooking his index finger over the bookshelves like a periscope. "That's . . . Oh wow." He lowered his face into his palms and remained like that for a long minute. "Oh wow."

Lorenzo spread his legs a little wider, propped his elbows on his knees, got his face down a little lower.

"You cannot hit her, you know that, right?"

"Hit her . . ." Billy's voice echoed off the cup of his hands. He raised his face, looking at Lorenzo head-on. "*That's* what you're here for?"

Lorenzo just stared.

"Hit her," he said, looking off, giving Lorenzo the impression that he was taking a moment to sort himself out, to restow all the things in his mental footlocker. When he finally began to speak again, Billy's voice had an entirely different register, still agitated but less fearful.

"What, she says she's a battered woman or something?" He looked off again, snorted. "Naw, man, that's . . ." He shook his head no, but suddenly tears began to drip down his cheeks, curve around his nose. "I never laid a *hand* on her."

"Ask my son, Lorenzo. Ask Shawn," Felicia called out from beyond the shelves.

"Shawn *never* saw me hit you."

"Yes he did."

Billy clucked in disgust. "She ain't no battered woman, are you kidding me? I ain't even from around here, but I will tell you, the people in this city? They *whack* their women. You go to the hospital, I'll *show* you battered women." There was nothing in Billy's expression or voice that seemed to accommodate the fact that he was crying. It was as if tears were blood, just a liquid that seeped from the body without needing a corresponding emotional acknowledgment.

Billy struggled to his feet, gangly and slack. He reached over the low bookshelf and, without actually looking at Felicia, trained the nearest chrome-plated gooseneck lamp on her face and bare arms, the light harsh and raw, bleaching her out. "You look at her. *Look* at her." Billy's voice was climbing, febrile, addressing Lorenzo as if Felicia were inanimate. "You look at her top to bottom. Where's the marks, where's the bruises, where's the broken bones, where's the black eyes."

In the spirit of her boyfriend's oddly impersonal aggression, Felicia refused to react to the glare of the light, her sullen eyes still fixed on the abstract TV snow.

For a long moment, Billy hung over the partition, one hand on the neck of the lamp, as if waiting for some acknowledgment of Exhibit A. Then, abruptly, he collapsed cross-legged on the mattress. "Hey, I grew up in a house, and my father, he was dead wrong in what he was doing, but I *know* what a battered woman looks like, all right? But while she's got you here? Why don't you ask her what she's done to *me*."

"Jesus Christ," Felicia groaned.

"See, she's doin' to me what my mother done to my father. Emasculating me, tearing me down, humiliating me."

"You cannot hit her," Lorenzo said quietly.

"Well." Billy slapped his bare legs. "I tell you what. She says she's gonna file a charge on me? Hey, I grew up in a house where you pull out that gun, you *shoot* or you leave it in your pocket. I grew up with *no* games."

"No games?" Felicia called out. "Then how come he made himself a *fort* in there."

"No games." Billy clenched his teeth.

"You cannot hit her," Lorenzo repeated evenly, feeling a headache coming on.

"So I say to her, 'You do what you got to do, but if that's the case, then you best be prepared to take it to the max because *I'm* gonna take it to the max too.' "

"Meaning what . . ." Lorenzo asked, suddenly more interested.

Billy's tears still dripped, as if disconnected to the face, the voice. "Meaning you file your charges, I'll file mine. But see, here's the dilemma for *me,* because I might have hit her once."

"Once?" a dull drawl from the other side of the room. "Try once a *night.*"

"Once," Billy repeated sharply. "But on my end, let me ask you. Is verbal humiliation indictable? Is, is, is tearing down my manhood indictable?"

"You cannot hit her," Lorenzo said evenly yet again, smiling, elbows on knees, eye to eye.

"Is, is spiritual castration indictable? And, like, right now, here we go again. Like, here *you* are, right? Now, I just saw you on Rolonda Watts last month. I'm watching you on the TV, and I like what you said, you know, about peer pressure on kids, the importance of role models. I was with you one hundred percent on that, and I said to her, 'That's your guy, right? I like his mentality.' She turns around to me, says, 'Oh yeah? Well, he don't like *you.*' "

"He's lying, Lorenzo," Felicia called out, a little louder this time.

"Man, you never even *met* me," Billy wailed.

"No, I haven't," Lorenzo said patiently, palming his scalp, tapping his feet.

"Now, tearin' me down to people I admire? People I don't even have a chance to make an impression on? Is that an indictable crime? No, right?"

"Billy, north, south, right, left, all conversation here between me and you begins with 'You can not hit her.' "

"Man, I never laid a *hand* on her."

"Yo brother! You just told me you did!" Lorenzo said, laughing like they were just hanging out. "C'mon there, Billy."

"Tearin' me down just because . . . Hey. You don't even . . . I was *good*. I graduated in the top fifteen percentile of my college class. I go over to Wall Street? They put me in some back room making cold calls. But I was the best they had, and how many other black brokers you think they had back there, because I didn't see anyone but *me*. Come lunchtime, I didn't even have nobody to talk to, but I was the *best*."

"Billy," Lorenzo said, not really following his flow, "you can not hit her." Along with Billy's seemingly disconnected tears, Lorenzo started to experience the man's self-contradicting words as just verbal smoke, as if his mind and mouth had a vested interest in not comparing notes.

"I mean I was rackin' it up. And let me tell you something, people pick up their phone and hear me? With *my* voice? *My* inflections? Trying to get them to invest their money and I do it better than any of those white boys? You *know* I had to be good."

"All right then." Lorenzo made a steeple of his splayed fingers. "But Billy—"

"And I still love her." He tilted his head toward the bookshelves, his facial expression finally, if fleetingly, in sync with his tears. "She is a very, very special woman, but if you try to emasculate me—"

"Emasculate." The word came sharply from over the border. "That's his favorite word, Lorenzo, emasculate."

"Look, you don't—" Billy abruptly cut himself off, taking such a violent swipe at the wetness under his eyes that it almost seemed like he was slapping himself.

"Last year, OK? I buried my father, and I lost my job."

"You better jump in there, Lorenzo," Felicia said. "He's gonna talk all night if you let him." Lorenzo winced at her timing.

"Now my mother is in the hospital with cancer, OK? In Paterson. I don't even have the carfare to go see her. She got a house in Plainfield? I don't even have the carfare to watch it for her."

"He's there all the time, Lorenzo. If he's so worried about saving the damn carfare, why doesn't he just move in, get out my hair *al*together." Lorenzo's left eye began to throb.

"Look," Billy said. "I'm not even from around here. I came up here to be with her. And now I don't even have nothing to go back to, you know what I'm sayin'? It's, like, *her* city, *her* friends, *she's* the one with the job, *she's* the one with the connections, *she's* the one can call *you* up, get you over here to intimidate me."

"I ain't intimidatin' you. I'm talking to you man to man and I just have one thing—"

"To say to me. I cannot *hit* her. And I agree. No debate on that, but let me tell you. Whether I hit her or not don't make any difference no more, because I am finished with her. I won't sleep with her, I won't break bread with her, I won't talk with her, I won't look at her. I am finished!"

"Good!" Felicia bellowed. "So move out! Lorenzo, tell him to move out. He livin' half the time in his mother's house anyhow, so tell him to get the other half of his ass over there too."

"I am over at my mother's house because my mother is *dying!*" Billy shouted at the floor. "I am over at my mother's house because that's the only place on Earth I got left where I can feel like a whole person!"

"Yeah, an' all he does when he comes back here after he's finished feeling like a whole person is to hole up in that hamster cage over there, drink beer, and feel sorry for himself because he's living off *me*." Billy started trembling, Lorenzo watching the rage bubble under his skin. "And you know, Lorenzo," Felicia added. "All due respect to his mother and whatnot—"

"Whatnot," Billy repeated through clenched teeth.

"But I *know* he's got some shorty over there. Tellin' me he's watchin' his mother's house . . . . Like what, the house is gonna run into the street? Nah, nah, he's knockin' boots over there, Lorenzo. I might be abused, but I'm not stupid. He wants to be treated like a man? Let him *act* like a man. Either move out or move in, because I can not take this *pup* tent in my house one day longer."

"*Her* house, *her* city, *her* friends, *her* friends, *her* money, *her* job, *her* connections, everybody on *her* side." Billy's face was a glistening river. "Man, you don't even know me. You don't . . . How can you not like me? I was watching you on TV. You made me feel good. You made me feel inspired."

"Well, look—" Lorenzo's beeper went off: Bump. "You and me. We know each other now, right?"

He handed Billy one of his cards. "You need me, you call me, same like her, 'cause now everybody knows me and I know everybody," he said, raising his voice to include Felicia. "So I'll be waiting for a call. And when I'm called, whoever calls me? I *will* come."

Billy nodded, mute now, as if not sure whether he was being validated or threatened. Lorenzo leaned forward and spoke in an intimate whisper, theatrically excluding Felicia. "How long you been living like this?"

"Just, you know, this week, a few days. I moved my stuff," Billy responded in Lorenzo's hushed, confidential tone.

"And you been hittin' her this week too."

"No."

"Yes, you have." Lorenzo inched away, speaking softly. Billy said nothing. "Yes, you have," Lorenzo repeated.

"It's been a bad week," Billy stammered. "You don't know."

"Uh-huh." Lorenzo kept close, waiting.

"I consider myself a gentleman."

"So." Billy stared at his hands. "You cannot hit her, brother."

"I know . . . I'm kind of out of my own depth right now."

Lorenzo nodded, and without moving his head, without turning his gaze, he reached across to the stack of neatly folded T-shirts, plucked one, and offered it to Billy so that he could wipe his eyes. Billy stared at the shirt for a moment, as if confused, then slipped it on, Lorenzo thinking, Damn . . .

"You talk about respect," Lorenzo continued in that quiet, forceful tone. "When you hit her, do you gain her respect? Or lose it."

"No doubt, no doubt." Billy's eyes were trained on the floor.

"Her son. What are you teaching him when he sees you—"

"I agree, I agree." Billy cut him off, as if the picture were too unbearable, too shameful.

"Do you want to leave her?" Lorenzo ducked his head a little, trying to lift Billy's eyes.

"No."

"Do you?"

Silence, then, "No."

" 'Cause if you do, I'll find you a place to stay."

"No."

"I can just pick up the phone and get you a room tonight, won't even cost you a penny." Lorenzo was getting carried away a little, but he didn't think Billy would go for it.

"No."

He gave the answer a few reflective seconds. "OK, then . . ." Billy's tears dripped in a lazy leak, like bathwater through a ceiling. Lorenzo put a hand on Billy's bare knee and moved in closer. "You're an intelligent, well-spoken young man, Billy. So, c'mon now. It's time for you to start collecting yourself, you know what I'm saying? We *need* you."

Billy's mouth worked wordlessly, his eyes brimming. "You are absolutely right," he finally said with tremulous conviction. "You have yet to meet the real *me*."

Lorenzo's beeper went off, this time the forensics lab, and he rose to his feet. "Well, I would look forward to meeting that individual."

Billy followed him out into the living room, hopping into a pair of jeans along the way. Felicia, sprawled on the couch, looked like she hadn't moved an inch in all the time that Lorenzo had spent behind the bookshelves in Billyworld. Lorenzo knew that she thought he had wound up taking Billy's side, but all he had done, as far as he was concerned, was to play to the man's vulnerability, stroking him into a state of at least temporary positiveness.

"Hey." Billy offered his hand, his breath yeasty and sweet. "I really enjoyed talking to you. I don't have too many full-bodied conversations with people these days."

"The feeling's mutual." Lorenzo smiled tightly, watching Felicia roll her eyes. "But just you all remember, I get a ring on my beeper? Whoever calls me, I am coming back."

"Good." Billy bobbed his head.

" 'Cause this isn't just about you and you. It's about . . ." Lorenzo chucked a thumb toward the other end of the apartment, toward Shawn's closed bedroom door. "That's the catastrophe."

"I agree." Billy bobbed his head again, passed a quick finger across a tear-mottled cheekbone.

Felicia twisted her lips way up on one side of her face, refused to look at either of them.

"You all have a good night now," Lorenzo said, lingering despite himself, feeling that, after all the back and forth, he and Billy hadn't really talked about shit. Finally taking his leave, Lorenzo stood quietly outside the apartment door, listening for the sharp sounds of a fight. After three minutes of hearing nothing but TV laugh track, he left the building.

Upon opening the door to his mother's apartment, where he intended to wait out the end of Karen Collucci's sit-down with Brenda Martin, he saw the answering machine winking redly at him from across the darkened living room. There were two messages, the first from Atlantic City, his mother calling to inform him that she had won two thousand dollars playing some kind of jackpot slot machine and was extending her stay with Lorenzo's aunts for however long it took to return the money to the casino. Lorenzo was vaguely amused that his mom seemed unaware of what had to be the hottest ongoing news event in the tristate area. But then he recalled from his one halfhearted trip to AC that the casinos had neither clocks nor windows.

The second call wasn't nearly so joyous or oblivious—his wife, Frankie. She was furious, in tears, one of the New York tabloids having run a sidebar on Jason, on the fact that the catching detective's kid was a twenty-two-year-old jailbird. Listening to his wife's distraught railing, he stood bobbing over the answering machine, mumbling, "I'll take care of it, I'll take care of it," knowing there was nothing he could do but eat it and move on.

When Frankie came to the end of her lament, Lorenzo became aware of a liquid tickle at the nape of his neck. Apparently, while listening to his wife, he had reopened the gash on the back of his head, vigorously scratching the barely formed scab until the blood was streaming down his back like water.

Changing into a fresh shirt, he pulled out his pager and saw the last number registered there: Forensics. Assuming Bump had paged him earlier simply for an update, Lorenzo returned the call to Forensics first, not really expecting any great revelation from them—Brenda's handbag, the last time he had laid eyes on it, was mashed and frosted with mud. As it turned out, he couldn't even raise anyone at that office to answer the phone.

Karen Collucci's call came a few minutes later, as Lorenzo was dozing off in front of the bathroom mirror, once again trying to dress his head wound. Karen gave him a thorough report—the taped message to Cody, the maps, the scent bag, and the dog. Regarding her gut take on Brenda, Karen was noncommittal, but she seemed to feel that it was imperative that the mother join them in the next day's grid search of the defunct Chase Institute and its abandoned campus grounds. Lorenzo asked her if she felt like they had any real chance of coming across Cody Martin tomorrow, and Karen responded to the question with a long, pointed silence. Then she said that, if all they were searching for was a body, they could just send out the damn dog. Lorenzo asked her for a few hours to think about it. Rapidly approaching the end of his tenure here as catching detective, he wanted at least one more crack at Brenda Martin himself.

Without any solid notion of a game plan, Lorenzo trudged up the stairs to Brenda's apartment. A stench akin to cooked diapers emanated from the ground-floor apartment, climbing along with him.

Jesse came to the door, Brenda's phone snug against her jawline. She was dumping to her editor and greeted him with a perfunctory nod.

Brenda sat on the couch. Her face was red from crying, and with her headphones on, she wasn't aware that he had come into her home.

"Brenda Martin's small apartment is broiling tonight . . . There are no air conditioners, no fans . . . and yet the windows remain shut . . . forthe cooler night air would be accompanied . . . by the cries and the entreaties of the crowd beneath her windows—no—the crowd below."

Jesse was full of shit. Someone, probably her brother, Lorenzo guessed, had come up with four fans and placed one in each corner of the living room. The air was still soupy in here, but at least it was circulating.

"Yet despite this suffocating heat . . . the Friends of Kent, four women and a man . . . sat in this room for over an hour . . . wearing the red satin baseball jackets—bomber jackets . . . that bear the logo of their organization."

Lorenzo took a dinette chair and brought it alongside Brenda on the couch. He could hear "Take Me to the River" coming through her phones, the beat pulsating around her head. He studied her, angling for a sign on how to proceed. His pager went off: Forensics playing phone tag.

"Their leader, Karen Collucci—two *L*'s, two *C*'s—has the fierce, unblinking eyes of a fanatic . . . but her cause is righteous."

He mimed slipping off the headphones, but Brenda was living behind her eyes, living inside her music.

"What's wrong with—you should see this. OK, zealot. How about zealot?" Jesse offered.

Lorenzo reached out to touch Brenda's knee, bring her into the world, but truly lost for an angle of approach he opted to step off. He rose from the dinette chair and retreated to the shadowed doorway, where, in order to buy some time, he again reached out to Forensics, this time successfully. The conversation lasted less than ten minutes, Lorenzo saying next to nothing, just listening, punctuating his silence with head bobs. When he hung up, he scrawled the name MAGDA BELLO on the cover of his notebook. The pen skittered in his fingers as if he had just received one of Chatterjee's asthma chasers. Considering himself armed now, motivated, though still without a plan, he finally called back Bump Rosen to get him started on finding Magda Bello and, more immediately, to simply ask his advice.

Bump's offering was pithy and sweet: "You genuinely feel for her, boss. Use it."

Lorenzo returned to the dinette chair, Brenda still off in the music, swaying in a rapture of avoidance. "I'm Your Puppet" was coming through the phones now, and all at once it occurred to him—the proper setting for their next encounter. He touched her knee and she levitated.

"Hold on," Jesse said to her editor. "I'll call you back."

"Brenda." Lorenzo leaned forward in the chair. "My boss says to me the FBI's gonna come in tomorrow on this. We kind of held them off because we thought we could do it just knockin' on doors." He paused to read her face: no real fear there, just exhaustion and misery. "But I'm startin' to think we need the, the expertise."

Brenda stared at him, then, as if seized up, abruptly bared her teeth. "He's killing me," she said, slowly tossing her head from side to side.

"Who's killing you," Lorenzo asked calmly, pretty sure he knew who she meant. But when she failed to respond, he refrained from pursuing it.

"Brenda, you getting any sleep?"

She looked at her lap. He turned to Jesse behind him. "She gettin' any sleep?"

Jesse stepped back toward the kitchen, raised her chin for him to follow. "I'm making some coffee, Brenda," she declared in a too-loud voice.

Lorenzo came into the small cooking space, unavoidably crowding her. "What's up."

"They had this cadaver dog?" Jesse put on water, let the tap run to cover conversation.

"Uh-huh."

"Guy says, 'Body,' the dog makes a beeline for under the dining table, starts rubbing its cheek on the carpet, you know, with its ass up in the air? Just rubbing, rubbing, acting all agitated like—" Jesse made a high-pitched whimpering sound.

"Huh." Lorenzo knew all this from his conversation with Karen, knew also that the dog's frantic reaction was inconclusive. The problem with these cross-trained animals, Lorenzo had been informed, was that sometimes you gave them the wrong trigger word. The trainer would be looking for a corpse, saying "Body," and the dog would discover drugs or a gun, then look back at the trainer, antsy and whining, as if to say, "Can we discuss this?"—wanting the "Seek" command instead.

Obviously there had been no corpse under the table, but Sherlock, a four-word all-star, could have picked up residual body fluids—blood, vomit, piss, or shit—or zeroed in on heroin, marijuana, cocaine. It was hard to say without taking a carpet sample, but there was definitely something of interest ground or spilled or rubbed into that fabric.

"Anything else?" Lorenzo blinked away sweat, the kitchen greasy and close.

"She's a bitch, that Karen Collucci."

"She's a zealot." Lorenzo smiled. "Anything else?"

"Yeah." Jesse shifted her weight and gestured to a milk glass on the side of the sink. It was half full of some kind of pale-green effervescent liquid, a ring of cakey sediment marking the waterline.

Lorenzo leaned over the glass and the raw, caustic fumes snapped his head back. "Whoa."

"What do you think?" Jesse paradiddled her nails on the stove.

Lorenzo looked through the cutout to Brenda, who was curled into her music on the couch. He took the glass and emptied it into the sink. Quietly rummaging around in her cutlery drawers, he came upon a box of Ziploc bags and dropped the glass into one.

"She talk about killing herself?"

"Nope, uh-uh."

Lorenzo grunted and slipped the glass into his jacket pocket.

"So what's up on your end?" Jesse yawned into her fist, a spasm of fatigue making her body shudder involuntarily.

"Nothing," Lorenzo lied. The kettle whistled and Jesse turned it off, not interested in coffee. "I want to take her for a ride," he said.

"A ride?" Jesse echoed, getting a little knotty.

"Yeah, and she might or might not be coming back," he added, answering the next question in advance.

"Can I ask where you're going?"

"Nope."

"We still got a contract, right?"

"Get some sleep," Lorenzo said, backing out of the kitchen. "Sleep near that phone there."

As Lorenzo rolled down late-night Jessup Avenue, Brenda softly sang to herself in the shotgun seat, Chuck Jackson's "Any Day Now." Her right temple was pressed to the passenger window, the headphone wires hanging jagged and kinked to the Discman in her lap. Lorenzo smiled nervously as he worked his way down the finger of land that was the city of Gannon, heading toward Gannon Bay. As he turned off Jessup onto F. X. Kiely Avenue, four blocks from the water, Brenda suddenly came to life, sitting up and slipping off her headphones. "Where are you taking me?"

"I'm taking you someplace peaceful," Lorenzo said, parking in front of a chain-link fence that was foaming with weeds and brush. "You need some serenity."

"Are you taking me to my son?" she asked, her voice hollow and stiff.

Lorenzo got out of the car, walked around to her side. "I wish I could, Brenda," he said, opening her door. "I truly wish I could." The gate was unlocked, so that Lorenzo had only to raise the hinged clasp. He offered Brenda his hand.

"Why are you taking me here." Brenda took a step back, her face chalky in the moonlight.

"Brenda," he said softly, holding the gate ajar with his foot.

"What's in there." She took another step back.

"History," he answered, carefully taking her by the hand.

Inside the gate, Lorenzo walked her along a quarter-mile curve of shattered macadam jutting out into the bay. A thin crescent of derelict pavement, it was flanked on one side by water the color of steel and, on the other, as far back as anyone could see, by abandoned acreage upon which—in no discernible pattern of plantings—humped, erratic man-made shapes cloaked in moonlit vegetation, rose from the ground like the overgrown ruins of some lost jungle civilization.

"You know about this place?" Lorenzo walked clumsily, dragging his heels in order to keep pace with her dazed, halting step.

"No," she said, looking out over the water, the black, lapping bay.

"It was called Freedomtown. It was like an American-history theme park—had all these rides and activities around American history, you know, like the Civil War, riverboats, old Model A Fords, like a Wild West street, a blacksmith shop. You sure you don't know this place?"

"I don't know. I heard of it."

"Yeah, OK. Well, they opened this up in like 1962, because a year or so before, over in New York? They had a place called Freedom*land*. And that was big-time. It was two hundred acres and it was in the exact shape of America, and everybody went to that. I remember, they had this jingle? For like a whole year, anytime I turned on the radio, the TV, I heard that jingle, some kid singing to his parents to take him to Freedomland.

"Anyways, it was real popular, so these guys over here? I think they were called the Hartoonian brothers, they said, Let's do it, so this was like only ten acres, but they figured all the people around Gannon, Jersey City, Bayonne, Dempsy, they might want to go to a place closer, so . . ."

They walked past the overgrown hummocks, Lorenzo speculating to himself about what lay at the heart of each one—a short-snouted Civil War mortar emplacement, an abandoned paddle wheel, the rotted hull of a Jean Laffite pirate ship, an overturned ticket booth, or maybe a pile of floorboards from a nineteenth-century beer garden—all of them transformed from cheap historical facsimiles to objects with archaeological validity of their own now, at rest under blankets of green.

One pile had a jagged wooden shingle thrust into its side, like the shaft of a shovel, the word *Information* still legible in ornate nineteenth-century-style lettering. Brenda kept her eyes toward the water and raised the volume on her Discman, which she carried like a plate or an offering across her two bandaged palms.

"See, the original Freedomland? Over in New York? That went belly-up after a few years because the '64 World's Fair opened out in Queens and took away all their business, and this joint here didn't last too much longer either. I think the brothers shut this down in like 1967 or something. The Hartoonians, they just disappeared, just walked away and left this like a carcass. People took all the stuff, it was like a free-for-all, everybody walking off with carousel horses, antique cars, pirate stuff, butter churns, cowboy hats, you name it. Me and my friends? I remember we took out a bar mirror they had in, like, this Tombstone saloon. We got it out, walked all the way back to Armstrong, gonna give it to my moms for Mother's Day? I dropped it in the hallway outside our apartment." Lorenzo hissed in disgust.

Brenda crooned the lyrics to "What's Your Name," a ballad Lorenzo hadn't heard, or thought about, in decades.

"Anyways," he forged on, his feet killing him from walking at her tippytoe pace. "The city? They came in here and just up and seized it for unpaid taxes, and, you know, over the years they were gonna make it into a park, sell it to private developers, make it a marina, condos, but, like, here you are."

Lorenzo couldn't tell if she was listening. He took her by the elbow, steering her onto a second walkway, deeper into the ruins, her back now to the water. She dug in, freeing her arm from his grip.

"What are you doing?" she wailed. "Please just say what you *want*."

"I just want to show you something," he said gently.

"Show me *what*."

Twenty yards off that second path, they stopped before a thirty-foot-high grayish plywood facade of a nineteenth-century urban boarding-house. It stood in the nighttime weeds like the forlorn, derelict screen of an abandoned drive-in theater. The front door, the cornices, pediments, lintels, flower boxes, and other detailing were simply painted on, and the windows, three stories high, three across, were rectangular cutouts without glass. But in one of the third-floor windows stood a wooden woman in turn-of-the-century dress, her torso and throat lazily ensnared by vines, her arms thrust high in a V, her eyebrows arched in terror, her mouth a pink-rimmed black hole, as if she had been frozen in the midst of screaming for help, the green creepers a host of snakes pulling her down into hell.

"This here is the Chicago Fire," Lorenzo said affectionately, noting how Brenda seemed transfixed by the moonlit dummy on the top floor. "See all these windows? There used to be gas jets behind the wall that would send out flames, you know, like turning on a burner? And you'd hear, like, a fire alarm go out over the whole park, and this old-time hand pumper would come out with these guys dressed like firemen. And one guy would have a megaphone, start yellin' for all the kids to come help. Kids came runnin', and, you know, they'd shoot water up to the windows, and about ten, fifteen minutes later? They'd turn off the gas, and it would be like the kids had put out the fire."

Lorenzo looked at the windows, trying to remember the crackle and smoke. The belching flames had been replaced by that conquering green, all nine windows spewing forth creepers, tendrils, and arms to heaven, a thick-stemmed, treelike weed whose uptipped double-leafed foliage seemed to mimic the gesture of the mannequin on the top floor.

Lorenzo followed Brenda's gaze upward, noticing now that the woman's left hand was gone and that the head and torso were chipped and riddled with bullet holes. "That's Timi Yuro." He muscled down a nervous yawn. "I don't know why, but we always called that lady Timi Yuro, even when we were kids."

Brenda, seemingly transfixed by the mannequin, appeared to be on the verge of saying something but finally looked off without comment.

Taking her by the elbow again, Lorenzo escorted her farther on, until they came to a low, moss-covered concrete ledge, a border of some kind. They sat there overlooking a ruptured, grass-veined field of cement, maybe a hundred feet square. At the far end of this seasick floor were the ruins of a hooded bandshell and the remains of a stage.

"See, now *this* is what I call American history. This isn't no re-creation like the rest. This is where history itself, was *made*."

"What history."

"My history." He waited until she turned to him. "See, when they opened up here? They had music, live music, and the people would dance out here on the floor, right? And the first year they had whatever was left of the big bands, or, or polka bands, or jumpin' jive, or whatever they called it—you know, stuff for your parents. But then later, when this place started to get in trouble? The Hartoonians aimed, like, a little younger, and they hooked up with Motown, started having Saturday-afternoon concerts with Motown singers, because back in those days? Like the early sixties? Motown wasn't real established yet, and they were probably sending their people out for next to nothing, you know, just to get the exposure. So, like, here comes the Miracles, the Four Tops, the Marvelettes, Marvin Gaye, and that was *fly*, except that what happened was, you start bookin' those kind of entertainers? Your amusement park is gonna start changing color on you. You're gonna start drawing a good deal of the public-housing kids from over in Dempsy, over in Darktown, see what I'm saying?

"Now, they closed this place up anyways, even though I personally don't feel they had to, financially, because they really started to pack the people in with the Motown shows. See, my theory was the city itself made them close down, you know, the councilmen, the retailers, the chamber of commerce, because they just didn't want all these D-Town niggers in here bustin' up the chifforobe."

Brenda lay back on the grass and, as if pulling the night up around her like a blanket, curled up on her side, facing away from him. But her eyes remained open and her Discman off.

"Now, see, me, I was part of the problem back then. Me and my boys, we would come over from Armstrong every Saturday afternoon and start kickin' it with, damn . . . Little Stevie Wonder, you know, 'Finger-tips' Stevie Wonder? The Contours, the Supremes—it was really something else. Man, I remember when Little Stevie Wonder came on? I was standing so close to the stage I could've just reached out and tied his shoelaces together, and, hey, we were no angels. We'd get in fights all the time, *all* the time, and, like, we'd get chased by some of the local white boys, you know, the Irish, the Italian, the Polish, but let me tell you, we'd *do* some of the chasing too. I mean, that was definitely a two-way street. But I got to say, the good memories here way outweigh the bad, *way* outweigh." Lorenzo nodded to himself, then turned to her. She was lying there moon-curled, a sack of pain.

"Brenda." He touched her shoulder. "You want to hear the best thing that ever happened to me out here? The, the highlight of my teenage years?" He waited. She seemed to shrivel before his tired eyes. "Brenda . . ." He touched her elbow.

"Don't stop," she said, her words muffled. Lorenzo was confused by that command, until she added, "Talk more."

"Yeah." Lorenzo rolled his head, hearing popping sounds and sliding gristle from the nape of his neck. "My greatest . . . I was here one Saturday with these three friends from Armstrong? And Mary, *Wells* was up on that stage, you remember her? 'The One Who Really Loves You,' 'You Beat Me to the Punch,' 'Two Lovers' . . . Yeah, well anyways, we were way up front by that stage there and she was, beautiful. To me, she was, oh man . . . And I was up there in front, like, not even hearin' her, just *look*in' . . . And she sees me, she's smilin', singin', I go off in a daydream, you know, like when you're kind of drivin' on a highway you just, like, go off? And next thing I know, somebody's pullin' on my wrist. And at first I thought someone was messin' with me. I wasn't all there, but I look up, and it's her . . . Mary. And she's pullin' on me, trying to get me up on the goddamn stage and I'm, like, Oh my God. She *gets* me up on the god-damn stage, me and my fourteen-year-old ass, and like, I'm dreamin' this, I'm *dreamin'* this. And she has me do a duet with her on 'Two Lovers,' you remember that?" Lorenzo, smiling at her back, sang haltingly, 'I got two lovers and I ain't ashamed . . .'

"I can't remember the rest, but, see, both lovers were the same guy split into two, kind and loving, and the other person, when he was treating her bad, messin' around on her, like, a split personality. But, you know, I swear, the older I get the more I think that song is about everybody, you know what I'm saying? How . . . I mean we're all two people. Damn, some people I can think of are at *least* two people. I think my wife she's, like, *seven* people, different one for each day of the week." Smiling, eyeing her—nothing.

He had no real idea what he was doing telling her all this out here in the midnight ruins of his teenaged heart, but he felt it was important to keep talking, to keep offering himself up. At some point it would be her turn.

"Anyways, I'm up there singing, and I got a voice back then? Fourteen years old, sound like someone's strangling a goose. I mean, people were falling down laughing, but I didn't care 'cause it was just a dream. And at the end of the song she kissed me. *Kissed* me. And I guess she meant to kiss me on the cheek, but she got me in the ear. You ever get kissed in the ear? It's loud, feels like someone stuck a bomb in your head, and it's got suction, a kiss like that. Feels like a toilet plunger or something, pull your eye right out through the ear hole."

Lorenzo paused, smiling. He had never used that one before, "feels like a toilet plunger." Everybody was always telling him he could have been a stand-up comic, but he liked the idea more of being a stand-up motivator, a stand-up interrogator.

"But, Brenda, as she did it? She put a hand on my neck, you know to draw me closer? And, I swear to God, what's this, like thirty-odd years later? I can still feel *exactly* where each of her five cool, cool fingers lay on me. And I can still smell her *hair spray,* her perfume . . . God almighty, that had to be the greatest day of my life. The greatest day of my *life!*" Lorenzo nodded, staring off at the stage, the nocturnal bandshell, the creeping green taking possession there, too, converting it into the world's largest planter.

The story, despite the number of the times he had told it, still had a powerfully sweet pull on him, especially here, in this place, and he was momentarily adrift, so much so that when he came back he was surprised to see Brenda sitting up again, tear-blind. Cry me a river, Lorenzo thought, marveling, moved, having never encountered a human being capable of shedding such an unrelenting stream of tears, day after day. But that's the thing, he thought, all she does is cry, Lorenzo praying, Please don't let me lose patience here.

"I have so much love in me," Brenda sobbed, shivering with the strain of her words. "So much love, you just can't know."

"Well, no," Lorenzo said. "You're wrong, 'cause I do know. And that's why I brought you here."

"Why . . ."

He tapped her Discman with a fingernail. "Gets you through the fire, don't it." She wiped away the tears, using the bandage as a sponge. "I hear what you listen to, Brenda, and I see how you live your life. I mean, who would *ever* work in the Armstrong Houses if they had any other option. Me," he said, touching his chest. "You. Why? Because we have the *love* to do it. We have the commitment. But me, I'm homegrown." He shrugged, clasped his hands across his belly. "You? Whoa, white girl from Gannon? And now your heart's breakin', your own family won't step up. Shunned in your hour of, of tribulation. So what do you do, where do you go." He nodded to the Discman. "You go to the music. You go to the music, and you go to the kids, talking about Kenya Taylor like she had been your own child, talking about Reginald Hackett, talking about *all* the kids in that shithole of a projects . . . *Much* love. *Much* love." Lorenzo paused, watching her rocking, a gentle bobbing back and forth now.

"The irony, the irony of it is, I can't think of one outsider—white, brown, black—who would be more, *pained* about what that projects is going through with this thing than you."

"I had no idea," she said brokenly. "I swear to God." The rocking became more pronounced, her hand pressed against her forehead.

"Let me ask you." Lorenzo kicked it into second gear. "George Howard, you know him from the Study Club?"

"Yeah."

"It wasn't George that jacked you, was it? I mean, you'd've recognized him if it was, right?"

"Sure. No. It wasn't him."

"Yeah, well, they got him all locked up."

"*Why.*" She bolted upright, the flush of her cheeks visible in the moonlight.

Lorenzo shrugged. "I guess he looked like the description you gave."

"Oh God *no.*"

"Busted him up bad too. I mean, it was half his own fault—boy should know how to dance by now—but—"

"It wasn't him, I swear."

"Yeah, I think they most likely know that by now, but things are kind of spinning out of people's hands. It's crazy mad over there. Bad, real bad. TV all over the place, people getting hotter and hotter, cops going off."

"Well, maybe this is good in a way," she said, not looking at him. Lorenzo waited. "You know, with the TV, people are kind of getting an audience for all their grievances finally. It's like sometimes things have to get worse before they get better."

Lorenzo kept his mouth shut, watching her close her eyes, shake her head, reject her own desperate construction.

"Anyways, given the music that's getting you through this? I thought you could draw some strength from this place." Lorenzo extended a hand toward the buckled field. "You know, the people who've performed here. It's kind of like, sacred ground for me, you know what I'm saying? And I kind of wanted to share this with you, you know, being who you are."

"It's not even mine," she muttered dejectedly, rocking again, her forehead on her knees.

"What isn't."

"The music."

"Naw, you can't think like that, Brenda," he said easily. "Music belongs to whoever needs it."

She shrugged off his generosity. They sat without words for a moment, the trees hissing softly above their heads.

"What's this." Lorenzo took the glass from her kitchen out of its Ziploc bag and held it up for her perusal. She stared blankly. "What's this," he said again, passing it under her nose, watching her rear back from the residual fumes. "What . . ." She wouldn't answer. "You weren't thinking of doing anything stupid, were you?"

"No," she said, her voice tiny and hoarse.

"You sure?" She didn't answer. "Please, Brenda." And then he forced himself to add, "When Cody comes back, he's gonna need you more than ever."

"No." She dragged the word out, crushing her eyes, rocking, almost spinning, Lorenzo's instincts telling him, Go, just go.

"You know that therapy group you told me about? You spent a lot of time looking back over your childhood, finding out how your parents messed you up, right?" No answer, Brenda undulating, rotating from the hips up. "Now I'm sure you know that most people in the world subscribe to the notion that, there comes a time in your life where you have to stop looking back at what was *done* to you all the time, you have to stop blaming your parents, your childhood, or whatnot, and you have to start taking responsibility for your own actions. And that's, like, the definition of manhood, or, or, womanhood. And this is not necessarily an unintelligent point of view, you know what I'm saying?" He could tell she wasn't listening yet. "My wife said that there was an article about me in the newspaper today. They picked up that my son is in the joint."

Brenda squinted at him. "What?"

"My youngest, Jason, he's in the state wing of County doing three to five for armed robbery. Used my gun too. Now, my friends, they all say to me, 'Yo, Lorenzo, that boy is his own independent self. Whatever he did to land where he landed, he's got to accept the mantle of responsibility. He din't have no pacifier in his mouth last ten years that *I* saw.' And I say, 'I know, I know.' But between you and me? It *is* my fault. I blame myself, because I wasn't there for him, I wasn't around to show him how to be, or, you know, I *did* show him how to be, which was"—he counted off on his fingers—"irresponsible, *high* most of the time, selfish, no self-control, out of the picture on a day-to-day basis, fighting with his moms when I *was* around.

"See, you ask anybody, I have this reputation of being like a father figure around this city, Dempsy. You know, help all the kids, do antidrug work, put on picnics in the summer, make sure everybody stays in school. People always asking me, people who didn't *know* me back in the day, sayin' to me, 'Lorenzo, of all the fathers in this city, how come *your* boy of all . . .'

"And I got like this stock response. You know, I say something like, 'Well, I was so busy being everybody else's daddy I forgot to be a father to my own blood sons.' It sounds good, but it's a lie. Back then I just didn't care, and now Jason's in jail and all I can do is be there for him, but it's kind of late in the game. He'll most likely be in and out of jail for the rest of his life. Funny thing is, *him* I get along with. It's his brother, straight-A student, never in trouble, teaches junior high math down in Camden . . . It's Reggie that won't talk to me, that cut me off dead . . . You know why?" Lorenzo intended to answer his own question, then realized that he didn't really know why.

"Man, I remember one night when Reggie was about eight, Jayce about six . . . I had walked out of the house about a year earlier and I was working in Secaucus for UPS, drunk more often than not. I get this call—Reggie's in the hospital, got appendicitis—so I go over to Dempsy Medical Center, and I'm chewing gum, you know, thinking that's gonna *fool* everybody. I go up and he's out of surgery a few hours, laying there, he's got his moms on one side of the bed holding his right hand, and his moms's boyfriend, Mark, this guy Mark Bosket, on the left, holding his other hand. This guy's like, looking all concerned, but it's for real. I see he's holding Reggie's hand, and his thumb is, like, rubbing the boy's knuckles—like how you kind of, unconciously touch someone to comfort him? Mark was for *real,* and I felt so bad, I felt so angry and bad that

I just turned on my heel, marched right out the room. So, like, I'm in the hallway now, and there's little Jason with his grandmother, my mother-in-law, and Jason sees me and, he like . . . *reaches* for me . . . just a little." Lorenzo stopped, his throat tight.

"Oh," Brenda whispered.

"Just a little gesture, but I was so mad that this other guy was holding Reggie's hand that I just blew past Jason, down the hallway, out the building. And now, I think back . . . Reggie, he was covered. His moms is there, Mark is there. He's covered. But Jason—his big brother's had surgery, his moms is behind the door in there, everybody all freakin' out—little Jason, he was *scared*. He needed me right then."

"Oh."

"He needed me, and I just . . ." Lorenzo looked off, blinking rapidly, gritting his teeth. "But let me tell you something," he plowed on. "With kids? No matter what you did, how badly you messed up, God will find some way of letting you get up to bat again. Might not be with that same child, but . . .

"Now, like I told you, these days people think of me out there like some kind of socially responsible Santa Claus or some damn thing. Big Daddy, that's what they call me. Even the hard-core young bloods call me that, you know, some of the jugglers. Hell, I know guys in the *joint* still call me that from when they was little, because I embrace all kids, I try to help 'em all. And I love both my sons now, one in jail, one not talking to me? I love them with more love, now that they're kind of out of reach, than I ever did when I could've picked them both up at the same time and held them in my arms all day long."

Lorenzo heard his voice starting to go flutey on him again and he quickly turned away, thinking, You just got *all* of it, thinking, You *owe* me.

"You see, Brenda, God's grace? It's like, retroactive. And every little kid out there is Jason for me, and every little kid out there is Reggie. See, we can always make amends, as long as we're honest, as long as we look in the mirror and say truly what we see. I *failed* him, I *hurt* him. I wasn't *there* for him. I didn't mean to, but I came up *short*. I admit it—I came up short. Right then and there you get your second wind, like God's breath right in your face, and as long as there's blood pumping in your veins there's a way to make it right, there's a way to make it *more* than right, because you did the hardest thing in the world, you looked in that mirror and you gave what you saw its rightful name. Hardest thing in the world. Took me years and years to do it, but I got more love in me now than I *ever* thought possible." Lorenzo looked at her full on. "Do you hear what I'm saying?"

She looked straight across the buckled dance floor to the shattered bandshell, gleaming in the moonlight like a crèche of bones, some of the adorning vine leaves fluttering in a sudden gust coming off the bay. Brenda's eyes were blurred stars, her lips forming half words, the beginnings of thoughts. Lorenzo watched her, waiting, waiting until he got the sense that she had floated off like an untethered balloon, sailing up and out of his grip in this sudden buffet of wind.

He tracked her gaze. She was looking beyond the bandshell to the upper windows of the Chicago Fire tenement facade, suddenly visible now through the wind-wafted upper branches of the trees. From where they were sitting, the mannequin in the third-story window seemed to sway with the foliage that alternately revealed and obscured her.

"Brenda, I got that . . . I got your handbag back from the forensics lab today?" She looked at him, attentive. "They couldn't really get any kind of prints off it. Not even yours. It was pretty smashed up."

"Huh."

"But they did find something, unusual about it." Lorenzo dug in, making her ask.

"What," she said, the word sounding like "Huh."

"Well, there's this hidden compartment, like this zippered . . . Well, you know what I'm talking about."

"What." Breathless.

"I don't know how we missed this, and I don't know who to blame, myself or Crime Scenes . . . I mean, it was right there."

"What."

Lorenzo took a breath. "Who's . . ." He looked at the name scrawled on the cover of his notebook. "Who's Magda Bello?"

"What," she said yet again, ignoring the question, demanding the punch line.

"You know anybody named Magda Bello? See, because they found a Social Security card and a driver's license for her in that zippered compartment."

"What are you saying . . ." She cocked her head, eyes fever-bright. Lorenzo kept silent. "What are you saying . . ." she asked again, this time a small catch in the back of her throat, a chirrup of tears.

"I'm just wondering how that could be."

"That's my bag," she said, sounding both hysterical and numb. "It's *mine*."

"Yeah, OK, well then, just tell me how those IDs got in there," he persisted, asking her almost tenderly.

"I don't know. How should *I* know."

She began to look around her immediate area with jerky intensity, as if she had just lost an earring, looking everywhere but at him.

"Brenda . . ." He laid a light hand on her arm. "This is kind of like our last, *quiet* talk . . . Do you understand what I'm saying to you?"

"I didn't do it," she said so flatly that at first Lorenzo thought he had misheard her.

"What?" he asked, then, "I never said you did." Then, with the sound of his own heartbeat drumming in his ears, he added, almost as an afterthought, "Didn't do what?"

18

A young boy, hands at his sides, stood on his head in a corner of Cody Martin's bedroom. Staring at him from under the covers of the lower bunk, Jesse was unable to move, too frightened by the child's unblinking upside-down eyes—doll's eyes, devil's eyes. Wrenching herself awake with a moan, she attempted both to seize the vision before it evaporated and to pry herself free of its exquisite grip. It was 5:00 A.M., the apartment so still she could hear it breathing.

The night before, when Lorenzo took Brenda out at around eleven o'clock, Jesse had quickly scanned over her first dispatch on Brenda, published in that evening's *Register*. Not a word of the Jose-filtered account stuck in her mind.

She had then prowled through the rooms, closets, and cabinets of the apartment like a thief, her major find a child's composition book in which Cody's name had been scripted, in precise columns, on seven continuous pages. The eighth page was torn out, the ninth blank but bearing the impression from the missing sheet of another word, not quite legible, that word, too, scripted in neat, obsessive rows.

Also in those exclusive hours, having finished pondering the notebook, Jesse had gotten down on all fours like the cadaver dog and sniffed that spot under the small dining table, absorbing a slight chemical pungency, some cleaning solution, a rug shampoo or deodorizer, any other scent beneath that too fine for her to pick up. As she crawled around the living room, she discovered that no other area of the carpet had quite that same synthetic tang.

At around midnight, with Lorenzo and Brenda still out, Danny Martin had called. Jesse had listened to his voice coming over Brenda's Friends of Kent answering machine, teary and raw: "Brenda, I'm going fucking crazy. Please talk to me. Please, Brenda, I love you. I'm sorry for whatever. Please let me help you. Please."

When Lorenzo had finally returned Brenda to the apartment a little before one, neither of them had looked at or spoken to Jesse—Lorenzo sullen and mute, immediately doing an about-face and leaving; Brenda, dazed and tottering, her eyes registering the tension of someone poised at the lip of a cliff. Within minutes of her return, Brenda dropped facedown on the pulled-out couch and plummeted into sleep.

At five o'clock, the bedroom had gathered enough light for Jesse to scratch out her nightmare vision of an inverted Cody, then review her postmidnight notes: "Boy's name written like a mantra. Other Name??? Ask. Danny on tape Please Please Please."

As the early hour attempted to reclaim her, Jesse's chicken scratch beginning to blur, she became aware of a soft hissing from the living room—whispered words, both intimate and fierce.

"I got more love in me now than I *ever* thought possible . . . *ever* thought possible."

Rolling out of bed, Jesse eased her way across the room. Standing in the doorway, she peered into the living room to see Brenda sitting cross-legged on the sheeted couch, rocking, gesturing, addressing the chalky darkness.

". . . *ever* thought possible. I got more love in me now . . ."

Jesse backstepped to the bunks, reached for her notebook, but then decided it would keep until true daylight.

By eight o'clock, even with the shades drawn, the sunlight powered its way into the living room like a brass band.

"Anything else going on out there?" Jesse half whispered into the phone. She sat perched on the arm of the opened convertible, Brenda staring at the far wall, laid out alongside her under multiple blankets.

"In the world or with this," Jose said, yawning.

"With this." Jesse dropped a hand into Brenda's hair, fingers sifting through the tangled crop to stroke the damp scalp underneath. Her stomach lurched as she came upon the crusted bump at the top of Brenda's head.

"Well." Jose yawned again. "Some cop got tuned up in Strongarm last night."

"Who."

"Chuck Rosen? Works the houses?"

"Bump? The guy they call Bump?"

"I believe so."

"Yeah? Is he OK?" Jesse held back her connection to Bump and his son.

"He'll live."

"Who's the actor?"

"Don't know."

"They catch the guy?"

"Guys, and nope."

"Shit. Why him?"

"It's the big *pay*back. Gotta git re*venge*."

"But why him?"

"Why ask why? Hey, I'm writing a book, *When Good Things Happen to Bad People*. What do you think?"

"What else."

"Well, *you* made the papers."

"Which." Her stomach hovered.

"Jersey Journal, New York Post."

"Why."

"You, the cop, Rolonda Watts, preferential treatment."

"What else." She couldn't pin down what she was asking for right now, the thing that was causing her to panic.

"What else? What else you looking for?"

"Read it to me."

"Don't have it. It's just sour grapes, forget about it. You going out with her on the search?"

"They're picking us up at nine."

"Don't lose her."

Jesse heard the clatter and snap of Brenda's Discman revving up. "Gotta go."

Twenty minutes later, after helping her get dressed, Jesse escorted Brenda down the gloomy stairs. Five sport-jacketed men carrying metallic suitcases passed them in the vestibule on their way up.

Brenda dug in by the mailboxes. "Are they here for me?"

Jesse, recalling the dull, molten look in Lorenzo's eyes when he returned Brenda to her apartment last night, knew that they were. "Don't worry about it," she said, thinking, Phase 2: The Search Warrant. She was sure that by the end of the day, there would be a press leak regarding the difficulty officials were having confirming Brenda's version of events.

Turning up the volume of her Discman for her, Jesse looped an arm through the crook of Brenda's elbow and walked her out into the sun. The press was barking blood from behind a police barricade, all questions and commentary melding into a vaguely hostile tumult of words. The day was blinding. Jesse raised a shading hand to her brow and was promptly whacked in the gut with a folded *Jersey Journal* flung newsboy-style, someone in the mob drawling, "Read all about it."

Without relinquishing her grip on Brenda's elbow, Jesse stooped to retrieve the paper, then scoured the crowd, not for the assailant but for their ride out of here. She spotted Louis, Karen's husband, sidestepping through the press, the sunlight bouncing off his brilliantined hair, turning it fluid and sparkling.

They rode in the back of the Friends of Kent van, the German shepherd in the shotgun seat. The dog stared at them crinkled-eyed, his tongue hanging out of his panting mouth, quivering and wet, like a dying fish. Already exhausted by the day, Brenda sat hunched over, burying herself in the music. Big Maybelle's "Candy" came through the phones loud enough for Louis to look back at them through his rearview mirror, his expression somewhere between suspicious and intrigued.

Ignoring both of them, Jesse pored over the *Journal,* looking to name her dread, skimming articles about the arrest of Curious George Howard, the liberation march in Armstrong, the prosecutor giving another press conference, Bump getting pounded. Jesse lingered over that one, stalling on the word "hospitalized," searching for the specific injuries. Then her eye caught the header she was really looking for, REPORTER-DETECTIVE LINK QUESTIONED, and she anxiously speed-read the graphs, the tone of the piece an objective whine. Coming to the end of it, she felt almost embarrassed, having feared that her childlessness would be newsworthy. Paranoia, in her experience, was almost always grandiose.

"Is the, is Lorenzo going to be there?" Brenda asked Jesse.

"I think he's busy doing other stuff on this today."

Brenda nodded.

"Hey, Brenda?" Jesse eased into it. "I saw you had this notebook

lying out last night. You know, with Cody's name in it? Was there another name in there? I couldn't—"

"It wasn't lying out," she said, low-keyed but sharp.

"I'm sorry, I was just, I just came across it, but was there another,
you know . . ."

Brenda let a half mile roll past before speaking again. "There's three
parts to your life," she announced quietly. "Before you have a child, after
you have a child . . . and when you have a child no more."

When Louis pulled into the parking lot of Saint Agnes Church, Jesse took
in what appeared to be a massive combination yard sale, bake sale, and
voter registration drive. From her vantage point in the rear of the parked
van, she began scrawling a quick inventory of what she saw—perhaps
two hundred people, hemmed in by card tables laden with coffee, pastries, Gatorade, pyramids of insect repellent, and stacks of cellophane-
wrapped white paper jumpsuits. There were two registration tables
manned by elderly women, the sign-in sheets bordered by piles of Cody-
feeding-the-goat buttons. A third table was covered with first aid
supplies—salt tablets, disinfectants, and various-sized gauze wrappings
and bandages.

"I think I'd like Lorenzo to be here," Brenda said gingerly. "His
name's Lorenzo, right?"

"Yeah, well, like I said, I believe he's doing his thing today," Jesse
said.

"Doing his thing," Brenda repeated with faint bitterness.

Louis sat patiently in the driver's seat, the three of them waiting for
Karen to come out of a hand-holding prayer circle with the other women
who had come to Brenda's house last night. This solemn ceremony was
taking place now in a far corner of the lot.

Jesse eyed a gray-haired woman in jeans standing to the side of the
medical supplies table, who seemed to be taking medical histories and
occasional blood pressure readings.

There were priests and Portosans, satellite trucks and shooters. A
soundman tripped and knocked over a cardboard barrel stuffed with
headless broomsticks, and Jesse was startled when Ben materialized out
of the crowd to right the merchandise. The barrel bore a gummed label:
GOD BLESS CODY MARTIN—TRUE VALUE HARDWARE.

"Do you believe in heaven and hell?" Brenda asked calmly.

"Me?" Jesse asked. "Why?"

"Jews don't believe in heaven and hell, right?"

"To tell you the truth? I have no idea. Why?" Brenda shrugged, closed her eyes.

From behind the lightly tinted window of the van, Jesse recognized herself in the other print reporters, every one of them looking slagged out, with faces the color of pancake batter, pants hanging wrinkled and shapeless over their shoes, as if they had been slept in. Clutching notebooks and Styrofoam cups of coffee, crullers, bananas, and muffins, they staggered around stuffing their faces with whatever was on the tables, eating and drinking as if by reflex—for strength, out of boredom.

"There just can't be nothing," Brenda said. "But how do you know . . ."

Jesse eyed three men tricked out in military camo, sporting sunglasses, rakish berets, and sheathed machetes. Another group of men, middle-aged, in jeans and sneakers, pored over Xeroxed maps, each man carrying a fat roll of neon-orange hazard tape. And then there were the kids, maybe two dozen, at least half of them blatantly handicapped. Some had the shuffling, tentative walk and sunken cheekbones that proclaimed Down's syndrome; others were in wheelchairs, palsied, curled into themselves; still others had something unnameable in the eye, the gait, the manner. Jesse looked away, frightened by them.

"He's doing his thing," Brenda muttered to herself. "Poppa's got a brand-new bag."

"Wait here. Let me get Karen." Louis left them in the van with the air conditioning running, the dog snuffling, settling into his paws in front of the vents.

Jesse tracked Louis through the crowd to where the prayer circle had just broken up, the women simultaneously stepping back from one another, eyes opening, chins rising. Louis touched the small of his wife's back, whispered in her ear. Jesse instantly sought out her brother by the broomsticks, watching him observe these small, unthinking intimacies, the look on his face both pained and fascinated. When she turned her eye back to Karen, the woman was already halfway across the lot, striding toward the van, smiling at and touching, kissing nearly everyone in her path.

"I'm such a coward," Brenda said quickly, breathlessly. "I always knew that about myself."

Karen rolled back the side panel and put a foot up on the inner step, an elbow across her knee. "How you doin' today, Brenda?" she asked, with the proprietary heartiness of a nurse just coming on duty. "Hey, Jesse, glad you could come," she added, cheery and dismissive, not interested in a response.

Brenda nodded without looking up from her lap. Karen studied her efforts to act as if she were alone, then reached across Jesse to turn off the Discman.

"Let me look at you." Brenda slowly raised her eyes, her entire frame jerking with fear of this woman. "OK." Karen looked down for a moment to organize her rap. "This is what's happening. I called for a press conference. I want you to issue a statement, an appeal, over there." She pointed to a corner of the rear wall of the church, where a copse of standing microphones was already set up. "OK? I want you to tell everybody how much you miss your son."

"That's obvious," Brenda sputtered.

Karen ignored the impotent protest. "You can address the kidnapper."

"He wasn't kidnapped."

"What do you mean?" Karen asked lightly, and then waited out a full minute of stubborn silence.

"He wasn't"—Brenda glared at the seat back in front of her—"he wasn't . . . The guy just took the car, he didn't—"

"OK. So talk to him. Talk to that guy."

Brenda looked at the carpet between her feet. "No." She sounded more dejected than defiant.

"Yes." Karen leaned closer to her, eyes wide with determination. Another silence held reign, Jesse unable to look at either of them. "I am trying to *help* you," Karen finally said with level forcefulness.

"Is, is Lorenzo here?" Brenda asked, addressing the carpet.

"No," Karen said.

"Can you get him here?"

"Why?" Karen looked off for a blink, scratched her nose. "Why, Brenda?"

"He knows me," she said, in a small yet willful voice.

"Do you want to be alone with him?" Karen asked. Jesse knew that she was really asking if Brenda was ready to give it up.

"No, I don't need to be alone with him," Brenda said. "But I won't leave this van unless I know he's coming."

Making a small show of controlling her impatience, Karen stepped away from the van, borrowed a cell phone from Louis, and at least acted out calling Lorenzo. Left alone for a few minutes, Jesse and Brenda avoided each other's eyes. Then Karen returned to her roost on the interior step of the open side panel.

"He's on his way."

Brenda expelled all the air from her frame, her shoulders seeming to drop into her ribs. "What can I say," she muttered almost inaudibly. Jesse didn't know if it was a question or a comment. Karen didn't seem to have that problem.

"To the people here?" she asked. "You can say what's in your heart. You feel like crying? *Cry.* Cry your eyes out. Make *them* cry. Make everybody out there cry. Make them believe you. If you make people believe you, they'll go all the way for you. They'll do anything you want, OK? Of course you miss him. Of course you want him back. Of course you love him. *Say* it. I don't care how obvious you think it is. People need to hear you *say* it."

Karen extended her hand past Jesse's face toward Brenda. Trapped, trembling, Brenda stood in a crouch to leave the van with her.

Dropping to the ground, Jesse was smacked again by the heat, wet and heavy. Momentarily dazed, she staggered backwards into the side of the van.

All activity in the parking lot came to a halt when Brenda appeared. Aware of the eyes, she seemed unable to move, stood rooted to the asphalt, hunched over as if she were still in the act of exiting the van, her eyes bugged and blind.

Then the shooters came running, though Louis, Ben, and a few of the women fended them off. Jesse heard her brother use his private-security voice—"Fellas, what was the deal here?"—a chiding, gently threatening tone that she hated. But when she caught his eye and threw him what was supposed to be a withering look, Ben, not interested in playing today, simply shrugged it off, leaving Jesse feeling helpless and abandoned.

Brenda's headphones began drawing some scowls—people confused, put off—and both Jesse and Karen reached for them at the same time. The press was assembled in a packed wedge facing the microphones, behind which now waited Marie, the intensely tan older woman from the night before, with an assemblage of children ranging in age from roughly four to twelve.

"What's with the kids?" Jesse asked Karen, that light-headed sensation growing stronger.

"They need to see children. I want them to see children," Karen answered, eyes on Brenda.

Two of the children on display were the ones with Down's syndrome; they stood bookended by two black six-year-olds, twin girls with buttery skin and clear eyes. Jesse wondered if they were Karen and Louis's daughters.

"What the hell can I possibly say?" Brenda beseeched Karen in a broken whisper.

"I told you. You say what's in your *heart*," Karen hissed back. "And *look* at them. You look right at them, otherwise they'll think you're hiding something and it'll come back to haunt you like you don't believe. *Go.*" Karen fairly shoved her forward, toward Marie, who opened her arms to gather her in, the choreography making Jesse think of trapeze artists.

While Brenda stood with her back to the crowd, Marie gently cupping her face, whispering to her eyes, Jesse found herself taking in all the handicapped kids at closer range, the lolling heads, the sunken pupils, the leg braces, the Velcro straps, the involuntary utterances. She felt both repelled and tender, heartbroken: the Friends of Kent knew their game. Weakened by all this pathos, she turned to say something conciliatory to Karen but was distracted by a young boy. He was amber-skinned with deep brown eyes and a soft, high corolla of kinky brown hair, a sober-looking kid, sitting in a wheelchair between her and Karen, studying her from under almost comically furrowed brows. Never knowing how to connect with kids in any natural way, Jesse nonetheless found herself smiling, even found herself thinking, Hey, I'm smiling, but then her eyes strayed to the boy's right hand—a boneless corkscrew of flesh curled into itself, no fingers, no nails, no articulation of any kind, a pigtail at the end of a wrist—and she vomited, dropped into a squat and vomited between her shoes. She stayed down there, eyes smarting.

People danced away from Jesse's mess, but the wheelchair stayed put, Jesse on eye level with the boy's legs, which were encased in some kind of hard plastic braces. When she finally stood up, ashamed, unable to look at the boy again, his dark, penetrating eyes, she wiped her mouth and turned to Karen.

"Oh God, I'm so sorry. I haven't been eating, I haven't—" She cut it short, cut the shit. "I'm sorry."

Karen regarded her with heavy-lidded stoniness. Jesse turned away, ready to move off, around to the other side of the crowd, but still seeing, behind her eyes, that solemn-faced boy with his mud-brown eyes, his tawny complexion. It was Karen's boy, Louis's boy, Jesse realized numbly; she was sure of it. She turned again to Karen—to confirm, to somehow find the words to apologize more deeply and personally. Before she could open her mouth, though, Karen simply gestured for her to turn back to the mikes, the show about to begin, and Jesse was more than willing to comply.

With Marie kneading her shoulders from behind, Brenda faced the crowd. Despite Karen's warning, her eyes were trained on the ground. Working her dry lips to no effect, blinking furiously, she clutched a microphone stand, her exhalations rasping out over the lot. Squinting in the heat, people waited patiently for Brenda's words, the air, Jesse sensed, reasonably free of judgment.

"I . . ." Brenda whispered, her body rippling under the accumulation of stares, "I'm . . ." Then, in a declarative burst: "I am nothing."

The crowd held back, poised for more.

"I am nothing." The statement was more fluid this time, more ardent, no hint of a second clause. "I am nothing."

To Jesse's eyes, it was as if the flesh obeyed the word, Brenda seeming to physically fade on the spot, her grayish atoms drifting free of one another into the sweltering air. A weighted silence fell over the lot, a moment of absorption punctuated by the swish of passing tires and the tinny report of an all-news radio station from inside the church.

When it settled over the volunteers that what had just been delivered to them was Brenda's message in its entirety, a scattered croon broke out, a soft moaning of "No" mingled with cries of support—"We're with you, Brenda," "It's not your fault, Brenda," "Don't think like that, Brenda"—these kindly, somewhat bewildered outbursts overlapping a current of murmurous exchanges between some of the searchers, whose faces and words registered confusion and distress. But not one comment within Jesse's earshot denoted anything but sympathy.

"Brenda, why are we looking where we're looking today?" one of the reporters shouted, but she had vacated her physical shell, and the lack of response provoked the pack to take off in a verbal free-for-all, the questions piling up unanswered at her feet.

Karen signaled for Marie to get Brenda out of there, the gesture, the flat of the hand sliding across the throat, straight out of show biz. As Brenda was escorted back to the van, Karen strode forward and commandeered the mikes.

"OK, this is great, this is great," she crowed, looking out over the crowd, the crouched, scuttling shooters. "Thank you. Thank you for coming."

With Brenda out of the spotlight, Jesse took in the volunteers, a real summertime mix, kids to seniors, Rambos to Sansabelts. Glancing back toward the van, Jesse saw Brenda being helped inside by Marie, semi-lifted up the side panel step like an invalid.

"OK, before I start"—Karen's voice turned Jesse back around—"does anybody have any second thoughts about going out today," she said, searching the assembled faces. "It's hotter than hell, and with what I'm going to make you wear once we get where we're going? You're gonna be hotter still. Anyone who wants to take a raincheck? Now's the time. It's no shame to back out. Your heart's in the right place but I would hate for it to stop ticking." There was a ripple of anxious laughter, the people antsy to just do it, get it on.

"I don't want casualties over there, and I don't want to have to hold up the search to bring someone out, OK? Someone who should've known better in the first place, OK?" She scanned the lot. "*Any*body." Karen continued to search the faces of the crowd, as did the women of her inner circle, who stood together behind her, leaning into the rear wall of the church, half of them smoking, two or three with a lazy, protective hand dropped down over the shoulders of their own kids. Teenie's girl was in a wheelchair too.

Jesse looked back to the van and saw Brenda in silhouette, slipping on her headphones.

"*Any*body," Karen repeated, and it became clear to Jesse that she wasn't going to proceed until she had flushed out at least one potential casualty. Finally, three people simultaneously began working their way toward the rear of the parking lot, an elderly couple and an obese teenage girl, who blushed furiously.

"Just give your names to the sign-in table," Karen called out, standing on tiptoe, as if they were already miles away, "and thank you for being honest with yourselves. Anybody else . . ."

For the first time that morning, Jesse noticed Elaine, the Kenter with the port-wine stain, standing slightly apart from the others by the church wall. Once again, she fixed Jesse with that expressionless stare.

"Anybody else . . ."

Slowly pivoting to avoid Elaine's flat gaze, Jesse wound up facing Louis, who sat on the low wall that ran behind the row of tables, his legs spread wide to accommodate the width of his son's wheelchair, which was parked directly beneath him. Louis was scanning the crowd, too, but he wasn't looking for self-doubters. Retired or not, he still had cop's eyes and he was looking for the actor. Jesse knew enough about criminal pathology to know that if Cody Martin was abducted purposefully, there was an excellent chance that the actor was in this crowd right now.

"OK," Karen finally relented. "Moving on. Does everybody have a team designation?" She raised a gin hand's worth of various-colored Post-its. "Everybody hold up your cards."

The crowd responded, raising a rainbow field of paper squares. Ben, still by the barrel of broomsticks, held up a green one.

"OK, anybody not assigned? No? OK. Now. These fellas here?" Karen swung a hand behind her to introduce the ten middle-aged men who had been poring over maps earlier. Most of them were balding, bespectacled, potbellied—indistinguishable from the other older men in the parking lot. "These fellas are your team leaders. Some of these guys go back with us five years, OK? They're Vietnam vets, they're cops, they're firemen, they're hunters. They know what they're doing. They know how to track, they know how to read the ground. You listen to them, they'll teach you how to use your eyes in there, OK? Now, what are we looking for. The boy? Sure. But *anything.* Clothes. Tin cans. Cigarette butts. Any sign of human habitation. Any sign of human, disruption. I'll leave it to your team leaders to break it down for you once you get in your groups, but there are a few things I need to say to you while we're all together."

Jesse forced herself to look back across the lot to Karen's son, who was sitting on his mobile throne between his father's knees. The hand didn't look that bad now, just a little goof-up. Jesse was disgusted with herself.

"*One.*" Karen held up a finger, waited for silence. "Once you're out there? Stay, with your group. The group stays together. Always. Going into those woods? It's pretty, it's peaceful, it's dangerous. Stay, together."

Looking back to the van again, Jesse saw a ponytailed reporter in knee socks and Bermuda shorts rapping on the side panel, trying to get at Brenda, coming on like the big, bad wolf. Jesse turned to signal Ben, but he was no longer over by the barrels. When she turned back to the van, she saw him already eighty-sixing the reporter, chest-bumping him backwards, toddling from side to side as the guy heatedly pleaded his case.

"*Two.*" Karen raised her fingers in a peace sign. "It's high tick season right now, and Lyme disease is *no joke.* So you're going to be using insect repellent, you're gonna be stuffing your cuffs into your socks, and you're going to be wearing this . . ." She slipped a paper body suit out of its cellophane wrapper and flapped it out full-length, booties to hood, a thin, pulp-textured outfit with a white plastic, crotch-to-throat zipper and elasticized wrists.

"One size fits all. Anybody trying to lose weight? Well, honey, just walk around in one of these for a few days and you'll be ten pounds lighter in no time at all, believe me," Karen said, patting her own hips, "I know."

That provoked another eager laugh from the crowd, the inner circle joining in this time, everyone but Louis and Elaine. Despite her tedious attempts at humor, Karen's grin never reached her eyes.

Jesse looked back to the van and saw three more reporters sniffing around like bears at a Dumpster.

"OK, we're almost, *I'm* almost finished. If you find an article of clothing or something that looks like it shouldn't be where it is? Whatever. Don't, touch. It's potential evidence. Do not, *touch.* Half of the group will stay with it, the other half will go and get help.

"Tape." Karen held up a roll of the neon-orange plastic. "You search an area? *Tag* it. I don't want three teams of searchers looking over the same stretch of woods. Let us know you been there. Your team leader will show you how. Another thing, very important. Look, *up.* I want at least one member of each team to look up, at branches, treetops. It's natural to look down, but like we all have seen in the movies, the party you might be looking down for might be looking down at *you. Anything* could be hanging in those trees—clothes, tools . . . You see a tree branch on the ground? How'd it break? Who broke it? Look, *up.*

"Sticks." She now pointed to the three barrels of broom handles. "Everyone will be issued a stick. Use it. Poke around. Push things aside, test the give of the ground. Never use your hands when you can use the stick.

"And *heroes.* A word for all you heroes out there. Remember, a hero ain't nothing but a sandwich. Stay, together. If you don't have a good feeling about something you're about to do? Don't do it. You're a little leery about someplace you're about to go? Don't, go. I don't want heroes, and I don't want martyrs." The inner circle all nodded on this one. "We have had broken legs, broken ankles, dog bites, rat bites, stitches. We've come up on pot parties, liquor parties, crack parties, people getting high in what we thought were deserted buildings—you name it. *No, heroes.*

"And last but not least, where do we pee . . ." The crowd laughed, and Karen took the opportunity to fire up a smoke. "There's four Portosans right here, a bathroom inside the church, and two more Portosans out where we're headed. I would prefer for everybody to go do their business before we head out, because I don't want anybody lagging behind, trying to get a little privacy, and winding up losing their group, OK?

"And this is Chris Konicki." Karen pointed out the woman who had been giving blood pressure readings. "She's a terrific nurse, been with us three years, and she'll be setting up a first aid station right out on the edge of the main road. If you start to feel exhausted, weak, nauseous, dehydrated, sing out. Let your leader know, and we'll get you right out to Chris, OK? And oh, to the members of the press. Fellas? We know you got a job to do and we want you to do that job. We want the coverage."

Jesse looked off, thinking, Fellas, thinking, an old-fashioned kind of gal.

"But you go out with us? You wear your tick suit, you grab your stick, and you stay with your group. No going off and shooting the sunlight coming down through the treetops, OK? This is not *National Geographic. Stay* with your *group.* And while you're out there? You got two eyes in your head just like everybody else. You see something off-kilter? You see something we should be looking at? Don't be shy, sing out, OK?" Karen turned to her husband. "Lou?"

Louis slid off the wall and steered his son's wheelchair to the microphone stand. Detaching the mike itself, he hunkered down and held it in front of the boy's face.

"Dear Jesus," the kid began, in a high, childish register. The tone of his voice surprised Jesse, who was expecting something with more bass in it. "Bless everybody here, give them a good day, and help us bring . . ." He faltered, his father whispering in his ear. "Help us bring Cody Martin home."

From two high windows inside the church, red, white, and blue balloons were suddenly released by an unseen hand and sailed out over the parking lot, drawing a croon of pleasure from the volunteers.

One red balloon impaled itself on a branch and dropped to the asphalt with what Jesse thought was a little more speed than was natural. Walking over to it, she saw attached to the string a prayer card to Saint Jude, the patron saint of impossible causes. She surveyed the parking lot, watching the volunteers, Post-its aloft, as they struggled to get past one another and group up with their team leaders. The kids were now being rolled into various custom wide vans, presumably to be driven home. She watched her brother handing out broomsticks, his eyes glistening, mouth wide open in some kind of expectant gape as Karen leaned into him and whispered in his ear. And she looked at the Friends of Kent van, encircled by frustrated, half-crazed shooters and reporters as if it were some kind of mysterious, power-granting shrine, Brenda somewhere inside, unreachable, stuffing her head full of rhythm and blues.

Saint Jude. Jesse tried to envision him—supernatural, celestial, beneficent—but no matter how hard she tried to believe in him, to see him, she had about as much faith in his intervention here today as she did in ever getting to meet Cody Martin and bounce him on her knee.

There was a flurry of activity at the Friends of Kent van as the women of the inner circle, save for Elaine, still leaning against the church wall, gave the hovering reporters the verbal bum's rush, evicting them from the immediate vicinity before unlocking the side panel and yanking it open to engage Brenda. Jesse watched as the women stooped before the shadowed maw of the interior, gesturing, hunching their shoulders as they presumably attempted to coax Brenda into the daylight again. They took turns leaning forward, reaching inside the van, hanging there, then grudgingly straightening up, each of them taking a crack at it, all to no avail. Marie finally stepped away and waved to Karen across the lot to give a hand.

Cutting herself free of her conversation with Ben, Karen strode through the crowd toward the red van, Jesse wheeling as she passed and following in her wake. Over Marie's shoulder, Jesse saw Brenda curled up into the van seat farthest from the door, her face swollen and streaming as she tried to ignore the entreaties of the women to come out and join the group.

"*Brenda.*" Karen wielded her name like a whip.

"*No.*" It was a disembodied bray. "Not without Lorenzo."

"I told you. He's coming."

"He's not *here.*"

"He'll *be* here."

Marie turned from the van again, almost mowing down Jesse, touched Karen's arm, and brought her a few steps away.

"I don't think she can cut it," Marie said quietly.

"She's coming," Karen said, with no flex at all. Then, looking straight at Jesse, as if expecting resistance: "She is coming."

19

Lorenzo awoke that morning at eight-thirty, the latest he'd slept since he'd stopped drinking eight years earlier. He dimly recalled a confused dream about Bump, then realized it wasn't a dream. The phone had rung at two-thirty—Bobby McDonald calling to inform him that his partner had got his ass kicked, been gang-jumped while walking to his car on Hurley Street, the final score three broken ribs, a fractured eye socket, and no positive IDs.

Flinching, Lorenzo now recalled that he had meant to jump out of bed and make it to his partner's bedside at the medical center, but he had obviously laid back down at the end of the conversation for what was intended as a few more minutes of shut-eye. His failure to rally for Bump left him feeling vaguely ashamed, but then another foul flashback, his long one-on-one with Brenda over in Freedomtown, left him feeling flat-out disgusted.

Earlier in the previous day, when they had had their long, hot God-versus-therapy pep talk in the empty apartment overlooking the crime scene, Lorenzo had considered Brenda's inability to give it up as a failure on his part; he had failed to get her to the place where she needed to be mentally in order to say the words. But last night, over in Freedomtown, he had done everything but show her his ass, and as far as he was concerned, she was the one who had come up short.

His only misgiving, in retrospect, was his declaration that this would be their last "quiet talk"; he might as well have told her straight-out to get herself a lawyer who would instruct her to shut her yap. But no matter now. His time was over and he was done with it, ready to hand the investigation, and Brenda, over to the FBI, as agreed. Finally rolling out of bed, he called McDonald and threw in the towel. They set up a meeting for eleven o'clock with the FBI, and running out of the house with a prepped toothbrush in one hand and two powdered doughnuts in the other, he figured he had just enough time for a bedside visit with his partner before his debriefing.

Driving over to the medical center, Lorenzo realized that he had forgotten to bring his asthma spray. The midmorning air was already dense with some kind of superheated toxic crud, and he had to pull over to a drugstore to buy an over-the-counter inhaler, the harsh solution and propellant of which, he quickly discovered, made him feel like he was taking deep drags off a cigar. Twenty minutes after making his purchase and after perfunctorily glad-handing his way through the reception area, the elevator, and the fourth-floor nurses' station, Lorenzo walked into Bump's semiprivate room. The bed was blocked from his sight by three visiting patients and a nurse.

At any given time there were always a goodly number of Armstrong tenants checked into the medical center, and apparently, once the word had gone out about the beating, at least these three had decided to make a call. They stood around the bed in thin hospital-issue seersucker bathrobes and cardboard slippers—two relatively young women, who Lorenzo knew were battling AIDS-related illnesses, and an older, heavier woman who suffered from diabetes. The nurse, too, was Armstrong-bred, born, raised, and still living there, her parents having moved in the day the houses opened for business back in 1955.

"Damn!" Lorenzo announced himself, after putting on his happy face in the hallway. "This like some, some *block* party in here!"

The three women greeted him loudly but the sight of Bump's face made Lorenzo go deaf. Broken blood vessels had turned the whites of his eyes a vivid red, and there was a bulge, as if someone had slipped a large marble under the skin between the corner of his left eye socket and his left temple, the bulk of it so pronounced that it gave that side of his face an Asiatic slant. The unearthly tint of his eyes, matched by the brilliant natural orange of his beard, made him look like a Scottish demon.

"Damn, boy!" Lorenzo locked in his grin. "You look like *Damien* or something."

"Ask Big Daddy, Kath," Bump addressed the nurse with a little too much animation. "Lorenzo, I'm trying to pull her coat about Shuckie. True or false, he's gettin' that little gangster man walk, right?" He turned his head back to the nurse before Lorenzo could respond. "I'm serious, Kath, I think it's high time you laid on some of that Mommy stick with him."

"Well, I tell you," she said in a low murmur of concentration. "You see him out there messin' up? You do your job."

"Hey"—Bump waved a hand—"that goes without saying, Kath, but what *I'm* sayin' is that the bud's gotta be nipped in the bud. It's gotta be handled in-*house*, otherwise me and Lorenzo, alls we can do is, you know, snip it as it grows, but the shit's gonna pop right back up again, you know what I'm saying?"

"I hear you." The woman was calm, as if she understood that Bump was just yakking to drown out the terror, busting a nut to act like he was still out there working Hurley and Gompers, patrolling the towers. "And he's got your schedule down cold, Kath. Nobody could ever accuse him of being a dummy."

"I hear you," she said again.

"A knucklehead yes, but not a dummy."

Lorenzo could hear the panic that fueled Bump's chatter, intuiting that it wasn't the trauma of the beating itself that was driving him now— the damage probably looked a lot worse than it was—but the fear of the unknown: potentially a diminished capacity to do the job, physically, mentally, or even the possibility of losing the job altogether. For a cop like Bump that would be the spiritual equivalent of death, the utter annihilation of identity.

"Big Daddy." One of the younger women, Lorraine Powell, spoke his name in a hoarse drawl, standing there dying, holding an unlit cigarette. "You best catch these niggers."

"I'm on it," he said absently, entertaining a nightmare vision of Bump over the coming years locked into lawsuit after lawsuit with the city.

"We *all* gonna be on it," said the other young woman, Doris Tate, three kids and a college degree, also dying.

"Y'all got some friends around here, boss." Lorenzo beamed down at him, took another hit of that caustic spray.

"You got *that* right," the older woman, Betty Castle, said, bobbing her head. "Like, no offense to the police in general, but I can't see hauling my behind out of a hospital bed to come down an' visit too many of y'all, if you want to know the truth."

Bump took Betty's hand. He started crying, covering his demonic eyes with a forearm, the sudden movement making his IV bag sway on its stand.

"Hey, Bump." Doris Tate put a hand on his chest. "I'll make you a deal. I'll take your beating, you take my virus, what you say."

Bump laughed, or at least stopped crying. "Let me talk to my man here, OK, ladies?" The women trailed out and Lorenzo watched them leave, his face averted from Bump, giving his partner time to regain his composure.

"Your family come by yet?" Lorenzo finally turned. Bump nodded slightly, looking off. Lorenzo pulled the curtain. "You know who did it?"

"Yup," Bump nodded tightly. Lorenzo waited. "Brenda Martin." There were no tears anymore.

"Who?" He took another hit of spray.

"She's killing us, Lorenzo." Bump wiped his blood-drowned eyes. "Either you wrap this fucker up or you give it over to someone who can."

"Done," Lorenzo mumbled, hating the taste that word left in his mouth.

Two blocks from the medical center it dawned on Lorenzo that he could've gotten his regular prescription Ventolin inhaler from Chatterjee or from any number of doctors in there whom he had come to know from years of rapes and assaults. Looking at his watch, he saw that he had just enough time to turn around and make a quick Ventolin run, but before he could manage a full 360, his cell phone rang.

"Lorenzo?"

"Who's this." He straightened out and headed back to the hospital.

"This is Karen Collucci."

"Hey. You off on the hunt yet?"

"What are you doing right now?" she asked, ignoring his question.

"I got a meet with the FBI."

"Do me, do your*self* a favor. Pull over to the curb, and hear me out."

A few minutes later, the Crown Victoria was heading off in yet a third direction, this time toward the parking lot of Saint Agnes, where the search party was in its final moments of shaping up before hitting the wrecked, overgrown campus of the William Howard Chase Institute. On the way over, Lorenzo called Bobby McDonald again, told him that Brenda had just asked to talk to him—not exactly true—and secured for himself another temporary reprieve before surrendering the investigation.

Karen Collucci had told him that Brenda refused to go out on the search unless he was part of it, but the leader of the Kenters still wanted Lorenzo to keep his distance from Brenda after she had seen his face. He could understand Karen's strategy of separating, in Brenda's mind, the centurions from the housewives, but since she had gone and asked for him . . .

Whatever the logic, Lorenzo knew that the only reason he so readily agreed to become part of this torturous and lung-searing exercise over the next few hours was the quickening of his blood when Karen had uttered her name, Brenda. He still wanted, craved, just one more encounter, and he'd take it any way he could.

But the price would be high, Lorenzo knew, envisioning the William Howard Chase Institute on a day like today, anticipating the interminable slog through a swelter of crumbled outbuildings, knee-high grass, sinkholes, and wild bramble—the visceral wallop of expected mortifications making him reach for his spray again.

The Chase Institute was in shambles, nothing more than an urban ghost town—half wilderness, half living menace—but Lorenzo had heard on more than one occasion from a local history buff, a lieutenant in Narcotics, that at its inception the Chase Institute for the Mentally and Physically Incapacitated had been a world-class showcase. The lieutenant had shown him archival photos of the 1904 ribbon-cutting ceremony, in which a top-hatted fat cat in a wicker-backed wheelchair, William Howard Chase himself, offered to the world a trim, bucolic seventy-five-acre campus consisting of ten residential cottages for adults, two larger dormitories for children, two workshops, a rehabilitation-oriented gymnasium, a Universalist chapel, a dining hall, a five-acre truck farm, and a small theater. The buildings had been constructed of limestone, the lieutenant had said, the grounds surrounded by lush forest, the air scented by the sea, the faculty idealistic, and the trust fund flush.

In its first few decades, the institute became the standard by which all other rehabilitation facilities were judged, but the crash of 1929 wiped out the institute's trust fund overnight, and the state of New Jersey, faced with the dispersion of seven hundred incapacitated patients, stepped in and took title. This, the lieutenant had said, was where the place became fascinating from the criminologist's point of view. By the mid-1930s the Chase Institute was more commonly referred to as William Howard Disgrace, a surly and abusive little corner of hell, greatly overpopulated and understaffed, owned and operated more by the poorly paid attendants than by the administrators, in the same intimate way that prisons are owned by the guards.

It became a dumping ground—the new influx of patients mostly abandoned by guilt-ridden, financially strapped families—and with this class of patients, this new breed of staff, there followed decade after decade of deteriorating service, murderous abuse, and two-fisted thievery. The once-pristine greens were overrun with weed and brush, the broad, flower-trimmed pathways cracked and potholed, and the limestone on many of the buildings seized and split by the tenacious growth of creeper vine. Ground-maintenance equipment disappeared, was reordered, and disappeared again. In the infirmary, drugs were more pilfered than administered, the staff finally taking to ordering directly for themselves. In the dining room, meat, canned goods, boxed goods, and dairy products were routinely resold to local supermarkets and groceries. The workshops were routinely stripped of tools and machinery.

Anything that could be requisitioned from the state—window glass, bedsheets, athletic supplies, Bibles, wheelchairs, shoes, roofing tiles—disappeared once it was received. There was organized pimping of the younger patients, both male and female. There were unexplained pregnancies, disappearances, deaths. Mildly retarded children grew to severely retarded adults without ever leaving the grounds.

Four decades of systematic plunder and mayhem finally came to a dead halt in the summer of 1967, when a reporter from the *Dempsy Register* going undercover as a newly hired orderly vanished three days into his assignment. Within a week, the institute was flooded with state investigators, local police, and the press.

Chase became a dark star—this Lorenzo remembered on his own—yielding weeks of national media coverage. After six months of investigation by the state, the gates of William Howard Disgrace were finally padlocked. It took another two years to truly shut it down, two more years to successfully relocate all of the three thousand patients who had been imprisoned there, including two old men who had come to Chase as children during the First World War. Within months of the last relocation, the forest began closing in again, reclaiming the campus with supernatural speed. By the early 1970s, the William Howard Chase Institute for the Mentally and Physically Incapacitated looked like nothing more than an overgrown outpost of Magna Graecia, most of the cottages and outbuildings barely visible from one to the other, lush veins of green bursting through the crumbling cement of a fifty-year-old pool, three times Olympic size, that had never seen a drop of water. And after all the hearings, investigations, audits, and commissions launched in 1967 came to an end, the reports published, the players dispersed, there was not one successfully pursued criminal prosecution, nor was the reporter ever found, even though half the grounds of the institute had been backhoed into a moonscape. This, too, as the lieutenant would have put it, was fascinating from the criminologist's point of view.

As Lorenzo pulled up alongside the church, he saw that the parking lot was overflowing with volunteers, the primary vibrations coming off that teeming square those of hyped boredom and physical distress, the people more than ready to roll.

As he hauled himself out of the car, the heat hit him like a hangover. Scanning the scene, he spotted a gaggle of Kenters hovering by the open side panel of their red van. Lorenzo assumed that Brenda was holed up in there, an animal trapped in its own burrow. Searching for Karen, he found Jesse instead, staring at him with concern from across the hood of his car.

"You look like shit," she said.

Lorenzo shrugged, then coughed, his lungs feeling as if they had been scoured with steel wool, the sensation having less to do with the asthma than with the promiscuous overuse of that piece-of-shit inhaler. He stood spread-legged, sun-dazed, staring straight through Jesse and breathing open-mouthed like a beached fish, as if his nostrils were inadequate for the task.

"Hey." Karen abruptly materialized before him from out of the mob. "Glad you could come. You ever do this before?"

Lorenzo wiped the sweat from his eyes. "Found a body in a junk yard once."

"Yeah?" Karen squinted. "Were you in Vietnam?"

"I believe I was." He massaged his chest. "But if I was, I was too high to remember any of it."

"You too, huh?" Karen laughed, a guttery rumble that, despite his distress, kind of piqued his interest.

"Where she at?" Lorenzo started to move for the red van. "In there?"

Karen reached out. "Hold on," she said, snagging his elbow. "We'll go over, say hello, but then like I told you on the phone, I want you to hang back today, OK? You can stay with me." Although he understood her motives, Lorenzo shot her a look both quizzical and territorial. "Trust me on this," she said. "It's enough she knows you're here."

A moment later, peering into the cool dark of the van, he saw Brenda pretty much as he had imagined her, raccoon-eyed and taut, fending off the world and all its treacherous kindness. "Hey," he wheezed, stooping over, his palms pressed into his kneecaps.

"Are you going out?" Brenda asked in a hoarse rasp of her own.

"I will if you will." He grinned encouragingly, his lungs feeling both puffed and dented. Standing back up, he tottered sideways, the parking lot coming at him like a dream, Lorenzo thinking, And this stuff here is paved.

The broad center drive of the Chase Institute campus, which began on the other side of an unlocked mesh fence three blocks from the church, was flanked by low brush; beyond that lay thick woods and the crumbling limestone remains of abandoned cottages. The procession of volunteers and media people stretched in an undulating formation that lurched, pinched, and bulged like heated wax. Despite the humidity-drunk straggle of the line, the volunteers had been specifically assigned placement in the march, shaped up by platoon in the order of designated search areas. Every fifty yards, the front two groups would peel off, one to each side of the road, then hop into their tick suits, broom handles clattering and rolling away from them, as their team leaders gave last-minute lectures.

Karen's group, smaller than the others, consisting of Marie, Teenie, Brenda, Jesse, Lorenzo, and Elaine, was at the tail end of the parade. Lorenzo overheard so many roadside briefings as they trudged along that after a while he felt he could lead a search party on his own. Shooters and reporters assigned to groups farther ahead in the procession tended to furtively drag their feet until they found themselves abreast of Brenda, then took some quick footage or barked some hit-and-run questions before Karen chased them off.

Brenda herself was in Discman mode again, staggering forward, her face opalescent, bubbling with sweat, incapable in Lorenzo's estimation, of finding a lump of coal in a snowball right now. Sporadically, she would throw him a nervous glance, but Lorenzo abided by Karen's request and kept his distance, only once getting close enough to hear the music leaking out of her headphones, different from the usual, religious and grand.

"How long you think this will take," Lorenzo asked Karen, as they reached the simmering crest of a long, tortuous rise in the road.

"That depends on Brenda," Karen said.

"I'm just asking—" Lorenzo cut himself off to conserve his wind, willing himself to refrain from taking another hit of his spray.

"OK, guys." Karen steered them to the edge of the road. All the squads that had been ahead of them were gone now, having suited up and followed their leaders into the woods.

Lorenzo watched as Jesse eased the packaged paper suit from beneath Brenda's elbow, dropped to one knee before her, and flapped it full-length out of its machine-precise fold. "Raise up." She patted Brenda's calf, waiting to work one leg of the suit over a sneaker. "Hold on to my shoulder." As ponderous as a circus elephant, Brenda lifted her left foot, lost her balance, and fell backwards onto a ledge of bramble. Jesse twisted around and looked up at Karen. "She's in no shape for this."

"Why don't you let Elaine help her out." Karen nodded to the woman whom Lorenzo considered the eeriest Kenter, trim, humorless, gray-haired, but with a startlingly young face, all eyes and clenched jaw muscles. When he had been introduced to her the night before, she neither shook his hand nor looked him in the eye.

"Jesse, you go with Teenie and Marie," Karen said. Jesse seemed stricken by the suggestion but was gently hustled away by the mother-daughter team before she could register a word of protest, the smooth play evoking in Lorenzo the notion of slick bouncers, top-notch people handlers, their one-track sense of mission granting them a kind of psychological brawn.

"So you never did this before, huh?" Karen asked Lorenzo, as she knelt before him and worked the suit up over a size-thirteen construction boot.

"Hell, no. I'm a city boy, born and bred," he drawled, embarrassed by Karen's having to help him suit up. "You do your canvass last night?"

"Yup." Karen worked on his second bootie, Lorenzo almost tipping over, his asthma making him feel, as it often did, like his body was some kind of inflated cage.

"And?"

"Nothing."

Lorenzo grunted.

"You surprised?" she murmured.

"Well, I'll tell you." He reached down and worked the suit up his legs. "Come this afternoon? FBI's gonna come in and take over."

"The Seventh Cavalry, huh?" Karen worked on her own suit.

"I don't know about all that," he muttered, experiencing once again how truly loath he was to hand Brenda over, call it quits.

"You see those three idiots with the machetes?"

Karen pointed out a trio of tricked-out rangers, replete with maroon berets, hacking their way through the brush about fifty yards away. "We always get a few like that," she said, zipping herself into the suit, then pulling up the hood. "Rambo knives, berets, full camo. I promise you, they'll be the first to fold. We got retirees out in these woods that are gonna last twice as long as those clowns."

Zipping himself in, Lorenzo felt the heat treble, trapped and recirculating inside the paper, felt even his shins dripping, the factory smell of the pulpy-textured material like shredded cedar, adding a layer of suffocation all its own.

"Yeah, there you go." Karen pulled up his hood for him, tying the drawstring under his chin. "We have something like a thousand of these in my basement. Didn't pay a dime. These broomsticks? The Gatorade? The buttons, the coffee, the fruit, the pastry? We pay for them with certificates of appreciation. Everybody wants to go to heaven."

Twenty yards away, Elaine was working the elasticized wrists of the suit over Brenda's bandaged hands. Swaddled in white, Brenda looked like a *penitenté.* Several yards beyond them, he saw Jesse, eyes trained anxiously on Brenda and Elaine, being worked into a suit by Marie.

"You sure I got to wear this?" Lorenzo licked his heat-caked lips. "Because I'm feeling a little cloudy in the chest."

"If you don't," Karen said, producing an aerosol can, "you'll be sorry. Close your mouth and cover your eyes." She sprayed Lorenzo's face with insect repellent, then the backs of his hands, Lorenzo getting a taste on his lips, bitter and wrong. "Here you go," she said, handing him a broomstick. "Walk where I walk."

Lorenzo saw, sliding through a break in the brush behind Karen, Elaine leading Brenda by the hand, steering her around brambles and stumps. Elaine was wearing jeans and, despite the heat, a turtleneck.

"Where's *her* suit?" Lorenzo asked, pointing.

Karen turned. "Elaine?" She fanned away something with wings. "Elaine doesn't wear suits. She says they get in the way of her instincts."

"Jesus," Marie muttered, her team catching up to them, Jesse bringing up the rear. "Anything taking a bite out of Elaine'd go insane."

"We kind of give Elaine her head," Teenie added.

"Yeah?" Lorenzo gasped. "Why is that." He realized within a few steps that he needed the stick as much for support as for exploration.

"Because," Karen said, "Elaine's son was, was abducted."

Lorenzo was surprised that Karen, of all people, had trouble saying that word. Teenie and Marie peeled off again, began staking out their turf, Jesse reluctantly tagging after them.

"About four years ago, in Nutley?" Karen began, her eyes searching the forest beneath her feet. "It was like our second or third kid. We were pretty raw, but we gave it our all. We combed every goddamned forest, field, drainpipe, creek, bay, everywhere, and she was with us every minute. And, you know, we still post flyers, get, you know, computer-generated portraits with age enhancements posted around, but Elaine, we kind of adopted her. She comes to us, says, 'If I can't find mine, let me help find someone else's,' goes out on every search, never gets tired, and, you know, off the record? I think we're the only thing that keeps her from doing herself in. Broke up with her husband, I don't even think she has custody of the kids. Maybe she does now, I'm not—"

"Why'd you put her with Brenda?" he asked, inhaling something that flew into his mouth, his eyes instantly filling with tears as he tried to bring it back up.

"You OK?"

"Why?" he persisted, in a hoarse strangle.

"Why?" Karen shrugged. "Sympathy." Lorenzo hunched over and coughed out something small and black, the effort jacking his pulmonary distress up another notch. "Let me tell you something about searches like this," Karen said, her eyes still trained on the ground. "This place, Chase, it looks enormous, right? It's not that bad. When you got a road like the one we just came off of? We usually never look more than two, three hundred feet from that road, you know, on either side." She poked through a thick mat of last year's fallen leaves until she hit the unbroken top soil. "I mean, basically, you just get off the road and look for the first line of heavy cover. You know, brush, overgrowth, whatever . . ."

Lorenzo could hear a mosquito singing inside his hood, slapped himself upside the head, then hunched over again, clutching his knees, taking five. Karen waited for him.

"We figure, somebody's gonna transport the body, they use a car, need a road. Then they're gonna have to go in somewheres where they can have privacy for twenty, thirty minutes for the burial. But if it's more than three hundred feet from the car, they have to be Superman, so they're going to look for a spot not *too* far but far enough. So ninety percent of the time? We're talking two, three hundred feet from the road. On the other hand"—she hesitated, drew a breath—"today I think we'll go into it a little deeper than usual."

"You tell people they're looking for a body?" He peered up at her from his resting crouch.

"Hell no. I tell them we're looking for clothes, we're looking for signs of human habitation, we're looking for any kind of, of discordance in nature. You never tell people you're looking for a body. Never."

Lorenzo watched Elaine lead Brenda down a slight berm to a shallow, brackish stream, Elaine clearing it in one stretched stride. Brenda, staring straight ahead, stumbled, went down on one knee into the water, stood up, and staggered on, docile and blind, the leg of her suit streaming a muddy drool.

"Hey." Lorenzo touched Karen's arm, laughed his angry laugh. "You see that? What you doin' to her?" he said, trying to come off affable.

"We're helping find her child," she answered evenly. "Watch your step."

Jesse, Marie, and Teenie came crackling through some underbrush, emerging a few yards from Lorenzo and Karen, mother and daughter tight-lipped with concentration, eyes trained like beams as they poked and sorted through the ground before them. Jesse had eyes only for Brenda, Lorenzo recognizing in her anxious, possessive gaze his own agitated sense of being off balance out here in this world of surly nature and hidden agendas.

Through the trees, he could see other volunteers, dozens of them working their respective turfs—walking, prodding, cautiously forging ahead in silence, the baggy-hooded white tick suits evoking in Lorenzo's mind a B-movie impression of soldier-scientists tentatively advancing on a meteorite or a downed spaceship. Karen stopped by a cluster of tin cans, their labels obliterated by a uniform orange coat of rust. Using her stick to separate them, she rejected her find: too old.

Picking up the drone of a nonstop mutter, Lorenzo turned to see Elaine, several yards to the left, leading Brenda by the wrist now and maintaining some kind of monologue. Brenda trailed her with a floppy skip, trying not to fall again. A finger of sweat sluiced its way from the nape of Lorenzo's neck to the waist of his boxers, then ran horizontally along the damp band. He took a small hit of spray, which did nothing but set his already inflamed bronchial passages on fire.

"You want to know how to look?" Karen asked, eyeing a downed candelabra of branches, then squinting up at the tree from which it had broken off. "It's easy, it's like meditation. You do it enough, your brain can go off, have sex or something, your eyes'll go on automatic pilot. First thing, you look for contrast—dark, light, smooth, rough. You look for rich grass, deep green, greasy-looking, fertile-looking, in a place where all the other grass is pale and scrubby. You look for flowers where you shouldn't expect to see them. Like here . . ." Karen took Lorenzo by the elbow, brought him over to a clump of tiger lilies growing on a slant off the raised lip of a depression. "What the hell are these doing here?" Karen asked, frowning at their ruddy splay. "It's not the kid. He's not going to grow flowers after only a few days, but that's the idea, see?"

She began to move on, but suddenly she backtracked to the tiger lilies, a scowl on her face. "Well, something's making this grow." She tore off two feet of orange hazard tape and tied it to the nearest tree. "We'll just put a dog-ear on that, come back later."

"Whoo . . ." Lorenzo exhaled softly, a cry for help made ineffective by pride.

"And you look for heel marks." Karen said, continuing her lesson. "A body is heavy. The guy's gonna sink a little carrying it, even if it's a child, because you got to remember they've been carrying that kid all the way from the car, so they're gonna start getting a little lead in the legs."

"Huh," Lorenzo said, seeing Brenda through the dapple, the very thought of breaking her down right now, the stamina that would require, making him buckle at the knees.

"You look for reddish soil—that's subsoil—clay balls. Guy digs a grave, he's flipping the layers of soil. You see any color that's different from the surrounding earth? Could be, could be. That's how we found Kent. I saw the, the red, I saw the clay balls, I saw—" Karen cut herself off, made the sign of the cross so quickly Lorenzo almost didn't catch it.

"See, let me explain something. Most people, they say we're trying . . . they say, like, we're crackpots. They try to cubbyhole us, try to dismiss our, our, commitment."

"Huh," Lorenzo grunted, not really listening, just trying to breathe.

"They say we're bored housewives, we're compensating, we're trying to make our own lives a little more interesting to ourselves. Well, I will grant them this. Finding a lost child? *Alive* occasionally? It does kind of make your day."

Off to the left, Lorenzo saw Brenda flop on a stump, her head between her knees, Elaine standing over her, mouth still going. Lorenzo could faintly pick up the monotonal flow, as steady and driving as the heat.

"Bored," Karen said acidly. "You see Teenie over there? Her daughter, her girl, has got Down's syndrome, OK? Teenie's brothers? She's got two brothers. Bobby, he's a lawyer, and James, he's retarded, he still lives at home with Marie, his mom. Another woman, Grace? She's in the hospital right now, her kid's got CP. My son, Pete?" Karen shot a quick glance in Jesse's direction, her face tightening. "The point is, Kent? The first boy we found? He had Down's syndrome too. Are you hearing this, Lorenzo? Down's syndrome, cerebral palsy, retardation—don't you think that each and every one of us has our hands full at home? Don't you think each and every one of us wouldn't kill for some kind of vacation? Go out, get bombed, sleep late, have a sex life, for Christ's sakes . . . But with Kent, with our own kids, it's the helplessness that gets to you. Some bastard taking advantage of that helplessness. So we do it out of rage . . . And we do it out of love."

Lorenzo saw Brenda hauled to her feet, Elaine half carrying her now, using the broom handle as a staff, talking, talking . . .

"Here, see that?" Karen pointed to a depression that seemed to be filled with dead leaves. Using her pole, she started flipping them aside, then saw that the ground at the base was the same color and texture as its surroundings—a natural sinkhole.

A faint breeze wafted through the woods, cooling, then chilling the perspiration inside his suit. He began to sweat again, the combination of humidity and asthma so debilitating that the simple untidiness of nature—a dip in land, a felled, half-rotted tree—seemed to him an insurmountable obstruction.

"And here." Karen tapped a downed branch that lay suspended over the ground, each end resting on a rock. "Does that look natural to you?"

"No way," he said mindlessly.

"Looks like somebody balanced it there, right? You look around, you see any other branches like that? Maybe somebody's trying to establish a perimeter. Maybe it's a little telltale trap to let the guy know his hideout's been discovered. Guy comes back, sees the branch is off the rock—he knows it's time to move on out. See what I'm saying? So you look for any unnatural symmetry, any patterns. This one bastard, he'd lay out twigs in a row like fallen dominoes, go out and do his thing, come back, see if anybody broke the line. You got to look for that."

"I got you," Lorenzo said, then chanced a last hit of spray.

There was a commotion far off to the left, white suits scurrying like snowmen in hell. She took a hand radio from inside her suit. "What's up."

"We had a little bit of a personal meltdown out here, Karen," a male voice answered.

"OK." She signed off.

Through the trees they watched two snowmen transport a third in a fireman's carry, followed by a fourth snowman with a shoulder-mounted Betacam.

"See these here?" Karen pointed to a crater maybe twenty feet across that hosted weeds, ferns, and the ubiquitous arms to heaven. "You know what this is? This is from when they were digging around for that reporter thirty years ago. There's something like fifty holes like this around here. Christ, talk about not dying in vain. The guy should be canonized. They closed this place down? It was like closing down Auschwitz. Do you have any idea of the generations of children, generation after generation of children that suffered in there?" Karen thrust her pole like a sword in the direction of the hospital grounds, which were not yet visible.

"Thousands, *thousands*, that, that, *died*, that were abused, neglected, forgotten, that just, just, pined away." Karen paused to brush some spittle from the corner of her mouth. "We find toys up there sometimes—old rubber dolls, a picture book, wooden blocks, forty, fifty, sixty years old." Karen's jaw locked at a slant. "Anyways, these craters? We don't go in them. We leave them for you guys, because these suits are great for bugs but they don't do shit against copperheads."

They worked their way through the woods, Lorenzo trudging after her like a hunchback, his booties totally gone from tramping through brackish rivulets and dry, rocky soil. To their left, Brenda and Elaine plodded on, Elaine as taut and tuned now as she was before they had entered these woods, Brenda, like Lorenzo, careening from tree to tree. As far as reading the lay of the land, Lorenzo remained blind, but Karen tagged three possibles—two patches of deep green grass and a small cluster of cigarette butts—explaining to him that digging a grave does bring on a case of the nerves, and a pile like that in a contained space suggested the spoor of a chain-smoker out here in the middle of nowhere.

The first of the institute's ruined buildings were now visible about a football field's length ahead, the cottages mostly camouflaged by vegeta-

tion but the more imposing children's dormitories behind them rising
above the tree line, high monolithic fortresses, shadowed and square,
standing between the forest and the afternoon sun.

"Look, see that?" Karen pointed out a scatter of boxes covering a
sandy patch of the forest floor, maybe a hundred or more. "Marie,"
Karen called, Marie coming over again, trailing Teenie and Jesse. Karen
used her stick to flip the lid, revealing snug stacks of roofing tiles—
brick-red, wave-patterned adobe-style shingles. "This used to be the
pickup spot when the staff was selling stuff out of the institute."

"You should've seen what we found out here five years ago," Marie
said, her chin over Karen's shoulder. "It was like a flea market. They
must've run like hell when the investigators started showing up."

"Just left everything."

"Blenders, sneakers, aspirin, silverware, garden tools."

"You know who took it all?" Karen wiped her face.

"The cops?" Lorenzo said reflexively, hunched over again, bug-eyed,
biting at the air, telling himself to be still, very still. From his crouch,
looking up, he tracked Jesse's distraught gaze to Brenda, sitting on yet
another stump, hands on knees, Elaine leaning over her, rubbing her
back, talking, talking, talking, Brenda starting to rock.

"Why'd you say you put Elaine with Brenda again?" Lorenzo asked in
a high wheeze.

"Sympathy."

"Sympathy," he repeated, waiting.

"I never lost a child, Lorenzo. Did you?"

"Not really," he said quietly, thinking, Not exactly.

"Anyways, the cops?" Karen continued. "Most of them, they're
friendly to us and all, but basically they don't really like us because they
think we're all, like, adrenaline over procedure, you know? And *we* think
they're a bunch of lazy bastards. You know—they put out a poster, call it
a day. Or, you know, they'll like this one possible perp, so they go after
him and if that doesn't pan out they fade. So what we got to do is keep
their interest up, you know, because otherwise . . . You got to keep it hot,
you got to keep it in the news, you got to keep coming up with fresh
stuff—a slipper, a brother-in-law, a jawbone. I swear, half the shit we
come up with? We just make it up—new witnesses, new evidence—just
to get it back in the news. But you know, some of those guys, the detectives? We know some great ones. These guys, they're like you, Lorenzo."

"Oh yeah?" Not having heard a word, Lorenzo was striving for that one elusive gulp of air, the one that would only be acquired if he could just get his pectoral muscles to rise up a tiny bit more.

"These detectives, there's only a few, but they never give up, *never*."

He shaped his lips into a straw, just wanting a sip, settling for a sip. He had been told that, when his father died of an asthma attack, his last words, spoken to his wife, were, "This the one, baby."

"Doesn't that sound like you, Lorenzo?"

Vaguely aware that she was trying to hustle him in some way, he managed to cast a glance toward Brenda and Elaine, then back up at Karen. "You know something?" he gasped. "With this heat out here? Brenda. I don't think she's gonna make it . . ." Nodding in agreement with himself, he sank to his knees, then flopped facedown onto the forest floor.

20

Jesse stepped out of the woods and stood before Cottage 9, one derelict two-story crumble among a dozen similar buildings scattered throughout a three-acre bowl of brush and high weeds. The cottages were sunk into the junkyard foliage like pumpkins in a field. Karen, Marie, and Teenie stood silently a few feet away from her, and Jesse saw that other squads, too, were emerging from the tree line at various spots on the circumference, popping out in billowing white clusters to regroup tentatively in front of the other cottages. Their team leaders squinted in the bald heat, sizing up the structures that lay before them.

Looking around for Brenda, Jesse spotted her in the distance, being marched around the circumference of the cottage clearing by Elaine. Brenda was leading with her knees, propelling herself forward in a fatigued duck walk. Jesse had yet to exchange a single word with her since they had left the parking lot; as soon as the search had begun, Marie and Teenie had hustled her away from Brenda, and Jesse quickly came to understand that part of the mother-daughter team's assignment today was keeping her distracted. They were trying to accomplish this with a nonstop stream of talk—a history of the group; tips on how to read the ground, the only items of interest that stuck with Jesse through the barrage of words; tidbits of information about Elaine, Brenda's new best friend and the mother of an abducted child herself, half crazed with mission and therefore considered by the others as holy.

After that initial swoop and shuffle, whenever Jesse would attempt to rejoin Brenda or at least to make it a threesome, one Kenter or another would quickly step up and whisk her away. This much was clear to her now: Brenda was with Elaine, and Elaine only, by design; something was shaping up out here in the jungle well beyond the hunt for Cody Martin.

The closest Jesse had gotten to reestablishing contact was the moment Lorenzo collapsed, all four women rushing to his aid, leaving a stuporous Brenda standing there by herself. When Jesse made her move, Brenda snapped to, throwing her a hard stare that made Jesse hesitate, and by the time she regained her footing, Elaine was back in possession. Everyone looked on as Teenie fed Lorenzo a few puffs of her own asthma inhaler, wondering aloud why the big dope didn't just say he was having trouble breathing from the beginning. Not only Teenie but Marie had packed prescription inhalers, to say nothing of the inhalers and even pure oxygen available at Chris Konicki's first aid station, which was only a few hundred yards away, out on the main road.

Cottage 9 was fronted by the remains of a gray wood porch, the painted-on number itself close to obliteration, fading into the weather-grooved handrail. The building was sand-colored, doorless, flanked by shatter-toothed window frames, yawning maws that even in the searing whiteness of the day revealed nothing of what was to be found inside.

Marie, stepping around an encrusted metal lawn chair that lay on its side in the high weeds, approached the house, Teenie and Karen almost simultaneously stepping back as if to give her elbow room. She put a hand on the porch rail but didn't step up on the weathered boards, just stood there motionless, the others waiting in silence until she finally turned to them.

"Forget it. We're not going in."

"Why not?" Jesse asked.

"Something doesn't feel right." Marie picked her way back to the group.

"What."

"I don't know, it just doesn't."

"If my mom says we don't go in, we don't go in," Teenie said.

"What . . . Why?"

"She just knows." Karen plucked a tick off Jesse's sleeve.

"There's something in there, but . . ." Marie pinched and fluttered the front of her paper suit. "Get Louis to do the dog."

Karen hauled out her hand radio again.

"Lou, where you at."

"What's up." Louis' voice came through static, distant and minute.

"We're at Cottage 9. Marie's got the willies."

"We did it this morning. Nothing there but rats. Don't go in."

"How about Cottage 8."

"Nothing. Just do the grounds."

"OK." Karen signed off, then gestured to Jesse. "Come here."

Taking Jesse by the hand she brought her to the edge of the porch. "Just . . ." Karen stood with her in silence. After a few seconds of acclimation, Jesse could hear the scuttling.

"He was in here?"

"The dog was," Karen said.

"So the place was searched already?"

"Oh yeah, Louis did the whole field this morning like six, seven o'clock. Him and a few of the guys."

"And?"

Karen shrugged.

"So you *know* the kid's not here."

"As far as the dog knows. There he is. You see him?" Karen pointed out Louis in the distance, the dog about twenty-five feet ahead of him. Louis was stepping high to clear the brush, the dog charging ahead. When it veered too far to the left or right, Louis whistled and the dog stopped, looking back. With an exaggerated sweeping gesture of his arm, Louis reined the dog in, keeping it moving in a straight line.

"So the kid's not here," Jesse said, watching Brenda on her walkabout—a medieval mortification, Elaine's heated words in her ear.

"Probably not," Karen said. "But you never know."

"You never know what?"

"Well, it's like this. We found a kid buried here . . . Christina Howell. When was it?" she said, turning to Marie.

"Four years July."

"Behind Cottage 6. The guy who did it? He used to be an orderly back in the late sixties here, before they shut the place down. Guy's out of a job, got no place to go, so he just moved into the woods, set up house. Guy had a whole elaborate system of twigs around his campsite that told him if anybody was nosing around.

"But so anyway, he got ahold of this kid Christina—she lived about two miles from here—*did* her, you know, killed her, buried her. We found her—well, the dog found her. Anyways, he's in Dannamora now for that, but we're pretty sure he did some other kids out here, missing kids we know about. They're buried around here somewheres—four, five kids, he won't say. Guy's name is Alex Rockwell, Alex . . . I write him every month, say, 'Look, you're not getting out of that place ever, no matter what, so square it with God. Where'd you bury the other kids. Their souls can't go to the Father unless we can give them a proper burial. C'mon, Alex, let them go home.' He never writes back but we know they're here. He had a few campsites, hideouts, in the woods around? The cops found dolls buried vertically, headfirst, about a dozen of them, which is exactly how he buried that kid Christina—straight down, headfirst. So what I'm saying is, a search like this? There's things to be found, Jesse. Maybe not what you think you're looking for, but . . . Hey, we never give up our kids. Plus, they're still looking for that reporter, right? So you never know."

Brenda was approaching that part of the perimeter closest to where they were all standing now, and Jesse was determined to hook up as they came around the horn. But before she could make her move there was a shriek from the forest: "I found him! I found him!" Someone else screeched: "His bones! Oh Jesus! His bones! His bones!" Then a babble rose from behind the trees, a few people breaking off from their groups in the cottage clearings. Some white-suited shooters hurdled the high weeds, their Betacams mounted like bazookas. "Jesus, Joseph, Mary, Mother of God his bones! His bones!" The hysteria was rising.

Taking her cue from her group, Jesse stood her ground, glancing anxiously from Karen and Marie to the frenzy in the woods.

"Bones," Karen said, then reached for her radio.

"This is Karen. What's up."

"Karen, this is Phil Caruso. We got bones here."

"OK."

"Stand the hell *back*," Caruso barked at his people. "Karen? Give me a second." A woman could be heard sobbing, "Oh my God, oh my God," through a blizzard of static. "Karen, give me a second."

"Take two." Karen looked off, shading her eyes from the sun, Marie and Teenie standing there quiet, waiting.

"Yeah, Karen?" Caruso was back on the radio.

"Go."

"Did the kid have hooves?"

"That's what I thought. Get everybody back with their group, OK?"

"Got it."

"I'm going over to see Brenda," Jesse announced.

"OK," Karen said. "We'll all go."

Leading the pack toward Brenda and Elaine, Jesse almost wished that Karen would try to stop her, but neither Karen nor anyone else made that move.

"Hey." Reaching out, Jesse laid a hand on Brenda's arm. Brenda threw her another of those icy glares, then moved on, Elaine holding her upright, holding her snug, an arm across the small of her back, fingers pressed into the far side of her rib cage. Jesse doggedly remained one step behind, observing Brenda, who was so physically gone that her head bobbed and lolled as if her neck was broken. Steering Brenda off their circular track, Elaine now led her toward the looming remains of the children's dormitories, Jesse at their heels, Teenie, Marie, and Karen bringing up the rear.

"The thing of it is, Brenda . . ." Elaine spoke in a low, forceful mutter that Jesse was close enough to overhear. "The thing of it is, I know who did it. I know who took him. Karen knows, the cops know. He doesn't know I know. I mean, he knows that he was a suspect, but he thinks he's in the clear, and I swear to you, if I live to be a hundred and one years old, I'll always be watching him. I'll always have my eyes and ears open. This guy, every time he leaves his house there's a chance he's going to visit my son's body. They *all* do. They bury in a place that's familiar to them and that's easy for them to get to, because they like to visit the grave, make sure everything's OK. See, *he* can visit the grave, that sick, evil bastard, but not me."

Caught up in Elaine's quiet rant, Jesse momentarily lost touch with the visual, and when she returned to the physical world, still a few feet behind the lead pair, it seemed to her that Brenda was floating along, her shoulders moving evenly despite the lolling of her head. And then she saw the veins standing taut and fat on the back of Elaine's hand, saw the rigidity in the arm that snaked around Brenda's back, and she realized that Elaine was literally carrying Brenda, the woman strong enough to power both herself and her charge through tangle and brush, the blinding sun irrelevant, the thickets no more than vapor and drift.

"Now this bastard, Brenda," Elaine plowed on, "he lives six doors down the street from me. Anytime I see him leave his house, and I know it's not the time for him to go in to his job? You know, like, it's night? Or, like, 7:00 A.M.? And he's the only one in the car? I'm right behind him. And we're neighbors so we talk, small talk, we say hello, and he's always uncomfortable around me, like, antsy, nervous, but that's his conscience, because I never do or say anything to let him know that I'm on to him. My husband was, like, 'Elaine, we got to move, we can't live in this house,' and I said, '*You* move. I'm not leaving my son behind. And I'm not leaving *him*.' "

Jesse felt a hand on her shoulder and jumped. It was Marie, smiling at her kindly, slowing her down, Elaine and Brenda suddenly out of ear-shot. "You know, Jesse, this weather, this bitch of a heat wave makes me think about something I haven't thought about in a dog's age. One time, maybe twenty-five, thirty years ago, I was with my mother in this shopping center. It must've been a hundred degrees outside. And we see this young woman, and this guy pulls up in a car, comes out, they kiss, and they go off holding hands. I say to my mother, 'Ma, it's nice to see a happily married couple for a change.' I was pregnant with Teenie or one of the boys at the time, I can't remember right now. And my mother says to me, 'They're not married.' I say, 'How can you tell?' She says, 'Married people never touch in a heat wave.' I'll never forget that. 'Married people never touch in a heat wave.' Anyway, Jesse, listen. Karen really needs you to keep your distance from Brenda right now."

"What, she's afraid I'm going to screw up Operation Gaslight?"

"Please."

Jesse backed off a step. Elaine, still supporting Brenda with that steel band of an arm, stopped at the last cottage leading out of the field, the others shaping up around her, quiet, eyes to the ground, Karen touching a knuckle to her lips. Jesse was thrown, the group going nowhere, doing nothing for the moment. Then they were on the move again, heading out of the field onto the potholed remains of a driveway.

"What was that?" Jesse asked Marie.

"What."

"Back there, the cottage."

"We always stop there. That's six."

"Six what?"

"Cottage 6. Where we found Christina. We always say hello when we're in the neighborhood."

To Jesse, they seemed to be rambling now, to have broken free of their assigned quadrant, following this potholed path in something of a different mood, both more and less intense, not as minutely observant of the landscape as before but with a charged alertness tied into some intangible. The only sound was Elaine's drilling monotone, which continued to pour unrelentingly into Brenda's ear. Ignoring Marie's request, Jesse stepped up close enough to hear again.

"Karen saved my life, Brenda. She came right up to my door, it wasn't even six hours into the police report. She sat me down, she took everything out of my head, put it on paper, hit the phones, said, 'Let's go.' I would go out with her until two in the morning. We had miner's helmets for the dark. Go home, go out again at six. Six till two, six till two. We went out seven days in a row like that. People would say to me, 'Elaine, you got to rest, you got to.' But how? You can't. You can never stop looking for your child. A mother never calls it quits. She's a hunter for all time. Tell me he's dead, I'll sleep for a week. But we can't stop. How can we say it's over until we know? I am telling you, Brenda, it's four years he's gone and every time I leave my house, every day, I look up the street, I look down the street. Maybe he's coming home. Three o'clock, the kids coming from school? I'm out there on the stoop. You can never stop."

Brenda's knees went out and Elaine had to seize her in a side-arm bear hug, legs spread wide to keep her from crashing to the ground. Jesse hurried to the opposite side to help, and Brenda's eyes, coming into focus, looked directly at her. "Don't you *touch* me," Brenda said, a passionate whisper.

Jesse, stunned, stepped back, leaving Elaine to struggle by herself, Brenda's body and mind completely separated now, her arms and legs flopping like a puppet with cut strings but her eyes still fleetingly clear. "You stay the fuck away from me."

Jesse, her stomach floating, continued to step back until she was with Marie again, then turned to her. "What did I do?"

Marie looked at her with mournful, almost apologetic regret. "I really think you need to stay away from her right now."

The group took a turn off the road, disappearing into the woods again, and by the time Jesse got a grip on herself, she had only the soundtrack of Elaine's harangue to guide her as she crashed through the thick underbrush. She finally came on them in a clearing atop a cement platform of some kind, a six-by-six square with two more encrusted metal lawn chairs, old food tins and beer cans littering the immediate area.

The women didn't seem that interested in the signs of habitation. They broke out cigarettes, unzipped the fronts of their paper suits, and took a breather, Elaine easing Brenda into one of the rusted chairs, squatting alongside her to be at eye level as she continued to pour words and visions into her ear. Jesse, bloated with anxiety, tried to catch Brenda's eye, but Brenda wasn't having any of it, gracefully raising a padded hand, palm out, in a shunning gesture that was almost regal.

"Hey, Jesse, come here." Karen beckoned with a cigarette, Jesse thinking, It's Karen I love. Putting an arm around Jesse's shoulder and walking her out of earshot again, Karen plowed through the foliage until they came to a mesh fence beyond which a massive crumbling swimming pool lay. Its size and proximity were so startling it was as if someone had led Jesse blindfolded to the lip of a cliff.

"What the hell . . ."

"Yeah." Karen hung a hand on the mesh.

The pool had to be a hundred and fifty feet long and fifty feet wide, its bottom a gentle, gradual slope from a few inches at the shallowest end to perhaps six feet at midpoint, after which it made a sheer perpendicular drop to twenty feet. Bisecting the front half, from the entrance to a few feet before the drop, was a rusted two-tiered rail. Jesse guessed it had been installed for the wheelchairs and the generally feeble. The pool had been painted bright blue at some point, but the color was almost gone now, bleached out by the sun, save for large blotches in the more shadowed areas. Vegetation foamed down from the surrounding edges, a cascade of ferns and vines and moss, making this ghost pool into yet another jungle ruin, its dimensions and sunken aspect suggesting a Mayan ball court or some other arena of a lost and forgotten people.

"Can you believe this?" Karen smiled at her tightly.

"Why is Brenda mad at me?" Jesse asked.

"What do you mean?" Karen lit a cigarette.

"She's staring daggers at me."

"Yeah?" Karen took a deep drag, then flicked the butt through the mesh and into the pool. "Maybe she's tired."

"What's going on here," Jesse impulsively demanded. "What kind of head fuck are you pulling on her?"

"You know what gets me?" Karen squinted at the pool. "This whole place, limestone, cement, brick, all falling to shit, but look . . ." She pointed to a lifeguard's chair standing directly across from them on the far side of the pool, the seat perched atop giraffe legs, impossibly slender and frail but intact.

"You know why that's still standing? It's never been sat in. This is a dummy pool. No pipes, no pump. Never had a drop of water in it. Somebody made out like a bandit."

Turning her gaze back to the cement platform, Jesse saw Brenda through the brush, ensconced in her rusted throne, Elaine still pumping her head full of madness.

"I remember this pool from when I was a kid," Karen said, turning Jesse back around. "I mean everyone knew it was some kind of boondoggle, that it never had any water in it, but it was supposed to be haunted. You know, somebody would tell you that they knew somebody who knew somebody who just happened to be walking by this fence one night and they heard the sound of splashing water, and when they looked, they saw a little girl or a little boy swimming and playing in there, you know, the thing all of a sudden filled with water. And then that little girl or boy would see the person and try to get them to jump in and play. And you know, occasionally, the story, it would be, like, somebody *did* jump in. And then they'd find them the next day dead with a broken neck or something, in the deep end of the empty pool, right? But the kicker was, when they did the autopsy? They found *water* in the lungs. Boom."

"Huh." Holding on to the mesh for support, Jesse turned again to Brenda and Elaine.

"You know, and when it shut down, this place? I was a teenager. We'd sneak in, climb the fence, go down in the pool, and get stoned. It was great for getting stoned, you know, with the vines, the *size* of it, the secrecy of it. Man, I had a blast here. Little did I know, huh?"

"What?" Jesse's head was on a swivel. "Yeah," she said, turning back to Brenda and Elaine. Then—thinking, Fuck it—she just walked away from Karen, and, as she headed for the cement platform, Karen let her go. Jesse joined Teenie and Marie's smoking circle, a respectful ten feet from Brenda but within earshot.

"Even your own family turns against you after a while." Elaine's low voice was raw and gravelly, her face immobile except for the fluid sheen of her eyes. "You become like a millstone. You come downstairs, the other kids are, like, 'Mommy? Are you going to be sad today?' That's the only thing that can bring you back to some, some charade of normal life—when it hits you what you're doing to your other children, to your marriage. But with me, I couldn't even rally for that. I couldn't fake it, I couldn't help it. This bastard, he took away my life, he took away my family." The mulberry splash that stained the side of Elaine's face seemed to deepen, darken, her lips thin as wafers now. "And my husband, he was, like, 'Elaine, think about the other kids, think about *me*. Elaine, we got to get on with the business of living.' That's what he called it, 'the business of living.'"

Brenda jackknifed, forehead to kneecap, rocking again, the ancient rusted metal of her chair squealing in a rhythm suggestive of sex. Jesse watched, fascinated.

"See, men, they always cave in. Talk to you about the business of living. Tell you to think about the others, the rest of us, *them*. And then they leave because they just don't have the heart, they just don't have the belly. *We* are the hunters. We . . . And, and, what can I say to my other children. They're with my husband now. All I can say to them is the truth. That if it had happened to either of them instead of their brother, I'd be the same way for them. I want them back, my family, I want them back, but until someone can tell me my son's gone? Here I am. And the thing that frightened me? Brenda? Is that I've been like this for four years, and I know I still have love in my heart, but if it goes on too much longer? I don't know if I'll have anything left for them. It's going to be too late."

Karen quietly sauntered up to join the others on the cement plat-form.

"Sometimes I just want to grab that murderous perverted son of a bitch," Elaine continued. "Say to him, 'Look, Jimmy, you did it. I know it, you know it. Now, don't say a word—just nod your head—is he dead, yes or no. Do that for me and I'll never bother you again. Nobody's gonna nail you for nodding your head and I swear, I'll go away, you'll never see me again. Is my son dead. Just nod your head.' " Brenda's knees trem-bled like jackhammers. "I need to *know*. I need to know *now*. Is he *dead*."

Marie and Teenie stood back off the platform, silent, smoking, waiting—everybody waiting.

"Sweet Christ in heaven, Jimmy, won't you please just tell me. Just nod your head." Brenda began to weep, Elaine kneading her neck. "A nod of the head. Such a little thing, and night becomes day." Brenda slumped between her knees, stayed there for a long moment, then came up groaning God's name, struggling to take possession of herself again.

Torn between wanting this to cease and wanting it to come to its natural conclusion, Jesse looked to Karen, who returned her glance with a steady eye, a finger pressed to her lips.

"Is he dead, Brenda. Yes or no. That's all I ask. Yes or no." Elaine's kneading hand slid down Brenda's back, massaging her spine.

Brenda straightened up from her crouch on the chair, then almost immediately slumped over again, her knees pressing into her rib cage, rocking again, Elaine whispering, "Put my heart at rest, Brenda, put my heart at rest," then falling into silence along with everyone else.

After a long moment, Brenda rose up from wherever she had gone, sat erect in the rusted chair again, a bandaged palm pressed into her left eye. "It's so hot," she said softly. "I feel like I'm in hell." The women remained silent, continuing to stare at her, but Jesse could feel it—the moment had passed and it was as if the air around them had somehow become deflated and slack.

"It's gonna be OK, Brenda." Elaine stood over her, tight-lipped, dry-eyed. "It's gonna be OK."

"Are we ready for the dorms?" Karen asked Elaine. "Think it's about that time?" Marie dropped her cigarette onto the cement, slowly crushing it with the toe of her sneaker.

Elaine looked at her hands a moment before answering, "I think we need to explore out here a little more." Rising to her feet, she grasped Brenda by the elbow. "Come on, you're almost done," she said, and hauled her up.

They were moving through the campus proper now, skirting the large, abandoned dormitories and sticking to the overgrown blacktop footpaths that linked the ruined buildings—the chapel, the gym, the theater—all of them boarded up, busted through, and boarded up again. The walkways were flanked by craters from the great manhunt of 1967, each bowl sprouting its own self-contained thicket.

There were no trees here, just the drilling whine of cicadas and the white-out heat. The Friends of Kent were basically going through the motions now, poking through the brush with their broomsticks in a desultory manner, as if biding their time.

Elaine took hold of Brenda again, and the group moved on. Jesse saw some of the other search parties emerge from the forest that separated the adult cottages from the rest of the grounds. Then she saw something else—Louis and the dog standing at the tree line, intercepting each group as it appeared and sending them back into the woods. He was waving everybody off, making sure that his wife's small party had the institute to themselves.

"You know, Brenda." Elaine abruptly stopped walking and, from inches away, spoke directly into her eyes. "When I said I just wanted to know if my son was dead or alive, that's not completely true." Brenda moved to put her headphones back over her ears, but Elaine slid them back down on her neck. "I would also want to be able to give him a proper burial in sanctified ground. The idea of him lying in some ditch, in some shallow grave in the forest, where the animals—" Brenda reared back and then plunged forward to vomit, bent at the waist, one hand across her midsection as if bowing. Jesse moved to her again, but Elaine still had possession, standing there, one hand on Brenda's spine, fending Jesse off with a fierce glare.

Marie collapsed. After staggering for a minute like a drunk, she dropped to her knees and listed sideways, managing to prop herself up at a forty-five-degree angle to the ground with an elbow-locked arm. Karen and Teenie swooped in on her, one on either side, Teenie unzipping her mother's paper suit, Karen feeding her a salt tablet and dousing her head with bottled water, then serving her sips of what remained.

"Christ." Marie laughed, looking around as if trying to remember where she was, what she was doing here.

"Ma, you want to go back?"

"No, I'm OK. Just help me up."

With everyone's attention focused on Marie, Jesse made her move, sliding up to Brenda and reaching for the headphones glued to the back of her neck. "Let me carry—" Brenda stepped away.

Elaine moved between them as if to shield Brenda from Jesse's overtures. "She said you told her you had a *son?*" Elaine flashed fire, giving Jesse the once-over, head to toe, then added, "You don't have any kids. How *dare* you."

Jesse turned to see Karen, stone-faced, take in this encounter, then shrug and look off. Jesse stared at the ground, almost smiling, thinking, Well, of course.

"I have to lay down," Brenda gasped between wrenching barks.

Elaine looked to Karen. "Let's do the dorms."

As the women moved off, Jesse hung back, absorbing what had just gone down and knowing that no one, including Brenda, especially Brenda, gave a damn if she continued on with them or just turned around and went home. She had done her job, had gotten Brenda out of the house and into these woods, had delivered her to Elaine's whispered assaults, and was now disposable. From the moment she had stepped inside Brenda's apartment that first night, flying the flag of Motherhood, Jesse had agonized over the immorality of her lie; but as it turned out, no one really cared about it, or her, in that way. The Friends of Kent saw Jesse's fictional child as a hook to get her to toe the line with them, then as a blade to sever her from Brenda once her services were no longer needed. These women were as ruthless, as manipulative, as driven as any reporter Jesse had ever known.

Letting the irony of the situation wash over her, Jesse watched Brenda and Karen and the others as they approached the black bulk of the dormitory, then found herself trotting after them, feeling lightheaded, liberated. Screwed, used, manipulated, she was still on the job, and the job was right here.

The children's dormitory was sealed off, the steps to the front door removed, and in order to get inside through a shattered window that was six feet above ground, the women had to boost one another up. Despite the comic possibilities, the clumsy climbing, the wobbly athletics, there was neither laughter nor wisecracks, just focus and effort, Brenda being airlifted from Elaine on the ground to Karen leaning out the window.

The interior of the building was as vast as an airplane hangar and dim, the meager light seeping in through filthy ground-level windows and swirling up into an amorphous darkness again. The great height of the building was apparent only by virtue of a hole that had been punched into the roof for a long-gone chimney, sunlight slanting through up there, too, projecting a slightly oblong disc against the highest section of wall.

The women were dwarfed by the emptiness, surrounded by rags, beer cans, crushed cigarette packs, and shards of plywood, all faintly illuminated by a poverty of watery sunlight fighting its way in through the grimy glass. There was graffiti on the walls—Fuck, Suck, satanic pentangles, genitalia, nicknames—random garbage for the eye. Something small ran past the group, too fast for anyone to react, Jesse thinking of the scuttling sounds inside Cottage 9.

"Stay together," Karen said, producing a flashlight and leading them onward. The sound of their cautious, shuffling gait, bouncing off the walls of this hollow hall, came back to them in a great scraping echo.

"I'm so tired." Brenda's words were as soft as breath, her head tilting back until her throat arched upwards. "What do you want from me."

Karen's flashlight picked up a child's patent leather dress shoe, laceless; a dead pigeon, its breast torn open, its wings splayed and matted with blood; another shoe, ancient in style but with an untrod sole. The women seemed to be consciously clustered around Brenda, as if they were all physically involved in propelling her forward, Jesse keeping separate, unable to tell if Brenda's feet were even touching the ground. There was another furry streak across the floor, and this time Jesse got a good look—not a rat, as she feared, but a cat.

They turned a corner; the building seemed to be composed of four long halls, and they came on a large pile of shoes, child-sized, with virgin soles and then on a pile of porcelain sinks. Along one wall, showerheads were affixed, spaced three feet apart, and against the opposite wall stood a row of toilet stalls, the heavily varnished saloon-style swinging doors dangling from their hinges, the toilets seatless, although one bowl was humming with flies.

"This is such a sad place," Karen said, playing her light across the floor, picking out more children's shoes, an empty wine bottle, another half-gutted bird. Brenda seemed to float behind shut lids, sleepwalking through the ruins, the women around her expressionless. Karen's flashlight picked out a pajama top, a bar of soap with teeth marks, the fire-curled pages of a telephone directory.

"Whenever I come here," Elaine whispered hoarsely, "I swear I can still hear them."

"Hear who?" Jesse asked, thinking, Whenever I come here? Another streak shot past and Jesse made out a flash of fur, the reflected gleam of an eye—another cat, the place crawling with them.

"Such a sad place," Karen repeated, her delivery overlarge, theatrical, her words caroming off the walls, mingling with the snare-drum shuffle of their steps. It's here, Jesse was thinking. Whatever they had been working toward, walking toward in the last few hours, it was right here.

They turned the corner again and came into what must have been the communal bedroom—a few white-enamel-painted iron bed frames scattered about upright and dozens of others piled in a jangle of rods and legs at the far ends of the room, as if a giant hand had swept them up and shoved them in the corners. Jesse could see that the beds had once been laid out in rows, the smudged impressions of the headboards still marking the long walls at regular intervals.

The sun, through dirt-laden windows, dappled the floors in this hall, too, revealing a fleet scatter of eyes and fur, the light gradually yielding to the walled darkness above. Then another gibbous disk beamed through a chimney hole in the roof, hanging over the floating darkness and barren sleep hall like a true moon suspended in a starless night.

Karen's flashlight picked out more mementos and debris—a washcloth stiffened into its folds, spray-paint cans, crumpled cigarette packs, a headless rubber doll, another doll with its eyes poked out, a Bible, a clip-on tie, a slipper, and another half-eaten pigeon, most likely the handiwork of the cats.

"God, I hate this place," Karen growled. "I swear they're still here." Jesse kept to the shadows, but stepping in something soft, she recoiled, edging out of the hall to the shadow line. Karen took Brenda's hand.

"We're gonna have a look around," she said to her. "It's a little dangerous, OK? Half these floorboards can go any minute, so I want you to stay in here and wait for us, OK?"

"Stay where."

"Make yourself comfortable." Karen, walking backwards, held Brenda's hands and led her to one of the upright beds, boosting her up on the bedsprings, leaving her legs dangling.

"What are you doing," Brenda asked, dreamily.

"Just wait for us," Karen said, backing away again.

"I can't be alone," Brenda said, half to herself, but when Jesse stepped back into the light of the sleep hall, Marie and Teenie gestured for her to stay put. The other women retreated to the shadows near Jesse, quietly toeing the debris, waiting, their faces tense, no eye contact. Brenda sat slumped on the edge of the bed alone, like an offering left on an altar, the hall seeming now to Jesse twice as vast and desolate, as if Brenda's lone presence gave it its true scale.

And then Jesse heard it. The crying. At first she thought it was Brenda, who sat with her back to them, but there were no corresponding convulsions in her frame. And again, crying—thin, plaintive, childlike wails that froze Jesse's heart. As the feeble cries grew in definition and volume, it occurred to Jesse that these ghostly lamentations hadn't just begun but were a constant presence in this building, which had over the decades housed thousands of forgotten children, and that she was only now hearing them because the Friends of Kent were, for the first time since entering this sound-sensitive hall, embracing silence.

The other women kept their eyes to the ground. Elaine started whispering to herself, an infinitesimal rant, with the cadence of a memorized, speedily delivered prayer. Karen lit a cigarette, extinguishing the match between her fingers.

Finally Brenda heard it. She sat up straight, jerked her head to either side, then slowly lifted her chin to the false moon, her mouth agape. The cries—tiny, penetrating—seemed to multiply. Brenda crossed her bandaged hands over her heart.

Frightened, Jesse turned to Karen but was fended off with an outthrust palm. Brenda slowly unrolled herself onto the rust-fused bedsprings until she was flat on her back. Inside the wails now, Jesse started hearing half-formed words, piteous entreaties. Brenda slid her headphones in place, blindly probed for the "Play" button. Marie, seeing this, hissed *"Fuck,"* but a moment later Brenda removed the phones and, still staring at that oblong moon, seemed to let the ghostly cries wash over her.

Then Jesse heard one word, distinctly, "Mommy," and it turned her blind. Karen, head bowed, closed her eyes and pressed a knuckle to her lips, as she had done standing in front of Cottage 6. She grabbed Elaine's hand. A cat flew past Jesse's feet, making her jump. Teenie walked deeper into the darkness, tugging at her collar and swallowing sobs. Brenda pressed her palms to her eyes, rolled onto her side, and curled up on the ungiving coils.

"Mommy." Again. No. And then it came to her: the cats. The goddamn cats, an endless soundtrack of mews and yowls that had been drowned out earlier by the hollow clamor of their footsteps and voices.

Brenda lay motionless, her hands between her thighs, and Jesse thought she might be asleep. They all watched her from the shadows as the hall filled with a mindless facsimile of disembodied longing, of inconsolable abandonment. Teenie returned from the dark, her face mottled from crying.

Slowly Brenda sat up. Stood up. She searched the walls, the spongy celestial blackness, then, calmly tearing apart her white tick suit as she went, she began to walk back toward the group with a shuffling step. Then she walked past them. Maintaining for a moment a discreet distance, the Friends of Kent then followed, Jesse bringing up the rear.

Outside, back in the pulverizing humidity, Brenda sat against a tree, her paper suit gone from the waist up. Jesse, Karen, and Elaine kneeled to the left of her, Teenie and Marie hanging back by the open window that had served as both entrance and exit. The women waited for Brenda to speak, no one daring to disturb her train of thought, Jesse badly frightened again, this time by the silence, how it would be broken.

"My son wasn't like those children in there," Brenda finally said, to no one, to everyone.

"OK." Karen ventured softly.

"He was loved."

"OK." There was a flutter in Karen's throat.

"He was cherished."

Karen said nothing this time, and Brenda seemed to withdraw. For a long moment, the air was filled with the lazy metallic razzle of cicadas.

"He's not here," she finally said, her voice heavy with surrender, then lowered her head and stared at her swaddled palms. "You're in the wrong park."

Part Three

Higher and Higher

21

The Dutch Oven diner sat midpoint on Route 13, a four-lane miracle mile running from Gannon through Dempsy to Bayonne—an ugly strip of highway flanked on either side by underpopulated malls, waterbed outlets, and carpet warehouses. The diner was considered a decent place to eat, so the wraparound parking lot was always full and it took Lorenzo, fingers still trembling from the hospital-fed oxygen, nerves shot, two slow circuits before he spotted the Friends of Kent van.

By the time Lorenzo had been brought into the medical center, his lungs were so seared and inflated from overuse of that store-bought spray they showed up on the X rays looking more like catcher's mitts than human organs. Enraged by his suicidal carelessness, Dr. Chatterjee had begun to shout at him, drawing stares from the other patients and medical personnel in the overcrowded emergency room. When the call from Karen Collucci came through on his cell phone, Lorenzo was sitting topless on a gurney, inhaling an Albuterol solution through a plastic face mask connected by a hose to a wall-mounted oxygen feed. The adrenaline brought on by the news from the Chase Institute made any continued treatment superfluous.

She had pulled it off, Karen—had pulled it off like he had prayed she would, and he felt embarrassed by the depth of his relief.

There were seven people waiting in the van: Louis in the driver's seat, Jesse alongside him, Teenie and Marie sandwiching Brenda in the middle row, and Elaine and Karen in the rear. No one was talking. Teenie and Marie each held one of Brenda's bandaged hands, Teenie gently stroking the raw-looking knuckles that protruded from the now-filthy gauze. Without looking at Brenda, Lorenzo quickly gestured for Karen to come outside, and she followed him up the steps to the vending-machine-lined vestibule of the diner.

"She said it was an accident." Karen's hands trembled as she lit a cigarette.

"OK." Lorenzo's hands still shook a little too.

"She said the kid is in Freedomtown, buried in Freedomtown."

"OK . . . Freedomtown?"

"She said he overdosed on Benadryl, liquid Benadryl. She wasn't even in the house."

"OK. I'll get that." Lorenzo fished in his pocket for his new prescription inhaler, dropped it, and felt the blood rush to his temples as he stooped to retrieve it.

"You OK?"

"What else you got," Lorenzo asked, deaf to an answer. His sheepish jubilation faded as he began racing through a feverish checklist in his head: take a quick statement right here, right now; call the medical examiner, pinpoint the burial site, notify Bobby McDonald, take her in for a deeper statement, avoid the word *arrest,* avoid the word *lawyer,* avoid the Mirandas, avoid the prosecutor, avoid the press, confirm the body, charge her with homicide, notify the prosecutor, coordinate the players, script a press conference, choreograph some proactive riot control, pray.

"You OK?" Karen repeated.

The head of the Dempsy board of education and one of the deputy mayors pushed through from the diner into the vestibule, both of them sucking on toothpicks. Lorenzo turned away, hoping they wouldn't recognize him, come over, and start shooting the shit. As the two men descended the steps to the parking lot, Lorenzo realized that he had picked the worst conceivable spot for a conversation of this nature.

"Real quick, did Jesse hear all this?"

"Yup." Three elderly women came into the vestibule, bitching about the no-smoking law, firing up Camels.

"She call it in?" Lorenzo asked.

"Nope."

"OK, good. Can you be with her a few more minutes?"

"Jesse?"

"No, Brenda. But send Jesse over to my car, OK?" Karen seemed to falter at the request, and Lorenzo, confused, was about to ask her what was wrong when she flung her arms around his neck and whispered, "Thank you, Jesus," sweet and husky in his ear. Lorenzo was physically staggered by the force behind her impulsive act of gratefulness.

"Hey. I should be thanking *you*," he said clumsily, her gratitude offered to Jesus, not his to reciprocate.

"Next time," she said with a smile, taking a swipe at her cheeks and heading back to the Blazer.

Sitting in his car waiting for Jesse to make it across the parking lot, he put a call in to the medical examiner's office, set up a rendezvous in Freedomtown, and before returning to an obsessive review of the tasks ahead of him, found himself reexperiencing Karen's ardent embrace. Then he saw, once again, Teenie and Marie, mother and daughter, each holding one of Brenda's hands in the backseat of the van—saw Teenie's small, soothing caresses—and he knew, absolutely knew that the overpowering mood of these people toward Brenda in the aftermath of her confession was one of great tenderness. Perhaps they felt more sympathy for her now that she had admitted to knowledge about her child's death than they had the day before, when they weren't quite sure of her innocence or guilt. In Lorenzo's imagination, Brenda was being treated not as if she had just confirmed death but as if she had given birth after a long, torturous labor, the encircling Kenters both family and delivery team.

Jesse crossed the parking lot, then slid into the passenger seat of the Crown Vic, the subsequent slamming of the door bringing him back into focus: time to kick it in gear. "Hey," she huffed, not looking at him, Lorenzo sensing that she did not feel like part of that family of midwives back in the Blazer.

"Yeah. How much time can you give me before running with this?" Lorenzo slid his hands in quarter circles around his steering wheel, then looked at his watch: twelve-twenty.

"How much time do you need?" Jesse asked with an odd flatness, staring out the passenger window toward the red van across the lot.

"I need enough time to get the body ID'd, take a statement, charge her, coordinate a press conference, and work out some crowd control."

"Just tell me how much time you need." Jesse cracked her window, took out a cigarette.

"I think you should remember that if it wasn't for me we wouldn't even be *needing* to have a conversation like this," Lorenzo said, touching her cigarette hand, then patting his chest.

"Just tell me." She tossed her unlit cigarette out the window, her toneless, defeated manner still throwing him.

"What time you go to press?"

"Five o'clock."

"Five o'clock." He nodded, figuring she was lying by an hour. "Give me till eight," Lorenzo said, taking back that hour, plus another, hoping to have it all wrapped and made public by seven.

"What's in it for me?"

"What's in it for you? Shit, I'll give you everything."

"Am I exclusive?"

"Exclusive as you want to be."

"I want to be the only paper carrying this tonight."

"Fine by me. I'm not saying shit till the press conference anyhow. You want to go to the exhumation?" he said, offering it like a treat.

"No. I want to hear her interview."

"Whoa, wait—"

"Just throw me in the men's room. Those walls are like cheesecloth."

"*Man.*" Lorenzo feigned outrage, laughing as if to mask anger. "You're, like, pushing the edge of the envelope here, Jess." He rapped a knuckle on his window. "You're goin' for the io*n*osphere with this."

"Oh c'mon, don't go all virginal on me. I won't run with nothing that'll trip you up, and I'll cover your ass completely." Jesse was hustling him now, coming back to life. "I've done this with your guys a million times before."

"My guys like who."

"*You'll* never know," she said, shrugging. "See what I'm saying?"

Brenda still sat in the middle row of the van, hemmed in by Teenie and Marie, sat there exuding presence—composed, alert, expectant, like a bride in the wings—and when Lorenzo leaned in through the open side-door panel and offered her his hand, she accepted it with a seamless grace, as if she had been waiting for him, for this moment, all the days of her life.

Bringing Brenda up and out into the parking lot, Lorenzo, still holding her hand, ducked back down and spoke to Karen in the van. "You want to keep us company?" Karen quickly gathered her stuff and joined them on the asphalt, Lorenzo assuming that she understood she was to be his corroborating witness for all that was to follow.

They returned to his car, Lorenzo, Brenda, and Karen, but after a long moment of agitated silence, Brenda said she needed to be on her feet, needed to be in the open air. They got out and walked to a shady corner of the parking lot, to a hangdog canopy of arms to heaven and other less identifiable rag trees that arched over the mesh fence separating the Dutch Oven diner from a Payless Shoe outlet. But there was a powerful reek of urine here, so after a moment they were on the move again, Brenda leading them ten steps this way, then twenty steps in the opposite direction, Lorenzo rolling with it for a minute or two, until he saw a look of mounting panic and disorientation come into her eyes. Gently, firmly, he led her back to his car.

"Now, I understand, Brenda, that you told Karen and those other ladies back there a different version of what happened to your son, other than the version you've been telling me." Brenda didn't seem to be listening. She eyed the customers climbing and descending the steps to the diner, as if she were in awe of their ability to come and go as they pleased. "Now, I don't know if you felt any particular kind of pressure out there this morning, you know, felt obliged to come up with something to get them off your back, and if that's the case, I can deal with that, but if what you're saying is the truth—"

"He's gone," she said flatly.

"Gone."

"He drank a bottle of Benadryl."

"He what?" She didn't repeat herself, just stared at the diner entrance across the lot. "When was this?"

"Two nights ago."

"The night you came into the hospital?"

"The night before that."

"OK." Lorenzo flicked a glance at Karen in the backseat. Eyes downcast, she sat twirling an unlit cigarette between her hands. "You say he drank a bottle of . . ." Lorenzo faltered. "How do you, did you see him—"

"No," she cut him off. "I wasn't there." The tone of this was in the spirit more of self-accusation than of alibi.

"Then how?"

"I found him."

"Was anybody else—"

"No," she said, cutting him off again. "He was by himself." Her voice began to break. "Nobody was there."

"So it was an accident," Lorenzo offered, to keep her verbal, give her at least a temporary out.

"An accident," she repeated tonelessly.

"Where's he now, Brenda?"

"In front of the Chicago Fire."

"The what?" He was momentarily thrown. "In Freedomtown?" She nodded. Karen snapped her cigarette in two.

Lorenzo hesitated before his next question. She had not said to him that the boy was dead. "Is he—"

"Buried there, yeah. Yes." The words were half throttled, escaping in a stuttery blurt. "Buried there."

"OK." He took a quick hit of Ventolin, smelled his own sweat. "Did you bury him?"

There was a minute's hesitation, then, "Yes."

"Yes?"

Despite the swelter, he was afraid to turn on the ignition, fearful of anything, any noise or movement, that would distract her, disrupt the flow.

"Am I under arrest?" she asked, almost apathetically.

"Whoa, hang on, hang on," he said easily. "I'm still trying to understand things here." Lorenzo was intent on stringing her out, keeping her talking as long as possible before having to Mirandize her. At the very least, he wanted to hold off charging her until she had personally taken him to her son's grave.

"If I go to jail"—Brenda exhaled the words, raising, then dropping her bandaged hands into her lap—"do I have to see people if they come to visit me?"

"Whoa, Brenda, you're way jumping the gun." Lorenzo made a blurring motion with his hand. "First thing we got to do is give your son a proper burial."

"Proper burial," she repeated.

"That's right." Lorenzo saw Ben roll up to the Friends of Kent van, saw Jesse exit the Blazer, then get in her brother's ride and just sit there, presumably waiting for Lorenzo to go somewhere.

"Let me ask you something," Brenda started out sharply. "How do you properly . . ." She trailed off, losing heart.

"Can you take me to him?"

"I *told* you where he is."

"Brenda, you're telling me such a different story now than what you told me before. How do I know—"

"Because you *know*," she answered sharply again, and she was right.

Fearing a confrontation at this delicate stage, Lorenzo moved to start up the car, intending to get her quickly to Freedomtown now, but the ignition wouldn't catch. "Hang on, just . . ." He closed his eyes and took another shot. The engine refused to turn over. Soaked through, buzzed with disbelief, Lorenzo tried it a third time, and finally the Crown Vic thrummed to life. He eased out of the parking lot and into traffic as smoothly and cautiously as if there were an open cup of coffee perched on the dashboard.

"You know, you get a high fever or you come down with a physical illness," Brenda said to no one in particular. "And you think you know what it is to be sick, but you don't. You have no clue."

Heading toward the ruined park, Lorenzo was afraid to open his mouth, say the wrong thing, make her balk at pointing out the burial site. Point—that was all she had to do. He risked a sideways glance and caught her anxiously stroking the headphone wires that ran down from her shoulders like strands of her hair. In the backseat, Karen stared out the window, her profile furrowed and brooding. But she was keeping it to herself, trying to come off invisible, doing it right.

Lorenzo, fully cognizant of the racial afterblast that would hit the city once Brenda's story—the fact that she had concocted the black man—leaked out, wondered why he wasn't feeling any particular anger toward her for what she had put people through, for what was yet to come. He conjectured that maybe, at this point, he was just too busy, physically and mentally, to let a particular emotion, a decisive mood settle in on him regarding Brenda. But he also experienced a distinct foreboding that this sense of ambiguity, this lack of emotional clarity might stay with him indefinitely. He allowed his thoughts to return to the more tangible issues, issues at hand—exhumation, confirmation, racing the media clock.

"Brenda," he said, turning to her. "You buried him?" She didn't answer, just sat there glassy-eyed, her hands curled dead in her lap. "What did you use?"

"What?"

"What did you use? What kind of tool?"

She stared back at him with defiant agitation, and he regretted not waiting with that question until he had her locked in. Then she raised her bandaged hands, palms out, nails curled inward like claws, like prongs on a garden tool.

Lorenzo had his doubts. He pushed it a little further. "Did you bury him deep?"

"No," she whispered, going off, coming back, repeating "No." Then, after a moment, abruptly leaning forward, her voice wobbly with panic, she asked, "Can you drive faster?"

Lorenzo got out of the car at the vine-ensnared gate, pulled it wide, then drove over the shattered footpath of Freedomtown to the Chicago Fire. There was a merciful breeze coming off the water, setting the foliage that embraced the boardinghouse facade to trembling, bringing it to life with a whispery sizzle of leaves. The buckshot effigy in the top window looked much more ravaged in the daylight, paint-flaked and weather-gouged like the detached maidenhead of a long-gone clipper ship.

The three of them got out and stood before the ruin, Lorenzo afloat in a riot of competing preoccupations: get the body up, Devil's Night to come, and lastly, what was this woman thinking the night before, walking right over her son's grave as he gave her the history of rhythm and blues? What the fuck was she thinking? Lorenzo studied her as she stood alongside him, stunned and rocking. As he was about to open his mouth, say something to prod her into action, Brenda abruptly lurched forward to the wall, a febrile charge that ended in a dazed halt, her eyes finally coming alive to scan the earth at the base of the facade.

"Brenda," Lorenzo called out softly, but she either didn't hear him or couldn't be bothered right now.

Stepping back a few paces from the wall, eyes still roaming the ground, she brought her hands to her temples, whispered, "Please," then bolted forward again to pace the width of the structure, moving in a humped crouch and wheeling quickly at the borders, like a dog trying to home in on its sweet spot, pacing and wheeling, pacing and wheeling. Lorenzo tried it again: "Brenda."

Hearing him this time, she came to a stop and shot upright, her eyes kaleidoscopes of panic. "I can't *find* him."

"Hold on, hold on," Lorenzo said, as much to himself as to Brenda, then reached for her arm, pulling her away from the wall, both of them standing back far enough to take in the entire facade without having to compartmentalize their gaze. "Where do you *think* you . . ." he said, striving for the right word, "you put him." Frowning, Karen quietly moved toward the wall.

"Under the angel," Brenda answered, eyes into eyes, Lorenzo smelling madness on her breath, thinking, The angel; thinking, Maybe this is all one nightmare of a hoax. "The angel." She gestured toward the figurehead. "Cody said she was an angel. I would come here with him." Her voice went off into a teary warble. "He said that she was an angel. I wanted to bury him under his angel, I *swear*."

"Hold on, hold on, hold on," Lorenzo chanted, envisioning this place twenty-four hours from now if Brenda couldn't find the grave—a backhoed pit the size of a bullring. "Hold on."

"Come here," Karen murmured. She was standing directly under the figurehead, her hands in her pockets, the toe of her shoe lightly digging into the earth under a tumbled mound of large oval stones, each one the diameter of a serving platter, most of this slapdash cairn obscured by tall weeds. Lorenzo, still holding Brenda by the elbow, approached the wall. Karen knelt down, slid a hand under the mound, and brought out a pinch of ruddy, crumble-textured dirt. "This is subsoil. It should be two feet under, not on the surface."

Lorenzo stared straight up the wall. The figurehead, from this point of view, loomed twice as large, the arms protruding from the window frame more like surreal elongated twists of wood than plausible representations of human limbs. Brenda settled on her knees and laid her cheek on one of the oval stones. She stared off into the weeds.

"This is it, Brenda?" She didn't answer. "This where you put him?" She closed her eyes. Lorenzo gently pulled her up off the stones.

"I need you to answer me."

"Yes."

"This is where he is."

"Yes."

"This is where you put him."

"Yes."

"And you dug out this piece here with your hands."

"Yes."

"And then what."

"What?"

"What did you do after that."

"I covered him."

"With . . ."

"Earth."

"Then what."

"What?"

"What you do then."

"What . . ." She was confused.

"What did you do after you covered him with earth?"

"I put the rocks on."

"You put the rocks on. *These* rocks?"

She gaped at him for a beat, then whispered, "Yes."

Lorenzo placed a hand on one of the larger stones, could feel its density. "You put all these stones here? All these rocks?"

"Yes," she said, sounding more emphatic this time.

He looked at Karen, who had her back turned to them but remained within earshot. Lorenzo wanted to push it a little, decided it could wait, then overruled himself. One more question. Maybe two.

"That's like a lot of work carrying these rocks. Where'd they come from?" Brenda made a vague gesture toward the wilderness behind the wall. "When you were looking for the, the spot, a few minutes ago, what were you looking for?"

"What? These." She touched a stone.

"You were looking for this pile of rocks."

"Yes."

"This big pile of rocks." She didn't answer and Lorenzo gave it a few seconds before adding, "Because if you know they're here, they're kind of hard to miss."

"My son is here."

"OK." Lorenzo tentatively acknowledged her claim.

"He's here." Lorenzo said nothing, just stared at her, demanding more, demanding the rest of it. Brenda crawled to the base of the wall, flattened a stand of weeds to reveal graffiti: I L Y was written with a black marker on the lowest plank of weather-beaten wood.

"Ily?" He pronounced it as a word. Brenda mumbled a corrected reading. "Say again?"

"I love you," she said in a defeated mutter, then, "I can't be here."

"We can take a walk," Lorenzo proposed lightly, warily, checking the time: one o'clock.

"Can we go back to the dance floor?"

"The what?" Lorenzo worried again, wondering who was home in her.

"Where the concerts were. Where you took me last night."

"Sure, no problem." Lorenzo offered her his hand.

Stuporous and wobbly, Brenda led Lorenzo, Karen following, to the old Motown stage, seating herself atop the section of low ledge where she had sat with Lorenzo the night before.

"This is good?" he asked. Karen took up her post behind them, leaning against a tree.

"Yeah," she said gingerly, but as soon as he made a move to sit next to her, she popped up again. "No. I don't want to leave him." She began marching back toward the Chicago Fire, Lorenzo and Karen exchanging glances, giving her this one last journey.

She sat cross-legged in front of the grave, and he dropped into a squat alongside her. "You tell me it was an accident, and I have no reason to disbelieve you," he said.

"I never said it was an accident."

"You said nobody was with him."

"That's right." She spoke to her hands, then jumped up. "I don't want to talk now." Lorenzo vigorously palmed his face and scalp, gearing up to Mirandize her, thinking, Shit, shit. "I can't be here," she said, starting to spin in a flat-footed way. "Please."

"Hey, I don't want to be here any more than you do."

"Please, I don't want a lawyer, I'll tell you everything, *please.*"

Lorenzo hesitated, bagging the Mirandizing for now. "Brenda," he said sorrowfully, "we have to wait for the medical examiner."

"What? *Why.*" She was gray-faced. "You're not going to make me watch them dig him up."

"No, no, no, I just have to show them."

"You can't make me do that."

Lorenzo began to make reassuring noises but was distracted by a blooming movement across the front of her jeans, and, before he could stop himself, he simply said it: "You just wet yourself." His voice was not unkind but unthinking. Lorenzo winced at his words, but she was oblivious to both the accident and the observation.

"I won't see him," she said, her voice vibrant with terror. "You can't make me do that."

"No, Brenda, please, I wouldn't. Look." He reached out to her, registering a thin, alkaline waft as he did. "If you want, we can wait outside the fence."

"Please," she said, her knees trembling now, "because I want to tell you what happened."

"OK." He stood up.

"I *want* to."

"All right." He extended his hand to her, but she backed away.

"Only you, though," she said, without looking at Karen. Karen stepped away from the painting of a ground-floor window she had been leaning against and waited, eyes to the ground. "I'm not going to say anything as long as she's here."

Without a word, Karen walked off in the direction of the front gate. At least, Lorenzo consoled himself, she could testify that Brenda had voluntarily declined her right to a lawyer.

"OK?" He smiled tightly, resisting the urge to look at the stain on her jeans again.

"OK," she answered shakily.

"OK." He hesitated, something not settled in his head. He looked up at the effigy, its arms reaching for the clouds, then dropped his gaze to the burial pile, a collapsed granite igloo, then finally came back to himself, to work.

"You want to get out of here?"

"Yes."

"Clear something up for me and we're gone."

"No." She hugged herself. "No more talking here. Take me outside, I'll tell you—"

"Brenda," he said, cutting her off. "You want to leave here, and I want to be able to take you out before the, the exhumation team comes by. I figure we got like twenty minutes at the most."

"No."

"Just straighten me out on this one thing and we're gone."

"No."

"Then here we stay. I'm sorry." He stood frowning down at the mound of stones, Brenda whirling in the weeds behind him, chained to his intransigence, working her fingertips as if on rosary beads. He looked at his watch—one-twenty—doing the math, something like six hours to wrap this up, then prep for Armageddon.

"*What . . .*" she blurted with enraged exasperation.

"Brenda," he said, turning to her, "you're gonna tell me the truth, right?" She nodded vigorously. "You're gonna make a clean breast of it, right?" She nodded again, feverish with distress. He turned back to the stones. "Where'd you say you got these?" She pointed to the woods behind the building front, Lorenzo not even bothering to look, thinking, Fuck it. "Come here for a second." He turned to her again, extended his hand. She took a step back. "Time is tight."

She finally stepped forward, without taking his hand. "He's there I swear."

"Do me . . ." Lorenzo hesitated, not wanting to tamper with a crime scene, but then thinking, Her word against mine. "Show me how you lifted these." He sank to his haunches and tapped one of the stones, jagged, mica-flecked. "Pick me up this rock right here."

Brenda made no move to do as he asked. He gave her a long, appraising glance, then, jerking up the knees of his jeans, he stooped and lifted the stone himself, instantly feeling it in his back, thinking, Seventy-five pounds if an ounce; thinking, Thirteen-inch-screen TV. He waddled over to her, the strain in his shoulders now, too, and held the stone between them.

"Take it from me." She looked away, her hands hanging lifeless, and after a long moment he just let it drop to the ground, the dull, muffled impact like a punctuation mark.

"Brenda," he said, arching his back, then reaching out to turn her face to him. "I have got to tell you. These last few days here, you have put me and a lot of other people through hell. People I care very much about. But despite what all went down? I swear to you, I also care for you. I feel for you. I don't know why, but I do. But so now here's the deal. When you start telling me the whole story? I want you to start by telling me who dug this grave, who put these rocks here, and please don't tell me it was you, because if you start with a lie? You have just lost the most important ally you ever had in your entire life, and I'm not even gonna bother to take a statement. I'm just gonna charge you and dump you in the system, let you tell your story to your lawyer." Fearful that he had just shot himself in the foot with this reading of the riot act, Lorenzo found himself sucking wind. Her lack of instantaneous protest, though, told him that he was on the money about a second player.

She turned away from him.

"Please, Brenda." Even given the shapeless drape of her jeans, he could see the tremor that coursed through her knees as clearly as if she were bare-legged. "Help me help you."

"Ho . . ." she exhaled.

"We could be here or we could be gone. It's up to you."

"He didn't have a choice." Brenda spoke the words so softly that Lorenzo felt he was reading her mind, not hearing her voice.

"He didn't want any part of it, but I scared him into helping me."

"Scared who."

"My son drank a bottle of Benadryl," she began carefully. "Nobody was there for him and he died." She recited these words with precision and controlled passion, as if they were the opening lines of an often-repeated prayer.

"*Who* didn't have a choice."

"I dug that grave with my hands. *I* did. I told myself I was making his bed for him one last time, that's how I got through it, but there was no way I could lay him down so I told Billy he had to do it for me. I told him he had to come to my house, take my son's body, bring it here, and lay him in the ground. I told him that he was responsible for what had happened, too, but it wasn't true. It was all me. It was always all me. But he had to do it for me. He had to—I had nobody else to turn to."

Her own blunt words seemed to have a calming effect on her. Lorenzo was taken by how much more composed she sounded now than at any other time over the last few days. Musing on this, Lorenzo forgot to ask her, Billy who?

"See, what I should have done," she continued in a conversational tone, "was go into the kitchen, fix myself a glass of Drano or Comet or laundry bleach, then lay down next to my son and go off with him, but I didn't have the belly for that, I didn't have the heart for that. I was too much of a coward, see what I'm saying?" She smiled blandly, looking him in the eye. "So I made Billy lay him down for me."

"Billy," Lorenzo finally said, then said it again. "Billy . . ." An open-ended question.

"Williams," she offered dejectedly.

"Billy Williams," he announced shakily, feeling stupid, the name not clicking.

"Felicia's boyfriend," Brenda said faintly as her gaze keyed in on something over Lorenzo's shoulder, her face nothing but eyes, Lorenzo saying the name again, this time to lock it in: "Billy Williams." Barricade Billy, crouched in his underwear, drowning in beer and tears, Billy Williams. Lorenzo finally turned to see what had seized her: the exhumation team. The work detail was composed of four homicide detectives, three bearing shovels, the fourth, a forensics kit; a heat-wilted coroner; and a Rastafarian-looking brother bearing a shoulder-mounted Betacam and a head full of dreadlocks. Lorenzo, still going south, wondered about grooming codes for civilian employees of the police department, then came back to himself, grabbing one of the Homicides by the arm, escorting him to the burial mound, saying, "This right here," giving the detective a perfunctory description of the boy—age, hair color, clothes—giving him his pager number, telling him to punch in three twos when the body came up, and even though he knew it would be close to an hour before any of the actual digging commenced, he whisked Brenda from the park, as if to spare her the sight of those shovels taking their first bites of earth.

22

Directly outside Freedomtown, Jesse sat in her brother's car waiting for Lorenzo and Brenda to return to the Crown Victoria, which was parked by the water's edge a few hundred feet inside the gate. The Chrysler had suffered heat stroke, and as Ben worked under the hood, feeding two quarts of bottled water into the radiator, Jesse reached out for her editor, the cell phone sweat-glued to the side of her face.

"Jose."

"Where you been."

"I need you to hold up the run."

"Why." Jesse didn't answer. "She gave it up?"

"I didn't say that." Ben slammed down the hood, making her jump.

"She gave it up," Jose said, marveling. "Fuckin' A."

"I didn't say that," Jesse said, working him. Karen Collucci appeared, walking down the footpath, passing Lorenzo's car and heading for the exit.

"Tell me what you got."

"Can you hold it for me till seven?" she said, watching Karen's approach.

"What do you got."

"Just hold it for me till seven."

"Tell me about the boyfriend."

Karen passed through the gate and Jesse hung up. "Hey." Karen leaned into Jesse's open window and nodded toward the phone. "You just call it in?"

"Of course not." Jesse shrugged.

"She didn't," Ben seconded.

"Shut up," Jesse snapped at her brother.

"Can you give me a lift?" Karen asked Ben.

"Whoa, I'm supposed to wait for Lorenzo," Jesse said quickly, panicking at the idea of missing them coming out, missing her payoff back in the Southern District men's room.

"Just drop me off on Jessup. It's like two minutes," Karen said. "They're gonna be a while yet."

As Ben pulled out into traffic, Jesse turned to Karen in the backseat.

"The body's in there?" Karen shrugged, lit a cigarette. "How's she holding up?"

Karen took a while returning her lighter to her purse before answering. "Hanging in."

"So what do you do from here?" Jesse asked, giving up.

"Me? Go home, hope the hot line doesn't ring."

"No news is good news?"

"You got that right," Ben answered for Karen.

"Tomorrow's Pete's birthday," Karen said, coughing into her fist. "I got to order the cake, buy the stuff for the party. He likes this Japanese computer pet or something—all the kids have them. They're like impossible to find. I mean the thing's a horror. It *dies* on you if you don't take care of it, which to me, of all people—"

"Who's Pete?" Jesse asked, thinking of Louis.

"My son," Karen said evenly. "You saw him."

The kid with the flipper hand. Jesse's head dropped to her chest. "Oh God, I'm so sorry," she mumbled.

"For what?" Jesse couldn't respond. "You mean what you did?" Karen answered for her. "Forget it. Pete's a tough kid. People like you, you know, react how you did. It's OK. It toughens him up, because that's the way it is, and me and Louis, we're not going to be around forever, and he's got to be ready, so when stuff like that happens? I consider that basic training. Pete's great. Pete's gonna be president."

"I just want you to understand—"

"Forget it," she said tersely, and Jesse was happy to oblige.

After they dropped Karen off at a cabstand, Jesse made a quick run into a deli for coffee and cigarettes. There were two Lotto customers ahead of her at the register, and as she danced in place, anxious to make it back to Freedomtown, she saw a black kid, nineteen, twenty, approaching the line from the rear of the store, a quart bottle of Coke in one hand and a box of Ring Dings in the other. Silk-screened across the chest of his white T-shirt was the police sketch of Brenda's jacker.

Jesse was so startled by the unexpected image that she straight-out accosted him. "Where'd you get that," she said, spooking the kid with her abruptness. "That's, somebody's selling that?"

"Guy on JFK," he answered cautiously.

"What guy."

"That your idea of a joke?" the deli owner, a heavyset man with a florid face and a full head of silver-white hair pitched in, glaring at the T-shirt as he processed a Lotto ticket.

"Ain't no joke," the black kid said, a little steadier. "Ain't nothing funny about it."

"So, what—that guy's a hero to you? A role model? Enlighten me, I'm too fucking stupid to understand." The kid looked off, tried to grin away his anger, his discomfort. "You know what that T-shirt represents?" The deli man addressed the second Lotto customer. "That T-shirt represents the death of intelligence, the death of decency."

The kid made a hissing sound, and Jesse saw him looking at his Coke and Ring Dings as if unsure what to do with them now.

"Decency is dead," the deli man answered, growing more red-faced. "All hail King Bullshit."

"This like Klan country," the kid muttered.

"This is what?" The deli man leaned across his counter. "Excuse me. This is what?" The silver of his hair intensified the blooming darkness of his face.

"You heard me," the kid said shakily, unconsciously stepping back. Jesse noticed a young cop back by the sandwich counter, the guy sporting the Hawaiian shirt and stonewashed jeans that screamed Gannon Narcotics.

"What . . ." The deli man continued to inflate. "You think we *owe* you something?"

The kid looked confused. "You hear me *ask* for something?"

"Everybody owes you, right? Everybody—we all fucking owe you." The kid looked at Jesse, his face twisted in irritated bewilderment. "Four hundred years," the deli man moaned, doing the Lawdy, Lawdy, rolling his eyes and wiggling his fingers toward heaven. "Four hundred years.

Well, I tell you what." He almost poked the kid in the chest from across the counter. "Let's just go back fifty. Who do you think did all the dying in World War II, huh? Just answer me that." Jesse had never heard that one before and was taken, almost captivated, by its sheer massiveness.

"Yeah? How about Vietnam?" the kid bounced back.

"Yo, George!" the cop half barked, half moaned, hungry.

"Vietnam?" The deli man reared up, then leaned across his counter again. "Let me tell you about Vietnam."

Jesse had to go but couldn't leave this back-and-forth right here; it was like putting her ear to the rail in order to hear the train coming, the news coming.

"You go down to the Wall, my friend," the deli man said, touching the kid's sternum, the contact charged. "You go down there and see who shows up to *weep*. Do a head count. Stand there for an hour and do a *head* count."

"A head count," the kid said dryly. "Like, us, them, us, them, like that?" He was getting into it now.

"You shit-skin smart-ass piece of shit," the deli man began to shout. "I'm three weeks in the hospital, you think I come back to work to put up with *you*? You think I come out of the hospital to deal with *you*?"

"Hey," the kid said, stepping back, hands up, playing it cool.

"Get the fuck out of my store," the deli man bellowed, extending a beefy, tanned arm toward the door, the faded blue ghost of an anchor tattoo visible inside his elbow.

"You want me to put these back on the shelves? Or can I just leave them here on the counter," the kid asked, fighting down a smirk, the winner.

The deli man made a big, windy move to come around the register, and the kid left.

Coming outside a moment later with a fresh pack of Winstons, Jesse saw the kid on a pay phone. She gestured to Ben, deciding to invest a few minutes in hanging around. Three drags into her first cigarette the cop came out, eating his sandwich on the hoof. "Hey, you," he barked, a food-garbled heads up directed to the kid on the phone.

The kid wheeled, made him for a cop, and returned to his conversation. The cop wolfed down the rest of his sandwich, waiting.

"Yo, *Mo,* gotta *go.*" The kid turned again. "Tell her you'll call her back in a minute," the cop said, wiping his lips with his thumb. The kid gave it ten, fifteen more seconds for good-bye, then hung up, the cop waving him forward. "That guy in there?" The cop looked off as he spoke. "George? He's an asshole." The kid said nothing, waiting for the punch line. "But I'm not too sure about your intellectual status either, my man. It's a free country and all, and I have a feeling I know where you might be coming from on this," he said, nodding at the T-shirt, "but I got to tell you, wearing something like that around here? It's . . ." He squinted, searching for the right word. "It's indelicate."

"Hey." The kid smiled, framed the jacker on his chest with the splayed fingers of both hands. "Don't you know who this is?"

"No." The cop wiped his lips with the side of his fist. "Pray tell."

"This is the boogie man." The kid's grin kicked up a notch. "This is *me.*"

Pulling up in front of Freedomtown again, Jesse saw one of the nondescript tan Crime Scene Unit minivans parked alongside Lorenzo's Crown Victoria. She had spent two weeks riding around in one of those death wagons a few summers back, and although the vehicle never transported the bodies, Jesse was convinced, by the third night out on the town, that the van interior reeked of fresh death, a sweetish, cloying aroma that hung in the air like smoke.

Within minutes of Jesse and Ben's return to the gate, Lorenzo, half carrying Brenda, came into view from around the first bend in the footpath. Without thinking, Jesse popped out of the car and began to approach them. Lorenzo waved her away furiously, and Brenda, once she recognized Jesse, turned her face into the big man's shoulder, as if attempting to avoid the press. Jesse got back in Ben's car and waited for Lorenzo to pull away.

Twenty minutes later, Ben dropped her off at the Southern District Station House. Head down, floating like a monk, she followed Lorenzo and Brenda into the lobby. She could tell, by the absolute silence that greeted them, that the word had gone out.

There was none of the usual bullshit and blather from the sergeant's desk, none of the jokes, small talk, or shout-outs, just a vibration of cold curiosity hiding behind a screen of petty activity. Lorenzo, without engaging any of the stares sent his way, hustled Brenda across the floor and up the stairs. Intent on collecting her due, Jesse continued to bring up the rear.

Ignoring Jesse, Lorenzo deposited Brenda in the third-floor inter-

view room, then quickstepped back into the hallway and rapped on
Bobby McDonald's door. Jesse positioned herself halfway up the stairs
to the fourth floor, so that when Lorenzo opened his boss's door she had
a clear shot of the office, Bobby McDonald in there wiping down his
glass-topped desk, a bottle of Fantastik in one hand, a bunched floret of
paper towel in the other.

"You charge her?" Bobby asked Lorenzo, eyes still trained on his
chore.

"Not yet. She's still talking to me."

"OK," Bobby said. "Good," he added, then *"Shit,"* tossing the paper
towels into a wastebasket. He sat on the edge of the desk, massaging his
temples. "Motherfucker."

"I hear you," Lorenzo said mildly. He was standing with his back to
Jesse, but from the stairs she could read his bobbling two-step in the
doorway just fine.

"We had no choice," McDonald addressed the air, explaining the
situation to the prosecutor, the cameras, himself. "There was a *child*
involved."

"That's right," Lorenzo said, straight-out dancing now.

"Fuck, man," McDonald hissed. "This is gonna be like the Night of
the Long Knives."

"May be." Lorenzo was almost doing jumping jacks. "I need to get in
there with her. You gonna be listening in?"

"Yeah." McDonald nodded toward the pig-nosed amp resting on his
desk. "But just me."

Thinking, Out of sight out of mind, Jesse made it into the third-floor
men's room before Lorenzo left his boss's office. A uniformed cop, enjoying a smoke, stood looking out an open window between a sink and a
urinal, and she swiftly moved to the nearest toilet stall, locking herself in
before he could react to her presence. Taking a seat on the toilet lid, she
found herself facing a graffiti-drizzled stall door centered with a bumper
sticker declaring POLICE!! DON'T MOVE!! It wasn't a joke, she knew, but a
ubiquitous reminder, plastered throughout the building, for cops to pro-
nounce "Police" distinctly when drawing down on an actor. The word,
when rushed, often sounded like "Please."

Jesse set up shop—cigarettes, lighter, pens, notepad. The wall behind the toilets was stripped to bare studs and a single layer of Sheetrock
on the far side, a renovation project frozen by budget cuts and a change
of administration. She could hear Brenda cough on the other side, the
sound making her feel a little skippy in the gut, then heard the door to

the interview room opening and closing, followed by a heavy shuffling tread—Lorenzo. Jesse pressed the side of her face to the smutty Sheetrock.

"Brenda," Lorenzo said, his voice muffled yet distinct, "before we start, can I get you something? Tea, soda, a sandwich?"

"You know—" Brenda began. But before she could complete her sentence, her voice was obliterated as the men's room door was thrown open to a stampede of cops. Jesse heard voices both male and female, hectic, competitive, racing for a piece of the bathroom wall—everybody, Jesse realized, wanting an earful on this one.

23

The interview room was traditionally barren—a Formica-topped card table, upon which rested an off-brand tape recorder and a six-pack of blank tape, and two chairs, a hardwood swivel-bottomed antique on casters for the interviewer and a metal going-nowhere folding chair for the interviewee. The long rectangular mirror beneath the wall clock fooled no one.

Brenda sat with her elbows on her knees, the CD player in her lap, headphones resting like an open choker at her throat. The heels of her palms were pressed into her eye sockets. Lorenzo, avoiding the table, sat facing her, a notebook on his crossed knee, the paper angled in such a way that she would be unable to see what he was writing. He had learned the hard way that nothing could sabotage the flow of a confession like a clear view of the note taking: the unconscious verbal slowdown to dictation speed often resulted in brooding or permanent withdrawal. He could still smell the cold reek of her accident but refrained from asking her if she wanted to freshen up.

"Brenda, before we start, can I get you something? Tea, soda, a sandwich?"

"You know, I have spent all my life, all my life, trying to get, like, maximum distance from everybody around me—my family, other people, *men*—ever since I was, ever since I can remember. Like, when I

was, I had to be three, four years old. Give me two clothespins I'll play
with them for an hour, doesn't, didn't make a difference; there could've
been a three-alarm fire ten feet away from me, I'm gone. I'm in the world
of those clothespins. I'd give them names, a sex, different voices, everything. My mother once took me to a hearing specialist because I
wouldn't ever turn to her when she called out my name, but I am telling
you, my ears were not the problem."

Lorenzo glanced at the mirror, which held them in profile, and wondered who and how many were behind it. "Brenda. I'd kind of like to
start out with what happened three nights ago."

"No," she said, holding up a hand. "You have to let me . . . I've been
thinking," Brenda took a deep breath, then a shallow breath. "Ever since
I met you, I've been thinking about how to, like, really, really *tell* you
about everything. And now you just have to let me do it."

Lorenzo nodded, gestured for her to proceed, clasped his hands over
his gut. It was two-ten, the clock a time bomb.

"With my family—my mother, my brother—school, cops, it was always, like, everybody, everybody please, just, go away. Leave me be. But
with a child, when you have a child, it's safe. It's *yours*. It's finally safe. I
mean, even that goddamn therapy group I was in, I mean everybody was
working so hard on their relationships, on their *peer* relationships; it was
so formal, so, like, earnest, everybody walking around with these gigantic
date books, making dates for everything, like two, three months in
advance—dinner dates, sleep-over dates, study dates, fuck dates, play
dates, music dates, sports dates, dog-walking dates. It was like, it was
like hiding in plain sight, do you know what I'm saying?"

He didn't really, but he felt it in some way, the urge to lie low,
mostly from his drinking days. Lorenzo was jumping ahead of himself,
half listening, wondering if there was a way he could call people—the
Reverend Longway, other clergymen, some councilmen, a few street
stars—give them a heads up on the possible postannouncement fallout,
without leaking the news.

"Even now, with the Study Clubs, you know, in Jefferson or in Armstrong or wherever, these kids that I'm—" she caught herself—"I was,
you know, involved with? Even, like, with Felicia and everybody? They're
the *other*, they're . . . It's *safe* to care for them, it's safe to put out for
them because, because they're not quite real to me. And if I had to
guess? I'd say I'm not quite real to them either."

"I don't follow," Lorenzo said, but he did.

"I'm white, they're black. They're black, I'm white. We're the *other* to each other. We're not quite *real*." She looked at him directly now. "Do you know what I'm saying?" She was almost begging him to agree.

"I hear you," he said mildly, but the observation scorched him, left him feeling betrayed in some vague way, and she knew it, her face taking on a stuck, stricken aspect.

"I *know* you know what I'm saying . . ."

"I'm right with you," he said, to get her going again.

"And, when I got pregnant? First I'm thinking, Get an abortion, who are you kidding . . . You know, I'm thinking, Hey, I'm my own baby. I mean, it never even occurred to me to have a child. *Me.* But all of a sudden, somehow I had a vision, long-range, of what it could be like—the, the companionship, the secret companionship. It was like, I saw a feeling. I saw, like, an emotional state that could be *mine*. You know what I'm—but then I remembered. This child has a father, too, and, I know this sounds sick but, like, in order to duck having to be with this guy? Ulysses? Like, as a family? I figured, have the abortion, then just adopt a kid with no strings attached. It wouldn't be mine, but it would be *mine*. And I liked Ulysses, too, but when he told me he was going back to Puerto Rico? I just busted out crying, and I'm sure he was thinking, you know, that I was crying, like, 'What Now My Love' or something, because he had kind of, you know, that smile, like, 'Look, she can't live without me.' But I swear to you, those tears? My tears? They were tears of joy. I mean it was too goddamn good to be true." She drifted off, staring past Lorenzo's shoulder. "Ulysses. If you think about it? Going back to Puerto Rico? He just, he just saved that baby's life." Her eyes strayed down to her hands, and she remained in that wilted, contemplative pose until Lorenzo felt the need to goose it along.

"Can I get you something?" He heard the coolness in his voice, knew it to be a reaction to her having assigned him to "other" status. He didn't have the luxury of reacting personally to that statement; all he could do here was withdraw emotionally, and so his pity began to drift.

"Four years," she muttered. "For four years, me and him, Cody, for four years I knew who I was. I was that boy's mother. What was that saying, that song? 'You Can't Touch This.' Remember that? For four years that was like my theme song, it was like my life was finally, you know, *good*."

Lorenzo became aware of a muffled shuffling sound from the wall opposite the one-way mirror, from the wall shared with the men's room. They were surrounded.

"But it wasn't enough, you see, just being with my son. It wasn't—you can't live on just that. You can try, but . . ." She began to withdraw again.

"Brenda." He spoke her name to bring her back.

"So Billy." She sighed, as if contemplating a steep flight of stairs. "Billy. I first met him—I had this thing at the Study Club where I would invite, like, adult role models for the kids. You know, show them people who got up and out, like in advertising, civil service, business, whatever. Anybody who the kids could eyeball and *see* it was possible to grow up and, you know, because you can't become something if you can't even visualize it. Like, you say, 'Chantal, you can become a lawyer,' and it's like, 'Become a what? Like who. I don't know no lawyers that look like me.'"

"Brenda," Lorenzo cut in, all her fervent compassion and empathy finally beginning to wear thin on him. "Brenda, Billy . . ."

"I know where I'm going."

"I just need you to get to Billy," he said, his voice warming up again despite himself. "Please."

"Billy. He came in because Felicia said to me, 'Yeah, I got someone for your role model show. I'll bring in my boyfriend. He was on Wall Street,' then something like, 'Get his ass out of the house.' So Billy comes in to talk to the kids, and he comes in in, like, a three-piece suit, wing-tip shoes, white shirt, tie, and I knew he was unemployed, and it was kind of sad, and, but he talked to the kids so, so earnestly about the stock market. He took this visit to the Study Club so seriously. And like, he's talking about stocks, bonds, hog bellies, pork bellies, buying on margin. I mean it was like, way over the kids' heads. I mean *I* didn't understand half the shit he said, but he was *trying*, he was so sweet, and he brought the *New York Times* and showed them how to read the, the stock listings. But you know, you could tell why he would have a hard time in life. I mean none of this was, I mean the kids were like, 'Huh?' and he wasn't picking up on it, but they liked him, liked his reaching out like that. And all the time he's talking, I look over at Felicia and she's rolling her eyes; it was like she had *had* it with him, this loser. I mean you could tell she had nothing left for him but contempt, and he had this look on his face when any of the kids were asking him something? His eyes would go all wide and his mouth would make like this O, like he didn't want to miss a word of what was being asked him, and I was just sitting there watching him in his unemployed Wall Street suit with that look on his face, and he had this little natty moustache and I just wanted to—

that moustache was just making everything worse, and I felt like I just wanted to peel it off his face, I just wanted to reach out . . ."

She went off again for a moment and so did Lorenzo, wondering when his pager would beep, needing that coded signal from the exhumation team coming up on his hip before he could charge her—charge her, tape her statement, then dump her, start making those calls.

"It was like, I could feel his weakness—like a flu, you know? And I just wanted to lie down with him, like, be sick with him, get better with him. I just understood him so well, so quickly. It was like—looking at him was like—he was *me*."

Lorenzo glanced at the clock again: two-thirty.

"Brenda. Billy, did he have anything to do with Cody's accident, other than—"

"He never even met Cody."

Lorenzo nodded, thinking, Pick him up, scare him with a conspiracy charge, see what comes out of his mouth.

"And so, like, at the end of his talk? The kids are all milling around, it's loud, it's crazy. I just went up to him and kind of took his hand for a second and he, like, jumped. He looked at me kind of startled, and, it was on. The whole thing took maybe ten seconds, and it was on."

Lorenzo nodded again, cast a glance at his blank pad.

"He just showed up at my apartment like two hours later. Cody was at some other kid's house to play, and Billy, he came in and he looked like, distracted, kind of worried, but you know, *hungry*. And we spent like an hour together, you know, sex, and, at the end of the hour I knew I was in big trouble, because I knew what was in store for me. I knew Billy would never lose that distracted, kind of worried vibration around me, and I knew, I knew that I would lose him. I mean, how you can lose something, or someone, you never had possession of to begin with, I don't know but it was like instant pain for me. Like a reminder of *why* I had structured my life around my son, focused my love on my son. But it was too late. I was, I had laid down with someone not a child; I had *held* someone not a child after all those years, and it was too late to go back. I had overabstained, and now I was in trouble."

Lorenzo heard someone coughing from behind the mirror, a ropy growl that just wouldn't quit.

"OK, so the day, that day? My son came home an hour after Billy had left, and I look at my boy, and for the first time in my life, in *his* life, he seemed, like, unlovely to me . . . And I knew I was in trouble.

"I don't, it wasn't the sex. It, that, I mean, it was OK. I mean, that's what you do, so you do it. But with me, with sex, if the guy is happy, I'm happy. If the guy feels good after, then OK, great, I feel good too. And Billy, he was no—he didn't—we didn't even, you know, every time. But I just couldn't wait to lay down with him again . . . For me, it was the arms, the holding."

She nodded, looking glassy, and Lorenzo began to feel for her again, lost some of his anger. He also knew he would never come back all the way with her.

"Do you want to know what I like in bed?" She asked him directly, eye to eye. "I like someone's hand right here . . ." She splayed a palm on the flat plane above her breasts, Lorenzo smiling, looking down at the table. "Right there, someone to press their hand right there. And I like a hand here." She pressed that same palm against her forehead as if she were checking for fever. "I like to lay on my back and close my eyes and feel someone's hand, not moving, just the pressure of it right here. It makes me feel safe, it makes me feel loved, physically loved . . . and I just float, float away."

"OK," Lorenzo said, trying to move her on.

"See, Billy didn't love me. I mean, so what, but—and I guess I didn't love him either, really, although I had that terror of loss that makes you feel like you love the person you're afraid of losing? But for Billy, I think he just liked being with someone who made him feel good about himself, and that was me. But there wasn't that much coming back from him. Billy's heart belonged to Mommy—you know, Felicia—and I guess I knew that from the gitty-up, but like I said, I went crazy and I was, like, in instant terror of losing him, which of course becomes—you know, what happens.

"We would get, we would see each other on the fly. He'd come up during the day if Cody was out at a friend's, or he'd come over late at night in Felicia's car and wait in the parking lot until Cody was asleep, and then I'd come down and we'd do stuff in the car or just talk, or sometimes I'd go over to his mother's house. He was house-sitting for his mother—she's in the hospital—so I'd drive out to Plainfield. But I guess most of the time I'd go down to Felicia's car at night, in front of my apartment. I wouldn't let him upstairs with Cody, in case he woke up. It was like I was cheating on Cody, or like I was sneaking out on one of my parents. Cody became like this, this . . .

"And for the first few weeks I could sort of control the panic, you know, of losing him, Billy, and kind of fake being a normal person having a normal sneaky, like, affair or whatever, but the dam, it just broke one night and, it was just pain, unbearable pain, being *with* Billy, being *away* from Billy, just second-by-second pain.

"It's like I got into this head where I had to interpret every gesture of his, every facial change, vocal change. If I came down into the parking lot and the car was clean, he loved me. If it had Felicia's shit all over? He was telling me something, sending me a message. And I couldn't sleep with him—I mean, fall asleep with him—because I was too busy analyzing how he was breathing, how he was lying. Was he curled away from me; was he going asleep to tune me out; why did he just turn on his side; is he faking being asleep; is his dream head telling him to get away from me . . .

"And sex? By the end, was unbearable because there was just too much stuff to decode, too many signals, too many . . . I'd just about have a nervous breakdown faking everything. And all the time I'm thinking, analyzing the talk, the touch, the time between talk and touch. And for Billy? I know that me being this way is, was bringing him down, making him unhappy with me; it's not, it wasn't, attractive. It wasn't, flattering. But I couldn't help it, I couldn't help it . . . And when I tried to, to mask it? The effort to hide it became just another . . .

"He couldn't put his finger on it, this hovering thing I'm laying on him, but he could *smell* it, you know? And, not now, but when I—in the beginning? He liked my sense of humor. I had this kind of low-key, mutter thing going that he liked, but I was aware he liked it and I was aware, like, for the first time how I did it, I was aware *that* I did it. So I would desperately try to get up this lay-back dryness for him, but *you* try desperately to, to fake . . . So *that* was shot. It was like everything, everything . . ."

Lorenzo physically readjusted himself, shifted his weight in the chair, attempting to get her moving faster toward the deed itself, but Brenda was oblivious to the signals.

"Billy, Billy was junk sickness, and, and the cure was the poison. And before Billy, it was all Cody for me. It was like, life was this cliff but I had kind of carved out this ledge for me and him, and I was happy, *more* than happy, but all of a sudden there was this gap . . ."

"Brenda," Lorenzo said.

"Like with my son, before Billy," she plowed on, the reintroduction of the boy settling him down again. "Before Billy, me and Cody—I would love watching videos with him or just like, lying down with him until he was asleep. But all of a sudden, I'm . . . It was terrible. I would look at my son's face in the, the TV light? And all of a sudden he's unprecious to me. And it was like, *videos?* I'm wasting critical minutes here like this. Billy's parked downstairs; I got to get this kid down. I *got* to before Billy loses patience and goes home. He did that once. But Cody, he takes—" She stopped, swallowed. "He takes," she continued, keeping it in the present tense, "twenty, thirty minutes, an hour sometimes to fall asleep, and I have to get the hell out of there before . . .

"And Cody, he can feel my tension and it keeps him awake, which makes me *more* crazy and that makes him *more* awake, but all I can think about is getting out that door, and sometimes I'd think he was asleep and I'd just make it to the hallway, you know, tippytoe, and it would be, like, at the last second, 'Mah-mee, Mah-mee . . .'" She used a braying sing-song. "And I'd be, like, "Get to *sleep!*" Brenda shouted it, eyes wide and gelid.

Lorenzo shifted in his seat again and glanced at the time bomb on the wall: two forty-five.

"And how fast would *you* fall asleep, you have this, this *giant* hanging over you, this half-insane giant who didn't *love* you anymore, didn't *want* you anymore; this person who used to treat you like the sun the moon and the stars, but no more, no more . . ."

She began to glaze and drift, the room becoming heavy with silence, a silence that Lorenzo knew to let be.

"So I started giving him Benadryl to put him out," she began again, her voice turgid with pain. "I started doping him, Cody, just to get him down, nothing more than you'd give a kid for a stuffed head . . . I was on a bus once, and I heard some woman talking to a friend about how she used it to get her kid to sleep every once in a while, so I tried it one night and it worked. It worked. I told him it was night vitamins, and it became a part of our bedtime routine.

"And the hell of it is, is that I *knew* about the gap between what I should feel and what I do, did feel. It's not like, well, you've been re-placed by Billy and that's the way it is. It *killed* me not to be moved by my son anymore."

Lorenzo coughed, resisting the impulse to check the time again, looking down at his blank book instead.

"But even at my worst, even at my worst there was a part of me that had the big picture still; there was a part of me that wanted to say to my son, Just let me get over this Billy guy, sweetheart, and I'll be right back. Just let me play this out to its miserable end, and we'll go back to watching the movies and having our talks . . . See, I *knew* about this, this, *seizure* by Billy. I recognized it, I could break it down, but I couldn't do anything to stop it. I was so . . . I am not a stupid person, but it was like, my intelligence—my experience with people—my intelligence was just standing on the shore . . ." She floated out a languid hand, signifying a river, he guessed.

"Let me—" He leaned forward, gearing up to intrude, to speed her along.

"See, Billy, with all his, his weakness, and, craziness, he was human—I mean, more human than *me,* because he had like a number of preoccupations. Love life, job hunt, whatever. But me, for me, it was all Billy, all Billy. And the thing is, right now talking to you? I can't even conjure up a picture of Billy's face."

"Brenda," Lorenzo began again, eyes irresistibly sliding to the time. "I hear everything you're saying, but right now I'm gonna need you to start talking about three nights ago. You got to start telling me about that."

She didn't respond at first, just sat there staring at Lorenzo's chest, lips moving, forming words that gradually became audible and coherent.

"He wouldn't go down, Cody . . . I had already dosed him, Billy was waiting in the car, but Cody just wouldn't go down. And *that* night, I knew that Billy was just on the verge of breaking it off with me, going back to Felicia whole hog, and I *had* to get down there. I had to talk to him but Cody just wouldn't fall asleep, and I just said, Fuck it, I got to go. And the thing of it is, I was even kind of relieved that Billy was finally dumping me. Kind of, you know, taking me out of my misery, so, it was probably the last time I'd ever leave him, my son, alone, it was probably the last . . ." She went away, came back. "But he wouldn't go down. He wouldn't. So after a while I just said to him, 'I have to go downstairs, you be a good boy and go to sleep.' And, he was, he was furious. He said to me, 'I don't want you to go,' but like a *man* would say it. He said, 'I know where you're going and I don't want you to go.'"

"I know where you're going . . ." Lorenzo repeated.

"The thing with Cody? You have to understand what it felt like for him. I had made him the center of my world, right? So like *his* whole world, was *me.* He has no father, I wouldn't let him see his grandmother, I wouldn't let him—I mean, he wasn't in school yet. Everything was me. It was not, it was love, but it was like crazy love, and now this wrap-around mother, me, his whole world, kind of cut out on him, and he was . . . He felt it right away with Billy. He got angry, he threw tantrums, he got withdrawn, he *knew*. He knew maybe not about Billy as Billy, but he *knew*. He felt it right away.

"And that night." She paused, rocking a little now, eyes fluttering. "That night he says, 'I know where you're going and I don't want you to go.' Like, standing there, kind of punchy with the Benadryl, and I want to say to him, 'Tonight is the last night. Just give me this one last . . .' But I don't say that, I'm too agitated, I'm, I say, 'You go to sleep, I'll be back up soon. I promise.' And he says to me, he says, 'If you go you'll be *sorry*.' Says it just like some jealous husband: 'If you go you'll be sorry.' And I'm, I almost didn't go. I almost . . . I had never heard that tone from him. It was so . . . If he had only sounded more babyish, or more pathetic, maybe I wouldn't have, but it was so *hard,* his voice, and it scared me. It, like, re*pell*ed me out of the house—but he was only four years old— nobody has to tell me that. And I remember thinking as I'm going down the stairs, *I* made him sound like that. I'm *making* him that way. And for maybe the millionth time since I'm with Billy, I'm thinking, like, just in general, I'm fucking up here, I'm really fucking up. Like, going down the stairs, This is bullshit. Total bullshit . . ." Her rocking picked up a notch.

"And I get downstairs, and there's Billy. And he tells me it's over. He can't handle both me and Felicia. And I knew this was coming, but I start yelling and crying, you know: 'You don't love her, she doesn't love you,' blah, blah, blah. And the thing is, I don't even know why I was kicking up such a fuss. Like I said, I was kind of relieved, but I guess I thought it was required of me or something, or maybe I just . . . So, blah, blah, blah, for like an hour, and Billy's a decent guy. He gives me my hour, he doesn't just, you know, 'Bye-bye, bitch.' He takes it from me. I guess he's feeling like he owes it to me.

"So we never leave the parking lot all that time, but finally Billy drives off. I'm, I can't go upstairs just yet, so I walk around for a while, you know, trying to cry, sort out what I'm supposed to be feeling. But finally I go upstairs and—I don't see him, Cody." Brenda's voice took on a fluttery cast. "I look in the bed, I'm, like, He's hiding." Lorenzo saw her legs starting to swing against each other.

"He's hiding. And, but, it's OK, because Billy's over and done with, and now I'm kind of, of lighthearted about it, relieved, and I know he's mad at me, Cody, and he's trying . . ." Her hands flew to her face, tamping tears. "He's trying to, you know, *scare* me or punish me, but it's OK, it's OK. I deserve it and, like I said, I'm kind of happy because now we're . . . It's gonna get *back* now, it's gonna be better, and I'm going, 'Cody, Cody,' like playing, like, 'Where are you-ou.' And then I see him. He's under the . . ." Brenda jammed up again, bared her teeth. "He's under the table and I'm . . . He's asleep, lying there. And I get down?"

She slipped off the chair and got on all fours, Lorenzo sliding back. "I go over to . . . First I thought I should just carry him to bed, then, no, I'm gonna wake him, and I crawl over and the *smell*. And I put my hand in something wet on the carpet. And I just like shot up under the table." Brenda sat up, unconsciously touching the crusty gash at the back of her head. "But the smell. The smell was, and then I saw the bottle laying there and . . . I never touched him, I never. The minute I saw that empty bottle I remembered, you know, 'If you leave you'll be sorry.' And I knew. I knew."

"Was he alive then?" Lorenzo helped her up to her chair, thinking, Aspiration of the stomach, the boy choking on his own vomit. She stared off, mouth working. "Brenda," he cautiously pushed. "Was he alive?"

"No," she whispered.

"How did you know," Lorenzo said, envisioning the boy blue and cold to the touch.

"He was not alive."

"Did you try to revive him?"

"He was not alive."

"Tell me how you knew he was not alive."

"Because I'm his *mom*." The words slipped out through clenched teeth, in a savagely peppy singsong, her eyes glittering, Lorenzo thinking, Suicide watch.

"I'm his *mom*," she repeated in that same sensuous, self-lacerating tone. "And us *moms*, we *know* these things."

"OK," Lorenzo said, retreating.

"He said, 'If you go you'll be sorry.' And he was right, he was right. What is that, suicide? No. He didn't know, he didn't . . . *I* set the pace, *I* showed him the way, taught him how to *be*, so you charge me with homicide, you *charge* me, you *fuck* me. You do whatever—"

"Whoa, whoa . . ." Lorenzo lurched forward, trapped her hands in his own, desperate to shut her up, then keep her talking, keep the information coming. "Brenda, Brenda . . ."

"He didn't know! He didn't know!" Her voice was a raw squawk, her eyes seeming to wobble in the sockets.

"Brenda!" Lorenzo barked, a verbal slap. "Brenda! Listen to me. You're talking about an accident. What you described to me, if it's true, was an accident." He withheld from her that, yes, she would initially be charged with homicide—to soothe the rage to come out on the streets tonight, to give the prosecutor a leg up on the plea bargaining. "A tragic accident, Brenda. What you say, it breaks my heart." Lorenzo stared at her, one hand holding both of hers, the other pressed to his chest. "But you can't go blaming yourself like that."

"Don't you *play* me," she snapped. "Don't you—"

"Brenda. We need to keep talking."

"About *what*. What else is there."

"I need for you to take me through the night."

"I'm done," she said, looking off furiously, vigorously scratching the side of her head. "So you *charge* me."

No way, not yet, Lorenzo thought, scrambling for the right tack. "Brenda, how do you feel about Billy now?"

"What?"

"How do you feel about him going to jail?"

"Why."

"Because if we stop talking right now? I have no choice but to lock him up for conspiracy," he said, leaving out the nature of that conspiracy: to commit murder. Lorenzo was avoiding that word at all costs right now. "Is that what you want to happen?" She sat up, a slow, reflective uncoiling.

"Now, if all he did was move a body, I need for you to lay it out for me, blow by blow, because I got to pick him up anyhow, and he can either go home tonight with a desk-appearance misdemeanor or he can go to jail." Lorenzo was lying to her—Billy would be going to County no matter what she revealed. "Now, what's gonna determine that judgment on my end is how well his story is gonna match yours. But if you don't *give* me a story? Then"—Lorenzo raised helpless hands, dropped them back down to his lap—"in he goes."

"Billy," she said.

Lorenzo gave her a few seconds. "Does he deserve to go to jail?"

"No," she said quietly.

"Then you got to help me keep him out." Brenda rested her forehead on the rickety card table. "Brenda?"

"I was driving. All I remember is putting my hand in something wet. I remember the smell and I remember whacking my head under the table, and then I was driving. I don't know how. I don't recall, like, leaving the house, but all of a sudden I'm in, I'm like somewhere in Jersey City. But I turn around and start driving home. I was thinking maybe it was a dream, seeing Cody like that, because I didn't have any memory of leaving the house, so maybe I wasn't even there, like I hallucinated the whole thing.

"So I park in the lot, I go up the stairs and—I don't go in. He's, I don't go in.

"Then I'm driving again. I'm thinking, Let me just crash, let me just . . . But I can't. So what do I do. I think about my mother, my brother, everybody that I have spent my entire life trying to escape from, all of these people staring at me, scrutinizing me, *knowing* me—everybody, like, converging on me. Like, locking me in. I mean, all my life these people . . . And I'm telling myself, Just crash the car. I'm, Just fucking *die*. But then I think, if I die, then he dies in *me*, within me, like . . ." She paused, then repeated, quoting herself with disgust, "He dies in me. Jesus Christ."

"Hey." Lorenzo offered her an open hand, restraining himself from saying something like, "Don't be so hard on yourself."

"And I'm in, like, this fog, this fog, and I find myself near Freedomtown. You have to understand, everything I do, everywhere I go, I'm—it's not like, it's like an animal. And I go in there, I'm in there, and I'm down on the ground, *clawing*, you know, making . . .

"And then I'm in front of my house again and I go upstairs. I go in, but I don't look at him. I can't. And then I'm out, I'm out, and I drive. I'm driving to Billy's house, his mother's house, but he's not there, and then I drive back and I call Felicia's house, and if—I'm hoping *he* picks up, because if Felicia picks up, but he does and when I said Cody, what happened to Cody, he hung up on me. He hung up, but he called me back, he called . . . and he believed me. He didn't, you know, challenge me. And I told him—I tried to—I think I tried to convince him it was his fault too. I don't remember exactly. I mean I'm floating, my body is floating, my mouth is floating . . . But he came, he came. I was watching from across the street and I saw him get out of a cab and I saw him go up to my house, up the stairs, and he came down with . . . And he got in my car and he drove off and he—I guess I told him where to go because . . ."

She made a vague gesture indicating, Lorenzo guessed, Freedomtown.

"The stones. I guess he did that. Made it proper." She was crying again. "And he had my car. I don't know what he did with it. And I couldn't go back up there. I, even with . . . So I took a cab to Jersey City and I checked into a motel near the tunnel and I was just sitting there in my room—my head's like—and I remember I went out about midnight and I'm going—I go into this 7-Eleven and I come out with a bottle of Clorox, I guess to, you know, but I couldn't do it, I couldn't. And I stayed up and, like, the room had two beds—it was one of those rooms with two big beds—and I just, I laid in one, then I laid in the other, I laid in one, I laid in the other. That's what I remember, going from bed to bed. I had the Clorox in the bathroom, and every hour or so I'd go in there. I turned on the TV one time, I remember that, you know, to see if . . . And the next day, I went to work. I just went to work. I had this weird—I just floated through the day. I couldn't, I was immune from everybody. Just floated. I can't remember much. I know I called him at his mother's house, Billy."

The thumbtack call, Lorenzo thought, envisioning her in the Study Club that day, her haunches embedded with pushpins, Shamiel crying.

"And Billy, he was sobbing. He was hysterical, but I can't tell you anything he said, because I just . . . And that night, I went back to the motel and I was just sitting there again and the cleaning lady, the maid? She had made the beds and whatever, and she left the Clorox in the bathroom. My bottle of Clorox, and in my mind it was like she knew that it was mine, not the hotel's, she knew *why* I had bought it, and she had left it there for me, like, 'Go ahead, do it, *do* it.' And I got so scared of dying, of *judgment* . . . and I got out of there and I just did what I did."

"What."

"I took a cab over to Armstrong and I just sat up on the Conrail tracks, and I must've figured out what I was going to do but I can't remember thinking about it. It was like automatic pilot. Like, I don't know whose handbag that was—you gave me the name. I thought it was empty. I saw it just lying there in the dirt by the parking lot of the motel. I had it with me, but I can't remember coming on it and thinking, like, Hey, I'll use that handbag. But I had it with me. I remember when I found it, it looked like someone had already backed over it in the motel lot, and so I took it with me and I was up there on the tracks and at some point I came down to the buildings and I walked over to the park there, Martyrs, and I tossed the bag in the dirt. I got down on my knees there and I just started jamming my hands in the shit. Just started scraping them, like, shoving them into the dirt, like . . . And they were fucked up from Freedomtown, you know, from digging in Freedom . . . And I just, just, mauled myself. I got—I wanted every fucking broken, rusted—I wanted it all in my skin, *all* of it. And then I walked up through the Bowl, and I guess I knew I was headed for the hospital, and I guess I knew what I was going to say when I got there, but I don't ever remember knowing the story—the, the *lie*—before it came out of my mouth. I was, I was just so scared of people, like, seeing me and *owning* me—my mother, my brother, everybody judging me—of being judged, and if I think of it now I would have to say somewhere in my head I knew that Armstrong . . ." She paused, exhaling heavily. "Judgment on Armstrong had been passed a long time ago.

"I mean, Armstrong was, like, *buckshot* with judgment. And so maybe it could absorb just one more hard knock. And that, that nobody, no individual would really get hurt by it, and that I could, like, go on, you know, in some way go on with some kind of life, but, no. No. You can't." Brenda shifted gears, spoke to his eyes now. "I never thought that all this would happen. The newspapers, I swear to you."

"OK."

"I would have *never*—"

"OK," Lorenzo said, not wanting to hear it. For a moment, a silence came down on them so absolute that Lorenzo began to imagine he could hear the breathing, the collective breathing that encircled this room.

"Billy," she said, breaking the spell. "The thing about Billy? That night at the hospital, when you came? You took me back to my apartment, and I hadn't, I hadn't been there since I saw Cody. And when we came in, I was expecting it to be, to have that *smell*. To have—I expected to *see* things there, still there. But the place was clean, it was clean, so Billy, he had to have come back to my place after. He had to have come back and cleaned up for me. I guess so that I wouldn't have to . . . that had to have been . . . he *did* that. For *me*. And what did that cost him, you know, take out of him, Billy. If I had to pick someone to get all bent out of shape over—I mean, coming back to my place like that? He had that in him, you see. He had that."

Lorenzo's pager finally went off. He glanced down and saw three twos coming up on his hip.

"What," Brenda said, flat and breathless.

"What?"

"What was that. They have Cody?"

"Brenda." Lorenzo reached out to touch her arm. "Listen, listen, listen . . ."

"Is he OK?"

"What?"

"What does he look like." Brenda inched forward on her chair, the skin around her eyes a papery gray.

"Brenda." Lorenzo reached for the tape recorder, thinking, Hurry.

"What did I do," she said with hollow awe.

"Brenda. This is not my call." Lorenzo quickly slipped in a tape. "This is coming from the prosecutor. But at this point I'm going to have to charge you with homicide. Now, personally, I have no reason to, to, disbelieve anything you told me."

"If you think about it, the whole planet is dying," she said quickly. "What's out there now. Pollution, AIDS, drugs. This is what's waiting for them out there." She was talking to the far wall, Lorenzo again thinking, Hurry.

"But because of all the, the obstruction you put in our paths, Brenda, this is what's required of me. Do you understand what I'm saying?" But she was elsewhere, inside herself or back out at the Chicago Fire. "Now, my guess is, in a few days, once the forensics is done? The charge is gonna get downgraded, but—"

"I think," Brenda interrupted, "I think I painted my son in kind of an idealized light, you know, because of what I did." Her voice was high and drifting. "He was a very difficult child, Cody. I'm not saying it was his fault that he was that way, but he was an angry child. He had a lot of anger."

"Now here's the thing." Lorenzo hurried past her words, rested a hand on the recorder. "We have to go on tape. And the reason we have to do this is because, if *I* say what your story was, you know, with no proof of your words, no documentation, people are gonna give us both the brush-off. Everybody is gonna say that I'm covering for you, that I feel sorry for you. See, I'm already in some hot water with a lot of people over this. People have been telling me all along I'm some kind of big-time fool for buying your *other* story. So for both our benefits, we got to get this down on tape, in your own words, OK?" She stared past him, whispering something, Lorenzo knowing he was saying all this just because this was how you did it. "Now, once we get it down, we'll play it back, listen to it. We can change, correct, add anything you want, OK? But this is the only way I can help you now, all right? Now once I got this going? Alls you got to do is tell me what happened, just like you already did. Just tell me again."

"Again," she said, the word weighing a ton.

He pressed Record. "This is Dempsy detective Lorenzo Council. I'm sitting here in the interview room of the Southern District station house on July the second at 2:55 P.M. With me is Brenda Martin, a white female, aged thirty-two, who resides at 16 Van Loon Street, Gannon, New Jersey, phone number 420-7210, Social Security number 183-40-3947."

Lorenzo tried to wink at her, as if to communicate that this was a scam they were pulling, him and her. "This statement is in relation to the death of Cody Martin, aged four."

Lorenzo hesitated as a ripple shot through her frame.

"Brenda? Now, once again, I have to advise you of your rights." His tone formal, for the prosecutor, for the walls.

"See, you have to understand something," she cut him off. "I wouldn't, I couldn't have always been there for him." She sounded reasonable, lucid—gone. Lorenzo was bumped off course more by her tone than by her words.

"Excuse me?"

And then all was lost to chaos. Brenda, wild-eyed, a horse in a burning stable, exploded out of her chair—her CD player clattering across the floor, the dislodged batteries rolling—and threw herself at the far wall as if there were an exit there that only she could see. Lorenzo, not having time to rise from his seat, instinctively snaked out an arm and caught her around the middle, intercepting her, bringing her down on his lap. Brenda flailed, squawking now, as Lorenzo hugged her from behind, his chair rearing back on its springs as if they were trying to land a marlin.

"Can I get some help in here?" Lorenzo barked in an oddly polite and formal tone, addressing the one-way mirror, the bathroom wall, the amp on Bobby McDonald's desk. Brenda whooped like a freight train as he struggled to restrain her, the tape recorder joining the CD player on the floor. With one of Lorenzo's hands around her waist, the other diagonally across her chest seizing her shoulder, Brenda whirled them both around the room on the caster-footed chair, propelling them sideways into a wall, Lorenzo repeating his request, this time with a little more snap: "Can I get some *help*."

24

The men's room had cleared out by the second call for help—the three remaining detectives who were listening in through the wall struggling past one another to leave—and Jesse was finally alone, still locked in her stall.

She could hear Brenda's muffled wails and entreaties mixing with the terse directives of the cops as they tried to restrain her, one of them calling out for Joyce Bannion, the only female detective on the tour. There would be no recorded statement this night, and Jesse's guess was that Brenda was headed for the hospital, not the jail. She would most likely be sedated, rehydrated, and left there overnight with a female cop on guard. In the morning, the judge, the prosecutor, and the public defender would come by for a bedside arraignment, and as soon as she was considered adequately recovered, Brenda would be transferred to County.

Jesse remained in the stall well past the time of Brenda's removal from the building. For the last hour, this room had hosted an endless procession of eavesdroppers, most of them hanging in only long enough to say that they had been there but one or another of them rattling the door of her stall every few minutes or so, so that Jesse's head was split between absorbing Brenda's tale and fending off discovery. The taut intensity of this double-jointed alertness had left her with a borderline migraine.

Jesse hadn't begun to appreciate the quality of the hatred that would soon rain down on Brenda until she overheard her asking Lorenzo, "Do you know what I like in bed?" and then, answering her own question, "I like someone's hand right here . . . And I like a hand here." No one in the bathroom could see where either "here" was, and, braced to absorb a medley of wisecracking speculations among the dozen or more cops who were listening in at that moment, Jesse was taken by surprise when not one of them mouthed off. In that silence she intuited complete condemnation: the sexual preferences of Brenda Martin received as morally offensive and repugnant information.

When the normal ambient racket descended once more on the third floor of the station house, Jesse started to punch in Jose, but she had to shut the phone down when two cops came in to use the facilities.

"You know what I'd do?" one asked the other over the sound of erratic splashings. "I'd tie her down in her cell, plaster the walls and ceilings with pictures of the kid, give it a week, then toss her a razor."

Jesse waited for the cops to leave, then slipped back out in the hallway. Blending into the general rush and buzz of the postarrest station house, she tried Jose again. He clipped the phone on the first ring.

"She get charged?"

"Yup," she said, keeping her head down, loitering in a sea of police.

"Homicide?"

"Yup."

"When's the presser?"

"Seven-thirty or so. They got to get their shit together, line up a few of the brothers to keep the peace. Let me just give you the dead nuts on the confession now. I'll do the write-up of the Friends of Kent search for tomorrow. No rush on that, right?"

"Go."

"She claims the kid—it was an accident. Said the boy drank a bottle of Benadryl."

"Sounds like an honest mistake. Go."

"It wasn't."

"What."

"A mistake."

"What?"

"Says the kid was mad at her."

"For . . ."

"Going out."

"Bullshit. Go."

"She goes out, comes back, the kid is dead."

"They recover the body?"

"In Freedomtown."

"Buried?"

"No, on a fuckin' Ferris wheel."

"Who's the man?"

"What?"

"You said 'going out.' With who."

She started to say, then realized that, although she knew the guy was Felicia Mitchell's boyfriend, all she had on him was a first name. In addition, she didn't know if Lorenzo was going to make the Billy end of things public information, and she didn't want to jam him up if he wasn't.

"I'll call you back in a minute."

"Jesse, wait—"

She hung up, eased herself into the squad room, and headed for Lorenzo, who was standing over his desk, salaaming into the phone.

"You were right. You were right. But I had to pursue the story as *told* to me. I had to do my *job*. That's the way it is, Rev. That's . . . You were right. I done *said* that about sixty times already, OK?"

Rev: Jesse guessed Longway, but it could have been Howell, McMichaels, or Bowers—lots of activist revs out there. Jesse eyed a crumpled pink dry-cleaning slip by Lorenzo's phone, the back of it inked with a scribbled list of twelve names, Lorenzo speed-humping his way through all of Dempsy's high-profile minority players.

"But now, here's the deal," Lorenzo said. "Are you going to help me tonight? 'Cause I need you up there. I need . . . Hey, I'm pissed too, I'm pissed as a motherfucker, but so now what do you want to happen to-night, huh? What, you want to see fireworks? You want Devil's Night? Who do you think's gonna . . . Who do you think's gonna get hurt most tonight if we don't . . . What . . . *Hey*. We're gonna have . . . Who do you think . . . Don't you think they're gonna be all set up for that?"

Jesse, practiced at reading upside down from years of talking to peo-ple from the visitor side of the desk, committed as many of the twelve names to memory as she could, the move for her here to hit some of these people before the presser, get herself a slew of first reactions, keep ahead of the story.

"Let me tell you something about tonight." Lorenzo lowered his voice, shifting into a tone of confidential menace. "They're most likely gonna have three, four hundred police out there in riot gear, a hundred, hundred fifty by Armstrong alone. Now, you ain't gonna *see* them unless something goes down, but my question to you is, given what I just told you, don't you think we got enough brothers in the joint as is? Or do you think we gotta lock up a whole 'nother busload tonight. Would that make you happy? Or how 'bout the medical center. Whose heads gonna get bust out there tonight? *Think,* Rev . . . Gannon? Naw, man, you want to see Gannon police tonight you got to go to Gannon. You want to see Gannon police for the next six *months?* You're gonna have to go to Gannon. That one's like money in the bank."

Or better still, Jesse thought, she would work on becoming part of the story, presenting herself as Lorenzo's secret liaison, hot out of the confession box: Detective Council thought you might need to know this about what Brenda Martin said; Lorenzo wants to know if you have any questions he can help you with. Make herself a human information bridge, runner to the stars. Jesse was counting on the scene being too hectic and emotional over the next twenty-four hours for anyone to take the time to check her credentials on this one.

"I agree. I agree." Lorenzo rubbed his eyes so vigorously that his glasses flew off. "So what's it gonna be . . . Naw, I can't cash in a maybe. Maybe's like a unsigned check. Well then, think about this. Me and you are talking right now, 'cause me and you are—I mean, we go back, man, we go . . . But I want you to think about who's *really* asking you for this favor. I want you to think about who'd be bending over backwards to kiss your ass in this city if only you'd get up there tonight. And then I want you to think about what you *need* around here . . . Right . . . Right. Man says to me, 'I'm sorry,' I say, 'How sorry *are* you? The swap line is open.'" Lorenzo laughed at the response to that, his fingers anxiously tapping the dry-cleaning slip.

Jesse caught Lorenzo's eye, signaled for a time-out, and got waved off.

"No gain without pain. No gain . . . Hey, you be as mad at me as you wanna be. Alls I'm asking is you think about who's gonna do the hurtin' tonight and who's gonna rake in the overtime . . . No. Long term too. Long term too . . . Then we got differing philosophies on our hands, brother. We got . . . Seven-thirty, abouts. In front of the courthouse . . . Well, if you got to think about it, you got to think about it. Alls I can say is, I'll be sorely disappointed to see you absent. No, I know you don't have to answer to me. Alls I'm doing is telling you how I'd feel. Hey, the only person we all got to answer to is the man in the mirror, brother. The man . . . Yeah, well, God too. I stand corrected." Lorenzo laughed again, furiously scratching his jaw this time. "I stand corrected. All right. All right." He finally hung up, the laugh vanishing as he ran his finger down the slip. He reached blindly for the phone again, whispering to himself the next number on the list.

"Who's Billy?" Jesse asked, causing him to misdial.

"Hang on." He dialed again, too pressed to look at her.

"Can I run with this Billy?"

"No, you cannot," Lorenzo declared flatly, still not looking at her. "Diane, hey," he said with a quick, nervous laugh. "Yeah, it's me. Is the rev in?" Lorenzo waited, taking the momentary pause to finally give her his eyes. "I believe we're even now, Jess. So you're gonna have to leave, OK?"

Ben was double-parked in front of the station house, and as Jesse headed for the car, a Chevy Nova pulled up, two detectives emerging from the rear seat, a tall, fleshy black man, maybe thirty years old, between them. Although uncuffed, this guy seemed to be definitely in the shit. His face was haggard, ripple-pouched, and his clothes looked like they had been thrown on in the dark—a clean but misbuttoned white shirt and a pair of charcoal dress slacks, sunlight glinting off the half-open fly. In that moment, he looked like nothing so much as an exhausted waiter, but Jesse picked up a vibe of education and some kind of slapdash white-collar résumé: computers, marketing, low-level management.

She gave it a shot. "Hey, Billy?" He turned to her with entreating, half-drowned eyes, then disappeared into the building.

Jesse decided to hit on the Reverend Longway first. As Ben drove her to Armstrong, she reconnected with Jose and filled him in on the confession, continuing to lay it out as Brenda had presented it—an accident followed by a panic attack—tamping the explanation for the bogus jacker down to a tight quote: "I was scared. I never thought any of this would happen." It was more or less what she had said, and, save for a cursory description of her giving it up to the Friends of Kent outside the abandoned children's dormitory earlier in the day, the tale of Brenda's auto-da-fé would have to keep for the next cycle.

Set in the community center, the Armstrong housing office was fronted by a glassed-in reception area. Jesse recognized the heavyset woman manning the phones, Betty something, a tenant working off her rent. She was normally a buoyant person, but when Jesse approached the perforated speak-through, Betty threw her a tight-mouthed glance, then turned away, focusing her attention on a portable TV, Jesse thinking, This is not good.

"Hey." Jesse propped her elbows on the small ledge beneath the speak-through. "Is the rev in? I have a message for him from Lorenzo Council."

"You can give it to me," Betty said, her eyes never leaving the rolling screen.

"Actually, I can't."

"Then you'll have to wait," she said tersely. "He's busy."

"It's kind of urgent."

"I said, he's busy."

"You a reporter?" The speaker was a teenager standing in the paint-chipped doorway behind the receptionist. The kid looked scared—fish-mouthed and blinky. "My father's on the phone, but you can come in if you're a reporter."

Longway's son steered her past a Xerox machine, past an out-of-order bathroom, past an empty room set up for the housing police, and into the deepest office. There were three desks and three phones, all being used now by people Jesse recognized from the job: Longway; another minister, Irvine Rainey; and a lay activist named Donald De Lauder. In mood and activity this humid, food-smelling room came off as a cloning of Lorenzo and his own desk earlier: the call going out farther and farther into the city.

"I'm Jesse Haus," she said to the son, the only one not engaged. "I'm with the *Register*." The kid kept his hands in the back pockets of his jeans and stared at her nervously, hungrily, his mouth agape. "I just . . ." She hated to waste questions on this terrorized boy. "I just came from . . . Did Lorenzo call you? He called you, right?" She was just saying it, knowing that he had.

"You have to talk to my father," the kid said, glancing anxiously at Longway, who, head down, was working the phone.

"I just came from hearing her confession, taking her statement, and Lorenzo asked me to come over and ask you if you needed to know anything," she said, stage-loud for the benefit of the phoners.

"Do *I?*" The kid touched his own chest, incredulous.

"Young lady," Donald De Lauder announced sonorously as he carefully hung up the phone. "Are you about to tell us how it is?" Longway's son gratefully stepped off.

"Well, I can tell you how it was—you know, how it went."

"You're going to tell me—us," he said, gesturing to the two other men on the phones, "the extenuating circumstances."

Gaunt, hollow-eyed and B-ball tall, De Lauder wore jeans, a dashiki, and, despite a haunted history, cop shoes—spit-shined, bulbous, and black. He was an ex-cop, a Newark PD undercover who in the late sixties had been accidentally shot during a police raid of a Black Panthers cell he had infiltrated.

"Well," Jesse said, his "young lady" now grating on her, "if you think it would be important for you to know, yeah, I can do that."

"Is she responsible for the death of her child?" he asked.

Jesse winced. "That's a tricky one."

"Well, how about we ask you a simpler question." The Reverend Longway abruptly joined in. "Was the child abducted from these houses?"

"No, he wasn't," Jesse said cleanly, knowing Longway had already been apprised of this fact.

"No," he repeated, declared. "Then you just told me all *I* need to know."

"Basically," Jesse plowed on, wanting more of a reaction, "the situation might not have been all that calculated."

"I'm not really interested." Longway folded his arms across his chest and settled on a corner of a desk, as if inviting her to take her best shot.

"Let me," he began, squinting into the middle distance, "let me tell you what you might have *seen* and *heard* over the last few days but apparently have not understood. And you might want to write this down, because I doubt if you're alone in your lack of comprehension in this city." Longway waited, demanding by his silence that she take dictation. Jesse was happy for the exclusive, the quotes, the whatever, but felt off balance. Why was he giving her this mini-interview when the whole world would be listening to him in a few hours?

"When you talk to the police," Longway began, "they will tell you that a child's life was at stake. They will tell you that they were operating on the information that they had received, that, that perception, comes before fact. That, that time, was of the essence."

Jesse was scrawling, murmuring, "OK."

"All good and well, all good and well," Longway sang, hands up. The last guy still on the phone, the Reverend Rainey, a handsome but gelatinous mountain of a young man, finished his call and lent an ear, the entire phone campaign coming to a halt.

"But let me propose to you another situation." Longway grinned. "And you tell *me* if this sounds plausible." Both Rainey and De Lauder were already nodding in affirmation, most likely having already heard what Longway was about to put forth, and suddenly Jesse got it, this whole exclusive one-on-one in the midst of high-pressure chaos. He was practicing on her; she was just a test run for the presser, an out-of-town audience, Jesse thinking, I'll take it.

"Can you imagine," Longway began. "Can you imagine if, if a *black* child. A black child from Armstrong had been abducted—was *said* to have been abducted—somewheres in the city of Gannon. Can you imagine the police department of Dempsy raiding that city in an effort to save that child?"

"Hell no!" Rainey exploded, Longway's son levitating off the floor.

"No, you cannot," Longway seconded.

"I hear you," Jesse murmured again, writing. Then she cut him off, the rest of his speech, asking, "So what's going to happen tonight?"

"What's going to happen?"

"Eight o'clock, nine o'clock, ten o'clock, midnight. In the physical world," Jesse pressed. "What is going to happen."

Longway hesitated, the question not on the dance card for now. De Lauder, losing interest, returned to working the phones. Rainey and the jumpy kid looked to Longway, waiting, like Jesse, for his response.

"Off the record?" he finally said in a more intimate tone, a sideways tone, and Jesse shut her notepad. "I honestly don't know."

"Nobody knows," the Reverend Rainey added soberly.

"What do *you* think's gonna happen?" Longway's son asked her, drawing the stares of Rainey and his father. Before she could respond, the kid, suddenly blushing, quickly headed for the door, where he bumped into a teenaged girl on her way in, the swift exchange of irritated clucking noises between them informing Jesse that they were brother and sister. The girl handed Longway a fat envelope, then left.

"Can I put it this way?" Jesse asked gingerly. "What, where, what do you think you'll be doing after the presser."

"Trying to, to get this city to call itself to account," the Reverend Rainey volunteered. "But without any more people of color getting hurt."

"We're gonna try to keep it cool," Longway added as he opened the envelope, which was stuffed with cash, "but maintain the *heat*."

Jesse nodded as if enlightened.

"We'll attempt," Rainey said, "to keep it under control, to keep it lawful."

"Attempt," Longway muttered, as he dumped the money on the desk. "That's the million-dollar verb here."

Jesse nodded to the crumpled mound of cash, small bills, mostly tens, fives, and ones. "For bail?"

"Yeah, I'm an old Boy Scout," he said as he began counting, his lips moving silently to the cadence of the math. "You know, 'Be prepared.'"

Halfway to a councilman's storefront office over on JFK, Jesse had a flash of how this next interview would most likely go and, rather than put herself through the ordeal, she had Ben pull to the curb. There were five people she wanted to hit on before the press conference, but as she sat there going over the list the whole exercise seemed like a waste of time. Jesse felt that she could almost make up her own quotes—attribute them at random to the various players and just feed the whole shebang over the phone to Jose without getting caught.

There was only one peripheral player whose responses she felt unable to predict: Felicia Mitchell. A sit-down with Felicia could be a wild ride, because Jesse was almost sure she hadn't received one of those heads-up phone calls from Lorenzo. And depending on how deep the word had gone out into the street by now, she might not have heard about the discovery of the body, Brenda's arrest, or any of it.

Jesse had Ben turn around and head for the Jefferson Houses. They hit heavy traffic—a three-car pileup on Route 13—and she spent the extra travel time phrasing and rephrasing her questions and disclosures, fretting over the right tone and wording of the bombshells she was about to lay in Felicia Mitchell's lap, trying to find the line between sincerity and opportunism that would allow her to walk out of there, once she was finished, with her head still on her shoulders and her sense of shame still in its cage.

It was four-twenty, and as Jesse entered the Study Club's double apartment, she saw that the rooms were almost deserted. Felicia was there, gazing out a window in the Pool Table Room, an aide was stowing away arts and crafts material in the Homework Room, and four children were huddled around a lime-green screen in the Computer

Room. Looking puffy-faced and distant, the head of the Study Club stood with her back to the door and peered out at the late afternoon haze as if it were the northern lights.

"Felicia?" Jesse crossed the room and came up alongside her at the window. "I'm Jesse Haus. Remember me?"

"No," she said too quickly, meaning yes. Jesse couldn't read her blue mood, gauge what, if anything, she knew. "I just came from Lorenzo; he sent me over and . . ." Jesse peered down the shotgun row of rooms, looking for an empty one. "Could we . . ." She gestured down the line. "It's really important."

Surrounded by four walls' worth of dos and don'ts, they sat on child-sized chairs in the Time-Out Room, their knees higher than their laps.

"What," Felicia said numbly.

Jesse hesitated, then took the plunge. "Felicia, they found Cody's body."

"His body?" She sat forward, allowing herself the fleeting luxury of incomprehension.

"He's dead," Jesse said, grimacing.

"Huh." Felicia grunted, stunned, taking stock, reading a poster on the wall, then abruptly spewing out a sob, as if her mouth had exploded—just one, a bitter blast of grief fading into a shivery intake of air. "Oh, that sweet child . . ."

"I'm sorry," Jesse said softly, feeling like shit.

"Sweet . . ." Felicia shook her head, breathing through her mouth now. "Brenda," she said, exhaling heavily. "Oh Jesus. Does Brenda know?"

Jesse was momentarily rocked. Having assumed that Felicia would instantly make the connection, she scrambled now to figure out how to phrase it. "Felicia." Jesse took her hand. "Brenda's under arrest."

"What?" she said quietly, disbelievingly. "She loved that child."

"It looks like it could have been an accident," Jesse said, sounding to herself like an undertaker smoothly offering his condolences.

"No." Felicia sat up, closed her mouth. "No. She loved him. I see parents, I see them with their kids all the time. *All* the time. She loved him. No."

"She confessed, Felicia. To Lorenzo." Jesse leaned forward. "Cody might have drunk something—you know, ingested—when she was out of the house."

"No." Felicia just not going for it. "I'm sorry."

"She comes back, sees the boy, gets crazy, gets scared, doesn't tell anybody, makes up that story."

"No."

"She confessed, Felicia." They sat in silence for a long moment, Jesse peeking at the time: five-forty. "She confessed."

"So all this with the carjacker . . ." Felicia's gaze was trained somewhere over Jesse's shoulder.

"She confessed." Jesse watched as the facts set up house, Felicia sinking back imperceptibly into the tiny chair—a subtle curling of the spine, as if air were escaping from a small puncture in the gut.

Finally, Felicia looked directly at Jesse. "She must have been so scared to do that. Tell that story and stick to it." She was forgiving Brenda, Jesse the shocked one now. "She loved that boy so much," Felicia said, letting herself cry.

Two of the remaining children came up, stood solemnly before Felicia, and ceremoniously, one by one, shook her hand. Unnerved by her glassy, teary state, the kids exited the Time-Out Room and then the front door, casting disturbed glances over their shoulders as they left.

"Do they know?" Jesse asked, thrown by the handshakes.

"No," Felicia said in a weepy whisper. "The kids got to shake somebody's hand before they leave, so we know when they're gone for the day." She sank into her thoughts again. "But they'll find out soon enough, huh?"

Jesse braced herself, trying to get up the stomach for the next blow, debating with herself if she even needed to go on—was allowed to go on—given that certain information was decreed off-limits to her.

"I have to go," Felicia abruptly announced, rising to her feet, and Jesse just said it.

"Felicia, do you know where Billy is now?"

She paused, turned, sat back down, and, after a quick moment of mental leapfrog, asked a simple question. "Did he hurt the child?"

"No," Jesse said, grateful for the big jump. "Didn't sound like it."

"Brenda," Felicia said in a voice filled with revelation, "Brenda." Then, looking directly at Jesse, she said it again: "Brenda," as if hammering a nail through a fact.

Leaving the high-rise that housed the Study Club, Jesse walked out into the late-afternoon heat, passing a fistful of teenagers perched on the top slat of a bench, all of them engaged in some kind of verbal dogfight. Jesse understood only every other word or so, keeping her head down and heading for the curb.

"Yo, yo, Miss." Jesse turned to the voice, a boy with the left leg of his jeans rolled to midcalf. "You a reporter, right? I know you."

"Yeah?" Jesse shielded her eyes from the sun.

"She gave it up, right?"

"Who . . ." Jesse making him spell it out.

"Who . . ." he repeated, in an acid drawl. "She gave it up."

"I can't say." With her hand above her eyes, Jesse looked like she was saluting him.

"You don't know? Or you can't say." Another kid pitched in. Jesse shrugged as if she didn't understand the question. Two and a half more hours until the official announcement.

"Nah, man," a third kid said. "That would be like all *over* the place by now."

Jesse walked on, thinking, It *is* all over the place by now. She heard one of the kids behind her mutter, "Bitch," but wasn't sure if he meant her, Brenda, or both of them.

A plastic Pepsi bottle went whizzing over her left shoulder as close to her cheek as a butterfly kiss and landed in a bobbling dance on the pavement several feet ahead. Jesse stopped, began to turn around, thought better of it, and—back tensed, braced for the possibility of another missile—casually escaped from the Jefferson Houses.

25

Lorenzo hung up the phone and checked his call list. Just two names left: the presidents of Invictus and Aspira, the black and Latino police associations. He needed to secure guarantees that some of their members, on their own time and in civilian clothes, would hang in at Armstrong and other potential flash points tonight. He hoped they could help keep things calm, although he assumed both organizations would balk at his request that everyone make the scene unarmed.

Just two more calls, then it would be time for his interview with Billy Williams, who had been stewing in solitude for a good forty-five minutes now.

When Billy had been brought into the Southern District station house at about three that afternoon, Lorenzo had told the detectives who'd picked him up to dump him in the interview room. Then Lorenzo had purposely left him in there unguarded, as if he wasn't worth the manpower it would take to baby-sit him.

While Billy sat staring at the walls, Lorenzo had continued working the phones, bullying, cajoling, begging, threatening, and lying to anyone he thought would help him keep the peace tonight. He promised all sorts of shit to people—civilian review boards, summer employment programs, neighborhood rehab initiatives, instant funding for pet development projects, more police, less police, and, the wildest promise of all, the introduction of ceiling-mounted video cameras in all five station houses, instituting around-the-clock film surveillance of in-house police conduct. No one was really falling for any of Lorenzo's cotton-candy promises, but most of the players responded positively, as he knew they would. They tacitly understood that something could be obtained from someone down the line, the city's day-to-day survival being largely underwritten by a vast and pervasive favor market.

Lorenzo made those last two calls on his hit list, ran some cold water over his face and scalp, then finally entered the interview room. Dropping heavily into the caster-footed chair and slouching down low, he gave Billy Williams a long, smoky look. "I oughta smack the shit out of you right here and now," Lorenzo muttered, sizing him up. Billy sat humped over and wretched, his clasped hands locked below his knees. "We could of had this thing sewn up tight, twenty-four hours ago." He let that sink in, working with long silent intervals for maximum claustrophobia.

"Twenty-four hours. You know what that boy looked like when we dug him up? You wouldn't even know he was ever human. Ever a child. Skin all, like, glossy, black"—making an educated guess—"peeling, stinking, bloated, gaseous. Got, like, maggots living in every orifice in his face and body."

Billy sighed, his clasped hands dropping toward his ankles. Lorenzo noticed that the tape recorder was cracked from Brenda's flip-out, one battery still on the floor. He'd have to snatch a fresh machine once this preinterview was concluded.

"You left him there. You left him there an extra twenty-four hours than had to be. You left him there, and you let Armstrong go all to hell an extra twenty-four hours than had to be, because when I came up to *see* you, you just plain turned to shit on me, talking about, respect, talking about—what was it?—emasculation. Emasculation. Man, you got that right, 'cause you sure as hell didn't have the balls to talk to me like a *man*. Tell the truth to me like a *man*."

"Look," Billy began gingerly. "You don't, you don't have to psychologize on me like I'm some kind of homey." He cringed at his own words. "I'm a college-educated individual. You know, for whatever it's worth."

"Oh, I'm sorry." Lorenzo lazily slung his chair from side to side. "Was I talking beneath you?"

"No, I'm just saying—"

"See, because I'd think even a ignorant illiterate—" Lorenzo shut himself down, not liking this particular line of hectoring. He sat up, rolled in close. "Let me ask you something . . . How did I treat you the other night, huh? Did I fuck you over? Did I disrespect you? I get an assault complaint like that, I'm supposed to come in and take you off to County, but I didn't, because you seemed to me like a reasonable, intelligent individual. I mean, I could've walked out of there and you could've turned around and beat Felicia half to death, and *I* would've been the one with his balls in a bear trap 'cause I let you slide. I trusted you. I trusted you with my *job*. See, but you messed up. You should have trusted me like I trusted you, because right now? I got some bad news for you, my man . . ."

"What . . ."

"Brenda? She's been charged with homicide. That's a done deal. But New Jersey? There's no accessory status in this state, so *you're* gettin' charged with homicide too."

"What?" In his panic, Billy began to unbutton his shirt.

"You should've opened up when you had the chance, boss."

"You think I *what?*" Billy rebuttoned his shirt, opened it again, his fingers flying up and down as if he were playing a clarinet. Lorenzo hoped he was good and soft now, unable to dissemble: nobody really interested in Billy except as a fact checker for Brenda's story.

"Yeah, we had her in here and she opened up like the Yellow Pages. That's why you're here, Billy."

"Oh, come *on.*" Billy's voice went liquid, his fingers crinkling the knees of his slacks now.

"The thing is," Lorenzo said, leaning in, an ally, "you got only *one* weapon to help yourself with, brother. Same one you always had. Except that weapon, it's getting less, potent by the hour. You know what that weapon is?"

Billy stared at him, as if he had no fucking idea what Lorenzo was talking about.

"The truth. You have the truth. But you tell me something after I found it out for myself? It don't count. It don't count. You got to come up with the *new* news, boss. You got to tell me something I *don't* know, and that's why that weapon's getting weaker and weaker. 'Cause I'm learning shit about what went down; I'm takin' in all kinds of information, and *your* data pool is just shrinking and shrinking and shrinking. So you tell me something fresh, you make me a believer. That's the only thing you can do for yourself, Billy, and you best begin like, *now.*"

Billy couldn't speak, Lorenzo's Halloween routine having done too good a job. Lorenzo would have to help him get it in gear.

"Are you a killer?"

"No."

"No?"

"No."

"Then how'd that boy die?"

"She said he drank some medicine."

"She said that?" Lorenzo began taking notes.

"Yeah. She called me at the apartment. Felicia's apartment."

"Said . . ."

"Said the boy, you know, he was dead. She was hysterical."

"Did you believe her?"

"Yeah, I guess I did. She was all sobbing. You should've heard her. It was—"

"What else she say."

"She said, oh man, she said that I had to come over, she's, like, all alone in the world, I'm her only friend, she can't touch the body. And I'm, like, 'Brenda, you got to call the police, Brenda.' She says she can't, begging me to help her. I say I can't *do* that. She says if I didn't come by she'd kill herself, and I'm like, 'Now wait a minute,' you know? I mean we had just broke up like two hours before, so at first I was thinking maybe she's scamming me, trying to get me to come over, so she could, like, get another shot at putting us together again, so I said, 'Just call the police.' She says, 'I'll kill myself,' and I just hung up but, like, I had this feeling right after . . . You know, Brenda, she's a serious person, she doesn't play like that. And it just didn't sound like something she'd cook up to . . . It sounded too crazy not to be real, so I called her back and—" Billy abruptly took five from his story, his face crumpling, shifting so effortlessly from sobriety to tears that at first Lorenzo thought he was simply imitating Brenda on the phone. Then he bawled, "Homicide," a hopeless wail, and Lorenzo knew to get parental, shift to Big Daddy.

"C'mon now, Billy," he said, patting his shoulder. Billy's tears abruptly stopped, and he picked up the story as cleanly as if he had simply turned his head to cough.

"Anyways, I call her back and she can't even speak. She's just like, noises, like, sobbing, strangling. I swear it was like listening to a broken heart direct. I mean, all I could make out was 'Please, Billy, please, Billy.' I mean, you had to be some kind of statue not to . . ." Billy sighed, his breath fluttering as he fought down another panic attack.

"So I went over. I went over, she wasn't there, but the door's wide open so I go in. The boy's laying there under the table, like on his side, and he's in his pajamas and his skin is, like, gray-blue and he's got like, vomit on his front and I just—I don't know—I just went robot on it. I got a garbage bag from under the sink? You know, one of those cinch sacks? And I got him out of there, like I was, it was a dream. I didn't, I had never seen him before, her son, and as I'm picking him up? I get hit with this, like, weird realization. I started thinking that I just couldn't ever remember picking up a child in my arms in my entire adult life. I mean, I *must* have, but—I mean, *I* don't have kids, Felicia's boy is mostly grown, I don't have nephews or nieces, so it was like maybe the first time I ever—"

"Then what."

Billy took a breath. "I'm like half out the door, and I stop myself. Where the fuck am I going? I mean, I don't even have a car. Felicia's . . . I didn't want to take her car. And I see on the table, the dining table, she had left me car keys and this note that said, 'Under his angel,' and I knew what she meant because she had taken me there, you know, over in Freedomtown a few weeks before, 'cause she's like the type of person, if she falls for you, you got taken on the tour of special places. You know—'This is where I grew up. This is where I got—I don't know—lost my virginity' or, like, 'This is the place I go to be with my thoughts.' She was, like, a sentimental person, and she had taken me there, Freedom-town, because I'm not from around here, and it was, like, 'This used to be my favorite place when I was a little kid, and *that* used to be the Chicago Fire, and Cody, my son, he calls that mannequin up there his angel, so I knew, but—" Billy suddenly reached out, touched Lorenzo's chair. "Detective Council, look into me. Look into my *heart* . . ."

"Just keep telling it, Billy," Lorenzo said gently. "You're doing good." Billy dropped his head between his knees, then came up talking.

"OK, so I go downstairs with the boy, and at first I was gonna go straight to the police, tell them something like, I found him some-wheres, you know. Just take it away from under her roof—maybe it wouldn't come back on her. But I got scared. I mean, how do I explain how I found this kid, and then it's, like, 'Oh, your girlfriend works with his mother? Huh, how 'bout dat.' It was like, the minute I had walked into that apartment, man, it was like, I was fucked. I mean, you just can't . . . So it was like, I *had* to do what she asked me. I had no choice. So I go to her car, I lay the boy down on the backseat. Now I'm thinking, I have to dig a grave, I have to . . . What am I gonna use, you know, and I straighten up from putting him in the backseat and I'm coming around to the front and I see her across the street in a doorway. She's all scrunched up, looks like some kind of wild animal, and I got scared of her. I didn't want her to come over, 'cause I didn't want to look into her face, you know, 'cause I swear I didn't think I could handle all that *madness* that came at me over the phone. So I'm desperate to get out of there before she can come across the street, and I'm so nervous I drop her keys, and I go bend down to pick them up and when I stand up? I look over to where she was? She was gone. And, like, I never saw her again. And, look." He touched Lorenzo's chair. "Alls I was doing was letting my heart go out. I never . . . And when you came over the last night? I was *scared*. It hit the news so big-time and here *you* come. I mean . . ." Billy shut his eyes, put a hand to his heart. "You be me last night, Detective. What would *you* do."

"You want me to understand you?" Lorenzo asked quietly.

"*Yes*," he said, bobbing his head.

"You want me to, to sympathize?"

"*Yes*."

"The more you tell me . . ." Lorenzo shrugged, leaning back.

Billy exhaled, got into it again. "So . . . I drive out to Freedomtown. I carry the boy to the, the spot. I didn't know what I'm gonna use, but I go there, and I could see where someone—Brenda, I guess—had tried to dig some kind of grave, but she must have used her bare hands to do it because it was real shallow—I'm talking maybe a few inches deep, and there were like, claw marks in the dirt, but she didn't tell me it was gonna *be* there. She didn't tell me about this already dug grave, and I almost had a heart attack that it was right there, like, waiting. And I knew it was for the boy because she had thrown in some, action figures, you know, dolls for boys? So I go look for something to dig with? And I find some broken plank laying there by the base of that fake building, and I kind of use it as a shovel, you know, make what she started deeper.

"And so then I go lay him in, and I didn't know whether to take him out of the garbage bag or not . . . I mean, you lay a child down like he's garbage? But I did it. I laid him in like that, because, because I didn't want to look at him." Billy started crying again, although the tears hadn't found their way into his voice yet.

"It's, like, if I just thought about it—like, all I'm doing here is burying a garbage bag—then I could *do* it, you know, then I could tell myself—" Billy stopped, looked away, his chin juddering against his hand. "Maybe I could do it, 'cause I got death all around me anyhow. My father's dead, my mother's in the hospital. I mean, it's everywhere I look . . ."

"OK," Lorenzo said, nudging.

"So." Billy took a deep breath. "So I close it up, and I get out of there."

"Close it up how."

"I covered him."

"With . . ."

"Earth."

"That's it?"

"Then I put some big rocks over him. I don't know why. I just, I guess I was thinking about, like, keeping the animals out, or I don't know . . . I don't know why I did that."

"So . . ." Lorenzo kept pushing him.

"So I drive back to her building. I was just going to leave the car and go, but when I got there, I started thinking about how she sounded over the phone and how she looked from across the street, and I just sat there in the car . . . Can I tell you the truth?"

"What you been doing all along?"

Billy ignored the question. "I kind of hoped she *did,* you know, kill herself, because nobody knew about me and her and, like, if she checked out? My ass was clear, right? And, I didn't want to go up there, but I did because I was, half expecting to find her like I found the boy. I mean, she was most definitely attached to that kid. I mean, you could tell. Anytime she was, nervous or uncomfortable with me, she'd always start talking about her son—what he had said yesterday, what had happened to him the night before, what movie they watched. He was like her security blanket, you know, out in the world, so I *knew* . . . Well, anyways I just wanted to see if—you know—go up there, not touch nothing but just see if she had . . ." Billy looked away, then came back.

"It wasn't, there was nobody there. It was just like I left it, door open . . . I didn't think she had ever come back, and I was there in that apartment thinking about I don't know what, and I just got down on my knees and started cleaning up under the table. I don't know why I did that either. Evidence? Getting rid of evidence? I don't know, I just . . . She had some cleaning shit under the kitchen sink, you know, like Comet? I didn't know where she was, or, even *if* she was, but I'm down there doing that, and then I go back downstairs, and I wasn't thinking too clearly, I guess, because I just got back into her car and drove myself over to my mother's house. It wasn't like, until I got in the driveway that I realized that I had taken her car, but that was that. I just put it in the garage, went in the house, started drinking, and fell out."

"Huh." Lorenzo was writing, thinking, In a garage, everybody scour-

ing the marshes and swamplands for it. He eyed the wall clock: four-
forty-five.

"And then, like, I woke up the next day—I *guess* I woke up the next
day—just kept drinking, fell out again, woke up the *second* day, turned
on the TV, and there she was. Opened up the paper, there she was.
Every which way I looked, there she was, there she was talking about
some *black* man did it, and at first I thought she meant me—like, set *me*
up—but then I just figured she was trying to get away with it and stack-
ing the deck in a way that everybody would buy in."

"Get away with what?"

"Her son."

"She kill him?"

"I wasn't there, but in my heart? No. I think she was telling me what
happened up front. I do. But I was scared anyhow. Scared of this here,"
he said, gesturing limply to the room, to Lorenzo. "And I just went back
to Felicia's house. I took my mother's car because I didn't want to get
back in that, Brenda's car, everybody looking for it. So I go back, I'm
nonstop drinking. I'm a beer drinker mostly, but . . . So I see Felicia and,
right from the jump I'm fighting with her because she starts in on me
with, you know, 'Who were you with last night? What's that bitch's
name?' And I just hit her. I'm no, I'm not . . . I just *whack*." He slapped
the back of his hand against an open palm. "I'm, my mind frame is like,
this whole thing is Felicia's fault. If she had only given me *respect*—as a
man, as a person—I would never have started in with Brenda to begin
with. And I just lost it. I'm like a crazy man. I start building up that
dugout for myself, you know." He blushed. "You saw that. And Felicia,
she's, like—I *hit* her. She keeps coming over, knocking my shit down,
we're yellin', screamin', I most likely hit her again, although I think we
got to check the videotape on that one. Finally she has to go off to work
and I built up my fortress of solitude. I was scared. I didn't want to go
out, I didn't want to stay in. I didn't want . . . My mother's dying in the
hospital." Billy turned away again, weepy.

"I mean, c'mon, man, you be *me*. I'm all holed up, I can't turn on the
TV, I can't—I don't know if they're coming for me or *what*. So Felicia
comes back in, we go at it again, *you* come by, I almost shit myself. I was
sure . . . But you started talking about something else, and like, now
you're saying to me, 'How come you didn't tell me what she did, what *I*
did.' But, it was like, if you didn't bring it up, maybe it didn't happen, you
know? I mean, what you expect me to say. 'Oh, by the way, that *kid* the
whole world is looking for? That *guy* the whole world got their *knives* out

for?' I mean, when you started in with that 'You cannot hit her' stuff, it was like, I just blocked on the other. I mean, I heard myself saying shit to you about . . . I just got into what *you* wanted to deal with. Straight up. You cannot tell me that's *so* hard to understand. But *homicide*. Jesus God, there's no proportion in that. I just, I just, she *needed* me. See, you . . . Mister Role Model. Your phone's most likely ringing off the hook nonstop, but look at me." He punched his chest. "Do you know how long it's been since anybody needed *me?* You look me in the eye and tell me you think I did a homicide."

Lorenzo had never thought that. He looked into Billy's weighted face, the features dragged downward, melting. "Hey, Billy," Lorenzo's tone gentle but unyielding. "Alls I can say is you should of talked to me when you had the chance."

"That's not answering my question."

"It's what the law requires, Billy," Lorenzo said, hunching forward, elbows on knees. "Do I believe what you just told me? Mostly I do. But you made me come get you, brother. You let this shit fester another twenty-four hours."

"Listen." Billy hunched forward too. "Didn't you think, don't you think I wanted to tell somebody? Don't you think I wanted to, to unload all this? How *bad* is what I did . . . ?" As Lorenzo got up and left the room, he could feel Billy's eyes tracking him with doglike alertness.

Bobby McDonald stood in the doorway of his office, Billy's now-solitary sighs and mutters emanating, crackling but audible, from the speaker on Bobby's desk.

Lorenzo grabbed a tape recorder from a secretary's cubicle and a phone from his own. "You getting her car?" he asked his boss on the fly, heading back to Billy in the box.

"On their way," McDonald said, returning to his desk.

Back in the interview room, Lorenzo plugged in the phone jack and, putting on a little performance for Billy, rang up the prosecutor's office—his name, on this day, getting him directly to Capra himself.

"Hey, what's up?" The prosecutor sounded cheery. "I hear you got the boyfriend."

"Billy Williams." Lorenzo, still standing, threw Billy what was supposed to be a reassuring nod, Billy's face heavy with anticipation. "I got him sitting here with me right now, and I was just wondering—he kind of made a clean breast of it, so is there anything we can do for him?"

"How bad do we want him?"

"Not too."

"So she's the one, still?"

Lorenzo hesitated, then said, "Yeah, as far as it goes."

"How's his story?"

"It's trackin'."

"No clinkers?"

"Not really."

"He's giving it his all?"

"And then some."

Billy closed his eyes, his lips moving in mute prayer.

"You're gonna be at the press conference, right?" Capra made it sound like it was something to look forward to—boys' night out.

"Hell yeah," Lorenzo answered in the same upbeat spirit. "So Billy—"

"OK, well, I mean I can't really do jack shit for him right now."

"I hear you."

"I mean, maybe we can do something down the road, but for now he's got to take a bad fall."

"Can we do something on bail?"

"He's full-tilt cooperating?"

"I'd say so."

"Nothing out of whack with her story?"

"Nope."

"Twenty-five thousand? How's that sound."

"Hold on." Lorenzo palmed the mouthpiece, turned to Billy. "Can you get ahold of twenty-five hundred dollars?"

Billy looked off, as if trying to remember something, then said, "I think so."

"OK," Lorenzo said into the phone.

"You got it."

"And yeah"—Lorenzo seized the moment—"can you do something about George Howard now?"

"Who?" Capra threw a squint into his voice.

Lorenzo gave himself a few heartbeats to calm down. "Curious George Howard," he said distinctly.

"I'm jerking your chain, Council," Capra said affably. "He's already out."

"Billy." Lorenzo inserted the blank tape from Brenda's aborted confession into the new recorder. "You ever, you never been in jail before?"

"No." He stared at the tape, at Lorenzo, as if watching a doctor prepare an injection.

"OK, here's what's gonna happen. You're gonna get charged with homicide and conspiracy to commit homicide, OK?" Billy jerked back. "Whoa, whoa, whoa." Lorenzo had a hand on his arm. "They're gonna set bail at twenty-five thousand. After a day or two, they'll give you the ten-percent option; alls you'll need is twenty-five hundred cash. Maybe you could put up your mom's house for the rest, get you out of the joint in two, three, maybe four days tops."

"My mother is *dying*."

"I'm sorry about that," Lorenzo answered politely, but he was starting to feel impatient—Billy was not a customer.

"Now, my guess is, in due time? If the forensics and the, the autopsy bear out your story? I think—I'm pretty sure—the charges are gonna be downgraded to something like improper disposal of a corpse. And that doesn't carry any jail time at all, but you're gonna at least have to go in for the next few days. Can you handle that?"

"How do *I* know." Billy's eyes vibrated with whatever images were scrolling through his mind right now. "Can I get protective custody?"

"Oh yeah. They'll do that as a matter of course, you know, because of all the publicity."

"My mother's dying." Lorenzo remained silent. "How'm I gonna get the mortgage for the house without her knowing all this?"

"That's not my department, Billy." Lorenzo glanced anxiously at the clock, the time sliding past his eye. "That's for you to figure out." Billy gripped his knees, shoulders bunched up by his ears. "Now, we're gonna go through all of this again, this time on tape."

"You know, Brenda, coming up with this, this black carjacker?" Billy said, his voice different now, reflective, as if he had, at least for the moment, accepted his short-term fate. "I got to say—above and beyond, I mean—that really threw me that she did that."

Although Lorenzo's immediate need was to take command of the dialogue, the shift in Billy's tone from desperate to oddly detached seemed worth a listen.

"I mean, I liked her. I mean, I couldn't *deal* with her, because she was, too all over me after a while, but she made me feel good about myself, she gave me respect. But this carjacker thing . . .

"See, I was raised, I was brought up to take people as they present themselves to you, you know, not to, to prejudge the gift by the wrapping. But I got to say I don't particularly *like* white people, and I'm not even talking about 1619, four hundred years and all that. I mean as company, as, as, like, to *talk* to. It's, like, I consider myself an educated individual, and the more education you have the more you're gonna interface with the, the world in its entirety out there, and, like, I don't know too many bald-faced crackers, to be honest. I mean . . . But still, it's, like, most white people—for me—I feel like they're not so much talking to me as they're *watch*ing themselves talking to me—like, admiring themselves talking to me—and I play this guessing game. How many minutes into this conversation, no matter what we're talking about right now—could be sports, the market, could be the weather—but how many minutes is it gonna take for *race* to come up. How long is it gonna take for the fact that it's a white person talking to a black person to take over and change the subject, turn the subject into something racial. It never fails. *Never.* And I don't know how you deal with it, but for me it's nerve-racking, and it's boring."

"I hear you," Lorenzo said automatically, his experience both better and worse. The job had introduced him to a bushel of straight-out rednecks, but there were others, like Bump, for whom he would risk his life.

"But I got to tell you," Billy plowed on. "Brenda? It never came up, the racial thing. With sex, with conversation, it never came up. As much as it was humanly possible, she treated me like—I mean, we were just two people."

"OK, Billy," Lorenzo said impatiently, knowing now that there wasn't anything here for him. He eyed the clock again: five-fifteen. The presser was less than three hours away, and they couldn't postpone it. The news of the arrest was probably already deep into the streets by now.

"So, like, with this carjacker she concocted?" Billy cruised on. "I'll tell you, knowing her as I do? If I didn't know what I know about what had happened, I'd've believed her in a heartbeat."

"Billy." Lorenzo pushed Record, officially ending the chat.

"I guess that shit is just bred in the bone," Billy said, gazing off.

"Billy—"

"I hate this fuckin' city." Billy's eyes went shiny again. "This city's got no heart."

"Billy? At this time I have to once again advise you of your rights—"

"This city just killed my mother."

26

Arriving at the press conference a few minutes before the announced starting time of seven-thirty, Jesse slipped into the crowd and regarded the local hitters assembled before and above her on the granite steps of the Dempsy City Hall. Backdropped by the neoclassical pillars, which lent the setting an almost operatic air, stood the mayor, the prosecutor, the chief of police, Bobby McDonald, Lorenzo Council, and that car-smacked off-kilter statue of the Dutchman, now lit a pinkish gold by the dying sun.

Behind this crew, elevated another few steps up the facade, stood a grim-faced municipal choir, which included eight of the twelve players who had been hit-listed on the back of Lorenzo's dry-cleaning slip. Rumors of Brenda's arrest had doubled the media presence, and a bristling army of shooters and reporters faced the microphones, backed by an even greater number of civilians.

On the border, between the media and the natives, Jesse saw that many of the locals displayed their allegiance with buttons or T-shirts, as if this were a political rally. Most whites and some blacks sported Cody-feeding-the-goat buttons; a good number of blacks wore those T-shirts emblazoned with the police sketch of the bogus jacker; and a few people wore both, which, to Jesse's mind, served only to underline the grimness of Brenda's scam.

The confession, edited to spare Lorenzo grief, would hit the streets in less than an hour, the *Dempsy Register* the only evening newspaper on either side of the Hudson to carry the arrest in tonight's news cycle.

And, given Brenda's "confession," Jose had held up Jesse's second diary installment, her account of the Friends of Kent visit to the apartment. Only the first one had run; the second, Jose felt, would need to be rewritten in the context of Brenda's culpability. Reflective in nature, it would keep for a few days, until the smoke cleared. More pressing now was Jesse's account of Brenda's breakdown in the ruins of the Chase Institute; he wanted that one for tomorrow evening's paper. But before she could sit herself down and begin her battle with blank-page malaise she wanted to see this here—*be* this here—and bodysurf the shock wave that would inevitably sweep through this crowd the minute the prosecutor made the announcement.

Turning back to view the crew on the steps of City Hall, she locked on Lorenzo, who was pacing like a cat, his vexed and fretful gaze trained on the back of the crowd. Jesse wheeled around again to see what he saw: a growing, percolating contingent that wore neither T-shirts nor buttons, a mob of D-Town youngbloods from the projects and JFK Boulevard. Loud and raucous, more and more of them slammed themselves into the back of the pack, a few heads abruptly popping up above the height of the crowd, as if squeezed vertically by the pressure of those around them. The milling agitation caused a surge that rippled straight through to the front lines of the press. Jesse bucked forward a few steps before she could check herself, then watched as those directly in front of her were forced into the same clumsy dance. Her eyes traveled back up to Lorenzo, who was just plain freaking now. Jesse knew that he was breaking down that rear guard into individuals, into followers and leaders, reviewing case histories to assess the potential for mayhem—knew that, in the coming half hour or so, she could use Lorenzo's face as a kind of rearview mirror.

"Good evening." Peter Capra, the county prosecutor, stepped up to bat, waiting out a last-second jostle of adjustment among the media people, then reading off a typed page: "At 2:30 P.M. today, the members of my office, working with the members of the Dempsy Police Department, recovered the remains of a male child believed to be Cody Martin." A low croon surged through the cluster of locals directly behind Jesse. "And in accordance," Capra said, then hesitated, Jesse chilled with expectancy, "and in accordance, charged Brenda Martin, the mother of Cody Martin, with homicide and conspiracy to commit homicide."

The reaction to this second verbal blow was a louder, more pervasive croon—of surprise, of betrayal—punctuated with scattered shouts. The woman directly behind Jesse barked "No!" Someone else shouted out an almost gleeful "Yes!" People swayed with emotion, the conversion of street buzz to stone-cold fact purging them of all tentativeness.

The prosecutor waited it out, then plowed on: "And charged William F. Williams, an acquaintance of Brenda Martin, also with homicide and conspiracy to commit homicide." Billy's arrest was almost ignored, or the response to it hard to gauge, because most people were still reacting to Brenda, to the death of Cody, the crowd whirling in place, cooing with anger, with horror, with satisfaction.

Jesse looked to Lorenzo, and his expression made her turn to the rear of crowd, where she saw some of that no-button, no-T-shirt mob lurch left, lurch right, then break off completely, like a chunk of ice worried by a strong current until it finally separates from the mother floe. Watching as a few dozen mobbers marched off, quiet but intent, Jesse wondered if they knew where they were going. Then she saw a few shooters shadowing them at a safe distance. Jesse wanted to go, too, but was stopped by the prosecutor's next words.

"Investigators were led to a burial site today at Foley's Point, Gannon, where the body of a child was exhumed, final identity of which is pending an autopsy." This last bit of information—graphic, specific— once again intensified the barking, the eerie cooing of the crowd. Jesse spotted a Cody button sailing off like a flying saucer, heard someone yelling, "I *told* you!" Lorenzo was up there on the steps, literally bouncing on the balls of his feet as he tried to follow the movements of that breakaway crew into the distance. Then he leaned into the ear of Ernie Hohner, the chief of police, a squat, pug-faced bulldog of a man, who nodded at Lorenzo's urgent whisperings and shrugged—a gesture not of indifference but of confidence. But Lorenzo looked none too convinced, anxiously rocking from side to side as if he were about to explode.

"What about Curious *George*," someone shouted from within the press pack.

A hoarse bellow came from the rear of the crowd: "The nigger was framed!"

"Mr. Howard was released on his own recognizance earlier this evening," Capra said evenly, "the charges pending against him to be adjudicated at a later date."

"Charges for *what*. He didn't *do* it, motherfucker!"

"Where she being held . . ." That came from up front.

The prosecutor plowed over the last question. "I want the people of this city to understand something." Jesse tracked Lorenzo's eyes to another break-off from the rim of the crowd. No one back there was listening to anything being said; mostly they were just rolling shoulders, talking with their eyes, waiting to see who was going to split next. "I would like the people of this city to understand that, given the initial accounts of Brenda Martin's story, we had no choice but to pursue the elements of that story as *told* to us." Capra read from a second typed page, Jesse recognizing Lorenzo's phone rap nearly word-for-word.

"I would like the people of this city to understand that, to the best of our knowledge, we were operating under the assumption that a child's *life* was at stake and we had to proceed with thoroughness and diligence in order to *save* that child's life, and that the, the heinousness of the crime committed is further compounded by the hoaxlike nature of Miss Martin's original story. Working with the false information given us regarding a carjacking at the Armstrong Houses, we recognize that this fabricated event might possibly have caused a series of well-intentioned but possibly overzealous police actions—"

"*Possibly?*" someone shouted, causing the prosecutor to drop a stitch.

"Police actions, to bring this investigation to a successful conclusion. And in response to that possibility"—the prosecutor continued, flipping the page, the Reverend Longway and a few others in the municipal choir shaking their heads in a gesture of theatrical cynicism—"there will be an independent commission established to investigate the actions of various members of the Dempsy County law enforcement community." Capra was speaking in a fast monotone now, a lawyer muttering his way through a contract. "And if there are any findings that any member of said law enforcement community transgressed in their *zeal* to apprehend a perpetrator, those findings will be brought forth before the grand jury and investigated thoroughly."

Jesse watched a number of reporters as they muscled their way to the back of the crowd to track the breakaway crews and document whatever bedlam was to follow.

"Hey." Ben sidled up next to her, breathing hard but smiling.

"Are they busting it up back there?" she asked.

"Nah," Ben growled happily. "They're loaded for bear."

"Who's loaded for bear."

"Tonight I feel there is a great, *hurting* in this city." The voice turned Jesse back to the microphone, the Reverend Longway up there now, doing his bit for world peace. "I feel there's a great, anger. It's an old anger, a righteous anger, an honorable anger."

Lorenzo, probably unable to bear it any longer, removed himself from the press conference, sliding off left, into the shadows, Jesse guessing he was heading straight to Armstrong.

"However," Longway continued, the crowd only half listening, "I feel that I must implore the, the bearers of this, this *rage* in the same way that I implore it of my*self*—to express it, constructively, to express it, *wisely*. I implore the wounded members of our community to bear it with dignity, because I promise you . . . We are owed, we are owed, and we will *collect*."

Despite the bombastic thump of his delivery, Longway looked shaky up there, Jesse thought, his facial expression registering an internal unsteadiness.

"However, that being said," Longway went on, mimicking the flat legalese of the prosecutor, "I would turn to the powers that be, assembled up here tonight behind me, and I would ask them as a token of their sincerity if they would, right here, right now, publicly apologize to the citizens of Armstrong for what had to be endured."

"Oh shit," Jesse whispered, unconsciously grinning, Longway pulling a fast one, making them eat it. The prosecutor, the chief of police, and the mayor instantly went stiff with anger.

"This is fucking great," Ben murmured.

The press conference had come to a dead stop, Longway standing there hogging the mikes, almost gathering them up in his arms, his body language implying that they would have to drag him away in front of all these cameras if no one responded to his challenge.

Capra finally took up the gauntlet, stepping forward and almost shouldering Longway off to the side as he leaned into the mikes. "As I *said*. The police reacted to the story as originally *told* to us. Also, as I said, there will be an investigation into all police activity, and any behavior deemed remiss will be investigated forthwith." No notes this time, the prosecutor's terse delivery heavy with rage.

"Is that an apology?" someone up front asked.

Capra gave it a full five seconds, staring at his interrogator. "I would characterize what I just said as a sincere and heartfelt explanation."

"*Fuck* you!" That come from what remained of the rear guard, who aimed a brace of raised middle-finger salutes the prosecutor's way. "Punk-ass bitch!"

Capra seemed to expand, his fury transforming him into something red, mean, and low to the ground. "I would also add that the law is the law," he said, addressing the rear mob directly now. "Tonight is no holiday *from* that law, and any criminalistic behavior, no matter from *what* quarter or stemming from *whatever* motivation, will be dealt with swiftly, and succinctly."

Jesse flinched, Capra busting them in advance.

"*Fuck* you!" came again from the rear, people turning, squinting, scowling, everybody getting spooked and confused.

"This press conference is over," Capra announced. "There'll be no more questions."

"Why not?" a reporter down front called out through cupped hands—Jesse laughing, One in every crowd.

With the conference at an end, the press split into two armies, Jesse joining the one crowding around Longway, the only player from the choir willing to talk. The other faction made a beeline for any black people in the crowd, cornering them, shoving cameras in their faces, and asking them if they thought Longway was right, if the prosecutor owed any apologies to anybody. The mad scramble was something like musical chairs, crews racing one another to lay claim to the limited number of blacks still hanging around, those crews unable to find their own subjects forced to piggyback on other impromptu interrogations, the losing shooter having to stand on tiptoe and raise the Betacam as high as he could, tilting it downward over the primary camera.

Jesse knew that very few of those man-on-the-street interviews would be usable, most of the people being filmed having rarely, if ever, been asked their opinions on anything. Now, suddenly thrust into the role of national spokesmen for racial injustice, they would come off either blinky and tongue-tied or profane and long-winded.

"It's the same ol' same ol'," Longway declared, shielding his eyes from the sun guns. "A *black* man did it, a *black* man did it. She knew her product and she knew her customers. A black man, boogie man, hottest item in the store, can't even keep it in stock. And the city of Gannon, the city of Dempsy were bumping each other in line to see who'd be the first to slap their money down and buy her story. Man, it sounded so good to them, they didn't even bat an eye, didn't even ask how much."

Jesse could actually hear the sound of writing. Bent over their pads, the reporters would sporadically snap upright, their heads swiveling almost a full 360 to track and locate any discordant bark, bang, or noise, everybody wired to the gills.

"But they should have inquired about the *price,* because an entire *race* has been maligned here these last few days," Longway declared. "And I will not give up until an apology, a public apology, comes out of somebody's mouth. I'll take it from the prosecutor, the mayor, or the chief of police and I'm gonna be *on* them, calling them out until I get it."

"What else do you want," Jesse asked Longway combatively, just to keep him lively, see if he'd repeat any of the rap he had practiced on her back in the housing office.

"What else do I want?" He reared back, his face suddenly turning ashy, his mouth hanging open. "I want everything *you* got," he said weakly, pointing a trembling finger at her.

"Like . . ." Jesse was egging him on but pretty much knew he wouldn't bite in the way she wanted.

"You're a bright lady." He popped what Jesse assumed was a nitro pill under his tongue. "You answer that for yourself."

With the presser over, Jesse wanted to cruise the city, take its temperature. As she and her brother rolled off in the Chrysler, the sky slowly changed from a brassy gold to a sullen violet, changed like a face. Within a few blocks, Jesse could almost see it, in the streets, the storefronts, the stoops and porches; in the mouths and eyes of the men and boys who moved toward Ben's car with a territorial saunter every time he stopped at a light, slowed down to take a corner. She could see it in the deepening purple of the air itself, the city like a balloon slowly filling with water, no one knowing when it would blow, where it would blow, no one, including those who would ultimately do the blowing.

Circling back toward City Hall, Ben drove Jesse past what seemed like a corral of teenagers. A good chunk of that rear mob from the press conference was now detained, in a deserted lot between two apartment houses, by a squad of helmeted cops, who were patting them down, checking IDs, and running their names through dashboard-mounted computers for outstanding warrants.

"Jesus," Jesse said mildly, assuming this was more about intimidation and dispersal than about making arrests.

"That's nothing," Ben crowed. He drove her to a bluff overlooking the Roosevelt Houses, the largest projects in Dempsy, where three police buses sat parked, engines running, the smoke from dozens of cigarettes wafting from the open windows, Jesse seeing rows of visored helmets, in silhouette, within. Ben then drove her to Bailey Street, three blocks from Armstrong, where the buses held roughly the same number of cops on standby. The ground beneath these bus windows, too, was littered with flicked butts, chain-smoking being Dempsy's idea of transcendental meditation. Ben parked the car a few hundred yards from the Bailey Street platoons and looked at his sister. It was eight-forty-five, the sky giving up all its nuanced shades and dropping into dead night.

There was only one place to go right now, and that was Armstrong. Jesse knew that her brother was too self-effacing, too polite to say that he was scared, to grant himself the right to say, "No way." Although she was afraid herself, she couldn't really help him out, because building in her all night long—from the tension of the presser, to the tour of the pregnant streets, to the reviewing of the shock troops—was that gnawing demand, that sweeping need to both lose and find herself in the big picture, to Be There. For tonight, Brenda was over. Brenda was about writing. Armstrong was Now.

They could smell the projects before they got there. It was a dull, penetrating stench that Jesse was unable to identify until she came within sight of the Bowl: a good number of the refrigerator crates planted out there were now on fire. Propelled by her own mandate, Jesse marched into the site through the high end, the Gompers Street outlet. Ben had no choice but to follow. From the nearest breezeway, that of Two Building, she could see five separate conflagrations on the slope of the Bowl, the tenants standing in jagged clusters around the burning crates and refrigerators, yelling at one another, crying, shouting indecipherable bulletins. Jesse identified at least a dozen black and Latino cops, all in civilian dress, trying to deal with it, calm everybody down. Some tenants looked heartsick, walleyed with despair, while others looked as if they'd just as soon level the entire site.

An ad hoc work crew of cops and tenants, their faces contorted by the heat and fumes, was busy putting out the flames with handheld extinguishers. Ben moved in to help but turned back, not wanting to leave his sister unguarded. Jesse waved him on. Then, struck with the realization that it wasn't against the law for her to lend a hand, she followed him. But before they could get to the nearest crate, they were inadvertently blindsided by Lorenzo. Holding a skinny twelve-year-old by the back of his neck, he barreled out of the shadows, charging across the Bowl toward a burning refrigerator as if to fling the kid into the flames but coming to a halt inches from disaster and shaking the boy like a kitten.

"What you *do* that for!" Lorenzo bellowed, his pendulous lower lip hanging open, eyes bugging behind his glasses, the sheer volume of his rage quieting the Bowl down so that the soft crackle of flame-licked wood was the predominant competing sound.

"What you *do* that for!" Lorenzo was crouched over, going eye to eye, people inching closer. "That's *yours,* you stupid motherfucker!" he said, flinging a hand to a destroyed refrigerator. Jesse read the kid's heavy-lidded nonreaction as paralysis. "That's for *you!* That's for your *family!*" Lorenzo maintained his close-range glare and bellow, the kid's eyes peeking out from behind tiny slits. Lorenzo waited for a response, but the kid, still speechless, answered with a small shrug.

"They're *laughing* at you!" Lorenzo roared into his dreamy face, Jesse overhearing someone say, "Who's *they.*"

The kid finally managed a small protest: "No they ain't."

"*What?*" Lorenzo got down even lower.

"They ain't laughing at me," he managed to murmur, looking at Jesse and Ben—white Dempsy. "They scared."

Jesse, off balance, vaguely embarrassed, turned away from the scene and took a few steps down the slope. From where she stood, she had adequate elevation to overlook all of Martyrs Park at the bottom of the projects and see a little into Gannon beyond the tree line. Although both the pocket park and that end of Hurley seemed peaceful, even deserted, there was something off down there. Jesse needed a long moment to nail what was throwing her. It was the absence of a Gannon cruiser in the abandoned mini-mall across the city line. Tonight, for the first time in years—tonight, when Gannon needed to guard its back more than on any other night in recent history—the Watch had been abandoned.

"That's, whoa . . ." Ben said, reading her mind.

At the refrigerators, someone had found either sand or cement mix and had trucked it to the Bowl in a wheelbarrow. Lorenzo, along with a number of others, was snatching up the grit in double-handed scoops and dumping it directly on the smoking crates. The kid Lorenzo had manhandled earlier was now seated in the dirt, his face calcified into a blank mask, his hands cuffed behind his back.

"I want to go over there." Jesse gestured to the mini-mall across the city line and began heading down the slope to Martyrs.

"Jesse, no." Ben reached out for her, laughing nervously. "No, Jesse."

But she wanted the mini-mall, and Ben, once again, had no choice.

Hitting Hurley Street at the base of the Bowl, they came up on a crew of teenagers who had been obscured from view back at the fires, five hard-core-looking kids hanging in the breezeway of Three Building, the high-rise closest to the park. These kids scoped them out with the almost leisurely assessing glare, cold and impersonal, that she and Ben had received all over town on their postpresser cruise. Scowling at his shoes, Ben muttered, "Shit," as if disgusted with himself, as if preview-ing the inevitable.

Jesse, musing on how much of her fear at times like this manifested itself as self-consciousness, felt incapable of pulling an embarrassing about-face. Briefly eyeing those who were openly eyeing her, she forged on into the leafy black mouth of the park, her brother dutifully bringing up the rear.

Inside Martyrs, the overhead lights were out, the park reduced to a humped silhouette of shrubs, swings, and slides. Only the sneakers, tied together and thrown into the trees bolo-style, were identifiable as such, swaying in minute arcs against the sky.

"It's fuckin' *dark*," Jesse hissed, too hyped to be scared anymore. The breezeway posse was out of sight and out of mind, her focus now the mystery across the city line.

"Just keep moving," Ben said with anxious heat, then, reversing the command, "Hold on." He seized her shoulder, cocking an ear, squinting back along the path to Hurley Street. "Just keep going," came a third command, as he gave her a weak push toward Gannon, then headed back alone toward Armstrong.

Once again on edge, not knowing what Ben was up to, Jesse stood her ground, listening, waiting for him to return along the path. All that could be heard from within the stillness was the distant shouting of the volunteer firemen up in the Bowl, the occasional slap of tires out on Jessup Avenue, Gannon-side, and the slow rolling crunch of rubble, as cars pulled in or out at the open end of Hurley.

The bronze memorial plaque of Martin, Malcolm, and Medgar that was bolted to a stout tree trunk gleamed dully but, without a light source, seemed to gleam from within, as if the three men in profile were reacting to what was going on around them. It scared the hell out of her. Overhead, above the trees, she could see the random grid of lighted windows in all five towers of Armstrong. Behind each one, lived a story, Jesse told herself, in an effort to calm down—a major goddamned story.

"Where she go to." The voice was blunt, all business, and Jesse turned to stone. Standing motionless off the paths, she decided that whatever was to happen to her now would be both earned and just. Her behavior with Brenda, her lies and verbal weaseling, her almost preda-tory reportage—whatever was about to go down, she informed herself, was deserved.

But no one came. Jesse scanned the murk and envisioned Brenda, forty-eight hours ago, somewhere within a few yards of here, down on her knees, ramming glass and metal under her skin—Brenda, as selfish, as uncaring, as predatory as any heartless hunter ever produced by these towers, as heartless as those blank-souled psychopaths who were probably stalking Jesse right now. Brenda, setting the world on fire to cover her own crimes, her own failings. Jesse, standing rigid, was finally filling with the loathing for her that had come so easily to everyone else in this city, feeling like the one who was conned, manipulated, sacrificed—standing here now, waiting to pay her tab.

But no one came. Wrestling herself free from her paralysis, she found her way to the skimpy playground enclosure a few dozen yards off the path—monkey bars, monkey barrels, a swing with no seat, a slide with only one climbing rail, seven cement Disney dwarfs, paint-flaked, useless. Perched on a dwarf, sweating, scared, her arms folded across her chest, Jesse said, "This is no place to raise a child." She said it out loud, and the responding crackle and crunch out on the footpath filled her chest with ice.

"Jesse?" It was her brother's voice, light-toned, OK. She flew out of the playground, intercepting him on the footpath. "Hey," Ben said, grinning, in shock, a slash running in a straight line from the edge of a nostril to the peak of a cheekbone. Jesse gawked, counting stitches. "So let's go," Ben said.

Lively, out of his mind, walking briskly ahead of his sister, Ben led the way out the Gannon end of the park. They crossed Jessup Avenue, a four-lane roadway that wasn't quite a highway, Jesse bringing up the rear, her own rattled mental state allowing her, for the moment, to consider Ben's dissociated peppiness as acceptable. They stood in the crusty bust-ass mini-mall parking lot, staring dumbly at nothing, at the absence of a police car. Jesse was the first to snap out of it.

"We have to take you to the medical center."

"No, I know," Ben said lightly, mopping his cheek with a raised shoulder, his blue shirt coming away purple with blood. "Anytime you're ready."

"Like now." Jesse took a step toward the roadway, then, faltering, unable to give it up, she came back and said, "Just give me thirty more seconds, OK?" Ben shrugged, took off his shirt, wadded it into a compress, held it against his opened face, and prepared to wait for her.

Quickly walking the length of the six vacant storefronts, Jesse turned the corner and saw nothing but a fly-buzzed Dumpster. She walked on, turning the next corner, and there they were: had to be seventy-five Gannon cops, with batons, Plexiglas shields, visored helmets, and what she assumed were plastic-pellet-filled shotguns. Everybody was smoking on this side of the city line, too, but maintaining complete silence; even the radios were turned down. The cop nearest Jesse pressed a finger to his lips, then chucked a thumb, telling her to blow.

Forty-five minutes later, in the overcrowded surgery room of the Dempsy Medical Center ER, Jesse, fascinated, watched a natty, fine-boned East Indian doctor, his name tag reading Chatterjee, sew up the side of Ben's face as casually as if he were lacing a boot.

She couldn't tell how many of the other punctures, gashes, slits, and discolorations waiting their turn along the walls were a result of tonight's presser, but one person she knew for sure, a Puerto Rican cop she had seen earlier, calming people down around the Armstrong Bowl. The guy was now holding a plastic bag of ice to his braised onion of an eye, a contrail of cement dust from the chunk that clipped him still lying in a powdery mist above his temple and down the blood-browned left side of his T-shirt.

Fucking Brenda, Jesse marveled to herself, recalling Jose's challenge over the phone: "Are you in love?"

"Helen of Troy, huh?" Chatterjee said, obviously to Jesse, although his eye never strayed from his embroidery. Ben remained glassy, oblivious.

"Excuse me?" Jesse said tentatively. But the doctor was distracted by a technician entering the room with an armful of readouts.

Across the room, Jesse spied a copy of tonight's *Dempsey Register*: SHE DID IT. The header was Jose's call, out of her hands. Buzzed about getting the wood, scoring the front page, Jesse scooped the paper up and skimmed her graphs—not great, not bad, just the reasonably objective facts, dressed in a gray suit of neutral prose. Although the headline was inaccurate—wasn't, strictly speaking, true—it filled Jesse with the hum of completion, made her think, It's this I love.

27

Since snatching up the first young firebug a few hours earlier, Lorenzo had made two more collars around the Bowl, one a sixteen-year-old boy, the other a sad-looking teenaged girl. He had no intention of processing these arrests, just wanted these kids immobilized for the duration. But the sight of the three of them sitting in the dirt with their hands cuffed behind their backs, was inflammatory, so he wound up herding them into the housing office and securing them to the desks in Longway's inner sanctum.

This vexing task took him less than fifteen minutes to perform, but when he reemerged from the building things had changed, the action having shifted from the Bowl to Hurley Street. The fires were more or less extinguished, the slope nearly deserted, but there were two Dempsy squad cars parked now at the open end of Hurley, the eight cops inside sporting flak jackets and visored helmets, the presumptuous riot gear like a self-fulfilling prophecy. Everybody was going crazy down on the cul-de-sac, most of the volunteer cops and the tenant leaders trying both to move the agitated mass back toward the Martyrs Park end of the street and to break up the crowd itself into smaller clusters.

Lorenzo, attempting to speed-read the situation, sensed something else going on, some in-house distress that was pulling people into face-to-face turmoil even without the visual provocation of the police cars. He tried to decipher this inner rumble by picking up on the voices and

the physical flow, but the energy was too diffuse, a cacophony of taunt-
ing shouts and heated conversations, people abruptly flying in and out of
the crowd like couriers in a combat zone. Decoding the street from
where Lorenzo stood was like trying to map the movements and motives
of fireflies.

Lorenzo grabbed some kid racing down the slope to Hurley. "What's
happening."

"They, they locked up the Convoys, man, the brothers? Raheem
Wallace too."

"For what." Lorenzo peered into the crowd again and keyed in on
Raheem's mother, Mary, a bird-small, round-faced woman in a housedress, pop-eyed and sweat-slick, standing at the heart of it, furious, loud,
pumping people up.

"Arrested for what," Lorenzo asked again, but the kid had booked.

Heading for Hurley, he had to drop into a quick squat as something
arced over his head, something thrown not at him but at the cop cars
behind him, whatever it was landing wet and lumpy on the windshield.
The driver used his wipers to clean the view, his straight-faced reaction
either fear or cool—Lorenzo couldn't tell which. Making his way to the
undulating front line of the crowd, Lorenzo joined the brace of volunteer
cops and tenants who were holding back some of the others.

"They locked up the Convoys?" he asked the cop to his right, who
was carefully leaning into some kids, goofing with them about it but
pushing them back.

"That's the word," the cop answered tensely.

"They got my son too," Mary Wallace bawled at him as she plowed
through the crowd, her hyperthyroid eyes accentuating her rage.

"For what," Lorenzo asked, calmly taking her measure. He was more
concerned right now with her incandescent anger than with her son,
cooling his heels at Juvie.

"They say he started a fire," she said, louder than necessary, talking
as much to the crowd as to Lorenzo.

"Fire in here?" Lorenzo glanced up the slope, at the smoky, stinking
Bowl.

"No, *not* in here," she snapped. "That's the *point*. They say he did
something in the Heights," she said, turning to the crowd full-on now.

"How many fires got started up there," she said, gesturing to the
Bowl. "Nobody gets arrested. Nobody. Why? 'Cause it's *in here*, it's *just
us*. They don't give a fuck what we do in here, right? But a child kicks up

over in some *white* neighborhood? They throw away the goddamn key on him."

Lorenzo had to get her the hell out of here.

"They just want some *black* kid to take the place of that jive-ass carjacker." She addressed the crowd like she owned them.

"*They* the ones who started shit. *They* the ones who fucked up, and now they just want to turn it back on us," she said, in a raw staccato growl. "It's like, even if we didn't do it, we *did* it."

"Mary—" Lorenzo reached out to her.

"And if they think they can take *my* son," she continued, "and make him their goddamn scapegoat for that *bitch*." Teary now, she wiped her nose with a quick flash of her palm, people grunting in sympathy, in anger. "If they think I will give them *my* son." Lorenzo itched to snatch her away, but he couldn't. "If they think . . ."

Some kind of missile took off from the crowd, a rock, a ball, something fist-sized; a few seconds later, a dull, metallic crump came from behind Lorenzo's back, the projectile most likely having landed on the hood of one of the police cars.

"Hey!" Lorenzo used the action to cut Mary off, reaching into the crowd as if to grab someone, coming out empty-handed, then taking over. "You *want* them coming in here?" he said, addressing the middle ranks.

"Fuck it," someone said, an invitation. Lorenzo couldn't quite get a fix on the voice, ignored it.

"Because I am telling you. I am *telling* you, you do *not*. Those two cars over there? They are *nothing*. That's like the tip of the iceberg. There's more police on call out there tonight than you got tenants, and you do *not* want them coming in your door."

"Fuck it." That same voice, but Lorenzo had everybody's attention and was not willing to lose it by going one-on-one.

"Now I'm gonna find out what's up, try to get them to back on out, because I don't want them here any more than you. But if anyone starts something?"

Lorenzo retreated from the crowd a few steps, shrugged in an exaggerated gesture of helplessness, then reached in at the last second to snag Mary Wallace by the elbow, catch her off balance. "Me and you we got to talk." He marched her out of the houses via the Hurley Street exit, Mary, overwhelmed by his mobile mass, trotting on tiptoe to keep up.

"Why don't you guys back up out of sight," he called to one of the riot-clad drivers, without breaking stride. "You're gonna *make* the trouble you think you're here to stop. Don't you see that?"

"Hey, Council," the driver tossed back, "ask me if I *want* to be here."

"Then call your boss," he said, hustling Mary around the bend and beneath the Conrail trestle, "before it's too late."

Backing Mary against the cool stone of the shadowed underpass, Lorenzo rested his hands on her shoulders. "All right, look, I'm gonna send someone over to Juvie, find out what happened, OK?" He exuded a reassuring calm that was a lie.

"He should have lit his fires up on the Bowl with the rest of them," she started in again. "He'd be free as a bird."

"Yeah, I hear you, Mary. I hear you," he said briskly. "But here's the thing. I do something for you, you got to do something for me. I cannot have you out here hopping around like Christ on a stick, gassin' up people's heads."

Lorenzo heard shattering glass, saw shards and nuggets skipping past the rear ends of the police cars. "You got to keep your mouth *shut*," he pressed on, talking fast now, desperate to get those cars out of here, " 'cause I promise you, all you're gonna be doing is bringing down more grief than you already got now." More glass, maybe tossed down from an apartment window. Lorenzo braced for the sound of slammed car doors, the cops on the move.

"Lorenzo, I don't even believe he did it." Her voice was more intimate now, plaintive and aggrieved. "They say he got a tire on fire and rolled it into that Chinese restaurant on Easter Avenue."

"A tire?" Lorenzo said, thinking, Aggravated arson.

"That doesn't sound like him, Lorenzo."

"That doesn't sound like *any*body," he said, then added, "Excuse me," and left her in the underpass, heading for the cop cars, Mary's voice echoing out from the stone-lined hollow, "He's a *scape*goat, Lorenzo."

As he came within conversation range of the cruisers—Lorenzo wanting to be hooked up on the radio with whoever had ordered them in—both cars abruptly clicked into reverse and, sweeping backwards in a half arc, shifted gears again and shot out of Hurley Street, flying up the hill that flanked the Bowl. Lorenzo was only partly relieved, the cars moving too fast to indicate a simple withdrawal from post.

Turning to Hurley, his anxiety grew stronger. The cul-de-sac was deserted now, the Bowl too. Then he saw them, the last of the street crowd racing into the breezeway of One Building up on Gompers, people charging into the lobby almost single file, like the tail of a mouse disappearing into its hole. By the time he had huffed his way up the slope, the lobby of the building was so thick with people, all of them seemingly barking and shouting, that he had to use his bulk and his elbows to force his way in through the door. He knew that somewhere in this teeming mob were at least four uniforms and a crew of medics, given the vehicles scatter parked in front of the building, but he couldn't see them.

The focus in the lobby seemed to be the elevator banks, people hopping in place and shouting out a dozen variations of what sounded like "Get him out." Spying a flash of blue, Lorenzo heard some cop, young, white, bawl back at them, "We got, to wait, for the mechanic!" Bulling his way deeper into the crowd, he finally caught sight of the elevator doors, both closed. A half dozen cops were attempting to clear some breathing space for themselves and the two medics there, a small wedge of air. The press of humanity was so dense that most people could only maneuver vertically, bouncing and bellowing, "Get him out!" over and over. The cops looked scared; the volunteer peacekeepers from the Invictus and Aspira organizations were as trapped as anyone else.

"We have, to wait, for the mechanic!" that same young cop bawled through cupped hands. "We don't, have, the key!"

"Then use the *white* key, motherfucker!" a deep male voice boomed from the back of the crowd.

A teenaged girl slipped into the cleared semicircle, slid in behind the cops and medics, and, pressing her body against one of the closed elevator doors, began hysterically jiggling in place, sobbing, slapping the unyielding greasy metal as if whoever was trapped on the other side could just open up and let her in. Again and again she brayed out a single name, Lorenzo fearing that, given the intensity of her trembling, the trapped party was her child. The cops nearest the elevator doors were too outwardly focused, too frazzled to take notice of her, only one of the medics giving her the once-over.

Some of the off-duty volunteers finally made their way to the clearing and began to push people back, but other police, late-arriving uniforms, were piling in from the breezeway, pushing people forward. Lorenzo was beginning to feel crushed. The sobbing girl continued slapping the elevator door, howling over and over, "Barry!" He could hear it clearly now. "Barry!" Scanning his mental directory, Lorenzo came up with three Barrys, none of them children.

"The mechanic, is on, his way!" That same cop, slowly bellowing it out, over and over, no one listening.

"Who's in there?" Lorenzo said loudly to those squirming and hopping around him. "Who's stuck?"

"Stuck!" one of the teenagers responded, turning to him with a look of half-crazed disdain. "Nobody's *stuck*. Motherfucker's up there on the ninth floor, push for the elevator, door opens, nigger's talking left, walkin' right, and steps in to the *shaft*. The motherfuckin' elevator ain't there, nigger, *drops*. And now he's in the black land. Nine motherfuckin' floors, layin' there all bust up in the basement, nine motherfuckin' floors . . . Nobody *stuck*."

"Who . . . ?"

The girl continued to slap the elevator door, howling "Barry!"

"My boy Watrous," the kid said. "Barry Watrous."

Lorenzo winced, knowing the girl now. Stephanie Watrous—her other brother had been killed just a few weeks back.

"Get him out!" Someone was booming it right in his ear, spraying the side of his face.

Lorenzo saw one of the Aspira volunteers, now up front, and catching his eye, gestured for him to take Stephanie out of there, up the stairs, anywhere but here. The cops by the elevators continued to push people back, while the cops still arriving from the street continued to push people forward. Lorenzo was wheezing like a bagpipe now, unable even to reach for his asthma spray. His own physical distress made him even more fearful for the rest of the crowd, fearful of their being smothered in here but also of their getting free, dispersing into the night with all this rage.

"Do something!" Lorenzo saw one of Barry's aunts pop out of the crowd, fists knotted at her side, a fat vein wriggling at her temple. "Pretend he's *white*."

"If you don't back up," a fear-fucked uniform said, thrusting a finger in her face, "you're going in."

Lorenzo shut his eyes, this asshole having just threatened the dead boy's aunt, who was so stunned by this response that she simply walked away.

"The mechanic, is on, the way!" that same cop howled. "We can't get in without the key!"

Lorenzo saw one of the medics light up a cigarette, probably meaning no disrespect, the guy having nothing to do except watch the needle climb higher and higher on this pressure cooker. But it looked bad, him lighting up in front of the crowd, really bad, and Lorenzo saw two of the man-boys in the crowd react, breaststroking their way forward, eyes on that medic. Lorenzo raced them, got there first, held them off with one hand, snatched the butt from the medic's lips with the other, the guy gasping in surprise, looking at Lorenzo as if he were just another D-Town goon.

In or out: there was no one in charge, and Lorenzo frantically tried to make the right call, wanting to keep the rage in here contained, or eject it into the street, the night, *this* night. He opted for an exodus, the crush just too dangerous.

"Get them *out*," he megaphoned over the heads of the crowd to the cops at the door, not sure any of them heard him. "Get them *out!*" No one in charge, his directive mingling with the crowd's chorus of "Get *him* out," a barnyard swirl of words vaporizing into the sopping air.

And then the mechanic arrived, just popped out of the front lines of the crowd, jockey-sized, sleep-smeared, his hair sticking out in unbrushed spikes. He seemed immune to the chaos, still groggy as he slipped into the clearing, a tool box in one hand and a heavy key ring in the other.

"Don't do nothing yet," Lorenzo said, crouching down to put his lips to the mechanic's ear. "Get them *out!*" he then boomed as loud as he could to the cops in the rear, waving everybody back with both hands, not wanting an open elevator shaft added to the mix, envisioning a forward surge, people pressing in to see the body at the bottom of the shaft, Barry Watrous lying twisted and mangled around the huge shock-absorber coils down there.

Either the mechanic didn't hear him or the guy just wanted to get back to bed, and within thirty seconds of his arrival the elevator doors were open. Lorenzo turned, ready to wring this little bastard's neck, but what he saw framed by the opened door froze him in place, froze everybody in place. A hush came over the lobby, punctuated by whispered awe, nonwords and groans.

The car that failed to meet Barry Watrous on nine had never left the ground floor. The impact of the body plummeting from that height had driven the car downwards, half its length, so that its roof, which now supported Barry's broken body, was at eye level with those who had been standing, shoving, shouting in the lobby.

Barry lay sprawled almost gracefully on his back, one leg twisted beneath him at a cartoon angle, his throat arched, his chin thrust upward, lips slightly apart, eyes shut, a flung hand now at rest, palm-out across his forehead in an attitude of almost languorous repose. His stunning proximity to the crowd had Lorenzo and everyone else struck dumb. The body lay before them like an offering, a tableau—a death for your contemplation, death itself for your contemplation, death displayed, death arrayed, death in all its inert majesty, in all its terrible absoluteness, death in your face, in your eye, a death to take your breath away—and for a long moment the air, what little there was to begin with, went out of the hall, no one talking, no one walking, the only signs of insistent life being the medic, quietly reaching in and feeling for a pulse in Barry's throat, and a seemingly sourceless ripple coursing through the unresisting crowd as the small mechanic worked his way, like a cat through tall grass, toward the lobby door and home.

The mechanic's exit brought Lorenzo back into focus: the elevator had killed someone, and there was no way that guy was going back to bed. Lorenzo began shoving his way toward the door, and a moment after that the rest of the lobby crowd came alive, too, with a rising mutter and buzz, people once again on the move, most of them heading for the street now, taking long last looks at the body on their way out, re-entering the night and all its possibilities.

Lorenzo was no longer worried about Armstrong's going off. Barry Watrous had taken the wind out of these houses, and he knew that for at least the next few hours Armstrong would grant both itself and the city a temporary stay of execution. The Crime Scene Unit, the county homicide squad, and a team from Emergency Services joined the uniforms and the medics still inside the lobby, and Lorenzo headed outside, mingling with the tenants in front of the building, a delayed weepiness now peppering the crowd, a low male drawl of mournful reflection.

As he was looking around for the retreating mechanic, Lorenzo heard someone out of his sight lines say, "Brenda Martin," just floating it out there, Lorenzo thinking, Brenda Martin, then having to say the name out loud to himself before he could remember who she was.

28

Jesse sat in the 4:00 A.M. waft and blear of a hot-sheet motel room and stared at the bubble-gum-blue screen of the laptop propped on the otherwise untouched bed. For the first time in days, Jesse was alone.

Three hours earlier, she had left her brother at the Medical Center. Ben was to be kept overnight, not for his slashed cheek but for exhaustion. In the surgery room, he had played dumb with the cops, affecting that overpolite, almost slavishly accommodating side of himself, but Jesse knew that, in this case, he was blowing smoke, knew that what was operating in him then was the Ben who paid the bills by serving subpoenas, the side of him that advertised itself on a business card as a "personal threat consultant," a stalker of stalkers, a counterintimidator of ex-husbands, ex-boyfriends, and any other type of restraining-order violator out there on the street.

A few weeks or months from now, Ben would have his payback on the boxcutter-wielding son of a bitch who had carved his face. The guy was destined for a hospital stay of his own, and although Jesse had no problem with Old Testament–style revenge, she didn't want to hear the details in advance, so she left her brother in the general-surgery room before the painkillers could make him chatty.

Now, with both her brother and Brenda tucked away for the night, with the streets finally quiet, Jesse had no choice but to get down to that most dreaded and much-delayed aspect of the job, the committing of thought to print. Jose needed both her piece on the Friends of Kent ordeal and the second installment of her vigil diary. He had asked her to come into the paper tonight and work at her cubicle, said he'd wait for her till whatever hour so they could have at least one face-to-face on this story. But Jesse liked Jose better over the phone—disembodied, omniscient, guiding, the good father—and she didn't want to go home to that jerry-rigged, flavored-coffee-reeking rip-off bachelorette. So she had checked into the Tunnel-View Motel in Jersey City, was trying to bang it out here, working under the light of the high-powered incandescent bulb that she always carried in her bag, squinting through her own smoke at the vacant gleam of the screen, but it just wasn't happening.

She could have blamed her lack of progress on many things—the voidish hour; the distraction of the hooker one room over, head-butting the shared wall and tonelessly lowing, or the East Indian motel manager, walking back and forth in his carpet slippers past her ground-floor window, coming off both aloof and curious. Jesse speculated that she was probably the only woman he had ever rented a room to who didn't earn her living with her mouth.

She could even have blamed her stall on Jose, who over the years had paper-trained her to write without personality or intimate observation. But the blank screen was about none of that. It was about Brenda. And it was about herself. Having begun this forty-eight-hour emotional car wash, drunk on intimacy and identification, Jesse had then pulled an abrupt about-face into anger and disdain, deciding that she had been lied to, manipulated, conned. These negatives were tricky for her to negotiate, given that she felt guilty of the very same hustles, and now here they were at the end of the ride, she and Brenda, and it just wouldn't come.

The hooker on the other side of the wall said either, "You're so big" or "You're a pig."

Jesse checked the time: four-fifteen. She reached for the phone.

"What." Jose picked up, sounding sleep-stuffed, pissed.

"Listen." She held the receiver to the wall above her headboard for a brief moment, the woman on the other side back to halfheartedly moaning.

"Jesus, that's my wife. Where are you."

"The No Tell Mo Tell."

"*Why.* What the fuck is wrong with you?"

"I'm shy," she said, feeling better now.

"You're almost finished, right?"

"Almost."

"You hear about the kid who died in Armstrong?"

"No."

"Elevator accident. Fell something like twelve stories."

"Jesus."

"They're making a movie about it. You know what it's called?"

"Shaft?"

"Very good."

"So what's the score," she asked.

"Eighteen. Arson, assault, disorderly, you name it. You hear about the kid who rolled a burning tire into the Chinese restaurant?"

"Is that a joke?"

"Nope."

"How'd they take the elevator accident at Armstrong?"

"Buggin'," he said. "But it stayed in-house."

"So, eighteen?" Jesse closed her eyes, fell asleep for a second.

"I'm telling you, we're like one lockup away from a riot. Come tomorrow night? It's gonna be like playing catch with a water balloon out there."

Jesse stared at the luminous blue sea of nothing propped on the bed. "So what's the early line on her," she asked.

"Criminally negligent homicide. Draw three to five—serve three or less if people forget, the full five if they don't."

"They're doing a bedside arraignment?" Jesse's yawns came down on her like snow.

"Yeah, but get this—they're doing a video feed of it into the court."

"From the hospital?" Jesse jumped, knowing instantly that she had to see that footage to kick out the jams on this piece, commit to a stance. "I thought they only video booked from the jail."

"She's a very special girl, our Brenda."

"I guess so," Jesse said evenly, needing her, feeling the old pull, but keeping it to herself.

"So it's going OK?" Jose inquired about the writing, sounding leery.

"Yeah, I'm almost done," Jesse said quickly.

"You're not thinking of going to the arraignment, are you?"

"No time," she murmured, not wanting to hear him say, Don't.

"Well, maybe you should," Jose said, coming on paternal and knowing now. "You know, like a wee hair of the dog."

At eight-forty-five in the morning, after little sleep and less writing, Jesse stood at the rear entrance to the Dempsy County judicial processing court, one of a long line of anxious reporters trying to secure a pass for Brenda's arraignment. The county clerk charged with overseeing the press passes was a frazzled, heavyset woman in matching coral top and slacks. She stood over a rickety card table that supported a joint-compound bucket filled with color-of-the-day buttons. There were more reporters than available seats, and the woman seemed prickly and over-whelmed. Jesse and most of the others familiar with this kind of situation knew that this lady was to be coddled and humored; any rudeness or ill temper on her part was to be swallowed with a smile. Jesse also understood that the same delicate obeisance would be required once inside the courtroom, the court officers on duty today under the fluorescent ceiling panels subject to the same high-pressure crankiness as this lady was out here under the climbing sun.

"Hey." Jesse felt the light clutch of a hand on her shoulder and turned to see the young bow-tied Jimmy Olsen look-alike she had briefly met in McCoy's bar now standing two places behind her in line. "Con-gratulations." He held up a copy of last night's *Dempsy Register.* "Nice work."

"Thanks, thank you." Jesse looked away, her eye falling on the head-line of a New York tabloid held by one of the other reporters. LIAR topped a photo of Brenda leaving her apartment house. The same paper, being read by someone else, displayed on page 3 a photo of Curious George. He was walking out of County; the header on that item read: FURIOUS GEORGE.

Judicial processing in Dempsy County had streamlined itself over the last year, doing away with the required physical presence of the ac-cused. The court had opted for arraignment via television, and a booking studio was set up in the county jail. The defendant would make his appearance on two video-screen monitors—one facing the judge, the other the benches—the judge, in turn, appearing before the accused on a jailhouse monitor. Both of them would also show up on their own screens, in a small, boxed "picture in picture."

The courtroom was standing room only, all eyes on the blank twenty-five-inch monitor angled at a slightly downward tilt from its ceil-ing mount. The glum, mostly stoic assembly of out-on-bail perps, family members, and Legal Aid lawyers who normally populated the benches was almost lost in the profane and anxious hum of professional court hounds, Jesse seated on the aisle, third row from the docket.

The hospital feed was unprecedented, but Jesse thought she knew where the prosecutor was coming from on this: offer up, in the most public way possible, the beginnings of Brenda Martin's mortification and, by doing so, possibly mollify some of the hotheads out there getting ready for Night Two.

"All rise." The court officer's voice was sonorous and automatic as the judge entered from offstage and took his seat—the honorable Joe Pisto, five feet even, with a too black hairpiece, a brace of gold chains under his judicial robes, and, parked out in the lot, Jesse knew, a custom-made El Dorado replete with champagne-pink pinstripe trim and a monogrammed driver's door.

"Be seated."

"Ladies and gentlemen of the media," Pisto began. "I assume you're here for the headline act, but unfortunately, sort of like pay-per-view boxing, you're going to have to sit through a mess of prelims in order to get to the Tyson fight, so please bear with us."

Among the members of the press, there was a barely perceptible rustle, a low-key bristling at the preemptive reproach. Jesse wasn't bothered, knowing that Judge Pisto's idea of a headline act was Judge Pisto and that he would be harrumphing and sardonically side-mouthing like this at every opportunity.

The first two names called were no-shows, so Pisto issued fugitive warrants, and then the monitor came to life, a bald switchblade of a man in the standard royal-blue jumpsuit of the county jail staring blankly into the camera. After a reading of the charges, and some preoccupied rote exchange with the prosecutor and the Legal Aid representative, Pisto addressed the monitor.

"Mr. Cortez."

"Hah?" A honk.

"I'm setting your bail at three hundred dollars."

"Hah?"

"Do you have three hundred dollars?" Pisto speaking to the TV.

"Hah?"

"I said, do you—" He cut himself off, then addressed the benches— "Is it him or me?"—people laughing like a TV audience.

"Can I go?" Cortez asked.

"Where would you like to go," Pisto responded, slowly and distinctly.

"Hah?" Cortez honked, bringing down the house.

Two more inmates showed up on video, and their bails were set; then a middle-aged man in a rumpled summer suit made a personal appearance to hear that his wife's assault charge against him had been downgraded to unlawful entry; then another video visit, the defendant filmed lumbering into the video room. Instead of taking a seat, he nosed up to within inches of the camera, his face fanning out as it filled the screen, fishbowl-style, Jesse thinking, Ernest Goes to Prison.

Once the last jailhouse video prisoner was disposed of, the screen flipped into a solid field of bright blue. A female court officer called out the name, charge, and docket number of another customer out on bail, the guy not in the room, and Pisto ordered yet another warrant.

The reporters were looking at one another now, growing impatient. Then, finally, Brenda's name rang out in a flat, blaring proclamation and was met with an abrupt jump in focus and energy out in the room, a poised tension, everybody working now. One of the assistant DAs approached the bench. It was John Savio, a popular, politically wired ex-cop prominent in the Dempsy County Save the Children fund, a guy who could put his heart into this one. Jesse watched him as he centered himself before the lectern, rolling his neck and shoulders as if he were waiting for the first-round bell.

The solid-blue overhead screen coughed in black and white before coming alive with a grainy, pixel-deficient image, the handheld camera seemingly trained on either a wall or a ceiling, then swinging in a blur before sharpening somewhat, finally focusing on a humped rumple of blankets, an IV tube sneaking in from a bedside drip stand, the picture in picture of Judge Pisto blocking out the foot of the bed. A thrum coursed through the benches, Jesse and everyone else inching forward in their seats, the court officers unconsciously criss-crossing one another's paths behind the rails as they glared vigilantly at the reporters.

Up on the screen, the camera pulled back to reveal a man standing bedside, the resolution once again too poor to identify the face. But the rumor had gone around, and the chest-length beard confirmed it: Brenda's lawyer was Paul Rosenbaum, champion of the poor, the down-trodden, the nonwhite, the addicted, the desperate, the technically guilty, the occasionally framed, the submoronic, the psychopathic, the abused turned abuser, the formerly innocent casualties of a racist free-enterprise system now fully grown to payback size; Rosenbaum, a world-class pain in the ass who turned every case into an indictment of the society into which both victim and victimizer had been involuntarily deposited at birth.

Two years earlier, during a front-page trial in which Rosenbaum was defending a cop shooter, Jesse had decided that the way to get close to him was by playing up her red-diaper pedigree, coming off as if she were more interested in justice than in getting the wood. He had gone for it, even given her his home phone number and asked her to keep tabs on the outside buzz for him. She had then misplayed her hand badly, though, calling him one evening to toss him a wild story that was making the rounds—that his client was in partnership with some cops in a drug deal—calling him not so much to give him a heads up on this ridiculous scenario but to provoke a quotable response from him. He had instantly seen through her gambit and mildly reproached her for abusing the privilege of having access to him, his voice registering as much disappointment in her as anger. Then he had excused himself, announcing that he was in the middle of putting his daughter to bed. And, upon hanging up, Jesse had retreated to hers, pulling down the shades and lying there in the dark from eight in the evening until the next morning.

Now, already feeling emotionally punchy and scoured-out by her marathons with Brenda, Jesse found the sight of the two of them up there on the screen together almost too much to bear. The reception worsened, Brenda somewhere in that electronic blizzard, the judge waiting until the video operator found his focus.

"Today is July the third, the time is 10:45 A.M., I'm Judge Joseph Pisto. Gentlemen?"

"Good morning, Judge," the prosecutor said, shifting his feet. "I'm John Savio, assistant district attorney of Dempsy County representing the state."

"Good morning, Judge." Rosenbaum took a step closer to the camera. "I'm Paul Rosenbaum of Rosenbaum, Winbarg, and I'm representing the defendant."

"Gentlemen? Are we ready to proceed?" Pisto's question was met with stereophonic affirmatives.

Rosenbaum: Jesse wondered who had done the reach out, taking a wild guess, coming up with someone who, under normal circumstances, would have preferred to see Rosenbaum befriended by one of his own clients in a jail cell; she guessed that the phone call to land Paul Rosenbaum had come from Danny Martin. The video operator tended to rock slightly from side to side, making Jesse seasick.

"Mr. Rosenbaum, is your client ready?"

"Yes she is, Judge."

"Can we see her?"

Rosenbaum peeled back a flap of blanket to reveal Brenda, cheek to the mattress, staring straight ahead. As the camera zoomed in, the screen was hit with another flurry of static, and it seemed to Jesse that Brenda was dissolving before her eyes, dematerializing into glazed, no-exit grief.

"Miss Martin?" the judge asked in a slightly louder than necessary voice. "Are you among us?"

"Yes she is, Your Honor," Rosenbaum answered for her.

Jesse could hear the sound of writing.

"I would like Miss Martin to respond."

"Yes," Brenda said, a sandpapery whistle, all faces in the courtroom angled to the monitor like flowers to the sun.

Jesse wondered why Rosenbaum was allowing Brenda to be arraigned publicly like this, then answered her own question: To be seen like this.

"How's your reception there, Counselor? Can you see us?"

"Yes we can, Your Honor."

"Miss Martin?" The judge's voice took on a somewhat measured, slightly loud tone again. "I have a complaint here, signed by Detective Lorenzo Council of the Dempsy Police Department, charging you with the homicide death of Cody Martin. Do you understand these charges as I have read them to you?"

The focus became sharper, but, simultaneously, something was affecting the film speed. The transmitted image slowed down just a hair, so that when Brenda limply raised, then dropped a hand in acknowledgment of the question, its trajectory seemed to move in minutely checked gradations—dream speed, like a progression of pages in a flip book.

"Miss Martin?" Pisto waited.

After another interminable silence, she croaked out another "Yes."

"And how do you plead."

"Not guilty, Your Honor," Rosenbaum responded with confident gusto, just as Jesse expected.

Earlier this morning, Jesse had made a few off-the-record breakfast-table calls to some detectives and lawyers around town, the general consensus being that the only way the prosecutor could make the straight-up homicide charge work was to prove the ingestion was forced—caustic burns around the mouth, caustic liquid in the boy's belly, the presence of some harsh toxic substance that no one would drink voluntarily, especially a child. But if the toxicology reports came back indicating that a sweetish-tasting substance had done the deed, then the prosecutor had a real job on his hands. Jose probably had it pegged about right last night: criminally negligent homicide.

"Gentlemen? I'll hear you on bail. Mr. Savio?"

Savio gently rocked from side to side, unconsciously miming the swaying of the image on the monitor. "Good morning, Your Honor."

"You said that."

"The state feels this is a heinous crime, the murder of a four-year-old child by his mother, and requests that bail be set in the amount of one million dollars, no cash option." A knowing whoosh ran through the pews; it was a sum fit for a terrorist. "Your Honor, we were initially told one story by the defendant, that story causing near chaos in this city; now we're about to hear another. Miss Martin went to great lengths not only to conceal the truth of what happened but also to dispose of the body in a most egregious manner."

"Egregious and Kathie Lee," someone behind Jesse whispered.

"Given the notoriety of this crime, the potential for, for mayhem set in motion by Miss Martin's actions, we consider her a menace to society, an expression I have rarely used in this courtroom before."

"Whoa, whoa." Pisto reared back. "Slow down there, hoss."

"In addition," Savio plowed on, "the state feels there's a reasonable question of flight, and if the defendant should skip out, I feel the anger in this city would reduce it to rubble."

"Mr. Savio." Pisto cracked his knuckles. "Despite the presence of so many reviewers out in our audience today, I would like to remind you that this is not the Winter Garden, and I would appreciate it, as of right this second, if you would kindly refrain from playing for the rear seats."

"Yes, Your Honor."

There was scribbling fever out in the benches, heads-down grins.

"Mr. Rosenbaum?"

Rosenbaum was no theatrical slouch either. During Savio's grim soliloquy, he had been slowly shaking his head with ostentatious dismay, the speed-hobbled image, with its infinitesimal stops and starts, converting that gesture into the head swivel of an automaton.

"Your Honor," he began, "Brenda Martin is an exemplary citizen, born, bred, and living in Dempsy County. A professional educator committed to the welfare of its people. She has never garnered so much as a parking ticket in the past, and, as far as being a menace to society, I would ask Your Honor to take a good look at my client and to consider what here is so particularly menacing to society or to anyone else. We respectfully ask for a bail of five thousand dollars."

"Mr. Rosenbaum, I believe when the state uses the expression "menace to society" they are not afraid of Miss Martin rising from her hospital bed and planting land mines, but I'm sure you know that." Pisto coughed into his fist, then vigorously rubbed his hands, as if anticipating some game of chance, some challenge. "All right, based on the nature of the crime, the publicity, and—as Mr. Savio has melodramatically but accurately pointed out—the number of lives affected by Miss Martin's actions, I'm going along with the prosecution's request. Bail is set at one million dollars, no cash option."

"Your Honor." Rosenbaum raised his hand but was plowed under.

"And if it's any consolation to you, Mr. Rosenbaum, I think jail right now is the safest place for your client to be. Thank you."

Pisto banged his gavel, and the room came alive with the hum of bottled information.

"OK." Pisto banged his gavel again, without any real impact, and his voice carried a trace of regret. "OK. Now that prime time is over, I'm giving our distinguished visitors three minutes to clear out. Anyone still in here after that better sit tight until lunch unless they care to see themselves on TV tomorrow"—he gestured toward the monitor—"live from county jail."

As the other reporters began to collect themselves, each one gearing up to blow on out of there as fast as he could, Brenda still lay in a sizzle of static, the video operator somehow not having gotten the message that transmission was no longer required. Brenda hovered over the courtroom like a wraith, floating in and out of sight through fields of electronic drift yet so inert within herself that, if not for the inexpert shakiness of the handheld camera, Jesse wouldn't have known that she was still staring at a live feed.

Those around her made for the doors, but Jesse, transfixed, kept her seat. As Brenda once again began slowly, unblinkingly to dissolve under another electronic swarm, Jesse was abruptly struck with the premonition that Brenda would not survive the summer—that what was up there on the monitor for all to see right now, if they cared to look, was a spirit photograph, a portent. Jesse was sure of it: Brenda was in her last days, and this arraignment, along with whatever was to follow, would all come to nothing.

29

Lorenzo stood to the rear of the small crowd that had collected outside Brenda's hospital room during the arraignment. He knew Paul Rosenbaum by reputation only and, as with many of the local personalities who affected life in the urban trenches, he was of at least two minds about him. But when Rosenbaum came out into the hallway after the arraignment, Lorenzo was flattered that the lawyer instantly recognized him, wading through the mob to shake his hand.

"How are you?" Rosenbaum smiled, giving him the once-over.

"Good," Lorenzo returned in kind, playing it close, save for one thing. "Here." He handed Rosenbaum a shopping bag containing Brenda's Discman, her CDs, and some fresh batteries thrown in for good measure. "She might want this."

"That's very thoughtful." Rosenbaum shook his hand again. "Be seeing you."

Last night, caught up in the death of Barry Watrous, Lorenzo had almost forgotten Brenda—how her criminal processing would continue to impact on this city, on himself—but once the body had been removed from the shaft, he had begun a slow return to a sober appreciation of the big picture, and before packing it in he had made a quick run to the Southern District station to gather and retrieve her musical gear. He had done this because he wanted her to remember him in a positive light, didn't want his handling of her during the investigation to be a liability to the prosecutor. But he also vaguely understood that there was more to the gesture than just professional prudence. She wouldn't be able to take the music into the jail, but at least she could have it for the duration of her stay in the hospital.

This hospital; he could have spent all day here visiting people—Brenda, Bump, Jesse's brother. But the person he wanted to see, the one he needed to see, was the rev. There were rumors floating about that, despite his latest hospitalization, Longway was attempting to put together some kind of protest march through Gannon tonight. Lorenzo thought the man had to be completely out of his mind. Last night's ultimate peace was a false one, purchased with a spectacular death from out of left field, but the rage out there was still on the build.

On his way over to the medical center this morning, Lorenzo had seen some of the local boneheads beginning to congregate at last night's hot spots, as if to be first in line for tonight's potential mayhem. And he knew from experience that the cops out there today would be jumpy as hell, treating every two-bit pullover and street-corner roll-up as if they were taking down terrorists, D-Town, as the thermometer climbed, a land of twitchy fists and hair-trigger emotions on both sides of the line.

Leaving Brenda behind him, he tripped down two flights of stairs to Longway's floor. Longway's room was unoccupied, although littered with signs of the rev's presence—a Walkman, imperfectly hidden under the pillow; a pack of Kools; a plastic liter of Coca-Cola; a Kangol cap, resting at the foot of the bed; and a pair of orthopedic shoes, moon-walk shoes, one atop the other in front of the small closet.

Out of reflex, Lorenzo ducked inside, tucked the Walkman out of sight, and removed the Kangol to the night table, a hat on the bed being a bad sign. Intent on hunting down Longway, Lorenzo stalked the corridors, so pulled into his own anxieties that he didn't notice Chatterjee until the doctor laid a hand on his arm.

"Hey," Lorenzo said flatly. "What you doing up here, hidin'?"

"Exactly," Chatterjee murmured.

"They driving you crazy down there?"

"I've had four reporters come in as patients today. Did I think she was faking it. What did she say. What did she do. What did her injuries look like."

"Yeah, huh?" Lorenzo's eyes were drawn to the flow of hallway traffic.

"My favorite? Do you think she's pregnant."

"Doc. I got to find the Reverend Longway. He's not in his room."

Beaming at Lorenzo for a long, teasing moment, Chatterjee finally took him by the elbow and walked him back the way he had just come, then around the corner to the adjoining corridor, the air filled with the astringent snap of alcohol. He brought him to the threshold of a ten-bed room, the barely restrained expression on the doctor's face that of someone ushering a birthday boy to a surprise party. "Look," he said, pointing to the far wall, to a patient laying immobile in a slash of sunlight. "They picked him up last night from the Randall Street shelter. I was going to call you, but here you are."

The offering was not Longway, as requested, but Mookie, killer-nephew of Mother Barrett and Uncle Theo, and the sight of him left Lorenzo light-headed, the rev momentarily fading on him as he began pacing the corridor, attempting to throw Mookie in the mix, clear his head for Mookie, old business abruptly rescued from a fading, disgruntled memory by a rush of blood and adrenaline.

Oblivious to the flow of the hallway, Lorenzo paced in a circuit that grew tighter and quicker, then tighter and quicker still, until, as if launching himself, he abruptly entered the sickroom, not convinced he was up for this, wondering if he could pull off some miracle of trickery right now. Coming up to the bedside, his mind a brimming blank, he saw Mookie's concave chest as revealed by the V-shaped furls of his unbuttoned pajama top—saw the purple lesions there, planted on the lusterless skin in a random scatter, like monstrous enlargements of what, in Lorenzo's imagination, Mookie's doctors had seen under the microscope.

Slowly turning his head from the light streaming through the window, then facing Lorenzo at the shadow side of his bed, Mookie took a few seconds to complete a blink of the eye, Lorenzo thinking that he probably had more dope in him now than he had ever had on the street. After another prolonged moment, Mookie finally nodded in recognition—a glacial bob of the head that ended a fifty-three-week nonconversation—then, touching one of his trilobite-shaped sarcomas, whispered, "He died for us."

Lorenzo thought the reference was to Uncle Theo, but then Mookie added, "Have you accepted him in your heart?"

Lorenzo gave it a beat, wiped his dry mouth. "Look at you," he whispered soothingly, struggling to keep the tremor out of his voice. "Look at you. You did it, boy. You just beat the system. No more jail. No more . . . You done got over, boss, you done got over." Mookie turned his head to the sunlight again. "Tell me you did it," Lorenzo whispered. "Tell me you did it." He decided in that moment, that, like the hat on the bed in Longway's room, coming on Mookie today was an omen, a tide changer. If he could just get Mookie to come clean now, then out on the streets tonight, the dove would prevail.

"Tell me you did it," Lorenzo murmured, a love call. Mookie closed his eyes. "C'mon now," Lorenzo cooed. "You talking to me about Jesus. Right now you're gonna meet the man with blood on your hands, don't you see that? C'mon, man, nobody's gonna mess with you now. You got over with it. Just tell me you did it." Mookie opened his eyes, closed them again. "Tell me you did it." Then, "C'mon now." Lorenzo was hovering. "C'mon now." Waiting, his legs trembling with renewed fatigue. "C'mon now . . ."

Mookie's lips parted, then hung there. He was asleep. Grinning like a good sport, Lorenzo straightened up, then began walking back through the room. He got as far as the door and, wheeling, charged back to Mookie's side. *"Fuck* you," Lorenzo hissed, leaning over him again. "You AIDS-ass mother*fucker.*"

Filled with a murderous despair, avoiding the dying eyes on either side of him, Lorenzo finally stalked out of the room and headed for the elevator banks. As he passed the fifth-floor visitors' lounge, he caught sight of the Reverend Longway sitting in his bathrobe, talking with two other ministers, the lay activist Donald De Lauder, and Curious George Howard.

De Lauder and the ministers coming by for a hospital visit didn't necessarily signify anything, but the presence of Curious George, this week's poster boy for racial injustice, was the closer. In Lorenzo's mind the march was a done deal. Standing in the doorway now, like an enraged cuckold, Lorenzo glared at them, Longway throwing him a weak wave, saying, "Speak of the devil."

"It's like this." Longway sat hunched over himself in the corduroy chair. "It's like, let's go over to *their* house, let's go barge in through *their* door, see how *they* like it."

Lorenzo tipped his chair back until his shoulders were gently bobbing against the wall. He regarded the Reverend Longway in his slippers and bathrobe, his sick-man skin the color of cigarette ash. The only others present now were Donald De Lauder and Curious George, who still bore the facial wounds from his go-round with Danny Martin. Hunkered down low on the couch, as if to duck the conversation on either side of him, George looked to Lorenzo as miserable in here as he did the other day, cuffed to the desk in Gannon.

"See, all this, this *rage* out there," Longway said. "If we don't, channel it? You know, make it articulate? It's just gonna be more self-destruction."

"Firing up those refrigerators at Armstrong," Donald De Lauder said, "that's like people getting mad at the landlord so they burn up their own homes. That's convict mentality, and that kind of thinking has got to be rerouted."

Lorenzo nodded in tentative agreement. Even given De Lauder's martyred history, he never felt comfortable around the guy. Perhaps unfairly, Lorenzo didn't trust anyone who had ever been shot; being that close to death permanently changed people, he believed, in unpredictable ways. In addition, De Lauder's personal trajectory was all over the psychic map. After surviving injuries from that raid on the Panthers headquarters back in the sixties, De Lauder sued the city of Newark, retired from the force, became a serious juicer, and, two years later, was arrested for armed robbery. He came out of jail four years after that—sober and pissed. Not one for public speaking, he had nonetheless created a mobile army of followers, the Justice Now League. A sort of quick-response team, a loan-out cadre working both sides of the Hudson, they were willing to bolster the local presence in the wake of any incident, exposé, or revelation perceived as racist in nature.

"Now nobody wants anyone hurt around here," De Lauder continued with his pitch, "but we want their anger. We can *work* with their anger."

Lorenzo bobbled against the wall, thinking, I'll give you anger—the people in this room suiting up in gasoline jackets to attend a bonfire. "Yeah, but like nonetheless, people *could* get hurt, right?"

"People *are* getting hurt." De Lauder shrugged, playing with his wedding ring. "And it's all that freelance improvising out there that's doing the damage."

"Why does it have to be tonight?" Lorenzo asked, beginning to find his voice. "You giving yourself next to no time to get it together."

"Why?" De Lauder again, Longway looking bad, slack-faced. "Because tonight's gonna be worse than last night. I mean, you got to know there's no way the police are gonna stand down again like that. Plus you got all those cameras out there, all those reporters. You got to strike while the iron's hot."

"While the iron's hot," Lorenzo said, starting to fume. "What if someone gets hurt?" Then, realizing he had already asked that, he added, "Some kid."

"Then they'd be gettin' hurt in front of the cameras."

"And that's gonna make it OK, because it's for the greater good of the community, right?"

"Look." Longway came back to life. "All I want, is Gannon acting like their natural selves." He rose to his feet, struggling to maintain his balance. "I want, I want them *on* TV screaming 'Nigger' at us. I want them waving watermelons. I want, I want them to show the world who they are by how they react to us. I don't want to do nothing on our end but show up, as advertised, and walk the walk."

"We're going to the zoo but that don't mean we got to act like the monkeys," De Lauder said, reaching up and gripping Longway's forearm to steady him. "Let the monkeys act like the monkeys. We're just going there to, to let the world see what our presence is gonna bring out in the people of Gannon. And you better believe the world *will* be watching, because this situation is a lot bigger than just Dempsy County. You gotta know *that*. I mean the stuff that happened here, that's like up and down the pike, that's endemic."

Curious George hissed like a radiator, threw Lorenzo a desperate get-me-out-of-here glance, much as he had two days earlier in Gannon.

"And like I told the reverend here, before you came in," De Lauder said, shaping his words with his hands. "Given the, the, high visibility we're gonna get on this, it's imperative that we do everything we can to make sure this thing goes off without a hitch on *our* end, all right?" Lorenzo held his peace, waiting. "Now, I am in no way shape or form looking to, to take over here, but I can offer you considerable help in your two greatest areas of potential liability, numbers and control.

"See, because from where I'm coming from, I think it would be a goddamn shame tonight if you had something like seventy-five people show up. I mean, you're gonna have more newsmen than that. But I'll tell you, historically? Dempsy's got a numbers problem. Dempsy County has always had a hard time getting black people to show up, to get their behinds on the line."

Curious George mumbled something about a phone call, stood up, and without waiting for anyone to clear out of his way he clumsily slid around the chairs and headed out, Longway and De Lauder watching him go.

"What's George gonna be," Lorenzo asked Longway. "Exhibit A?"

"You best believe it," Longway responded without irony.

"Yeah, well good luck on that."

"All right, like I was saying." De Lauder turned them back to him. "Numbers . . . I'm going to deliver to you one hundred and twenty-five members of my organization, eighteen to eighty years of age. They believe, they're experienced, and they know how to conduct themselves in a situation like this. They are disciplined. Which brings us to the second issue. Control . . . Now, I have every confidence in my own people being able to, to maintain, no matter what provocation is thrown in their path. We even have our own, what we call security ushers. But on your end, you're not sure *who's* gonna show, and you don't know *why* they're gonna show. Some might be there to stand up and be counted. Beautiful. Some might show 'cause they like all the TV business. And some, might be two, might be a dozen, they're gonna be there 'cause they want to set it off. They want to bust it up, they want to *light* it up, and *those* brothers, as far as I'm concerned, might as well be wearing white sheets for all the damage they're gonna do us. But that's why I'm so glad to see *you* here, Lorenzo."

Lorenzo leaned back, crossed his arms.

"See, I don't even know how you feel about this march tonight, whether you approve or disapprove. My guess is you're kind of on the fence, and I know what your job is in the world, especially vis-à-vis this particular situation, so if you said to me, to us, 'Back off,' I would have no choice but to respect that. But if you *did* decide to come on board? Well, then I can't think of anyone else be better to help us on the X-factor end of things. Can you?" he asked Longway, who was eyeing Lorenzo as if amused by his resistance. "And I'm not even referring to the symbolic significance of having the arresting detective on this marching along with us," De Lauder said. "I'm talking about straight-out nuts-and-bolts crowd control. Because experience tells me it's gonna be harder for any of the local knuckleheads to act up if they got someone they know ridin' shotgun on them."

"Where the hell did George go." Longway abruptly sat up. "He best not have flown the coop."

"Fuck George," Lorenzo blurted, embarrassing himself and drawing mild stares from the others. "I'll go get him," he muttered, and left the room—basically, to leave the room.

George was down the hall, squawking into a pay phone. "I said, where my motherfuckin' *tape* at," he sputtered, spraying the receiver. "What you mean you lent it to Keisha. Where you come to lent out *my* got-damn tape . . . Naw, naw, naw." He cast an anxious glance back to the lounge he had just escaped from. "Well I'm gonna come get it right now . . . *Right* now . . . Well, you best go get it then . . . You best go get it or I'm gonna jump in your motherfuckin' chest, you *hear* me?" George slammed down the receiver and bolted for the stairs, Lorenzo making no move to stop him.

Returning to the lounge, Lorenzo found Longway by himself now, De Lauder having left for parts unknown. They sat in the cool of the room, each waiting for the other to kick it off.

"George in the wind?" Longway asked, as if not interested in the answer.

"How come I got to hear about this secondhand," Lorenzo said sharply.

"I didn't want to put you on the spot."

"*What* spot."

"You being the detective that broke the case. I didn't want to put you in a awkward situation."

"Bullshit."

Longway shrugged, done with it, and the silence resumed, Lorenzo momentarily lost again in the fog of his own worries. "This thing comes off," he asked the rev in a less emotional tone, "what do you think you're gonna get for it."

"Hey." The rev raised and dropped a floppy hand. "You get what you can get. You know how it goes. Citizen review board, more black cops, more jobs, a goddamn basketball tournament. You get whatever you can get. You know how it works around here."

Lorenzo envisioned promises, getting promises. Maybe some figure-head review board. Useless. Worse than useless, because then the powers that be can point to that and say, "See what we did for you?"

"So you coming on board?" Longway asked.

"I don't know. If I do you'll see me there."

"All right."

"How the hell you gonna lead a march tonight. You look sicker than shit."

"Are you kidding me? I been waitin' my whole life for something like this."

"*I,*" Lorenzo repeated reproachfully, but Longway ignored it.

"And I'll tell you," the rev added, "if something *does* go wrong and someone gets hurt? I hope to God it's me." Lorenzo shut his eyes and palmed his face. *"What . . ."* Longway demanded irritably.

"Naw, I hear what you're sayin'."

"How come most times people get ready to make a move around here, you always go to grab the backs of their shirt for them."

"Well, look," Lorenzo said, feeling a little more focused, "there's moves and there's moves. Most times I got to roll a body is because someone thought they were making a move."

"Aw c'mon with that crap." Longway waved him off. "How could you *not* step up in a situation like this." Lorenzo felt himself sinking, physically, mentally. "What is it, Lorenzo?" Longway asked almost tenderly— the pastor now, the old friend—and, moved by the quiet earnestness in his voice, Lorenzo felt himself unclench.

"I just want to keep people safe," he said, his voice almost sensuous with conviction.

"Safe." Longway leaned back in his chair, let his hands flop on his thighs. "Safe for what?"

Leaving the hospital, Lorenzo was surprised to see Bobby McDonald in the lobby, the presence of his boss here, at this particular time, putting him on edge.

"Hey." McDonald smiled. "There you are."

"Here I am," Lorenzo said, waiting.

"How's the rev?"

"OK. Getting discharged today, I guess."

"Good, good." Bobby squinted into the sun. "You gonna finish up the arrest reports today?"

"On my way in."

" 'Cause I should've gotten them yesterday, but I understand, you know, it's like one thing on top of the other here."

"They'll be done today." Waiting.

"Excellent." McDonald coughed into his fist. "So let me ask you, what do you think of this march tonight?"

There you go. "It's better than burnin' down the house," Lorenzo said, shrugging.

"Yeah?" His boss sounded like he truly wanted to believe that. "Are you taking, are you participating?"

"I might, you know, like to help keep things under control."

"Yeah, huh?" McDonald winced. "I don't know. I just, I had a feeling that . . ." He exhaled heavily. "I don't know, Lorenzo, you did such an ace job closing this out, trying to keep everything in check last night. I mean, whether you know it or not, you made a lot of new friends out there."

"OK." Waiting again.

"I mean, it's a free country and all, but . . . I don't know, brother, there's like two seconds left on the game clock here. Why would you want to throw shit in the mix now?"

Lorenzo remained in the lobby until McDonald was gone, then headed out to the parking lot. Once inside his car, he decided to blow off the promised reports and return to his mother's apartment for a few more hours of sleep. He was unable to sort himself out right now, except to understand that he had finally shot his wad and should not be around people. There was no more give in him, no more flex, and he knew without a doubt that if he didn't take himself out of circulation for a while, he would most definitely go off and that, when he did, the eruption would probably be directed at the wrong people.

Pulling into the Hurley Street cul-de-sac, he saw the mayor's Town Car pulling out—the chief of police, in his own ride, bringing up the rear—and remembered being told earlier this morning, by another cop outside Brenda's hospital room, that after last night's press conference and arrests, the theme around town today would be Open City, Dempsy setting itself up like one big civic workshop, putting on a show for both the locals and the press. There was to have been a tenants meeting with the mayor and the chief of police at Armstrong this morning, that one apparently just having come to an end; a Keep Cool workshop for the teenagers here; a Stop the Violence rally at Roosevelt; an all-faiths inter-racial healing session at Saint Michael's; a meeting of Invictus for black cops; a meeting at City Hall to begin the process of setting up a civilian review board for police conduct; and, later, a visit to Miss Dotson's apartment, the mayor and anyone else he could intimidate or persuade going to make peace with the family of Curious George Howard.

As Lorenzo began trudging toward Five Building, toward his childhood bed in his childhood bedroom, he envisioned the entire trick-bag day as a high-stakes version of Brenda's Fruit Salad game, all the hitters in town endlessly passing one another in the elevators, the hallways, the parking lots, heading in or out of meetings—all of it, as far as he was concerned, wall-to-wall horseshit.

"My name is Isaac Hathaway and I'm here, today, because I *love* you."

This opening declaration came from the ground-level day-care room off to the side of the elevators in Five Building, and Lorenzo reluctantly dragged himself across the lobby to get a peek inside. He saw roughly two dozen Armstrong teenagers and a few of the younger kids sitting in a wide circle facing the speaker, a thirtyish-looking light-skinned black man who had the scrubbed, ego-chastened look of the ex-addict, ex-jailbird a few years into Recovery. His cheap short-sleeved button-down shirt and slacks were starched, fresh, anonymous, and he was bright-voiced and clear of eye, but an unnatural dent marked his left temple and a six-inch knife scar lay like a blanched leech inside his forearm.

"Let me say that again." He paused to wait out the wisecracks, the embarrassment. "My name is Isaac Hathaway and I'm here, today, because I *love* you." The guy beamed at them, the boys sniggering. "I love *you,* I love *you,* I love *you.*" Isaac Hathaway methodically went around the horn, Lorenzo furious, immediately realizing that someone had fucked up and arranged a Self-Esteem workshop instead of a Keep Cool workshop, somebody always fucking up like that around here.

"I love *you,* I love *you,* and I even love the brother sittin' under the window pretending he's asleep over there." Hathaway's voice carried a heightened buoyancy now as he gestured toward a glower-faced fifteen-year-old leaning up against the wall. The boy's name was Daniel Bennett, and as Lorenzo watched him sitting knees to chin, he was suddenly gripped by a disturbingly powerful desire to march over and smack Daniel—not a bad kid—on his head.

"But most important," Hathaway said, then paused. "I love *me.*" He withstood another wave of sputtery ridicule, Lorenzo still standing in the doorway fuming.

"See I'm *from* here. I'm from here just like you. But I don't live here now. Unh-uh. Unh-uh. I got me a house. I got me a small house over in Jersey City. It's small, but it's mine. I got me a wife, a son, and I got me a roof over my head. I got out," he said, grinning at them. "I got out. And you may ask me, 'How'd you get out, Isaac? How'd you do it?' And I'll tell you. I got out because I got me an education. Did I go to Twenty-two School like you all? *No.* Me? I went to the school of hard knocks. Let me show you my diplomas." Hathaway held up the knife-scarred arm. "Here's my bachelor's degree." He stared at them, the kids attentive now, half smiles of interest on their faces. Hathaway removed his tie and unbuttoned the front of his shirt, popping out his left shoulder, touching a starred bullet wound. "Here's my master's."

"Ho!" one of the boys barked. Lorenzo was disgusted: this type of show-and-tell invariably backfired, the kids always winding up jazzed instead of "woken up."

"And here"—he lifted the belly of his shirt to reveal another long vertical knife scar above his navel—"here's my Ph.D."

"Damn!" All the boys were grinning now, the girls speaking to one another behind a screen of hands.

"Either you *change*," he announced, "or you ex-*pire*."

"You *change* your new *tire*," one wiseguy whispered loudly, cracking up the kids nearest to him.

"Now, we're gonna get into something here, but first I want to know who *you* are, so I want you all to go around the horn, tell me your name, and after you say your name? I want you to say, 'And I *love* myself.' OK? I'll go first, 'cause I *love* saying how much I love myself, so my name is Isaac Hathaway and I *love* myself. G'head—this girl first."

"Ex*cuse* me," Lorenzo exploded, paralyzing his audience. "I got to *go*, but I would like to give you kids some *tips* on the next few nights out here. I'd like to give you some tips on survival. No theories, no speeches. *Facts*." Prowling the room, Lorenzo glared at them. "*Facts*. The police, is angry. The police, is scared. And the ones you're gonna see around here tonight? Tomorrow night? They don't *know* you. They don't know what's in your head, who your mother is, if you're a good kid, bad kid, all they know is they're living on the edge of their own nerves, *just like you*.

"*Freeze* means *freeze*. It don't mean take another step. It don't mean wave your arms, it don't mean turn your back, and it don't mean show your girlfriend how brave you are. *Freeze* means *freeze*. *Listen* to the police officer, because you just might be the straw that breaks the camel's back." Lorenzo was bellowing, his voice cracking. "Any way a person can die, I've seen it, and I'm tired of it. I'm tired of going to autopsies and funerals of kids who look *just like you*. You want the *best* advice for these next few days? Stay *home*. Watch TV. Read a book. Don't mess up. *Thank* you."

"Thank *you*," Isaac Hathaway said with a cautious positiveness. Angry to the point of tears, Lorenzo finally left the room.

A moment later, Lorenzo found himself prowling the breezeway, enraged by that useless workshop and enraged at Longway, De Lauder, Curious George, and at himself. He was enraged, too, at the cops, at the *idea* of the cops who would ring these high-rises again at nightfall—

wired, scared, ready for anything, expecting the worst—those kids in there having done nothing to merit the danger of this armed edginess but having the misfortune, in the wake of Brenda's hoax, to call this place home.

Pacing, livid, liberated, Lorenzo finally hopped off the fence, coming down on Longway's side, thinking, The rev is right; it's *their* goddamned turn.

30

After Brenda's video arraignment, Jesse took off in Ben's car, heading for the medical center to check in on him. She dreaded the visit, knowing he would fall all over himself to take the blame for his own slashing, offering her a free pass on that one, a pass she'd most likely accept.

As she rolled along JFK Boulevard, the loud, dull crack of something thrown at the car had her swerving wildly, then whipping the Chrysler down side street after side street, and it wasn't until she pulled into the medical center parking lot that she ventured a glance at the fractured star that had been her brother's passenger-side window. Jesse was sure that Ben would figure out a way to take the blame for that one too.

Climbing the broad steps leading to the main lobby, she ran into Willy Hernandez, the cop whom she had last seen safeguarding the double-shooting crime scene on the night she first met Brenda. Willy was descending the steps, his left hand thickly bandaged.

"What happened to you?" Jesse asked, welcoming the delay.

"I'm in Roosevelt last night. You know, the volunteer peacekeeper thing?" Willy stood with his feet planted on separate steps. "I'm there all goddamn night, tense as a motherfucker, right? But we keep it all tucked in—no violence, no arrests—straight through till sunup. I go home? Within like, five minutes of stepping into my own house, I break a freakin' juice glass, wind up filleting my palm. Fifteen stitches, I'll proba-bly never play the violin again."

"Jesus," Jesse said, not really listening. "You OK?" Willy just stared at her. "So what's the word on tonight?"

"Tonight?" Willy shrugged. "Word is we might be ducking us a bullet. Word is they're taking it out of town."

"Who is."

"Longway, some others. They're gearing up for a march into Gannon, if you can believe it."

"No." Jesse put that one on hold.

"And me," Willy said, "I can't decide if *that's* fucked up, or *I'm* fucked up for thinking that's fucked up."

After Willy continued on his way, Jesse decided to forestall her visit further by taking a seat on the hospital steps and returning to work on the second installment of her diary piece. Her desire to put off seeing Ben made her unself-consciously productive for once, lost in her own written voice. She wrote, and rewrote, for close to an hour, just banging it out, the work only coming to a halt when she saw Paul Rosenbaum, Brenda's lawyer, exit the building, flanked by aides and trailing reporters.

Rosenbaum made his way to the lowest landing and then came to a halt, holding his briefcase to his chest like a schoolgirl as the reporters who had been following him—Jesse among them now, and others coming up from the street—formed their usual packed wedge, the lawyer smiling patiently as he waited for his audience to settle in. "What's going on here is both grotesque and inhuman," he began without preamble. "There was no homicide. The police, looking for a scapegoat to blame for their own unconscionable and racist misconduct, have keyed in on the *one* person who suffers most horribly and inconsolably as a result of this tragic accident."

As if he was unaware of the infernal racket of the lunchtime city around him, Rosenbaum's delivery was both soft and measured, and after realizing that they were missing half of what he was saying, the reporters became perfectly still in order to catch his words—still and attentive. Jesse knew Rosenbaum well enough to recognize that this was a calculated act on his part, this choosing a clamorous setting to deliver half-murmured words, gently forcing his audience to truly listen to what he had to say and, by extension, to slow down in their rush to judgment.

"Our office has been deluged with more letters and phone calls regarding the plight of Brenda Martin than for any other client we have ever represented . . . And I would have to say, some of the, the outpourings, some of the offerings that have come our way constitute the most heartrending and compassionate missives I have ever read or heard in my life."

He came to a full stop, slowly scanning his audience, face by face, throwing Jesse the briefest smile of recognition.

"However," he continued, "to those, who have been writing obscene letters, writing death threats, phoning in death threats . . ." He paused again, the crowd motionless. "If you're trying to, to, make her feel any more miserable than she is now . . . If you're trying to make her suffer, any more than she is suffering now . . . It is not a productive expenditure of your time.

"Over the last four, hellish days she has been desperately, desperately trying to, to fend off the reality, of her son's death. But as of yesterday, her last illusion has been exploded . . . And the place in which she now dwells, is unspeakable.

"Consider, consider the endurance required by her illusion, the, the enormity of it. Consider the great number of people caught up in the *web* of this illusion. Consider the chain reaction of grief, and pain, provoked by this most desperate of desperate fantasies." Rosenbaum came to a dead stop again. "And then consider the engine of *denial*, that drove this tortured woman, as she struggled to confront the loss of the most precious person in her life."

Jesse, fighting to hold on to her detachment, told herself she was impressed. Most lawyers would have ducked the carjacker scam; Rosenbaum was embracing it.

"At present, she is shunned by family, by friends, and by those quarters of the community to which she has dedicated her entire adult working life. From the hospital, later today or early tomorrow, when they deem her, healthy, she will be transferred to the Dempsy County jail and put in isolation—put in a six-by-fourteen-foot cell, under twenty-four-hour video surveillance reinforced every fifteen minutes around the clock by guard visitations. She will be issued paper clothing and perhaps given a Bible.

"They call this protective custody, but both the guards and inmates will subject her to incessant verbal abuse. Her food will be spat in, and she will hear through the ventilation ducts of her cell a constant stream of threats and taunts from the other cells, which are linked by the air-conditioning system of the prison. A perennial favorite, for tormenting accused child killers," Rosenbaum said, taking another searching pause, "is the imitating, of a baby's cry."

Jesse knew this but flinched nonetheless. She heard someone grunt in sympathy.

"But nothing, *nothing* that they can inflict on her comes anywhere near what she will inflict on herself for not being able to save her son's life. They will put her in protective custody and say it's for her own welfare. But physical violence, mental violence, even the possibility of violent death, will be *nothing* compared to the torment of living the rest of her life without her son.

"Homicide . . ." Rosenbaum tasted the word, the outrage. "Homicide. We will prove in court that the death of Cody Martin was accidental, but I will tell you something. The crushing sense of guilt this woman is now beginning to experience is like a slow-motion homicide unto itself.

"I understand the district attorney has decided not to ask for the death penalty, but if he changes his mind, let him rest assured, that if he's looking for an executioner, Brenda Martin will be happy to pull the switch herself." Rosenbaum took a step back from the wedge. "The prosecutor's office should be ashamed of itself. And I hope to see all of you at the trial."

As the presser shifted into Q and A, Jesse wandered off. There would be no trial, Jesse betting on a plea deal, criminally negligent homicide still the odds-on favorite. But Rosenbaum was right: manslaughter, reckless endangerment, homicide, criminally negligent or not—what difference would it make? Brenda would be her own jailer, and a merciless one at that. As the group interview droned on, Jesse suddenly felt a cold whistle of panic in her belly, felt in some vague way responsible for Brenda's agony. She and Brenda, they had played each other, Jesse told herself, each working the lie they needed to put forth in order to get over. It was a straight swap.

"Jesse." Rosenbaum's voice jerked her around. "I liked what you wrote about being alone with her. I'm sure it wasn't an easy experience." He was smiling as if glad to see her, his presence exuding a mild air of moral benediction every bit as proprietary as Karen Collucci's scorched-earth briskness. "She asks about you," Rosenbaum said.

"What do you mean . . ." Jesse was excited by this news but also wary, braced for some kind of pitch here, some kind of setup.

"You were kind of her only friend."

"Huh." Jesse sure of it now, deciding that he was softening her up, wanting her as a witness for the defense. She wondered if Brenda had told him about her fictional child, had to tell him, this prissy, self-righteous bastard who had busted Jesse on her shit once before, this moral blackmailer with his soft-steel humanism.

"Are you OK?" he asked.

"Never better," she said, and giving Rosenbaum her back, she trotted up the remaining steps to the hospital entrance. A visit with her brother suddenly felt like the least of all evils.

The rental TV mounted over Ben's hospital bed was turned to CNN, which was rolling earlier footage from outside the arraignments court, the reporters interviewing anyone wearing either a jacker T-shirt or a Cody button. Jesse's entrance caught Ben by surprise, and despite the fact that he was hooked up to an IV, he bolted upright in bed, scrambling for the remote, knowing how his sister couldn't abide hearing the words.

He blushed, embarrassed, and touched the broad square patch on his stitched cheek. "It was my own stupid fault."

"Aw fuck you."

"Why fuck me?" He seemed bewildered rather than hurt.

"Just . . ." Jesse felt sick. "Never mind."

A silence came down on them as they stared rigidly at the CNN report with unseeing eyes. "You know, Jesse," Ben finally said, "if I ever got mad at you like you get mad at me, you'd break like glass."

Numbed by Ben's words, his even-toned observation itself provoking a demonstration of its truth, Jesse quickly mumbled, "I'm sorry."

"No, I'm just saying . . ." Ben retreated.

"I'm sorry," Jesse repeated, feeling self-revulsed, weak, her eyes filling with tears.

"Jesse, c'mon, I didn't mean anything."

A silver twitch coming off the screen took her out of her self-pity before she could examine it, CNN now showing an amateur video of Brenda and Cody hanging together in the Study Club.

"Jesus," Jesse exhaled, leaning into the side of her brother's bed.

The shaky footage, still on mute, showed mother and son seated at a table, side by side, working on the construction of a glue-sloppy Popsicle house. Brenda, hunched over the child-height table, kept flicking a self-conscious eye toward the camera as older kids darted in and out of the background. Cody, oblivious, frowned at the task before him, occasionally scratching his nose or touching his mother's arm. Brenda's every gesture, glance, twitch of the mouth or the eye, in light of recent events, seemed freighted with menace.

Jesse, used to this type of postcrime twenty-twenty hindsight, felt unchilled by the footage of Brenda, but she found herself totally unprepared for the wallop that seeing Cody Martin as a living, breathing child delivered.

Cody had been to her an abstraction, his existence conjectural, confined to photos, anecdotes, and a vacant bedroom. Now, the unthinking sideways glances at his mother, the look of mingled fascination and shyness that crossed his face when an older Armstrong boy abruptly leaned across the worktable, the splay of his fingers as he brushed a gluey palm against the chest of his T-shirt, all of it, any of it, was just too much, too much, and Jesse, caught off guard, felt this boy rushing into her for the first time—and by extension, the horror, the absolute horror of his death.

And along with Cody came Brenda again, every fragmented memory of her over the last few days—her stark gray eyes, her wracked sleep, her staggering gait in the punishing heat, the cold, damp feel of her skin, too, all of that, in the context of the living child she had lost, came rushing in, and what Jesse felt right now was love, a precious and fearsome love for both of them, like the Infilling gone mad. They had invaded her, set up house in her, had become part of her, Jesse understanding that this seizure of her heart was permanent and would persist impervious to all exterior judgments, moral, criminal, or social.

"How'd they, where'd they get that video?" she asked mildly.

"You want me to find out?" Ben, as always, ready to help.

The image shifted again, this time showing a mass of people, standing in groups or alone, before the facade of the Chicago Fire in Freedomtown, standing with their arms folded across their chests, or taking snapshots, or wiping tears, rocking from foot to foot, no one really moving, the trampled earth smothered in flowers, toys, and balloons.

Jesse reached for the remote and turned up the volume. "The local residents here, Tim, have already dubbed this sad place the Wailing Wall." And Jesse was out of there.

With the previous day's announcement of Brenda's arrest and that day's arraignment, the media invasion had metastasized yet again—more sat trucks, more news vans, more camera crews streaming out of the Holland and Lincoln tunnels from the east and pulling off the New Jersey

State Turnpike and Garden State Parkway from the south—the new reporters and shooters hitting the streets of Gannon and Dempsy like tourists piling out of a charter bus. It was easy for Jesse to tell who was fresh; it was in the crease of the slacks and the avidness of the eyes, an anxious, fevered look, as the new troops scrambled to absorb the world of this story in a few quick gulps, get physically and mentally centered in the scene as swiftly as possible and start the search for unexplored angles.

Dempsy County itself had changed, at least temporarily, taking on the aspect of an open-air museum of horror: This is where she said she was carjacked; this is where she lived; this is where the boyfriend lived. This is where she worked. This is where she rented movies. This is where the refrigerators were burned. This is where she confessed, where *he* confessed—each mundane and dreary location taking on an air of sinister holiness. But indisputably, the greatest attraction of all was the burial site in the ruins of Freedomtown. The weather-beaten facade of the Chicago Fire had been transformed into a tragic magnet for both journalists and civilians, the vast number of people—the curious, the grief-stricken, and the titillated—who felt compelled to stand beneath the ravaged mannequin generating its own unique sidebar.

The earth, carpeted with tributes, and the wall, the lowest eight feet of which had simply vanished behind a shaggy paper coat of personal messages—poems, letters, prayers, to the boy, to the family, to the public, to God, secured with thumbtacks, pushpins, tape, or simply stuffed into the splits and cracks of the half-rotted boards—conspired to camouflage this forlorn ground, change it into a happy place, a festive place, a positive place, the loneliness of it, the bottomless abandoned quality of it obscured by a blizzard of bright colors and human chatter, by sunlight bouncing off the bay, a picnic with tears.

As Jesse drifted through the crowd, she noticed that most people tended to stay in one spot, stood rooted, holding their youngest kids in their arms, or slightly tilted into one another. The only restless activity was the attempts of the mobile kids, the three- and four-year-olds, bored and bewildered, to get at the memorial toys—the Flintstone action figures, the G.I. Joe and Lion King and Hercules dolls that lay amid the bouquets and Styrofoam crosses. The kids strained to get at the Mickey Mouse balloons and the Mattel Hot Wheels, their mothers, grandmothers yanking on their arms, crouching down and going blaze-eyed, hissing, shaking fingers as if the kids were acting up in church, each child, in his own inarticulate way, responding: "Then why did you bring me here?"

Jesse saw that the stones were gone, Billy's cairn most likely disassembled and spirited away by souvenir hunters, along with the yellow crime scene tape, the empty film canisters, and discarded rubber gloves, all the detritus of an exhumation swiftly falling into the hands of the first wave of pilgrims. The scooped earth of the grave itself seemed to have been taken too, fistful by fistful, until the hole had become three times its original size, that gaping pit instantly filled with flowers.

Jesse wandered through the site as if it were a field hospital, compulsively scrawling down sights and sounds with blank alertness: a man in a suit crying into a cell phone; a staked crayon drawing of Jesus beckoning, arm extended, "Come, my child" written above his head in a word balloon; a green plastic telephone glued to a Styrofoam heart, JESUS CALLED printed underneath.

She watched at a discreet distance, as a young blond woman, her face red and puffy, asked the two-year-old girl in her arms, "Can you say, 'Jesus loves me'?" The baby curled herself deeper into her mother. The woman asked again, her voice cracking, "Can you say it for Mommy?" The baby's continuing refusal made the mother's voice climb even higher, to a teary whisper. "Please?"

Another mother, stooping to be on eye level with her little boy, whispered into his face, "See what they do to you if you don't behave?"

Jesse slowly worked her way to the wall, the voices washing over her.

"I heard that child was sexually abused."

"By who, her?"

"No, the boyfriend. That's why they killed him."

"God makes good things come out of bad. You watch."

"I'm telling you, her story cannot be told yet."

"She should of just told the father, '*Take* the damn kid, it's *your* turn.'"

"I guess the sound of that little boy saying, 'Mommy I love you' wasn't enough for her."

"God gave a son too, you know."

Another little boy, looking up at his mother, commented in a confused yet sober tone, "I thought they killed kids with swords."

Enough. Jesse flipped her pad shut and scanned the celestial bulletin board, reading a poem in Magic Marker:

> *It doesn't end in this muddy sod*
> *Little Cody Martin is in the arms of God*
> *So go, littlest angel, go romp and play*
> *We'll all be together on Judgment Day.*

Next to that, was an announcement, neatly typed:

This child's sacrifice was not in vain. It brings us all together black and white in our common bond of sadness. It reminds us how human we all are and how hurt and pain touches us all. Go to God now, little angel, and thank you.

Then, from behind her, Jesse heard some woman say, "I couldn't help it either. It gets away from you." Spooked, she turned but saw no one within earshot who looked like they could have said that. Feeling a hand on her shoulder, she turned back to the wall again and found herself facing a beautiful blue-black man, tall, an archangel.

"Why are you here?" he asked softly.

"What?" Jesse blinked.

"What brings you here?"

Jesse just stared, wondering if this was real. "What do you mean?"

"I'm with the *Dispatch.*" The hallucination held up its reporter's pad.

"Fuck off," Jesse said, flashing her own, then began wading her way out through the splashy sorrow, a barely perceptible whiff of rot following her to the car.

31

The march was called for five in the evening, the collection point the Hurley Street cul-de-sac at the base of the Bowl.

It was hoped that the heat and humidity would have dipped to a tolerable level by five and that, if the march took off any time near the designated hour, there would be enough of the day left for the event to end in some kind of natural light. No one wanted a massive dispersal in the dark, the breakup being the most unpredictable moment in any demonstration of this nature.

But things were off. At four-forty-five, the humidity was still slap hammering the world, and as Lorenzo scanned the basin of Hurley Street, he counted as many media types as marchers in the crowd. He was cheating, too, adding in the dozens of little kids from the houses— some of them running around barefoot, going nowhere—and all the knuckleheads lurking in the building lobbies, every one of them back-stepping into the shadowed void of the stairwells whenever he was able to make eye contact. Donald De Lauder and his 125 followers were no-where to be seen.

Over the next half hour, though, the cars continued to roll in, the public buses dropped off more and more bodies—some from Dempsy, others from wherever—and by five-fifteen, five-thirty, Lorenzo had to admit what they had here was a bona fide presence. Most of the peo-ple he was happy to see—families, seniors, males of a certain age and carriage—but some looked like potential trouble, and Lorenzo found himself bracing carload after carload of young men, immediately going up in their faces, saying, "You fellas here for the demonstration?" Giving them cop's eyes, saying, "I'm Detective Lorenzo Council." Shaking their hands one by one. "And I'm glad for your support."

The crowd continued to grow—more cars, more drop-offs, two city council members—Lorenzo breathing a little easier, but still no sign of De Lauder. Between two parked cars in the shadow of the Conrail retaining wall, the Reverend Longway, somewhat slag-faced from his hospital stay, formed a circle with three other ministers, all of them holding hands, chin to chest, praying. That group was circled by three crouching, duck-walking shooters and filmed from above by a fourth, dangling over the edge of the fence that topped the Conrail wall, his free hand clutching the mesh as he got his aerial of the ministers' scalps.

Lorenzo saw Tariq Wilkins, the kid who had tried to rappel out of his bedroom window that first night, make his way down from the high end of the projects, swinging on his crutches as he cut through the Bowl, his grandmother bringing up the rear. Then Teacher Timmons appeared, the kid Danny Martin had clocked that same night, coming down to Hurley now with his mother. The one person he didn't see, the one he decided he needed to see, was Curious George Howard.

Another wrecking crew rolled up, twelve guys, all sporting baggy camo, emerging from three Jeeps bearing New York plates. Lorenzo did it again, giving them the iron-eyed glad hand, then spying a bulge in one guy's fatigues. "What you got there, boss?" The kid, stocky, shaved head, about eighteen, fished out a glass bottle of Coca-Cola. Lorenzo asked him to drink it now, then toss away the bottle, the others half pivoting with glee at the request, all high-pitched sniggers and "Ho shits," their boy showdowned straight out of the car. The kid smirked at Lorenzo, trying to step up, saying, "I ain't thirsty yet."

Before Lorenzo could strategize a second, half-friendly directive, his eye caught a brace of hard bright blue gleams winking through the foliage of Martyrs Park. Stepping away to get a better view, he spied a phalanx of Gannon motorcycle cops across the city line, the hard blue of their crash helmets glinting in the sunset. Lorenzo forgot the Coke-bottle showdown, wondering, worrying if Gannon was planning to make a goal-line stand. The time was five-forty-five, the crowd large enough now to draw a crowd, but still no De Lauder.

"Why are you marching?" Lorenzo turned to face a Betacam, then saw, over the shoulder of the accompanying reporter, Millrose Carter. "What?" Lorenzo watched Millrose, the Man Who Never Sleeps, worked his way down the Bowl to Hurley, calling out, "Hey!"—grinning, silver-eyed with liquor, briskly rubbing his hands. "I'm here," he said. "Let's go! Let's go!" Lorenzo was laughing suddenly, buoyant.

"Are you marching against your brother officers?" the reporter persisted.

"I'm just here to help things go off right," Lorenzo said distantly, dancing a little, as usual. Finally seeing Curious George emerge from his grandmother's building, he said, "Awright, George" under his breath, happy.

"But you *are* marching, so how do you feel about the march?"

"Hey, I'm like, if you're right? Be you white, black, green, police, or whatever, I'll back you one hundred percent. But if you're wrong, I'm gonna be *on* you one hundred percent," Lorenzo said, doing the word mambo, then, noticing the Convoy brothers coming down the Bowl, ending the interview with a faint "Excuse me."

"You guys coming along?" he asked Eric and Caprice, smiling his warning smile.

"Hell, yeah." Eric shrugged. "We got to represent." Lorenzo shook Eric's hand, held on to it.

"Who else is coming?"

"I don't know," Eric said, shrugging again. "Maybe Corey and them?"

"You guys know it's a *march*, right?" Lorenzo's eyes strayed to Martyrs Park.

"Like, what, check your Uzis at the door?"

"What?" Lorenzo said. He was distracted again, unable to keep his eyes off those blue gleams peeking through the trees.

Coming out of Martyrs, Gannon-side, Lorenzo stood before a dozen motorcycles, the cops nodding to him but laying back behind their silvered shades.

"Hey, fellas." Lorenzo put his hands in his pockets, jingled his change.

"Evening," one of them said.

"I guess you know they're coming." He gave it a grin.

"That's what the drums say," the same cop answered. Lorenzo didn't know any of them, or at least couldn't ID them in all that headgear.

"I hope you're not gonna try to stop us coming through."

"Free country," another cop said.

" 'Cause we got the press, we got families, senior citizens . . ."

"No problem."

" 'Cause I don't want nobody hurt."

"Us neither."

"Here *or* there." Lorenzo gestured ahead and behind him, meaning black or white.

"Amen to that," the cop who mentioned drums said, bobbing his head.

Lorenzo stood his ground for a second, as if there were something else to say.

"All right, then . . ." He finally turned back to the park.

"Hey, Council?" One of the cops, he didn't know which one, turned him around. "Thanks for the overtime, bro."

A few steps back inside the park, Lorenzo dropped to one knee to retie a sneaker.

"Some fun, huh, Jess?" he said without looking at her. She was half hidden, leaning against the low stone wall that marked the Gannon-side perimeter.

"I didn't want to get in your way," Jesse said, pushing herself up, embarrassed.

"Hey." He switched downed knees, began retying the other sneaker. "You go where you want. Just when I start blastin'? Try to stay out of my line of fire."

"Yeah, OK," she mumbled, and followed him back out into the potholed Armstrong side of things.

Three steps into Hurley Street the Reverend Longway came hustling up, looking antsy and hot.

"How you feeling, Rev," Lorenzo asked.

"Let's go, let's go." Longway ignored the query.

"De Lauder ain't here."

"Well, shit." The reverend thrust a curled wrist in Lorenzo's face: five past six. "He had a *watch* on last time I saw."

As if on cue, three yellow school buses pulled into the cul-de-sac, all of Hurley Street breaking out in spontaneous applause in reaction to this infusion of so many new heads.

The bus doors opened with a pneumatic sigh, and De Lauder's people began piling out—*kufis* and Kangols, more seniors than middle-aged, more middle-aged than young, like in church. A third of the people carried homemade signs.

Some of the men coming off the bus wore mustard-colored armbands emblazoned with the letters JNL, Lorenzo assuming that these were the "security ushers" that De Lauder had mentioned in the hospital, nothing more imposing about them than a uniform look of sober alertness. De Lauder appeared in the doorway of the last bus, and Longway was up in his face, flashing him the time before the man could even set foot to ground. De Lauder shrugged helplessly, gestured to the small army of marchers that he had had to collect, then said something to make Longway smile. With the rev mollified, De Lauder stepped off the bus and began to look around him, eyeing the locals as if assessing their mettle.

"Hey," De Lauder acknowledged Lorenzo, swinging out an arm in a lazy arc and snagging his hand in a loose, waggling grip. "Glad you made it."

"Glad *you* made it," Lorenzo said with a little edge. De Lauder caught sight of the motorcycles through the trees. "Don't worry about it," Lorenzo said.

"If you say so," De Lauder said, then made a lassoing gesture that took in all of Hurley Street. "You know everybody here?"

" 'Bout half."

"All right, let me run it down to you. We're gonna shape up about six across. The ministers, the victims, their families up front, and get, like, the cameras in front of *them,* you know, walking backwards, gettin' us coming on. Now I'd like my people to line up like, flanking the others, kind of containing them, help us keep it orderly. And me and my men? We're gonna be, like, every half dozen rows, flanking the flankers, have a couple of guys bringing up the rear. But *you,* I'd like you to be sort of a free safety, you know, like a free-range prowler, 'cause you know who to be watching around here up front. This is like a big X-factor situation and we just don't have the local information."

"All right." Lorenzo, fighting down a hit of panic, said the words almost daintily, a small, tense smile on his face.

"You ever ride shotgun on something like this?"

"Not really." Lorenzo gave him that small, overwhelmed smile again.

"It's like this . . ." De Lauder took a breath, as if to set himself. "This gig, it's kind of like a *wall*eyed gig. Like, you ever see a hammerhead shark? Got his eyes coming out the side of his head where his ears should be? You got to be kind of like a hammerhead shark, 'cause you got to be looking right and left, at the same time. You got to be eyeing *our* people on the *in*side, and you got to keep an eye on *their* people watchin' us go by. And I tell you, you just hope the police over there are on the job tonight, 'cause without them helping out, what we got to deal with is always just this side of too much, you know what I'm saying? I mean, shit can and will come from *any*where."

"All right," Lorenzo said softly, his chest rising with every breath.

"Like on the inside? Our people? You keep an eye on the young people, check out their hands, see if they're carrying anything. Could be a brick, a sap, a kitchen knife. Worst thing is a lightbulb. You hear a lightbulb pop, you think it's gunfire and it's on. So you're always watching their hands. Pat 'em down if you have to, give 'em a warning up front before we get out the gate. I ain't worried about hurtin' people's feelings, because this is life and *death*. The other thing is the juicers, can't abide the juicers. You smell liquor on anybody's breath? See it in their face? Out they go. Out they go. Last thing we want to do is pour alcohol on a flammable situation."

"I hear you," Lorenzo said faintly, recalling Millrose Carter's liquored eyes, knowing he didn't have the heart to bounce the guy from the march.

"Now *out*side? The Gannon people? Not much you can do. Like I said, shit can come from anywhere. You want to keep an eye on the windows, the rooftops, so you can catch that chunk of cement, but basically, and this is what I'm saying, you got to hope the local cops are on the case.

"Now, the locals right up on the sidewalk? The sidelines? You know, the nigger shouters, the watermelon wavers, the spitters—you just ignore them 'cause they're showing all their cards up front. The watermelon waver, he's *doin'* his thing. The spitter? He's busy spittin'. The nigger shouter, he's busy shoutin' nigger. What you got to keep an eye on is the quiet ones. You keep an eye on the ones who's pacing us, like, ducking behind the front lines and keeping parallel to us. They might have something in their back pockets or under their shirts and just be waitin' for the right time. It's *hard*. This ain't no Macy's parade and just because you're paranoid don't mean someone's *not* out to nail your ass, you know what I'm sayin'?"

"Yes, I do." Lorenzo was wheezing a little, wondering if his suddenly labored breathing was asthma, anxiety, or both; wondering if it would pass once they were all on the move or if it would hobble him every step of the way.

As De Lauder began corralling his people, Lorenzo scanned the crowd. There had to be at least three hundred people here, maybe more, *many* people he didn't know—Lorenzo looking for new crews, potential trouble, and then seeing her, Brenda, leaning against the stone retaining wall under the Conrail fence.

The way the woman was standing, he couldn't see more than a quarter profile, but it was her, pale, thin, rumpled, leaning into the wall as if for support, as if she were too weak to stand on her own. Brenda, Brenda—Lorenzo palming his heart—he would swear to it.

"NO JUS-TICE . . . ," an unseen voice cried out, expectant, demanding.

"NO PEACE," half the crowd responded.

"NO JUS-TICE . . ."

"NO PEACE." Everybody in on this one.

"WHAT DO WE WANT . . ." Again, that long, trailing, muezzin-like call.

"JUSTICE!"

"WHEN DO WE WANT IT . . ."

"NOW!" The word was like the basso exhalation of a nation.

The Reverend Longway was assisted to a flat ledge of shale six feet above the cul-de-sac, a natural platform jutting out of the eroded earth that climbed from the asphalt of Hurley Street to the breezeways of the lower buildings.

"You know." Longway grinned his "I've had it" grin, his voice strong enough, despite his illness, to project out over the entire assemblage. "The police department of Gannon, they say they came in here because there was a child's *life* at stake. They say they were operating on the information they had, received. That, that perception comes before hard information. That, that *time* was of the essence . . . All good and well, all good and well." The reverend shoved his glasses up his nose with a thumb. "But let me propose to you . . . another situation. And *you* tell *me* if it sounds, plausible."

Scoping out the rev's listeners, Lorenzo spied Curious George standing apart from everyone else, talking to himself, unhappy, Lorenzo feeling sorry for his profoundly apolitical ass.

"Can you imagine, can you imagine if, if a *black* child, a black child from Armstrong, had been abducted, was *said* to have been abducted somewheres in the city of Gannon . . . Can you imagine the police department of Dempsy *raiding* that city in an effort to save that child?"

"No!" The word barked sharp, over and over, like scattered shot on a pistol range.

"No." Longway nodded emphatically. "No. You most definitely cannot."

Lorenzo spotted Jesse and saw that she was grinning, closely following Longway's words with an amused smirk on her mug, and he had no idea what to make of that.

"The police department of the city of Gannon, they come into these houses the way they did, do you know why?"

"Why," the crowd responded.

"Do you know *why?*" Longway was pumping it. "Because they knew, that they *could.* They saw us as, defenseless. They saw us as, helpless. And they knew that they could. But do you know what? I don't *see* no defenseless people out here tonight."

"No!"

"I don't *see* no, no *help*less people out here tonight."

"No!"

"They came in here, because they knew that they could, and *this* city, *our* city, said, 'Come on in. Come on in.'"

People cried out "No," "Yes," and other, less articulate sentiments. Lorenzo checked out De Lauder, a mirror image of Lorenzo himself, ceaselessly eyeballing the crowd, immune to the rev's words, working.

"You know, my mother," Longway continued, downshifting, "was a great, believer in courtesy."

"Yess . . ." A lone voice, expectant, hanging in the air.

"And one of the courtesies, that she believed in honoring, was that if someone came a-calling to your house, it was only right, that at the appropriate time, you return the visit."

"Awright . . ." people called out, some clapping in appreciation of the metaphor to come.

"See, my mother would not have approved of the Gannon police, because when they came a-calling here, they didn't even bother to knock, they just shouldered their way through the door like a push-in mugger, but now *we* are gonna be more dignified than that. *We,* are gonna be in control of ourselves, our passions, our, physicality. But nonetheless, a visit's a visit, and now it's time for us to return the call."

Lorenzo finally found himself clapping, appreciating the artful way Longway had said it: Watch it, don't fuck up.

"NO JUS-TICE . . ." That unseen muezzin was calling out again.

"NO PEACE." Hurley Street rumbled out the refrain in a tight huff, Lorenzo moved by the power behind it, the coordinated passion.

The JNL security ushers more or less took over, beginning the task of shaping people up six across, pushing, pulling, arranging people in the order of their significance to the tale—the injured, their families, the high visibles up front; De Lauder's other bus people, knowing the drill, automatically lining up single file on either side of the Dempsy people; the JNL security guards then flanking the flankers, everyone pumped, ready to roll.

De Lauder came up to Lorenzo, passed him a JNL armband, saying, "You should wear this," then jogged off.

Lorenzo, feeling a little light in the gut, bunched the mustard-colored fabric in his fist and started on his own trot up and down the line, ducking in here and there, all the time with one eye on the hard bright blue that winked at him through the trees.

"WHOSE STREETS . . ."

"OUR STREETS."

As the marchers, their progress cadenced to the call and response, began working their way around the benches and playground fixtures of Martyrs Park—some reaching up and touching the bronze plaque of Martin, Malcolm, and Medgar, as if for luck—the motorcycles that had been fronting the city line neatly parted into two rows, which then flowed out into Gannon alongside the emerging procession. The guzzling rumble of the choppers almost drowned out the one-two call-out of the marchers, and this unsolicited police escort, combined with the furiously crab-scuttling and back-stepping presence of the shooters, nearly doubled the width of the march.

The protesters, about three hundred strong, marched on Jessup Avenue toward the heart of Gannon.

At every cross-street for the first few hundred yards over the city line, more choppers appeared, melding into the motorcade, lengthening it, loudening it. And at the first major intersection, a Brinks-like Emergency Services truck cut in front of the advance guard of backtracking shooters and the oncoming, arm-linked reverends. This fortress on wheels then slowed to a crawl in order to maintain a steady twenty-foot distance between itself and the front lines.

The sector of Gannon that abutted Martyrs Park was the neglected northern end of Jessup Avenue, a bleak urban plain, four lanes wide, flanked by sex and dope motels, third-tier fast-food franchises, and discount gas stations. The more vital residential and retail districts didn't begin for a good half mile deeper into the city, and so, with at least ten blocks of hoofing it until they hit their target area, the protesters already found themselves completely boxed in by police, heading for downtown like an imprisoned yet mobile millipede.

Concerned about Longway's heart, Lorenzo periodically jogged up to the front to take an eyeball read, but there was just too much static in the air for him to make any kind of meaningful assessment. The rev was positioned dead center in the front row, his arms linked tightly with the ever-miserable Curious George on one side, Tariq Wilkins's grandmother on the other. He plowed ahead like a fullback without moves—his face set in cement, mouth a pugnacious line—marching tensed and bunched as if, any second, he would have to smash his way through a physical barrier.

Lorenzo, by contrast, continued to dart, working out his anxiety by worrying the length of the procession like a sheepdog, darting forward, darting in, darting out, ignoring the motorcycles, focusing on the innermost rows of marchers, trying to key in on those who weren't chanting along with the rest. He first eyed their hands, their clothes, looking for bulges, then their faces, tracking their gazes—who was looking at who, was there any silent communication going on, were there any secret game plans in the mix. Lorenzo put a mental dog-ear on a few people, but it was hard to know without straight-up bracing them, and the momentum of the crowd made that nearly impossible now.

The motorcycle cops were coming off fairly serene, but the pedestrian pace they were forced to sustain made for some fishtailing in order to maintain balance, and Lorenzo envisioned someone's foot getting run over, envisioned all kinds of accidental shit.

The march followed Jessup Avenue until it reached the northern edge of central Gannon. Now they could see the locals waiting for them, beginning about four intersections down the line, where the retail district began in earnest, block after block of Laundromats, bars, travel agencies, and dry cleaners, all the way to the bay. The locals were out there, the sidewalks dense with humanity.

A whoosh of anticipation fired through the marchers, and Lorenzo could literally see a corresponding ripple surge through the figures in the distance, a rooted undulation, like the effect of heavy surf on ocean-bed vegetation.

"NO JUS-TICE . . ."

"NO PEACE"—the sight of Gannon waiting for them provoking a tighter, deeper response.

But something was wrong down there on the sidewalks of Jessup, Lorenzo taking the better part of a block to figure out what was bugging him, then nailing it: there were no placards among the spectators, no homemade signs. The marchers were fairly bristling with oak-tag sentiments held high, pennants of anger, but there was no corresponding artwork, there were none of the written counterpoints he had been expecting. As they came within two blocks of the hot zone, still too far away to pick up any vocalizations, counterchants, catcalls, he saw something else that made him want to dig in his heels—beach chairs, collapsible vinyl and aluminum beach chairs, dotted the curbs, some occupied, others vacant, the kind you would drag out on a hot summer day to watch the circus come into town.

When they finally came within earshot of the locals, all that could be heard was a conversational murmur, people talking to one another rather than addressing the intruders, rude but not enraged. The locals leaned against storefronts, sprawled in those low-slung chairs, tilted out of second- and third-story windows, forearms propped on pillows or towels, faces sullen. There were no epithets, no profanities, nothing coming back to the marchers. Lorenzo felt both relieved and unnerved, Gannon seemingly handling this situation by giving Armstrong the silent treatment, the cold shoulder, offering the cameras nothing but hard stares.

HEY, GANNON,
HAVE YOU HEARD
ARMSTRONG AIN'T
JOHANNESBURG

Lorenzo settled into the center of the right flank, one eye on Gannon, the other on the marchers, the rumble of the motorcycles making it hard to focus.

Occasionally one or another of the motorcycle cops would wave to someone on the sidewalk, exchange a friendly word with a buddy or a neighbor, even the security detail treating this march as a nonevent. He saw Jesse drift out of the procession and slip into the truculent crowd, presumably to check out the Gannon mind-set. Lorenzo caught her eye, and Jesse, as if reading his thoughts, returned his gaze with a shrug of bewilderment, Lorenzo thinking that he truly liked Jesse, always had.

"WHAT DO WE WANT."

"JUSTICE."

"WHEN DO WE WANT IT."

"NOW."

Walking backwards, Lorenzo almost tripped over a shooter who was also walking backwards, but in the opposite direction. Regaining his balance, he returned his attention to the marchers, keying in on hands, eyes, noticing a young muscular kid in matching striped shirt and shorts holding a brown paper bag folded tight against itself—could be a sandwich, a brick, could be anything. Lorenzo also spied a leather-bound sap peeking out of another kid's shirt, the black-stitched business end nesting in his back-turned palm, the grip running up the length of his forearm, hidden by the long sleeves of a sky-blue Carolina Panthers jersey. Lorenzo made a move to cut into the crowd, have a word with the kid, but he was distracted by one of the motorcycle cops chatting up the JNL teenager marching nearest to his wheels.

"Yo, how much you pay for that Tommy Hilfiger. My kid wants that." The boy looked at the cop, then looked away.

Donald De Lauder, whirling, walleyed, spun past Lorenzo on his way to the front.

Peering into the crowd of marchers again, Lorenzo couldn't find either the kid with the sap or the other kid with the tightly wrapped paper bag. On the sidewalk, someone let loose with an explosive sneeze, Lorenzo whipping his head to the noise, taking in the people sitting splay-legged on those beach chairs, then catching movement on a roof—pigeons—then seeing John Mahler, the Gannon chief of police, standing in the crowd, arms folded across his chest, talking to Jesse, shrugging about something, a surly *C'est la vie* kind of gesture.

"Come on, yo, how much that set you back?" the cop still ragged the kid.

"Hey, whyn't you just cap yourself a nigger tonight, get one free, OK?"

"Now, now," the cop said, waggling a gloved finger.

And then Lorenzo saw her again—Brenda, about ten rows ahead of him, walking on the opposite flank. He still couldn't see more than the curve of her cheek, the jut of her jaw, but that chopped shock of hair, that knotted rope of a spine climbing to the nape beneath a small, low-slung army-green backpack.

In his frazzled state, Lorenzo thought it made sense, her being here—that she *would* be here on an issue like this—then caught himself, his dizzy ruminations abruptly supplanted by dread: the backpack. What was in that backpack.

HEY, GANNON,
HAVE YOU HEARD,
ARMSTRONG AIN'T
JOHANNESBURG

This time the chant came from a group of Gannon teenagers draped on a stoop, the kids chanting it again, fists in the air, then, in harmony, bellowing, "Fight the power!" They were fucking with people, drawing some hard stares both from the other spectators and from the marchers. The shooters came to life, finally having the makings of an incident, Eric Convoy drawling, "Yeah, you be fightin' the power in a *min*ute," Gannon's white homeys, hearing this, arching eyebrows high, saying "Yo, sorry, brother, sorry," then cracking up again, Lorenzo tense until a Gannon bookie stepped over to have a word with them, the kids finally going quiet.

That backpack. Lorenzo sliced into the march, getting close enough to hear her voice, faint and listless: "No peace." Reaching past people to get to her, he rested a hand on the small of someone's back for support and felt a gun—this marcher packin'. Lorenzo kept his hand on the piece, his other hand now on the guy's right arm.

"Hey," Lorenzo said softly in his ear. The young man—dashikied, bearded, bespectacled—reflexively gripped the wrist of the hand that rested on his gun, wheeling around.

"Easy, easy," Lorenzo murmured, engaging the hand that seized his. "What's with the gat, boss?"

The guy said nothing, just stared into Lorenzo's face until Lorenzo ID'd him—a new kid in Narcotics, apparently working undercover today. Seeing the recognition come into Lorenzo's eyes, the young cop tilted his chin to the left, to the rear, silently indicating a few other Dempsy undercovers scattered about. Lorenzo nodded, sliding back out to the flanks, thinking, Guns, we got guns in here today—forgetting his second Brenda sighting, that backpack, just wanting this to be over, having to admit to himself that, as in combat, the ultimate goal for him here, right now, was for everyone to make it back home intact.

The procession was six blocks deep into downtown, still getting no reaction. Some of the marchers began to fall out of their ranks, just wandering a bit into the security lanes, the JNL ushers, sour-faced now, nudging them back into formation.

"WHOSE STREETS"

"OUR STREETS."

No, their streets, Lorenzo thought, overhearing the two motorcycle cops nearest him discuss Aruba, time shares.

The Emergency Services Unit truck had developed a bit of an exhaust malfunction and was spewing back a faintly yellow plume, another joke, another head fuck. Lorenzo saw Longway and De Lauder lock eyes, both of them furious. Longway seized De Lauder's forearm to speak into his ear over the racket of the motorcycles. De Lauder nodded animatedly, then quickly sidestepped back out to the security flank, passing the reverend's directive on to one of his ushers, that man quickly turning and passing it on to the JNL man behind him, the whisper chain stretching back six rows in so many seconds, not quite reaching Lorenzo. At the next intersection, Longway, still linked to Curious George and Tariq's grandmother, abruptly veered left into a side street, De Lauder and the other left-flank ushers stepping to the curb to wave the marchers into this impromptu detour. The entire procession turned left like a magic trick—the ESU truck suddenly by itself a half block up Jessup, the motorcycles unable to continue the escort service because the side street was too narrow to accommodate them—and within minutes Armstrong had returned the head fuck, finessing the cops, the tight-faced spectators, marching now unchecked on Father L. Mullane Street, a tremor of triumph and joy shooting through the ranks, the motorcycles forced to form a rear-guard convoy.

Lorenzo felt it too, that rush of glee, but it was quickly dispelled by a sense of insignificance, of pettiness—Lorenzo disgusted, thinking, This is what passes for a victory these days, all payoffs boiling down to a quick hit, here and gone, the beat going on. He was finally more angry than anxious, finally—if only for a moment—wanting more from today than everyone's safe return home.

The new, slightly giddy route took them past the Mary Bethune Houses, the only public housing project in Gannon, and at the sight of black Gannon faces hanging out of the aluminum-framed windows the marchers became ebullient, started coming on like victorious combat troops entering a liberated hill town. Bellows went up: "Come on down!" "We marchin' for you!" The thrust fists of unity were returned with shouts and waves from the windows, a few of the Bethune kids hanging in front of their buildings hurling themselves into the ranks, each of them backslapped into the fold, everybody buzzed now except the motorcycle cops, who continued dutifully to bring up the rear.

At the next intersection, the marchers took a right; a block later they turned right again, and soon they found themselves on narrow Father Pitino Street, which emptied out into Jessup Avenue again. The ESU truck was waiting for them at the intersection. There seemed to be an effort on De Lauder's part to pull off an about-face, but that proved too chaotic, putting the motorcycle cops in front and the reverends in the rear. Since there was no room to make even a tight U-turn on Father Pitino, it was decided to march back out on Jessup, the marchers' point made—Armstrong finally having rattled Gannon's cage. But as the front ranks headed for the intersection, the ESU truck just sat there, blocking the mouth of the street. The abrupt halt this provoked, combined with the oblivious forward motion of the rear ranks, caused a rippling clash of bodies, the front wheels of the motorcycles abruptly offering seats to the last two rows of protesters, everybody else bumping one another forward until the very first line, the reverends and the families, were inadvertently shoved into the side panels of the truck.

Lorenzo saw it in a blink: disaster. The marchers were trapped in a narrow canyon of brick, people starting to turn in place, some of them popping up from the bustle to get a look-see. A mutter rose, a few shouts, people yelling for the ESU truck to move out of the way. Lorenzo could see the driver, red-faced, working the ignition, the gears; the fucking thing was stalled. The shouts got louder, panic taking hold, someone's Betacam hitting the wall with a hollow clatter, the motorcycles not knowing what was happening or where to go, the ESU driver shouting into his radio.

Abruptly, from the mob of spectators waiting on Jessup, at least two dozen Gannon cops materialized, jeans and Hawaiian shirts, high-tops and cutoffs, every one of them racing to the intersection, the sidewalk crowd apparently riddled with cops, each one putting a shoulder to the rear of the truck now, digging in and pushing its deadweight out of the way. The marchers were pouring through the widening gap, back onto Jessup, Lorenzo, De Lauder, and the entire armbanded security force trying to control the spillage into that broader street, trying to maintain formation until the marchers turned left and proceeded once again down the main drag, leaving Lorenzo damp and spent. The ushers, desperate to get everyone refocused, called out through cupped hands, "WHOSE STREETS."

The marchers, shaking off a pinwheel of emotions, roared back, "OUR STREETS," the Gannon locals greeting this reemergence of the invaders with a smattering of polite, sarcastic applause.

Three blocks south of Jessup and Pitino, at the intersection of Jessup and Hruska, the crowds of spectators abruptly came to an end, even though the marchers' goal was the front lawn of the Municipal Building, which housed the police department, a mere four blocks farther south at Jessup and Sisto. It was as if the line had been drawn and, once the marchers passed Cavanaugh's Bar on the east corner of Jessup, and Hruska and DeFillipo's Bakery on the west corner, they found themselves entering a well-tended ghost town, each step bringing them deeper and deeper into isolation, that eerie sense of abandonment peaking at their destination.

The march came to a ragged halt at a crossroads unlike any other on that low-slung, bustling strip. Broad, spacious lawns fronted vast civic and spiritual temples—the Municipal Building, Saint Anselm's, the main branch of the Gannon Public Library, and the middle school. There were no shops, no homes, and no people, save for the motorcycle cops, the ever-present shooters, and a handful of renegade locals who had broken away from the sidewalk crowd. The silent aggregation of colonnades, spires, and uniform rows of dead-eyed windows seemed not only to isolate but to diminish the marchers, who were now re-forming in a rough square before Longway. The reverend stood above them on the front steps of the building, forced to preach to the converted. Taking five, the cops straddled their parked bikes under a line of trees across the street, joined by the shooters, who were finally cooling out, firing up smokes, this part of the gig the visual equivalent of a grounder.

Angry and humiliated, Lorenzo was deaf to anything being said by Longway up on the steps. Looking back up to the populated side of Jessup and Hruska, he could see the locals coming off the sidewalks and mingling in the streets now, the body language and the odd raucous squawk or guttering laugh that made it down to Sisto suggesting a block party or some other kind of celebration. He had to admit it: Gannon had him tripping. It was as if they had allowed Armstrong in, then walked out of their own house.

Spotting Jesse making her way alone down the deserted stretch of Jessup to the demonstration, Lorenzo gestured for her to join him at the back of the crowd. Sidling up alongside him, she did a half-whispered impersonation of Mahler, the Gannon chief: "Well, the Reverend Longway called up, said he was coming over, said it was gonna be a nonviolent demonstration, and, you know, we've known and respected the reverend for years, so we're taking him at his word, but . . ." Jesse paused, grimacing, pouring it on. "Look, personally, I feel they're exploiting the tragic death of a child to push forward on some agenda and, you know, speaking personally again, I feel offended by that, but . . ."

"Shit," Lorenzo hissed in disgust.

Jesse looked at him with sympathy. "They seen you comin'."

The motorcycles abruptly kicked up again, Longway's speech had come to an end, and the marchers were once again on the move, heading back up Jessup to Armstrong, to home. Halfheartedly assisting in the shape-up, Lorenzo could see the plainclothes cops up there on the populated side of Jessup, pushing the locals back to the sidewalks, clearing the shop-lined street for the return march. He read in the distant choreography that some of the locals didn't seem too happy about having to surrender their main drag a second time, and as he trotted up to the front rank, a part of him almost wished that Gannon would try to make a stand, create some kind of physical blockade, offer him something into which he could sink his teeth.

When the marchers came within shouting distance of Hruska again, a yellow-and-white Gannon fire truck crawled out of a side street and cut in front of them, taking over from the stalled ESU vehicle.

One of the motorcycles pulled out and came abreast of the front line, the visored, faceless cop addressing Longway: "Hey, Rev, I don't know how you're holding up today with coming out of the hospital and all, but if you need to, be happy to give you a ride in the fire truck." The cop said it straight-faced, but the offer was met with a molten silence.

The procession moved slowly back through the heart of downtown Gannon, the marchers quiet, almost sullen now that the march, from Gannon's point of view, was heading in the right direction. In contrast, the spectators seemed looser, slightly festive, people talking loudly to one another, a few of them making exaggerated waves of fare-thee-well, as if the marchers were about to head up a gangplank and set sail to ports unknown—the overall vibration Gannon 1, Armstrong 0.

Although now was the time for him to be most vigilant—one town a steaming river of humiliation and disappointment, the other standing on the banks, high on victory—Lorenzo felt lead-footed, apathetic, looking neither at the crowds nor at the protesters, his eyes half-mast and filled with resentment.

As the silent marchers reentered that urban wilderness sector of Jessup Avenue that fronted Armstrong, Gannon's fire truck and motorcycles continued to box them in. The internal order of the ranks was falling apart now, some people tired from the tension; others, mostly the seniors, tired from the physical march itself; most everybody, Lorenzo figured, feeling burned and unsatisfied. The fire truck led them all the way to the Gannon entrance of Martyrs Park, where it finally peeled off, and the motorcycles re-formed into those two defensive lines facing the projects. Lorenzo stood at the mouth of the park, watching the truck growl its way back downtown, then panned the impassively alert faces of the motorcycle cops. Lorenzo stepped in place, fuming, frustrated: Gannon was herding Armstrong back into Dempsy again, just like they always did.

"WHOSE STREETS," someone called out, trying to boost the mood.

"OUR STREETS." The response was slack and desultory as people entered Martyrs and began the juke and weave around benches and kiddie swings again. They ducked under the summer-heavy boughs, focused on the effort to maintain the physical flow of so many bodies through this small obstacle course, any further impulse to chant stopped cold by the bald sight of the Armstrong towers as the marchers came through the foliage to be smacked in the face with the reality of where they lived—came to it from Gannon's point of view.

Lorenzo stood at the park's entrance as if holding open a door, his right hand extended toward Armstrong, pointing the way, his left stretched back to the marchers still in Gannon, the fingers unconsciously flexing in a beckoning speed-it-up gesture as he frisked the faces that went past him, gauging the potential for trouble. This close to home, his natural state of anxiety overwhelmed his anger at Gannon, and he found himself thinking, This is where I am, this is what I do. Stand at the door, straddle the fence—Lorenzo admitted to himself once again that this was all he ever truly cared about, keeping people out of harm's way, physically safe, day by day, hour by hour, minute by minute. And as the protesters poured past him, he came to the realization that, in his own way, he was as bad as any knucklehead out here, perpetually surrendering to a craving for instant gratification, too fixated on the here and now to ever truly think about the future, the big picture. Revolution, rhetoric, confrontation, demonstration, agitation, manifesto, mandate—in his heart, Lorenzo cared for none of it, his credo, now and always, To Hover and Protect.

Standing there volunteer supervising the exodus, he became aware of Jesse, who was behind and a little to the left of him, one foot in each city. She was shadowing him, riding his perspective, and it set him on edge, Lorenzo wanting her safely over the line too. But as he turned to her it happened. One of the motorcycle cops said, "You all have a good night now," putting a slightly down-home spin on it. Upon hearing this Gannon farewell, Millrose Carter, the Man Who Never Sleeps, stopped dead. One foot in Dempsy, he slowly arched his back, chin pointing skyward, face drawn into a tired grimace, looking like a man who had just remembered some tedious undone chore. Then he turned back toward Gannon, breasting his way through the Armstrong-bound marchers until he came to stand in front of the motorcycles.

"Can I help you?" one of the cops asked evenly.

Lorenzo knew what was going to happen next. He might have had a second or two to keep it from going down, but he just watched it happen. Millrose punched that cop flush in the mouth, knocking him backwards off his bike, and within a heartbeat the world turned upside down, the Man Who Never Sleeps disappearing under a pile of blue helmets. The marchers on either side of the assault, after a moment's confusion, began smashing into one another as they raced either to safety or to further set things off. Motorcycles toppled like dominoes as people were bulled into trees, fences, benches, the video shooters scrambling just like everybody else—to safety or toward the fray—the sky breaking up into peals of panic and impulse, emotion and radio squawk.

Lorenzo's first act of commitment was yoking Eric Convoy, catching him across the throat with a forearm as he high-stepped toward the action, taking him off his feet. The kid came down flat on his back, Lorenzo not sure what to do with him next, settling for getting down in his face, aiming a finger, and saying, "I *see* you."

Coming upright, Lorenzo clotheslined another kid, Corey Miller, flinging him back toward Armstrong, then another, then another, feeling like a manic, overtaxed goalie, getting into a rhythm of interceptions, keeping the Armstrong hotheads off the Gannon cops, and keeping those same cops from locking up half the high-rises.

Back across the line in Gannon, Lorenzo saw Jesse dancing in and out of harm's way, as if daring herself to rub up against the rage, craving the rage, the physical communion. He saw a couple of the Armstrong knuckleheads stomping on downed choppers; saw Daniel Bennett, the sulky kid from the self-esteem workshop, catch a baton across the midsection, then curtsey to the pain; saw one of the satellite-truck antennas crack and topple; saw two of Dempsy's black undercovers basically doing what he was doing, running interference; saw one of them, the dashikied bearded kid from Narcotics, being backed into the motorcycles by an onrush and catching yet another Gannon baton, thrust like a bayonet between the ribs, then dropping on all fours like a dog, Lorenzo remembering feeling that kid's gun as he slid across the parade ranks in pursuit of Brenda, Lorenzo thinking, Guns, guns, attempting to radio for help, having held off earlier, sure someone else had done so already, then stopping midtransmission to grab Eric's brother Caprice, getting spun around by him, and losing his radio.

He saw a Betacam skitter across the four-lane Gannon roadway, heard sirens, saw a satellite truck peel out, then change its mind, running over a motorcycle as it backed up closer to the action.

More sirens: Gannon coming, Dempsy coming. Lorenzo turned back to the Hurley Street cul-de-sac and saw the Reverend Longway, looking angry but dazed, restrained from the fray by Teacher Timmons's mother and another minister; saw Donald De Lauder and the JNL security ushers forming a cordon, calmly escorting their own marchers back onto the yellow buses, the people moving swiftly, quietly. De Lauder was impassive, tight-lipped, repeating Lorenzo's shepherding gesture, one arm outstretched toward the open bus doors, the other extended toward his people, fingers flexing in a gesture of urgency.

The Gannon cops, deserting their motorcycles, withdrew into a tight defensive square, unconsciously stepping over and obscuring a sprawled body as they did, no one rushing them now, just tossing shit—rocks, bottles—going after the sat trucks and cameras, the shooters filming as they retreated. Lorenzo saw a group of Armstrong hotheads and others he didn't know bypass both the cops and the media, running blindly back into Gannon as if to destroy it with their bare hands. But there was nothing out there in this part of the city—it was a paved prairie, just highway and sky—so they wound up running toward the heart of Jessup Avenue, a half mile away, running like it was a race. Where you going, Lorenzo thought, seeing in the distance the flying blue misery lights, a convoy of Gannon cruisers and Crown Victorias coming in. Lorenzo looked away: Save your wind, boys, Gannon's coming to you.

Through a shifting human screen, Lorenzo caught sight of that sprawled body again, lost it in the defensive shuffle of the cops, then got another peek. It was Millrose Carter, flat on his back, mouth agape, eyes rolled in frozen revelation, a creeping fan of blood beneath his head, the Man Who Never Sleeps having finally come to rest. Lorenzo made a move to claim him, his body, then saw two teenagers crawling like cougars over a mountain range of slant-parked Crown Vics, crawling toward Jesse, saw her eyes fill with knowledge as she braced to pay her tab. Lorenzo stood there, flat-footed with indecision now, Jesse wide right; Millrose, lying in his stained halo, wide left; Daniel Bennett directly before him, forehead to the asphalt, retching in pain; the black Dempsy undercover curled on his side now, softly moaning.

Lorenzo, overwhelmed, in a state of detached awe, stood before the offspring of Brenda Martin's desperate reflex, a teeming litter of incident and outrage, enough fodder here for a dozen more marches, charges, countercharges, commissions, investigations, indictments, headlines, midnight negotiations, and political swap meets, Lorenzo sagging, so tired, thinking, To Hover and Protect, choosing his words carefully as he addressed himself: It's an impractical motto.

As he turned back toward Armstrong, Lorenzo's mouth abruptly filled with the taste of coins. He lost his sight and slid into a daydream. When his vision returned a few seconds or a few minutes later, he touched his scalp and his hand came away sticky. He took a stagger step backwards and slipped on an unopened glass bottle of Coke covered with blood. Moving like an old man now, he eased himself down on a Martyrs Park bench, looked up, and saw that camo-wearing son of a bitch he had braced before the march, the one he'd asked to drink his soda right then, the one who'd responded, "I ain't thirsty yet." The kid, meeting Lorenzo's brain-drunk gaze, cringed as if in apology, the thrown bottle most likely intended for someone else. Then one of his crew hauled on his arm and he vanished.

Lorenzo sat there on the bench, blacked out, came to, blacked out, came to again and again, each state lasting only seconds. He saw a number of things, not sure if they were from inside his concussed head or from the real world: he saw the Reverend Longway sitting in the dirt of the park, slump-shouldered and stunned; saw Jesse, in the manner of someone about to spew toothpaste into a sink, thrust her head forward, cheeks bulging, and drool blood into her cupped palms; saw Curious George, ducking the drama, leaning out Miss Dotson's window, sipping a beer and tapping cigarette ash onto his grandmother's mound of butts down below; saw Brenda Martin or that Brenda Martin–looking woman as she strolled out along Hurley Street, turned a corner, and disappeared; and finally, just before the last black wave put him to sleep for the better part of the next thirty-six hours, he saw the Conrail train, roaring past Armstrong, and it was on fire.

He didn't know if it was truly on fire or if the train was just coming directly out of the sunset, but it appeared to him, right then, as a monstrous flaming arrow, arching toward Newark like an omen, a portent.

You do what you can do—Lorenzo going down now, his inner voice coming at him, dozy and distant—that's all you can do . . .

Part Four

Steal Away

32

The wake for Cody Martin was held on Saturday, the Fourth of July, from nine to noon, restricted to family and friends. The Manganaro Funeral Home looked as if it were hosting a movie premiere, the short red carpet that ran from the curb to the glass doors lined six-deep with media and civilians.

To be admitted, guests had to wear the orange Velcro disc that had been delivered to their homes the evening before, and this admissions procedure yielded a sparse, erratic procession of gray-faced middle-aged couples—aunts and uncles, Jesse assumed, maybe a few retired cops, cronies of Brenda's late father. There were also a number of younger, Danny Martin–aged cops, accompanied by their wives or girlfriends. No one brought children.

Jesse saw at least two reporters sporting pilfered Velcro buttons, both of them heads-down, solemn-faced, as they crashed the show.

Most of the local people in the crowd, murmuring and nodding, seemed to recognize the invited mourners, but the media response to their arrival was subdued. When Danny Martin finally pulled up front, exiting the car and swinging around the front end to open the door for his mother, there was a great surge forward to preserve the moment on film. Danny wore a bronze-toned, too-long double-breasted suit, the cuffs brushing his knuckles. As a result of his dustup with Curious George, the bridge of his nose was cross-taped and there were broad sepia swaths under his eyes. He seemed to have grown jowls overnight, and he needed a shave.

Brenda's mother, Elaine, hid behind makeup and enormous sunglasses as her son escorted her to the door. Jesse noticed that her mouth hung open, like that of an elderly person trying to negotiate breathing and walking at the same time.

Five minutes after Danny and his mother arrived, the Gannon chief of police, the chief of detectives, and the mayor rolled up in separate cars. These men seemed to be the last of the invitees, and the press wound up staring at one another across the red carpet, a few turning to pump one of the funeral directors, who had come outside to check the action. The guy seemed to be enjoying all the drama, but was apologetically unwilling to give any details about what was going on inside the chapel.

Glancing across the divide of the red carpet to the other half of the crowd, Jesse spotted a vaguely familiar face, an olive-skinned man, late thirties, forty, possibly Latino, whose goatee and short hair were shot through with streaks of gray. As if sensing Jesse's attention, he looked directly at her, and she recalled who he was—bachelor number two, the second possible deep throat from McCoy's, the one who had bolted out of the bar when she approached his table. On the heels of this recognition came an intuitive epiphany, Jesse knowing without a doubt that this guy was Ulysses Maldonado, Cody's biological father, the man who was supposed to be somewhere in Puerto Rico.

Jesse made a move to cross the carpet, to approach him, but, as if reading her mind, Ulysses locked eyes with her, shook his head no, and held up a hand, signaling her to keep away.

As she stepped back in place—the other reporters circling the funeral director, trying to squeeze him for details, for images—a tricked-out Range Rover pulled up to the curb, three black men inside. The one in the shotgun seat yelled out, "Yeah, see how many a you motherfuckers gonna show up for *Mill*rose's funeral," the driver, leaning across to the passenger window, adding, "That bitch killed Millrose *too*."

The locals reacted instantly, throwing garbage, stones, tin cans, whatever was at hand, and the Range Rover had to floor it.

Edwin "Millrose" Carter: there would be hell to pay for last night's lone fatality, not so much for the death itself but for the difficulty in assigning blame. The blow that had caved in Millrose's skull could have come from a number of things, and although the smart money was on a

Gannon baton, he could just as easily have been clocked by a chunk of cement, a hurled bottle like the one that clocked Lorenzo—And eyewitnesses had testified that the victim himself had set off the free-for-all by punching the cop, the coroner adding to the tangle by announcing that the body had close to six shots of hard liquor in its system, or a bottle and a half of wine.

It had been less than twelve hours since the medical examiner's pronouncement, but already Jesse could predict that the debate over culpability would go on for years, the trench between the two cities, between the cops and the projects people growing just a little bit wider for it, a little bit deeper.

A few minutes later, in the wake of the verbal ambush from the men in the Range Rover, a distant report of staccato pops and cracks had some of the crowd turning in anxious circles. Jesse, too, felt a bubble of panic until she heard someone say dryly, "Fourth of July." Once the crowd, laughing a little, settled down again, Jesse glanced across the carpeted divide to eyeball Ulysses, to mutely plead for a sit-down, but found that he was no longer there. As she brooded over the lost encounter, two of the younger, bulked-up dark-suited mourners emerged from the funeral home to cop a smoke. The cameras drove them back indoors, one of the guys muttering, "Vultures," the shooter next to Jesse responding, "Original."

The Friends of Kent van then pulled up, Louis at the wheel, Karen and the others—Marie, Teenie, and Elaine—piling out. The women all wore dark skirt suits or dresses, gold Friends of Kent pins catching the sun on their shoulders or at their throats. They made no effort to enter the funeral home, just attached themselves to the rear of the crowd and stood in silence.

Jesse worked her way back to them, touching Karen on the arm. "Hey," she whispered, feeling slightly breathless.

"Hey, Jesse," Karen responded, her voice subdued but still holding an edge of ownership. The other women nodded and smiled, Marie leaning over and giving Jesse a dry peck on the cheek.

"Are you going in?" Jesse was still whispering, although they were outdoors at the rear of a thick crowd.

"Nah." Karen shrugged.

"You're not on the list?"

"Nope." Karen shrugged again. "It's OK. We'll pay our respects from here. So how are you doing, Jesse?"

Touched by the inquiry, Jesse began to gush. "Good. Did you read what I, any of what—"

"No, I'm not, they don't sell the *Register* by me."

"Good. I got—you know, I've been writing about this all along—and actually I got three job offers." The offers were more like preliminary feelers, but Jesse, hearing herself, was unable to stop her mouth.

"Good for you," Karen said mildly.

"Yeah, one in Colorado, one—"

"That's great." Karen's eyes were elsewhere.

"And," Jesse went on, begging herself to just shut up, "two in the Sunbelt or something. But I'm not, you know, this is where . . . it's flattering, but . . ."

"Good for you."

"I hope, I think I did you justice."

"I'm sure you did."

"You know, maybe, like, I could do a piece on you, the organization. I think it would make, you know . . ."

"Yeah, sure."

"I mean, once the smoke clears," Jesse said, having no intention of writing something like that. "I think it would help you."

"Everything helps." Karen reached for a tissue, blew her nose.

"Right, well . . ." Mortified, Jesse moved away.

After some time, there was an abrupt exodus from the funeral home—seemingly everybody—Danny and his mother bringing up the rear, the guests offering up mottled and stony faces, no one crying, not one tear but plenty of rage. Puzzled, Jesse checked her watch, confirming that there was still an hour left for the wake. Taking an educated guess about what was happening, she quietly circled around to the rear of the home, where the mortuary wagons made their deliveries, hoisted herself up on a concrete abutment that lay in tree shadow, and waited. To occupy herself, she ran down a postriot tally.

Last night's violence had produced only ten arrests. But by this morning, in order to douse any residual embers that might still be glowing out there, the prosecutor had downgraded all the charges to disorderly persons, a matter of desk appearances and fines, seven of the arrestees walking, the remaining three held on outstanding warrants for earlier, unrelated crimes. There were also ten hospitalizations: Lorenzo, concussion; four marchers suffering various cuts and fractures, including a broken ankle and a broken collarbone; three Gannon cops, two treated for back injuries, one for a scratched cornea; Jesse herself, who had received eight stitches inside her cheek; and lastly, that black Dempsy undercover whose spleen had been ruptured by a Gannon baton.

Hot, fly-buzzed, tired of it all, Jesse let the numbers go and drifted into free association until roughly twenty minutes later, when, as she had anticipated, the Department of Corrections van pulled up to the rear of the mortuary. She watched from the shadows as two sheriffs exited the grill-windowed wagon, came around to the side panel, shoved it back, and literally lifted Brenda, who was shackled at the waist, wrists, and ankles, a single heavy chain running through all the restraint junctions—just hoisted her out of the van and set her down on the asphalt. Two corrections officers came out after her, the four cops together forming a protective diamond. Walking slowly to accommodate her chain-toddling gait, they escorted her to the delivery bay.

Brenda appeared to be grinning and Jesse was glad that there were no cameras back here, the grin nothing more than a frozen rictus. And, as Danny Martin had seemed to have grown jowls in the last forty-eight hours, Brenda appeared to have greatly thickened through the middle. Jesse was startled by this new bulk before realizing that what had caught her eye was a bulletproof vest.

Jesse had been hanging around the funeral home since eight o'clock in the morning, figuring that County would have trucked Brenda over then, an hour before the wake was scheduled to begin. That strategy made a lot more sense than showing up in the middle of the service like this, forcing the family to leave the premises, to simply stand around and ponder Brenda, in there all by herself, which only created grief on top of grief, rage on top of rage. Knowing something about the bureaucracy over at the correctional center, though, Jesse could also imagine that Brenda had sat parked in front of the jail for a good couple of hours earlier this morning, waiting for someone to secure a few more signatures on the various temporary release forms.

Brenda was given exactly twenty-two minutes to say good-bye to her son, and in that time, as word of her arrival leaked out, Jesse was slowly enveloped by the crowd of locals and shooters that had been standing in front. When Brenda finally reappeared with her four-man escort, she was pelted with all the predictable cries: Baby Killer, Bitch, Whore, Die, Baby Killer, Animal, Pig, Die, Die, Baby Killer, Baby Killer.

Whatever Brenda had experienced inside the Manganaro chapel

over the past twenty-two minutes had deepened her involuntary grin, her mouth seeming locked open, her upper and lower jaws slightly askew.

"Look at her, she's laughing," the woman standing next to Jesse sputtered.

Brenda raised her face to that, looked directly at Jesse without really seeing her. Jesse impulsively whispered, "Hi," her heart tumbling with incontestable love, the woman saying it again: "She's *laughing.*" Jesse ignored Brenda's jagged joker mouth, stared at her eyes instead; they were wild, like trapped birds, desperate to escape their imprisoning sockets.

After the wake, not wanting to go home and be alone, Jesse came into the newsroom for the first time in a week. There were a few staffers who congratulated her on her work of the last few days, but most kept their distance, a time-conditioned response to her lone-wolf routine. On some days, the cold shoulder bothered her, on others she couldn't care less; today it felt bad.

Jose was not around. She sat in her cubicle and reread the last installment of her at-home vigil with Brenda, scheduled to run in that evening's edition. She scanned her account of the visit from Karen Collucci and the Friends of Kent—the slow collection of Cody's clothes for the scent bag, Brenda being persuaded to leave a message for her dead son on the tape recorder, the surprise appearance of the cadaver dog. In hindsight, every uttered word, every glance, every tormented second of Brenda's lie came back to her in excruciatingly precise detail, and she was awed by Brenda's having held out on her confession for as long as she had.

She recalled Paul Rosenbaum's expression, "engine of denial"; at the time, it had seemed easy to dismiss as the facile hyperbole of a media manipulator. Over the last four days, Jesse had never thought that Brenda was doing anything but straight-out, conscious lying. But as she reviewed her written observations now, in the aftermath of the confession, the march, the riot, the wake, Jesse wondered for the first time if she had understood anything at all of what she experienced at 16 Van Loon Street or in the steaming ruins of the Chase Institute.

After a few moments of reflection, the ringing of the phone came as a relief.

"Yeah."

"Hey." It was Ben.

"What."

"Nothing. I'm at the hospital. They have to resew me, the guy fucked up the stitches or something." Jesse waited. "You know who I ran into here? That cop, Bump. He's getting out tomorrow. We got to talking. Nice guy."

"And . . ." Jesse lit a cigarette.

"Jess?" he began gingerly. "Did you ever, you didn't ever . . . it's not my place, but did you ever interview his son? You kind of promised."

"Tell him I need a day or two."

"I mean, it's not my place—"

"I can't talk now, I'm working."

A few seconds later the phone rang again. Annoyed, expecting her brother again, Jesse picked up. She heard a computer-generated female-toned word collage telling her she had a collect call from—and then a small razzle of static, punctuating the transition to a true voice, coming through now, hesitant and small—"Brenda Martin."

Jesse arrived at the county jail visitors' center at three o'clock that after-noon. As the sergeant pored over her credentials, a corrections van backed up to a heavy door and unloaded six young black women in royal-blue prison scrubs, each with a rolled Islamic prayer rug under her arm. Jesse guessed that they were returning from sentence hearings, the three of them flashing fingers to another female inmate, who was swabbing the floor around the reception desk. Jesse guessed again that the num-ber of fingers signified the number of years they had just received. One heavyset woman shot out two, in a peace sign; another, looking stunned, splayed out a full five.

Because of Brenda's celebrity, the visit was set up in the privacy of the guards' lounge. Jesse was escorted into the harshly lit room, deserted for the moment, the walls lined with vending machines, pay phones, and three bulletin boards, all heavily papered with union-related notices, an-nouncements of schedule changes, and jail-theme cartoons clipped from various newspapers and magazines. Her escort set up two facing folding chairs as far away as possible from the other furniture, then stepped back and gestured for her to have a seat.

Physically isolated, enveloped by silence, Jesse sat dry-mouthed, fingers fluttering. By the time that Brenda, escorted by two guards, shuffled into the room, she had dropped her pen four times.

Wearing the same royal-blue scrubs as the women Jesse had seen coming off the prison van, Brenda looked like an exhausted surgeon, her skin unhealthily pearlescent. But the tea-stained pouches under her eyes seemed to have receded.

"Hey," they both said simultaneously, then smiled, Brenda's smile the broader of the two. Jesse felt unnerved, felt that something was deeply, dangerously wrong with Brenda, nailing it quickly: she was too happy.

Brenda crossed one leg over the other. She wore paper slippers with cardboard soles.

"How are you doing?" Jesse asked automatically.

"How am I doing?" Brenda repeated the question thoughtfully. "I'm OK," she said slowly, seriously. Then, "Better than OK."

"Are they giving you a hard time in here?"

Brenda shrugged. "I don't care."

"OK." Jesse nodded, vaguely alarmed. Then, as if to bring Brenda back to a more appropriate frame of mind, she asked, "Were you OK at the wake?"

"I want to give you this." Brenda ignored the question, handing Jesse four folded sheets of lined paper, the left vertical edges frilled from being torn out of a child's composition book. "It's a dream I had last night."

"OK," Jesse said, accepting it, sliding the paper into her shoulder bag.

"Because for you?" Brenda gestured to the steno pad. "Writing about this? You haven't the words."

"Words, for . . ." Jesse let it hang, staring, demanding more, then catching herself, becoming confused, not sure if she was here to work or to talk.

"For what it felt, *feels* like. 'Were you OK at the wake . . .' " she quoted Jesse, with faint ridicule. "You just can't . . ." She nodded to the notepad again. "You don't have the words. You can't possibly . . . just run the dream. Dreams are like, who you are. What really drives you, under all the bullshit. If people want to know about me? I don't know." Brenda looked off. "You should just run the dream or something."

"OK. I mean, it's not my call, but . . ." Jesse trailed off, not knowing what else to say.

"And I want to give you this," Brenda said, handing over a fifth piece of paper. "This is for you in private. It's a list of my favorite songs. I told you I'd make you a tape but I never did, so this is the best I can do now, you know, in here."

Jesse scanned the sheet, Brenda's block writing large and schoolgirl-ish, the Ss scooped and curved like the necks of swans, the Is haloed instead of dotted, line after line written in a bold, frenetic hand:

FOR YOUR PRECIOUS LOVE—Linda Jones
HIGHER AND HIGHER—Jackie Wilson
STEAL AWAY—Jimmy Hughes
WHEN SOMETHING IS WRONG WITH MY BABY—Sam and Dave
ANY DAY NOW—Chuck Jackson
COME TO ME (DON'T YOU FEEL LIKE CRYING)—Solomon Burke
CRY BABY—Garnett Mims
YOUR GOOD THING IS ABOUT TO END—Mabel John
WHEN MY LOVE COMES DOWN—Ruby Johnson
I CAN'T STAND THE RAIN—Ann Peebles
LITTLE BLUEBIRD—Johnny Taylor
TRAMP—Otis and Carla
THE GREATEST LOVE—Judy Clay
HAVE MERCY—Don Covay
ARE YOU LONESOME FOR ME, BABY—Freddie Scott
HELLO STRANGER—Barbara Lewis

Beneath this hit parade of lamentation, Brenda had begun a second type of music listing but either had lost interest or was finished after only a few names:

Joe Tex—THE HEALER
Percy Sledge—THE CRY BABY
Curtis Mayfield—SWEET PAIN
Al Green—
Aaron Neville—

"Thank you," Jesse said quietly, disturbed by this second gift coming on the heels of the written dream—Brenda giving away the store now. "Thanks." They sat in silence for a moment, Jesse perusing the song titles in order to avoid Brenda's eyes.

"You know," Brenda finally said, "I sit in there, the cell, and I'm, I get very still, inside, outside. I get . . . and I go back to places, you know, times, days that, I kind of forgot about but they were good. Certain people, certain moments . . ."

Brenda went off, looked through Jesse, then came back brightly: "I want to tell you about this one day."

"OK," Jesse said, bracing herself for another giveaway, for whatever intimacies were about to land in her lap. "Please."

"Five years ago December," Brenda began. "That fall? I got a job teaching ESL, English as a Second Language, at this community college in New York. This school, the students, they were from all over the map. And, at the time I was living at home. I had been through this therapy in New York, moved back to New Jersey, and at this point I was like on the tail end of a cocaine . . . I was still doing it, but I was getting, you know, I couldn't stand myself. I mean, a cokehead living at home with her mother, so . . ." She leaned forward, hugging herself. "I got this job. They called it adjunct instructor. It was bullshit. I had one year of college but I told them I was going for a master's somewhere or other and they didn't bother to check. They were desperate for teachers. It wasn't even, I mean, you got paid by the hour like a baby-sitter. Anyways, they gave me this class, five mornings a week, eight in the morning. And at first, I'd show up, just, I'd just throw on some clothes, stagger out of the house, take the PATH into the city, get in there, and, this class, the *smell* of this class . . ."

Jesse began writing.

"Just listen to me, OK?" Brenda put out a hand, and Jesse stopped.

"The smell—you walk in, these people, my students, it would be like, cologne, makeup, perfume, hair spray, suits, skirts. It was like walking into a nightclub first thing in the morning, everybody dressed to kill. But, they'd *be* there, wanting it, you know, *Teach* me. Very serious, like, focused, hungry for knowledge, for, for, betterment. I mean, we were all the same age, me and them, twenties, early thirties, and they had, you know, families, children, jobs, and still they were coming in 8:00 A.M. on the dime five days a week for me. *Me.* And, honestly, I didn't have shit. I didn't have, I had no idea what I was doing there, I had no idea what I was doing *any*where.

"I was like, like *egg* yolk. I was a live-at-home, cokehead, fuckup fuck-all. And so like the term starts, and I'd stumble into class five minutes late, ten minutes, half asleep, open this color-by-numbers textbook the ESL department gave me, and I couldn't diagram a sentence if you paid me, and, well, that's what they were doing, paying me, but I was, I'd just wing it—vocabulary words, the difference between T-O, T-O-O, T-W-O, whatever.

"And, at the end of the first week, this Puerto Rican guy in the class comes up to me, my age, a little older, says to me, 'Do you want us to respect you?' And what do you say. 'Sure. Yes.' And, he like, *flicks* the bottom of my shirt, like . . ." Brenda reached across to Jesse's midriff and soundlessly snapped her fingers as if trying to remove something odious from the tips. He says to me, 'Then you start respecting us . . .'

"He walks out and I'm freaked. I know what he's talking about, but it's even worse. I look down to where he touched my shirt? And I see that I came into school that day still wearing my pajama top. I was so ashamed, I just . . .

"OK. The next Monday, I come in on time, I'm dressed decent, I hadn't done coke over the weekend, I still don't know how to teach this class, but I'm, I want to *try*. The guy? He's not there. He's gone. I find out he requested a transfer to another ESL section.

"OK. So I started to try to teach. I start—subject, predicate, objective clause, unobjective clause—who gives a shit. But I come onto something. We were talking in class, and, I don't know how it came up but we were talking about abortion, something in the paper that day, and the students went nuts, arguing, mostly against abortion, but not all. But I noticed that if they got, *hot* about something they somehow found the words they needed. So that's what I did; every week I'd write something on the blackboard to make them go crazy, some issue like welfare, curse or cure; death penalty, yes or no; school prayer, castration for rapists, whatever. And on Mondays? We'd just talk, yell, argue, get it all out. On Tuesdays they'd write down their arguments—first draft—I'd read it, make notes to them. Wednesday second draft—I'd read it, make notes. Thursday final draft. Friday you read your stuff out loud to the class. It was, it was definitely engaging.

"They still, I mean, after two months of being in my class, this woman leaves me this note: 'I am please to be excuse for tomorrow I am to be a doctors appointment.' So there's *that* . . .

"And on the home front? Me? By, say, early October? I had pretty much cleaned up on coke, managed to move out of the house again, got a one-room on the Lower East Side, walk to work, and, the class is fun. I'm never late, I'm not coming in like a pig. Then in mid-October? I run into that guy who transferred out on me. I see him in a coffee shop across from the school, and I can tell, just the way he's looking at me, smiling at me, that he knows. He knows what I've been through, the changes I made, and his eyes, it's like, 'Good for you. Bravo,' and I started to cry."

Brenda broke it off, a trembling finger sliding along her cheekbone.

"I'm sitting there crying, he comes over, sits down, and, what can I say. By mid-November? I'm pregnant. This is Ulysses I'm telling you about, this ex-student of mine. I go in to teach every day, I never had morning sickness, I don't know why not, and I don't tell him.

"I don't tell anybody. I'm thinking, Should I abort? Should I keep the baby? Should I keep the baby and lose Ulysses? But he's the father. Should I abort, then adopt, so I'd be free of any kind of marriage? I even have this fantasy of opening it up to the class—you know, hot-button topic for the week—although this class, my students, they're like the most conservative people I ever met in my life, you know, coming over here, starting from the bottom, climbing up, up. So, I don't know. I don't know what to do.

"But so the last week of school? December 15. Ten to eight in the morning. I'm walking to class: Should I have an abortion—yes, no, yes, no, yes, no. I'm losing my mind. I'm walking, and all of a sudden Ulysses has a hand on my arm and he pulls me into a stairwell. He's got something to tell me. Very solemn, very, he's truly sorry, but he's decided to go back to Puerto Rico. He got a good job offer down there. Ever so sorry. So he goes, and I never told him, I never, I'm like, *thank* you, God. I go into class that day, Monday, I'm feeling great, and I tell the class, I say, this coming Friday? The last day of school? The hell with it. Let's just have a little Christmas party. Let's just have a party in class, it's been a tough semester, blah, blah . . .

"OK. So, I come in that Friday, ten to eight in the morning, the entire class is in there waiting for me and like, they had showed up, for a *party*. I just meant we'll all have coffee and cake, salute each other, but, no. They showed up, like, suits, dresses, hairdos, wine, a boom box, music, popcorn, pretzels, cousins, children, parents. I mean, they wanted to celebrate. They had, I mean for them it was—coming through this class—it was an accomplishment, a watermark, their first term as a college student and they . . ."

Brenda leaned forward, touched Jesse's hand.

"Jesse, I had no idea. Anyways, we were dancing, I posed for pictures shaking their hands, shaking their cousins' hands, holding their babies, we're all laughing, hugging, kissing, we're all teary, and at some point near the end, they stopped the music and they presented me with a wristwatch. Like a thank you present for being their teacher—you know, *To Sir with Love*. And, I remember accepting that watch and I had no illusions about being a *good* teacher, but thinking, Today I'm a teacher.

"And not only that, but my family? At least the Italian side, my mother's side? They were the students in here, in a class like this, what, seventy years ago? Eighty years ago?

"And here *I* am, and I'm, I've brought my own family full circle, I've brought us around the room to the teacher's desk. And my students? Now it, it's their turn to start up the generations. And I just remember standing there, taking that wristwatch, and feeling so—I knew *who* I was, I knew *where* I was, I had my baby inside me, my students around me, it was Christmas . . . ."

A silence came over the room. Jesse looked at her hands, absorbing the fullness of the picture Brenda was painting, getting lost in it, and was a while in becoming aware that the silence enveloping them was false, not a silence at all. And when she looked up, she saw that Brenda was streaming tears, hand to forehead, her mouth locked open in a yawning, soundless gawp. Jesse had no idea what to do, how to help, so she just sat there until Brenda regained control of herself, palming the look of suffocating grief from her face as if by a parlor trick.

"How long did you teach there, Brenda?" Jesse asked calmly.

"That was it," she said. "I wasn't rehired." She looked away, shrugged. "You can't fool everybody."

One of the guards coughed, startling Jesse, who realized that she had been oblivious to their presence, three of them standing there in plain sight against the walls.

"Jesse," Brenda said, almost brightly, "You know who comes to see me?" Jesse waited. "My mother. She comes . . ." Brenda looked off before continuing in a comic huff. "*Now* she comes."

Jesse gave it a small smile, disturbed by how quickly Brenda was able to lighten her tone.

"But I'm glad to see her. I never thought I would say this, but I'm glad to see her."

"Yeah?"

"She's my mother. You got to have *some*body in your corner, right?"

Jesse fought the urge to say, "What about me?" She had decided that this was no longer an interview.

"Listen. That detective, Lorenzo? Do you ever see him?" Brenda's slipper flapped against her heel as she nervously flexed her crossed leg.

"Sure," Jesse said. "Can I help you with something, Brenda?"

"When you see him? Tell him, tell him that I thought he was very patient with me. He was, he saw right through me, but he was so patient. He didn't have to be that way. He didn't . . . tell him . . ." Brenda's eyes shone with a bright, trembling sadness, an oddly buoyant despair. "Tell him, tell him I *love* him." Her voice became feathery, broken. "I love him for how he dealt with me."

"Brenda," Jesse half whispered, having no idea what to say beyond her name but reaching out, touching her knee.

"And I need for you to tell him I'm sorry." Brenda forged on, then added in a husky whisper, "and that I'm ashamed." A farewell speech. "And Jesse," she said, "there's something I need to tell *you*." She gripped Jesse's wrist, her fingers cold, slightly damp, her touch unbearable. "I was thinking about you telling me—you know—lying to me about having a child?"

"Yes." Jesse said it as both a question and a confession.

"I just wanted to tell you that I don't, I know you had a job to do so, I mean, I don't even remember how it came up. I mean, I don't remember a lot of things but I just, it came about. It just came about, and I don't think of you as a ruthless individual or anything, and I think you feel bad about it, and, don't. It's OK."

Another farewell speech, another parting gift. Jesse eased her hand free. "Brenda, are you going somewhere?"

"What?" She cocked her head, an alert half smile on her face.

"What . . ." Jesse challenged her, leaned forward.

Brenda's eyes fixed on Jesse's hands. Her smile expanded meaninglessly. Jesse hunched forward even further, lowered her voice. "Read my mind, Brenda. What am I thinking . . ."

"Don't worry about it," Brenda said, her voice dropping to Jesse's murmurous level. "They're way ahead of you." She nodded in the direction of the guards. "That's why they call it suicide watch."

Jesse sat in Ben's car and read Brenda's dream.

Unlike the bold, almost juvenile hand that had block printed the list of favorite songs, Brenda's script was cramped low to the line and uniform, charging across the page like an army of ants.

I'm in bed with a man and this man, while asleep, is shoving me off the bed in a dream-induced impersonal fit of revulsion and I am overcome with a wave of sadness and abandonment.

My tears, soft and visible only to me.

Then, still in his sleep the man changes course and lifts me back up to the bed. Then he wakes up and holds me in full and conscious tenderness and I am filled with this feeling of cloudlike happiness and love.

I say "I love you" in a soft voice that is strange to me in its conviction. Then we both sink into this grateful tenderness with each other. It's joy for now and ever after.

Then I hear a child calling out from another room. "It's dark."

I say to the man, still in that strange soft voice, "I'll get him."

I go to this child who is laying in his pajamas on a couch in a living room, who I thought was my own son but is not, who is a child that Ulysses has had with another woman. But they must have lost or abandoned him because I know that he's parentless now, this boy in front of me, but then I think, at least he's got me (even though I am not a blood relation let alone his birth mother), and I tenderly bring this boy into bed with us and I say to him "Do you like him?" meaning the man.

The boy says "I like him."

I say "Would you like him to be your new daddy if I marry him?"

The boy says "Oh yes!" in this Candyland voice, but sincere.

"It's our secret but we're going to be a family," I say.

This boy is beside himself with heart-joy as am I, as is the man.

Then we are mounting an elephant. The three of us are high up wrapped in elephant skin, elephant ears, and we are so together, so whole, that the air is singing and then it hits me—if I have a baby with this new man of mine, this child right here, so recently inducted into our "whole love," will go crazy with fear of it all being jeopardized; the balance of things, and this new family could even turn dangerous to him, terrorize him with loss-fear.

But then I think he's got nine months to get more secure with our family, so maybe he'll be on more solid ground by then. At least nine months because I haven't had sex yet, haven't made love to this man yet, this dream of a man.

I decide that I'll worry about this boy's possible freak-out down the line.

Right now, all I know is that I'm aching with tenderness, with wholeness, like a singing in my blood.

The rest of what Brenda had written was directly addressed to Jesse.

Dear Jesse,

I know about the march and I know about the fight by Martyrs Park. All I can do to make amends is lay myself out to people, not to justify or even explain but to show who I am. I believe our true reality lies in our dreams.

Sincerely,
Brenda Martin

Carefully refolding the pages, Jesse was thrown by Brenda's calling the melee in Martyrs Park a "fight." She wondered if Brenda knew how intense that fight had been, that a life had been lost. Reflecting on it, she decided that she preferred to think of her as being in the dark on that one; nothing would be gained by making sure Brenda had the full list of casualties.

Pulling out of the parking lot, Jesse also found herself pondering what Brenda considered the happiest day in her life. If the man at the wake this morning was Ulysses, as Jesse was almost sure that he was, then those remembered golden hours of five years ago were based on a misconception—that Cody's father was unaware of the boy's existence, that, as he announced his abrupt travel plans to Brenda that day in the community college stairwell, he was unaware of her pregnancy.

As for Brenda's dream-missive, which lay now on the passenger seat, the pages fluttering and trembling in the fan-whipped air like a beating heart, Jesse didn't know what to make of it beyond the obvious—Brenda's yearning for some kind of magically instant family rapture. But she did know this: a dream was all that it would ever be, given that Brenda was condemned to live in one glass house or another for as long as she chose to remain on earth.

33

Walking into the paper at noon the next day, Jesse saw it in all the faces that stared at her with expectant fascination: Brenda was dead.

Across the cluttered, windowless expanse of the newsroom, she spotted Jose in silhouette, struggling to his feet behind the frosted glass wall of his office. Before he could enter the open room and lay eyes on her, Jesse was on her way back down the stairs to the street.

Exiting the building via the freight entrance in order to duck her brother, who was parked out front, Jesse wandered through what remained of Dempsy's downtown district—a few Moorish movie palaces turned money-hustling revival temples; a flock of beat-up black-and-orange taxis clustered in front of the main PATH station, their Sikh drivers hanging out on the convergence of hoods; a forlorn row of card tables, almost two blocks long, an open market featuring off-brand chocolate bars, tube socks, ski hats, and tin windup frogs.

A half hour of this walkabout was all Jesse could stand. Leaning against the off-kilter Dutchman in front of City Hall, she reached out to Jose.

"Jesse?" he said, speaking her name into the phone with uncharacteristic tentativeness.

"So what happened," she finally asked.

The story coming out of County was that Brenda had strangled herself in plain view of her guards. The two-piece cotton scrubs she had worn for Jesse's visit were loaners, allowed only for that journey out of her cell. Normally she wore a paper jumpsuit meant to foil any plans for hanging herself. But what she had done was to get under her blankets, remove the jumpsuit, tie the arms in a knot to the left side of her bed-springs, and tie the legs tightly around her throat, all this knot work obscured by the blanket pulled up to her chin. Then, once both ends were secured, she had leaned hard to the right, cutting off her air until she blacked out. The choke hold had asphyxiated her within a matter of minutes.

Despite the suicide watch, Brenda's death went undiscovered for twelve hours. The guards, thinking she was asleep, had let her go without breakfast, and it wasn't until the arrival of the lunch tray that anyone tried to rouse her.

After laying it all out for Jesse, Jose asked if she wanted to write Brenda's obituary or take a crack at an editorial, some kind of summing up. She declined, and to his credit, he didn't ask twice. Instead, he simply tossed her back into the pool, briefing her regarding an ongoing situation over the line in Gannon. The owner of the Hair and Now beauty parlor there had apparently flipped and was holding himself hostage, threatening to blow his head off if any of the cops, strung out along the street and on the rooftops opposite, attempted to enter his bankrupt and, as of this morning, self-vandalized salon.

At first Jesse was grateful to Jose, the embracing of fresh drama the only way she could imagine getting past Brenda right now. But the more she thought about it, the cooler she felt, realizing that making the scene over there would entail hopping into the Benmobile, working the Gannon cops, schmoozing and dry humping her way to the information. She took a pass in order to continue her walkabout, spending the rest of the day alternately envisioning and obliterating Jose's rendition of Brenda's final hours, alternately allowing the tragedy to come inside her and reassuring herself that none of it was her fault.

Her brother found her at the tail end of twilight, coming up in the Chrysler, cruising parallel to her path on the sidewalk, then gassing it a little before stopping a half block ahead and leaning across the front seat to push open the passenger door. Jesse surrendered, letting her brother drive her wherever, and was surprised when he pulled up outside the gates of Freedomtown—surprised by the rightness of his instincts.

"I hear Lorenzo's out of the hospital," he said as Jesse stepped from the car. "Maybe you should call him tonight." Ben, both obeisant and controlling, on the money.

"Could you call him for me?" Jesse asked politely, an attempt to take back some control over the moment.

Even given the darkness—it was pushing nine o'clock by now—Ben didn't try to escort his sister into the park. He knew to wait, to sit outside the vine-wreathed fence and reread the paper, sip coffee, or do whatever else he did when Jesse had no real need of him.

Although there were still a few people maintaining a vigil before the Chicago Fire, now known as the Wailing Wall—a young pregnant woman with a serious shiner who sat cross-legged on a blanket; an older man, squatting on his haunches, talking to himself; and a trio of loud, possibly drunk or stoned young reporters, who were animatedly attempting to suss out the exact footpath taken by Billy Williams from his car to the open grave—Jesse was struck by the abject desolation of this spot.

Gone were the crowds and their sorrowful chatter, gone, too, the buoyant affect of sunlight splashing off a carpet of floral tributes and primary-colored toys. Now it was the moon that held court, its cold albino rays embracing the easel-propped Styrofoam Bibles and crucifixes, making them gleam like scattered bones, that same underworld light finding the silvered balloons and transforming them into a random flotilla of gently bobbling skulls.

From behind the wall, beyond the clumped, hulking silhouette of the trees, Jesse could hear a sixteen-wheeler growling its way south on an otherwise silent turnpike. From the north, she heard the deep junkyard baying of a large dog, and from directly behind her came the incessant whisper of the black, lapping bay. It was a terrible place—remote, devoid of consolation—and by the time Lorenzo, wearing a beret to cover his stitches, finally showed up, Jesse almost jumped on his back with relief.

The two of them sat off to one side of the wall and, for a long stretch, quietly watched the visitors who arrived to pray, to deposit small gifts, or just to rubberneck recent history.

"I heard you went and visited her yesterday," Lorenzo said.

"Yeah, I did."

"Did she know someone had got killed over all this?"

"I'm not sure," Jesse said. "Maybe. What was his name? Millrose?"

"Millrose." Lorenzo nodded. "Millrose Carter."

"They gonna be able to hang that on anybody?"

Lorenzo shrugged, made a noise. "The state attorney general's office supposed to be looking at videotape right now but, hey, you know how it goes. We shall see what we shall see. Meanwhile, the rev and some others are thinking about gearing up for another march through Gannon."

"For Millrose?"

"For Millrose."

They drifted into silence. The three boisterous reporters left the park.

Jesse returned to the moment. "She said for me to tell you that she thought you were kind and patient with her."

"OK." Lorenzo nodded, smiling guardedly.

"And that she loves, loved you for it."

"OK." He gave another quick nod.

Jesse stared at the wall again, thinking of Brenda and her son, both gone now, and she started to cry, a crinkled facial spasm that could easily be confused with laughing. "Shit." She delicately tongued her stitched cheek. "That hurts."

"You hear what happened with Danny Martin?" Lorenzo asked. Jesse waited. "Yesterday, after the wake? Danny just took off, went on down to the shore, like, Wildwood, Asbury Park, somewheres down there, got himself good and oiled, and about three or four this morning? He got pulled over by state troopers on the Garden State, said he was doing close to ninety and fishtailing all over the place, right? They pull him over, see he's a cop, so alls they're gonna do is take him off the road, let him sleep it off at the barracks—you know, like a professional courtesy.

"But Danny, Danny's all like, 'Kiss my ass,' and they start getting pissed, but they see he's way out of control so they're like, still ready to do him the courtesy, but then he's like, 'Keep your fuckin' hands off me, I'll kick you teeth down your—' You know. So this morning the troopers call Gannon, say, 'Come on down and get him.'

"So Leo Sullivan goes down to bring him home? Says Danny's face looked like a bunch of grapes. Those ol' boys wound up doing a *dance* on him. They still didn't charge him, just tuned him up, and when they found out who he was, you know, in relation to this stuff up here? They even felt bad about doing that, but . . ."

"Sounds like he was looking to get his ass kicked."

"Yeah." Lorenzo bobbed his head slowly, brought his hands around his raised knees. "I'd go along with that. I think he was looking for some kind of, you know, outlet or something."

Lorenzo touched his beret. "You think I look French? Everybody's calling me Frenchy today, but I tell you, you do not want to see what I got underneath this thing."

"She wrote down a dream she had." Jesse retrieved Brenda's four-page missive from the rear pocket of her jeans and offered it to Lorenzo. "Do you want to read it?"

"Nope." He looked off, smiling. "Not really."

They sat in silence again, taking in the flowers and balloons, the wall itself, its lower third still shagged with a white beard of notes, poems, and other outpourings but also, as of this evening, sporting a flyer posted by a carpenter looking for work, his phone number hanging at the bottom on dozens of tear-away fringes.

"Jesse . . . Do you believe in the, the psychology of dreams?"

"You dream about what's on your mind." She shrugged.

"Yeah? Because where I grew up, the only thing dreams was good for was giving you a number to play the next morning."

"Huh." Jesse made an acknowledging noise, Lorenzo's last comment striking her as a little too self-consciously folksy.

"But I had me a dream in the hospital?" He exhaled heavily, shook his head once. "Man."

"What."

Lorenzo hesitated, smiled nervously, then jumped in. "I dreamed that there was this riot goin' on over in the new county jail? And they were callin' in everybody. Sheriffs, city police, county police, prosecutor's office, bosses. I mean, everybody," he said, sweeping the air with a downturned palm. "It was like, all hands on deck. And I was there, you know, suitin' up in the reception area along with everybody else, gettin' ready to go in. And I was scared, because, you know, my son, Jason, is in County. He truly is. In the, the state-run wing."

"I know."

"And like, here *I* was, grabbin' pepper spray, a pellet gun, a, a, billy club. And what if my son . . ." Lorenzo cleared his throat, passed a quick thumb under his eye.

"Jesus." Jesse watched him trying not to cry.

"But then all of a sudden the warden or somebody high up comes in, says, 'Hold up, boys, we got like a deal goin' on.' Says, 'The inmates, they say they'll stop tearin' up the place and release all hostages if we come meet with them.' Well, it wasn't like, *meet*. It's like, they wanted to put on a show for us. And we had to go into, like, some kind of dining hall, where they're gonna put on this show.

"So all the cops, we go in and there's like this long runway in there, like a fashion runway, and we sit around this runway, and all these brothers come out. Black, the black inmates, and they're dressed like

African warriors, got on all kinds of shit like Zulu warriors, but it's just to show us, like, this is who we are, this is where we come from. Like a racial-pride thing, like, 'Respect us, this is our blood,' and I'm like, All right, all right, I get it. It's about respect. The inmates are gonna make us sit there and acknowledge their ethnic heritage or something. But it's like a fashion show too. It's all fucked up. Well, shit, it's a dream, so OK.

"Sure enough, here comes the next crew out on the runway, and this time it's the Hispanics, the Latinos, and these guys, they're all dressed up like Zorro or matadors or, or, I don't know, what do you call them? Conquistadors and, and Indian chiefs, Indian warriors, and it's like, 'This is who *we* are,' and hey," Lorenzo said, chin to his chest, "anything's better than violence in my book. So, we're all sittin' there, like, no problem, on with the show, and then out comes this third bunch, and these guys—"

Lorenzo broke off to cough, and Jesse once again had the sense that he was masking the impulse to cry.

"These guys, they were wearin'—at first I thought they were wearin' *dresses,* like, dirty white dresses, and so I figured they were representing the women in there, the Maytags, you know what I'm saying? And then I saw, I saw my *son* come out in one of those dresses, and I'm, like, 'Oh my God, he's done turned into a jailhouse woman,' and it's, like, the *worst.* And then I look in his face and there's no expression on it, no, no light in it. I mean, Jason—" Lorenzo coughed again. "Jason sometimes has got, like, this *light* in his face, but—and then I see none of these jailhouse women got any kind of light, or life in their eyes. And I take a closer look at what they're wearing?"

He waited it out, swallowing, "They ain't women, and they ain't wearing dresses. They're wearing winding sheets. They're wearing shrouds. They're the dead." Lorenzo abruptly started bawling. "They're the dead, and there's Jason, there's my son, and he's walking, talking, but he's *dead.* And I can't *do* anything for him. I can't help him, I can't save him, I can't teach him. I mean, there was a time when *yes,* but I fucked up, I fucked up . . ."

Lorenzo sneezed tears, a congestion of grief, Jesse looking away.

"And now he's out of reach. He's right there in front of me, but he's stone out of reach."

"But he's OK?" Jesse's voice was lighter than air, the question meaningless, polite, and Lorenzo rightly ignored it.

"You know this past week, all this week people were saying to me, 'Big Daddy, what's up with you and that *child* killer, man? Stop strokin' and start swingin.'" He rubbed his swollen face, getting himself under control. "Well, yeah, I knew what she did. Shit, I knew before anybody. But I knew how she felt too. And like, that story she threw us? That was like, unconscionable, and I cannot tell you why she said it except it was like a white-mind reflex, but I am telling you—she started paying for it right from the *door*. Believe me, I *know*. And hey, I'm sorry . . ." He momentarily lost control again, his voice catching. "I'm sorry, but my heart went out to her. I mean, there was no way she was gonna walk on this, and, well, now she's dead, you can't get much more payback than that. So now everybody can just shut the fuck up about it and get on with their lives, you know what I'm saying? I mean, politically, we'll see what kind of water we can squeeze out of the rock, but—"

Lorenzo stopped cold, seemed to look at himself through Jesse's eyes. "I can't believe you had me crying." He began to laugh now, playing.

"Me?" Jesse squawked, grateful for the change-up.

"That's more intimate than sex."

Jesse thought about it for a moment—her and Lorenzo. No. "Yeah, I heard you guys rather punch than munch."

"What's *that* supposed to mean."

"You figure it out."

Exhausted by the talk, they took a breather, watching three white teenagers plop down on the grass, one of them firing up a fat blunt, taking a deep hit, and passing it to his left.

"So I hear you got a job offer out in Tombstone, Arizona," Lorenzo said calmly, eyeing that joint, the smell reaching them.

"Tucson," Jesse said, then corrected herself. "I mean Phoenix."

Lorenzo laughed. "You *sure*, now."

"Nope."

"When you going?"

"Never."

"Well, if you did decide to go, I'd miss you," he said, with no bantering undertone.

"Me too," Jesse fumbled, thrown by Lorenzo's sincerity.

"Let me ask you. If you did decide to, you know, go there, start over, would you bring your brother with you?"

"Nope." Safe to say, since she wasn't going anywhere.

"Uh-oh! Uh-oh!" Lorenzo shifted gears again, throwing all his ragged emotions into animated clowning now, the three stoned kids looking their way.

"Hey, birds got to swim, fish got to fly."

"Yeah, I hear you," he said, calming down. Then he called out to the kids, "I'm gonna count to ten. If that blunt ain't shredded and stomped on, your ass is mine," not bothering to show any ID, his tone of voice his ID, the three of them complying, then vanishing.

"She could have fucked me good," Jesse said.

"Who." Lorenzo asked openly. Jesse realized that he didn't know of her bogus-child scam on Brenda; no reason to tell him now.

"So what's on your plate?" she asked, steering him away.

"Me? They're talking about starting up this curfew program, city-wide curfew for the, the minors—get everybody off the street by 11:00 P.M. Word is the mayor asked for me personally to run the operation, and, like, I'm thinking about it, but I don't even know if I agree with it. I mean, there's arguments to be made on either side. I mean, you know, they're not worried about the Irish or the Italian kids up in the Heights, right? Which leaves *who*. But *I* don't want them fifteen-year-old knuckleheads out on JFK at two in the morning either. But like, we're talking July August here . . . Hot, muggy, no school, no one wants to stay inside. So, I don't know, it's complicated."

Jesse envisioned it, getting a ride-along on the first night a summertime curfew went into effect, a dream assignment.

"And I'll tell you, if I *do* do it? I'm gonna insist that Bump comes in with me on this, 'cause he's hooked in every bit as good as me out there."

"He's OK?"

"Bump? Yeah, he came out the hospital like two days ago. He's all right. Alls he got to do is wear like these protective goggles out there, you know, like Kareem Abdul Jabbar used to wear? He's gonna be OK, though." Lorenzo turned to her then, his voice becoming more personal and slightly chiding. "You ever gonna do that article on his son like you promised?"

"This week." Jesse crossed her heart, thinking, Maybe. See what comes over the scanner.

Grunting, Lorenzo struggled to his feet, one hand holding his beret in place. "Already I got some people calling me Curfew Council. What do you think of that, Curfew Council."

"It beats Frenchy," she said, rising too, swiping the dirt from the rear of her jeans, "I can tell you that much."

"Yeah, huh?" Lorenzo arched his back, yawned. "As long as those kids up in the Heights is fair game too."

As they left Freedomtown, Lorenzo saw Ben waiting for his sister and he became knotty at the thought of losing Jesse's company right now.

"Take a ride with me," he murmured, touching Jesse's elbow. To his relief, after she had a brief conversation with her brother, Jesse hopped into the Crown Vic. Despite his need for her company, his need to keep talking, he then felt overcome with an odd shyness and became verbally strangled.

Jesse, apparently under the same choke-mouthed spell, was no help. And for want of any other way to commune with her about the last few days, Lorenzo began cruising past all the stations of the cross—the route of the march in Gannon, Brenda's apartment complex on Van Loon, the Southern District station house back in Dempsy—hoping for some kind of release, some kind of clearance. But each site now seemed to him a disappointment, seemed in some way over the last couple of days to have physically shrivelled.

As he cut across JFK on his way to revisit Armstrong, one of the street shmoes—a stocky blur of a man, late thirties, hanging in front of a bar—caught Lorenzo's eye, Lorenzo thinking, I don't need to see this, I do not need to see this. But he was also grateful for the opportunity to open his mouth again, start nibbling on the world again.

"Dexter!" he barked out the window, the car rocking to a stop. The guy got all blinky, managing to rear back and lean forward at the same time, not too happy about seeing Lorenzo either.

"Get over here." Disengaging himself from two gaunt middle-aged women, Dexter reluctantly shuffled up to the car, his eyes puffed and slitted. "Where the fuck you supposed to be."

"Jail." Dexter shrugged and looked away. His crossed hands, dangling inside the window now, were swollen to the size of woolen gloves.

"That's right," Lorenzo said. "At what time?"

"Six."

"Yeah, huh? My watch says ten-thirty."

"I missed the bus."

"You supposed to be out here looking for a *job*. What the fuck you doing hanging on the corner."

Dexter, still humped into the window, looked off again, gave it another shrug.

"*Did* you look for a job?" Lorenzo said, coming on like a rolling-pin wife.

"Nope."

"Why not."

"Because I had me some *sex*. I been in County six months. I was over*due*."

"Nobody gives a fuck about your sex life. You supposed to be looking for a job."

"Everything's closed."

"McDonald's ain't closed."

"Yeah? You work at McDonald's."

Jesse laughed. Lorenzo took a moment to massage his temples, this routine scolding unusually wearing on him right now, like sweeping leaves on a windy day.

Dexter checked out Jesse in the passenger seat. "How you doin'?"

"I've been better," Jesse answered pleasantly, the sound of her voice unexpectedly picking up Lorenzo's spirits, making him think that she might be getting a little bit of her appetite back too.

"Lorenzo, can you lend me some money for the bus?" Dexter asked. "You right, I gotta get going."

Lorenzo threw him the thousand-yard stare, then shook his head in disgust. "Get the fuck in back."

As Lorenzo drove Dexter to jail, the car quickly became saturated with a musk of liquor-scented sweat, the odor such that, despite the air-conditioning, Lorenzo had to open his window to breathe. And try as he might, he couldn't quite recall the powerful allure that alcohol had once held for him. He glared at the fuckup in his rearview, but Dexter was oblivious to the vibrations, his eyes continuously pulled to the passing scenery.

"Dexter," Jesse said, turning around, glancing at his sausage-fat fingers. "What are you on, work release?"

"Work release?" he said after a while. "Nah, it's like *job*-hunt release. They let you out like nine in the morning, you supposed to look for a job for when your sentence is up, then you come back in the evening."

"*Early* evening," Lorenzo scolded—just couldn't help it.

Lorenzo pulled up to the Dempsy County Correctional Center, and the prisoner exited from the backseat without a word. He shuffled toward the main entrance, Lorenzo muttering, "You're welcome," staying put until he had seen the official sign-in through the glass double doors.

With Dexter safely tucked in, Lorenzo headed back toward the streets of Dempsy and felt the muteness come down on him again, felt it come down on Jesse, too, the air heavy with things unsaid. He began slowing down at green lights, stopping at yellows, bewildered, thwarted, resisting the impulse to call it a night.

"Go back to what you were doing," Jesse said, quietly breaking the ice. "That was good."

And so Lorenzo resumed their visitation to the stations, cruising the Dempsy Medical Center, then rolling past the now-silent Saint Agnes parking lot, launch site of the Friends of Kent search party, then the haunted grounds of the former Chase Institute itself, the rust-eaten, shatter-ribbed gates creaking and banging, a horror-movie cliché masking a half century's worth of true horror. Slowly Lorenzo came to understand that what they were really doing now, he and Jesse, was saying good-bye—to Brenda and, in a way, to each other.

Lorenzo pulled up to the Gannon side of Martyrs Park, the scene of the crime, the scene of the melee. They left the car and strolled together through the humid, jungly pocket park to the Armstrong side, the towers there looking both ramshackle and indestructible. Maintaining their silent communion, they walked the length of the cul-de-sac, Lorenzo ducking some kids hanging in the breezeway of Four Building, avoiding the obligatory verbal sparring match. It wasn't until they approached the Bowl that he felt compelled to speak, the sight of those refrigerators still just sitting out there first disorienting, then enraging him.

"Look at this," he said, laughing, pissed, as he gestured to the field of crates. "After all that shit, right? They *still* got these goddamned things just laying out here like nothing happened."

"I hear you," Jesse said automatically, then, "Listen, on the curfew? When you do your first night roundup . . ." She was speaking gingerly now. "Do you think I can get a ride along?"

"What?" Lorenzo's agitation had turned him deaf.

Jesse's cell phone rang and she stepped back, putting Lorenzo on hold. Grousing to himself, he began stomping through the Bowl, glaring at the refrigerators as if they were responsible for their own immobility. He worked out his exasperation in a crisscross pattern, almost making it to the high end of the slope before his asthma caught up with him and forced him to take a seat on the edge of a scorched crate.

Momentarily done in, his scalp on fire beneath its protective beret, he dropped his head between his knees, then came up and took a hit of spray. Down below on Hurley, he saw Jesse, still on the horn, pacing back and forth across the rubbled cul-de-sac with unappeasable energy.

Sensing a closer presence, Lorenzo sat up a little more and saw a boy—nine, ten years old—perched like a cat on the crate to his immediate left.

"What you doin' down here," Lorenzo said, with reflexive sharpness.

"What you doin' down here." the boy repeated in pitch-perfect mockery. He had wide, intelligent eyes and a copper cast to his skin.

"It's eleven o'clock," Lorenzo wheezed. "Get your behind upstairs."

"Get *your* behind upstairs," the boy said easily.

"If you make me stand up you're gonna be sorry."

"You're gonna be sorry." The kid aped Lorenzo's expression, enjoying the conversation, the attention.

Attempting to regain his feet, Lorenzo made it halfway up before he found himself seated again, skull pulsing like a gong, his asthma resurrecting itself past the medication.

"Are you high?" the boy asked, without malice, without judgment.

"I'm OK," Lorenzo answered quietly, just sitting there now, massaging his temples. "But it's late," he added, making a great effort to maintain a gentle tone. "So I want you to go on home . . ."